The Monster-Maker and Other Science Fiction Classics

THE Monster-Maker AND Other Science Fiction Classics

COMPILED BY MICHAEL KELAHAN

FALL RIVER PRESS

Fall River Press
122 Fifth Avenue
New York, NY 10011

ISBN 978-1-4351-2507-0

Printed and bound in the United States of America

1 3 5 7 9 10 8 6 4 2

Contents

For

ELLEN DATLOW,

who has seen the light and

dark sides of science fiction

Introduction

The first science fiction magazine, *Amazing Stories*, debuted at newsstands with an April 1926 date on its cover. The term "science fiction" was not coined until several years later to describe the fiction genre that *Amazing Stories* promoted. How, then, do we explain the contents of this anthology, whose selections comfortably fit the template of the science fiction tale yet date almost entirely to the first two decades of the twentieth century—or earlier?

The explanation is simple: Long before it was formally named, or codified as a literary genre, science fiction existed as a popular approach to storytelling. The novel that many scholars consider the first work of science fiction, Mary Shelley's *Frankenstein; or, the Modern Prometheus* (1818), was one of the last gasps of the Gothic era, which took root in the late eighteenth century, shortly after the novel emerged as a popular storytelling form. For her novel, Shelley took a theme popular in supernatural fiction—the reanimated dead—and gave it a scientific rationale. Thus, the science fiction approach to storytelling dates back almost to the emergence of narrative fiction as a storytelling form.

In hindsight, the publication of Mary Shelley's science fiction novel in the early years of the nineteenth century was as prescient as it was visionary. The nineteenth and early twentieth centuries saw a pace of scientific progress hitherto unprecedented in human civilization—not just in terms of scientific advances, but in terms of how those advances translated into inventions, processes, and systems that touched the lives of all who lived in developed nations and transformed how they lived, thought, and saw their world. In such a hothouse environment, stories that extrapolated science imaginatively, or that speculated where and what the scientific advances of today might lead to in the future, were inevitable. Indeed, *Amazing Stories* acknowledged the significance of these stories and the literary tradition that they established by reprinting in its first issue stories by Edgar Allan Poe, Jules Verne, and H.G. Wells—all of whom are represented in this volume, and all of whom had written influential works of science fiction before the turn of the twentieth century.

The Monster-Maker and Other Science Fiction Classics taps the full reservoir of speculative stories written before science fiction got its name. Its contents represent some of the most imaginative work produced at that time in America, England, and Europe. Some of these stories appeared in leading literary periodicals of their day, others in pulp fiction magazines that catered to readers interested in the sensational and the fantastic. Several seem quaintly of their time. Mary Shelley's "The Mortal Immortal," concerned with the unnatural prolonging of a lifespan through alchemical means, introduces a theme that would become technologically more sophisticated in later science fiction. Similarly, Edgar Allan Poe's "A Tale of the Ragged Mountains" might be thought of as a time travel tale written before the notion of a time machine evolved. The ideas behind most of these stories, though, gave rise to themes on which the science fiction genre was founded and continue to serve as touchstones in science fiction today.

In the nineteenth century, John Cleve Symmes, Jr.'s theories of a Hollow Earth, whose interior was accessible though points of egress at the North and South Poles, gained traction in fringe circles of science. Symmes's farfetched idea clearly is behind George Griffith's "From Pole to Pole," which envisions some of the scientific challenges that scientific exploration of a channel through the Earth might pose. In his novel *At the Earth's Core*, Edgar Rice Burroughs elaborated Symmes's theory even further, imagining a subterranean world with its own sun and a lost race to whom it is home.

Counterbalancing these stories of marvels inside our own world are stories that look with wonder to outer space. H.G. Wells' "The Crystal Egg" is set on Earth, but its titular artifact proves to be a portal to an extraplanetary realm. H.P. Lovecraft's "The Colour out of Space," likewise, is set on our own planet, but insofar as it depicts of an alien influence that comes to our planet aboard a meteor and that blights the landscape it leaches into, it can be read a tale of extraterrestrial invasion.

The idea that earth is home to higher life forms other than human beings was one of the most popular themes in early science fiction. In George Allan England's "The Thing from Outside" and A. Merritt's "The Moon Pool," these life forms are predatory and hostile (although when Merritt later turned his story into the opening chapters of a novel-length sequel, the fearsome being of light that terrorizes his explorers proves to be something more benign than the events of the short story would suggest). In Francis Stevens' "Unseen, Unfeared," an entire universe of repellant life forms lives clandestinely among us, their appearance mercifully obscured to all but those who pry scientifically into their existence. J.H. Rosny, in "The Sixth

Sense, or Another World," imagines a world invisible to ordinary human eyes whose beings assume a variety of fascinating biological and geometric shapes. In "The Diamond Lens," Fitz-James O'Brien shows how, to some people, the microscopic life forms that live in a drop of water might seem preferable to human life.

Artificial life was another topic that invited imaginative speculation in the nineteenth century. W.C. Morrow's "The Monster-Maker," concerned with a megalomaniacal scientist who experiments with human remains, is a direct descendant of Mary Shelley's *Frankenstein*. In "Moxon's Master," an early tale of robotics, Ambrose Bierce translates ideas from Shelley's novel into a cautionary tale about the creation of artificial intelligence. Indeed, for all their scientific marvels and sense of wonder, it is interesting to see how many of these stories explore the dark side of science and technology. The theoretical realm of science proves dangerous to human existence in John Buchan's "Space." Technology proves destined to be misused with amusing consequences in Harriet Prescott Spofford's "The Ray of Displacement," or abused to cause pain and suffering in Franz Kafka's "In the Penal Colony." In Jack London's "The Shadow and the Flash," a scientific breakthrough becomes a weapon in the hands of fallible, competitive scientists. Science is revealed to be dangerous when it is mishandled by experimenters who have no idea how dangerously it can run amok in Jules Verne's "Doctor Ox's Experiment" and Sir Arthur Conan Doyle's "The Los Amigos Fiasco."

Just as science has advanced considerably in the century or more since these stories were written, so has science fiction evolved as a literature. Regardless, these stories share with the science fiction of today an imaginative audacity that distinguishes them from other types of fiction, and a speculative sweep that begins with the simple proposition, "What if . . . ?"

—Michael Kelahan
New York, 2012

The Mortal Immortal

MARY SHELLEY

Mary Shelley's (1797–1851) Gothic novel Frankenstein; or, The Modern Prometheus *(1851) is regarded by most scholars as the first tale of science fiction. Readers of Shelley's account of Victor Frankenstein's experiment to create life by animating a monstrous creature stitched together from corpse parts will recall that Victor first studied the teachings of alchemist Cornelius Agrippa (a.k.a. Paracelsus) en route to acquiring the more sophisticated scientific training that made his experiment succeed. This short story, which first appeared in the 1834 issue of* The Keepsake, *is the narrative of a student of Agrippa's and revisits some of the themes of Shelley's landmark novel.*

JULY 16, 1833.—This is a memorable anniversary for me; on it I complete my three hundred and twenty-third year!

The Wandering Jew?—certainly not. More than eighteen centuries have passed over his head. In comparison with him, I am a very young Immortal.

Am I, then, immortal? This is a question which I have asked myself, by day and night, for now three hundred and three years, and yet cannot answer it. I detected a grey hair amidst my brown locks this very day—that surely signifies decay. Yet it may have remained concealed there for three hundred years—for some persons have become entirely white-headed before twenty years of age.

I will tell my story, and my reader shall judge for me. I will tell my story, and so contrive to pass some few hours of a long eternity, become so wearisome to me. For ever! Can it be? to live for ever! I have heard of enchantments, in which the victims were plunged into a deep sleep, to wake, after a hundred years, as fresh as ever: I have heard of the Seven Sleepers—thus to be immortal would not be so burthensome: but, oh! the weight of never-ending time—the tedious passage of the still-succeeding hours! How happy was the fabled Nourjahad!—But to my task.

All the world has heard of Cornelius Agrippa. His memory is as immortal as his arts have made me. All the world has also heard of his scholar, who, unawares, raised the foul fiend during his master's absence, and was destroyed by him. The report, true or false, of this accident, was attended with many inconveniences to the renowned philosopher. All his scholars at once deserted him—his servants disappeared. He had no one near him to put coals on his ever-burning fires while he slept, or to attend to the changeful colours of his medicines while he studied. Experiment after experiment failed, because one pair of hands was insufficient to complete them: the dark spirits laughed at him for not being able to retain a single mortal in his service.

I was then very young—very poor—and very much in love. I had been for about a year the pupil of Cornelius, though I was absent when this accident took place. On my return, my friends implored me not to return to the alchymist's abode. I trembled as I listened to the dire tale they told; I required no second warning; and when Cornelius came and offered me a purse of gold if I would remain under his roof, I felt as if Satan himself tempted me. My teeth chattered—my hair stood on end—I ran off as fast as my trembling knees would permit.

My failing steps were directed whither for two years they had every evening been attracted—a gently bubbling spring of pure living water, beside which lingered a dark-haired girl, whose beaming eyes were fixed on the path I was accustomed each night to tread. I cannot remember the hour when I did not love Bertha; we had been neighbours and playmates from infancy—her parents, like mine, were of humble life, yet respectable—our attachment had been a source of pleasure to them. In an evil hour, a malignant fever carried off both her father and mother, and Bertha became an orphan. She would have found a home beneath my paternal roof, but, unfortunately, the old lady of the near castle, rich, childless, and solitary, declared her intention to adopt her. Henceforth Bertha was clad in silk—inhabited a marble palace—and was looked on as being highly favoured by fortune. But in her new situation among her new associates, Bertha remained true to the friend of her humbler days; she often visited the cottage of my father, and when forbidden to go thither, she would stray towards the neighbouring wood, and meet me beside its shady fountain.

She often declared that she owed no duty to her new protectress equal in sanctity to that which bound us. Yet still I was too poor to marry, and she grew weary of being tormented on my account. She had a haughty but an impatient spirit, and grew angry at the obstacles that prevented our union. We met now after an absence, and she had been sorely beset while I was away; she complained bitterly, and almost reproached me for being poor. I replied hastily—

"I am honest, if I am poor!—were I not, I might soon become rich!"

This exclamation produced a thousand questions. I feared to shock her by owning the truth, but she drew it from me; and then, casting a look of disdain on me, she said—

"You pretend to love, and you fear to face the Devil for my sake!"

I protested that I had only dreaded to offend her; while she dwelt on the magnitude of the reward that I should receive. Thus encouraged—shamed by her—led on by love and hope, laughing at my late fears, with quick steps and a light heart, I returned to accept the offers of the alchymist, and was instantly installed in my office.

A year passed away. I became possessed of no insignificant sum of money. Custom had banished my fears. In spite of the most painful vigilance, I had never detected the trace of a cloven foot; nor was the studious silence of our abode ever disturbed by demoniac howls. I still continued my stolen interviews with Bertha, and Hope dawned on me—Hope—but not perfect joy; for Bertha fancied that love and security were enemies, and her pleasure was to divide them in my bosom. Though true of heart, she was somewhat of a coquette in manner; and I was jealous as a Turk. She slighted me in a thousand ways, yet would never acknowledge herself to be in the wrong. She would drive me mad with anger, and then force me to beg her pardon. Sometimes she fancied that I was not sufficiently submissive, and then she had some story of a rival, favoured by her protectress. She was surrounded by silk-clad youths—the rich and gay. What chance had the sad-robed scholar of Cornelius compared with these?

On one occasion, the philosopher made such large demands upon my time, that I was unable to meet her as I was wont. He was engaged in some mighty work, and I was forced to remain, day and night, feeding his furnaces and watching his chemical preparations. Bertha waited for me in vain at the fountain. Her haughty spirit fired at this neglect; and when at last I stole out during the few short minutes allotted to me for slumber, and hoped to be consoled by her, she received me with disdain, dismissed me in scorn, and vowed that any man should possess her hand rather than he who could not be in two places at once for her sake. She would be revenged! And truly she was. In my dingy retreat I heard that she had been hunting, attended by Albert Hoffer. Albert Hoffer was favoured by her protectress, and the three passed in cavalcade before my smoky window. Methought that they mentioned my name; it was followed by a laugh of derision, as her dark eyes glanced contemptuously towards my abode.

Jealousy, with all its venom and all its misery, entered my breast. Now I shed a torrent of tears, to think that I should never call her mine; and, anon, I imprecated a thousand curses on her inconstancy. Yet, still I must stir the fires of the alchymist, still attend on the changes of his unintelligible medicines.

Cornelius had watched for three days and nights, nor closed his eyes. The progress of his alembics was slower than he expected: in spite of his anxiety, sleep weighed upon his eyelids. Again and again he threw off drowsiness with more than human energy; again and again it stole away his senses. He eyes his crucibles wistfully. "Not ready yet," he murmured; "will another night pass before the work is accomplished? Winzy, you are vigilant—you are faithful—you have slept, my boy—you slept last night. Look at that glass vessel. The liquid it contains is of a soft rose-colour: the moment it begins to change its hue, awaken me—till then I may close my eyes. First, it will turn white, and then emit golden flashes; but wait not till then; when the rose-colour fades, rouse me." I scarcely heard the last words, muttered, as they were, in sleep. Even then he did not quite yield to nature. "Winzy, my boy," he again said, "do not touch the vessel—do not put it to your lips; it is a philter—a philter to cure love; you would not cease to love your Bertha—beware to drink!"

And he slept. His venerable head sunk on his breast, and I scarce heard his regular breathing. For a few minutes I watched the vessel—the rosy hue of the liquid remained unchanged. Then my thoughts wandered—they visited the fountain, and dwelt on a thousand charming scenes never to be renewed—never! Serpents and adders were in my heart as the word "Never!" half formed itself on my lips. False girl!—false and cruel I never more would she smile on me as that evening she smiled on Albert. Worthless, detested woman! I would not remain unrevenged—she should see Albert expire at her feet—she should die beneath my vengeance. She had smiled in disdain and triumph—she knew my wretchedness and her power. Yet what power had she?—the power of exciting my hate—my utter scorn—my—oh, all but indifference! Could I attain that—could I regard her with careless eyes, transferring my rejected love to one fairer and more true, that were indeed a victory!

A bright flash darted before my eyes. I had forgotten the medicine of the adept; I gazed on it with wonder: flashes of admirable beauty, more bright than those which the diamond emits when the sun's rays are on it, glanced from the surface of the liquid; an odour the most fragrant and grateful stole over my sense; the vessel seemed one globe of living radiance, lovely to the eye, and most inviting to the

4

taste. The first thought, instinctively inspired by the grosser sense, was, I will—I must drink. I raised the vessel to my lips. "It will cure me of love—of torture!" Already I had quaffed half of the most delicious liquor ever tasted by the palate of man, when the philosopher stirred. I started—I dropped the glass—the fluid flamed and glanced along the floor, while I felt Cornelius's gripe at my throat, as he shrieked aloud, "Wretch! you have destroyed the labour of my life!"

The philosopher was totally unaware that I had drunk any portion of his drug. His idea was, and I gave a tacit assent to it, that I had raised the vessel from curiosity, and that, frighted at its brightness, and the flashes of intense light it gave forth, I had let it fall. I never undeceived him. The fire of the medicine was quenched—the fragrance died away—he grew calm, as a philosopher should under the heaviest trials, and dismissed me to rest.

I will not attempt to describe the sleep of glory and bliss which bathed my soul in paradise during the remaining hours of that memorable night. Words would be faint and shallow types of my enjoyment, or of the gladness that possessed my bosom when I woke. I trod air—my thoughts were in heaven. Earth appeared heaven, and my inheritance upon it was to be one trance of delight. "This it is to be cured of love," I thought; "I will see Bertha this day, and she will find her lover cold and regardless; too happy to be disdainful, yet how utterly indifferent to her!"

The hours danced away. The philosopher, secure that he had once succeeded, and believing that he might again, began to concoct the same medicine once more. He was shut up with his books and drugs, and I had a holiday. I dressed myself with care; I looked in an old but polished shield, which served me for a mirror; methought my good looks had wonderfully improved. I hurried beyond the precincts of the town, joy in my soul, the beauty of heaven and earth around me. I turned my steps towards the castle—I could look on its lofty turrets with lightness of heart, for I was cured of love. My Bertha saw me afar off, as I came up the avenue. I know not what sudden impulse animated her bosom, but at the sight, she sprung with a light fawn-like bound down the marble steps, and was hastening towards me. But I had been perceived by another person. The old high-born hag, who called herself her protectress, and was her tyrant, had seen me also; she hobbled, panting, up the terrace; a page, as ugly as herself, held up her train, and fanned her as she hurried along, and stopped my fair girl with a "How, now, my bold mistress? whither so fast? Back to your cage—hawks are abroad!"

Bertha clasped her hands—her eyes were still bent on my approaching figure. I saw the contest. How I abhorred the old crone who checked the kind impulses of my Bertha's softening heart. Hitherto, respect for her rank had caused me to avoid the lady of the castle; now I disdained such trivial considerations. I was cured of love, and lifted above all human fears; I hastened forwards, and soon reached the terrace. How lovely Bertha looked! her eyes flashing fire, her cheeks glowing with impatience and anger, she was a thousand times more graceful and charming than ever. I no longer loved—Oh no! I adored—worshipped—idolized her!

She had that morning been persecuted, with more than usual vehemence, to consent to an immediate marriage with my rival. She was reproached with the encouragement that she had shown him—she was threatened with being turned out of doors with disgrace and shame. Her proud spirit rose in arms at the threat; but when she remembered the scorn that she had heaped upon me, and how, perhaps, she had thus lost one whom she now regarded as her only friend, she wept with remorse and rage. At that moment I appeared. "Oh, Winzy!" she exclaimed, "take me to your mother's cot; swiftly let me leave the detested luxuries and wretchedness of this noble dwelling—take me to poverty and happiness."

I clasped her in my arms with transport. The old dame was speechless with fury, and broke forth into invective only when we were far on our road to my natal cottage. My mother received the fair fugitive, escaped from a gilt cage to nature and liberty, with tenderness and joy; my father, who loved her, welcomed her heartily; it was a day of rejoicing, which did not need the addition of the celestial potion of the alchymist to steep me in delight.

Soon after this eventful day, I became the husband of Bertha. I ceased to be the scholar of Cornelius, but I continued his friend. I always felt grateful to him for having, unawares, procured me that delicious draught of a divine elixir, which, instead of curing me of love (sad cure! solitary and joyless remedy for evils which seem blessings to the memory), had inspired me with courage and resolution, thus winning for me an inestimable treasure in my Bertha.

I often called to mind that period of trance-like inebriation with wonder. The drink of Cornelius had not fulfilled the task for which he affirmed that it had been prepared, but its effects were more potent and blissful than words can express. They had faded by degrees, yet they lingered long—and painted life in hues of splendour. Bertha often wondered at my lightness of heart and unaccustomed gaiety; for, before, I had been rather serious, or even sad, in my disposition. She loved me the better for my cheerful temper, and our days were winged by joy.

Five years afterwards I was suddenly summoned to the bedside of the dying Cornelius. He had sent for me in haste, conjuring my instant presence. I found him stretched on his pallet, enfeebled even to death; all of life that yet remained animated his piercing eyes, and they were fixed on a glass vessel, full of a roseate liquid.

"Behold," he said, in a broken and inward voice, "the vanity of human wishes! a second time my hopes are about to be crowned, a second time they are destroyed. Look at that liquor—you remember five years ago I had prepared the same, with the same success; then, as now, my thirsting lips expected to taste the immortal elixir— you dashed it from me! and at present it is too late."

He spoke with difficulty, and fell back on his pillow. I could not help saying—

"How, revered master, can a cure for love restore you to life?"

A faint smile gleamed across his face as I listened earnestly to his scarcely intelligible answer.

"A cure for love and for all things—the Elixir of Immortality. Ah! if now I might drink, I should live for ever!"

As he spoke, a golden flash gleamed from the fluid; a well-remembered fragrance stole over the air; he raised himself, all weak as he was—strength seemed miraculously to re-enter his frame—he stretched forth his hand—a loud explosion startled me—a ray of fire shot up from the elixir, and the glass vessel which contained it was shivered to atoms! I turned my eyes towards the philosopher; he had fallen back—his eyes were glassy—his features rigid—he was dead!

But I lived, and was to live for ever! So said the unfortunate alchymist, and for a few days I believed his words. I remembered the glorious intoxication that had followed my stolen draught. I reflected on the change I had felt in my frame—in my soul. The bounding elasticity of the one—the buoyant lightness of the other. I surveyed myself in a mirror, and could perceive no change in my features during the space of the five years which had elapsed. I remembered the radiant hues and grateful scent of that delicious beverage—worthy the gift it was capable of bestowing— I was, then, IMMORTAL!

A few days after I laughed at my credulity. The old proverb, that "a prophet is least regarded in his own country," was true with respect to me and my defunct master. I loved him as a man—I respected him as a sage—but I derided the notion that he could command the powers of darkness, and laughed at the superstitious fears with which he was regarded by the vulgar. He was a wise philosopher, but had no acquaintance with any spirits but those clad in flesh and blood. His science was simply human; and human science, I soon persuaded myself, could never conquer nature's laws so far as to imprison the soul for ever within its carnal habitation. Cornelius had brewed a soul-refreshing drink—more inebriating than wine—sweeter and more fragrant than any fruit: it possessed probably strong medicinal powers, imparting gladness to the heart and vigour to the limbs; but its effects would wear out; already were they diminished in my frame. I was a lucky fellow to have quaffed health and joyous spirits, and perhaps long life, at my master's hands; but my good fortune ended there: longevity was far different from immortality.

I continued to entertain this belief for many years. Sometimes a thought stole across me—Was the alchymist indeed deceived? But my habitual credence was, that I should meet the fate of all the children of Adam at my appointed time—a little late, but still at a natural age. Yet it was certain that I retained a wonderfully youthful look. I was laughed at for my vanity in consulting the mirror so often, but I consulted it in vain—my brow was untrenched—my cheeks—my eyes—my whole person continued as untarnished as in my twentieth year.

I was troubled. I looked at the faded beauty of Bertha—I seemed more like her son. By degrees our neighbours began to make similar observations, and I found at last that I went by the name of the Scholar bewitched. Bertha herself grew uneasy. She became jealous and peevish, and at length she began to question me. We had no children; we were all in all to each other; and though, as she grew older, her vivacious spirit became a little allied to ill-temper, and her beauty sadly diminished, I cherished her in my heart as the mistress I had idolized, the wife I had sought and won with such perfect love.

At last our situation became intolerable: Bertha was fifty—I twenty years of age. I had, in very shame, in some measure adoped the habits of a more advanced age; I no longer mingled in the dance among the young and gay, but my heart bounded along with them while I restrained my feet; and a sorry figure I cut among the Nestors of our village. But before the time I mention, things were altered—we were universally shunned; we were—at least, I was—reported to have kept up an iniquitous acquaintance with some of my former master's supposed friends. Poor Bertha was pitied, but deserted. I was regarded with horror and detestation.

What was to be done? we sat by our winter fire—poverty had made itself felt, for none would buy the produce of my farm; and often I had been forced to journey twenty miles, to some place where I was not known, to dispose of our property. It is true, we had saved something for an evil day—that day was come.

We sat by our lone fireside—the old-hearted youth and his antiquated wife. Again Bertha insisted on knowing the truth; she recapitulated all she had ever heard said about me, and added her own observations. She conjured me to cast off the spell; she described how much more comely grey hairs were than my chestnut locks; she descanted on the reverence and respect due to age—how preferable to the slight regard paid to mere children: could I imagine that the despicable gifts of youth and good looks outweighed disgrace, hatred, and scorn? Nay, in the end I should be burnt as a dealer in the black art, while she, to whom I had not deigned to communicate any portion of my good fortune, might be stoned as my accomplice. At length she insinuated that I must share my secret with her, and bestow on her like benefits to those I myself enjoyed, or she would denounce me—and then she burst into tears.

Thus beset, methought it was the best way to tell the truth. I revealed it as tenderly as I could, and spoke only of a very long life, not of immortality—which representation, indeed, coincided best with my own ideas. When I ended, I rose and said—

"And now, my Bertha, will you denounce the lover of your youth?—You will not, I know. But it is too hard, my poor wife, that you should suffer from my ill-luck and the accursed arts of Cornelius. I will leave you—you have wealth enough, and friends will return in my absence. I will go; young as I seem, and strong as I am, I can work and gain my bread among strangers, unsuspected and unknown. I loved you in youth; God is my witness that I would not desert you in age, but that your safety and happiness require it."

I took my cap and moved towards the door; in a moment Bertha's arms were round my neck, and her lips were pressed to mine. "No, my husband, my Winzy," she said, "you shall not go alone—take me with you; we will remove from this place, and, as you say, among strangers we shall be unsuspected and safe. I am not so very old as quite to shame you, my Winzy; and I daresay the charm will soon wear off, and, with the blessing of God, you will become more elderly-looking, as is fitting; you shall not leave me."

I returned the good soul's embrace heartily. "I will not, my Bertha; but for your sake I had not thought of such a thing. I will be your true, faithful husband while you are spared to me, and do my duty by you to the last."

The next day we prepared secretly for our emigration. We were obliged to make great pecuniary sacrifices—it could not be helped. We realized a sum sufficient, at least, to maintain us while Bertha lived; and, without saying adieu to any one, quitted our native country to take refuge in a remote part of western France.

It was a cruel thing to transport poor Bertha from her native village, and the friends of her youth, to a new country, new language, new customs. The strange secret of my destiny rendered this removal immaterial to me; but I compassionated her deeply, and was glad to perceive that she found compensation for her misfortunes in a variety of little ridiculous circumstances. Away from all tell-tale chroniclers, she sought to decrease the apparent disparity of our ages by a thousand feminine arts—rouge, youthful dress, and assumed juvenility of manner. I could not be angry. Did not I myself wear a mask? Why quarrel with hers, because it was less successful? I grieved deeply when I remembered that this was my Bertha, whom I had loved so fondly, and won with such transport—the dark-eyed, dark-haired girl, with smiles of enchanting archness and a step like a fawn—this mincing, simpering, jealous old woman. I should have revered her grey locks and withered cheeks; but thus!—It was my work, I knew; but I did not the less deplore this type of human weakness.

Her jealousy never slept. Her chief occupation was to discover that, in spite of outward appearances, I was myself growing old. I verily believe that the poor soul loved me truly in her heart, but never had woman so tormenting a mode of displaying fondness. She would discern wrinkles in my face and decrepitude in my walk, while I bounded along in youthful vigour, the youngest looking of twenty youths. I never dared address another woman. On one occasion, fancying that the belle of the village regarded me with favouring eyes, she brought me a grey wig. Her constant discourse among her acquaintances was, that though I looked so young, there was ruin at work within my frame; and she affirmed that the worst symptom about me was my apparent health. My youth was a disease, she said, and I ought at all times to prepare, if not for a sudden and awful death, at least to awake some morning white-headed and bowed down with all the marks of advanced years. I let her talk— I often joined in her conjectures. Her warnings chimed in with my never-ceasing speculations concerning my state, and I took an earnest, though painful, interest in listening to all that her quick wit and excited imagination could say on the subject.

Why dwell on these minute circumstances? We lived on for many long years. Bertha became bedrid and paralytic; I nursed her as a mother might a child. She grew peevish, and still harped upon one string—of how long I should survive her. It has ever been a source of consolation to me, that I performed my duty scrupulously towards her. She had been mine in youth, she was mine in age; and at last, when I heaped the sod over her corpse, I wept to feel that I had lost all that really bound me to humanity.

Since then how many have been my cares and woes, how few and empty my enjoyments! I pause here in my history—I will pursue it no further. A sailor without rudder or compass, tossed on a stormy sea—a traveller lost on a widespread heath, without landmark or stone to guide him—such have I been: more lost, more hopeless than either. A nearing ship, a gleam from some far cot, may save them; but I have no beacon except the hope of death.

Death! mysterious, ill-visaged friend of weak humanity! Why alone of all mortals have you cast me from your sheltering fold? Oh, for the peace of the grave! the deep silence of the iron-bound tomb! that thought would cease to work in my brain, and my heart beat no more with emotions varied only by new forms of sadness!

Am I immortal? I return to my first question. In the first place, is it not more probable that the beverage of the alchymist was fraught rather with longevity than eternal life? Such is my hope. And then be it remembered, that I only drank half of the potion prepared by him. Was not the whole necessary to complete the charm to have drained half the Elixir of Immortality is but to be half-immortal—my For-ever is thus truncated and null.

But again, who shall number the years of the half of eternity? I often try to imagine by what rule the infinite may be divided. Sometimes I fancy age advancing upon me. One grey hair I have found. Fool! do I lament? Yes, the fear of age and death often creeps coldly into my heart; and the more I live, the more I dread death, even while I abhor life. Such an enigma is man—born to perish—when he wars, as I do, against the established laws of his nature.

But for this anomaly of feeling surely I might die: the medicine of the alchymist would not be proof against fire—sword—and the strangling waters. I have gazed upon the blue depths of many a placid lake, and the tumultuous rushing of many a mighty river, and have said, peace inhabits those waters; yet I have turned my steps away, to live yet another day. I have asked myself, whether suicide would be a crime in one to whom thus only the portals of the other world could be opened. I have done all, except presenting myself as a soldier or duellist, an object of destruction to my—no, not my fellow-mortals, and therefore I have shrunk away. They are not my fellows. The inextinguishable power of life in my frame, and their ephemeral existence, places us wide as the poles asunder. I could not raise a hand against the meanest or the most powerful among them.

Thus I have lived on for many a year—alone, and weary of myself—desirous of death, yet never dying—a mortal immortal. Neither ambition nor avarice can enter my mind, and the ardent love that gnaws at my heart, never to be returned—never to find an equal on which to expend itself—lives there only to torment me.

This very day I conceived a design by which I may end all—without self-slaughter, without making another man a Cain—an expedition, which mortal frame can never survive, even endued with the youth and strength that inhabits mine. Thus I shall put my immortality to the test, and rest for ever—or return, the wonder and benefactor of the human species.

Before I go, a miserable vanity has caused me to pen these pages. I would not die, and leave no name behind. Three centuries have passed since I quaffed the fatal beverage; another year shall not elapse before, encountering gigantic dangers—warring with the powers of frost in their home—beset by famine, toil, and tempest—I yield this body, too tenacious a cage for a soul which thirsts for freedom, to the destructive elements of air and water; or, if I survive, my name shall be recorded as one of the most famous among the sons of men; and, my task achieved, I shall adopt more resolute means, and, by scattering and annihilating the atoms that compose my frame, set at liberty the life imprisoned within, and so cruelly prevented from soaring from this dim earth to a sphere more congenial to its immortal essence.

A Tale of the Ragged Mountains

EDGAR ALLAN POE

Edgar Allan Poe (1809–1849) is usually thought of as a writer of horror fiction, but many of his short stories are laced with scientific speculations and feature plots involving mesmerism, phrenology, and other pseudo-sciences. This tale, which was first published in the April 1844 issue of Godey's Lady's Book, *is typical of much of Poe's writing, insofar as it leaves ambiguous whether the dislocations in time and space experienced by its narrator are explicable in scientific or supernatural terms.*

During the fall of the year 1827, while residing near Charlottesville, Virginia, I casually made the acquaintance of Mr. Augustus Bedloe. This young gentleman was remarkable in every respect, and excited in me a profound interest and curiosity. I found it impossible to comprehend him either in his moral or his physical relations. Of his family I could obtain no satisfactory account. Whence he came, I never ascertained. Even about his age—although I call him a young gentleman—there was something which perplexed me in no little degree. He certainly *seemed* young—and he made a point of speaking about his youth—yet there were moments when I should have had little trouble in imagining him a hundred years of age. But in no regard was he more peculiar than in his personal appearance. He was singularly tall and thin. He stooped much. His limbs were exceedingly long and emaciated. His forehead was broad and low. His complexion was absolutely bloodless. His mouth was large and flexible, and his teeth were more wildly uneven, although sound, than I had ever before seen teeth in a human head. The expression of his smile, however, was by no means unpleasing, as might be supposed; but it had no variation whatever. It was one of profound melancholy—of a phaseless and unceasing gloom. His eyes were abnormally large, and round like those of a cat. The pupils, too, upon any accession or diminution of light, underwent contraction or dilation, just such as is observed in the feline tribe. In moments of excitement the orbs grew bright to a degree almost inconceivable; seeming to emit luminous rays, not of a reflected but of an intrinsic lustre, as does a candle or the sun; yet their ordinary condition was so totally vapid, filmy, and dull as to convey the idea of the eyes of a long-interred corpse.

These peculiarities of person appeared to cause him much annoyance, and he was continually alluding to them in a sort of half explanatory, half apologetic strain, which, when I first heard it, impressed me very painfully. I soon, however, grew accustomed to it, and my uneasiness wore off. It seemed to be his design rather to insinuate than directly to assert that, physically, he had not always been what he was—that a long series of neuralgic attacks had reduced him from a condition of more than usual personal beauty, to that which I saw. For many years past he had been attended by a physician, named Templeton—an old gentleman, perhaps seventy years of age—whom he had first encountered at Saratoga, and from whose attention, while there, he either received, or fancied that he received, great benefit. The result was that Bedloe, who was wealthy, had made an arrangement with Dr. Templeton, by which the latter, in consideration of a liberal annual allowance, had consented to devote his time and medical experience exclusively to the care of the invalid.

Doctor Templeton had been a traveller in his younger days, and at Paris had become a convert, in great measure, to the doctrines of Mesmer. It was altogether by means of magnetic remedies that he had succeeded in alleviating the acute pains of his patient; and this success had very naturally inspired the latter with a certain degree of confidence in the opinions from which the remedies had been educed. The Doctor, however, like all enthusiasts, had struggled hard to make a thorough convert of his pupil, and finally so far gained his point as to induce the sufferer to submit to numerous experiments. By a frequent repetition of these, a result had arisen, which of late days has become so common as to attract little or no attention, but which, at the period of which I write, had very rarely been known in America. I mean to say, that between Doctor Templeton and Bedloe there had grown up, little by little, a very distinct and strongly marked *rapport,* or magnetic relation. I am not prepared to assert, however, that this rapport extended beyond the limits of the simple sleep-producing power, but this power itself had attained great intensity. At the first attempt to induce the magnetic somnolency, the mesmerist entirely failed.

14

In the fifth or sixth he succeeded very partially, and after long continued effort. Only at the twelfth was the triumph complete. After this the will of the patient succumbed rapidly to that of the physician, so that, when I first became acquainted with the two, sleep was brought about almost instantaneously by the mere volition of the operator, even when the invalid was unaware of his presence. It is only now, in the year 1845, when similar miracles are witnessed daily by thousands, that I dare venture to record this apparent impossibility as a matter of serious fact.

The temperament of Bedloe was, in the highest degree sensitive, excitable, enthusiastic. His imagination was singularly vigorous and creative; and no doubt it derived additional force from the habitual use of morphine, which he swallowed in great quantity, and without which he would have found it impossible to exist. It was his practice to take a very large dose of it immediately after breakfast each morning—or, rather, immediately after a cup of strong coffee, for he ate nothing in the forenoon—and then set forth alone, or attended only by a dog, upon a long ramble among the chain of wild and dreary hills that lie westward and southward of Charlottesville, and are there dignified by the title of the Ragged Mountains.

Upon a dim, warm, misty day, toward the close of November, and during the strange *interregnum* of the seasons which in America is termed the Indian Summer, Mr. Bedloe departed as usual for the hills. The day passed, and still he did not return.

About eight o'clock at night, having become seriously alarmed at his protracted absence, we were about setting out in search of him, when he unexpectedly made his appearance, in health no worse than usual, and in rather more than ordinary spirits. The account which he gave of his expedition, and of the events which had detained him, was a singular one indeed.

"You will remember," said he, "that it was about nine in the morning when I left Charlottesville. I bent my steps immediately to the mountains, and, about ten, entered a gorge which was entirely new to me. I followed the windings of this pass with much interest. The scenery which presented itself on all sides, although scarcely entitled to be called grand, had about it an indescribable and to me a delicious aspect of dreary desolation. The solitude seemed absolutely virgin. I could not help believing that the green sods and the gray rocks upon which I trod had been trodden never before by the foot of a human being. So entirely secluded, and in fact inaccessible, except through a series of accidents, is the entrance of the ravine, that it is by no means impossible that I was indeed the first adventurer—the very first and sole adventurer who had ever penetrated its recesses.

"The thick and peculiar mist, or smoke, which distinguishes the Indian Summer, and which now hung heavily over all objects, served, no doubt, to deepen the vague impressions which these objects created. So dense was this pleasant fog, that I could at no time see more than a dozen yards of the path before me. This path was excessively sinuous, and as the sun could not be seen, I soon lost all idea of the direction in which I journeyed. In the meantime the morphine had its customary effect—that of enduing all the external world with an intensity of interest. In the quivering of a leaf—in the hue of a blade of grass—in the shape of a trefoil—in the humming of a bee—in the gleaming of a dew-drop—in the breathing of the wind—in the faint odors that came from the forest—there came a whole universe of suggestion—a gay and motly train of rhapsodical and immethodical thought.

"Busied in this, I walked on for several hours, during which the mist deepened around me to so great an extent that at length I was reduced to an absolute groping of the way. And now an indescribable uneasiness possessed me—a species of nervous hesitation and tremor. I feared to tread, lest I should be precipitated into some abyss. I remembered, too, strange stories told about these Ragged Hills, and of the uncouth and fierce races of men who tenanted their groves and caverns. A thousand vague fancies oppressed and disconcerted me—fancies the more distressing because vague. Very suddenly my attention was arrested by the loud beating of a drum.

"My amazement was, of course, extreme. A drum in these hills was a thing unknown. I could not have been more surprised at the sound of the trump of the Archangel. But a new and still more astounding source of interest and perplexity arose. There came a wild rattling or jingling sound, as if of a bunch of large keys—and upon the instant a dusky-visaged and half-naked man rushed past me with a shriek. He came so close to my person that I felt his hot breath upon my face. He bore in one hand an instrument composed of an assemblage of steel rings, and shook them vigorously as he ran. Scarcely had he disappeared in the mist before, panting after him, with open mouth and glaring eyes, there darted a huge beast. I could not be mistaken in its character. It was a hyena.

"The sight of this monster rather relieved than heightened my terrors—for I now made sure that I dreamed, and endeavored to arouse myself to waking consciousness. I stepped boldly and briskly forward. I rubbed my eyes. I called aloud. I pinched my limbs. A small spring of water presented itself to my view, and here, stooping, I bathed my hands and my head and neck. This seemed to dissipate the equivocal sensations which had hitherto annoyed me. I arose, as I thought, a new man, and proceeded steadily and complacently on my unknown way.

"At length, quite overcome by exertion, and by a certain oppressive closeness of the atmosphere, I seated myself beneath a tree. Presently there came a feeble gleam of sunshine, and the shadow of the leaves of the tree fell faintly but definitely upon

16

the grass. At this shadow I gazed wonderingly for many minutes. Its character stupefied me with astonishment. I looked upward. The tree was a palm.

"I now arose hurriedly, and in a state of fearful agitation—for the fancy that I dreamed would serve me no longer. I saw—I felt that I had perfect command of my senses—and these senses now brought to my soul a world of novel and singular sensation. The heat became all at once intolerable. A strange odor loaded the breeze. A low continuous murmur, like that arising from a full, but gently-flowing river, came to my ears, intermingled with the peculiar hum of multitudinous human voices.

"While I listened in an extremity of astonishment which I need not attempt to describe, a strong and brief gust of wind bore off the incumbent fog as if by the wand of an enchanter.

"I found myself at the foot of a high mountain, and looking down into a vast plain, through which wound a majestic river. On the margin of this river stood an Eastern-looking city, such as we read of in the Arabian Tales, but of a character even more singular than any there described. From my position, which was far above the level of the town, I could perceive its every nook and corner, as if delineated on a map. The streets seemed innumerable, and crossed each other irregularly in all directions, but were rather long winding alleys than streets, and absolutely swarmed with inhabitants. The houses were wildly picturesque. On every hand was a wilderness of balconies, of verandas, of minarets, of shrines, and fantastically carved oriels. Bazaars abounded; and in these were displayed rich wares in infinite variety and profusion—silks, muslins, the most dazzling cutlery, the most magnificent jewels and gems. Besides these things, were seen, on all sides, banners and palanquins, litters with stately dames close veiled, elephants gorgeously caparisoned, idols grotesquely hewn, drums, banners, and gongs, spears, silver and gilded maces. And amid the crowd, and the clamor, and the general intricacy and confusion—amid the million of black and yellow men, turbaned and robed, and of flowing beard, there roamed a countless multitude of holy filleted bulls, while vast legions of the filthy but sacred ape clambered, chattering and shrieking, about the cornices of the mosques, or clung to the minarets and oriels. From the swarming streets to the banks of the river, there descended innumerable flights of steps leading to bathing places, while the river itself seemed to force a passage with difficulty through the vast fleets of deeply-burthened ships that far and wide encountered its surface. Beyond the limits of the city arose, in frequent majestic groups, the palm and the cocoa, with other gigantic and weird trees of vast age; and here and there might be seen a field of rice, the thatched hut of a peasant, a tank, a stray temple, a gypsy camp, or a solitary graceful maiden taking her way, with a pitcher upon her head, to the banks of the magnificent river.

"You will say now, of course, that I dreamed; but not so. What I saw—what I heard—what I felt—what I thought—had about it nothing of the unmistakable idiosyncrasy of the dream. All was rigorously self-consistent. At first, doubting that I was really awake, I entered into a series of tests, which soon convinced me that I really was. Now, when one dreams, and, in the dream, suspects that he dreams, the suspicion *never fails to confirm itself,* and the sleeper is almost immediately aroused. Thus Novalis errs not in saying that 'we are near waking when we dream that we dream.' Had the vision occurred to me as I describe it, without my suspecting it as a dream, then a dream it might absolutely have been, but, occurring as it did, and suspected and tested as it was, I am forced to class it among other phenomena."

"In this I am not sure that you are wrong," observed Dr. Templeton, "but proceed. You arose and descended into the city."

"I arose," continued Bedloe, regarding the Doctor with an air of profound astonishment "I arose, as you say, and descended into the city. On my way I fell in with an immense populace, crowding through every avenue, all in the same direction, and exhibiting in every action the wildest excitement. Very suddenly, and by some inconceivable impulse, I became intensely imbued with personal interest in what was going on. I seemed to feel that I had an important part to play, without exactly understanding what it was. Against the crowd which environed me, however, I experienced a deep sentiment of animosity. I shrank from amid them, and, swiftly, by a circuitous path, reached and entered the city. Here all was the wildest tumult and contention. A small party of men, clad in garments half-Indian, half-European, and officered by gentlemen in a uniform partly British, were engaged, at great odds, with the swarming rabble of the alleys. I joined the weaker party, arming myself with the weapons of a fallen officer, and fighting I knew not whom with the nervous ferocity of despair. We were soon overpowered by numbers, and driven to seek refuge in a species of kiosk. Here we barricaded ourselves, and, for the present were secure. From a loop-hole near the summit of the kiosk, I perceived a vast crowd, in furious agitation, surrounding and assaulting a gay palace that overhung the river. Presently, from an upper window of this place, there descended an effeminate-looking person, by means of a string made of the turbans of his attendants. A boat was at hand, in which he escaped to the opposite bank of the river.

"And now a new object took possession of my soul. I spoke a few hurried but energetic words to my companions, and, having succeeded in gaining over a few of them to my purpose made a frantic sally from the kiosk. We rushed amid the crowd that surrounded it. They retreated, at first, before us. They rallied, fought madly, and retreated again. In the mean time we were borne far from the kiosk, and became bewildered and entangled among the narrow streets of tall, overhanging houses, into the recesses of which the sun had never been able to shine. The rabble pressed impetuously upon us, harrassing us with their spears, and overwhelming us with flights of arrows. These latter were very remarkable, and resembled in some respects the writhing creese of the Malay. They were made to imitate the body of a creeping serpent, and were long and black, with a poisoned barb. One of them struck me upon the right temple. I reeled and fell. An instantaneous and dreadful sickness seized me. I struggled—I gasped—I died."

"You will hardly persist *now*," said I smiling, "that the whole of your adventure was not a dream. You are not prepared to maintain that you are dead?"

When I said these words, I of course expected some lively sally from Bedloe in reply; but, to my astonishment, he hesitated, trembled, became fearfully pallid, and remained silent. I looked toward Templeton. He sat erect and rigid in his chair—his teeth chattered, and his eyes were starting from their sockets. "Proceed!" he at length said hoarsely to Bedloe.

"For many minutes," continued the latter, "my sole sentiment—my sole feeling—was that of darkness and nonentity, with the consciousness of death. At length there seemed to pass a violent and sudden shock through my soul, as if of electricity. With it came the sense of elasticity and of light. This latter I felt—not saw. In an instant I seemed to rise from the ground. But I had no bodily, no visible, audible, or palpable presence. The crowd had departed. The tumult had ceased. The city was in comparative repose. Beneath me lay my corpse, with the arrow in my temple, the whole head greatly swollen and disfigured. But all these things I felt—not saw. I took interest in nothing. Even the corpse seemed a matter in which I had no concern. Volition I had none, but appeared to be impelled into motion, and flitted buoyantly out of the city, retracing the circuitous path by which I had entered it. When I had attained that point of the ravine in the mountains at which I had encountered the hyena, I again experienced a shock as of a galvanic battery, the sense of weight, of volition, of substance, returned. I became my original self, and bent my steps eagerly homeward—but the past had not lost the vividness of the real—and not now, even for an instant, can I compel my understanding to regard it as a dream."

"Nor was it," said Templeton, with an air of deep solemnity, "yet it would be difficult to say how otherwise it should be termed. Let us suppose only, that the soul of the man of to-day is upon the verge of some stupendous psychal discoveries. Let us content ourselves with this supposition. For the rest I have some explanation to make. Here is a watercolor drawing, which I should have shown you before, but which an unaccountable sentiment of horror has hitherto prevented me from showing."

We looked at the picture which he presented. I saw nothing in it of an extraordinary character; but its effect upon Bedloe was prodigious. He nearly fainted as he gazed. And yet it was but a miniature portrait—a miraculously accurate one, to be sure—of his own very remarkable features. At least this was my thought as I regarded it.

"You will perceive," said Templeton, "the date of this picture—it is here, scarcely visible, in this corner—1780. In this year was the portrait taken. It is the likeness of a dead friend—a Mr. Oldeb—to whom I became much attached at Calcutta, during the administration of Warren Hastings. I was then only twenty years old. When I first saw you, Mr. Bedloe, at Saratoga, it was the miraculous similarity which existed between yourself and the painting which induced me to accost you, to seek your friendship, and to bring about those arrangements which resulted in my becoming your constant companion. In accomplishing this point, I was urged partly, and perhaps principally, by a regretful memory of the deceased, but also, in part, by an uneasy, and not altogether horrorless curiosity respecting yourself.

"In your detail of the vision which presented itself to you amid the hills, you have described, with the minutest accuracy, the Indian city of Benares, upon the Holy River. The riots, the combat, the massacre, were the actual events of the insurrection of Cheyte Sing, which took place in 1780, when Hastings was put in imminent peril of his life. The man escaping by the string of turbans was Cheyte Sing himself. The party in the kiosk were sepoys and British officers, headed by Hastings. Of this party I was one, and did all I could to prevent the rash and fatal sally of the officer who fell, in the crowded alleys, by the poisoned arrow of a Bengalee. That officer was my dearest friend. It was Oldeb. You will perceive by these manuscripts," (here the speaker produced a note-book in which several pages appeared to have been freshly written,) "that at the very period in which you fancied these things amid the hills, I was engaged in detailing them upon paper here at home."

In about a week after this conversation, the following paragraphs appeared in a Charlottesville paper:

"We have the painful duty of announcing the death of Mr. AUGUSTUS BEDLO, a gentleman whose amiable manners and many virtues have long endeared him to the citizens of Charlottesville.

"Mr. B., for some years past, has been subject to neuralgia, which has often threatened to terminate fatally; but this can be regarded only as the mediate cause of his decease. The proximate cause was one of especial singularity. In an excursion to the Ragged Mountains, a few days since, a slight cold and fever were contracted, attended with great determination of blood to the head. To relieve this, Dr. Templeton resorted to topical bleeding. Leeches were applied to the temples. In a fearfully brief period the patient died, when it appeared that in the jar containing the leeches, had been introduced, by accident, one of the venomous vermicular sangsues which are now and then found in the neighboring ponds. This creature fastened itself upon a small artery in the right temple. Its close resemblance to the medicinal leech caused the mistake to be overlooked until too late.

"N. B. The poisonous sangsue of Charlottesville may always be distinguished from the medicinal leech by its blackness, and especially by its writhing or vermicular motions, which very nearly resemble those of a snake."

I was speaking with the editor of the paper in question, upon the topic of this remarkable accident, when it occurred to me to ask how it happened that the name of the deceased had been given as Bedlo.

"I presume," I said, "you have authority for this spelling, but I have always supposed the name to be written with an *e* at the end."

"Authority?—no," he replied. "It is a mere typographical error. The name is Bedlo with an *e,* all the world over, and I never knew it to be spelt otherwise in my life."

"Then," said I mutteringly, as I turned upon my heel, "then indeed has it come to pass that one truth is stranger than any fiction—for Bedloe, without the *e,* what is it but Oldeb conversed! And this man tells me that it is a typographical error."

The Diamond Lens

Fitz-James O'Brien

Fitz-James O'Brien (1828–1862) was born in Ireland but emigrated to the United States while in his twenties. A journalist, poet, and fiction writer, he wrote prolifically for the New York Times, Putnam's Magazine, Vanity Fair, Harper's, and other popular periodicals. A number of his stories tread the boundary between supernatural and science fiction, among them this tale, a fanciful extrapolation of optics and microscopy that appeared in the January 1858 issue of the Atlantic Monthly. Its theme of an infinitesimally small world that exists inside a speck of matter would become a staple of science fiction in the twentieth century.

I

THE BENDING OF THE TWIG

From a very early period of my life the entire bent of my inclinations had been toward microscopic investigations. When I was not more than ten years old, a distant relative of our family, hoping to astonish my inexperience, constructed a simple microscope for me by drilling in a disk of copper a small hole in which a drop of pure water was sustained by capillary attraction. This very primitive apparatus, magnifying some fifty diameters, presented, it is true, only indistinct and imperfect forms, but still sufficiently wonderful to work up my imagination to a preternatural state of excitement.

Seeing me so interested in this rude instrument, my cousin explained to me all that he knew about the principles of the microscope, related to me a few of the wonders which had been accomplished through its agency, and ended by promising to send me one regularly constructed, immediately on his return to the city. I counted the days, the hours, the minutes that intervened between that promise and his departure.

Meantime, I was not idle. Every transparent substance that bore the remotest resemblance to a lens I eagerly seized upon, and employed in vain attempts to realize that instrument the theory of whose construction I as yet only vaguely comprehended. All panes of glass containing those oblate spheroidal knots familiarly known as "bull's-eyes" were ruthlessly destroyed in the hope of obtaining lenses of marvelous power. I even went so far as to extract the crystalline humor from the eyes of fishes and animals, and endeavored to press it into the microscopic service. I plead guilty to having stolen the glasses from my Aunt Agatha's spectacles, with a dim idea of grinding them into lenses of wondrous magnifying properties—in which attempt it is scarcely necessary to say that I totally failed.

At last the promised instrument came. It was of that order known as Field's simple microscope, and had cost perhaps about fifteen dollars. As far as educational purposes went, a better apparatus could not have been selected. Accompanying it was a small treatise on the microscope—its history, uses, and discoveries. I comprehended then for the first time the "Arabian Nights' Entertainments." The dull veil of ordinary existence that hung across the world seemed suddenly to roll away, and to lay bare a land of enchantments. I felt toward my companions as the seer might feel toward the ordinary masses of men. I held conversations with nature in a tongue which they could not understand. I was in daily communication with living wonders such as they never imagined in their wildest visions, I penetrated beyond the external portal of things, and roamed through the sanctuaries. Where they beheld only a drop of rain slowly rolling down the window-glass, I saw a universe of beings animated with all the passions common to physical life, and convulsing their minute sphere with struggles as fierce and protracted as those of men. In the common spots of mould, which my mother, good housekeeper that she was, fiercely scooped away from her jam pots, there abode for me, under the name of mildew, enchanted gardens, filled with dells and avenues of the densest foliage and most astonishing verdure, while from the fantastic boughs of these microscopic forests hung strange fruits glittering with green, and silver, and gold.

It was no scientific thirst that at this time filled my mind. It was the pure enjoyment of a poet to whom a world of wonders has been disclosed. I talked of my solitary pleasures to none. Alone with my microscope, I dimmed my sight, day after day and night after night, poring over the marvels which it unfolded to me. I was like one who, having discovered the ancient Eden still existing in all its primitive glory, should resolve to enjoy it in solitude, and never betray to mortal the secret of its locality. The rod of my life was bent at this moment. I destined myself to be a microscopist.

Of course, like every novice, I fancied myself a discoverer. I was ignorant at the time of the thousands of acute intellects engaged in the same pursuit as myself, and with the advantage of instruments a thousand times more powerful than mine. The names of Leeuwenhoek, Williamson, Spencer, Ehrenberg, Schultz, Dujardin, Schact, and Schleiden were then entirely unknown to me, or, if known, I was ignorant of their patient and wonderful researches. In every fresh specimen of cryptoga-mia which I placed beneath my instrument I believed that I discovered wonders of which the world was as yet ignorant. I remember well the thrill of delight and admiration that shot through me the first time that I discovered the common wheel animalcule (*Rotifera vulgaris*) expanding and contracting its flexible spokes and seem-ingly rotating through the water. Alas! as I grew older, and obtained some works treating of my favorite study, I found that I was only on the threshold of a science to the investigation of which some of the greatest men of the age were devoting their lives and intellects.

As I grew up, my parents, who saw but little likelihood of anything practical resulting from the examination of bits of moss and drops of water through a brass tube and a piece of glass, were anxious that I should choose a profession. It was their desire that I should enter the counting-house of my uncle, Ethan Blake, a prosper-ous merchant, who carried on business in New York. This suggestion I decisively combated. I had no taste for trade; I should only make a failure; in short, I refused to become a merchant.

But it was necessary for me to select some pursuit. My parents were staid New England people, who insisted on the necessity of labor, and therefore, although, thanks to the bequest of my poor Aunt Agatha, I should, on coming of age, inherit a small fortune sufficient to place me above want, it was decided that, instead of waiting for this, I should act the nobler part, and employ the intervening years in rendering myself independent.

After much cogitation, I complied with the wishes of my family, and selected a profession. I determined to study medicine at the New York Academy. This disposi-tion of my future suited me. A removal from my relatives would enable me to dispose of my time as I pleased without fear of detection. As long as I paid my Academy fees, I might shirk attending the lectures if I chose; and, as I never had the remotest intention of standing an examination, there was no danger of my being "plucked."

Besides, a metropolis was the place for me. There I could obtain excellent instruments, the newest publications, intimacy with men of pursuits kindred with my own—in short, all things necessary to ensure a profitable devotion of my life to my beloved science. I had an abundance of money, few desires that were not bounded by my illuminating mirror on one side and my object-glass on the other; what, therefore, was to prevent my becoming an illustrious investigator of the veiled worlds? It was with the most buoyant hope that I left my New England home and established myself in New York.

II

THE LONGING OF A MAN OF SCIENCE

My first step, of course, was to find suitable apartments. These I obtained, after a couple of days' search, in Fourth Avenue; a very pretty second floor, unfurnished, containing sitting-room, bedroom, and a smaller apartment which I intended to fit up as a laboratory. I furnished my lodgings simply, but rather elegantly, and then devoted all my energies to the adornment of the temple of my worship. I visited Pike, the celebrated optician, and passed in review his splendid collection of microscopes— Field's Compound, Hingham's, Spencer's, Nachet's Binocular (that founded on the principles of the stereoscope), and at length fixed upon that form known as Spencer's Trunnion Microscope, as combining the greatest number of improvements with an almost perfect freedom from tremor. Along with this I purchased every possible accessory—draw-tubes, micrometers, a *camera-lucida,* lever-stage, achromatic condensers, white cloud illuminators, prisms, parabolic condensers, polarizing apparatus, forceps, aquatic boxes, fishing-tubes, with a host of other articles, all of which would have been useful in the hands of an experienced microscopist, but, as I afterward discovered, were not of the slightest present value to me. It takes years of practice to know how to use a complicated microscope. The optician looked suspiciously at me as I made these valuable purchases. He evidently was uncertain whether to set me down as some scientific celebrity or a madman. I think he was inclined to the latter belief. I suppose I was mad. Every great genius is mad upon the subject in which he is greatest. The unsuccessful madman is disgraced and called a lunatic.

Mad or not, I set myself to work with a zeal which few scientific students have ever equaled. I had everything to learn relative to the delicate study upon which I had embarked—a study involving the most earnest patience, the most rigid analytic powers, the steadiest hand, the most untiring eye, the most refined and subtle manipulation.

For a long time half my apparatus lay inactively on the shelves of my laboratory, which was now most amply furnished with every possible contrivance for facilitating my investigations. The fact was that I did not know how to use some of my scientific implements—never having been taught microscopics—and those whose use I understood theoretically were of little avail until by practice I could attain the necessary delicacy of handling. Still, such was the fury of my ambition, such the untiring perseverance of my experiments, that, difficult of credit as it may be, in the course of one year I became theoretically and practically an accomplished microscopist.

During this period of my labors, in which I submitted specimens of every substance that came under my observation to the action of my lenses, I became a discoverer—in a small way, it is true, for I was very young, but still a discoverer. It was I who destroyed Ehrenberg's theory that the *Volvox globator* was an animal, and proved that his "monads" with stomachs and eyes were merely phases of the formation of a vegetable cell, and were, when they reached their mature state, incapable of the act of conjugation, or any true generative act, without which no organism rising to any stage of life higher than vegetable can be said to be complete. It was I who resolved the singular problem of rotation in the cells and hairs of plants into ciliary attraction, in spite of the assertions of Wenham and others that my explanation was the result of an optical illusion.

But notwithstanding these discoveries, laboriously and painfully made as they were, I felt horribly dissatisfied. At every step I found myself stopped by the imperfections of my instruments. Like all active microscopists, I gave my imagination full play. Indeed, it is a common complaint against many such that they supply the defects of their instruments with the creations of their brains. I imagined depths beyond depths in nature which the limited power of my lenses prohibited me from exploring. I lay awake at night constructing imaginary microscopes of immeasurable power, with which I seemed to pierce through all the envelopes of matter down to its original atom. How I cursed those imperfect mediums which necessity through ignorance compelled me to use! How I longed to discover the secret of some perfect lens, whose magnifying power should be limited only by the resolvability of the object, and which at the same time should be free from spherical and chromatic aberrations—in short, from all the obstacles over which the poor microscopist finds himself continually stumbling! I felt convinced that the simple microscope, composed of a single lens of such vast yet perfect power, was possible of construction. To attempt to bring the compound microscope up to such a pitch would have been commencing at the wrong end; this latter being simply a partially successful endeavor to remedy those very defects of the simplest instrument, which, if conquered, would leave nothing to be desired.

It was in this mood of mind that I became a constructive microscopist. After another year passed in this new pursuit, experimenting on every imaginable substance—glass, gems, flints, crystals, artificial crystals formed of the alloy of various vitreous materials—in short, having constructed as many varieties of lenses as Argus had eyes—I found myself precisely where I started, with nothing gained save an extensive knowledge of glass-making. I was almost dead with despair. My parents were surprised at my apparent want of progress in my medical studies (I had not attended one lecture since my arrival in the city), and the expenses of my mad pursuit had been so great as to embarrass me very seriously.

I was in this frame of mind one day, experimenting in my laboratory on a small diamond—that stone, from its great refracting power, having always occupied my attention more than any other—when a young Frenchman who lived on the floor above me, and who was in the habit of occasionally visiting me, entered the room.

I think that Jules Simon was a Jew. He had many traits of the Hebrew character: a love of jewelry, of dress, and of good living. There was something mysterious about him. He always had something to sell, and yet went into excellent society. When I say sell, I should perhaps have said peddle; for his operations were generally confined to the disposal of single articles—a picture, for instance, or a rare carving in ivory, or a pair of duelling-pistols, or the dress of a Mexican *caballero*. When I was first furnishing my rooms, he paid me a visit, which ended in my purchasing an antique silver lamp, which he assured me was a Cellini—it was handsome enough even for that—and some other knick-knacks for my sitting-room. Why Simon should pursue this petty trade I never could imagine. He apparently had plenty of money, and had the *entrée* of the best houses in the city—taking care, however, I suppose, to drive no bargains within the enchanted circle of the Upper Ten. I came at length to the conclusion that this peddling was but a mask to cover some greater object, and even went so far as to believe my young acquaintance to be implicated in the slave-trade. That, however, was none of my affair.

On the present occasion, Simon entered my room in a state of considerable excitement.

"*Ah! mon ami!*" he cried, before I could even offer him the ordinary salutation, "it has occurred to me to be the witness of the most astonishing things in the world. I promenade myself to the house of Madame ———. How does the little animal—*le renard*—name himself in the Latin?"

"Vulpes," I answered.

"Ah! yes—Vulpes. I promenade myself to the house of Madame Vulpes."

"The spirit medium?"

"Yes, the great medium. Great heavens! what a woman! I write on a slip of paper many of questions concerning affairs of the most secret—affairs that conceal themselves in the abysses of my heart the most profound; and behold! by example! what occurs? This devil of a woman makes me replies the most truthful to all of them. She talks to me of things that I do not love to talk of to myself. What am I to think? I am fixed to the earth!"

"Am I to understand you, M. Simon, that this Mrs. Vulpes replied to questions secretly written by you, which questions related to events known only to yourself?"

"Ah! more than that, more than that," he answered, with an air of some alarm. "She related to me things— But," he added after a pause, and suddenly changing his manner, "why occupy ourselves with these follies? It was all the biology, without doubt. It goes without saying that it has not my credence.—But why are we here, *mon ami?* It has occurred to me to discover the most beautiful thing as you can imagine—a vase with green lizards on it, composed by the great Bernard Palissy. It is in my apartment; let us mount. I go to show it to you."

I followed Simon mechanically; but my thoughts were far from Palissy and his enameled ware, although I, like him, was seeking in the dark a great discovery. This casual mention of the spiritualist, Madame Vulpes, set me on a new track. What if, through communication with more subtle organisms than my own, I could reach at a single bound the goal which perhaps a life, of agonizing mental toil would never enable me to attain?

While purchasing the Palissy vase from my friend Simon, I was mentally arranging a visit to Madame Vulpes.

III

THE SPIRIT OF LEEUWENHOEK

Two evenings after this, thanks to an arrangement by letter and the promise of an ample fee, I found Madame Vulpes awaiting me at her residence alone. She was a coarse-featured woman, with keen and rather cruel dark eyes, and an exceedingly sensual expression about her mouth and under jaw. She received me in perfect silence, in an apartment on the ground floor, very sparsely furnished. In the centre of the room, close to where Mrs. Vulpes sat, there was a common round mahogany table. If I had come for the purpose of sweeping her chimney, the woman could not have looked more indifferent to my appearance. There was no attempt to inspire the visitor with awe. Everything bore a simple and practical aspect. This intercourse with the spiritual world was evidently as familiar an occupation with Mrs. Vulpes as eating her dinner or riding in an omnibus.

"You come for a communication, Mr. Linley?" said the medium, in a dry, businesslike tone of voice.

"By appointment—yes."

"What sort of communication do you want?—a written one?"

"Yes—I wish for a written one."

"From any particular spirit?"

"Yes."

"Have you ever known this spirit on this earth?"

"Never. He died long before I was born. I wish merely to obtain from him some information which he ought to be able to give better than any other."

"Will you seat yourself at the table, Mr. Linley," said the medium, "and place your hands upon it?"

I obeyed—Mrs. Vulpes being seated opposite to me, with her hands also on the table. We remained thus for about a minute and a half, when a violent succession of raps came on the table, on the back of my chair, on the floor immediately under my feet, and even on the window-panes. Mrs. Vulpes smiled composedly.

"They are very strong to-night," she remarked. "You are fortunate." She then continued, "Will the spirits communicate with this gentleman?"

Vigorous affirmative.

"Will the particular spirit he desires to speak with communicate?"

A very confused rapping followed this question.

"I know what they mean," said Mrs. Vulpes, addressing herself to me; "they wish you to write down the name of the particular spirit that you desire to converse with. Is that so?" she added, speaking to her invisible guests.

That it was so was evident from the numerous affirmatory responses. While this was going on, I tore a slip from my pocket-book and scribbled a name under the table.

"Will this spirit communicate in writing with this gentleman?" asked the medium once more.

After a moment's pause, her hand seemed to be seized with a violent tremor, shaking so forcibly that the table vibrated. She said that a spirit had seized her hand and would write. I handed her some sheets of paper that were on the table and a pencil. The latter she held loosely in her hand, which presently began to move over the paper with a singular and seemingly involuntary motion. After a few moments had elapsed, she handed me the paper, on which I found written, in a large, uncultivated hand, the words, "He is not here, but has been sent for." A pause of a minute or so ensued, during which Mrs. Vulpes remained perfectly silent, but the raps continued at regular intervals. When the short period I mention had elapsed, the hand of the medium was again seized with its convulsive tremor, and she wrote, under this strange influence, a few words on the paper, which she handed to me. They were as follows:—

"I am here. Question me.

LEEUWENHOEK"

I was astounded. The name was identical with that I had written beneath the table, and carefully kept concealed. Neither was it at all probable that an uncultivated woman like Mrs. Vulpes should know even the name of the great father of microscopics. It may have been biology; but this theory was soon doomed to be destroyed. I wrote on my slip—still concealing it from Mrs. Vulpes—a series of questions which, to avoid tediousness, I shall place with the responses, in the order in which they occurred:

I.—Can the microscope be brought to perfection?

SPIRIT.—Yes.

I.—Am I destined to accomplish this great task?

SPIRIT.—You are.

I.—I wish to know how to proceed to attain this end. For the love which you bear to science, help me!

SPIRIT.—A diamond of one hundred and forty carats, submitted to electro-magnetic currents for a long period, will experience a rearrangement of its atoms *inter se,* and from that stone you will form the universal lens.

I.—Will great discoveries result from the use of such a lens?

SPIRIT.—So great that all that has gone before is as nothing.

I.—But the refractive power of the diamond is so immense that the image will be formed within the lens. How is that difficulty to be surmounted?

SPIRIT.—Pierce the lens through its axis, and the difficulty is obviated. The image will be formed in the pierced space, which will itself serve as a tube to look through. Now I am called. Good night.

I can not at all describe the effect that these extraordinary communications had upon me. I felt completely bewildered. No biological theory could account for the *discovery* of the lens. The medium might, by means of biological *rapport* with my mind, have gone so far as to read my questions and reply to them coherently. But biology could not enable her to discover that magnetic currents would so alter the crystals of the diamond as to remedy its previous defects and admit of its being polished into a perfect lens. Some such theory may have passed through my head, it is true; but if so, I had forgotten it. In my excited condition of mind there was no course left but to become a convert, and it was in a state of the most painful nervous exaltation that I left the medium's house that evening. She accompanied me to the door, hoping that I was satisfied. The raps followed us as we went through the hall, sounding on the balusters, the flooring, and even the lintels of the door. I hastily expressed my satisfaction, and escaped hurriedly into the cool night air. I walked home with but one thought possessing me—how to obtain a diamond of the immense size required. My entire means multiplied a hundred times over would have been inadequate to its purchase. Besides, such stones are rare, and become historical. I could find such only in the regalia of Eastern or European monarchs.

IV

THE EYE OF MORNING

There was a light in Simon's room as I entered my house. A vague impulse urged me to visit him. As I opened the door of his sitting-room unannounced, he was bending, with his back toward me, over a carcel lamp, apparently engaged in minutely examining some object which he held in his hands. As I entered, he started suddenly, thrust his hand into his breast pocket, and turned to me with a face crimson with confusion.

"What!" I cried, "poring over the miniature of some fair lady? Well, don't blush so much; I won't ask to see it."

Simon laughed awkwardly enough, but made none of the negative protestations usual on such occasions. He asked me to take a seat.

"Simon," said I, "I have just come from Madame Vulpes."

This time Simon turned as white as a sheet, and seemed stupefied, as if a sudden electric shock had smitten him. He babbled some incoherent words, and went hastily to a small closet where he usually kept his liquors. Although astonished at his emotion, I was too preoccupied with my own idea to pay much attention to anything else.

"You say truly when you call Madame Vulpes a devil of a woman," I continued. "Simon, she told me wonderful things to-night, or rather was the means of telling

31

me wonderful things. Ah! if I could only get a diamond that weighed one hundred and forty carats!"

Scarcely had the sigh with which I uttered this desire died upon my lips when Simon, with the aspect of a wild beast, glared at me savagely, and, rushing to the mantelpiece, where some foreign weapons hung on the wall, caught up a Malay creese, and brandished it furiously before him.

"No!" he cried in French, into which he always broke when excited. "No! you shall not have it! You are perfidious! You have consulted with that demon, and desire my treasure! But I will die first! Me, I am brave! You can not make me fear!"

All this, uttered in a loud voice, trembling with excitement, astounded me. I saw at a glance that I had accidentally trodden upon the edges of Simon's secret, whatever it was. It was necessary to reassure him.

"My dear Simon," I said, "I am entirely at a loss to know what you mean. I went to Madame Vulpes to consult with her on a scientific problem, to the solution of which I discovered that a diamond of the size I just mentioned was necessary. You were never alluded to during the evening, nor, so far as I was concerned, even thought of. What can be the meaning of this outburst? If you happen to have a set of valuable diamonds in your possession, you need fear nothing from me. The diamond which I require you could not possess; or, if you did possess it, you would not be living here."

Something in my tone must have completely reassured him; for his expression immediately changed to a sort of constrained merriment, combined however, with a certain suspicious attention to my movements. He laughed, and said that I must bear with him; that he was at certain moments subject to a species of vertigo, which betrayed itself in incoherent speeches, and that the attacks passed off as rapidly as they came. He put his weapon aside while making this explanation, and endeavored, with some success, to assume a more cheerful air.

All this did not impose on me in the least. I was too much accustomed to analytical labors to be baffled by so flimsy a veil. I determined to probe the mystery to the bottom.

"Simon," I said, gayly, "let us forget all this over a bottle of Burgundy. I have a case of Lausseure's *Clos Vougeot* downstairs, fragrant with the odors and ruddy with the sunlight of the Côte d'Or. Let us have up a couple of bottles. What say you?"

"With all my heart," answered Simon smilingly.

I produced the wine and we seated ourselves to drink. It was of a famous vintage, that of 1848, a year when war and wine throve together—and its pure but powerful juice seemed to impart renewed vitality to the system. By the time we had half finished the second bottle, Simon's head, which I knew was a weak one, had begun to yield, while I remained calm as ever, only that every draught seemed to send a flush of vigor through my limbs. Simon's utterance became more and more indistinct. He took to singing French *chansons* of a not very moral tendency. I rose suddenly from the table just at the conclusion of one of those incoherent verses, and, fixing my eyes on him with a quiet smile, said, "Simon, I have deceived you. I learned your secret this evening. You may as well be frank with me. Mrs. Vulpes, or rather, one of her spirits, told me all."

He started with horror. His intoxication seemed for the moment to fade away, and he made a movement toward the weapon that he had a short time before laid down, I stopped him with my hand.

"Monster!" he cried passionately, "I am ruined! What shall I do? You shall never have it! I swear by my mother!"

"I don't want it," I said; "rest secure, but be frank with me. Tell me all about it."

The drunkenness began to return. He protested with maudlin earnestness that I was entirely mistaken—that I was intoxicated; then asked me to swear eternal secrecy, and promised to disclose the mystery to me. I pledged myself, of course, to all. With an uneasy look in his eyes, and hands unsteady with drink and nervousness, he drew a small case from his breast and opened it. Heavens! How the mild lamplight was shivered into a thousand prismatic arrows as it fell upon a vast rose-diamond that glittered in the case! I was no judge of diamonds, but I saw at a glance that this was a gem of rare size and purity. I looked at Simon with wonder and—must I confess it?—with envy. How could he have obtained this treasure? In reply to my questions, I could just gather from his drunken statements (of which, I fancy, half the incoherence was affected) that he had been superintending a gang of slaves engaged in diamond-washing in Brazil; that he had seen one of them secrete a diamond, but, instead of informing his employers, had quietly watched the negro until he saw him bury his treasure; that he had dug it up and fled with it, but that as yet he was afraid to attempt to dispose of it publicly—so valuable a gem being almost certain to attract too much attention to its owner's antecedents—and he had not been able to discover any of those obscure channels by which such matters are conveyed away safely. He added, that, in accordance with oriental practice, he had named his diamond with the fanciful title of "The Eye of Morning."

While Simon was relating this to me, I regarded the great diamond attentively. Never had I beheld anything so beautiful. All the glories of light ever imagined or described seemed to pulsate in its crystalline chambers. Its weight, as I learned from Simon, was exactly one hundred and forty carats. Here was an amazing coincidence.

The hand of destiny seemed in it. On the very evening when the spirit of Leeuwenhoek communicates to me the great secret of the microscope, the priceless means which he directs me to employ start up within my easy reach! I determined, with the most perfect deliberation, to possess myself of Simon's diamond.

I sat opposite to him while he nodded over his glass, and calmly revolved the whole affair. I did not for an instant contemplate so foolish an act as a common theft, which would of course be discovered, or at least necessitate flight and concealment, all of which must interfere with my scientific plans. There was but one step to be taken—to kill Simon. After all, what was the life of a little peddling Jew in comparison with the interests of science? Human beings are taken every day from the condemned prisons to be experimented on by surgeons. This man, Simon, was by his own confession a criminal, a robber, and I believed on my soul a murderer. He deserved death quite as much as any felon condemned by the laws: why should I not, like government, contrive that his punishment should contribute to the progress of human knowledge?

The means for accomplishing everything I desired lay within my reach. There stood upon the mantel-piece a bottle half full of French laudanum. Simon was so occupied with his diamond, which I had just restored to him, that it was an affair of no difficulty to drug his glass. In a quarter of an hour he was in a profound sleep.

I now opened his waistcoat, took the diamond from the inner pocket in which he had placed it, and removed him to the bed, on which I laid him so that his feet hung down over the edge. I had possessed myself of the Malay creese, which I held in my right hand, while with the other I discovered as accurately as I could by pulsation the exact locality of the heart. It was essential that all the aspects of his death should lead to the surmise of self-murder. I calculated the exact angle at which it was probable that the weapon, if levelled by Simon's own hand, would enter his breast; then with one powerful blow I thrust it up to the hilt in the very spot which I desired to penetrate. A convulsive thrill ran through Simon's limbs. I heard a smothered sound issue from his throat, precisely like the bursting of a large air-bubble sent up by a diver when it reaches the surface of the water; he turned half round on his side, and, as if to assist my plans more effectually, his right hand, moved by some mere spasmodic impulse, clasped the handle of the creese, which it remained holding with extraordinary muscular tenacity. Beyond this there was no apparent struggle. The laudanum, I presume, paralyzed the usual nervous action. He must have died instantly.

There was yet something to be done. To make it certain that all suspicion of the act should be diverted from any inhabitant of the house to Simon himself, it was necessary that the door should be found in the morning *locked on the inside.* How to do this, and afterward escape myself? Not by the window; that was a physical impossibility. Besides, I was determined that the windows *also* should be found bolted. The solution was simple enough. I descended softly to my own room for a peculiar instrument which I had used for holding small slippery substances, such as minute spheres of glass, etc. This instrument was nothing more than a long, slender hand-vice, with a very powerful grip, and a considerable leverage, which last was accidentally owing to the shape of the handle. Nothing was simpler than, when the key was in the lock, to seize the end of its stem in this vise, through the keyhole, from the outside, and so lock the door. Previously, however, to doing this, I burned a number of papers on Simon's hearth. Suicides almost always burn papers before they destroy themselves. I also emptied some more laudanum into Simon's glass—having first removed from it all traces of wine—cleaned the other wine-glass, and brought the bottles away with me. If traces of two persons drinking had been found in the room, the question naturally would have arisen, Who was the second? Besides, the wine-bottles might have been identified as belonging to me. The laudanum I poured out to account for its presence in his stomach, in case of a *post-mortem* examination. The theory naturally would be that he first intended to poison himself, but, after swallowing a little of the drug, was either disgusted with its taste, or changed his mind from other motives, and chose the dagger. These arrangements made, I walked out, leaving the gas burning, locked the door with my vise, and went to bed.

Simon's death was not discovered until nearly three in the afternoon. The servant, astonished at seeing the gas burning—the light streaming on the dark landing from under the door—peeped through the keyhole and saw Simon on the bed. She gave the alarm. The door was burst open, and the neighborhood was in a fever of excitement.

Every one in the house was arrested, myself included. There was an inquest; but no clew to his death beyond that of suicide could be obtained. Curiously enough, he had made several speeches to his friends the preceding week that seemed to point to self-destruction. One gentleman swore that Simon had said in his presence that "he was tired of life." His landlord affirmed that Simon, when paying him his last month's rent, remarked that "he should not pay him rent much longer." All the other evidence corresponded—the door locked inside, the position of the corpse, the burnt papers. As I anticipated, no one knew of the possession of the diamond by Simon, so that no motive was suggested for his murder. The jury, after a prolonged examination, brought in the usual verdict, and the neighborhood once more settled down to its accustomed quiet.

V

ANIMULA

The three months succeeding Simon's catastrophe I devoted night and day to my diamond lens. I had constructed a vast galvanic battery, composed of nearly two thousand pairs of plates,—a higher power I dared not use, lest the diamond should be calcined. By means of this enormous engine I was enabled to send a powerful current of electricity continually through my great diamond, which it seemed to me gained in lustre every day. At the expiration of a month I commenced the grinding and polishing of the lens, a work of intense toil and exquisite delicacy. The great density of the stone, and the care required to be taken with the curvatures of the surfaces of the lens, rendered the labor the severest and most harassing that I had yet undergone.

At last the eventful moment came; the lens was completed. I stood trembling on the threshold of new worlds. I had the realization of Alexander's famous wish before me. The lens lay on the table, ready to be placed upon its platform. My hand fairly shook as I enveloped a drop of water with a thin coating of oil of turpentine, preparatory to its examination—a process necessary in order to prevent the rapid evaporation of the water. I now placed the drop on a thin slip of glass under the lens, and throwing upon it, by the combined aid of a prism and a mirror, a powerful stream of light, I approached my eye to the minute hole drilled through the axis of the lens. For an instant I saw nothing save what seemed to be an illuminated chaos, a vast, luminous abyss. A pure white light, cloudless and serene, and seemingly limitless as space itself, was my first impression. Gently, and with the greatest care, I depressed the lens a few hair's-breadths. The wondrous illumination still continued, but as the lens approached the object a scene of indescribable beauty was unfolded to my view.

I seemed to gaze upon a vast space, the limits of which extended far beyond my vision. An atmosphere of magical luminousness permeated the entire field of view. I was amazed to see no trace of animalculous life. Not a living thing, apparently, inhabited that dazzling expanse. I comprehended instantly that, by the wondrous power of my lens, I had penetrated beyond the grosser particles of aqueous matter, beyond the realms of infusoria and protozoa, down to the original gaseous globule, into whose luminous interior I was gazing as into an almost boundless dome filled with a supernatural radiance.

It was, however, no brilliant void into which I looked. On every side I beheld beautiful inorganic forms, of unknown texture, and colored with the most enchanting hues. These forms presented the appearance of what might be called, for want of a more specific definition, foliated clouds of the highest rarity—that is, they undulated and broke into vegetable formations, and were tinged with splendors compared with which the gilding of our autumn woodlands is as dross compared with gold. Far away into the illimitable distance stretched long avenues of these gaseous forests, dimly transparent, and painted with prismatic hues of unimaginable brilliancy. The pendent branches waved along the fluid glades until every vista seemed to break through half-lucent ranks of many-colored drooping silken pennons. What seemed to be either fruits or flowers, pied with a thousand hues, lustrous and ever varying, bubbled from the crowns of this fairy foliage. No hills, no lakes, no rivers, no forms animate or inanimate, were to be seen, save those vast auroral copses that floated serenely in the luminous stillness, with leaves and fruits and flowers gleaming with unknown fires, unrealizable by mere imagination.

How strange, I thought, that this sphere should be thus condemned to solitude! I had hoped, at least, to discover some new form of animal life—perhaps of a lower class than any with which we are at present acquainted, but still some living organism. I found my newly discovered world, if I may so speak, a beautiful chromatic desert.

While I was speculating on the singular arrangements of the internal economy of Nature, with which she so frequently splinters into atoms our most compact theories, I thought I beheld a form moving slowly through the glades of one of the prismatic forests. I looked more attentively, and found that I was not mistaken. Words can not depict the anxiety with which I awaited the nearer approach of this mysterious object. Was it merely some inanimate substance, held in suspense in the attenuated atmosphere of the globule? or was it an animal endowed with vitality and motion? It approached, flitting behind the gauzy, colored veils of cloud-foliage, for seconds dimly revealed, then vanishing. At last the violet pennons that trailed nearest to me vibrated; they were gently pushed aside, and the form floated out into the broad light.

It was a female human shape. When I say human, I mean it possessed the outlines of humanity—but there the analogy ends. Its adorable beauty lifted it illimitable heights beyond the loveliest daughter of Adam.

I cannot, I dare not, attempt to inventory the charms of this divine revelation of perfect beauty. Those eyes of mystic violet, dewy and serene, evade my words. Her long, lustrous hair following her glorious head in a golden wake, like the track sown in heaven by a falling star, seems to quench my most burning phrases with its splendors. If all the bees of Hybla nestled upon my lips, they would still sing but hoarsely the wondrous harmonies of outline that enclosed her form.

She swept out from between the rainbow-curtains of the cloud-trees into the broad sea of light that lay beyond. Her motions were those of some graceful naiad, cleaving, by a mere effort of her will, the clear, unruffled waters that fill the chambers of the sea. She floated forth with the serene grace of a frail bubble ascending through the still atmosphere of a June day. The perfect roundness of her limbs formed suave and enchanting curves. It was like listening to the most spiritual symphony of Beethoven the divine, to watch the harmonious flow of lines. This, indeed was a pleasure cheaply purchased at any price. What cared I if I had waded to the portal of this wonder through another's blood. I would have given my own to enjoy one such moment of intoxication and delight.

Breathless with gazing on this lovely wonder, and forgetful for an instant of everything save her presence, I withdrew my eye from the microscope eagerly— alas! As my gaze fell on the thin slide that lay beneath my instrument, the bright light from mirror and from prism sparkled on a colorless drop of water! There, in that tiny bead of dew, this beautiful being was forever imprisoned. The planet Neptune was not more distant from me than she. I hastened once more to apply my eye to the microscope.

Animula (let me now call her by that dear name which I subsequently bestowed on her) had changed her position. She had again approached the wondrous forest, and was gazing earnestly upward. Presently one of the trees—as I must call them— unfolded a long ciliary process, with which it seized one of the gleaming fruits that glittered on its summit, and, sweeping slowly down, held it within reach of Animula. The sylph took it in her delicate hand and began to eat. My attention was so entirely absorbed by her that I could not apply myself to the task of determining whether this singular plant was or was not instinct with volition.

I watched her, as she made her repast, with the most profound attention. The suppleness of her motions sent a thrill of delight through my frame; my heart beat madly as she turned her beautiful eyes in the direction of the spot in which I stood. What would I not have given to have had the power to precipitate myself into that luminous ocean and float with her through those grooves of purple and gold! While I was thus breathlessly following her every movement, she suddenly started, seemed to listen for a moment, and then cleaving the brilliant ether in which she was floating, like a flash of light, pierced through the opaline forest, and disappeared.

Instantly a series of the most singular sensations attacked me. It seemed as if I had suddenly gone blind. The luminous sphere was still before me, but my daylight had vanished. What caused this sudden disappearance? Had she a lover or a husband? Yes, that was the solution! Some signal from a happy fellow-being had vibrated through the avenues of the forest, and she had obeyed the summons.

The agony of my sensations, as I arrived at this conclusion, startled me. I tried to reject the conviction that my reason forced upon me. I battled against the fatal conclusion—but in vain. It was so. I had no escape from it. I loved an animalcule!

It is true that, thanks to the marvelous power of my microscope, she appeared of human proportions. Instead of presenting the revolting aspect of the coarser creatures, that live and struggle and die, in the more easily resolvable portions of the water-drop, she was fair and delicate and of surpassing beauty. But of what account was all that? Every time that my eye was withdrawn from the instrument it fell on a miserable drop of water, within which, I must be content to know, dwelt all that could make my life lovely.

Could she but see me once! Could I for one moment pierce the mystical walls that so inexorably rose to separate us, and whisper all that filled my soul, I might consent to be satisfied for the rest of my life with the knowledge of her remote sympathy. It would be something to have established even the faintest personal link to bind us together—to know that at times, when roaming through these enchanted glades, she might think of the wonderful stranger who had broken the monotony of her life with his presence and left a gentle memory in her heart!

But it could not be. No invention of which human intellect was capable could break down the barriers that nature had erected. I might feast my soul upon her wondrous beauty, yet she must always remain ignorant of the adoring eyes that day and night gazed upon her, and, even when closed, beheld her in dreams. With a bitter cry of anguish I fled from the room, and, flinging myself on my bed, sobbed myself to sleep like a child.

VI

THE SPILLING OF THE CUP

I arose the next morning almost at daybreak, and rushed to my microscope, I trembled as I sought the luminous world in miniature that contained my all. Animula was there. I had left the gas-lamp, surrounded by its moderators, burning when I went to bed the night before. I found the sylph bathing, as it were, with an expression of pleasure animating her features, in the brilliant light which surrounded her. She tossed her lustrous golden hair over her shoulders with innocent coquetry. She lay at full length in the transparent medium, in which she supported herself with ease, and gambolled with the enchanting grace that the nymph Salmacis might have exhibited when she sought to conquer the modest Hermaphroditus. I tried an experiment to satisfy myself if her powers of reflection were developed. I lessened the lamp-light considerably. By the dim light that remained, I could see an expression of pain flit across her face. She looked upward suddenly, and her brows contracted. I flooded the stage of the microscope again with a full stream of light, and her whole expression changed. She sprang forward like some substance deprived of all weight. Her eyes sparkled and her lips moved. Ah! if science had only the means of conducting and reduplicating sounds, as it does rays of light, what carols of happiness would then have entranced my ears! what jubilant hymns to Adonais would have thrilled the illumined air!

I now comprehended how it was that the Count de Cabalis peopled his mystic world with sylphs—beautiful beings whose breath of life was lambent fire, and who sported forever in regions of purest ether and purest light. The Rosicrucian had anticipated the wonder that I had practically realized.

How long this worship of my strange divinity went on thus I scarcely know. I lost all note of time. All day from early dawn, and far into the night, I was to be found peering through that wonderful lens. I saw no one, went nowhere, and scarce allowed myself sufficient time for my meals. My whole life was absorbed in contemplation as rapt as that of any of the Romish saints. Every hour that I gazed upon the divine form strengthened my passion—a passion that was always overshadowed by the maddening conviction that, although I could gaze on her at will, she never, never could behold me!

At length I grew so pale and emaciated, from want of rest and continual brooding over my insane love and its cruel conditions, that I determined to make some effort to wean myself from it. "Come," I said, "this is at best but a fantasy. Your imagination has bestowed on Animula charms which in reality she does not possess. Seclusion from female society has produced this morbid condition of mind. Compare her with the beautiful women of your own world, and this false enchantment will vanish."

I looked over the newspapers by chance. There I beheld the advertisement of a celebrated *danseuse* who appeared nightly at Niblo's. The Signorina Caradolce had the reputation of being the most beautiful as well as the most graceful woman in the world. I instantly dressed and went to the theatre.

The curtain drew up. The usual semicircle of fairies in white muslin were standing on the right toe around the enameled flower-bank, of green canvas, on which the belated prince was sleeping. Suddenly a flute is heard. The fairies start. The trees open, the fairies all stand on the left toe, and the queen enters. It was the Signorina. She bounded forward amid thunders of applause, and, lighting on one foot, remained poised in the air. Heavens! was this the great enchantress that had drawn monarchs at her chariot-wheels? Those heavy, muscular limbs, those thick ankles, those cavernous eyes, that stereotyped smile, those crudely painted cheeks! Where were the vermeil blooms, the liquid, expressive eyes, the harmonious limbs of Animula?

The Signorina danced. What gross, discordant movements! The play of her limbs was all false and artificial Her bounds were painful athletic efforts; her poses were angular and distressed the eye. I could bear it no longer; with an exclamation of disgust that drew every eye upon me, I rose from my seat in the very middle of the Signorina's *pas-de-fascination,* and abruptly quitted the house.

I hastened home to feast my eyes once more on the lovely form of my sylph. I felt that henceforth to combat this passion would be impossible. I applied my eyes to the lens. Animula was there—but what could have happened? Some terrible change seemed to have taken place during my absence. Some secret grief seemed to cloud the lovely features of her I gazed upon. Her face had grown thin and haggard; her limbs trailed heavily; the wondrous lustre of her golden hair had faded. She was ill!—ill, and I could not assist her! I believe at that moment I would have forfeited all claims to my human birthright if I could only have been dwarfed to the size of an animalcule, and permitted to console her from whom fate had forever divided me.

I racked my brain for the solution of this mystery. What was it that afflicted the sylph? She seemed to suffer intense pain. Her features contracted, and she even writhed, as if with some internal agony. The wondrous forests appeared also to have lost half their beauty. Their hues were dim and in some places faded away altogether. I watched Animula for hours with a breaking heart, and she seemed absolutely to wither away under my very eye. Suddenly I remembered that I had not looked at the water-drop for several days. In fact, I hated to see it; for it reminded me of the natural barrier between Animula and myself. I hurriedly looked down on the stage of the microscope. The slide was still there—but, great heavens! the water-drop had vanished! The awful truth burst upon me; it had evaporated, until it had become so minute as to be invisible to the naked eye; I had been gazing on its last atom, the one that contained Animula—and she was dying!

I rushed again to the front of the lens and looked through. Alas! the last agony had seized her. The rainbow-hued forests had all melted away, and Animula lay struggling feebly in what seemed to be a spot of dim light. Ah! the sight was horrible: the limbs once so round and lovely shriveling up into nothings; the eyes—those eyes that shone like heaven—being quenched into black dust; the lustrous golden hair now lank and discolored. The last throe came. I beheld that final struggle of the blackening form—and I fainted.

When I awoke out of a trance of many hours, I found myself lying amid the wreck of my instrument, myself as shattered in mind and body as it. I crawled feebly to my bed, from which I did not rise for many months.

They say now that I am mad; but they are mistaken. I am poor, for I have neither the heart nor the will to work; all my money is spent, and I live on charity. Young men's associations that love a joke invite me to lecture on optics before them, for which they pay me, and laugh at me while I lecture. "Linley, the mad microscopist," is the name I go by. I suppose that I talk incoherently while I lecture. Who could talk sense when his brain is haunted by such ghastly memories, while ever and anon among the shapes of death I behold the radiant form of my lost Animula!

Doctor Ox's Experiment

JULES VERNE

One of the founding fathers of science fiction, French writer Jules Verne (1828–1905) wrote more than fifty wildly speculative novels, dubbed "Voyages extraordinaire," among them A Journey to the Center of the Earth *(1864),* Twenty Thousand Leagues Under the Sea *(1869–1870), and* Around the World in Eighty Days *(1873). This rare shorter story was first serialized in the March through May 1872 issues of* Musées des Familles. *Verne is said to have confided later that the "science" on which the story's events are based was totally made up, but that doesn't make his tale seem any less imaginative or provocative.*

I

HOW IT IS USELESS TO SEEK, EVEN ON THE BEST MAPS, FOR THE SMALL TOWN OF QUIQUENDONE

If you try to find, on any map of Flanders, ancient or modern, the small town of Quiquendone, probably you will not succeed. Is Quiquendone, then, one of those towns which have disappeared? No. A town of the future? By no means. It exists in spite of geographies, and has done so for some eight or nine hundred years. It even numbers two thousand three hundred and ninety-three souls, allowing one soul to each inhabitant. It is situated thirteen and a half kilometres north-west of Oudenarde, and fifteen and a quarter kilometres south-east of Bruges, in the heart of Flanders. The Vaar, a small tributary of the Scheldt, passes beneath its three bridges, which are still covered with a quaint mediaeval roof, like that at Tournay. An old château is to be seen there, the first stone of which was laid so long ago as 1197, by Count Baldwin, afterwards Emperor of Constantinople; and there is a Town Hall, with Gothic windows, crowned by a chaplet of battlements, and surrounded by a turreted belfry, which rises three hundred and fifty-seven feet above the soil. Every hour you may hear there a chime of five octaves, a veritable aerial piano, the renown of which surpasses that of the famous chimes of Bruges. Strangers—if any ever come to Quiquendone—do not quit the curious old town until they have visited its "Stadtholder's Hall," adorned by a full-length portrait of William of Nassau, by Brandon; the loft of the Church of Saint Magloire, a masterpiece of sixteenth century architecture; the cast-iron well in the spacious Place Saint Ernuph, the admirable ornamentation of which is attributed to the artist-blacksmith, Quentin Metsys; the tomb formerly erected to Mary of Burgundy, daughter of Charles the Bold, who now reposes in the Church of Notre Dame at Bruges; and so on. The principal industry of Quiquendone is the manufacture of whipped creams and barley-sugar on a large scale. It has been governed by the Van Tricasses, from father to son, for several centuries. And yet Quiquendone is not on the map of Flanders! Have the geographers forgotten it, or is it an intentional omission? That I cannot tell; but Quiquendone really exists; with its narrow streets, its fortified walls, its Spanish-looking houses, its market, and its burgomaster—so much so, that it has recently been the theatre of some surprising phenomena, as extraordinary and incredible as they are true, which are to be recounted in the present narration.

Surely there is nothing to be said or thought against the Flemings of Western Flanders. They are a well-to-do folk, wise, prudent, sociable, with even tempers, hospitable, perhaps a little heavy in conversation as in mind; but this does not explain why one of the most interesting towns of their district has yet to appear on modern maps.

This omission is certainly to be regretted. If only history, or in default of history the chronicles, or in default of chronicles the traditions of the country, made mention of Quiquendone! But no; neither atlases, guides, nor itineraries speak of it. M. Joanne himself, that energetic hunter after small towns, says not a word of it. It might be readily conceived that this silence would injure the commerce, the industries, of the town. But let us hasten to add that Quiquendone has neither industry nor commerce, and that it does very well without them. Its barley-sugar and whipped cream are consumed on the spot; none is exported. In short, the Quiquendonians have no need of anybody. Their desires are limited, their existence is a modest one; they are calm, moderate, phlegmatic—in a word, they are Flemings; such as are still to be met with sometimes between the Scheldt and the North Sea.

II

IN WHICH THE BURGOMASTER VAN TRICASSE AND THE COUNSELOR NIKLAUSSE CONSULT ABOUT THE AFFAIRS OF THE TOWN

"You think so?" asked the burgomaster.

"I—think so," replied the counsellor, after some minutes of silence.

"You see, we must not act hastily," resumed the burgomaster.

"We have been talking over this grave matter for ten years," replied the Counsellor Niklausse, "and I confess to you, my worthy Van Tricasse, that I cannot yet take it upon myself to come to a decision."

"I quite understand your hesitation," said the burgomaster, who did not speak until after a good quarter of an hour of reflection, "I quite understand it, and I fully share it. We shall do wisely to decide upon nothing without a more careful examination of the question."

"It is certain," replied Niklausse, "that this post of civil commissary is useless in so peaceful a town as Quiquendone."

"Our predecessor," said Van Tricasse gravely, "our predecessor never said, never would have dared to say, that anything is certain. Every affirmation is subject to awkward qualifications."

The counsellor nodded his head slowly in token of assent; then he remained silent for nearly half an hour. After this lapse of time, during which neither the counsellor nor the burgomaster moved so much as a finger, Niklausse asked Van Tricasse whether his predecessor—of some twenty years before—had not thought of suppressing this office of civil commissary, which each year cost the town of Quiquendone the sum of thirteen hundred and seventy-five francs and some centimes.

"I believe he did," replied the burgomaster, carrying his hand with majestic deliberation to his ample brow; "but the worthy man died without having dared to make up his mind, either as to this or any other administrative measure. He was a sage. Why should I not do as he did?"

Counsellor Niklausse was incapable of originating any objection to the burgomaster's opinion.

"The man who dies," added Van Tricasse solemnly, "without ever having decided upon anything during his life, has very nearly attained to perfection."

This said, the burgomaster pressed a bell with the end of his little finger, which gave forth a muffled sound, which seemed less a sound than a sigh. Presently some light steps glided softly across the tile floor. A mouse would not have made less noise, running over a thick carpet. The door of the room opened, turning on its well-oiled

45

hinges. A young girl, with long blonde tresses, made her appearance. It was Suzel Van Tricasse, the burgomaster's only daughter. She handed her father a pipe, filled to the brim, and a small copper brazier, spoke not a word, and disappeared at once, making no more noise at her exit than at her entrance.

The worthy burgomaster lighted his pipe, and was soon hidden in a cloud of bluish smoke, leaving Counsellor Niklausse plunged in the most absorbing thought.

The room in which these two notable personages, charged with the government of Quiquendone, were talking, was a parlour richly adorned with carvings in dark wood. A lofty fireplace, in which an oak might have been burned or an ox roasted, occupied the whole of one of the sides of the room; opposite to it was a trellised window, the painted glass of which toned down the brightness of the sunbeams. In an antique frame above the chimney-piece appeared the portrait of some worthy man, attributed to Memling, which no doubt represented an ancestor of the Van Tricasses, whose authentic genealogy dates back to the fourteenth century, the period when the Flemings and Guy de Dampierre were engaged in wars with the Emperor Rudolph of Hapsburgh.

This parlour was the principal apartment of the burgomaster's house, which was one of the pleasantest in Quiquendone. Built in the Flemish style, with all the abruptness, quaintness, and picturesqueness of Pointed architecture, it was considered one of the most curious monuments of the town. A Carthusian convent, or a deaf and dumb asylum, was not more silent than this mansion. Noise had no existence there; people did not walk, but glided about in it; they did not speak, they murmured. There was not, however, any lack of women in the house, which, in addition to the burgomaster Van Tricasse himself, sheltered his wife, Madame Brigitte Van Tricasse, his daughter, Suzel Van Tricasse, and his domestic, Lotchè Janshéu. We may also mention the burgomaster's sister, Aunt Hermance, an elderly maiden who still bore the nickname of Tatanémance, which her niece Suzel had given her when a child. But in spite of all these elements of discord and noise, the burgomaster's house was as calm as a desert.

The burgomaster was some fifty years old, neither fat nor lean, neither short nor tall, neither rubicund nor pale, neither gay nor sad, neither contented nor discontented, neither energetic nor dull, neither proud nor humble, neither good nor bad, neither generous nor miserly, neither courageous nor cowardly, neither too much nor too little of anything—a man notably moderate in all respects, whose invariable slowness of motion, slightly hanging lower jaw, prominent eyebrows, massive forehead, smooth as a copper plate and without a wrinkle, would at once have betrayed to a physiognomist that the burgomaster Van Tricasse was phlegm personified. Never, either from anger or passion, had any emotion whatever hastened the beating of this man"s heart, or flushed his face; never had his pupils contracted under the influence of any irritation, however ephemeral. He invariably wore good clothes, neither too large nor too small, which he never seemed to wear out. He was shod with large square shoes with triple soles and silver buckles, which lasted so long that his shoemaker was in despair. Upon his head he wore a large hat which dated from the period when Flanders was separated from Holland, so that this venerable masterpiece was at least forty years old. But what would you have? It is the passions which wear out body as well as soul, the clothes as well as the body; and our worthy burgomaster, apathetic, indolent, indifferent, was passionate in nothing. He wore nothing out, not even himself, and he considered himself the very man to administer the affairs of Quiquendone and its tranquil population.

The town, indeed, was not less calm than the Van Tricasse mansion. It was in this peaceful dwelling that the burgomaster reckoned on attaining the utmost limit of human existence, after having, however, seen the good Madame Brigitte Van Tricasse, his wife, precede him to the tomb, where, surely, she would not find a more profound repose than that she had enjoyed on earth for sixty years.

This demands explanation.

The Van Tricasse family might well call itself the "Jeannot family." This is why:—

Every one knows that the knife of this typical personage is as celebrated as its proprietor, and not less incapable of wearing out, thanks to the double operation, incessantly repeated, of replacing the handle when it is worn out, and the blade when it becomes worthless. A precisely similar operation had been going on from time immemorial in the Van Tricasse family, to which Nature had lent herself with more than usual complacency. From 1340 it had invariably happened that a Van Tricasse, when left a widower, had remarried a Van Tricasse younger than himself; who, becoming in turn a widow, had married again a Van Tricasse younger than herself; and so on, without a break in the continuity, from generation to generation. Each died in his or her turn with mechanical regularity. Thus the worthy Madame Brigitte Van Tricasse had now her second husband; and, unless she violated her every duty, would precede her spouse—he being ten years younger than herself—to the other world, to make room for a new Madame Van Tricasse. Upon this the burgomaster calmly counted, that the family tradition might not be broken. Such was this mansion, peaceful and silent, of which the doors never creaked, the windows never rattled, the floors never groaned, the chimneys never roared, the weathercocks never grated, the furniture never squeaked, the locks never clanked, and the occupants never made more noise than their shadows. The god Harpocrates would certainly have chosen it for the Temple of Silence.

III

IN WHICH THE COMMISSARY PASSAUF ENTERS AS NOISILY AS UNEXPECTEDLY

When the interesting conversation which has been narrated began, it was a quarter before three in the afternoon. It was at a quarter before four that Van Tricasse lighted his enormous pipe, which could hold a quart of tobacco, and it was at thirty-five minutes past five that he finished smoking it.

All this time the two comrades did not exchange a single word.

About six o'clock the counsellor, who had a habit of speaking in a very summary manner, resumed in these words—

"So we decide—"

"To decide nothing," replied the burgomaster.

"I think, on the whole, that you are right, Van Tricasse."

"I think so too, Niklausse. We will take steps with reference to the civil commissary when we have more light on the subject—later on. There is no need for a month yet."

"Nor even for a year," replied Niklausse, unfolding his pocket-handkerchief and calmly applying it to his nose.

There was another silence of nearly a quarter of an hour. Nothing disturbed this repeated pause in the conversation; not even the appearance of the house-dog Lento, who, not less phlegmatic than his master, came to pay his respects in the parlour. Noble dog!— a model for his race. Had he been made of pasteboard, with wheels on his paws, he would not have made less noise during his stay.

Towards eight o'clock, after Lotchè had brought the antique lamp of polished glass, the burgomaster said to the counsellor—

"We have no other urgent matter to consider?"

"No, Van Tricasse; none that I know of."

"Have I not been told, though," asked the burgomaster, "that the tower of the Oudenarde gate is likely to tumble down?"

"Ah!" replied the counsellor; "really, I should not be astonished if it fell on some passer-by any day."

"Oh! before such a misfortune happens I hope we shall have come to a decision on the subject of this tower."

"I hope so, Van Tricasse."

"There are more pressing matters to decide."

"No doubt; the question of the leather-market, for instance."

"What, is it still burning?"

"Still burning, and has been for the last three weeks."

"Have we not decided in council to let it burn?"

"Yes, Van Tricasse—on your motion."

"Was not that the surest and simplest way to deal with it?"

"Without doubt."

"Well, let us wait. Is that all?"

"All," replied the counsellor, scratching his head, as if to assure himself that he had not forgotten anything important.

"Ah!" exclaimed the burgomaster, "haven't you also heard something of an escape of water which threatens to inundate the low quarter of Saint Jacques?"

"I have. It is indeed unfortunate that this escape of water did not happen above the leather-market! It would naturally have checked the fire, and would thus have saved us a good deal of discussion."

"What can you expect, Niklausse? There is nothing so illogical as accidents. They are bound by no rules, and we cannot profit by one, as we might wish, to remedy another."

It took Van Tricasse's companion some time to digest this fine observation.

"Well, but," resumed the Counsellor Niklausse, after the lapse of some moments, "we have not spoken of our great affair!"

"What great affair? Have we, then, a great affair?" asked the burgomaster.

"No doubt. About lighting the town."

"O yes. If my memory serves me, you are referring to the lighting plan of Doctor Ox."

"Precisely."

"It is going on, Niklausse," replied the burgomaster. "They are already laying the pipes, and the works are entirely completed."

"Perhaps we have hurried a little in this matter," said the counsellor, shaking his head.

"Perhaps. But our excuse is, that Doctor Ox bears the whole expense of his experiment. It will not cost us a sou."

49

"That, true enough, is our excuse. Moreover, we must advance with the age. If the experiment succeeds, Quiquendone will be the first town in Flanders to be lighted with the oxy—What is the gas called?"

"Oxyhydric gas."

"Well, oxyhydric gas, then."

At this moment the door opened, and Lotchè came in to tell the burgomaster that his supper was ready.

Counsellor Niklausse rose to take leave of Van Tricasse, whose appetite had been stimulated by so many affairs discussed and decisions taken; and it was agreed that the council of notables should be convened after a reasonably long delay, to determine whether a decision should be provisionally arrived at with reference to the really urgent matter of the Oudenarde gate.

The two worthy administrators then directed their steps towards the street-door, the one conducting the other. The counsellor, having reached the last step, lighted a little lantern to guide him through the obscure streets of Quiquendone, which Doctor Ox had not yet lighted. It was a dark October night, and a light fog overshadowed the town.

Niklausse's preparations for departure consumed at least a quarter of an hour; for, after having lighted his lantern, he had to put on his big cow-skin socks and his sheep-skin gloves; then he put up the furred collar of his overcoat, turned the brim of his felt hat down over his eyes, grasped his heavy crow-beaked umbrella, and got ready to start.

When Lotchè, however, who was lighting her master, was about to draw the bars of the door, an unexpected noise arose outside.

Yes! Strange as the thing seems, a noise—a real noise, such as the town had certainly not heard since the taking of the donjon by the Spaniards in 1513—terrible noise, awoke the long-dormant echoes of the venerable Van Tricasse mansion.

Some one knocked heavily upon this door, hitherto virgin to brutal touch! Redoubled knocks were given with some blunt implement, probably a knotty stick, wielded by a vigorous arm. With the strokes were mingled cries and calls. These words were distinctly heard:—

"Monsieur Van Tricasse! Monsieur the burgomaster! Open, open quickly!"

The burgomaster and the counsellor, absolutely astounded, looked at each other speechless.

This passed their comprehension. If the old culverin of the château, which had not been used since 1385, had been let off in the parlour, the dwellers in the Van Tricasse mansion would not have been more dumbfounded.

Meanwhile, the blows and cries were redoubled. Lotchè, recovering her coolness, had plucked up courage to speak.

"Who is there?"

"It is I! I! I!"

"Who are you?"

"The Commissary Passauf!"

The Commissary Passauf! The very man whose office it had been contemplated to suppress for ten years. What had happened, then? Could the Burgundians have invaded Quiquendone, as they did in the fourteenth century? No event of less importance could have so moved Commissary Passauf, who in no degree yielded the palm to the burgomaster himself for calmness and phlegm.

On a sign from Van Tricasse—for the worthy man could not have articulated a syllable—the bar was pushed back and the door opened.

Commissary Passauf flung himself into the antechamber. One would have thought there was a hurricane.

"What's the matter, Monsieur the commissary?" asked Lotchè, a brave woman, who did not lose her head under the most trying circumstances.

"What's the matter!" replied Passauf, whose big round eyes expressed a genuine agitation. "The matter is that I have just come from Doctor Ox's, who has been holding a reception, and that there—"

"There?"

"There I have witnessed such an altercation as—Monsieur the burgomaster, they have been talking politics!"

"Politics!" repeated Van Tricasse, running his fingers through his wig.

"Politics!" resumed Commissary Passauf, "which has not been done for perhaps a hundred years at Quiquendone. Then the discussion got warm, and the advocate, André Schut, and the doctor, Dominique Custos, became so violent that it may be they will call each other out."

"Call each other out!" cried the counsellor. "A duel! A duel at Quiquendone! And what did Advocate Schut and Doctor Custos say?"

"Just this: 'Monsieur advocate,' said the doctor to his adversary, 'you go too far, it seems to me, and you do not take sufficient care to control your words!'"

The Burgomaster Van Tricasse clasped his hands—the counsellor turned pale and let his lantern fall—the commissary shook his head. That a phrase so evidently irritating should be pronounced by two of the principal men in the country!

"This Doctor Custos," muttered Van Tricasse, "is decidedly a dangerous man—a hare-brained fellow! Come, gentlemen!"

On this, Counsellor Niklausse and the commissary accompanied the burgomaster into the parlour.

IV

IN WHICH DOCTOR OX REVEALS HIMSELF AS A PHYSIOLOGIST OF THE FIRST RANK, AND AS AN AUDACIOUS EXPERIMENTALIST

Who, then, was this personage, known by the singular name of Doctor Ox?

An original character for certain, but at the same time a bold *savant,* a physiologist, whose works were known and highly estimated throughout learned Europe, a happy rival of the Davys, the Daltons, the Bostocks, the Menzies, the Godwins, the Vierordts—of all those noble minds who have placed physiology among the highest of modern sciences.

Doctor Ox was a man of medium size and height, aged—: but we cannot state his age, any more than his nationality. Besides, it matters little; let it suffice that he was a strange personage, impetuous and hot-blooded, a regular oddity out of one of Hoffmann"s volumes, and one who contrasted amusingly enough with the good people of Quiquendone. He had an imperturbable confidence both in himself and in his doctrines. Always smiling, walking with head erect and shoulders thrown back in a free and unconstrained manner, with a steady gaze, large open nostrils, a vast mouth which inhaled the air in liberal draughts, his appearance was far from unpleasing. He was full of animation, well proportioned in all parts of his bodily mechanism, with quicksilver in his veins, and a most elastic step. He could never stop still in one place, and relieved himself with impetuous words and a superabundance of gesticulations.

Was Doctor Ox rich, then, that he should undertake to light a whole town at his expense? Probably, as he permitted himself to indulge in such extravagance—and this is the only answer we can give to this indiscreet question.

Doctor Ox had arrived at Quiquendone five months before, accompanied by his assistant, who answered to the name of Gédéon Ygène; a tall, dried-up, thin man, haughty, but not less vivacious than his master.

And next, why had Doctor Ox made the proposition to light the town at his own expense? Why had he, of all the Flemings, selected the peaceable Quiquendonians, to endow their town with the benefits of an unheard-of system of lighting? Did he not, under this pretext, design to make some great physiological experiment by operating *in animâ vili?* In short, what was this original personage about to attempt? We know not, as Doctor Ox had no confidant except his assistant Ygène, who, moreover, obeyed him blindly.

In appearance, at least, Doctor Ox had agreed to light the town, which had much need of it, "especially at night," as Commissary Passauf wittily said. Works for producing a lighting gas had accordingly been established; the gasometers were ready for use, and the main pipes, running beneath the street pavements, would soon appear in the form of burners in the public edifices and the private houses of certain friends of progress. Van Tricasse and Niklausse, in their official capacity, and some other worthies, thought they ought to allow this modern light to be introduced into their dwellings.

If the reader has not forgotten, it was said, during the long conversation of the counsellor and the burgomaster, that the lighting of the town was to be achieved, not by the combustion of common carburetted hydrogen, produced by distilling coal, but by the use of a more modern and twenty-fold more brilliant gas, oxyhydric gas, produced by mixing hydrogen and oxygen.

The doctor, who was an able chemist as well as an ingenious physiologist, knew how to obtain this gas in great quantity and of good quality, not by using manganate of soda, according to the method of M. Tessie du Motay, but by the direct decomposition of slightly acidulated water, by means of a battery made of new elements, invented by himself. Thus there were no costly materials, no platinum, no retorts, no combustibles, no delicate machinery to produce the two gases separately. An electric current was sent through large basins full of water, and the liquid was decomposed into its two constituent parts, oxygen and hydrogen. The oxygen passed off at one end; the hydrogen, of double the volume of its late associate, at the other. As a necessary precaution, they were collected in separate reservoirs, for their mixture would have produced a frightful explosion if it had become ignited. Thence the pipes were to convey them separately to the various burners, which would be so placed as to prevent all chance of explosion. Thus a remarkably brilliant flame would be obtained, whose light would rival the electric light, which, as everybody knows, is, according to Cassellmann's experiments, equal to that of eleven hundred and seventy-one wax candles—not one more, nor one less.

It was certain that the town of Quiquendone would, by this liberal contrivance, gain a splendid lighting; but Doctor Ox and his assistant took little account of this, as will be seen in the sequel.

The day after that on which Commissary Passauf had made his noisy entrance into the burgomaster's parlour, Gédéon Ygène and Doctor Ox were talking in the laboratory which both occupied in common, on the ground-floor of the principal building of the gas-works.

"Well, Ygène, well," cried the doctor, rubbing his hands. "You saw, at my reception yesterday, the cool-bloodedness of these worthy Quiquendonians. For animation they are midway between sponges and coral! You saw them disputing and irritating each other by voice and gesture? They are already metamorphosed, morally and physically! And this is only the beginning. Wait till we treat them to a big dose!"

"Indeed, master," replied Ygène, scratching his sharp nose with the end of his forefinger, "the experiment begins well, and if I had not prudently closed the supply-tap, I know not what would have happened."

"You heard Schut, the advocate, and Custos, the doctor?" resumed Doctor Ox. "The phrase was by no means ill-natured in itself, but, in the mouth of a Quiquendonian, it is worth all the insults which the Homeric heroes hurled at each other before drawing their swords. Ah, these Flemings! You'll see what we shall do some day!"

"We shall make them ungrateful," replied Ygène, in the tone of a man who esteems the human race at its just worth.

"Bah!" said the doctor; "what matters it whether they think well or ill of us, so long as our experiment succeeds?"

"Besides," returned the assistant, smiling with a malicious expression, "is it not to be feared that, in producing such an excitement in their respiratory organs, we shall somewhat injure the lungs of these good people of Quiquendone?"

"So much the worse for them! It is in the interests of science. What would you say if the dogs or frogs refused to lend themselves to the experiments of vivisection?"

It is probable that if the frogs and dogs were consulted, they would offer some objection; but Doctor Ox imagined that he had stated an unanswerable argument, for he heaved a great sigh of satisfaction.

"After all, master, you are right," replied Ygène, as if quite convinced. "We could not have hit upon better subjects than these people of Quiquendone for our experiment."

"We—could—not," said the doctor, slowly articulating each word.

"Have you felt the pulse of any of them?"

"Some hundreds."

"And what is the average pulsation you found?"

"Not fifty per minute. See—this is a town where there has not been the shadow of a discussion for a century, where the carmen don't swear, where the coachmen don't insult each other, where horses don't run away, where the dogs don't bite, where the cats don't scratch—a town where the police-court has nothing to do from one year"s end to another—a town where people do not grow enthusiastic about anything, either about art or business—a town where the gendarmes are a sort of myth, and in which an indictment has not been drawn up for a hundred years—a town, in short, where for three centuries nobody has struck a blow with his fist or so much as exchanged a slap in the face! You see, Ygène, that this cannot last, and that we must change it all."

"Perfectly! perfectly!" cried the enthusiastic assistant; "and have you analyzed the air of this town, master?"

"I have not failed to do so. Seventy-nine parts of azote and twenty-one of oxygen, carbonic acid and steam in a variable quantity. These are the ordinary proportions."

"Good, doctor, good!" replied Ygène. "The experiment will be made on a large scale, and will be decisive."

"And if it is decisive," added Doctor Ox triumphantly, "we shall reform the world!"

V

IN WHICH THE BURGOMASTER AND THE COUNSELOR PAY A VISIT TO DOCTOR OX, AND WHAT FOLLOWS

The Counsellor Niklausse and the Burgomaster Van Tricasse at last knew what it was to have an agitated night. The grave event which had taken place at Doctor Ox's house actually kept them awake. What consequences was this affair destined to bring about? They could not imagine. Would it be necessary for them to come to a decision? Would the municipal authority, whom they represented, be compelled to interfere? Would they be obliged to order arrests to be made, that so great a scandal should not be repeated? All these doubts could not but trouble these soft natures; and on that evening, before separating, the two notables had "decided" to see each other the next day.

On the next morning, then, before dinner, the Burgomaster Van Tricasse proceeded in person to the Counsellor Niklausse's house. He found his friend more calm. He himself had recovered his equanimity.

"Nothing new?" asked Van Tricasse.

"Nothing new since yesterday," replied Niklausse.

"And the doctor, Dominique Custos?"

"I have not heard anything, either of him or of the advocate, André Schut."

After an hour"s conversation, which consisted of three remarks which it is needless to repeat, the counsellor and the burgomaster had resolved to pay a visit to Doctor Ox, so as to draw from him, without seeming to do so, some details of the affair.

Contrary to all their habits, after coming to this decision the two notables set about putting it into execution forthwith. They left the house and directed their steps towards Doctor Ox's laboratory, which was situated outside the town, near the Oudenarde gate—the gate whose tower threatened to fall in ruins.

They did not take each other's arms, but walked side by side, with a slow and solemn step, which took them forward but thirteen inches per second. This was, indeed, the ordinary gait of the Quiquendonians, who had never, within the memory of man, seen any one run across the streets of their town.

From time to time the two notables would stop at some calm and tranquil crossway, or at the end of a quiet street, to salute the passers-by.

"Good morning, Monsieur the burgomaster," said one.

"Good morning, my friend," responded Van Tricasse.

"Anything new, Monsieur the counsellor?" asked another.

"Nothing new," answered Niklausse.

But by certain agitated motions and questioning looks, it was evident that the altercation of the evening before was known throughout the town. Observing the direction taken by Van Tricasse, the most obtuse Quiquendonians guessed that the burgomaster was on his way to take some important step. The Custos and Schut affair was talked of everywhere, but the people had not yet come to the point of taking the part of one or the other. The Advocate Schut, having never had occasion to plead in a town where attorneys and bailiffs only existed in tradition, had, consequently, never lost a suit. As for the Doctor Custos, he was an honourable practitioner, who, after the example of his fellow-doctors, cured all the illnesses of his patients, except those of which they died—a habit unhappily acquired by all the members of all the faculties in whatever country they may practise.

On reaching the Oudenarde gate, the counsellor and the burgomaster prudently made a short detour, so as not to pass within reach of the tower, in case it should fall; then they turned and looked at it attentively.

"I think that it will fall," said Van Tricasse.

"I think so too," replied Niklausse.

"Unless it is propped up," added Van Tricasse. "But must it be propped up? That is the question."

"That is—in fact—the question."

Some moments after, they reached the door of the gasworks.

"Can we see Doctor Ox?" they asked.

Doctor Ox could always be seen by the first authorities of the town, and they were at once introduced into the celebrated physiologist's study.

Perhaps the two notables waited for the doctor at least an hour; at least it is reasonable to suppose so, as the burgomaster—a thing that had never before happened in his life—betrayed a certain amount of impatience, from which his companion was not exempt.

Doctor Ox came in at last, and began to excuse himself for having kept them waiting; but he had to approve a plan for the gasometer, rectify some of the machinery—But everything was going on well! The pipes intended for the oxygen were already laid. In a few months the town would be splendidly lighted. The two notables might even now see the orifices of the pipes which were laid on in the laboratory.

Then the doctor begged to know to what he was indebted for the honour of this visit.

"Only to see you, doctor; to see you," replied Van Tricasse. "It is long since we have had the pleasure. We go abroad but little in our good town of Quiquendone. We count our steps and measure our walks. We are happy when nothing disturbs the uniformity of our habits."

Niklausse looked at his friend. His friend had never said so much at once—at least, without taking time, and giving long intervals between his sentences. It seemed to him that Van Tricasse expressed himself with a certain volubility, which was by no means common with him. Niklausse himself experienced a kind of irresistible desire to talk.

As for Doctor Ox, he looked at the burgomaster with sly attention.

Van Tricasse, who never argued until he had snugly ensconced himself in a spacious armchair, had risen to his feet. I know not what nervous excitement, quite foreign to his temperament, had taken possession of him. He did not gesticulate as yet, but this could not be far off. As for the counsellor, he rubbed his legs, and breathed with slow and long gasps. His look became animated little by little, and he had "decided" to support at all hazards, if need be, his trusty friend the burgomaster.

Van Tricasse got up and took several steps; then he came back, and stood facing the doctor.

"And in how many months," he asked in a somewhat emphatic tome, "do you say that your work will be finished?"

"In three or four months, Monsieur the burgomaster," replied Doctor Ox.

"Three or four months—it's a very long time!" said Van Tricasse.

"Altogether too long!" added Niklausse, who, not being able to keep his seat, rose also.

"This lapse of time is necessary to complete our work," returned Doctor Ox. "The workmen, whom we have had to choose in Quiquendone, are not very expeditious."

"How not expeditious?" cried the burgomaster, who seemed to take the remark as personally offensive.

"No, Monsieur Van Tricasse," replied Doctor Ox obstinately. "A French workman would do in a day what it takes ten of your workmen to do; you know, they are regular Flemings!"

"Flemings!" cried the counsellor, whose fingers closed together. "In what sense, sir, do you use that word?"

"Why, in the amiable sense in which everybody uses it," replied Doctor Ox, smiling.

"Ah, but doctor," said the burgomaster, pacing up and down the room, "I don't like these insinuations. The workmen of Quiquendone are as efficient as those of any other town in the world, you must know; and we shall go neither to Paris nor London for our models! As for your project, I beg you to hasten its execution. Our streets have been unpaved for the putting down of your conduit-pipes, and it is a hindrance to traffic. Our trade will begin to suffer, and I, being the responsible authority, do not propose to incur reproaches which will be but too just."

Worthy burgomaster! He spoke of trade, of traffic, and the wonder was that those words, to which he was quite unaccustomed, did not scorch his lips. What could be passing in his mind?

"Besides," added Niklausse, "the town cannot be deprived of light much longer."

"But," urged Doctor Ox, "a town which has been un-lighted for eight or nine hundred years—"

"All the more necessary is it," replied the burgomaster, emphasizing his words. "Times alter, manners alter! The world advances, and we do not wish to remain behind. We desire our streets to be lighted within a month, or you must pay a large indemnity for each day of delay; and what would happen if, amid the darkness, some affray should take place?"

"No doubt," cried Niklausse. "It requires but a spark to inflame a Fleming! Fleming! Flame!"

"Apropos of this," said the burgomaster, interrupting his friend, "Commissary Passauf, our chief of police, reports to us that a discussion took place in your drawing-room last evening, Doctor Ox. Was he wrong in declaring that it was a political discussion?"

"By no means, Monsieur the burgomaster," replied Doctor Ox, who with difficulty repressed a sigh of satisfaction.

"So an altercation did take place between Dominique Gustos and André Schut?"

"Yes, counsellor; but the words which passed were not of grave import."

"Not of grave import!" cried the burgomaster. "Not of grave import, when one man tells another that he does not measure the effect of his words! But of what stuff are you made, monsieur? Do you not know that in Quiquendone nothing more is needed to bring about extremely disastrous results? But monsieur, if you, or any one else, presume to speak thus to me—"

"Or to me," added Niklausse.

As they pronounced these words with a menacing air, the two notables, with folded arms and bristling air, confronted Doctor Ox, ready to do him some violence, if by a gesture, or even the expression of his eye, he manifested any intention of contradicting them.

But the doctor did not budge.

"At all events, monsieur," resumed the burgomaster, "I propose to hold you responsible for what passes in your house. I am bound to insure the tranquillity of this town, and I do not wish it to be disturbed. The events of last evening must not be repeated, or I shall do my duty, sir! Do you hear? Then reply, sir."

The burgomaster, as he spoke, under the influence of extraordinary excitement, elevated his voice to the pitch of anger. He was furious, the worthy Van Tricasse, and might certainly be heard outside. At last, beside himself, and seeing that Doctor Ox did not reply to his challenge, "Come, Niklausse," said he.

And, slamming the door with a violence which shook the house, the burgomaster drew his friend after him.

Little by little, when they had taken twenty steps on their road, the worthy notables grew more calm. Their pace slackened, their gait became less feverish. The flush on their faces faded away; from being crimson, they became rosy. A quarter of an hour after quitting the gasworks, Van Tricasse said softly to Niklausse, "An amiable man, Doctor Ox! It is always a pleasure to see him!"

VI

IN WHICH FRANTZ NIKLAUSSE AND SUZEL VAN TRICASSE
FORM CERTAIN PROJECTS FOR THE FUTURE

Our readers know that the burgomaster had a daughter, Suzel But, shrewd as they may be, they cannot have divined that the counsellor Niklausse had a son, Frantz; and had they divined this, nothing could have led them to imagine that Frantz was the betrothed lover of Suzel. We will add that these young people were made for each other, and that they loved each other, as folks did love at Quiquendone.

It must not be thought that young hearts did not beat in this exceptional place; only they beat with a certain deliberation. There were marriages there, as in every other town in the world; but they took time about it. Betrothed couples, before engaging in these terrible bonds, wished to study each other; and these studies lasted at least ten years, as at college. It was rare that any one was "accepted" before this lapse of time.

Yes, ten years! The courtships last ten years! And is it, after all, too long, when the being bound for life is in consideration? One studies ten years to become an engineer or physician, an advocate or attorney, and should less time be spent in acquiring the knowledge to make a good husband? Is it not reasonable? and, whether due to temperament or reason with them, the Quiquendonians seem to us to be in the right in thus prolonging their courtship. When marriages in other more lively and excitable cities are seen taking place within a few months, we must shrug our shoulders, and hasten to send our boys to the schools and our daughters to the *pensions* of Quiquendone.

For half a century but a single marriage was known to have taken place after the lapse of two years only of courtship, and that turned out badly!

Frantz Niklausse, then, loved Suzel Van Tricasse, but quietly, as a man would love when he has ten years before him in which to obtain the beloved object. Once every week, at an hour agreed upon, Frantz went to fetch Suzel, and took a walk with her along the banks of the Vaar. He took good care to carry his fishing-tackle, and Suzel never forgot her canvas, on which her pretty hands embroidered the most unlikely flowers.

Frantz was a young man of twenty-two, whose cheeks betrayed a soft, peachy down, and whose voice had scarcely a compass of one octave.

As for Suzel, she was blonde and rosy. She was seventeen, and did not dislike fishing. A singular occupation this, however, which forces you to struggle craftily with a barbel. But Frantz loved it; the pastime was congenial to his temperament. As patient as possible, content to follow with his rather dreamy eye the cork which bobbed on the top of the water, he knew how to wait; and when, after sitting for six hours, a modest barbel, taking pity on him, consented at last to be caught, he was happy—but he knew how to control his emotion.

On this day the two lovers—one might say, the two betrothed—were seated upon the verdant bank. The limpid Vaar murmured a few feet below them. Suzel quietly drew her needle across the canvas. Frantz automatically carried his line from left to right, then permitted it to descend the current from right to left. The fish made capricious rings in the water, which crossed each other around the cork, while the hook hung useless near the bottom.

From time to time Frantz would say, without raising his eyes—

"I think I have a bite, Suzel."

"Do you think so, Frantz?" replied Suzel, who, abandoning her work for an instant, followed her lover's line with earnest eye.

"N-no," resumed Frantz; "I thought I felt a little twitch; I was mistaken."

"You *will* have a bite, Frantz," replied Suzel, in her pure, soft voice. "But do not forget to strike at the right moment. You are always a few seconds too late, and the barbel takes advantage to escape."

"Would you like to take my line, Suzel?"

"Willingly, Frantz."

"Then give me your canvas. We shall see whether I am more adroit with the needle than with the hook."

And the young girl took the line with trembling hand, while her swain plied the needle across the stitches of the embroidery. For hours together they thus exchanged soft words, and their hearts palpitated when the cork bobbed on the water. Ah, could they ever forget those charming hours, during which, seated side by side, they listened to the murmurs of the river?

The sun was fast approaching the western horizon, and despite the combined skill of Suzel and Frantz, there had not been a bite. The barbels had not shown themselves complacent, and seemed to scoff at the two young people, who were too just to bear them malice.

"We shall be more lucky another time, Frantz," said Suzel, as the young angler put up his still virgin hook.

"Let us hope so," replied Frantz.

Then walking side by side, they turned their steps towards the house, without exchanging a word, as mute as their shadows which stretched out before them. Suzel became very, very tall under the oblique rays of the setting sun. Frantz appeared very, very thin, like the long rod which he held in his hand.

They reached the burgomaster's house. Green tufts of grass bordered the shining pavement, and no one would have thought of tearing them away, for they deadened the noise made by the passers-by.

As they were about to open the door, Frantz thought it his duty to say to Suzel—

"You know, Suzel, the great day is approaching?"

"It is indeed, Frantz," replied the young girl, with downcast eyes.

"Yes," said Frantz, "in five or six years—"

"Good-bye, Frantz," said Suzel.

"Good-bye, Suzel," replied Frantz.

And, after the door had been closed, the young man resumed the way to his father's house with a calm and equal pace.

VII

IN WHICH THE ANDANTES BECOME ALLEGROS,
AND THE ALLEGROS VIVACES

The agitation caused by the Schut and Custos affair had subsided. The affair led to no serious consequences. It appeared likely that Quiquendone would return to its habitual apathy, which that unexpected event had for a moment disturbed.

Meanwhile, the laying of the pipes destined to conduct the oxyhydric gas into the principal edifices of the town was proceeding rapidly. The main pipes and branches gradually crept beneath the pavements. But the burners were still wanting; for, as it required delicate skill to make them, it was necessary that they should be fabricated abroad. Doctor Ox was here, there, and everywhere; neither he nor Ygène, his assistant, lost a moment, but they urged on the workmen, completed the delicate mechanism of the gasometer, fed day and night the immense piles which decomposed the water under the influence of a powerful electric current. Yes, the doctor was already making his gas, though the pipe-laying was not yet done; a fact which, between ourselves, might have seemed a little singular. But before long—at least there was reason to hope so—before long Doctor Ox would inaugurate the splendours of his invention in the theatre of the town.

For Quiquendone possessed a theatre—a really fine edifice, in truth—the interior and exterior arrangement of which combined every style of architecture. It was at once Byzantine, Roman, Gothic, Renaissance, with semicircular doors, pointed windows, flamboyant rose-windows, fantastic bell-turrets—in a word, a specimen of all sorts, half a Parthenon, half a Parisian Grand Café. Nor was this surprising, the theatre having been commenced under the burgomaster Ludwig Van Tricasse, in 1175, and only finished in 1837, under the burgomaster Natalis Van Tricasse. It had required seven hundred years to build it, and it had, been successively adapted to the architectural style in vogue in each period. But for all that it was an imposing structure; the Roman pillars and Byzantine arches of which would appear to advantage lit up by the oxyhydric gas.

Pretty well everything was acted at the theatre of Quiquendone; but the opera and the opera comique were especially patronized. It must, however, be added that the composers would never have recognized their own works, so entirely changed were the "movements" of the music.

In short, as nothing was done in a hurry at Quiquendone, the dramatic pieces had to be performed in harmony with the peculiar temperament of the Quiquendonians. Though the doors of the theatre were regularly thrown open at four o'clock and closed again at ten, it had never been known that more than two acts were played during the six intervening hours. "Robert le Diable," "Les Huguenots," or "Guillaume Tell" usually took up three evenings, so slow was the execution of these masterpieces. The *vivaces,* at the theatre of Quiquendone, lagged like real *adagios.* The *allegros* were "long-drawn out" indeed. The demisemiquavers were scarcely equal to the ordinary semibreves of other countries. The most rapid runs, performed according to Quiquendonian taste, had the solemn march of a chant. The gayest shakes were languishing and measured, that they might not shock the ears of the *dilettanti.* To give an example, the rapid air sung by Figaro, on his entrance in the first act of *Le Barbier de Séville*, lasted fifty-eight minutes—when the actor was particularly enthusiastic.

Artists from abroad, as might be supposed, were forced to conform themselves to Quiquendonian fashions; but as they were well paid, they did not complain, and willingly obeyed the leader's baton, which never beat more than eight measures to the minute in the *allegros.*

But what applause greeted these artists, who enchanted without ever wearying the audiences of Quiquendone! All hands clapped one after another at tolerably long intervals, which the papers characterized as "frantic applause;" and sometimes nothing but the lavish prodigality with which mortar and stone had been used in the twelfth century saved the roof of the hall from falling in.

Besides, the theatre had only one performance a week, that these enthusiastic Flemish folk might not be too much excited; and this enabled the actors to study their parts more thoroughly, and the spectators to digest more at leisure the beauties of the masterpieces brought out.

Such had long been the drama at Quiquendone. Foreign artists were in the habit of making engagements with the director of the town, when they wanted to rest after their exertions in other scenes; and it seemed as if nothing could ever change these inveterate customs, when, a fortnight after the Schut-Custos affair, an unlooked-for incident occurred to throw the population into fresh agitation.

It was on a Saturday, an opera day. It was not yet intended, as may well be supposed, to inaugurate the new illumination. No; the pipes had reached the hall, but, for reasons indicated above, the burners had not yet been placed, and the waxcandles still shed their soft light upon the numerous spectators who filled the theatre. The doors had been opened to the public at one o'clock, and by three the hall was half full. A queue had at one time been formed, which extended as far as the end of the Place Saint Ernuph, in front of the shop of Josse Lietrinck the apothecary. This eagerness was significant of an unusually attractive performance.

"Are you going to the theatre this evening?" inquired the counsellor the same morning of the burgomaster.

"I shall not fail to do so," returned Van Tricasse, "and I shall take Madame Van Tricasse, as well as our daughter Suzel and our dear Tatanemance, who all dote on good music."

"Mademoiselle Suzel is going then?"

"Certainly, Niklausse."

"Then my son Frantz will be one of the first to arrive," said Niklausse.

"A spirited boy, Niklausse," replied the burgomaster sententiously; "but hot-headed! He will require watching!"

"He loves, Van Tricasse—he loves your charming Suzel."

"Well, Niklausse, he shall marry her. Now that we have agreed on this marriage, what more can he desire?"

"He desires nothing, Van Tricasse, the dear boy! But, in short—we'll say no more about it—he will not be the last to get his ticket at the box-office."

"Ah, vivacious and ardent youth!" replied the burgomaster, recalling his own past. "We have also been thus, my worthy counsellor! We have loved—we too! We have danced attendance in our day! Till to-night, then, till to-night! By-the-bye, do you know this Fiovaranti is a great artist? And what a welcome he has received among us! It will be long before he will forget the applause of Quiquendone!"

The tenor Fiovaranti was, indeed, going to sing; Fiovaranti, who, by his talents as a virtuoso, his perfect method, his melodious voice, provoked a real enthusiasm among the lovers of music in the town.

For three weeks Fiovaranti had been achieving a brilliant success in *Les Huguenots.* The first act, interpreted according to the taste of the Quiquendonians, had occupied an entire evening of the first week of the month.—Another evening in the second week, prolonged by infinite *andantes,* had elicited for the celebrated singer a real ovation. His success had been still more marked in the third act of Meyerbeer's masterpiece. But now Fiovaranti was to appear in the fourth act, which was to be performed on this evening before an impatient public. Ah, the duet between Raoul and Valentine, that pathetic love-song for two voices, that strain so full of *crescendos, stringendos,* and *più crescendos*—all this, sung slowly, compendiously, interminably! Ah, how delightful!

At four o'clock the hall was full. The boxes, the orchestra, the pit, were overflowing. In the front stalls sat the Burgomaster Van Tricasse, Mademoiselle Van Tricasse,

Madame Van Tricasse, and the amiable Tatanemance in a green bonnet; not far off were the Counsellor Niklausse and his family, not forgetting the amorous Frantz. The families of Custos the doctor, of Schut the advocate, of Honore Syntax the chief judge, of Norbet Sontman the insurance director, of the banker Collaert, gone mad on German music, and himself somewhat of an amateur, and the teacher Rupp, and the master of the academy, Jerome Resh, and the civil commissary, and so many other notabilities of the town that they could not be enumerated here without wearying the reader's patience, were visible in different parts of the hall.

It was customary for the Quiquendonians, while awaiting the rise of the curtain, to sit silent, some reading the paper, others whispering low to each other, some making their way to their seats slowly and noiselessly, others casting timid looks towards the bewitching beauties in the galleries.

But on this evening a looker-on might have observed that, even before the curtain rose, there was unusual animation among the audience. People were restless who were never known to be restless before. The ladies' fans fluttered with abnormal rapidity. All appeared to be inhaling air of exceptional stimulating power. Every one breathed more freely. The eyes of some became unwontedly bright, and seemed to give forth a light equal to that of the candles, which themselves certainly threw a more brilliant light over the hall. It was evident that people saw more clearly, though the number of candles had not been increased. Ah, if Doctor Ox's experiment were being tried! But it was not being tried, as yet.

The musicians of the orchestra at last took their places. The first violin had gone to the stand to give a modest la to his colleagues. The stringed instruments, the wind instruments, the drums and cymbals, were in accord. The conductor only waited the sound of the bell to beat the first bar.

The bell sounds. The fourth act begins. The *allegro appassionato* of the inter-act is played as usual, with a majestic deliberation which would have made Meyerbeer frantic, and all the majesty of which was appreciated by the Quiquendonian *dilettanti*.

But soon the leader perceived that he was no longer master of his musicians. He found it difficult to restrain them, though usually so obedient and calm. The wind instruments betrayed a tendency to hasten the movements, and it was necessary to hold them back with a firm hand, for they would otherwise outstrip the stringed instruments; which, from a musical point of view, would have been disastrous. The bassoon himself, the son of Josse Lietrinck the apothecary, a well-bred young man, seemed to lose his self-control.

Meanwhile Valentine has begun her recitative, "I am alone," &c.; but she hurries it.

The leader and all his musicians, perhaps unconsciously, follow her in her *cantabile,* which should be taken deliberately, like a 12/8 as it is. When Raoul appears at the door at the bottom of the stage, between the moment when Valentine goes to him and that when she conceals herself in the chamber at the side, a quarter of an hour does not elapse; while formerly, according to the traditions of the Quiquendone theatre, this recitative of thirty-seven bars was wont to last just thirty-seven minutes.

Saint Bris, Nevers, Cavannes, and the Catholic nobles have appeared, somewhat prematurely, perhaps, upon the scene. The composer has marked *allegro pomposo* on the score. The orchestra and the lords proceed *allegro* indeed, but not at all *pomposo,* and at the chorus, in the famous scene of the "benediction of the poniards," they no longer keep to the enjoined *allegro.* Singers and musicians broke away impetuously. The leader does not even attempt to restrain them. Nor do the public protest; on the contrary, the people find themselves carried away, and see that they are involved in the movement, and that the movement responds to the impulses of their souls.

> "Will you, with me, deliver the land,
> From troubles increasing, an impious band?"

They promise, they swear. Nevers has scarcely time to protest, and to sing that "among his ancestors were many soldiers, but never an assassin." He is arrested. The police and the aldermen rush forward and rapidly swear "to strike all at once." Saint Bris shouts the recitative which summons the Catholics to vengeance. The three monks, with white scarfs, hasten in by the door at the back of Nevers's room, without making any account of the stage directions, which enjoin on them to advance slowly. Already all the artists have drawn sword or poniard, which the three monks bless in a trice. The soprani tenors, bassos, attack the *allegro furioso* with cries of rage, and of a dramatic 6/8 time they make it 6/8 quadrille time. Then they rush out, bellowing—

> "At midnight,
> Noiselessly,
> God wills it,
> Yes,
> At midnight."

At this moment the audience start to their feet. Everybody is agitated—in the boxes, the pit, the galleries. It seems as if the spectators are about to rush upon the stage, the Burgomaster Van Tricasse at their head, to join with the conspirators and annihilate the Huguenots, whose religious opinions, however, they share. They applaud, call before the curtain, make loud acclamations! Tatanemance grasps her bonnet with feverish hand. The candles throw out a lurid glow of light.

Raoul, instead of slowly raising the curtain, tears it apart with a superb gesture and finds himself confronting Valentine.

At last! It is the grand duet, and it starts off *allegro vivace*. Raoul does not wait for Valentine's pleading, and Valentine does not wait for Raoul''s responses.

The fine passage beginning, "Danger is passing, time is flying," becomes one of those rapid airs which have made Offenbach famous, when he composes a dance for conspirators. The *andante amoroso*, "Thou hast said it, aye, thou lovest me," becomes a real *vivace furioso*, and the violoncello ceases to imitate the inflections of the singer's voice, as indicated in the composer's score. In vain Raoul cries, "Speak on, and prolong the ineffable slumber of my soul." Valentine cannot "prolong." It is evident that an unaccustomed fire devours her. Her *b's* and her *c's* above the stave were dreadfully shrill. He struggles, he gesticulates, he is all in a glow.

The alarum is heard; the bell resounds; but what a panting bell! The bell-ringer has evidently lost his self-control. It is a frightful tocsin, which violently struggles against the fury of the orchestra.

Finally the air which ends this magnificent act, beginning, "No more love, no more intoxication, O the remorse that oppresses me!" which the composer marks *allegro con moto*, becomes a wild *prestissimo*. You would say an express-train was whirling by. The alarum resounds again. Valentine falls fainting. Raoul precipitates himself from the window.

It was high time. The orchestra, really intoxicated, could not have gone on. The leader's baton is no longer anything but a broken stick on the prompter's box. The violin strings are broken, and their necks twisted. In his fury the drummer has burst his drum. The counter-bassist has perched on the top of his musical monster. The first clarionet has swallowed the reed of his instrument, and the second hautboy is chewing his reed keys. The groove of the trombone is strained, and finally the unhappy cornist cannot withdraw his hand from the bell of his horn, into which he had thrust it too far.

And the audience! The audience, panting, all in a heat, gesticulates and howls. All the faces are as red as if a fire were burning within their bodies. They crowd each other, hustle each other to get out—the men without hats, the women without mantles! They elbow each other in the corridors, crush between the doors, quarrel, fight! There are no longer any officials, any burgomaster. All are equal amid this infernal frenzy!

Some moments after, when all have reached the street, each one resumes his habitual tranquillity, and peaceably enters his house, with a confused remembrance of what he has just experienced.

The fourth act of *Les Huguenots*, which formerly lasted six hours, began, on this evening at half-past four, and ended at twelve minutes before five.

It had only lasted eighteen minutes!

VIII

IN WHICH THE ANCIENT AND SOLEMN GERMAN WALTZ BECOMES A WHIRLWIND

But if the spectators, on leaving the theatre, resumed their customary calm, if they quietly regained their homes, preserving only a sort of passing stupefaction, they had none the less undergone a remarkable exaltation, and overcome and weary as if they had committed some excess of dissipation, they fell heavily upon their beds.

The next day each Quiquendonian had a kind of recollection of what had occurred the evening before. One missed his hat, lost in the hubbub; another a coat-flap, torn in the brawl; one her delicately fashioned shoe, another her best mantle. Memory returned to these worthy people, and with it a certain shame for their unjustifiable agitation. It seemed to them an orgy in which they were the unconscious heroes and heroines. They did not speak of it; they did not wish to think of it. But the most astounded personage in the town was Van Tricasse the burgomaster.

The next morning, on waking, he could not find his wig. Lotchè looked everywhere for it, but in vain. The wig had remained on the field of battle. As for having it publicly claimed by Jean Mistrol, the town-crier—no, it would not do. It were better to lose the wig than to advertise himself thus, as he had the honour to be the first magistrate of Quiquendone.

The worthy Van Tricasse was reflecting upon this, extended beneath his sheets, with bruised body, heavy head, furred tongue, and burning breast. He felt no desire to get up; on the contrary; and his brain worked more during this morning than it had probably worked before for forty years. The worthy magistrate recalled to his mind all the incidents of the incomprehensible performance. He connected them with the events which had taken place shortly before at Doctor Ox's reception. He tried to discover the causes of the singular excitability which, on two occasions, had betrayed itself in the best citizens of the town.

"What *can* be going on?" he asked himself. "What giddy spirit has taken possession of my peaceable town of Quiquendone? Are we about to go mad, and must

we make the town one vast asylum? For yesterday we were all there, notables, counsellors, judges, advocates, physicians, schoolmasters; and ail, if my memory serves
me—all of us were assailed by this excess of furious folly! But what was there in that
infernal music? It is inexplicable! Yet I certainly ate or drank nothing which could
put me into such a state. No; yesterday I had for dinner a slice of overdone veal, several spoonfuls of spinach with sugar, eggs, and a little beer and water—that couldn't
get into my head! No! There is something that I cannot explain, and as, after all, I am
responsible for the conduct of the citizens, I will have an investigation."

But the investigation, though decided upon by the municipal council, produced
no result. If the facts were clear, the causes escaped the sagacity of the magistrates.
Besides, tranquillity had been restored in the public mind, and with tranquillity, forgetfulness of the strange scenes of the theatre. The newspapers avoided speaking of
them, and the account of the performance which appeared in the "Quiquendone
Memorial," made no allusion to this intoxication of the entire audience.

Meanwhile, though the town resumed its habitual phlegm, and became apparently Flemish as before, it was observable that, at bottom, the character and temperament of the people changed little by little. One might have truly said, with
Dominique Custos, the doctor, that "their nerves were affected."

Let us explain. This undoubted change only took place under certain conditions.
When the Quiquendonians passed through the streets of the town, walked in the
squares or along the Vaar, they were always the cold and methodical people of former
days. So, too, when they remained at home, some working with their hands and others with their heads—these doing nothing, those thinking nothing—their private
life was silent, inert, vegetating as before. No quarrels, no household squabbles, no
acceleration in the beating of the heart, no excitement of the brain. The mean of
their pulsations remained as it was of old, from fifty to fifty-two per minute.

But, strange and inexplicable phenomenon though it was, which would have
defied the sagacity of the most ingenious physiologists of the day, if the inhabitants of
Quiquendone did not change in their home life, they were visibly changed in their
civil life and in their relations between man and man, to which it leads.

If they met together in some public edifice, it did not "work well," as Commissary
Passauf expressed it. On 'change, at the town-hall, in the amphitheatre of the academy, at
the sessions of the council, as well as at the reunions of the *savants*, a strange excitement
seized the assembled citizens. Their relations with each other became embarrassing
before they had been together an hour. In two hours the discussion degenerated
into an angry dispute. Heads became heated, and personalities were used. Even at
church, during the sermon, the faithful could not listen to Van Stabel, the minister,

in patience, and he threw himself about in the pulpit and lectured his flock with far more than his usual severity. At last this state of things brought about altercations more grave, alas! than that between Custos and Schut, and if they did not require the interference of the authorities, it was because the antagonists, after returning home, found there, with its calm, forgetfulness of the offences offered and received.

This peculiarity could not be observed by these minds, which were absolutely incapable of recognizing what was passing in them. One person only in the town, he whose office the council had thought of suppressing for thirty years, Michael Passauf, had remarked that this excitement, which was absent from private houses, quickly revealed itself in public edifices; and he asked himself, not without a certain anxiety, what would happen if this infection should ever develop itself in the family mansions, and if the epidemic—this was the word he used—should extend through the streets of the town. Then there would be no more forgetfulness of insults, no more tranquillity, no intermission in the delirium; but a permanent inflammation, which would inevitably bring the Quiquendonians into collision with each other.

"What would happen then?" Commissary Passauf asked himself in terror. "How could these furious savages be arrested? How check these goaded temperaments? My office would be no longer a sinecure, and the council would be obliged to double my salary—unless it should arrest me myself, for disturbing the public peace!"

These very reasonable fears began to be realized. The infection spread from "change, the theatre, the church, the town-hall, the academy, the market, into private houses, and that in less than a fortnight after the terrible performance of *Les Huguenots*."

Its first symptoms appeared in the house of Collaert, the banker.

That wealthy personage gave a ball, or at least a dancing-party, to the notabilities of the town. He had issued, some months before, a loan of thirty thousand francs, three quarters of which had been subscribed; and to celebrate this financial success, he had opened his drawing-rooms, and given a party to his fellow-citizens.

Everybody knows that Flemish parties are innocent and tranquil enough, the principal expense of which is usually in beer and syrups. Some conversation on the weather, the appearance of the crops, the fine condition of the gardens, the care of flowers, and especially of tulips; a slow and measured dance, from time to time, perhaps a minuet; sometimes a waltz, but one of those German waltzes which achieve a turn and a half per minute, and during which the dancers hold each other as far apart as their arms will permit—such is the usual fashion of the balls attended by the aristocratic society of Quiquendone. The polka, after being altered to four time, had tried to become accustomed to it; but the dancers always lagged behind the orchestra, no matter how slow the measure, and it had to be abandoned.

These peaceable reunions, in which the youths and maidens enjoyed an honest and moderate pleasure, had never been attended by any outburst of ill-nature. Why, then, on this evening at Collaert the banker's, did the syrups seem to be transformed into heady wines, into sparkling champagne, into heating punches? Why, towards the middle of the evening, did a sort of mysterious intoxication take possession of the guests? Why did the minuet become a jig? Why did the orchestra hurry with its harmonies? Why did the candles, just as at the theatre, burn with unwonted refulgence? What electric current invaded the banker's drawing-rooms? How happened it that the couples held each other so closely, and clasped each other's hands so convulsively, that the "cavaliers seuls" made themselves conspicuous by certain extraordinary steps in that figure usually so grave, so solemn, so majestic, so very proper?

Alas! what Œdipus could have answered these unsolvable questions? Commissary Passauf, who was present at the party, saw the storm coming distinctly, but he could not control it or fly from it, and he felt a kind of intoxication entering his own brain. All his physical and emotional faculties increased in intensity. He was seen, several times, to throw himself upon the confectionery and devour the dishes, as if he had just broken a long fast.

The animation of the ball was increasing all this while. A long murmur, like a dull buzzing, escaped from all breasts. They danced—really danced. The feet were agitated by increasing frenzy. The faces became as purple as those of Silenus. The eyes shone like carbuncles. The general fermentation rose to the highest pitch.

And when the orchestra thundered out the waltz in *Der Freyschuetz*—when this waltz, so German, and with a movement so slow, was attacked with wild arms by the musicians—ah! it was no longer a waltz, but an insensate whirlwind, a giddy rotation, a gyration worthy of being led by some Mephistopheles, beating the measure with a firebrand! Then a galop, an infernal galop, which lasted an hour without any one being able to stop it, whirled off, in its windings, across the halls, the drawing-rooms, the antechambers, by the staircases, from the cellar to the garret of the opulent mansion, the young men and young girls, the fathers and mothers, people of every age, of every weight, of both sexes; Collaert, the fat banker, and Madame Collaert, and the counsellors, and the magistrates, and the chief justice, and Niklausse, and Madame Van Tricasse, and the Burgomaster Van Tricasse, and the Commissary Passauf himself, who never could recall afterwards who had been his partner on that terrible evening.

But *she* did not forget! And ever since that day she has seen in her dreams the fiery commissary, enfolding her in an impassioned embrace! And "she"—was the amiable Tatanémance!

IX

IN WHICH DOCTOR OX AND YGÈNE, HIS ASSISTANT, SAY A FEW WORDS

"Well, Ygène?"

"Well, master, all is ready. The laying of the pipes is finished."

"At last! Now, then, we are going to operate on a large scale, on the masses!"

X

IN WHICH IT WILL BE SEEN THAT THE EPIDEMIC INVADES THE ENTIRE TOWN, AND WHAT EFFECT IT PRODUCES

During the following months the evil, in place of subsiding, became more extended. From private houses the epidemic spread into the streets. The town of Quiquendone was no longer to be recognized.

A phenomenon yet stranger than those which had already happened, now appeared; not only the animal kingdom, but the vegetable kingdom itself, became subject to the mysterious influence.

According to the ordinary course of things, epidemics are special in their operation. Those which attack humanity spare the animals, and those which attack the animals spare the vegetables. A horse was never inflicted with smallpox, nor a man with the cattle-plague, nor do sheep suffer from the potato-rot. But here all the laws of nature seemed to be overturned. Not only were the character, temperament, and ideas of the townsfolk changed, but the domestic animals—dogs and cats, horses and cows, asses and goats—suffered from this epidemic influence, as if their habitual equilibrium had been changed. The plants themselves were infected by a similar strange metamorphosis.

In the gardens and vegetable patches and orchards very curious symptoms manifested themselves. Climbing plants climbed more audaciously. Tufted plants became more tufted than ever. Shrubs became trees. Cereals, scarcely sown, showed their little green heads, and gained, in the same length of time, as much in inches as formerly, under the most favourable circumstances, they had gained in fractions. Asparagus attained the height of several feet; the artichokes swelled to the size of melons, the melons to the size of pumpkins, the pumpkins to the size of gourds, the gourds to the size of the belfry bell, which measured, in truth, nine feet in diameter. The cabbages were bushes, and the mushrooms umbrellas.

The fruits did not lag behind the vegetables. It required two persons to eat a strawberry, and four to consume a pear. The grapes also attained the enormous proportions of those so well depicted by Poussin in his *Return of the Envoys to the Promised Land.*

It was the same with the flowers: immense violets spread the most penetrating perfumes through the air; exaggerated roses shone with the brightest colours; lilies formed, in a few days, impenetrable copses; geraniums, daisies, camelias, rhododendrons, invaded the garden walks, and stifled each other. And the tulips—those dear liliaceous plants so dear to the Flemish heart, what emotion they must have caused to their zealous cultivators! The worthy Van Bistrom nearly fell over backwards, one day, on seeing in his garden an enormous *Tulipa gesneriana*, a gigantic monster, whose cup afforded space to a nest for a whole family of robins!

The entire town flocked to see this floral phenomenon, and renamed it the *Tulipa quiquendonia.*

But alas! if these plants, these fruits, these flowers, grew visibly to the naked eye, if all the vegetables insisted on assuming colossal proportions, if the brilliancy of their colours and perfume intoxicated the smell and the sight, they quickly withered. The air which they absorbed rapidly exhausted them, and they soon died, faded, and dried up.

Such was the fate of the famous tulip, which, after several days of splendour, became emaciated, and fell lifeless.

It was soon the same with the domestic animals, from the house-dog to the stable pig, from the canary in its cage to the turkey of the back-court. It must be said that in ordinary times these animals were not less phlegmatic than their masters. The dogs and cats vegetated rather than lived. They never betrayed a wag of pleasure nor a snarl of wrath. Their tails moved no more than if they had been made of bronze. Such a thing as a bite or scratch from any of them had not been known from time immemorial. As for mad dogs, they were looked upon as imaginary beasts, like the griffins and the rest in the menagerie of the apocalypse.

But what a change had taken place in a few months, the smallest incidents of which we are trying to reproduce! Dogs and cats began to show teeth and claws. Several executions had taken place after reiterated offences. A horse was seen, for the first time, to take his bit in his teeth and rush through the streets of Quiquendone; an ox was observed to precipitate itself, with lowered horns, upon one of his herd; an ass was seen to turn himself ever, with his legs in the air, in the Place Saint Ernuph, and bray as ass never brayed before; a sheep, actually a sheep, defended valiantly the cutlets within him from the butcher's knife.

Van Tricasse, the burgomaster, was forced to make police regulations concerning the domestic animals, as, seized with lunacy, they rendered the streets of Quiquendone unsafe.

But alas! if the animals were mad, the men were scarcely less so. No age was spared by the scourge. Babies soon became quite insupportable, though till now so easy to bring up; and for the first time Honore Syntax, the judge, was obliged to apply the rod to his youthful offspring.

There was a kind of insurrection at the high school, and the dictionaries became formidable missiles in the classes. The scholars would not submit to be shut in, and, besides, the infection took the teachers themselves, who overwhelmed the boys and girls with extravagant tasks and punishments.

Another strange phenomenon occurred. All these Quiquendonians, so sober before, whose chief food had been whipped creams, committed wild excesses in their eating and drinking. Their usual regimen no longer sufficed. Each stomach was transformed into a gulf, and it became necessary to fill this gulf by the most energetic means. The consumption of the town was trebled. Instead of two repasts they had six. Many cases of indigestion were reported. The Counsellor Niklausse could not satisfy his hunger. Van Tricasse found it impossible to assuage his thirst, and remained in a state of rabid semi-intoxication.

In short, the most alarming symptoms manifested themselves and increased from day to day. Drunken people staggered in the streets, and these were often citizens of high position.

Dominique Custos, the physician, had plenty to do with the heartburns, inflammations, and nervous affections, which proved to what a strange degree the nerves of the people had been irritated.

There were daily quarrels and altercations in the once deserted but now crowded streets of Quiquendone; for nobody could any longer stay at home. It was necessary to establish a new police force to control the disturbers of the public peace. A prison-cage was established in the Town Hall, and speedily became full, night and day, of refractory offenders. Commissary Passauf was in despair.

A marriage was concluded in less than two months—such a thing had never been seen before. Yes, the son of Rupp, the schoolmaster, wedded the daughter of Augustine de Rovere, and that fifty-seven days only after he had petitioned for her hand and heart!

Other marriages were decided upon, which, in old times, would have remained in doubt and discussion for years. The burgomaster perceived that his own daughter, the charming Suzel, was escaping from his hands.

As for dear Tatanémance, she had dared to sound Commissary Passauf on the subject of a union, which seemed to her to combine every element of happiness, fortune, honour, youth!

At last—to reach the depths of abomination—a duel took place! Yes, a duel with pistols—horse-pistols—at seventy-five paces, with ball-cartridges. And between whom? Our readers will never believe!

Between M. Frantz Niklausse, the gentle angler, and young Simon Collaert, the wealthy banker's son.

And the cause of this duel was the burgomaster's daughter, for whom Simon discovered himself to be fired with passion, and whom he refused to yield to the claims of an audacious rival!

XI

IN WHICH THE QUIQUENDONIANS ADOPT A HEROIC RESOLUTION

We have seen to what a deplorable condition the people of Quiquendone were reduced. Their heads were in a ferment. They no longer knew or recognized themselves. The most peaceable citizens had become quarrelsome. If you looked at them askance, they would speedily send you a challenge. Some let their moustaches grow, and several—the most belligerent—curled them up at the ends.

This being their condition, the administration of the town and the maintenance of order in the streets became difficult tasks, for the government had not been organized for such a state of things. The burgomaster—that worthy Van Tricasse whom we have seen so placid, so dull, so incapable of coming to any decision—the burgomaster became intractable. His house resounded with the sharpness of his voice. He made twenty decisions a day, scolding his officials, and himself enforcing the regulations of his administration.

Ah, what a change! The amiable and tranquil mansion of the burgomaster, that good Flemish home—where was its former calm? What changes had taken place in your household economy! Madame Van Tricasse had become acrid, whimsical, harsh. Her husband sometimes succeeded in drowning her voice by talking louder than she, but could not silence her. The petulant humour of this worthy dame was excited by everything. Nothing went right. The servants offended her every moment. Tatanémance, her sister-in-law, who was not less irritable, replied sharply to her. M. Van Tricasse naturally supported Lotchè, his servant, as is the case in all good households; and this permanently exasperated Madame, who constantly disputed, discussed, and made scenes with her husband.

"What on earth is the matter with us?" cried the unhappy burgomaster. "What is this fire that is devouring us? Are we possessed with the devil? Ah, Madame Van Tricasse, Madame Van Tricasse, you will end by making me die before you, and thus violate all the traditions of the family!"

The reader will not have forgotten the strange custom by which M. Van Tricasse would become a widower and marry again, so as not to break the chain of descent.

Meanwhile, this disposition of all minds produced other curious effects worthy of note. This excitement, the cause of which has so far escaped us, brought about unexpected physiological changes. Talents, hitherto unrecognized, betrayed themselves. Aptitudes were suddenly revealed. Artists, before common-place, displayed new ability. Politicians and authors arose. Orators proved themselves equal to the most arduous debates, and on every question inflamed audiences which were quite ready to be inflamed. From the sessions of the council, this movement spread to the public political meetings, and a club was formed at Quiquendone; whilst twenty newspapers, the "Quiquendone Signal," the "Quiquendone Impartial," the "Quiquendone Radical," and so on, written in an inflammatory style, raised the most important questions.

But what about? you will ask. Apropos of everything, and of nothing; apropos of the Oudenarde tower, which was falling, and which some wished to pull down, and others to prop up; apropos of the police regulations issued by the council, which some obstinate citizens threatened to resist; apropos of the sweeping of the gutters, repairing the sewers, and so on. Nor did the enraged orators confine themselves to the internal administration of the town. Carried on by the current they went further, and essayed to plunge their fellow-citizens into the hazards of war.

Quiquendone had had for eight or nine hundred years a *casus belli* of the best quality; but she had preciously laid it up like a relic, and there had seemed some probability that it would become effete, and no longer serviceable.

This was what had given rise to the *casus belli*.

It is not generally known that Quiquendone, in this cosy corner of Flanders, lies next to the little town of Virgamen. The territories of the two communities are contiguous.

Well, in 1185, some time before Count Baldwin's departure to the Crusades, a Virgamen cow—not a cow belonging to a citizen, but a cow which was common property, let it be observed—audaciously ventured to pasture on the territory of Quiquendone. This unfortunate beast had scarcely eaten three mouthfuls; but the offence, the abuse, the crime—whatever you will—was committed and duly indicted, for the magistrates, at that time, had already begun to know how to write.

"We will take revenge at the proper moment," said simply Natalis Van Tricasse, the thirty-second predecessor of the burgomaster of this story, "and the Virgamenians will lose nothing by waiting."

The Virgamenians were forewarned. They waited thinking, without doubt, that the remembrance of the offence would fade away with the lapse of time; and really, for several centuries, they lived on good terms with their neighbours of Quiquendone.

But they counted without their hosts, or rather without this strange epidemic, which, radically changing the character of the Quiquendonians, aroused their dormant vengeance.

It was at the club of the Rue Monstrelet that the truculent orator Schut, abruptly introducing the subject to his hearers, inflamed them with the expressions and metaphors used on such occasions. He recalled the offence, the injury which had been done to Quiquendone, and which a nation "jealous of its rights" could not admit as a precedent; he showed the insult to be still existing, the wound still bleeding: he spoke of certain special head-shakings on the part of the people of Virgamen, which indicated in what degree of contempt they regarded the people of Quiquendone; he appealed to his fellow-citizens, who, unconsciously perhaps, had supported this mortal insult for long centuries; he adjured the "children of the ancient town" to have no other purpose than to obtain a substantial reparation. And, lastly, he made an appeal to "all the living energies of the nation!"

With what enthusiasm these words, so new to Quiquendonian ears, were greeted, may be surmised, but cannot be told. All the auditors rose, and with extended arms demanded war with loud cries. Never had the Advocate Schut achieved such a success, and it must be avowed that his triumphs were not few.

The burgomaster, the counsellor, all the notabilities present at this memorable meeting, would have vainly attempted to resist the popular outburst. Besides, they had no desire to do so, and cried as loud, if not louder, than the rest—

"To the frontier! To the frontier!"

As the frontier was but three kilometers from the walls of Quiquendone, it is certain that the Virgamenians ran a real danger, for they might easily be invaded without having had time to look about them.

Meanwhile, Josse Liefrinck, the worthy chemist, who alone had preserved his senses on this grave occasion, tried to make his fellow-citizens comprehend that guns, cannon, and generals were equally wanting to their design.

They replied to him, not without many impatient gestures, that these generals, cannons, and guns would be improvised; that the right and love of country sufficed, and rendered a people irresistible.

Hereupon the burgomaster himself came forward, and in a sublime harangue made short work of those pusillanimous people who disguise their fear under a veil of prudence, which veil he tore off with a patriotic hand.

At this sally it seemed as if the hall would fall in under the applause.

The vote was eagerly demanded, and was taken amid acclamations.

The cries of "To Virgamen! to Virgamen!" redoubled.

The burgomaster then took it upon himself to put the armies in motion, and in the name of the town he promised the honours of a triumph, such as was given in the times of the Romans to that one of its generals who should return victorious.

Meanwhile, Josse Liefrinck, who was an obstinate fellow, and did not regard himself as beaten, though he really had been, insisted on making another observation. He wished to remark that the triumph was only accorded at Rome to those victorious generals who had killed five thousand of the enemy.

"Well, well!" cried the meeting deliriously.

"And as the population of the town of Virgamen consists of but three thousand five hundred and seventy-five inhabitants, it would be difficult, unless the same person was killed several times—"

But they did not let the luckless logician finish, and he was turned out, hustled and bruised.

"Citizens," said Pulmacher the grocer, who usually sold groceries by retail, "whatever this cowardly apothecary may have said, I engage by myself to kill five thousand Virgamenians, if you will accept my services!"

"Five thousand five hundred!" cried a yet more resolute patriot.

"Six thousand six hundred!" retorted the grocer.

"Seven thousand!" cried Jean Orbideck, the confectioner of the Rue Hemling, who was on the road to a fortune by making whipped creams.

"Adjudged!" exclaimed the burgomaster Van Tricasse, on finding that no one else rose on the bid.

And this was how Jean Orbideck the confectioner became general-in-chief of the forces of Quiquendone.

XII

IN WHICH YGÈNE, THE ASSISTANT, GIVES A REASONABLE PIECE OF ADVICE, WHICH IS EAGERLY REJECTED BY DOCTOR OX

"Well, master," said Ygène next day, as he poured the pails of sulphuric acid into the troughs of the great battery.

"Well," resumed Doctor Ox, "was I not right? See to what not only the physical developments of a whole nation, but its morality, its dignity, its talents, its political sense, have come! It is only a question of molecules."

"No doubt; but—"

"But—"

"Do you not think that matters have gone far enough, and that these poor devils should not be excited beyond measure?"

"No, no!" cried the doctor; "no! I will go on to the end!"

"As you will, master; the experiment, however, seems to me conclusive, and I think it time to—"

"To—"

"To close the valve."

"You'd better!" cried Doctor Ox. "If you attempt it, I'll throttle you!"

XIII

IN WHICH IT IS ONCE MORE PROVED THAT BY TAKING HIGH GROUND ALL HUMAN LITTLENESSES MAY BE OVERLOOKED

"You say?" asked the Burgomaster Van Tricasse of the Counsellor Niklausse.

"I say that this war is necessary," replied Niklausse, firmly, "and that the time has come to avenge this insult."

"Well, I repeat to you," replied the burgomaster, tartly, "that if the people of Quiquendone do not profit by this occasion to vindicate their rights, they will be unworthy of their name."

"And as for me, I maintain that we ought, without delay, to collect our forces and lead them to the front."

"Really, monsieur, really!" replied Van Tricasse. "And do you speak thus to *me?*"

"To yourself, monsieur the burgomaster; and you shall hear the truth, unwelcome as it may be."

"And you shall hear it yourself, counsellor," returned Van Tricasse in a passion, "for it will come better from my mouth than from yours! Yes, monsieur, yes, any delay would be dishonourable. The town of Quiquendone has waited nine hundred years for the moment to take its revenge, and whatever you may say, whether it pleases you or not, we shall march upon the enemy."

"Ah, you take it thus!" replied Niklausse harshly. "Very well, monsieur, we will march without you, if it does not please you to go."

"A burgomaster's place is in the front rank, monsieur!"

"And that of a counsellor also, monsieur."

"You insult me by thwarting all my wishes," cried the burgomaster, whose fists seemed likely to hit out before long.

"And you insult me equally by doubting my patriotism," cried Niklausse, who was equally ready for a tussle.

"I tell you, monsieur, that the army of Quiquendone shall be put in motion within two days!"

"And I repeat to you, monsieur, that forty-eight hours shall not pass before we shall have marched upon the enemy!"

It is easy to see, from this fragment of conversation, that the two speakers supported exactly the same idea. Both wished for hostilities; but as their excitement disposed them to altercation, Niklausse would not listen to Van Tricasse, nor Van Tricasse to Niklausse. Had they been of contrary opinions on this grave question, had the burgomaster favoured war and the counsellor insisted on peace, the quarrel would not have been more violent. These two old friends gazed fiercely at each other. By the quickened beating of their hearts, their red faces, their contracted pupils, the trembling of their muscles, their harsh voices, it might be conjectured that they were ready to come to blows.

But the striking of a large clock happily checked the adversaries at the moment when they seemed on the point of assaulting each other.

"At last the hour has come!" cried the burgomaster.

"What hour?" asked the counsellor.

"The hour to go to the belfry tower."

"It is true, and whether it pleases you or not, I shall go, monsieur."

"And I too."

"Let us go!"

"Let us go!"

It might have been supposed from these last words that a collision had occurred, and that the adversaries were proceeding to a duel; but it was not so. It had been agreed that the burgomaster and the counsellor, as the two principal dignitaries of the town, should repair to the Town Hall, and there show themselves on the high tower which overlooked Quiquendone; that they should examine the surrounding country, so as to make the best strategetic plan for the advance of their troops.

Though they were in accord on this subject, they did not cease to quarrel bitterly as they went. Their loud voices were heard resounding in the streets; but all the passers-by were now accustomed to this; the exasperation of the dignitaries seemed quite natural, and no one took notice of it. Under the circumstances, a calm man would have been regarded as a monster.

The burgomaster and the counsellor, having reached the porch of the belfry, were in a paroxysm of fury. They were no longer red, but pale. This terrible discussion, though they had the same idea, had produced internal spasms, and every one knows that paleness shows that anger has reached its last limits.

At the foot of the narrow tower staircase there was a real explosion. Who should go up first? Who should first creep up the winding steps? Truth compels us to say that there was a tussle, and that the Counsellor Niklausse, forgetful of all that he owed to his superior, to the supreme magistrate of the town, pushed Van Tricasse violently back, and dashed up the staircase first.

Both ascended, denouncing and raging at each other at every step. It was to be feared that a terrible climax would occur on the summit of the tower, which rose three hundred and fifty-seven feet above the pavement.

The two enemies soon got out of breath, however, and in a little while, at the eightieth step, they began to move up heavily, breathing loud and short.

Then—was it because of their being out of breath?—their wrath subsided, or at least only betrayed itself by a succession of unseemly epithets. They became silent, and, strange to say, it seemed as if their excitement diminished as they ascended higher above the town. A sort of lull took place in their minds. Their brains became cooler, and simmered down like a coffee-pot when taken away from the fire. Why?

We cannot answer this "why"; but the truth is that, having reached a certain landing-stage, two hundred and sixty-six feet above ground, the two adversaries sat down and, really more calm, looked at each other without any anger in their faces.

"How high it is!" said the burgomaster, passing his handkerchief over his rubicund face.

"Very high!" returned the counsellor. "Do you know that we have gone fourteen feet higher than the Church of Saint Michael at Hamburg?"

"I know it," replied the burgomaster, in a tone of vanity very pardonable in the chief magistrate of Quiquendone.

The two notabilities soon resumed their ascent, casting curious glances through the loopholes pierced in the tower walls. The burgomaster had taken the head of the procession, without any remark on the part of the counsellor. It even happened that at about the three hundred and fourth step, Van Tricasse being completely tired out, Niklausse kindly pushed him from behind. The burgomaster offered no resistance to this, and, when he reached the platform of the tower, said graciously—

"Thanks, Niklausse; I will do the same for you one day."

A little while before it had been two wild beasts, ready to tear each other to pieces, who had presented themselves at the foot of the tower; it was now two friends who reached its summit.

The weather was superb. It was the month of May. The sun had absorbed all the vapours. What a pure and limpid atmosphere! The most minute objects over a broad space might be discerned. The walls of Virgamen, glistening in their whiteness,—its red, pointed roofs, its belfries shining in the sunlight—appeared a few miles off. And this was the town that was foredoomed to all the horrors of fire and pillage!

The burgomaster and the counsellor sat down beside each other on a small stone bench, like two worthy people whose souls were in close sympathy. As they recovered breath, they looked around; then, after a brief silence—

"How fine this is!" cried the burgomaster.

"Yes, it is admirable!" replied the counsellor. "Does it not seem to you, my good Van Tricasse, that humanity is destined to dwell rather at such heights, than to crawl about on the surface of our globe?"

"I agree with you, honest Niklausse," returned the burgomaster, "I agree with you. You seize sentiment better when you get clear of nature. You breathe it in every sense! It is at such heights that philosophers should be formed, and that sages should live, above the miseries of this world!"

"Shall we go around the platform?" asked the counsellor.

"Let us go around the platform," replied the burgomaster.

And the two friends, arm in arm, and putting, as formerly, long pauses between their questions and answers, examined every point of the horizon.

"It is at least seventeen years since I have ascended the belfry tower," said Van Tricasse.

"I do not think I ever came up before," replied Niklausse; "and I regret it, for the view from this height is sublime! Do you see, my friend, the pretty stream of the Vaar, as it winds among the trees?"

"And, beyond, the heights of Saint Hermandad! How gracefully they shut in the horizon! Observe that border of green trees, which Nature has so picturesquely arranged! Ah, Nature, Nature, Niklausse! Could the hand of man ever hope to rival her?"

"It is enchanting, my excellent friend," replied the counsellor. "See the flocks and herds lying in the verdant pastures,—the oxen, the cows, the sheep!"

"And the labourers going to the fields! You would say they were Arcadian shepherds; they only want a bagpipe!"

"And over all this fertile country the beautiful blue sky, which no vapour dims! Ah, Niklausse, one might become a poet here! I do not understand why Saint Simeon Stylites was not one of the greatest poets of the world."

"It was because, perhaps, his column was not high enough," replied the counsellor, with a gentle smile.

At this moment the chimes of Quiquendone rang out. The clear bells played one of their most melodious airs. The two friends listened in ecstasy.

Then in his calm voice, Van Tricasse said,—

"But what, friend Niklausse, did we come to the top of this tower to do?"

"In fact," replied the counsellor, "we have permitted ourselves to be carried away by our reveries—"

"What did we come here to do?" repeated the burgomaster.

"We came," said Niklausse, "to breathe this pure air, which human weaknesses have not corrupted."

"Well, shall we descend, friend Niklausse?"

"Let us descend, friend Van Tricasse."

They gave a parting glance at the splendid panorama which was spread before their eyes; then the burgomaster passed down first, and began to descend with a slow and measured pace. The counsellor followed a few steps behind. They reached the landing-stage at which they had stopped on ascending. Already their cheeks began to redden. They tarried a moment, then resumed their descent.

In a few moments Van Tricasse begged Niklausse to go more slowly, as he felt him on his heels, and it "worried him." It even did more than worry him; for twenty steps lower down he ordered the counsellor to stop, that he might get on some distance ahead.

The counsellor replied that he did not wish to remain with his leg in the air to await the good pleasure of the burgomaster, and kept on.

Van Tricasse retorted with a rude expression.

The counsellor responded by an insulting allusion to the burgomaster's age, destined as he was, by his family traditions, to marry a second time.

The burgomaster went down twenty steps more, and warned Niklausse that this should not pass thus.

Niklausse replied that, at all events, he would pass down first; and, the space being very narrow, the two dignitaries came into collision, and found themselves in utter darkness. The words "blockhead" and "booby" were the mildest which they now applied to each other.

"We shall see, stupid beast!" cried the burgomaster,—"we shall see what figure you will make in this war, and in what rank you will march!"

"In the rank that precedes yours, you silly old fool!" replied Niklausse.

Then there were other cries, and it seemed as if bodies were rolling over each other. What was going on? Why were these dispositions so quickly changed? Why were the gentle sheep of the tower's summit metamorphosed into tigers two hundred feet below it?

However this might be, the guardian of the tower, hearing the noise, opened the door, just at the moment when the two adversaries, bruised, and with protruding eyes, were in the act of tearing each other's hair—fortunately they wore wigs.

"You shall give me satisfaction for this!" cried the burgomaster, shaking his fist under his adversary's nose.

"Whenever you please!" growled the Counsellor Niklausse, attempting to respond with a vigorous kick.

The guardian, who was himself in a passion—I cannot say why—thought the scene a very natural one. I know not what excitement urged him to take part in it, but he controlled himself, and went off to announce throughout the neighbourhood that a hostile meeting was about to take place between the Burgomaster Van Tricasse and the Counsellor Niklausse.

XIV

IN WHICH MATTERS GO SO FAR THAT THE INHABITANTS OF QUIQUENDONE, THE READER, AND EVEN THE AUTHOR, DEMAND AN IMMEDIATE DENOUEMENT

The last incident proves to what a pitch of excitement the Quiquendonians had been wrought. The two oldest friends in the town, and the most gentle—before the advent of the epidemic, to reach this degree of violence! And that, too, only a few minutes after their old mutual sympathy, their amiable instincts, their contemplative habit, had been restored at the summit of the tower!

On learning what was going on, Doctor Ox could not contain his joy. He resisted the arguments which Ygène, who saw what a serious turn affairs were taking, addressed to him. Besides, both of them were infected by the general fury. They were not less excited than the rest of the population, and they ended by quarrelling as violently as the burgomaster and the counsellor.

Besides, one question eclipsed all others, and the intended duels were postponed to the issue of the Virgamenian difficulty. No man had the right to shed his blood uselessly, when it belonged, to the last drop, to his country in danger. The affair was, in short, a grave one, and there was no withdrawing from it.

The Burgomaster Van Tricasse, despite the warlike ardour with which he was filled, had not thought it best to throw himself upon the enemy without warning him. He had, therefore, through the medium of the rural policeman, Hottering, sent to demand reparation of the Virgamenians for the offence committed, in 1195, on the Quiquendonian territory.

The authorities of Virgamen could not at first imagine of what the envoy spoke, and the latter, despite his official character, was conducted back to the frontier very cavalierly.

Van Tricasse then sent one of the aides-de-camp of the confectioner-general, citizen Hildevert Shuman, a manufacturer of barley-sugar, a very firm and energetic man, who carried to the authorities of Virgamen the original minute of the indictment drawn up in 1195 by order of the Burgomaster Natalis Van Tricasse.

The authorities of Virgamen burst out laughing, and served the aide-de-camp in the same manner as the rural policeman.

The burgomaster then assembled the dignitaries of the town.

A letter, remarkably and vigorously drawn up, was written as an ultimatum; the cause of quarrel was plainly stated, and a delay of twenty-four hours was accorded to the guilty city in which to repair the outrage done to Quiquendone.

The letter was sent off, and returned a few hours afterwards, torn to bits, which made so many fresh insults. The Virgamenians knew of old the forbearance and equanimity of the Quiquendonians, and made sport of them and their demand, of their *casus belli* and their *ultimatum*.

There was only one thing left to do—to have recourse to arms, to invoke the God of battles, and, after the Prussian fashion, to hurl themselves upon the Virgamenians Before the latter could be prepared.

This decision was made by the council in solemn conclave, in which cries, objurgations, and menacing gestures were mingled with unexampled violence. An assembly of idiots, a congress of madmen, a club of maniacs, would not have been more tumultuous.

As soon as the declaration of war was known, General Jean Orbideck assembled his troops, perhaps two thousand three hundred and ninety-three combatants from a population of two thousand three hundred and ninety-three souls. The women, the children, the old men, were joined with the able-bodied males. The guns of the town had been put under requisition. Five had been found, two of which were without cocks, and these had been distributed to the advance-guard. The artillery was composed of the old culverin of the château, taken in 1339 at the attack on Quesnoy, one of the first occasions of the use of cannon in history, and which had not been fired off for five centuries. Happily for those who were appointed to take it in charge there were no projectiles with which to load it; but such as it was, this engine might well impose on the enemy. As for side-arms, they had been taken from the museum of antiquities—flint hatchets, helmets, Frankish battle-axes, javelins, halberds, rapiers, and so on; and also in those domestic arsenals commonly known as "cupboards" and "kitchens." But courage, the right, hatred of the foreigner, the yearning for vengeance, were to take the place of more perfect engines, and to replace—at least it was hoped so—the modern mitrailleuses and breech-loaders.

The troops were passed in review. Not a citizen failed at the roll-call. General Orbideck, whose seat on horseback was far from firm, and whose steed was a vicious beast, was thrown three times in front of the army; but he got up again without injury, and this was regarded as a favourable omen. The burgomaster, the counsellor, the civil commissary, the chief justice, the school-teacher, the banker, the rector—in short, all the notabilities of the town—marched at the head. There were no tears shed, either by mothers, sisters, or daughters. They urged on their husbands, fathers, brothers, to the combat, and even followed them and formed the rear-guard, under the orders of the courageous Madame Van Tricasse.

The crier, Jean Mistrol, blew his trumpet; the army moved off, and directed itself, with ferocious cries, towards the Oudenarde gate.

★   ★   ★

At the moment when the head of the column was about to pass the walls of the town, a man threw himself before it.

"Stop! stop! Fools that you are!" he cried. "Suspend your blows! Let me shut the valve! You are not changed in nature! You are good citizens, quiet and peaceable! If you are so excited, it is my master, Doctor Ox's, fault! It is an experiment! Under the pretext of lighting your streets with oxyhydric gas, he has saturated—"

The assistant was beside himself; but he could not finish. At the instant that the doctor's secret was about to escape his lips, Doctor Ox himself pounced upon the unhappy Ygène in an indescribable rage, and shut his mouth by blows with his fist.

It was a battle. The burgomaster, the counsellor, the dignitaries, who had stopped short on Ygène's sudden appearance, carried away in turn by their exasperation, rushed upon the two strangers, without waiting to hear either the one or the other.

Doctor Ox and his assistant, beaten and lashed, were about to be dragged, by order of Van Tricasse, to the round-house, when—

XV

IN WHICH THE DENOUEMENT TAKES PLACE

When a formidable explosion resounded. All the atmosphere which enveloped Quiquendone seemed on fire. A flame of an intensity and vividness quite unwonted shot up into the heavens like a meteor. Had it been night, this flame would have been visible for ten leagues around.

The whole army of Quiquendone fell to the earth, like an army of monks. Happily there were no victims; a few scratches and slight hurts were the only result. The confectioner, who, as chance would have it, had not fallen from his horse this time, had his plume singed, and escaped without any further injury.

What had happened?

Something very simple, as was soon learned; the gasworks had just blown up. During the absence of the doctor and his assistant, some careless mistake had no doubt been made. It is not known how or why a communication had been established between the reservoir which contained the oxygen and that which enclosed the hydrogen. An explosive mixture had resulted from the union of these two gases, to which fire had accidentally been applied.

This changed everything; but when the army got upon its feet again, Doctor Ox and his assistant Ygène had disappeared.

XVI

IN WHICH THE INTELLIGENT READER SEES THAT HE HAS GUESSED CORRECTLY, DESPITE ALL THE AUTHOR'S PRECAUTIONS

After the explosion, Quiquendone immediately became the peaceable, phlegmatic, and Flemish town it formerly was.

After the explosion, which indeed did not cause a very lively sensation, each one, without knowing why, mechanically took his way home, the burgomaster leaning on the counsellor's arm, the advocate Schut going arm in arm with Custos the doctor, Frantz Niklausse walking with equal familiarity with Simon Collaert, each going tranquilly, noiselessly, without even being conscious of what had happened, and having already forgotten Virgamen and their revenge. The general returned to his confections, and his aide-de-camp to the barley-sugar.

Thus everything had become calm again; the old existence had been resumed by men and beasts, beasts and plants; even by the tower of Oudenarde gate, which the explosion—these explosions are sometimes astonishing—had set upright again!

And from that time never a word was spoken more loudly than another, never a discussion took place in the town of Quiquendone. There were no more politics, no more clubs, no more trials, no more policemen! The post of the Commissary Passauf became once more a sinecure, and if his salary was not reduced, it was because the burgomaster and the counsellor could not make up their minds to decide upon it.

From time to time, indeed, Passauf flitted, without any one suspecting it, through the dreams of the inconsolable Tatanémance.

As for Frantz's rival, he generously abandoned the charming Suzel to her lover, who hastened to wed her five or six years after these events.

And as for Madame Van Tricasse, she died ten years later, at the proper time, and the burgomaster married Mademoiselle Pelágie Van Tricasse, his cousin, under excellent conditions—for the happy mortal who should succeed him.

XVII

IN WHICH DOCTOR OX'S THEORY IS EXPLAINED

What, then, had this mysterious Doctor Ox done? Tried a fantastic experiment—nothing more.

After having laid down his gas-pipes, he had saturated, first the public buildings, then the private dwellings, finally the streets of Quiquendone, with pure oxygen, without letting in the least atom of hydrogen.

This gas, tasteless and odorless, spread in generous quantity through the atmosphere, causes, when it is breathed, serious agitation to the human organism. One who lives in an air saturated with oxygen grows excited, frantic, burns!

You scarcely return to the ordinary atmosphere before you return to your usual state. For instance, the counsellor and the burgomaster at the top of the belfry were themselves again, as the oxygen is kept, by its weight, in the lower strata of the air.

But one who lives under such conditions, breathing this gas which transforms the body physiologically as well as the soul, dies speedily, like a madman.

It was fortunate, then, for the Quiquendonians, that a providential explosion put an end to this dangerous experiment, and abolished Doctor Ox's gas-works.

To conclude: Are virtue, courage, talent, wit, imagination—are all these qualities or faculties only a question of oxygen?

Such is Doctor Ox's theory; but we are not bound to accept it, and for ourselves we utterly reject it, in spite of the curious experiment of which the worthy old town of Quiquendone was the theatre.

The Monster-Maker

W.C. Morrow

William Chambers Morrow (1853–1923) lived most of his life in the San Francisco area where he was an acquaintance of Ambrose Bierce and sold stories regularly to William Randolph Hearst's San Francisco Examiner. *This story, which was first published in the October 15, 1887 issue of* The Argonaut, *builds on some of the same concepts of scientific reanimation of the dead first addressed in Mary Shelley's* Frankenstein; or, The Modern Prometheus. *Like Shelley's tale, Morrow's is a skillful fusion of horror and science fiction.*

A young man of refined appearance, but evidently suffering great mental distress, presented himself one morning at the residence of a singular old man, who was known as a surgeon of remarkable skill. The house was a queer and primitive brick affair, entirely out of date, and tolerable only in the decayed part of the city in which it stood. It was large, gloomy, and dark, and had long corridors and dismal rooms; and it was absurdly large for the small family—man and wife—that occupied it. The house described, the man is portrayed—but not the woman. He could be agreeable on occasion, but, for all that, he was but animated mystery. His wife was weak, wan, reticent, evidently miserable, and possibly living a life of dread or horror—perhaps witness of repulsive things, subject of anxieties, and victim of fear and tyranny; but there is a great deal of guessing in these assumptions. He was about sixty-five years of age and she about forty. He was lean, tall, and bald, with thin, smooth-shaven face, and very keen eyes; kept always at home, and was slovenly. The man was strong, the woman weak; he dominated, she suffered.

Although he was a surgeon of rare skill, his practice was almost nothing, for it was a rare occurrence that the few who knew of his great ability were brave enough to penetrate the gloom of his house, and when they did so it was with deaf ear turned to sundry ghoulish stories that were whispered concerning him. These were, in great part, but exaggerations of his experiments in vivisection; he was devoted to the science of surgery.

The young man who presented himself on the morning just mentioned was a handsome fellow, yet of evident weak character and unhealthy temperament—sensitive, and easily exalted or depressed. A single glance convinced the surgeon that his visitor was seriously affected in mind, for there was never bolder skull-grin of melancholia, fixed and irremediable.

A stranger would not have suspected any occupancy of the house. The street door—old, warped, and blistered by the sun—was locked, and the small, faded-green window-blinds were closed. The young man rapped at the door. No answer. He rapped again. Still no sign. He examined a slip of paper, glanced at the number on the house, and then, with the impatience of a child, he furiously kicked the door. There were signs of numerous other such kicks. A response came in the shape of a shuffling footstep in the hall, a turning of the rusty key, and a sharp face that peered through a cautious opening in the door.

"Are you the doctor?" asked the young man.

"Yes, yes! Come in," briskly replied the master of the house.

The young man entered. The old surgeon closed the door and carefully locked it. "This way," he said, advancing to a rickety flight of stairs. The young man followed. The surgeon led the way up the stairs, turned into a narrow, musty-smelling corridor at the left, traversed it, rattling the loose boards under his feet, at the farther end opened a door at the right, and beckoned his visitor to enter. The young man found himself in a pleasant room, furnished in antique fashion and with hard simplicity.

"Sit down," said the old man, placing a chair so that its occupant should face a window that looked out upon a dead wall about six feet from the house. He threw open the blind, and a pale light entered. He then seated himself near his visitor and directly facing him, and with a searching look, that had all the power of a microscope, he proceeded to diagnosticate the case.

"Well?" he presently asked.

The young man shifted uneasily in his seat.

"I—I have come to see you," he finally stammered, "because I'm in trouble."

"Ah!"

"Yes; you see, I—that is—I have given it up."

90

"Ah!" There was pity added to sympathy in the ejaculation.

"That's it. Given it up," added the visitor. He took from his pocket a roll of banknotes, and with the utmost deliberation he counted them out upon his knee. "Five thousand dollars," he calmly remarked. "That is for you. It's all I have; but I presume—I imagine—no; that is not the word—*assume*—yes; that's the word— assume that five thousand—is it really that much? Let me count." He counted again. "That five thousand dollars is a sufficient fee for what I want you to do."

The surgeon's lips curled pityingly—perhaps disdainfully also. "What do you want me to do?" he carelessly inquired.

The young man rose, looked around with a mysterious air, approached the surgeon, and laid the money across his knee. Then he stooped and whispered two words in the surgeon's ear.

These words produced an electric effect. The old man started violently; then, springing to his feet, he caught his visitor angrily, and transfixed him with a look that was as sharp as a knife. His eyes flashed, and he opened his mouth to give utterance to some harsh imprecation, when he suddenly checked himself. The anger left his face, and only pity remained. He relinquished his grasp, picked up the scattered notes, and, offering them to the visitor, slowly said:

"I do not want your money. You are simply foolish. You think you are in trouble. Well, you do not know what trouble is. Your only trouble is that you have not a trace of manhood in your nature. You are merely insane—I shall not say pusillanimous. You should surrender yourself to the authorities, and be sent to a lunatic asylum for proper treatment."

The young man keenly felt the intended insult, and his eyes flashed dangerously.

"You old dog—you insult me thus!" he cried. "Grand airs, these, you give yourself! Virtuously indignant, old murderer, you! Don't want my money, eh? When a man comes to you himself and wants it done, you fly into a passion and spurn his money; but let an enemy of his come and pay you, and you are only too willing. How many such jobs have you done in this miserable old hole? It is a good thing for you that the police have not run you down, and brought spade and shovel with them. Do you know what is said of you? Do you think you have kept your windows so closely shut that no sound has ever penetrated beyond them? Where do you keep your infernal implements?"

He had worked himself into a high passion. His voice was hoarse, loud, and rasping. His eyes, bloodshot, started from their sockets. His whole frame twitched, and his fingers writhed. But he was in the presence of a man infinitely his superior.

Two eyes, like those of a snake, burned two holes through him. An overmastering, inflexible presence confronted one weak and passionate. The result came.

"Sit down," commanded the stern voice of the surgeon.

It was the voice of father to child, of master to slave. The fury left the visitor, who, weak and overcome, fell upon a chair.

Meanwhile, a peculiar light had appeared in the old surgeon's face, the dawn of a strange idea; a gloomy ray, strayed from the fires of the bottomless pit; the baleful light that illumines the way of the enthusiast. The old man remained a moment in profound abstraction, gleams of eager intelligence bursting momentarily through the cloud of sombre meditation that covered his face. Then broke the broad light of a deep, impenetrable determination. There was something sinister in it, suggesting the sacrifice of something held sacred. After a struggle, mind had vanquished conscience.

Taking a piece of paper and a pencil, the surgeon carefully wrote answers to questions which he peremptorily addressed to his visitor, such as his name, age, place of residence, occupation, and the like, and the same inquiries concerning his parents, together with other particular matters.

"Does any one know you came to this house?" he asked.

"No."

"You swear it?"

"Yes."

"But your prolonged absence will cause alarm and lead to search."

"I have provided against that."

"How?"

"By depositing a note in the post, as I came along, announcing my intention to drown myself."

"The river will be dragged."

"What then?" asked the young man, shrugging his shoulders with careless indifference. "Rapid undercurrent, you know. A good many are never found."

There was a pause.

"Are you ready?" finally asked the surgeon.

"Perfectly." The answer was cool and determined.

The manner of the surgeon, however, showed much perturbation. The pallor that had come into his face at the moment his decision was formed became intense. A nervous tremulousness came over his frame. Above it all shone the light of enthusiasm.

"Have you a choice in the method?" he asked.

"Yes; extreme anaesthesia."

"With what agent?"

"The surest and quickest."

"Do you desire any—any subsequent disposition?"

"No; only nullification; simply a blowing out, as of a candle in the wind; a puff—then darkness, without a trace. A sense of your own safety may suggest the method. I leave it to you."

"No delivery to your friends?"

"None whatever."

Another pause.

"Did you say you are quite ready?" asked the surgeon.

"Quite ready."

"And perfectly willing?"

"Anxious."

"Then wait a moment."

With this request the old surgeon rose to his feet and stretched himself. Then with the stealthiness of a cat he opened the door and peered into the hall, listening intently. There was no sound. He softly closed the door and locked it. Then he closed the window-blinds and locked them. This done, he opened a door leading into an adjoining room, which, though it had no window, was lighted by means of a small skylight. The young man watched closely. A strange change had come over him. While his determination had not one whit lessened, a look of great relief came into his face, displacing the haggard, despairing look of a half-hour before. Melancholic then, he was ecstatic now.

The opening of the second door disclosed a curious sight. In the centre of the room, directly under the skylight, was an operating-table, such as is used by demonstrators of anatomy. A glass case against the wall held surgical instruments of every kind. Hanging in another case were human skeletons of various sizes. In sealed jars, arranged on shelves, were monstrosities of divers kinds preserved in alcohol. There were also, among innumerable other articles scattered about the room, a manikin, a stuffed cat, a desiccated human heart, plaster casts of various parts of the body, numerous charts, and a large assortment of drugs and chemicals. There was also a lounge, which could be opened to form a couch. The surgeon opened it and moved the operating-table aside, giving its place to the lounge.

"Come in," he called to his visitor.

The young man obeyed without the least hesitation.

"Take off your coat."

He complied.

"Lie down on that lounge."

In a moment the young man was stretched at full length, eyeing the surgeon. The latter undoubtedly was suffering under great excitement, but he did not waver; his movements were sure and quick. Selecting a bottle containing a liquid, he carefully measured out a certain quantity. While doing this he asked:

"Have you ever had any irregularity of the heart?"

"No."

The answer was prompt, but it was immediately followed by a quizzical look in the speaker's face.

"I presume," he added, "you mean by your question that it might be dangerous to give me a certain drug. Under the circumstances, however, I fail to see any relevancy in your question."

This took the surgeon aback; but he hastened to explain that he did not wish to inflict unnecessary pain, and hence his question.

He placed the glass on a stand, approached his visitor, and carefully examined his pulse.

"Wonderful!" he exclaimed.

"Why?"

"It is perfectly normal."

"Because I am wholly resigned. Indeed, it has been long since I knew such happiness. It is not active, but infinitely sweet."

"You have no lingering desire to retract?"

"None whatever."

The surgeon went to the stand and returned with the draught.

"Take this," he said, kindly.

The young man partially raised himself and took the glass in his hand. He did not show the vibration of a single nerve. He drank the liquid, draining the last drop. Then he returned the glass with a smile.

"Thank you," he said; "you are the noblest man that lives. May you always prosper and be happy! You are my benefactor, my liberator. Bless you, bless you! You reach down from your seat with the gods and lift me up into glorious peace and rest. I love you—I love you with all my heart!"

These words, spoken earnestly, in a musical, low voice, and accompanied with a smile of ineffable tenderness, pierced the old man's heart. A suppressed convulsion swept over him; intense anguish wrung his vitals; perspiration trickled down his face. The young man continued to smile.

"Ah, it does me good!" said he.

The surgeon, with a strong effort to control himself, sat down upon the edge of the lounge and took his visitor's wrist, counting the pulse.

"How long will it take?" the young man asked.

"Ten minutes. Two have passed." The voice was hoarse.

"Ah, only eight minutes more! . . . Delicious, delicious! I feel it coming. . . . What was that? . . . Ah, I understand. Music. . . . Beautiful! . . . Coming, coming. . . . Is that—that—water? . . . Trickling? Dripping? Doctor!"

"Well?"

"Thank you, . . . thank you. . . . Noble man, . . . my saviour, . . . my bene . . . bene . . . factor. . . . Trickling, . . . trickling . . . Dripping, dripping . . . Doctor!"

"Well?"

"Doctor!"

"Past hearing," muttered the surgeon.

"Doctor!"

"And blind."

Response was made by a firm grasp of the hand.

"Doctor!"

"And numb."

"Doctor!"

The old man watched and waited.

"Dripping, . . . dripping."

The last drop had run. There was a sigh, and nothing more.

The surgeon laid down the hand.

"The first step," he groaned, rising to his feet; then his whole frame dilated. "The first step—the most difficult, yet the simplest. A providential delivery into my hands of that for which I have hungered for forty years. No withdrawal now! It is possible, because scientific; rational, but perilous. If I succeed—*if?* I *shall* succeed. I *will* succeed. . . . And after success—what? . . . Yes; what? Publish the plan and the result? The gallows . . . . So long as *it* shall exist, . . . and *I* exist, the gallows. That much. . . . But how account for its presence? Ah, that pinches hard! I must trust to the future."

He tore himself from the revery and started.

"I wonder if *she* heard or saw anything."

With that reflection he cast a glance upon the form on the lounge, and then left the room, locked the door, locked also the door of the outer room, walked down two or three corridors, penetrated to a remote part of the house, and rapped at a

95

door. It was opened by his wife. He, by this time, had regained complete mastery over himself.

"I thought I heard some one in the house just now," he said, "but I can find no one."

"I heard nothing."

He was greatly relieved.

"I did hear some one knock at the door less than an hour ago," she resumed, "and heard you speak, I think. Did he come in?"

"No."

The woman glanced at his feet and seemed perplexed.

"I am almost certain," she said, "that I heard foot-falls in the house, and yet I see that you are wearing slippers."

"Oh, I had on my shoes then!"

"That explains it," said the woman, satisfied; "I think the sound you heard must have been caused by rats."

"Ah, that was it!" exclaimed the surgeon. Leaving, he closed the door, reopened it, and said, "I do not wish to be disturbed to-day." He said to himself, as he went down the hall, "All is clear there."

He returned to the room in which his visitor lay, and made a careful examination.

"Splendid specimen!" he softly exclaimed; "every organ sound, every function perfect; fine, large frame; well-shaped muscles, strong and sinewy; capable of wonderful development—if given opportunity. . . . I have no doubt it can be done. Already I have succeeded with a dog—a task less difficult than this, for in a man the cerebrum overlaps the cerebellum, which is not the case with a dog. This gives a wide range for accident, with but one opportunity in a lifetime! In the cerebrum, the intellect and the affections; in the cerebellum, the senses and the motor forces; in the medulla oblongata, control of the diaphragm. In these two latter lie all the essentials of simple existence. The cerebrum is merely an adornment; that is to say, reason and the affections are almost purely ornamental. I have already proved it. My dog, with its cerebrum removed, was idiotic, but it retained its physical senses to a certain degree."

While thus ruminating he made careful preparations. He moved the couch, replaced the operating-table under the skylight, selected a number of surgical instruments, prepared certain drug-mixtures, and arranged water, towels, and all the accessories of a tedious surgical operation. Suddenly he burst into laughter.

"Poor fool!" he exclaimed. "Paid me five thousand dollars to kill him! Didn't have the courage to snuff his own candle! Singular, singular, the queer freaks these madmen have! You thought you were dying, poor idiot! Allow me to inform you, sir, that you are as much alive at this moment as ever you were in your life. But it will be all the same to you. You shall never be more conscious than you are now; and for all practical purposes, so far as they concern you, you are dead henceforth, though you shall live. By the way, how should you feel *without a head?* Ha, ha, ha! . . . But that's a sorry joke."

He lifted the unconscious form from the lounge and laid it upon the operating-table.

★   ★   ★

About three years afterwards the following conversation was held between a captain of police and a detective:

"She may be insane," suggested the captain.

"I think she is."

"And yet you credit her story!"

"I do."

"Singular!"

"Not at all. I myself have learned something."

"What!"

"Much, in one sense; little, in another. You have heard those queer stories of her husband. Well, they are all nonsensical—probably with one exception. He is generally a harmless old fellow, but peculiar. He has performed some wonderful surgical operations. The people in his neighborhood are ignorant, and they fear him and wish to be rid of him; hence they tell a great many lies about him, and they come to believe their own stories. The one important thing that I have learned is that he is almost insanely enthusiastic on the subject of surgery—especially experimental surgery; and with an enthusiast there is hardly such a thing as a scruple. It is this that gives me confidence in the woman's story."

"You say she appeared to be frightened?"

"Doubly so—first, she feared that her husband would learn of her betrayal of him; second, the discovery itself had terrified her."

"But her report of this discovery is very vague," argued the captain. "He conceals everything from her. She is merely guessing."

"In part—yes; in other part—no. She heard the sounds distinctly, though she did not see clearly. Horror closed her eyes. What she thinks she saw is, I admit, preposterous; but she undoubtedly saw something extremely frightful. There are many peculiar little circumstances. He has eaten with her but few times during the last three years, and nearly always carries his food to his private rooms. She says that he either consumes an enormous quantity, throws much away, or is feeding something that eats prodigiously. He explains this to her by saying that he has animals with which he experiments. This is not true. Again, he always keeps the door to these rooms carefully locked; and not only that, but he has had the doors doubled and otherwise strengthened, and has heavily barred a window that looks from one of the rooms upon a dead wall a few feet distant."

"What does it mean?" asked the captain.

"A prison."

"For animals, perhaps."

"Certainly not."

"Why!"

"Because, in the first place, cages would have been better; in the second place, the security that he has provided is infinitely greater than that required for the confinement of ordinary animals."

"All this is easily explained: he has a violent lunatic under treatment."

"I had thought of that, but such is not the fact."

"How do you know?"

"By reasoning thus: He has always refused to treat cases of lunacy; he confines himself to surgery; the walls are not padded, for the woman has heard sharp blows upon them; no human strength, however morbid, could possibly require such resisting strength as has been provided; he would not be likely to conceal a lunatic's confinement from the woman; no lunatic could consume all the food that he provides; so extremely violent mania as these precautions indicate could not continue three years; if there is a lunatic in the case it is very probable that there should have been communication with some one outside concerning the patient, and there has been none; the woman has listened at the keyhole and has heard no human voice within; and last, we have heard the woman's vague description of what she saw."

"You have destroyed every possible theory," said the captain, deeply interested, "and have suggested nothing new."

"Unfortunately, I cannot; but the truth may be very simple, after all. The old surgeon is so peculiar that I am prepared to discover something remarkable."

"Have you suspicions?"

"I have."

"Of what?"

"A crime. The woman suspects it."

"And betrays it?"

"Certainly, because it is so horrible that her humanity revolts; so terrible that her whole nature demands of her that she hand over the criminal to the law; so frightful that she is in mortal terror; so awful that it has shaken her mind."

"What do you propose to do?" asked the captain.

"Secure evidence. I may need help."

"You shall have all the men you require. Go ahead, but be careful. You are on dangerous ground. You would be a mere plaything in the hands of that man."

Two days afterwards the detective again sought the captain.

"I have a queer document," he said, exhibiting torn fragments of paper, on which there was writing. "The woman stole it and brought it to me. She snatched a handful out of a book, getting only a part of each of a few leaves."

These fragments, which the men arranged as best they could, were (the detective explained) torn by the surgeon's wife from the first volume of a number of manuscript books which her husband had written on one subject—the very one that was the cause of her excitement. "About the time that he began a certain experiment three years ago," continued the detective, "he removed everything from the suite of two rooms containing his study and his operating-room. In one of the bookcases that he removed to a room across the passage was a drawer, which he kept locked, but which he opened from time to time. As is quite common with such pieces of furniture, the lock of the drawer is a very poor one; and so the woman, while making a thorough search yesterday, found a key on her bunch that fitted this lock. She opened the drawer, drew out the bottom book of a pile (so that its mutilation would more likely escape discovery), saw that it might contain a clew, and tore out a handful of the leaves. She had barely replaced the book, locked the drawer, and made her escape when her husband appeared. He hardly ever allows her to be out of his sight when she is in that part of the house."

The fragments read as follows: ". . . the motory nerves. I had hardly dared to hope for such a result, although inductive reasoning had convinced me of its possibility, my only doubt having been on the score of my lack of skill. Their operation has been only slightly impaired, and even this would not have been the case had the operation been performed in infancy, before the intellect had sought and obtained recognition as an essential part of the whole. Therefore I state, as a proved fact, that the cells of the motory nerves have inherent forces sufficient to the purposes of those nerves. But hardly so with the sensory nerves. These latter are, in fact, an offshoot of the former, evolved from them by natural (though not essential) heterogeneity, and to a certain extent are dependent on the evolution and expansion of a contemporaneous tendency, that developed into mentality, or mental function. Both of these latter tendencies, these evolvements, are merely refinements of the motory system, and not independent entities; that is to say, they are the blossoms of a plant that propagates from its roots. The motory system is the first . . . nor am I surprised that such prodigious muscular energy is developing. It promises yet to surpass the wildest dreams of human strength. I account for it thus: The powers of assimilation had reached their full development. They had formed the habit of doing a certain amount of work. They sent their products to all parts of the system. As a result of my operation the consumption of these products was reduced fully one-half; that is to say, about one-half of the demand for them was withdrawn. But force of habit required the production to proceed. This production was strength, vitality, energy. Thus double the usual quantity of this strength, this energy, was stored in the remaining . . . developed a tendency that did surprise me. Nature, no longer suffering the distraction of extraneous interferences, and at the same time being cut in two (as it were), with reference to this case, did not fully adjust herself to the new situation, as does a magnet, which, when divided at the point of equilibrium, renews itself in its two fragments by investing each with opposite poles; but, on the contrary, being severed from laws that theretofore had controlled her, and possessing still that mysterious tendency to develop into something more potential and complex, she blindly (having lost her lantern) pushed her demands for material that would secure this development, and as blindly used it when it was given her. Hence this marvellous voracity, this insatiable hunger, this wonderful ravenousness; and hence also (there being nothing but the physical part to receive this vast storing of energy) this strength that is becoming almost hourly herculean, almost daily appalling. It is becoming a serious . . . narrow escape to-day. By some means, while I was absent, it unscrewed the stopper of the silver feeding-pipe (which I have already herein termed 'the artificial mouth'), and, in one of its curious antics, allowed all the chyle to escape from its stomach through the tube. Its hunger then became intense—I may say furious. I placed my hands upon it to push it into a chair, when, feeling my touch, it caught me, clasped me around the neck, and would have crushed me to death instantly had I not slipped from its powerful grasp. Thus I always had to be on my guard. I have provided the screw stopper with a spring catch, and . . . usually docile when not hungry; slow and heavy in its movements, which are, of course, purely unconscious; any apparent excitement in movement being due to local irregularities in the blood-supply of the cerebellum, which, if I did not have it enclosed in a silver case that is immovable, I should expose and . . ."

The captain looked at the detective with a puzzled air.

"I don't understand it at all," said he.

"Nor I," agreed the detective.

"What do you propose to do?"

"Make a raid."

"Do you want a man?"

"Three. The strongest men in your district."

"Why, the surgeon is old and weak!"

"Nevertheless, I want three strong men; and for that matter, prudence really advises me to take twenty."

★   ★   ★

At one o'clock the next morning a cautious, scratching sound might have been heard in the ceiling of the surgeon's operating-room. Shortly afterwards the skylight sash was carefully raised and laid aside. A man peered into the opening. Nothing could be heard.

"That is singular," thought the detective.

He cautiously lowered himself to the floor by a rope, and then stood for some moments listening intently. There was a dead silence. He shot the slide of a dark-lantern, and rapidly swept the room with the light. It was bare, with the exception of a strong iron staple and ring, screwed to the floor in the centre of the room, with a heavy chain attached. The detective then turned his attention to the outer room; it was perfectly bare. He was deeply perplexed. Returning to the inner room, he called softly to the men to descend. While they were thus occupied he re-entered the outer room and examined the door. A glance sufficed. It was kept closed by a spring attachment, and was locked with a strong spring-lock that could be drawn from the inside.

"The bird has just flown," mused the detective. "A singular accident! The discovery and proper use of this thumb-bolt might not have happened once in fifty years, if my theory is correct."

By this time the men were behind him. He noiselessly drew the spring-bolt, opened the door, and looked out into the hall. He heard a peculiar sound. It was as though a gigantic lobster was floundering and scrambling in some distant part of the old house. Accompanying this sound was a loud, whistling breathing, and frequent rasping gasps.

These sounds were heard by still another person—the surgeon's wife; for they originated very near her rooms, which were a considerable distance from her husband's. She had been sleeping lightly, tortured by fear and harassed by frightful dreams. The conspiracy into which she had recently entered, for the destruction of

101

her husband, was a source of great anxiety. She constantly suffered from the most gloomy forebodings, and lived in an atmosphere of terror. Added to the natural horror of her situation were those countless sources of fear which a fright-shaken mind creates and then magnifies. She was, indeed, in a pitiable state, having been driven first by terror to desperation, and then to madness.

Startled thus out of fitful slumber by the noise at her door, she sprang from her bed to the floor, every terror that lurked in her acutely tense mind and diseased imagination starting up and almost overwhelming her. The idea of flight—one of the strongest of all instincts—seized upon her, and she ran to the door, beyond all control of reason. She drew the bolt and flung the door wide open, and then fled wildly down the passage, the appalling hissing and rasping gurgle ringing in her ears apparently with a thousandfold intensity. But the passage was in absolute darkness, and she had not taken a half-dozen steps when she tripped upon an unseen object on the floor. She fell headlong upon it, encountering in it a large, soft, warm substance that writhed and squirmed, and from which came the sounds that had awakened her. Instantly realizing her situation, she uttered a shriek such as only an unnamable terror can inspire. But hardly had her cry started the echoes in the empty corridor when it was suddenly stifled. Two prodigious arms had closed upon her and crushed the life out of her.

The cry performed the office of directing the detective and his assistants, and it also aroused the old surgeon, who occupied rooms between the officers and the object of their search. The cry of agony pierced him to the marrow, and a realization of the cause of it burst upon him with frightful force.

"It has come at last!" he gasped, springing from his bed.

Snatching from a table a dimly-burning lamp and a long knife which he had kept at hand for three years, he dashed into the corridor. The four officers had already started forward, but when they saw him emerge they halted in silence. In that moment of stillness the surgeon paused to listen. He heard the hissing sound and the clumsy floundering of a bulky, living object in the direction of his wife's apartments. It evidently was advancing towards him. A turn in the corridor shut out the view. He turned up the light, which revealed a ghastly pallor in his face.

"Wife!" he called.

There was no response. He hurriedly advanced, the four men following quietly. He turned the angle of the corridor, and ran so rapidly that by the time the officers had come in sight of him again he was twenty steps away. He ran past a huge, shapeless object, sprawling, crawling, and floundering along, and arrived at the body of his wife.

He gave one horrified glance at her face, and staggered away. Then a fury seized him. Clutching the knife firmly, and holding the lamp aloft, he sprang toward the ungainly object in the corridor. It was then that the officers, still advancing cautiously, saw a little more clearly, though still indistinctly, the object of the surgeon's fury, and the cause of the look of unutterable anguish in his face. The hideous sight caused them to pause. They saw what appeared to be a man, yet evidently was not a man; huge, awkward, shapeless; a squirming, lurching, stumbling mass, completely naked. It raised its broad shoulders. *It had no head,* but instead of it a small metallic ball surmounting its massive neck.

"Devil!" exclaimed the surgeon, raising the knife.

"Hold, there!" commanded a stern voice.

The surgeon quickly raised his eyes and saw the four officers, and for a moment fear paralyzed his arm.

"The police!" he gasped.

Then, with a look of redoubled fury, he sent the knife to the hilt into the squirming mass before him. The wounded monster sprang to its feet and wildly threw its arms about, meanwhile emitting fearful sounds from a silver tube through which it breathed. The surgeon aimed another blow, but never gave it. In his blind fury he lost his caution, and was caught in an iron grasp. The struggling threw the lamp some feet toward the officers, and it fell to the floor, shattered to pieces. Simultaneously with the crash the oil took fire, and the corridor was filled with flame. The officers could not approach. Before them was the spreading blaze, and secure behind it were two forms struggling in a fearful embrace. They heard cries and gasps, and saw the gleaming of a knife.

The wood in the house was old and dry. It took fire at once, and the flames spread with great rapidity. The four officers turned and fled, barely escaping with their lives. In an hour nothing remained of the mysterious old house and its inmates but a blackened ruin.

The Los Amigos Fiasco

SIR ARTHUR CONAN DOYLE

Before he became a professional writer and earned renown as the creator of Sherlock Holmes, Sir Arthur Conan Doyle (1859–1930) practiced medicine for nearly a decade. This story, which first appeared in the December 1892 issue of The Idler, *is a tongue-in-cheek study of the then-unexplored consequences of electrocution as a means of capital punishment. Doyle later collected it in* Round the Red Lamp *(1894), a collection of his stories based on medical themes.*

I used to be the leading practitioner of Los Amigos. Of course, everyone has heard of the great electrical generating gear there. The town is wide spread, and there are dozens of little townlets and villages all round, which receive their supply from the same centre, so that the works are on a very large scale. The Los Amigos folk say that they are the largest upon earth, but then we claim that for everything in Los Amigos except the gaol and the death-rate. Those are said to be the smallest.

Now, with so fine an electrical supply, it seemed to be a sinful waste of hemp that the Los Amigos criminals should perish in the old-fashioned manner. And then came the news of the eleotrocutions in the East, and how the results had not after all been so instantaneous as had been hoped. The Western Engineers raised their eyebrows when they read of the puny shocks by which these men had perished, and they vowed in Los Amigos that when an irreclaimable came their way he should be dealt handsomely by, and have the run of all the big dynamos. There should be no reserve, said the engineers, but he should have all that they had got. And what the result of that would be none could predict, save that it must be absolutely blasting and deadly. Never before had a man been so charged with electricity as they would charge him. He was to be smitten by the essence of ten thunderbolts. Some prophesied combustion, and some disintegration and disappearance. They were waiting eagerly to settle the question by actual demonstration, and it was just at that moment that Duncan Warner came that way.

Warner had been wanted by the law, and by nobody else, for many years. Desperado, murderer, train robber and road agent, he was a man beyond the pale of human pity. He had deserved a dozen deaths, and the Los Amigos folk grudged him so gaudy a one as that. He seemed to feel himself to be unworthy of it, for he made two frenzied attempts at escape. He was a powerful, muscular man, with a lion head, tangled black locks, and a sweeping beard which covered his broad chest. When he was tried, there was no finer head in all the crowded court. It's no new thing to find the best face looking from the dock. But his good looks could not balance his bad deeds. His advocate did all he knew, but the cards lay against him, and Duncan Warner was handed over to the mercy of the big Los Amigos dynamos.

I was there at the committee meeting when the matter was discussed. The town council had chosen four experts to look after the arrangements. Three of them were admirable. There was Joseph M'Conner, the very man who had designed the dynamos, and there was Joshua Westmacott, the chairman of the Los Amigos Electrical Supply Company, Limited. Then there was myself as the chief medical man, and lastly an old German of the name of Peter Stulpnagel. The Germans were a strong body at Los Amigos, and they all voted for their man. That was how he got on the committee. It was said that he had been a wonderful electrician at home, and he was eternally working with wires and insulators and Leyden jars; but, as he never seemed to get any further, or to have any results worth publishing he came at last to be regarded as a harmless crank, who had made science his hobby. We three practical men smiled when we heard that he had been elected as our colleague, and at the meeting we fixed it all up very nicely among ourselves without much thought of the old fellow who sat with his ears scooped forward in his hands, for he was a trifle hard of hearing, taking no more part in the proceedings than the gentlemen of the press who scribbled their notes on the back benches.

We did not take long to settle it all. In New York a strength of some two thousand volts had been used, and death had not been instantaneous. Evidently their shock had been too weak. Los Amigos should not fall into that error. The charge should be six times greater, and therefore, of course, it would be six times more effective. Nothing could possibly be more logical. The whole concentrated force of the great dynamos should be employed on Duncan Warner.

So we three settled it, and had already risen to break up the meeting, when our silent companion opened his month for the first time.

"Gentlemen," said he, "you appear to me to show an extraordinary ignorance upon the subject of electricity. You have not mastered the first principles of its actions upon a human being."

The committee was about to break into an angry reply to this brusque comment, but the chairman of the Electrical Company tapped his forehead to claim its indulgence for the crankiness of the speaker.

"Pray tell us, sir," said he, with an ironical smile, "what is there in our conclusions with which you find fault?"

"With your assumption that a large dose of electricity will merely increase the effect of a small dose. Do you not think it possible that it might have an entirely different result? Do you know anything, by actual experiment, of the effect of such powerful shocks?"

"We know it by analogy," said the chairman, pompously. "All drugs increase their effect when they increase their dose; for example—for example——"

"Whisky," said Joseph M'Connor.

"Quite so. Whisky. You see it there."

Peter Stulpnagel smiled and shook his head.

"Your argument is not very good," said he. "When I used to take whisky, I used to find that one glass would excite me, but that six would send me to sleep, which is just the opposite. Now, suppose that electricity were to act in just the opposite way also, what then?"

We three practical men burst out laughing. We had known that our colleague was queer, but we never had thought that he would be as queer as this.

"What then?" repeated Philip Stulpnagel.

"We'll take our chances," said the chairman.

"Pray consider," said Peter, "that workmen who have touched the wires, and who have received shocks of only a few hundred volts, have died instantly. The fact is well known. And yet when a much greater force was used upon a criminal at New York, the man struggled for some little time. Do you not clearly see that the smaller dose is the more deadly?"

"I think, gentlemen, that this discussion has been carried on quite long enough," said the chairman, rising again. "The point, I take it, has already been decided by the majority of the committee, and Duncan Warner shall be electrocuted on Tuesday by the full strength of the Los Amigos dynamos. Is it not so?"

"I agree," said Joseph M'Connor.

"I agree," said I.

"And I protest," said Peter Stulpnagel.

"Then the motion is carried, and your protest will be duly entered in the minutes," said the chairman, and so the sitting was dissolved.

The attendance at the electrocution was a very small one. We four members of the committee were, of course, present with the executioner, who was to act under their orders. The others were the United States Marshal, the governor of the gaol, the chaplain, and three members of the press. The room was a small brick chamber, forming an outhouse to the Central Electrical station. It had been used as a laundry, and had an oven and copper at one side, but no other furniture save a single chair for the condemned man. A metal plate for his feet was placed in front of it, to which ran a thick, insulated wire. Above, another wire depended from the ceiling, which could be connected with a small metallic rod projecting from a cap which was to be placed upon his head. When this connection was established Duncan Warner's hour was come.

There was a solemn hush as we waited for the coming of the prisoner. The practical engineers looked a little pale, and fidgeted nervously with the wires. Even the hardened Marshal was ill at ease, for a mere hanging was one thing, and this blasting of flesh and blood a very different one. As to the pressmen, their faces were whiter than the sheets which lay before them. The only man who appeared to feel none of the influence of these preparations was the little German crank, who strolled from one to the other with a smile on his lips and mischief in his eyes. More than once he even went so far as to burst into a shout of laughter, until the chaplain sternly rebuked him for his ill-timed levity.

"How can you so far forget yourself, Mr. Stulpnagel," said he, "as to jest in the presence of death?"

But the German was quite unabashed.

"If I were in the presence of death I should not jest," said he, "but since I am not I may do what I choose."

This flippant reply was about to draw another and a sterner reproof from the chaplain, when the door was swung open and two warders entered leading Duncan Warner between them. He glanced round him with a set face, stepped resolutely forward, and seated himself upon the chair.

"Touch her off!" said he.

It was barbarous to keep him in suspense. The chaplain murmured a few words in his ear, the attendant placed the cap upon his head, and then, while we all held our breath, the wire and the metal were brought in contact.

"Great Scott!" shouted Duncan Warner.

He had bounded in his chair as the frightful shock crashed through his system. But he was not dead. On the contrary, his eyes gleamed far more brightly than they had done before. There was only one change, but it was a singular one. The black had passed from his hair and beard as the shadow passes from a landscape. They were both as white as snow. And yet there was no other sign of decay. His skin was smooth and plump and lustrous as a child's.

The Marshal looked at the committee with a reproachful eye.

"There seems to be some hitch here, gentlemen," said he.

We three practical men looked at each other.

Peter Stulpnagel smiled pensively.

"I think that another one should do it," said I.

Again the connection was made, and again Duncan Warner sprang in his chair and shouted, but, indeed, were it not that he still remained in the chair none of us would have recognised him. His hair and his beard had shredded off in an instant, and the room looked like a barber's shop on a Saturday night. There he sat, his eyes still shining, his skin radiant with the glow of perfect health, but with a scalp as bald as a Dutch cheese, and a chin without so much as a trace of down. He began to revolve one of his arms, slowly and doubtfully at first, but with more confidence as he went on.

"That jint," said he, "has puzzled half the doctors on the Pacific Slope. It's as good as new, and as limber as a hickory twig."

"You are feeling pretty well?" asked the old German.

"Never better in my life," said Duncan Warner cheerily.

The situation was a painful one. The Marshal glared at the committee. Peter Stulpnagel grinned and rubbed his hands. The engineers scratched their heads. The bald-headed prisoner revolved his arm and looked pleased.

"I think that one more shock——" began the chairman.

"No, sir," said the Marshal "we've had foolery enough for one morning. We are here for an execution, and a execution we'll have."

"What do you propose?"

"There's a hook handy upon the ceiling. Fetch in a rope, and we'll soon set this matter straight."

There was another awkward delay while the warders departed for the cord. Peter Stulpnagel bent over Duncan Warner, and whispered something in his ear. The desperado started in surprise.

"You don't say?" he asked.

The German nodded.

"What! No ways?"

Peter shook his head, and the two began to laugh as though they shared some huge joke between them.

The rope was brought, and the Marshal himself slipped the noose over the criminal's neck. Then the two warders, the assistant and he swung their victim into the air. For half an hour he hung—a dreadful sight—from the ceiling. Then in solemn silence they lowered him down, and one of the warders went out to order the shell to be brought round. But as he touched ground again what was our amazement when Duncan Warner put his hands up to his neck, loosened the noose, and took a long, deep breath.

"Paul Jefferson's sale is goin' well," he remarked, "I could see the crowd from up yonder," and he nodded at the hook in the ceiling.

"Up with him again!" shouted the Marshal, "we'll get the life out of him somehow."

In an instant the victim was up at the hook once more.

They kept him there for an hour, but when he came down he was perfectly garrulous.

"Old man Plunket goes too much to the Arcady Saloon," said he. "Three times he's been there in an hour; and him with a family. Old man Plunket would do well to swear off."

It was monstrous and incredible, but there it was. There was no getting round it. The man was there talking when he ought to have been dead. We all sat staring in amazement, but United States Marshal Carpenter was not a man to be euchred so easily. He motioned the others to one side, so that the prisoner was left standing alone.

"Duncan Warner," said he, slowly, "you are here to play your part, and I am here to play mine. Your game is to live if you can, and my game is to carry out the sentence of the law. You've beat us on electricity. I'll give you one there. And you've beat us on hanging, for you seem to thrive on it. But it's my turn to beat you now, for my duty has to be done."

He pulled a six-shooter from his coat as he spoke, and fired all the shots through the body of the prisoner. The room was so filled with smoke that we could see

109

nothing, but when it cleared the prisoner was still standing there, looking down in disgust at the front of his coat.

"Coats must be cheap where you come from," said he. "Thirty dollars it cost me, and look at it now. The six holes in front are bad enough, but four of the balls have passed out, and a pretty state the back must be in."

The Marshal's revolver fell from his hand, and he dropped his arms to his sides, a beaten man.

"Maybe some of you gentlemen can tell me what this means," said he, looking helplessly at the committee.

Peter Stulpnagel took a step forward.

"I'll tell you all about it," said he.

"You seem to be the only person who knows anything."

"I *am* the only person who knows anything. I should have warned these gentlemen; but, as they would not listen to me, I have allowed them to learn by experience. What you have done with your electricity is that you have increased this man's vitality until he can defy death for centuries."

"Centuries!"

"Yes, it will take the wear of hundreds of years to exhaust the enormous nervous energy with which you have drenched him. Electricity is life, and you have charged him with it to the utmost. Perhaps in fifty years you might execute him, but I am not sanguine about it."

"Great Scott! What shall I do with him?" cried the unhappy Marshal.

Peter Stulpnagel shrugged his shoulders.

"It seems to me that it does not much matter what you do with him now," said he.

"Maybe we could drain the electricity out of him again. Suppose we hang him up by the heels?"

"No, no, it's out of the question."

"Well, well, he shall do no more mischief in Los Amigos, anyhow," said the Marshal, with decision. "He shall go into the new gaol. The prison will wear him out."

"On the contrary," said Peter Stulpnagel, "I think that it is much more probable that he will wear out the prison."

It was rather a fiasco and for years we didn't talk more about it than we could help, but it's no secret now and I thought you might like to jot down the facts in your case-book.

The Sixth Sense, or Another World

J.H. ROSNY

Although little of their work was translated into English in their lifetime, the Belgian brothers Joseph Henri Honoré Boex (1856–1940) and Séraphin Justin François Boex, who signed their collaborations "J.H. Rosny," are acknowledged as early founders of modern science fiction. This tale, which appeared in an 1895 issue of Revue Parisenne *and was translated into English for the August 1896 issue of* The Chatauquan, *is a semi-humorous inquiry into the invisible forms of life that might inhabit the world around us.*

I came into the world with a unique organism. From the very first I was an object of astonishment. Not that I appeared deformed. I am told that I was in face and form more graceful than one generally is at birth. But I had the most extraordinary tint—a species of pale violet. By the light of lamps, especially oil lamps, that tint became still paler; became of a strange whiteness like a lily submerged in water. This is at least the view of other men, for I see myself differently, as I see all objects of this world differently.

I became stranger and stranger by my tastes, by my habits, and by my qualities. At six years old I lived almost entirely on alcohol. I rarely took a few mouthfuls of vegetables or fruit. I grew prodigiously fast. I was incredibly lean and light— I mean light from the point of view of specific gravity, which is exactly the contrary of lean people generally. Thus I swam without the slightest difficulty and floated like a poplar plank. My head sank in the water hardly any more than the rest of my body.

I was nimble in proportion to my lightness. I ran with the rapidity of a hare and easily jumped over ditches and obstacles that no child twice my age would have tried to cross. I could climb to the top of a poplar tree in the twinkling of an eye or, what was still more surprising, I could jump onto the roof of our farmhouse. On the other hand, the slightest weight was too much for me.

If I saw certain things not so well as other people did I saw a great many that nobody but myself saw. This difference showed itself especially in colors. Everything that is called red, orange, yellow, green, blue, and indigo appeared to me of a blackish gray, while I perceived the violet and the series of colors beyond it—the colors which are only darkness for ordinary men. I have found out since that I distinguish thus at least thirty colors just as different as, for example, the yellow and the green.

In the second place transparency did not show itself to my eye under ordinary conditions. I did not see very well through a window pane or through water. Many crystals called translucent were more or less opaque to me. On the contrary a great number of bodies called opaque did not stop my vision.

This difference of my vision from that of other men was little noticed by my neighbors. People thought I was poor at distinguishing the colors and that was all. It is a defect too common to attract attention.

The faculty of seeing through the clouds, of seeing the stars during the most obscure nights, of seeing through a wooden door what is passing in a neighboring room—what is all that in comparison with the perception of a living world?—a world with animated beings moving by the side of, and about, man, without man having any consciousness of it and without his being warned by any sort of immediate contact. What is all that in comparison with the revelation that there exists upon this earth another fauna than our fauna?—a fauna without resemblance either of form or of organization or of manners or of mode of growth or of birth and death with ours—a fauna which lives by the side of ours and through ours, influences the elements which surround us, and is vivified and influenced by these elements without our suspecting its presence—a living world as various as our own, as powerful as ours.

At about eight years of age I was perfectly aware that there were beings distinguished from the atmospheric phenomena as much as the animals of our realm are. In the rapture that this discovery caused me I tried to express it. I never could succeed. My speech was almost incomprehensible and my extraordinary vision made people distrust me. No one stopped to try to untangle my notions and my phrases, nor yet to admit that I could see through closed doors, though I had given many proofs of it.

I fell into discouragement and dreaming. I became a sort of little recluse. I caused ill will, and felt the same, in the company of other children of my age. I was not exactly their victim, for my swiftness placed me out of the reach of their childish malice and gave me the means of avenging myself with ease. However many of them there might be never did an urchin succeed in striking me. They took me for both a simpleton and a wizard, but they thought my witchcraft only to be scorned, so my life became meditative and was spent largely out of doors. Nothing kept me human but the love of my mother.

I will describe briefly some scenes of my tenth year. My father said one day, "He will never be able to talk." My mother looked at me with compassion, convinced that I was a simpleton. I followed my mother to the farmyard. The cattle came toward her. I looked at them with interest and loved them, but round about me the other realm was moving and was captivating my soul—the mysterious realm which I alone am acquainted with. On the brown earth several forms are spread out. They move, they palpitate on a level with the soil. They are of several sorts, different in outline, in motion, and especially in the arrangement, the design, and colors of the stripes which are upon them. These stripes make up on the whole the principles of their being, and, child that I was, I perceived it very well. While the mass of their form is dull and grayish, the stripes are almost always sparkling. They constitute very complicated networks. They emanate from centers. They radiate others until they are lost, becoming indistinct. Their colors are innumerable, their curves infinite.

I have seen all that very well since, although I am incapable of defining it. An adorable charm possesses me in contemplating these *Mœdigen* (this is the name that I spontaneously gave them during my childhood).

These terrestrial *Mœdigen* are not the only intangible beings. There is a population in the air of marvelous splendor and subtlety, of varied and incomparable brilliancy. By the side of it the most beautiful birds are slow and heavy. Here again it is an outline and stripes, but the background is not grayish. It is strangely luminous. It sparkles like the sun and the stripes separate themselves into vibrating nerves. Their centers palpitate violently. The *Vuren*, as I call them, are of more irregular form than the terrestrial *Mœdigen* and they generally move systematically, crossing and recrossing one another.

I make my way across a recently mown meadow. The combat of one *Mœdigen* with another draws my attention. These combats are frequent. Sometimes it is a combat between equals. More frequently it is the attack of a strong one upon a weak one. In the present case the weak one, after a short defense, takes to flight, swiftly pursued by his assailant. In spite of the rapidity of their movements I follow them. I succeed in keeping them in sight until the moment when the strife begins again. They rush one against the other, harshly, even rigidly, seeming to be solid to each other. In the combat the lines phosphoresce, and directing themselves toward the point of combat their centers become paler and smaller. At first the struggle is kept up with some equality; the weaker displays the more intense energy and succeeds in obtaining from his adversary a truce. He profits by this to flee again, but is quickly overtaken and attacked with force and finally seized, that is to say, held fast in the fold of the outline of the other. This is exactly what he had sought to avoid. Now I see all his lines tremble. His centers struggle desperately and as the lines grow paler the centers become indistinct. After some minutes his liberty is given back and he withdraws slowly, being much weakened. His antagonist on the contrary sparkles more than ever. His lines are more colored and his centers more clearly marked. This struggle moved me profoundly. I confusedly understood that the *Mœdigen* do not kill each other, that the conqueror contents himself with taking some strength at the expense of the conquered.

I was a very poor pupil. My writing is nothing but a hasty trace, shapeless and illegible. My speech remains incomprehensible. My absent-mindedness is evident. My schoolmasters were continually crying out to me, "Karel, will you stop watching the motion of the flies?"

At seventeen years of age life became to me decidedly unendurable. I was weary of dreaming. What good was it for me to be acquainted with things more marvelous than other men were aware of, since this knowledge was to die with me? Several times I dreamed of writing, but what reader would not think me insane?—and writing was difficult for me, almost similar to what it would be for an ordinary man to be obliged to engrave his thought upon marble tablets with a large pair of scissors and a wooden mallet. So I had no courage to write and yet I hoped ardently for some unknown person and for some happy, remarkable destiny.

I grew still leaner so that I became fantastic. The people in the village called me a ghost. My silhouette was as trembling as that of a young poplar tree, as light as a shadow, and withal I was reaching the stature of a giant. Slowly a project began to be born. Was I not in myself an object of curiosity? The physical aspects of my nature were worthy of analysis. I obtained from my parents the permission to go to Amsterdam, free to come back if fortune were unfavorable to me.

I set out one morning. The distance was sixty-six miles. I easily made it in two hours on foot. I went into an inn along the magnificent canal and inquired for a hospital, saying I was sick. I was directed to the hospital and there inquired for the doctor—Dr. van den Heuvel—and told him I wanted to be studied. He smiled with an approving air and put to me the usual question that everybody puts:

"Can you see with those eyes of yours?"

"Very well. I often see through wood and clouds."

But I had spoken too swiftly. He cast an anxious look at me. I went on, sweating great drops:

"I see even through wood and clouds."

"Indeed, that would be extraordinary. Well, what do you see through that door there?" He pointed toward a closed door.

"A large bookcase with glass doors and a carved wooden table."

"Indeed!" he replied stupefied. He remained silent a few minutes and then said, "You speak with great difficulty."

"Rather, I speak too fast. I cannot speak slowly."

"Very well, speak a little in your own way."

I related to him how I came to Amsterdam. He listened with close attention with an air of intelligent observation that I had never met with among my equals. He did not understand a word that I said, but he showed the sagacity of an analyzer.

"I am not mistaken. You pronounce from twenty to thirty syllables every second. That is to say, six times as many as the human ear can take in. Besides your voice is much sharper than anything I ever heard in the way of a human voice. Your gestures are of excessive rapidity and correspond to your speech. Your whole organization is probably more rapid than ours."

"I run," said I, "swifter than the hare. I write ——"

"Ah," he interrupted, "let's see your writing."

I scratched a few words on a notebook that he held out to me. The first were quite legible, but the others more and more tangled up.

"Indeed," said he, "I believe I shall have reason to congratulate myself upon meeting you. Certainly it will be interesting to study you. If only we could find an easy process of communication." He walked back and forth with his long eyebrows contracted. Suddenly he said, "I have it! You shall learn stenography."

A smiling expression appeared upon his face. "I have forgotten the phonograph. It will suffice to unroll it more slowly when listening to it than when inscribing it. You will stay with me during your sojourn at Amsterdam."

I agreed. The next day the doctor wrote to my parents, got me a professor of stenography, and secured some phonographs. As he was very rich and devoted to science there is no experiment which he did not propose to make. My sight, my hearing, my muscles, the color of my skin, were subjected to scrupulous investigations over which he became more and more enthusiastic, exclaiming, "That partakes of prodigy."

He was first occupied with the swiftness of my perception. He was able to satisfy himself that the subtlety of my hearing corresponded with the swiftness of my speech. The words of ten or fifteen people talking all at once, all of whom I perfectly understood, proved this point. The swiftness of my sight was proved as well. A handful of shot thrown into the air was accurately counted by me before falling. As to color, I was able to prove that I see the violet, and beyond the violet a scale of shades at least double the spectrum which exists from the red to the violet. This astonished the doctor more than all the rest.

We labored patiently the whole year without my mentioning the *Mœdigen*. I wished absolutely to convince my host and give him innumerable proofs of my faculty of sight before venturing upon his confidence. At last when I related to him about the creatures I saw in the air and on the earth, he suspected occultism and could not help saying,

"The world of the fourth estate, the souls, the phantoms of spirits."

"No, no. Nothing of the kind. A world of living beings like ourselves, condemned to a short life, to organic needs, to birth, growth, and struggle."

I do not know whether Van den Heuvel believed me. He was certainly under a lively emotion.

"Are they fluids?" he asked.

"I do not know, for their peculiarities are too contradictory for the idea that we have of matter. The earth is as irresistible to them as to us. Likewise most of the minerals. Again, they are totally impenetrable in their relation one to another. But they do traverse, although at times with some difficulty, plants, animals, and organic tissues, and we likewise traverse them. Their form has this strange thing about it— that they have hardly any thickness and their shape varies infinitely. I have known some that are 100 meters long. With some nutrition takes place at the expense of the earth and all the meteors; with others at the expense of meteors and of individuals of their realm, yet without its being a cause of death as with us, since it is sufficient for the stronger to take strength from the weaker, and this strength may be drawn out without destroying the source of life."

"Are they numerous everywhere?"

"Yes, and hardly less numerous in the city than in the country, in the house than in the street."

"Will you describe one to me—a special one of large size?"

"I see one near that tree. Its form is greatly elongated and rather irregular. It is convex on the right and concave on the left with some wrinkles and folds, but its structure is not characteristic of the gens, for the structure varies extremely from one species to another. Its infinitesimal thinness, however, is a quality general to all of them. It can hardly surpass a tenth of a millimeter, while its length reaches five feet and its greatest breadth is forty centimeters. What mainly defines it and all its class are the lines which cross it in every direction, ending in networks. Every system of lines is provided with a center—a sort of spot, slightly crumpled above the mass of the body, but sometimes, on the contrary, it is hollow. These centers have no fixed form. Sometimes they are almost circular or elliptical. Sometimes they are spiral. They are extremely mobile and their size varies from time to time. The edge of them palpitates greatly with a sort of transverse undulation. Generally the lines which project from them are broad. They end in infinitely delicate traces which gradually disappear. These lines have the faculty of changing their places in the body, and of varying their curves."

I was silent. The doctor caused my words to be twice repeated by our faultless instrument. Then he remained a longtime in silence. At last he murmured, "You have overwhelmed me."

We have now been pursuing our labors five years. They are far from reaching their end. The first publication of our discoveries will hardly appear yet for a long time. I have made it a rule to do nothing in haste. We have no other investigator to get ahead of us and no ambition to satisfy. We are living passionately, always on the border of marvelous discoveries.

I have recently had an experience which adds profound interest to my life and which fills me with infinite joy. You know how homely I am from the human point of view and how apt to terrify young women; yet I have found a companion who adapts herself to me and is happy over it. It is a hysterical, nervous young girl whom we met one day in a hospital in Amsterdam. They say her appearance is miserable, of the paleness of plaster, with hollow cheeks and wandering eyes. For me the sight of her is agreeable and her company charming. My presence, far from astonishing her, as it does all the rest, appeared from the very first to please and comfort her. I was so much touched by it that I went to see her again along with the doctor. He was not slow in perceiving that I had upon her health and upon her well-being a beneficent action. Examination proved that I influenced her magnetically. When I approached and when I laid my hands upon her, I communicated a gaiety and serenity to her that had a curative effect. In return I felt happiness near her. Her face appeared pretty to me. Her paleness and her leanness were only delicacy. Her eyes, which were capable of seeing the gleam of magnets, like the eyes of many hyperaesthetics, had for me none of the character of wandering that people reproached her with. I was resolved to marry her and thanks to the good will of my friends I easily succeeded in my purpose. Our union is happy. My wife's health is restored, although she remains extremely sensitive and frail. For the past six months my fate has been especially enviable. A child is born to us and that child combines all the characteristics of my constitution—color, sight, hearing, and extreme rapidity of motion. He promises to be an exact second edition of my own organism. The doctor is watching his growth with delight.

The Crystal Egg

H.G. WELLS

One of the greatest and most influential writers of science fiction, Herbert George Wells (1866–1946) is the author of The Time Machine *(1895),* The Island of Dr. Moreau *(1896),* The Invisible Man *(1897),* The First Men in the Moon *(1901), and countless other science fiction classics. In the opening paragraphs of his landmark novel* The War of the Worlds *(1898), Wells wrote how the planet Earth had been under study by the invading Martians for some time. This story, published a year earlier in the May issue of* The New Review, *reveals just how that study was achieved.*

There was, until a year ago, a little and very grimy-looking shop near Seven Dials, over which, in weather-worn yellow lettering, the name of "C. Cave, Naturalist and Dealer in Antiquities," was inscribed. The contents of its window were curiously variegated. They comprised some elephant tusks and an imperfect set of chessmen, beads and weapons, a box of eyes, two skulls of tigers and one human, several moth-eaten stuffed monkeys (one holding a lamp), an old-fashioned cabinet, a fly-blown ostrich egg or so, some fishing-tackle, and an extraordinarily dirty, empty glass fish-tank. There was also, at the moment the story begins, a mass of crystal, worked into the shape of an egg and brilliantly polished. And at that two people who stood outside the window were looking, one of them a tall, thin clergyman, the other a black-bearded young man of dusky complexion and unobtrusive costume. The dusky young man spoke with eager gesticulation, and seemed anxious for his companion to purchase the article.

While they were there, Mr. Cave came into his shop, his beard still wagging with the bread and butter of his tea. When he saw these men and the object of their regard, his countenance fell. He glanced guiltily over his shoulder, and softly shut the door. He was a little old man, with pale face and peculiar watery blue eyes; his hair was a dirty grey, and he wore a shabby blue frock-coat, an ancient silk hat, and carpet slippers very much down at heel. He remained watching the two men as they talked. The clergyman went deep into his trouser pocket, examined a handful of money, and showed his teeth in an agreeable smile. Mr. Cave seemed still more depressed when they came into the shop.

The clergyman, without any ceremony, asked the price of the crystal egg. Mr. Cave glanced nervously towards the door leading into the parlour, and said five pounds. The clergyman protested that the price was high, to his companion as well as to Mr. Cave—it was, indeed, very much more than Mr. Cave had intended to ask when he had stocked the article—and an attempt at bargaining ensued. Mr. Cave stepped to the shop door, and held it open. "Five pounds is my price," he said, as though he wished to save himself the trouble of unprofitable discussion. As he did so, the upper portion of a woman's face appeared above the blind in the glass upper panel of the door leading into the parlour, and stared curiously at the two customers. "Five pounds is my price," said Mr. Cave, with a quiver in his voice.

The swarthy young man had so far remained a spectator, watching Cave keenly. Now he spoke. "Give him five pounds," he said. The clergyman glanced at him to see if he were in earnest, and when he looked at Mr. Cave again, he saw that the latter's face was white. "It's a lot of money," said the clergyman, and, diving into his pocket, began counting his resources. He had little more than thirty shillings, and he appealed to his companion, with whom he seemed to be on terms of considerable intimacy. This gave Mr. Cave an opportunity of collecting his thoughts, and he began to explain in an agitated manner that the crystal was not, as a matter of fact, entirely free for sale. His two customers were naturally surprised at this, and inquired why he had not thought of that before he began to bargain. Mr. Cave became confused, but he stuck to his story, that the crystal was not in the market that afternoon, that a probable purchaser of it had already appeared. The two, treating this as an attempt to raise the price still further, made as if they would leave the shop. But at this point the parlour door opened, and the owner of the dark fringe and the little eyes appeared.

She was a coarse-featured, corpulent woman, younger and very much larger than Mr. Cave; she walked heavily, and her face was flushed. "That crystal *is* for sale," she said. "And five pounds is a good enough price for it. I can't think what you're about, Cave, not to take the gentleman's offer!"

Mr. Cave, greatly perturbed by the irruption, looked angrily at her over the rims of his spectacles, and, without excessive assurance, asserted his right to manage his business in his own way. An altercation began. The two customers watched the scene with interest and some amusement, occasionally assisting Mrs. Cave with suggestions. Mr. Cave, hard driven, persisted in a confused and impossible story of an inquiry for the crystal that morning, and his agitation became painful. But he stuck to his point with extraordinary persistence. It was the young Oriental who ended this curious controversy. He proposed that they should call again in the course of two days—so as to give the alleged inquirer a fair chance. "And then we must insist," said the clergyman. "Five pounds." Mrs. Cave took it on herself to apologise for her husband, explaining that he was sometimes "a little odd," and as the two customers left, the couple prepared for a free discussion of the incident in all its bearings.

Mrs. Cave talked to her husband with singular directness. The poor little man, quivering with emotion, muddled himself between his stories, maintaining on the one hand that he had another customer in view, and on the other asserting that the crystal was honestly worth ten guineas. "Why did you ask five pounds?" said his wife. "*Do* let me manage my business my own way!" said Mr. Cave.

Mr. Cave had living with him a step-daughter and a step-son, and at supper that night the transaction was re-discussed. None of them had a high opinion of Mr. Cave's business methods, and this action seemed a culminating folly.

"It's my opinion he's refused that crystal before," said the step-son, a loose-limbed lout of eighteen.

"But *Five Pounds*!" said the step-daughter, an argumentative young woman of six-and-twenty.

Mr. Cave's answers were wretched; he could only mumble weak assertions that he knew his own business best. They drove him from his half-eaten supper into the shop, to close it for the night, his ears aflame and tears of vexation behind his spectacles. Why had he left the crystal in the window so long? The folly of it! That was the trouble closest in his mind. For a time he could see no way of evading sale.

After supper his step-daughter and step-son smartened themselves up and went out and his wife retired upstairs to reflect upon the business aspects of the crystal, over a little sugar and lemon and so forth in hot water. Mr. Cave went into the shop, and stayed there until late, ostensibly to make ornamental rockeries for gold-fish cases, but really for a private purpose that will be better explained later. The next day Mrs. Cave found that the crystal had been removed from the window, and was lying behind some second-hand books on angling. She replaced it in a conspicuous position. But she did not argue further about it, as a nervous headache disinclined her from debate. Mr. Cave was always disinclined. The day passed disagreeably. Mr. Cave was, if anything, more absent-minded than usual, and uncommonly irritable withal. In the afternoon, when his wife was taking her customary sleep, he removed the crystal from the window again.

The next day Mr. Cave had to deliver a consignment of dog-fish at one of the hospital schools, where they were needed for dissection. In his absence Mrs. Cave's mind reverted to the topic of the crystal, and the methods of expenditure suitable to a windfall of five pounds. She had already devised some very agreeable expedients, among others a dress of green silk for herself and a trip to Richmond, when a jangling of the front door bell summoned her into the shop. The customer was an examination coach who came to complain of the non-delivery of certain frogs asked for the previous day. Mrs. Cave did not approve of this particular branch of Mr. Cave's business, and the gentleman, who had called in a somewhat aggressive mood, retired after a brief exchange of words—entirely civil, so far as he was concerned. Mrs. Cave's eye then naturally turned to the window; for the sight of the crystal was an assurance of the five pounds and of her dreams. What was her surprise to find it gone!

She went to the place behind the locker on the counter, where she had discovered it the day before. It was not there; and she immediately began an eager search about the shop.

When Mr. Cave returned from his business with the dogfish, about a quarter to two in the afternoon, he found the shop in some confusion, and his wife, extremely exasperated and on her knees behind the counter, routing among his taxidermic material. Her face came up hot and angry over the counter, as the jangling bell announced his return, and she forthwith accused him of "hiding it."

"Hid *what*?" asked Mr. Cave.

"The crystal!"

At that Mr. Cave, apparently much surprised, rushed to the window. "Isn't it here?" he said. "Great Heavens! what has become of it?"

Just then Mr. Cave's step-son re-entered the shop from the inner room—he had come home a minute or so before Mr. Cave—and he was blaspheming freely. He was apprenticed to a second-hand furniture dealer down the road, but he had his meals at home, and he was naturally annoyed to find no dinner ready.

But when he heard of the loss of the crystal, he forgot his meal, and his anger was diverted from his mother to his step-father. Their first idea, of course, was that he had hidden it. But Mr. Cave stoutly denied all knowledge of its fate, freely offering his bedabbled affidavit in the matter—and at last was worked up to the point of accusing, first, his wife and then his step-son of having taken it with a view to a private sale. So began an exceedingly acrimonious and emotional discussion, which ended for Mrs. Cave in a peculiar nervous condition midway between hysterics and amuck, and caused the step-son to be half-an-hour late at the furniture establishment in the afternoon. Mr. Cave took refuge from his wife's emotions in the shop.

In the evening the matter was resumed, with less passion and in a judicial spirit, under the presidency of the step-daughter. The supper passed unhappily and culminated in a painful scene. Mr. Cave gave way at last to extreme exasperation, and went out banging the front door violently. The rest of the family, having discussed him with the freedom his absence warranted, hunted the house from garret to cellar, hoping to light upon the crystal.

The next day the two customers called again. They were received by Mrs. Cave almost in tears. It transpired that no one *could* imagine all that she had stood from Cave at various times in her married pilgrimage. . . . She also gave a garbled account of the disappearance. The clergyman and the Oriental laughed silently at one another, and said it was very extraordinary. As Mrs. Cave seemed disposed to give them the complete history of her life they made to leave the shop. Thereupon Mrs. Cave, still clinging to hope, asked for the clergyman's address, so that, if she could get anything out of Cave, she might communicate it. The address was duly given, but apparently was afterwards mislaid. Mrs. Cave can remember nothing about it.

In the evening of that day the Caves seem to have exhausted their emotions, and Mr. Cave, who had been out in the afternoon, supped in a gloomy isolation that contrasted pleasantly with the impassioned controversy of the previous days. For some time matters were very badly strained in the Cave household, but neither crystal nor customer reappeared.

Now, without mincing the matter, we must admit that Mr. Cave was a liar. He knew perfectly well where the crystal was. It was in the rooms of Mr. Jacoby Wace, Assistant Demonstrator at St. Catherine's Hospital, Westbourne Street. It stood on the sideboard partially covered by a black velvet cloth, and beside a decanter of American whisky. It is from Mr. Wace, indeed, that the particulars upon which this narrative is based were derived. Cave had taken off the thing to the hospital hidden in the dog-fish sack, and there had pressed the young investigator to keep it for him. Mr. Wace was a little dubious at first. His relationship to Cave was peculiar. He had a taste for singular characters, and he had more than once invited the old man to smoke and drink in his rooms, and to unfold his rather amusing views of life in general and of his wife in particular. Mr. Wace had encountered Mrs. Cave, too, on occasions when Mr. Cave was not at home to attend to him. He knew the constant interference to which Cave was subjected, and having weighed the story judicially, he decided to give the crystal a refuge. Mr. Cave promised to explain the reasons for his remarkable affection for the crystal more fully on a later occasion, but he spoke distinctly of seeing visions therein. He called on Mr. Wace the same evening.

He told a complicated story. The crystal he said had come into his possession with other oddments at the forced sale of another curiosity dealer's effects, and not knowing what its value might be, he had ticketed it at ten shillings. It had hung upon his hands at that price for some months, and he was thinking of "reducing the figure," when he made a singular discovery.

At that time his health was very bad—and it must be borne in mind that, throughout all this experience, his physical condition was one of ebb—and he was in considerable distress by reason of the negligence, the positive ill-treatment even, he received from his wife and step-children. His wife was vain, extravagant, unfeeling, and had a growing taste for private drinking; his step-daughter was mean and over-reaching; and his step-son had conceived a violent dislike for him, and lost no chance of showing it. The requirements of his business pressed heavily upon him, and Mr. Wace does not think that he was altogether free from occasional intemperance. He had begun life in a comfortable position, he was a man of fair education, and he suffered, for weeks at a stretch, from melancholia and insomnia. Afraid to disturb his family, he would slip quietly from his wife's side, when his thoughts became intolerable, and wander about the house. And about three o'clock one morning, late in August, chance directed him into the shop.

The dirty little place was impenetrably black except in one spot, where he perceived an unusual glow of light. Approaching this, he discovered it to be the crystal egg, which was standing on the corner of the counter towards the window. A thin ray smote through a crack in the shutters, impinged upon the object, and seemed as it were to fill its entire interior.

It occurred to Mr. Cave that this was not in accordance with the laws of optics as he had known them in his younger days. He could understand the rays being refracted by the crystal and coming to a focus in its interior, but this diffusion jarred with his physical conceptions. He approached the crystal nearly, peering into it and round it, with a transient revival of the scientific curiosity that in his youth had determined his choice of a calling. He was surprised to find the light not steady, but writhing within the substance of the egg, as though that object was a hollow sphere of some luminous vapour. In moving about to get different points of view, he suddenly found that he had come between it and the ray, and that the crystal none the less remained luminous. Greatly astonished, he lifted it out of the light ray and carried it to the darkest part of the shop. It remained bright for some four or five minutes, when it slowly faded and went out. He placed it in the thin streak of daylight, and its luminousness was almost immediately restored.

So far, at least, Mr. Wace was able to verify the remarkable story of Mr. Cave. He has himself repeatedly held this crystal in a ray of light (which had to be of a less diameter than one millimetre). And in a perfect darkness, such as could be produced by velvet wrapping, the crystal did undoubtedly appear very faintly phosphorescent. It would seem, however, that the luminousness was of some exceptional sort, and not equally visible to all eyes; for Mr. Harbinger—whose name will be familiar to the scientific reader in connection with the Pasteur Institute—was quite unable to see any light whatever. And Mr. Wace's own capacity for its appreciation was out of comparison inferior to that of Mr. Cave's. Even with Mr. Cave the power varied very considerably: his vision was most vivid during states of extreme weakness and fatigue.

Now, from the outset, this light in the crystal exercised a curious fascination upon Mr. Cave. And it says more for his loneliness of soul than a volume of pathetic writing could do, that he told no human being of his curious observations. He seems to have been living in such an atmosphere of petty spite that to admit the existence of a pleasure would have been to risk the loss of it. He found that as the dawn advanced, and the amount of diffused light increased, the crystal became to all appearance non-luminous. And for some time he was unable to see anything in it, except at night-time, in dark corners of the shop.

But the use of an old velvet cloth, which he used as a background for a collection of minerals, occurred to him, and by doubling this, and putting it over his head and hands, he was able to get a sight of the luminous movement within the crystal even in the day-time. He was very cautious lest he should be thus discovered by his wife, and he practised this occupation only in the afternoons, while she was asleep upstairs, and then circumspectly in a hollow under the counter. And one day, turning the crystal about in his hands, he saw something. It came and went like a flash, but it gave him the impression that the object had for a moment opened to him the view of a wide and spacious and strange country; and turning it about, he did, just as the light faded, see the same vision again.

Now it would be tedious and unnecessary to state all the phases of Mr. Cave's discovery from this point. Suffice that the effect was this: the crystal, being peered into at an angle of about 137 degrees from the direction of the illuminating ray, gave a clear and consistent picture of a wide and peculiar country-side. It was not dream-like at all: it produced a definite impression of reality, and the better the light the more real and solid it seemed. It was a moving picture: that is to say, certain objects moved in it, but slowly in an orderly manner like real things, and, according as the direction of the lighting and vision changed, the picture changed also. It must, indeed, have been like looking through an oval glass at a view, and turning the glass about to get at different aspects.

Mr. Cave's statements, Mr. Wace assures me, were extremely circumstantial, and entirely free from any of that emotional quality that taints hallucinatory impressions. But it must be remembered that all the efforts of Mr. Wace to see any similar clarity in the faint opalescence of the crystal were wholly unsuccessful, try as he would. The difference in intensity of the impressions received by the two men was very great, and it is quite conceivable that what was a view to Mr. Cave was a mere blurred nebulosity to Mr. Wace.

The view, as Mr. Cave described it, was invariably of an extensive plain, and he seemed always to be looking at it from a considerable height, as if from a tower or a mast. To the east and to the west the plain was bounded at a remote distance by vast reddish cliffs, which reminded him of those he had seen in some picture; but what the picture was Mr. Wace was unable to ascertain. These cliffs passed north and south—he could tell the points of the compass by the stars that were visible of a night—receding in an almost illimitable perspective and fading into the mists of the distance before they met. He was nearer the eastern set of cliffs; on the occasion of his first vision the sun was rising over them, and black against the sunlight and pale against their shadow appeared a multitude of soaring forms that Mr. Cave regarded as birds. A vast range of buildings spread below him; he seemed to be looking down upon them; and as they approached the blurred and refracted edge of the picture they became indistinct. There were also trees curious in shape, and in colouring a deep mossy green and an exquisite grey, beside a wide and shining canal. And something great and brilliantly coloured flew across the picture. But the first time Mr. Cave saw these pictures he saw only in flashes, his hands shook, his head moved, the vision came and went, and grew foggy and indistinct. And at first he had the greatest difficulty in finding the picture again once the direction of it was lost.

His next clear vision, which came about a week after the first, the interval having yielded nothing but tantalising glimpses and some useful experience, showed him the view down the length of the valley. The view was different, but he had a curious persuasion, which his subsequent observations abundantly confirmed, that he was regarding the strange world from exactly the same spot, although he was looking in a different direction. The long facade of the great building, whose roof he had looked down upon before, was now receding in perspective. He recognised the roof. In the front of the facade was a terrace of massive proportions and extraordinary length, and down the middle of the terrace, at certain intervals, stood huge but very graceful masts, bearing small shiny objects which reflected the setting sun. The import of these small objects did not occur to Mr. Cave until some time after, as he was describing the scene to Mr. Wace. The terrace overhung a thicket of the most luxuriant and graceful vegetation, and beyond this was a wide grassy lawn on which certain broad creatures, in form like beetles but enormously larger, reposed. Beyond this again was a richly decorated causeway of pinkish stone; and beyond that, and lined with dense *red* weeds, and passing up the valley exactly parallel with the distant cliffs, was a broad and mirror-like expanse of water. The air seemed full of squadrons of great birds, manœuvring in stately curves; and across the river was a multitude of splendid buildings, richly coloured and glittering with metallic tracery and facets, among a forest of moss-like and lichenous trees. And suddenly something flapped repeatedly across the vision, like the fluttering of a jewelled fan or the beating of a wing, and a face, or rather the upper part of a face with very large eyes, came as it were close to his own and as if on the other side of the crystal. Mr. Cave was so startled and so impressed by the absolute reality of these eyes that he drew his head back from the crystal to look behind it. He had become so absorbed in watching that he was quite surprised to find himself in the cool darkness of his little shop, with its familiar odour of methyl, mustiness, and decay. And as he blinked about him, the glowing crystal faded and went out.

Such were the first general impressions of Mr. Cave. The story is curiously direct and circumstantial. From the outset, when the valley first flashed momentarily on his senses, his imagination was strangely affected, and as he began to appreciate the details of the scene he saw, his wonder rose to the point of a passion. He went about his business listless and distraught, thinking only of the time when he should be able to return to his watching. And then a few weeks after his first sight of the valley came the two customers, the stress and excitement of their offer, and the narrow escape of the crystal from sale, as I have already told.

Now, while the thing was Mr. Cave's secret, it remained a mere wonder, a thing to creep to covertly and peep at, as a child might peep upon a forbidden garden. But Mr. Wace has, for a young scientific investigator, a particularly lucid and consecutive habit of mind. Directly the crystal and its story came to him, and he had satisfied himself, by seeing the phosphorescence with his own eyes, that there really was a certain evidence for Mr. Cave's statements, he proceeded to develop the matter systematically. Mr. Cave was only too eager to come and feast his eyes on this wonderland he saw, and he came every night from half-past eight until half-past ten, and sometimes, in Mr. Wace's absence, during the day. On Sunday afternoons, also, he came. From the outset Mr. Wace made copious notes, and it was due to his scientific method that the relation between the direction from which the initiating ray entered the crystal and the orientation of the picture were proved. And, by covering the crystal in a box perforated only with a small aperture to admit the exciting ray, and by substituting black holland for his buff blinds, he greatly improved the conditions of the observations; so that in a little while they were able to survey the valley in any direction they desired.

So having cleared the way, we may give a brief account of this visionary world within the crystal. The things were in all cases seen by Mr. Cave, and the method of working was invariably for him to watch the crystal and report what he saw, while Mr. Wace (who as a science student had learnt the trick of writing in the dark) wrote a brief note of his report. When the crystal faded, it was put into its box in the proper position and the electric light turned on. Mr. Wace asked questions, and suggested observations to clear up difficult points. Nothing, indeed, could have been less visionary and more matter-of-fact.

The attention of Mr. Cave had been speedily directed to the bird-like creatures he had seen so abundantly present in each of his earlier visions. His first impression was soon corrected, and he considered for a time that they might represent a diurnal species of bat. Then he thought, grotesquely enough, that they might be cherubs. Their heads were round and curiously human, and it was the eyes of one of them that had so startled him on his second observation. They had broad, silvery wings, not feathered, but glistening almost as brilliantly as new-killed fish and with the same subtle play of colour, and these wings were not built on the plan of bird-wing or bat, Mr. Wace learned, but supported by curved ribs radiating from the body. (A sort of butterfly wing with curved ribs seems best to express their appearance.) The body was small, but fitted with two bunches of prehensile organs, like long tentacles, immediately under the mouth. Incredible as it appeared to Mr. Wace, the persuasion at last became irresistible that it was these creatures which owned the great quasi-human buildings and the magnificent garden that made the broad valley so splendid. And Mr. Cave perceived that the buildings, with other peculiarities, had no doors, but that the great circular windows, which opened freely, gave the creatures egress and entrance. They would alight upon their tentacles, fold their wings to a smallness almost rod-like, and hop into the interior. But among them was a multitude of smaller-winged creatures, like great dragon-flies and moths and flying beetles, and across the greensward brilliantly-coloured gigantic ground-beetles crawled lazily to and fro. Moreover, on the causeways and terraces, large-headed creatures similar to the greater winged flies, but wingless, were visible, hopping busily upon their hand-like tangle of tentacles.

Allusion has already been made to the glittering objects upon masts that stood upon the terrace of the nearer building. It dawned upon Mr. Cave, after regarding one of these masts very fixedly on one particularly vivid day that the glittering object there was a crystal exactly like that into which he peered. And a still more careful scrutiny convinced him that each one in a vista of nearly twenty carried a similar object.

Occasionally one of the large flying creatures would flutter up to one, and folding its wings and coiling a number of its tentacles about the mast, would regard the crystal fixedly for a space—sometimes for as long as fifteen minutes. And a series of observations, made at the suggestion of Mr. Wace, convinced both watchers that, so far as this visionary world was concerned, the crystal into which they peered actually stood at the summit of the end-most mast on the terrace, and that on one occasion at least one of these inhabitants of this other world had looked into Mr. Cave's face while he was making these observations.

So much for the essential facts of this very singular story. Unless we dismiss it all as the ingenious fabrication of Mr. Wace, we have to believe one of two things: either that Mr. Cave's crystal was in two worlds at once, and that while it was carried about in one, it remained stationary in the other, which seems altogether absurd; or else that it had some peculiar relation of sympathy with another and exactly similar crystal in this other world, so that what was seen in the interior of the one in this world was, under suitable conditions, visible to an observer in the corresponding crystal in the other world; and *vice versa*. At present, indeed, we do not know of any way in which two crystals could so come *en rapport*, but nowadays we know enough to understand that the thing is not altogether impossible. This view of the crystals as *en rapport* was the supposition that occurred to Mr. Wace, and to me at least it seems extremely plausible. . . .

And where was this other world? On this, also, the alert intelligence of Mr. Wace speedily threw light. After sunset, the sky darkened rapidly—there was a very brief twilight interval indeed—and the stars shone out. They were recognisably the same as those we see, arranged in the same constellations. Mr. Cave recognised the Bear, the Pleiades, Aldebaran, and Sirius; so that the other world must be somewhere in the solar system, and, at the utmost, only a few hundreds of millions of miles from our own. Following up this clue, Mr. Wace learned that the midnight sky was a darker blue even than our midwinter sky, and that the sun seemed a little smaller. *And there were two small moons!* "like our moon but smaller, and quite differently marked," one of which moved so rapidly that its motion was clearly visible as one regarded it. These moons were never high in the sky, but vanished as they rose: that is, every time they revolved they were eclipsed because they were so near their primary planet. And all this answers quite completely, although Mr. Cave did not know it, to what must be the condition of things on Mars.

Indeed, it seems an exceedingly plausible conclusion that peering into this crystal Mr. Cave did actually see the planet Mars and its inhabitants. And if that be the case, then the evening star that shone so brilliantly in the sky of that distant vision was neither more nor less than our own familiar earth.

For a time the Martians—if they were Martians—do not seem to have known of Mr. Cave's inspection. Once or twice one would come to peer, and go away very shortly to some other mast, as though the vision was unsatisfactory. During this time Mr. Cave was able to watch the proceedings of these winged people without being disturbed by their attentions, and although his report is necessarily vague and fragmentary, it is nevertheless very suggestive. Imagine the impression of humanity a Martian observer would get who, after a difficult process of preparation and with considerable fatigue to the eyes, was able to peer at London from the steeple of St. Martin's Church for stretches, at longest, of four minutes at a time. Mr. Cave was unable to ascertain if the winged Martians were the same as the Martians who hopped about the causeways and terraces, and if the latter could put on wings at will. He several times saw certain clumsy bipeds, dimly suggestive of apes, white and partially translucent, feeding among certain of the lichenous trees, and once some of these fled before one of the hopping, round-headed Martians. The latter caught one in its tentacles, and then the picture faded suddenly and left Mr. Cave most tantalisingly in the dark. On another occasion a vast thing, that Mr. Cave thought at first was some gigantic insect, appeared advancing along the causeway beside the canal with extraordinary rapidity. As this drew nearer Mr. Cave perceived that it was a mechanism of shining metals and of extraordinary complexity. And then, when he looked again, it had passed out of sight.

After a time Mr. Wace aspired to attract the attention of the Martians, and the next time that the strange eyes of one of them appeared close to the crystal Mr. Cave cried out and sprang away, and they immediately turned on the light and began to gesticulate in a manner suggestive of signalling. But when at last Mr. Cave examined the crystal again the Martian had departed.

Thus far these observations had progressed in early November, and then Mr. Cave, feeling that the suspicions of his family about the crystal were allayed, began to take it to and fro with him in order that, as occasion arose in the daytime or night, he might comfort himself with what was fast becoming the most real thing in his existence.

In December Mr. Wace's work in connection with a forthcoming examination became heavy, the sittings were reluctantly suspended for a week, and for ten or eleven days—he is not quite sure which—he saw nothing of Cave. He then grew anxious to resume these investigations, and, the stress of his seasonal labours being abated, he went down to Seven Dials. At the corner he noticed a shutter before a bird fancier's window, and then another at a cobbler's. Mr. Cave's shop was closed.

He rapped and the door was opened by the step-son in black. He at once called Mrs. Cave, who was, Mr. Wace could not but observe, in cheap but ample widow's weeds of the most imposing pattern. Without any very great surprise Mr. Wace learnt that Cave was dead and already buried. She was in tears, and her voice was a little thick. She had just returned from Highgate. Her mind seemed occupied with her own prospects and the honourable details of the obsequies, but Mr. Wace was at last able to learn the particulars of Cave's death. He had been found dead in his shop in the early morning, the day after his last visit to Mr. Wace, and the crystal had been clasped in his stone-cold hands. His face was smiling, said Mrs. Cave, and the velvet cloth from the minerals lay on the floor at his feet. He must have been dead five or six hours when he was found.

This came as a great shock to Wace, and he began to reproach himself bitterly for having neglected the plain symptoms of the old man's ill-health. But his chief thought was of the crystal. He approached that topic in a gingerly manner, because he knew Mrs. Cave's peculiarities. He was dumfounded to learn that it was sold.

Mrs. Cave's first impulse, directly Cave's body had been taken upstairs, had been to write to the mad clergyman who had offered five pounds for the crystal, informing him of its recovery; but after a violent hunt, in which her daughter joined her, they were convinced of the loss of his address. As they were without the means required to mourn and bury Cave in the elaborate style the dignity of an old Seven Dials inhabitant demands, they had appealed to a friendly fellow-tradesman in Great Portland Street. He had very kindly taken over a portion of the stock at a valuation. The valuation was his own, and the crystal egg was included in one of the lots. Mr. Wace, after a few suitable condolences, a little off-handedly proffered perhaps, hurried at once to Great Portland Street. But there he learned that the crystal egg had already been sold to a tall, dark man in grey. And there the material facts in this curious, and to me at least very suggestive, story come abruptly to an end. The Great Portland Street dealer did not know who the tall dark man in grey was, nor had he observed him with sufficient attention to describe him minutely. He did not even know which way this person had gone after leaving the shop. For a time Mr. Wace remained in the shop, trying the dealer's patience with hopeless questions, venting his own exasperation. And at last, realising abruptly that the whole thing had passed out of his hands, had vanished like a vision of the night, he returned to his own rooms, a little astonished to find the notes he had made still tangible and visible upon, his untidy table.

His annoyance and disappointment were naturally very great. He made a second call (equally ineffectual) upon the Great Portland Street dealer, and he resorted to advertisements in such periodicals as were lively to come into the hands of a *bric-a-brac* collector. He also wrote letters to *The Daily Chronicle* and *Nature*, but both those periodicals, suspecting a hoax, asked him to reconsider his action before they printed, and he was advised that such a strange story, unfortunately so bare of supporting evidence, might imperil his reputation as an investigator. Moreover, the calls of his proper work were urgent. So that after a month or so, save for an occasional reminder to certain dealers, he had reluctantly to abandon the quest for the crystal egg, and from that day to this it remains undiscovered. Occasionally, however, he tells me, and I can quite believe him, he has bursts of zeal, in which he abandons his more urgent occupation and resumes the search.

Whether or not it will remain lost for ever, with the material and origin of it, are things equally speculative at the present time. If the present purchaser is a collector, one would have expected the enquiries of Mr. Wace to have reached him through the dealers. He has been able to discover Mr. Cave's clergyman and "Oriental"—no other than the Rev. James Parker and the young Prince of Bosso-Kuni in Java. I am obliged to them for certain particulars. The object of the Prince was simply curiosity—and extravagance. He was so eager to buy because Cave was so oddly reluctant to sell. It is just as possible that the buyer in the second instance was simply a casual purchaser and not a collector at all, and the crystal egg, for all I know, may at the present moment be within a mile of me, decorating a drawing-room or serving as a paper-weight—its remarkable functions all unknown. Indeed, it is partly with the idea of such a possibility that I have thrown this narrative into a form that will give it a chance of being read by the ordinary consumer of fiction.

My own ideas in the matter are practically identical with those of Mr. Wace. I believe the crystal on the mast in Mars and the crystal egg of Mr. Cave's to be in some physical, but at present quite inexplicable, way *en rapport*, and we both believe further that the terrestrial crystal must have been—possibly at some remote date—sent hither from that planet, in order to give the Martians a near view of our affairs. Possibly the fellows to the crystals on the other masts are also on our globe. No theory of hallucination suffices for the facts.

Moxon's Master

Ambrose Bierce

Ambrose Bierce (1842–1914?) was best known a writer of macabre fiction and stories drawn from his experiences in the American Civil War. Occasionally, he explored science fiction themes, as in this early tale of robotics, which first appeared in the April 16, 1899 issue of The San Francisco Examiner. *Bierce's tale may have been inspired by "Maelzel's Chess Player" (1836), an essay Edgar Allan Poe wrote exposing a supposed chess-playing automaton as a hoax.*

"Are you serious?—do you really believe that a machine thinks?"

I got no immediate reply; Moxon was apparently intent upon the coals in the grate, touching them deftly here and there with the fire-poker till they signified a sense of his attention by a brighter glow. For several weeks I had been observing in him a growing habit of delay in—answering even the most trivial of commonplace questions. His air, however, was that of preoccupation rather than deliberation: one might have said that he had "something on his mind."

Presently he said:

"What is a 'machine?' The word has been variously defined. Here is one definition from a popular dictionary: 'Any instrument or organization by which power is applied and made effective, or a desired effect produced.' Well, then, is not a man a machine? And you will admit that he thinks—or thinks he thinks."

"If you do not wish to answer my question," I said, rather testily, "why not say so?—all that you say is mere evasion. You know well enough that when I say 'machine' I do not mean a man, but something that man has made and controls."

"When it does not control him," he said, rising abruptly and looking out of a window, whence nothing was visible in the blackness of a stormy night. A moment later he turned about and with a smile said: "I beg your pardon; I had no thought of evasion. I considered the dictionary man's unconscious testimony suggestive and worth something in the discussion. I can give your question a direct answer easily enough: I do believe that a machine thinks about the work that it is doing."

That was direct enough, certainly. It was not altogether pleasing, for it tended to confirm a sad suspicion that Moxon's devotion to study and work in his machine-shop had not been good for him. I knew, for one thing, that he suffered from insomnia, and that is no light affliction. Had it affected his mind? His reply to my question seemed to me then evidence that it had; perhaps I should think differently about it now. I was younger then, and among the blessings that are not denied to youth is ignorance. Incited by that great stimulant to controversy, I said:

"And what, pray, does it think with—in the absence of a brain?"

The reply, coming with less than his customary delay, took his favorite form of counter-interrogation:

"With what does a plant think—in the absence of a brain?"

"Ah, plants also belong to the philosopher class! I should be pleased to know some of their conclusions; you may omit the premises."

"Perhaps," he replied, apparently unaffected by my foolish irony, "you may be able to infer their convictions from their acts. I will spare you the familiar examples of the sensitive mimosa, the several insectivorous flowers and those whose stamens bend down and shake their pollen upon the entering bee in order that he may fertilize their distant mates. But observe this. In an open spot in my garden I planted a climbing vine. When it was barely above the surface I set a stake into the soil a yard away. The vine at once made for it, but as it was about to reach it after several days I removed it a few feet. The vine at once altered its course, making an acute angle, and again made for the stake. This manœuvre was repeated several times, but finally, as if discouraged, the vine abandoned the pursuit and ignoring further attempts to divert it traveled to a small tree, further away, which it climbed.

"Roots of the eucalyptus will prolong themselves incredibly in search of moisture. A well-known horticulturist relates that one entered an old drain pipe and followed it until it came to a break, where a section of the pipe had been removed to make way for a stone wall that had been built across its course. The root left the drain and followed the wall until it found an opening where a stone had fallen out. It crept through and following the other side of the wall back to the drain, entered the unexplored part and resumed its journey."

"And all this?"

"Can you miss the significance of it? It shows the consciousness of plants. It proves that they think."

"Even if it did—what then? We were speaking, not of plants, but of machines. They may be composed partly of wood—wood that has no longer vitality—or wholly of metal. Is thought an attribute also of the mineral kingdom?"

"How else do you explain the phenomena, for example, of crystallization?"

"I do not explain them."

"Because you cannot without affirming what you wish to deny, namely, intelligent cooperation among the constituent elements of the crystals. When soldiers form lines, or hollow squares, you call it reason. When wild geese in flight take the form of a letter V you say instinct. When the homogeneous atoms of a mineral, moving freely in solution, arrange themselves into shapes mathematically perfect, or particles of frozen moisture into the symmetrical and beautiful forms of snowflakes, you have nothing to say. You have not even invented a name to conceal your heroic unreason."

Moxon was speaking with unusual animation and earnestness. As he paused I heard in an adjoining room known to me as his "machine-shop," which no one but himself was permitted to enter, a singular thumping sound, as of some one pounding upon a table with an open hand. Moxon heard it at the same moment and, visibly agitated, rose and hurriedly passed into the room whence it came. I thought it odd that any one else should be in there, and my interest in my friend—with doubtless a touch of unwarrantable curiosity—led me to listen intently, though, I am happy to say, not at the keyhole. There were confused sounds, as of a struggle or scuffle; the floor shook. I distinctly heard hard breathing and a hoarse whisper which said "Damn you!" Then all was silent, and presently Moxon reappeared and said, with a rather sorry smile:

"Pardon me for leaving you so abruptly. I have a machine in there that lost its temper and cut up rough."

Fixing my eyes steadily upon his left cheek, which was traversed by four parallel excoriations showing blood, I said:

"How would it do to trim its nails?"

I could have spared myself the jest; he gave it no attention, but seated himself in the chair that he had left and resumed the interrupted monologue as if nothing had occurred:

"Doubtless you do not hold with those (I need not name them to a man of your reading) who have taught that all matter is sentient, that every atom is a living, feeling, conscious being. *I* do. There is no such thing as dead, inert matter: it is all alive; all instinct with force, actual and potential; all sensitive to the same forces in its environment and susceptible to the contagion of higher and subtler ones residing in such superior organisms as it may be brought into relation with, as those of man when he is fashioning it into an instrument of his will. It absorbs something of his intelligence and purpose—more of them in proportion to the complexity of the resulting machine and that of its work.

"Do you happen to recall Herbert Spencer's definition of 'Life'? I read it thirty years ago. He may have altered it afterward, for anything I know, but in all that time I have been unable to think of a single word that could profitably be changed or added or removed. It seems to me not only the best definition, but the only possible one.

"'Life,' he says, 'is a definite combination of heterogeneous changes, both simultaneous and successive, in correspondence with external coexistences and sequences.'"

"That defines the phenomenon," I said, "but gives no hint of its cause."

"That," he replied, "is all that any definition can do. As Mill points out, we know nothing of cause except as an antecedent—nothing of effect except as a consequent. Of certain phenomena, one never occurs without another, which is dissimilar: the first in point of time we call cause, the second, effect. One who had many times seen a rabbit pursued by a dog, and had never seen rabbits and dogs otherwise, would think the rabbit the cause of the dog.

"But I fear," he added, laughing naturally enough, "that my rabbit is leading me a long way from the track of my legitimate quarry: I'm indulging in the pleasure of the chase for its own sake. What I want you to observe is that in Herbert Spencer's definition of 'life' the activity of a machine is included—there is nothing in the definition that is not applicable to it. According to this sharpest of observers and deepest of thinkers, if a man during his period of activity is alive, so is a machine when in operation. As an inventor and constructor of machines I know that to be true."

Moxon was silent for a long time, gazing absently into the fire. It was growing late and I thought it time to be going, but somehow I did not like the notion of leaving him in that isolated house, all alone except for the presence of some person of whose nature my conjectures could go no further than that it was unfriendly, perhaps malign. Leaning toward him and looking earnestly into his eyes while making a motion with my hand through the door of his workshop, I said:

"Moxon, whom have you in there?"

Somewhat to my surprise he laughed lightly and answered without hesitation:

"Nobody; the incident that you have in mind was caused by my folly in leaving a machine in action with nothing to act upon, while I undertook the interminable task of enlightening your understanding. Do you happen to know that Consciousness is the creature of Rhythm?"

"O bother them both!" I replied, rising and laying hold of my overcoat. "I'm going to wish you good night; and I'll add the hope that the machine which you inadvertently left in action will have her gloves on the next time you think it needful to stop her."

Without waiting to observe the effect of my shot I left the house.

Rain was falling, and the darkness was intense. In the sky beyond the crest of a hill toward which I groped my way along precarious plank sidewalks and across miry, unpaved streets I could see the faint glow of the city's lights, but behind me nothing was visible but a single window of Moxon's house. It glowed with what seemed to me a mysterious and fateful meaning. I knew it was an uncurtained aperture in my friend's "machine-shop," and I had little doubt that he had resumed the studies interrupted by his duties as my instructor in mechanical consciousness and the fatherhood of Rhythm. Odd, and in some degree humorous, as his convictions seemed to me at that time, I could not wholly divest myself of the feeling that they had some tragic relation to his life and character—perhaps to his destiny—although I no longer entertained the notion that they were the vagaries of a disordered mind. Whatever might be thought of his views, his exposition of them was too logical for that. Over and over, his last words came back to me: "Consciousness is the creature of Rhythm." Bald and terse as the statement was, I now found it infinitely alluring. At each recurrence it broadened in meaning and deepened in suggestion. Why, here, (I thought) is something upon which to found a philosophy. If consciousness is the product of rhythm all things *are* conscious, for all have motion, and all motion is rhythmic. I wondered if Moxon knew the significance and breadth of his thought— the scope of this momentous generalization; or had he arrived at his philosophic faith by the tortuous and uncertain road of observation?

That faith was then new to me, and all Moxon's expounding had failed to make me a convert; but now it seemed as if a great light shone about me, like that which fell upon Saul of Tarsus; and out there in the storm and darkness and solitude I experienced what Lewes calls "The endless variety and excitement of philosophic thought." I exulted in a new sense of knowledge, a new pride of reason. My feet seemed hardly to touch the earth; it was as if I were uplifted and borne through the air by invisible wings.

Yielding to an impulse to seek further light from him whom I now recognized as my master and guide, I had unconsciously turned about, and almost before I was aware of having done so found myself again at Moxon's door. I was drenched with rain, but felt no discomfort. Unable in my excitement to find the doorbell I instinctively tried the knob. It turned and, entering, I mounted the stairs to the room that I had so recently left. All was dark and silent; Moxon, as I had supposed, was in the adjoining room—the "machine-shop." Groping along the wall until I found the communicating door I knocked loudly several times, but got no response, which I attributed to the uproar outside, for the wind was blowing a gale and dashing the rain against the thin walls in sheets. The drumming upon the shingle roof spanning the unceiled room was loud and incessant.

I had never been invited into the machine-shop—had, indeed, been denied admittance, as had all others, with one exception, a skilled metal worker, of whom no one knew anything except that his name was Haley and his habit silence. But in my spiritual exaltation, discretion and civility were alike forgotten and I opened the door. What I saw took all philosophical speculation out of me in short order.

Moxon sat facing me at the farther side of a small table upon which a single candle made all the light that was in the room. Opposite him, his back toward me, sat another person. On the table between the two was a chessboard; the men were playing. I knew little of chess, but as only a few pieces were on the board it was obvious that the game was near its close. Moxon was intensely interested—not so much, it seemed to me, in the game as in his antagonist, upon whom he had fixed so intent a look that, standing though I did directly in the line of his vision, I was altogether unobserved. His face was ghastly white, and his eyes glittered like diamonds. Of his antagonist I had only a back view, but that was sufficient; I should not have cared to see his face.

He was apparently not more than five feet in height, with proportions suggesting those of a gorilla—a tremendous breadth of shoulders, thick, short neck and broad, squat head, which had a tangled growth of black hair and was topped with a crimson fez. A tunic of the same color, belted tightly to the waist, reached the seat—apparently a box—upon which he sat; his legs and feet were not seen. His left forearm appeared to rest in his lap; he moved his pieces with his right hand, which seemed disproportionately long.

I had shrunk back and now stood a little to one side of the doorway and in shadow. If Moxon had looked farther than the face of his opponent he could have observed nothing now, except that the door was open. Something forbade me either to enter or to retire, a feeling— I know not how it came—that I was in the presence

138

of an imminent tragedy and might serve my friend by remaining. With a scarcely conscious rebellion against the indelicacy of the act I remained.

The play was rapid. Moxon hardly glanced at the board before making his moves, and to my unskilled eye seemed to move the piece most convenient to his hand, his motions in doing so being quick, nervous and lacking in precision. The response of his antagonist, while equally prompt in the inception, was made with a slow, uniform, mechanical and, I thought, somewhat theatrical movement of the arm, that was a sore trial to my patience. There was something unearthly about it all, and I caught myself shuddering. But I was wet and cold.

Two or three times after moving a piece the stranger slightly inclined his head, and each time I observed that Moxon shifted his king. All at once the thought came to me that the man was dumb. And then that he was a machine—an automaton chess-player! Then I remembered that Moxon had once spoken to me of having invented such a piece of mechanism, though I did not understand that it had actually been constructed. Was all his talk about the consciousness and intelligence of machines merely a prelude to eventual exhibition of this device—only a trick to intensify the effect of its mechanical action upon me in my ignorance of its secret?

A fine end, this, of all my intellectual transports—my "endless variety and excitement of philosophic thought!" I was about to retire in disgust when something occurred to hold my curiosity. I observed a shrug of the thing's great shoulders, as if it were irritated: and so natural was this—so entirely human—that in my new view of the matter it startled me. Nor was that all, for a moment later it struck the table sharply with its clenched hand. At that gesture Moxon seemed even more startled than I: he pushed his chair a little backward, as in alarm.

Presently Moxon, whose play it was, raised his hand high above the board, pounced upon one of his pieces like a sparrow-hawk and with the exclamation "checkmate!" rose quickly to his feet and stepped behind his chair. The automaton sat motionless.

The wind had now gone down, but I heard, at lessening intervals and progressively louder, the rumble and roll of thunder. In the pauses between I now became conscious of a low humming or buzzing which, like the thunder, grew momentarily louder and more distinct. It seemed to come from the body of the automaton, and was unmistakably a whirring of wheels. It gave me the impression of a disordered mechanism which had escaped the repressive and regulating action of some controlling part—an effect such as might be expected if a pawl should be jostled from the teeth of a ratchet-wheel. But before I had time for much conjecture as to its nature my attention was taken by the strange motions of the automaton itself.

A slight but continuous convulsion appeared to have possession of it. In body and head it shook like a man with palsy or an ague chill, and the motion augmented every moment until the entire figure was in violent agitation. Suddenly it sprang to its feet and with a movement almost too quick for the eye to follow shot forward across table and chair, with both arms thrust forth to their full length—the posture and lunge of a diver. Moxon tried to throw himself backward out of reach, but he was too late: I saw the horrible thing's hands close upon his throat, his own clutch its wrists. Then the table was overturned, the candle thrown to the floor and extinguished, and all was black dark. But the noise of the struggle was dreadfully distinct, and most terrible of all were the raucous, squawking sounds made by the strangled man's efforts to breathe. Guided by the infernal hubbub, I sprang to the rescue of my friend, but had hardly taken a stride in the darkness when the whole room blazed with a blinding white light that burned into my brain and heart and memory a vivid picture of the combatants on the floor, Moxon underneath, his throat still in the clutch of those iron hands, his head forced backward, his eyes protruding, his mouth wide open and his tongue thrust out; and—horrible contrast!—upon the painted face of his assassin an expression of tranquil and profound thought, as in the solution of a problem in chess! This I observed, then all was blackness and silence.

Three days later I recovered consciousness in a hospital. As the memory of that tragic night slowly evolved in my ailing brain recognized in my attendant Moxon's confidential workman, Haley. Responding to a look he approached, smiling.

"Tell me about it," I managed to say, faintly—"all about it."

"Certainly," he said; "you were carried unconscious from a burning house—Moxon's. Nobody knows how you came to be there. You may have to do a little explaining. The origin of the fire is a bit mysterious, too. My own notion is that the house was struck by lightning."

"And Moxon?"

"Buried yesterday—what was left of him."

Apparently this reticent person could unfold himself on occasion. When imparting shocking intelligence to the sick he was affable enough. After some moments of the keenest mental suffering I ventured to ask another question:

"Who rescued me?"

"Well, if that interests you—I did."

"Thank you, Mr. Haley, and may God bless you for it. Did you rescue, also, that charming product of your skill, the automaton chess-player that murdered its inventor?"

The man was silent a long time, looking away from me. Presently he turned and gravely said:

"Do you know that?"

"I do," I replied; "I saw it done."

That was many years ago. If asked to-day I should answer less confidently.

The Shadow
and the Flash

JACK LONDON

In his popular tales of adventure—notably the classic novels The Call of the Wild *(1903) and* White Fang *(1906)—Jack London (1876– 1916) contrasted civilization and savagery as it manifests in the lives of his modern characters. This story, which appeared in the June 1903 issue of* The Bookman, *is one of a handful in which London explored science fiction concepts. Though set in a world of recondite and sophisticated science, its rival characters wage battle with the same ferocity shown by the primitives in London's wilderness adventures.*

When I look back, I realize what a peculiar friendship it was. First, there was Lloyd Inwood, tall, slender, and finely knit, nervous and dark. And then Paul Tichlorne, tall, slender, and finely knit, nervous and blond. Each was the replica of the other in everything except color. Lloyd's eyes were black; Paul's were blue. Under stress of excitement, the blood coursed olive in the face of Lloyd, crimson in the face of Paul. But outside this matter of coloring they were as like as two peas. Both were high-strung, prone to excessive tension and endurance, and they lived at concert pitch.

But there was a trio involved in this remarkable friendship, and the third was short, and fat, and chunky, and lazy, and, loath to say, it was I. Paul and Lloyd seemed born to rivalry with each other, and I to be peacemaker between them. We grew up together, the three of us, and full often have I received the angry blows

142

each intended for the other. They were always competing, striving to outdo each other, and when entered upon some such struggle there was no limit either to their endeavors or passions.

This intense spirit of rivalry obtained in their studies and their games. If Paul memorized one canto of "Marmion," Lloyd memorized two cantos, Paul came back with three, and Lloyd again with four, till each knew the whole poem by heart. I remember an incident that occurred at the swimming hole—an incident tragically significant of the life-struggle between them. The boys had a game of diving to the bottom of a ten-foot pool and holding on by submerged roots to see who could stay under the longest. Paul and Lloyd allowed themselves to be bantered into making the descent together. When I saw their faces, set and determined, disappear in the water as they sank swiftly down, I felt a foreboding of something dreadful. The moments sped, the ripples died away, the face of the pool grew placid and untroubled, and neither black nor golden head broke surface in quest of air. We above grew anxious. The longest record of the longest-winded boy had been exceeded, and still there was no sign. Air bubbles trickled slowly upward, showing that the breath had been expelled from their lungs, and after that the bubbles ceased to trickle upward. Each second became interminable, and, unable longer to endure the suspense, I plunged into the water.

I found them down at the bottom, clutching tight to the roots, their heads not a foot apart, their eyes wide open, each glaring fixedly at the other. They were suffering frightful torment, writhing and twisting in the pangs of voluntary suffocation; for neither would let go and acknowledge himself beaten. I tried to break Paul's hold on the root, but he resisted me fiercely. Then I lost my breath and came to the surface, badly scared. I quickly explained the situation, and half a dozen of us went down and by main strength tore them loose. By the time we got them out, both were unconscious, and it was only after much barrel-rolling and rubbing and pounding that they finally came to their senses. They would have drowned there, had no one rescued them.

When Paul Tichlorne entered college, he let it be generally understood that he was going in for the social sciences. Lloyd Inwood, entering at the same time, elected to take the same course. But Paul had had it secretly in mind all the time to study the natural sciences, specializing on chemistry, and at the last moment he switched over. Though Lloyd had already arranged his year's work and attended the first lectures, he at once followed Paul's lead and went in for the natural sciences and especially for chemistry. Their rivalry soon became a noted thing throughout the university. Each was a spur to the other, and they went into chemistry deeper than did ever students before—so deep, in fact, that ere they took their sheepskins they could have stumped any chemistry or "cow college" professor in the institution, save "old" Moss, head of the department, and even him they puzzled and edified more than once. Lloyd's discovery of the "death bacillus" of the sea toad, and his experiments on it with potassium cyanide, sent his name and that of his university ringing round the world; nor was Paul a whit behind when he succeeded in producing laboratory colloids exhibiting amoeba-like activities, and when he cast new light upon the processes of fertilization through his startling experiments with simple sodium chlorides and magnesium solutions on low forms of marine life.

It was in their undergraduate days, however, in the midst of their profoundest plunges into the mysteries of organic chemistry, that Doris Van Benschoten entered into their lives. Lloyd met her first, but within twenty-four hours Paul saw to it that he also made her acquaintance. Of course, they fell in love with her, and she became the only thing in life worth living for. They wooed her with equal ardor and fire, and so intense became their struggle for her that half the student-body took to wagering wildly on the result. Even "old" Moss, one day, after an astounding demonstration in his private laboratory by Paul, was guilty to the extent of a month's salary of backing him to become the bridegroom of Doris Van Benschoten.

In the end she solved the problem in her own way, to everybody's satisfaction except Paul's and Lloyd's. Getting them together, she said that she really could not choose between them because she loved them both equally well; and that, unfortunately, since polyandry was not permitted in the United States she would be compelled to forego the honor and happiness of marrying either of them. Each blamed the other for this lamentable outcome, and the bitterness between them grew more bitter.

But things came to a head enough. It was at my home, after they had taken their degrees and dropped out of the world's sight, that the beginning of the end came to pass. Both were men of means, with little inclination and no necessity for professional life. My friendship and their mutual animosity were the two things that linked them in any way together. While they were very often at my place, they made it a fastidious point to avoid each other on such visits, though it was inevitable, under the circumstances, that they should come upon each other occasionally.

On the day I have in recollection, Paul Tichlorne had been mooning all morning in my study over a current scientific review. This left me free to my own affairs, and I was out among my roses when Lloyd Inwood arrived. Clipping and pruning and tacking the climbers on the porch, with my mouth full of nails, and Lloyd following me about and lending a hand now and again, we fell to discussing the mythical race of invisible people, that strange and vagrant people the traditions of which have come down to us. Lloyd warmed to the talk in his nervous, jerky fashion, and was soon interrogating the physical properties and possibilities of invisibility. A perfectly black object, he contended, would elude and defy the acutest vision.

"Color is a sensation," he was saying. "It has no objective reality. Without light, we can see neither colors nor objects themselves. All objects are black in the dark, and in the dark it is impossible to see them. If no light strikes upon them, then no light is flung back from them to the eye, and so we have no vision-evidence of their being."

"But we see black objects in daylight," I objected.

"Very true," he went on warmly. "And that is because they are not perfectly black. Were they perfectly black, absolutely black, as it were, we could not see them— ay, not in the blaze of a thousand suns could we see them! And so I say, with the right pigments, properly compounded, an absolutely black paint could be produced which would render invisible whatever it was applied to."

"It would be a remarkable discovery," I said non-committally, for the whole thing seemed too fantastic for aught but speculative purposes.

"Remarkable!" Lloyd slapped me on the shoulder. "I should say so. Why, old chap, to coat myself with such a paint would be to put the world at my feet. The secrets of kings and courts would be mine, the machinations of diplomats and politicians, the play of stock-gamblers, the plans of trusts and corporations. I could keep my hand on the inner pulse of things and become the greatest power in the world. And I—" He broke off shortly, then added, "Well, I have begun my experiments, and I don't mind telling you that I'm right in line for it."

A laugh from the doorway startled us. Paul Tichlorne was standing there, a smile of mockery on his lips.

"You forget, my dear Lloyd," he said.

"Forget what?"

"You forget," Paul went on—"ah, you forget the shadow."

I saw Lloyd's face drop, but he answered sneeringly, "I can carry a sunshade, you know." Then he turned suddenly and fiercely upon him. "Look here, Paul, you'll keep out of this if you know what's good for you."

A rupture seemed imminent, but Paul laughed good-naturedly. "I wouldn't lay fingers on your dirty pigments. Succeed beyond your most sanguine expectations, yet you will always fetch up against the shadow. You can't get away from it. Now I shall go on the very opposite tack. In the very nature of my proposition the shadow will be eliminated—"

"Transparency!" ejaculated Lloyd, instantly. "But it can't be achieved."

"Oh, no; of course not." And Paul shrugged his shoulders and strolled off down the briar-rose path.

This was the beginning of it. Both men attacked the problem with all the tremendous energy for which they were noted, and with a rancor and bitterness that made me tremble for the success of either. Each trusted me to the utmost, and in the long weeks of experimentation that followed I was made a party to both sides, listening to their theorizings and witnessing their demonstrations. Never, by word or sign, did I convey to either the slightest hint of the other's progress, and they respected me for the seal I put upon my lips.

Lloyd Inwood, after prolonged and unintermittent application, when the tension upon his mind and body became too great to bear, had a strange way of obtaining relief. He attended prize fights. It was at one of these brutal exhibitions, whither he had dragged me in order to tell his latest results, that his theory received striking confirmation.

"Do you see that red-whiskered man?" he asked, pointing across the ring to the fifth tier of seats on the opposite side. "And do you see the next man to him, the one in the white hat? Well, there is quite a gap between them, is there not?"

"Certainly," I answered. "They are a seat apart. The gap is the unoccupied seat."

He leaned over to me and spoke seriously. "Between the red-whiskered man and the white-hatted man sits Ben Wasson. You have heard me speak of him. He is the cleverest pugilist of his weight in the country. He is also a Caribbean negro, full-blooded, and the blackest in the United States. He has on a black overcoat buttoned up. I saw him when he came in and took that seat. As soon as he sat down he disappeared. Watch closely; he may smile."

I was for crossing over to verify Lloyd's statement, but he restrained me. "Wait," he said.

I waited and watched, till the red-whiskered man turned his head as though addressing the unoccupied seat; and then, in that empty space, I saw the rolling whites of a pair of eyes and the white double-crescent of two rows of teeth, and for the instant I could make out a negro's face. But with the passing of the smile his visibility passed, and the chair seemed vacant as before.

"Were he perfectly black, you could sit alongside him and not see him," Lloyd said; and I confess the illustration was apt enough to make me well-nigh convinced.

I visited Lloyd's laboratory a number of times after that, and found him always deep in his search after the absolute black. His experiments covered all sorts of pigments, such as lamp-blacks, tars, carbonized vegetable matters, soots of oils and fats, and the various carbonized animal substances.

"White light is composed of the seven primary colors," he argued to me. "But it is itself, of itself, invisible. Only by being reflected from objects do it and the objects become visible. But only that portion of it that is reflected becomes visible. For instance, here is a blue tobacco-box. The white light strikes against it, and, with one exception, all its component colors—violet, indigo, green, yellow, orange, and red— are absorbed. The one exception is *blue*. It is not absorbed, but reflected. Wherefore the tobacco-box gives us a sensation of blueness. We do not see the other colors because they are absorbed. We see only the blue. For the same reason grass is *green*. The green waves of white light are thrown upon our eyes."

"When we paint our houses, we do not apply color to them," he said at another time. "What we do is to apply certain substances that have the property of absorbing from white light all the colors except those that we would have our houses appear. When a substance reflects all the colors to the eye, it seems to us white. When it absorbs all the colors, it is black. But, as I said before, we have as yet no perfect black. *All* the colors are not absorbed. The perfect black, guarding against high lights, will be utterly and absolutely invisible. Look at that, for example."

He pointed to the palette lying on his work-table. Different shades of black pigments were brushed on it. One, in particular, I could hardly see. It gave my eyes a blurring sensation, and I rubbed them and looked again.

"That," he said impressively, "is the blackest black you or any mortal man ever looked upon. But just you wait, and I'll have a black so black that no mortal man will be able to look upon it—*and see it!*"

On the other hand, I used to find Paul Tichlorne plunged as deeply into the study of light polarization, diffraction, and interference, single and double refraction, and all manner of strange organic compounds.

"Transparency: a state or quality of body which permits all rays of light to pass through," he defined for me. "That is what I am seeking. Lloyd blunders up against the shadow with his perfect opaqueness. But I escape it. A transparent body casts no shadow; neither does it reflect light-waves—that is, the perfectly transparent does not. So, avoiding high lights, not only will such a body cast no shadow, but, since it reflects no light, it will also be invisible."

We were standing by the window at another time. Paul was engaged in polishing a number of lenses, which were ranged along the sill. Suddenly, after a pause in the conversation, he said, "Oh! I've dropped a lens. Stick your head out, old man, and see where it went to."

Out I started to thrust my head, but a sharp blow on the forehead caused me to recoil. I rubbed my bruised brow and gazed with reproachful inquiry at Paul, who was laughing in gleeful, boyish fashion.

"Well?" he said.

"Well?" I echoed.

"Why don't you investigate?" he demanded. And investigate I did. Before thrusting out my head, my senses, automatically active, had told me there was nothing there, that nothing intervened between me and out-of-doors, that the aperture of the window opening was utterly empty. I stretched forth my hand and felt a hard object, smooth and cool and flat, which my touch, out of its experience, told me to be glass. I looked again, but could see positively nothing.

"White quartzose sand," Paul rattled off, "sodic carbonate, slaked lime, cutlet, manganese peroxide—there you have it, the finest French plate glass, made by the great St. Gobain Company, who made the finest plate glass in the world, and this is the finest piece they ever made. It cost a king's ransom. But look at it! You can't see it. You don't know it's there till you run your head against it.

"Eh, old boy! That's merely an object-lesson—certain elements, in themselves opaque, yet so compounded as to give a resultant body which is transparent. But that is a matter of inorganic chemistry, you say. Very true. But I dare to assert, standing here on my two feet, that in the organic I can duplicate whatever occurs in the inorganic.

"Here!" He held a test-tube between me and the light, and I noted the cloudy or muddy liquid it contained. He emptied the contents of another test-tube into it, and almost instantly it became clear and sparkling.

"Or here!" With quick, nervous movements among his array of test-tubes, he turned a white solution to a wine color, and a light yellow solution to a dark brown. He dropped a piece of litmus paper into an acid, when it changed instantly to red, and on floating it in an alkali it turned as quickly to blue.

"The litmus paper is still the litmus paper," he enunciated in the formal manner of the lecturer. "I have not changed it into something else. Then what did I do? I merely changed the arrangement of its molecules. Where, at first, it absorbed all colors from the light but red, its molecular structure was so changed that it absorbed red and all colors except blue. And so it goes, ad infinitum. Now, what I purpose to do is this." He paused for a space. "I purpose to seek—ay, and to find—the proper reagents, which, acting upon the living organism, will bring about molecular changes analogous to those you have just witnessed. But these reagents, which I shall find, and for that matter, upon which I already have my hands, will not turn the living body to blue or red or black, but they will turn it to transparency. All light will pass through it. It will be invisible. It will cast no shadow."

A few weeks later I went hunting with Paul. He had been promising me for some time that I should have the pleasure of shooting over a wonderful dog—the most wonderful dog, in fact, that ever man shot over, so he averred, and continued to aver till my curiosity was aroused. But on the morning in question I was disappointed, for there was no dog in evidence.

"Don't see him about," Paul remarked unconcernedly, and we set off across the fields.

I could not imagine, at the time, what was ailing me, but I had a feeling of some impending and deadly illness. My nerves were all awry, and, from the astounding tricks they played me, my senses seemed to have run riot. Strange sounds disturbed me. At times I heard the swish-swish of grass being shoved aside, and once the patter of feet across a patch of stony ground.

"Did you hear anything, Paul?" I asked once.

But he shook his head, and thrust his feet steadily forward.

While climbing a fence, I heard the low, eager whine of a dog, apparently from within a couple of feet of me; but on looking about me I saw nothing.

I dropped to the ground, limp and trembling.

"Paul," I said, "we had better return to the house. I am afraid I am going to be sick."

"Nonsense, old man," he answered. "The sunshine has gone to your head like wine. You'll be all right. It's famous weather."

But, passing along a narrow path through a clump of cottonwoods, some object brushed against my legs and I stumbled and nearly fell. I looked with sudden anxiety at Paul.

"What's the matter?" he asked. "Tripping over your own feet?"

I kept my tongue between my teeth and plodded on, though sore perplexed and thoroughly satisfied that some acute and mysterious malady had attacked my nerves. So far my eyes had escaped; but, when we got to the open fields again, even my vision went back on me. Strange flashes of vari-colored, rainbow light began to appear and disappear on the path before me. Still, I managed to keep myself in hand, till the vari-colored lights persisted for a space of fully twenty seconds, dancing and flashing in continuous play. Then I sat down, weak and shaky.

"It's all up with me," I gasped, covering my eyes with my hands. "It has attacked my eyes. Paul, take me home."

But Paul laughed long and loud. "What did I tell you?—the most wonderful dog, eh? Well, what do you think?"

He turned partly from me and began to whistle. I heard the patter of feet, the panting of a heated animal, and the unmistakable yelp of a dog. Then Paul stooped down and apparently fondled the empty air.

"Here! Give me your fist."

And he rubbed my hand over the cold nose and jowls of a dog. A dog it certainly was, with the shape and the smooth, short coat of a pointer.

Suffice to say, I speedily recovered my spirits and control. Paul put a collar about the animal's neck and tied his handkerchief to its tail. And then was vouchsafed us the remarkable sight of an empty collar and a waving handkerchief cavorting over the fields. It was something to see that collar and handkerchief pin a bevy of quail in a clump of locusts and remain rigid and immovable till we had flushed the birds.

Now and again the dog emitted the vari-colored light-flashes I have mentioned. The one thing, Paul explained, which he had not anticipated and which he doubted could be overcome.

"They're a large family," he said, "these sun dogs, wind dogs, rainbows, halos, and parhelia. They are produced by refraction of light from mineral and ice crystals, from mist, rain, spray, and no end of things; and I am afraid they are the penalty I must pay for transparency. I escaped Lloyd's shadow only to fetch up against the rainbow flash."

A couple of days later, before the entrance to Paul's laboratory, I encountered a terrible stench. So overpowering was it that it was easy to discover the source—a mass of putrescent matter on the doorstep which in general outlines resembled a dog.

Paul was startled when he investigated my find. It was his invisible dog, or rather, what had been his invisible dog, for it was now plainly visible. It had been playing about but a few minutes before in all health and strength. Closer examination revealed that the skull had been crushed by some heavy blow. While it was strange that the animal should have been killed, the inexplicable thing was that it should so quickly decay.

"The reagents I injected into its system were harmless," Paul explained. "Yet they were powerful, and it appears that when death comes they force practically instantaneous disintegration. Remarkable! Most remarkable! Well, the only thing is not to die. They do not harm so long as one lives. But I do wonder who smashed in that dog's head."

Light, however, was thrown upon this when a frightened housemaid brought the news that Gaffer Bedshaw had that very morning, not more than an hour back, gone violently insane, and was strapped down at home, in the huntsman's lodge, where he raved of a battle with a ferocious and gigantic beast that he had encountered in the Tichlorne pasture. He claimed that the thing, whatever it was, was invisible, that with his own eyes he had seen that it was invisible; wherefore his tearful wife and daughters shook their heads, and wherefore he but waxed the more violent, and the gardener and the coachman tightened the straps by another hole.

Nor, while Paul Tichlorne was thus successfully mastering the problem of invisibility, was Lloyd Inwood a whit behind. I went over in answer to a message of his to come and see how he was getting on. Now his laboratory occupied an isolated situation in the midst of his vast grounds. It was built in a pleasant little glade, surrounded on all sides by a dense forest growth, and was to be gained by way of a winding and erratic path. But I have travelled that path so often as to know every foot of it, and conceive my surprise when I came upon the glade and found no laboratory. The quaint shed structure with its red sandstone chimney was not. Nor did it look as if it ever had been. There were no signs of ruin, no débris, nothing.

I started to walk across what had once been its site. "This," I said to myself, "should be where the step went up to the door." Barely were the words out of my mouth when I stubbed my toe on some obstacle, pitched forward, and butted my head into something that *felt* very much like a door. I reached out my hand. It *was* a door. I found the knob and turned it. And at once, as the door swung inward on its hinges, the whole interior of the laboratory impinged upon my vision. Greeting Lloyd, I closed the door and backed up the path a few paces. I could see nothing of the building. Returning and opening the door, at once all the furniture and every detail of the interior were visible. It was indeed startling, the sudden transition from void to light and form and color.

"What do you think of it, eh?" Lloyd asked, wringing my hand. "I slapped a couple of coats of absolute black on the outside yesterday afternoon to see how it worked. How's your head? You bumped it pretty solidly, I imagine."

"Never mind that," he interrupted my congratulations. "I've something better for you to do."

While he talked he began to strip, and when he stood naked before me he thrust a pot and brush into my hand and said, "Here, give me a coat of this."

It was an oily, shellac-like stuff, which spread quickly and easily over the skin and dried immediately.

"Merely preliminary and precautionary," he explained when I had finished; "but now for the real stuff."

I picked up another pot he indicated, and glanced inside, but could see nothing.

"It's empty," I said.

"Stick your finger in it."

I obeyed, and was aware of a sensation of cool moistness. On withdrawing my hand I glanced at the forefinger, the one I had immersed, but it had disappeared.

151

I moved and knew from the alternate tension and relaxation of the muscles that I moved it, but it defied my sense of sight. To all appearances I had been shorn of a finger; nor could I get any visual impression of it till I extended it under the skylight and saw its shadow plainly blotted on the floor.

Lloyd chuckled. "Now spread it on, and keep your eyes open."

I dipped the brush into the seemingly empty pot, and gave him a long stroke across his chest. With the passage of the brush the living flesh disappeared from beneath. I covered his right leg, and he was a one-legged man defying all laws of gravitation. And so, stroke by stroke, member by member, I painted Lloyd Inwood into nothingness. It was a creepy experience, and I was glad when naught remained in sight but his burning black eyes, poised apparently unsupported in mid-air.

"I have a refined and harmless solution for them," he said. "A fine spray with an air-brush, and presto! I am not."

This deftly accomplished, he said, "Now I shall move about, and do you tell me what sensations you experience."

"In the first place, I cannot see you," I said, and I could hear his gleeful laugh from the midst of the emptiness. "Of course," I continued, "you cannot escape your shadow, but that was to be expected. When you pass between my eye and an object, the object disappears, but so unusual and incomprehensible is its disappearance that it seems to me as though my eyes had blurred. When you move rapidly, I experience a bewildering succession of blurs. The blurring sensation makes my eyes ache and my brain tired."

"Have you any other warnings of my presence?" he asked.

"No, and yes," I answered. "When you are near me I have feelings similar to those produced by dank warehouses, gloomy crypts, and deep mines. And as sailors feel the loom of the land on dark nights, so I think I feel the loom of your body. But it is all very vague and intangible."

Long we talked that last morning in his laboratory; and when I turned to go, he put his unseen hand in mine with nervous grip, and said, "Now I shall conquer the world!" And I could not dare to tell him of Paul Tichlorne's equal success.

At home I found a note from Paul, asking me to come up immediately, and it was high noon when I came spinning up the driveway on my wheel. Paul called me from the tennis court, and I dismounted and went over. But the court was empty. As I stood there, gaping open-mouthed, a tennis ball struck me on the arm, and as I turned about, another whizzed past my ear. For aught I could see of my assailant, they came whirling at me from out of space, and right well was I peppered with them. But when the balls already flung at me began to come back for a second whack, I realized the situation. Seizing a racquet and keeping my eyes open, I quickly saw a rainbow flash appearing and disappearing and darting over the ground. I took out after it, and when I laid the racquet upon it for a half-dozen stout blows, Paul's voice rang out:

"Enough! Enough! Oh! Ouch! Stop! You're landing on my naked skin, you know! Ow! O-w-w! I'll be good! I'll be good! I only wanted you to see my metamorphosis," he said ruefully, and I imagined he was rubbing his hurts.

A few minutes later we were playing tennis—a handicap on my part, for I could have no knowledge of his position save when all the angles between himself, the sun, and me, were in proper conjunction. Then he flashed, and only then. But the flashes were more brilliant than the rainbow—purest blue, most delicate violet, brightest yellow, and all the intermediary shades, with the scintillant brilliancy of the diamond, dazzling, blinding, iridescent.

But in the midst of our play I felt a sudden cold chill, reminding me of deep mines and gloomy crypts, such a chill as I had experienced that very morning. The next moment, close to the net, I saw a ball rebound in mid-air and empty space, and at the same instant, a score of feet away, Paul Tichlorne emitted a rainbow flash. It could not be he from whom the ball had rebounded, and with sickening dread I realized that Lloyd Inwood had come upon the scene. To make sure, I looked for his shadow, and there it was, a shapeless blotch the girth of his body, (the sun was overhead), moving along the ground. I remembered his threat, and felt sure that all the long years of rivalry were about to culminate in uncanny battle.

I cried a warning to Paul, and heard a snarl as of a wild beast, and an answering snarl. I saw the dark blotch move swiftly across the court, and a brilliant burst of vari-colored light moving with equal swiftness to meet it; and then shadow and flash came together and there was the sound of unseen blows. The net went down before my frightened eyes. I sprang toward the fighters, crying:

"For God's sake!"

But their locked bodies smote against my knees, and I was overthrown.

"You keep out of this, old man!" I heard the voice of Lloyd Inwood from out of the emptiness. And then Paul's voice crying, "Yes, we've had enough of peacemaking!"

From the sound of their voices I knew they had separated. I could not locate Paul, and so approached the shadow that represented Lloyd. But from the other side came a stunning blow on the point of my jaw, and I heard Paul scream angrily, "Now will you keep away?"

Then they came together again, the impact of their blows, their groans and gasps, and the swift flashings and shadow-movings telling plainly of the deadliness of the struggle.

I shouted for help, and Gaffer Bedshaw came running into the court. I could see, as he approached, that he was looking at me strangely, but he collided with the combatants and was hurled headlong to the ground. With despairing shriek and a cry of "O Lord, I've got 'em!" he sprang to his feet and tore madly out of the court.

I could do nothing, so I sat up, fascinated and powerless, and watched the struggle. The noonday sun beat down with dazzling brightness on the naked tennis court. And it was naked. All I could see was the blotch of shadow and the rainbow flashes, the dust rising from the invisible feet, the earth tearing up from beneath the straining foot-grips, and the wire screen bulge once or twice as their bodies hurled against it. That was all, and after a time even that ceased. There were no more flashes, and the shadow had become long and stationary; and I remembered their set boyish faces when they clung to the roots in the deep coolness of the pool.

They found me an hour afterward. Some inkling of what had happened got to the servants and they quitted the Tichlorne service in a body. Gaffer Bedshaw never recovered from the second shock he received, and is confined in a madhouse, hopelessly incurable. The secrets of their marvellous discoveries died with Paul and Lloyd, both laboratories being destroyed by grief-stricken relatives. As for myself, I no longer care for chemical research, and science is a tabooed topic in my household. I have returned to my roses. Nature's colors are good enough for me.

The Ray of Displacement

HARRIET PRESCOTT SPOFFORD

Harriet Prescott Spofford (1835–1921) placed her tales of science fiction and the supernatural—like her non-fantasy fiction—in leading periodicals of the nineteenth and twentieth centuries. This story, from the October 1903 issue of Metropolitan Magazine, *shows the type of amusing paradoxes writers could conjure in tales of science run amok.*

"We should have to reach the Infinite to arrive at the Impossible."

It would interest none but students should I recite the circumstances of the discovery. Prosecuting my usual researches, I seemed rather to have stumbled on this tremendous thing than to have evolved it from formulæ.

Of course, you already know that all molecules, all atoms, are separated from each other by spaces perhaps as great, when compared relatively, as those which separate the members of the stellar universe. And when by my Y-ray I could so far increase these spaces that I could pass one solid body through another, owing to the differing situation of their atoms, I felt no disembodied spirit had wider, freer range than I. Until my discovery was made public my power over the material universe was practically unlimited.

Le Sage's theory concerning ultra-mundane corpuscles was rejected because corpuscles could not pass through solids. But here were corpuscles passing through solids. As I proceeded, I found that at the displacement of one one-billionth of a centimeter the object capable of passing through another was still visible, owing to the refraction of the air, and had the power of communicating its polarization; and that at two one-billionths the object became invisible, but that at either displacement the subject, if a person, could see into the present plane; and all movement and direction were voluntary. I further found my Y-ray could so polarize a substance that its touch in turn temporarily polarized anything with which it came in contact, a negative current moving atoms to the left, and a positive to the right of the present plane.

My first experience with this new principle would have made a less determined man drop the affair. Brant had been by way of dropping into my office and laboratory when in town. As I afterwards recalled, he showed a signal interest in certain toxicological experiments. "Man alive!" I had said to him once, "let those crystals alone! A single one of them will send you where you never see the sun!" I was uncertain if he brushed one off the slab. He did not return for some months. His wife, as I heard afterwards, had a long and baffling illness in the meantime, divorcing him on her recovery; and he had remained out of sight, at last leaving his native place for the great city. He had come in now, plausibly to ask my opinion of a stone—a diamond of unusual size and water.

I put the stone on a glass shelf in the next room while looking for the slide. You can imagine my sensation when that diamond, with something like a flash of shadow, so intense and swift it was, burst into a hundred rays of blackness and subsided—a pile of carbon! I had forgotten that the shelf happened to be negatively polarized, consequently everything it touched sharing its polarization, and that in pursuing my experiment I had polarized myself also, but with the opposite current; thus the atoms of my fingers passing through the spaces of the atoms of the stone already polarized, separated them negatively so far that they suffered disintegration and returned to the normal. "Good heavens! What has happened!" I cried before I thought. In a moment he was in the rear room and bending with me over the carbon. "Well," he said straightening himself directly, "you gave me a pretty fright. I thought for a moment that was my diamond."

"But it is!" I whispered.

"Pshaw!" he exclaimed roughly. "What do you take me for? Come, come, I'm not here for tricks. That's enough damned legerdemain. Where's my diamond?"

With less dismay and more presence of mind I should have edged along to my batteries, depolarized myself, placed in vacuum the tiny shelf of glass and applied my Y-ray; and with, I knew not what, of convulsion and flame the atoms might have slipped into place. But, instead, I stood gasping. He turned and surveyed me; the low order of his intelligence could receive but one impression.

"Look here," he said, "you will give me back my stone! Now! Or I will have an officer here!"

My mind was flying like the current through my coils. How could I restore the carbon to its original, as I must, if at all, without touching it, and how could I gain time without betraying my secret? "You are very short," I said. "What would you do with your officer?"

"Give you up! Give you up, appear against you, and let you have a sentence of twenty years behind bars."

"Hard words, Mr. Brant. You could say I had your property. I could deny it. Would your word outweigh mine? But return to the office in five minutes—if it is a possible thing you shall——"

"And leave you to make off with my jewel! Not by a long shot! I'm a bad man to deal with, and I'll have my stone or——"

"Go for your officer," said I.

His eye, sharp as a dagger's point, fell an instant. How could he trust me? I might escape with my booty. Throwing open the window to call, I might pinion him from behind, powerful as he was. But before he could gainsay, I had taken half a dozen steps backward, reaching my batteries.

"Give your alarm," I said. I put out my hand, lifting my lever, turned the current into my coils, and blazed up my Y-ray for half a heart-beat, succeeding in that brief time in reversing and in receiving the current that so far changed matters that the thing I touched would remain normal, although I was left still so far subjected to the ray of the less displacement that I ought, when the thrill had subsided, to be able to step through the wall as easily as if no wall were there. "Do you see what I have here?" I most unwisely exclaimed. "In one second I could annihilate you——" I had no time for more, or even to make sure I was correct, before, keeping one eye on me, he had called the officer.

"Look here," he said again, turning on me. "I know enough to see you have something new there, some of your damned inventions. Come, give me my diamond, and if it is worth while I'll find the capital, go halves, and drop this matter."

"Not to save your life!" I cried.

"You know me, officer," he said, as the blue coat came running in. "I give this man into custody for theft."

"It is a mistake, officer," I said. "But you will do your duty."

"Take him to the central station," said Mr. Brant, "and have him searched. He has a jewel of mine on his person."

"Yer annar's sure it's not on the primmises?" asked the officer.

"He has had no time——"

"Sure, if it's quick he do be he's as like to toss it in a corner——"

I stretched out my hand to a knob that silenced the humming among my wires, and at the same time sent up a thread of white fire whose instant rush and subsidence hinted of terrible power behind. The last divisible particle of radium—their eyeballs throbbed for a week.

"Search," I said. "But be careful about shocks. I don't want murder here, too."

Apparently they also were of that mind. For, recovering their sight, they threw my coat over my shoulders and marched me between them to the station, where I was searched, and, as it was already late, locked into a cell for the night.

I could not waste strength on the matter. I was waiting for the dead middle of the night. Then I should put things to proof.

I confess it was a time of intense breathlessness while waiting for silence and slumber to seal the world. Then I called upon my soul, and I stepped boldly forward and walked through that stone wall as if it had been air.

Of course, at my present displacement I was perfectly visible, and I slipped behind this and that projection, and into that alley, till sure of safety. There I made haste to my quarters, took the shelf holding the carbon, and at once subjected it to the necessary treatment. I was unprepared for the result. One instant the room seemed full of a blinding white flame, an intolerable heat, which shut my eyes and singed my hair and blistered my face.

"It is the atmosphere of a fire-dissolving planet," I thought. And then there was darkness and a strange odor.

I fumbled and stumbled about till I could let in the fresh air; and presently I saw the dim light of the street lamp. Then I turned on my own lights—and there was the quartz slab with a curious fusing of its edges, and in the center, flashing, palpitating, lay the diamond, all fire and whiteness. I wonder if it were not considerably larger; but it was hot as if just fallen from Syra Vega; it contracted slightly after subjection to dephlogistic gases.

It was near morning when, having found Brant's address, I passed into his house and his room, and took my bearings. I found his waistcoat, left the diamond in one of its pockets, and returned. It would not do to remain away, visible or invisible. I must be vindicated, cleared of the charge, set right before the world by Brant's appearing and confessing his mistake on finding the diamond in his pocket.

Judge Brant did nothing of the kind. Having visited me in my cell and in vain renewed his request to share in the invention which the habit of his mind convinced him must be of importance, he appeared against me. And the upshot of the business was that I went to prison for the term of years he had threatened.

I asked for another interview with him; but was refused, unless on the terms already declined. My lawyer, with the prison chaplain, went to him, but to no purpose. At last I went myself, as I had gone before, begging him not to ruin the work of my life. He regarded me as a bad dream, and I could not undeceive him without betraying my secret. I returned to my cell and again waited. For to escape was only to prevent possible vindication. If Mary had lived—but I was alone in the world.

The chaplain arranged with my landlord to take a sum of money I had, and to keep my rooms and apparatus intact till the expiration of my sentence. And then I put on the shameful and degrading prison garb and submitted to my fate.

It was a black fate. On the edge of the greatest triumph over matter that had ever been achieved, on the verge of announcing the actuality of the Fourth Dimension of Space, and of defining and declaring its laws, I was a convict laborer at a prison bench.

One day Judge Brant, visiting a client under sentence of death, in relation to his fee, made pretext to look me up, and stopped at my bench. "And how do you like it as far as you've gone?" he said.

"So that I go no farther," I replied. "And unless you become accessory to my taking off, you will acknowledge you found the stone in your pocket——"

"Not yet, not yet," he said, with an unctuous laugh. "It was a keen jest you played. Regard this as a jest in return. But when you are ready, I am ready."

The thing was hopeless. That night I bade good-bye to the life that had plunged me from the pinnacle of light to the depths of hell.

When again conscious I lay on a cot in the prison hospital. My attempt had been unsuccessful. St. Angel sat beside me. It was here, practically, he came into my life—alas! that I came into his.

In the long nights of darkness and failing faintness, when horror had me by the throat, he was beside me, and his warm, human touch was all that held me while I hung over the abyss. When I swooned off again his hand, his voice, his bending face recalled me. "Why not let me go, and then an end?" I sighed.

"To save you from a great sin," he replied. And I clung to his hand with the animal instinct of living.

I was well, and in my cell, when he said. "You claim to be an honest man——"

"And yet?"

"You were about taking that which did not belong to you."

"I hardly understand "

"Can you restore life once taken?"

"Oh, life! That worthless thing!"

"Lent for a purpose."

"For torture!"

"If by yourself you could breathe breath into any pinch of feathers and toss it off your hand a creature—but, as it is, life is a trust. And you, a man of parts, of power, hold it only to return with usury."

"And stripped of the power of gathering usury! Robbed of the work about to revolutionize the world!"

"The world moves on wide waves. Another man will presently have reached your discovery."

As if that were a thing to be glad of! I learned afterwards that St. Angel had given up the sweetness of life for the sake of his enemy. He had gone to prison, and himself worn the stripes, rather than the woman he loved should know her husband was the criminal. Perhaps he did not reconcile this with his love of inviolate truth. But St. Angel had never felt so much regard for his own soul as for the service of others. Self-forgetfulness was the dominant of all his nature.

"Tell me," he said, sitting with me, "about your work."

A whim of trustfulness seized me. I drew an outline, but paused at the look of pity on his face. He felt there was but one conclusion to draw—that I was a madman.

"Very well," I said, "you shall see." And I walked through the wall before his amazed eyes, and walked back again.

For a moment speechless, "You have hypnotic power," then he said. "You made me think I saw it."

"You did see it. I can go free any day I choose."

"And you do not?"

"I must be vindicated." And I told exactly what had taken place with Brant and his diamond. "Perhaps that vindication will never come," I said at last. "The offended amour propre, and the hope of gain, hindered in the beginning. Now he will find it impossible."

"That is too monstrous to believe!" said St. Angel. "But since you can, why not spend an hour or two at night with your work?"

"In these clothes! How long before I should be brought back? The first way-farer—oh, you see!"

St. Angel thought a while. "You are my size," he said then. "We will exchange clothes. I will remain here. In three hours return, that you may get your sleep. It is fortunate the prison should be in the same town."

Night after night then I was in my old rooms, the shutters up, lost in my dreams and my researches, arriving at great ends.

Night after night I reappeared on the moment, and St. Angel went his way.

I had now found that molecular displacement can be had in various directions. Going further, I saw that gravity acts on bodies whose molecules are on the same plane, and one of the possible results of the application of the Y-ray was the suspension of the laws of gravity. This possibly accounted for an almost inappreciable buoyancy and the power of directing one's course. My last studies showed that a substance thus treated has the degenerative power of attracting the molecules of any norm into its new orbit—a disastrous possibility. A chair might disappear into a table previously treated by a Y-ray. In fact, the outlook was to infinity. The change so slight—the result so astonishing! The subject might go into molecular interstices as far removed, to all essential purpose, as if billions of miles away in interstellar space. Nothing was changed, nothing disrupted; but the thing had stepped aside to let the world go by. The secrets of the world were mine. The criminal was at my mercy. The lover had no reserves from me. And as for my enemy, the Lord had delivered him into my hand. I could leave him only a puzzle for the dissectors. I could make him, although yet alive, a conscious ghost to stand or wander in his altered shape through years of nightmare alone and lost. What wonders of energy would follow this ray of displacement. What withdrawal of malignant growth and deteriorating tissue was to come. "To what heights of succor for humanity the surgeon can rise with it!" said St. Angel, as, full of my enthusiasm, I dilated on the marvel.

"He can work miracles!" I exclaimed. "He can heal the sick, walk on the deep, perhaps—who knows—raise the dead!"

I was at the height of my endeavor when St. Angel brought me my pardon. He had so stated my case to the Governor, so spoken of my interrupted career, and of my prison conduct, that the pardon had been given. I refused to accept it. "I accept," I said, "nothing but vindication, if I stay here till the day of judgment!"

"But there is no provision for you now," he urged. "Officially you no longer exist."

"Here I am," I said, "and here I stay."

"At any rate," he continued, "come out with me now and see the Governor, and see the world and the daylight outdoors, and be a man among men a while!"

With the stipulation that I should return, I put on a man's clothes again and went out the gates.

It was with a thrill of exultation that, exhibiting the affairs in my room to St. Angel, finally I felt the vibrating impulse that told me I had received the ray of the larger displacement. In a moment I should be viewless as the air.

"Where are you?" said St. Angel, turning this way and that. "What has become of you?"

"Seeing is believing," I said. "Sometimes not seeing is the naked truth."

"Oh, but this is uncanny!" he exclaimed. "A voice out of empty air."

"Not so empty! But place your hand under the second coil. Have no fear. You hear me now," I said. "I am in perhaps the Fourth Dimension. I am invisible to any one not there—to all the world, except, presently, yourself. For now you, you also, pass into the unseen. Tell me what you feel."

"Nothing," he said. "A vibration—a suspicion of one. No, a blow, a sense of coming collapse, so instant it has passed."

"Now," I said, "there is no one on earth with eyes to see you but myself!"

"That seems impossible."

"Did you see me? But now you do. We are on the same plane. Look in that glass. There is the reflection of the room, of the window, the chair. Do you see me? Yourself?"

"Powers of the earth and air, but this is ghastly!" said St. Angel.

"It is the working of natural law. Now we will see the world, ourselves unseen."

"An unfair advantage."

"Perhaps. But there are things to accomplish to-day." What things I never dreamed; or I had stayed on the threshold.

I wanted St. Angel to know the manner of man this Brant was. We went out, and arrested our steps only inside Brant's office.

"This door is always blowing open!" said the clerk, and he returned to a woman standing in a suppliant attitude. "The Judge has gone to the races," he said, "and he's left word that Tuesday morning your goods'll be put out of the house if you don't pay up!" The woman went her way weeping.

Leaving, we mounted a car; we would go to the races ourselves. I doubt if St. Angel had ever seen anything of the sort. I observed him quietly slip a dime into the conductor's pocket—he felt that even the invisible, like John Gilpin, carried a right. "This opens a way for the right hand undreamed of the left," he said to me later.

It was not long before we found Judge Brant, evidently in an anxious frame, his expanse of countenance white with excitement. He had been plunging heavily, as I learned, and had big money staked, not upon the favorite but upon Hannan, the black mare. "That man would hardly put up so much on less than a certainty," I thought. Winding our way unseen among the grooms and horses, I found what I suspected—a plan to pocket the favorite. "But I know a game worth two of that," I said. I took a couple of small smooth pebbles, previously prepared, from the chamois bag into which I had put them with some others and an aluminum wafer treated for the larger displacement, and slipped one securely under the favorite's saddle-girth. When he warmed to his work he should be, for perhaps half an hour, at the one-billionth point, before the virtue expired, and capable of passing through every obstacle as he was directed.

"Hark you, Danny," then I whispered in the jockey's ear.

"Who are you? What—I—I—don't——" looking about with terror.

"It's no ghost," I whispered hurriedly. "Keep your nerve. I am flesh and blood—alive as you. But I have the property which for half an hour I give you—a new discovery. And knowing Bub and Whittler's game, it's up to you to knock 'em out. Now, remember, when they try the pocket ride straight through them!"

Other things kept my attention; and when the crucial moment came I had some excited heart-beats. And so had Judge Brant. It was in the instant when Danny, having held the favorite well in hand for the first stretch, Hannan and Darter in the lead and the field following, was about calling on her speed, that suddenly Bub and Whittler drew their horses' heads a trifle more closely together, in such wise that it was impossible to pass on either side, and a horse could no more shoot ahead than if a stone wall stood there. "Remember, Danny!" I shouted, making a trumpet of my hands. "Ride straight through!"

And Danny did. He pulled himself together, and set his teeth as if it were a compact with powers of evil, and rode straight through without turning a hair, or disturbing either horse or rider. Once more the Y-ray was triumphant.

But about Judge Brant the air was blue. It would take a very round sum of money to recoup the losses of those few moments. I disliked to have St. Angel hear him; but it was all in the day's work.

The day had not been to Judge Brant's mind, as at last he bent his steps to the club. As he went it occurred to me to try upon him the larger ray of displacement, and I slipped down the back of his collar the wafer I had ready. He would not at once feel its action, but in the warmth either of walking or dining, its properties should be lively for nearly an hour. I had curiosity to see if the current worked not only through all substances, but through all sorts and conditions.

"I should prefer a better pursuit," said St. Angel, as we reached the street. "Is there not something ignoble in it?"

"In another case. Here it is necessary to hound the criminal, to see the man entirely. A game not to be played too often, for there is work to be done before establishing the counteracting currents that may ensure reserves and privacies to people. To-night let us go to the club with Judge Brant, and then I will back to my cell."

As you may suppose, Brant was a man neither of imagination nor humor. As you have seen, he was hard and cruel, priding himself on being a good hater, which in his contention meant indulgence of a preternaturally vindictive temper when prudence allowed. With more cunning than ability, he had achieved some success in his profession, and he secured admission to a good club, recently crowning his efforts, when most of the influential members were absent, by getting himself made one of its governors.

It would be impossible to find a greater contrast to this wretch than in St. Angel—a man of delicate imagination and pure fancy, tender to the child on the street, the fly on the wall; all his atmosphere that of kindness. Gently born, but too finely bred, his physical resistance was so slight that his immunity lay in not being attacked. His clean, fair skin, his brilliant eyes, spoke of health, but the fragility of frame did not speak of strength. Yet St. Angel's life was the active principle of good; his neighborhood was purification.

I was revolving these things while we followed Judge Brant, when I saw him pause in an agitated manner, like one startled out of sleep. A quick shiver ran over his strong frame; he turned red and pale, then with a shrug went on. The displacement had occurred. He was now on the plane of invisibility, and we must have a care ourselves.

Wholly unconscious of any change, the man pursued his way. The street was as usual. There was the boy who always waited for him with the extra but to-night was oblivious; and failing to get his attention the Judge walked on. A shower that had been threatening began to fall, the sprinkle becoming a downpour, with umbrellas spread and people hurrying. The Judge hailed a car; but the motorman was as blind as the newsboy. The shower stopped as suddenly as it had begun, but he went on some paces before perceiving that he was perfectly dry, for as he shut and shook his umbrella not a drop fell, and as he took off his hat and looked at it, not an atom of moisture was to be found there. Evidently bewildered, and looking about shamefacedly, I fancied I could hear him saying, with his usual oaths, "I must be deucedly overwrought, or this is some blue devilment."

As the Judge took his accustomed seat in the warm and brilliantly lighted room, and picking up the evening paper, looked over the columns, the familiar every-day affair quieting his nerves so that he could have persuaded himself he had been half asleep as he walked, he was startled by the voice, not four feet away, of one of the old officers who made the Kings County their resort. Something had ruffled the doughty hero. "By the Lord Harry, sir," he was saying in unmodulated tones, "I should like to know what this club is coming to when you can spring on it the election of such a man as this Brant! Judge? What's he Judge of? Beat his wife, too, didn't he? The governors used to be gentlemen!"

"But you know, General," said his vis-à-vis, "I think no more of him than you do; but when a man lives at the Club——"

"Lives here!" burst in the other angrily. "He hasn't anywhere else to live! Is there a decent house in town open to him? Well, thank goodness, I've somewhere else to go before he comes in! The sight of him gives me a fit of the gout!" And the General stumped out stormily.

"Old boy seems upset!" said some one not far away. "But he's right. It was sheer impudence in the fellow to put up his name."

I could see Brant grow white and gray with anger, as surprised and outraged, wondering what it meant—if the General intended insult—if Scarsdale—but no, apparently they had not seen him. The contemptuous words rankled; the sweat stood on his forehead.

Had not the moment been serious, there were a thousand tricks to play. But the potency of the polarization was subsiding and in a short time the normal molecular plane would be re-established. It was there that I made my mistake. I should not have allowed him to depolarize so soon. I should have kept him bewildered and foodless till famished and weak. Instead, as ion by ion the effect of the ray decreased, his shape grew vague and misty, and then one and another man there rubbed his eyes, for Judge Brant was sitting in his chair and a waiter was hastening towards him.

It had all happened in a few minutes. Plainly the Judge understood nothing of the circumstances. He was dazed, but he must put the best face on it; and he ordered his dinner and a pony of brandy, eating like a hungry animal.

He rose, after a time, refreshed, invigorated, and all himself. Choosing a cigar, he went into another room, seeking a choice lounging place, where for a while he could enjoy his ease and wonder if anything worse than a bad dream had befallen. As for the General's explosion, it did not signify; he was conscious of such opinion; he was overliving it; he would be expelling the old cock yet for conduct unbecoming a gentleman.

Meanwhile, St. Angel, tiring of the affair, and weary, had gone into this room, and in an arm-chair by the hearth was awaiting me—the intrusive quality of my observations not at all to his mind. He had eaten nothing all day, and was somewhat faint. He had closed his eyes, and perhaps fallen into a light doze when he must have been waked by the impact of Brant's powerful frame, as the latter took what seemed to him the empty seat. I expected to see Brant at once flung across the rug by St. Angel's natural effort in rising. Instead, Brant sank into the chair as into down pillows.

I rushed, as quickly as I could, to seize and throw him off, "Through him! Pass through him! Come out! Come to me!" I cried. And people to-day remember that voice out of the air, in the Kings County Club.

It seemed to me that I heard a sound, a sob, a whisper, as if one cried with a struggling sigh, "Impossible!" And with that a strange trembling convulsed Judge Brant's great frame, he lifted his hands, he thrust out his feet, his head fell forward, he groaned gurglingly, shudder after shudder shook him as if every muscle quivered with agony or effort, the big veins started out as if every pulse were a red-hot iron. He was wrestling with something, he knew not what, something as antipathetic to him as white is to black; every nerve was concentrated in rebellion, every fiber struggled to break the spell.

The whole affair was that of a dozen heart-beats—the attempt of the opposing molecules each to draw the other into its own orbit. The stronger physical force, the greater aggregation of atoms was prevailing. Thrust upward for an instant, Brant fell back into his chair exhausted, the purple color fading till his face shone fair as a girl's, sweet and smiling as a child's, white as the face of a risen spirit—Brant's!

Astounded, I seized his shoulder and whirled him about. There was no one else in the chair. I looked in every direction. There was no St. Angel to be seen. There was but one conclusion to draw—the molecules of Brant's stronger material frame had drawn into their own plane the molecules of St. Angel's.

I rushed from the place, careless if seen or unseen, howling in rage and misery. I sought my laboratory, and in a fiend's fury depolarized myself, and I demolished every instrument, every formula, every vestige of my work. I was singed and scorched and burned, but I welcomed any pain. And I went back to prison, admitted by the officials who hardly knew what else to do. I would stay there, I thought, all my days. God grant they should be few! It would be seen that a life of imprisonment and torture were too little punishment for the ruin I had wrought.

It was after a sleepless night, of which every moment seemed madness, that, the door of my cell opening, I saw St. Angel. St. Angel? God have mercy on me, no, it was Judge Brant I saw!

He came forward, with both hands extended, a grave, imploring look on his face. "I have come," he said, a singular sweet overtone in his voice that I had never heard before, yet which echoed like music in my memory, "to make you all the reparation in my power. I will go with you at once before the Governor, and acknowledge that I have found the diamond. I can never hope to atone for what you have suffered. But as long as I live, all that I have, all that I am, is yours!"

There was a look of absolute sweetness on his face that for a dizzy moment made me half distraught. "We will go together," he said. "I have to stop on the way and tell a woman whose mortgage comes due to-day that I have made a different disposition; and, do you know," he added brightly, after an instant's hesitation, "I think I shall help her pay it!" and he laughed gayly at the jest involved.

"Will you say that you have known my innocence all these years?" I said sternly.

"Is not that," he replied, with a touching and persuasive quality of tone, "a trifle too much? Do you think this determination has been reached without a struggle? If you are set right before the world, is not something due to—Brant?"

"If I did not know who and what you are," I said, "I should think the soul of St. Angel had possession of you!"

The man looked at me dreamily. "Strange!" he murmured. "I seem to have heard something like that before. However," as if he shook off a perplexing train of thought, "all that is of no consequence. It is not who you are, but what you do. Come, my friend, don't deny me, don't let the good minute slip. Surely the undoing of the evil of a lifetime, the turning of that force to righteousness, is work outweighing all a prison chaplain's——"

My God, what had the intrusion of my incapable hands upon forbidden mysteries done!

"Come," he said. "We will go together. We will carry light into dark places—there are many waiting——"

"St. Angel!" I cried, with a loud voice, "are you here?"

And again the smile of infinite sweetness illuminated the face even as the sun shines up from the depths of a stagnant pool.

From Pole to Pole

*An account of a journey through the axis of the earth;
collated from the diaries of the late Professor Haffkin
and his niece, Mrs. Arthur Princeps*

GEORGE GRIFFITH

*One of the best-known writers of science fiction in his day, British writer
George Griffith (1857–1906) placed this story in the October 1904 issue of
the* Windsor Magazine. *It is one of the more provocative treatments on
the theme of the hollow earth, a concept whose origins are in antiquity but
whose leading proponent in the nineteenth century, John Cleeves Symmes,
Jr., proposed accessing the planet's interior from the North Pole much as
Griffith's scientific adventurers do via the South Pole.*

"Well, Professor, what is it? Something pretty important, I suppose, from the
wording of your note. What is the latest achievement? Have you solved the problem of serial navigation, or got a glimpse into the realms of the fourth dimension,
or what?"

"No, not any of those as yet, my friend, but something that may be quite as
wonderful of its sort," replied Professor Haffkin, putting his elbows down on the
table and looking keenly across it under his shaggy, iron-grey eyebrows at the young
man who was sitting on the opposite side pulling meditatively at a good cigar and
sipping a whisky-and-soda.

"Well, if it is something really extraordinary and at the same time practicable—as you know, my ideas of the practicable are fairly wide—I'm there as far as the financial part goes. As regards the scientific end of the business, if you say 'Yes,' it is 'Yes.' "

Mr. Arthur Princeps had very good reasons for thus "going blind" on a project of which he knew nothing save that it probably meant a sort of scientific gamble to the tune of several thousands of pounds. He had had the good fortune to sit under the Professor when he was a student at the Royal School of Mines, and being possessed of that rarest of all gifts, an intuitive imagination, he had seen vast possibilities through the meshes of the verbal network of the Professor's lectures.

Further, the kindly Fates had blessed him with a twofold dowry. He had a keen and insatiable thirst for that kind of knowledge which is satisfied only by the demonstration of hard facts. He was a student of physical science simply because he couldn't help it; and his grandfather had left him ground-rents in London, Birmingham, and Manchester, and coal and iron mines in half-a-dozen counties, which produced an almost preposterous income.

At the same time, he had inherited from his mother and his grandmother that kind of intellect which enabled him to look upon all this wealth as merely a means to an end.

Later on, Professor Haffkin had been his examiner in Applied Mathematics at London University, and he had done such an astonishing paper that he had come to him after he had taken his D.Sc. degree and asked him in brief but pregnant words for the favour of his personal acquaintance. This had led to an intellectual intimacy which not only proved satisfactory from the social and scientific points of view, but also materialised on many profitable patents.

The Professor was a man rich in ideas, but comparatively poor in money. Arthur Princeps had both ideas and money, and as a result of this conjunction of personalities the man of science had made thousands out of his inventions, while the scientific man of business had made tens of thousands by exploiting them; and that is how matters stood between them on this particular evening when they were dining tête-à-tête in the Professor's house in Russell Square.

When dinner was over, the Professor got up and said—

"Bring your cigar up into the study, Mr. Princeps. I want a pipe, and I can talk more comfortably there than here. Besides, I've something to show you."

"All right, Professor ; but if you're going to have a pipe, I'll do the same. One can think better with a pipe than a cigar. It takes too much attention."

He tossed the half of his Muria into the grate and followed the Professor up to his sanctum, which was half study, half laboratory, and withal a very comfortable apartment. There was a bright wood-and-coal fire burning in the old-fashioned grate, and on either side of the hearth there was a nice, deep, cosy armchair.

"Now, Mr. Princeps," said the Professor, when they were seated, "I am going to ask you to believe something which I dare say you will think impossible."

"My dear sir, if you think it possible, that is quite enough for me," replied Princeps. "What is it?"

The Professor took a long pull at his pipe, and then, turning his head so that his eyes met his guest's, he replied—

"It's a journey through the centre of the earth."

Arthur Princeps bit the amber of his pipe clean through, sat bolt upright, caught the pipe in his hand, spat the pieces of amber into the fireplace, and said—

"I beg your pardon, Professor—through the centre of the earth? That's rather a large order, isn't it? I've just been reading an article in one of the scientific papers which goes to show that the centre of the earth—the kernel of the terrestrial nut, as it were— is a rigid, solid body harder and denser than anything we know on the surface."

"Quite so, quite so," replied the Professor. "I have read the article myself, and I admit that the reasoning is sound as far as it goes; but I don't think it goes quite far enough—I mean far enough back. However, I think I can show you what I mean in a much shorter time than I can tell you."

As he said this, he got up from his chair and went to a little cupboard in a big bureau which stood in a recess beside the fireplace. He took out a glass vessel about six inches in diameter and twelve in height, and placed it gently on a little table which stood between the easy-chairs.

Princeps glanced at it and saw that it was filled with a fluid which looked like water. Exactly half-way between the surface of the fluid and the bottom of the glass there was a spherical globule of a brownish-yellow colour, and about an inch in diameter. As the Professor set the glass on the table, the globule oscillated a little and then came to a rest. Princeps looked at it with a little lift of his eyelids, but said nothing. His host went back to the cupboard and took out a long, thin, steel needle with a little disc of thin white metal fixed about three inches from the end. He lowered it into the fluid in the glass and passed it through the middle of the globule, which broke as the disc passed into it, and then re-shaped itself again in perfectly spherical form about it.

The Professor looked up and said, just as though he were repeating a portion of one of his lectures—

"This is a globule of coloured oil. It floats in a mixture of alcohol and water which is of exactly the same specific gravity as its own. It thus represents as nearly as possible the earth in its former molten condition, floating in space. The earth had then, as now, a rotary action on its own axis. This needle represents that axis. I give it a rotary motion, and you will see here what happened millions of years ago to the infant planet Terra."

As he said this, he began to twirl the needle swiftly but very steadily between the forefingers of his right and left hand. The globule flattened and spread out laterally until it became a ring, with the needle and the disc in the centre of it. Then the twirling slowed down. The ring became a globule again, but it was flattened at either pole, and there was a clearly defined circular hole through it from pole to pole. The Professor deftly withdrew the needle and disc through the opening, and the globule continued to revolve round the hole through its centre.

"That is what I mean," he said. "Of course, I needn't go into detail with you. There is the earth as I believe it to be today, with certain exceptions which you will readily see.

"The exterior crust has cooled. Inside that there is probably a semi-fluid sphere, and inside that again, possibly, the rigid body, the core of the earth. But I don't believe that that hole has been filled, simply because it must have been there to begin with. Granted also that the pull of gravitation is towards the centre, still, if there is a void from Pole to Pole, as I hold there must be, as a natural consequence of the centrifugal force generated by the earth's revolution, the mass of the earth would pull equally in all directions away from that void."

"I think I see," said Princeps, upon whom the astounding possibilities of this simple demonstration had been slowly breaking. "I see. Granted a passage like that from Pole to Pole—call it a tunnel—a body falling into it at one end would be drawn towards the centre. It would pass it at a tremendous velocity and be carried towards the other end; but as the attraction of the mass of the earth would be equal on all sides of it, it would take a perfectly direct course—I mean, it wouldn't smash itself to bits against the sides of the tunnel.

"The only difficulty that I see is that, suppose that the body were dropped into the tunnel at the North Pole, it wouldn't quite reach the South Pole. It would stop and turn back, and so it would oscillate like a pendulum with an ever-decreasing swing until it finally came to rest in the middle of the tunnel—or, in other words, the centre of the earth."

You've only got to tell me that you really think it possible, and I'm with you. If you like to undertake the details, you can draw on me up to a hundred thousand; and when you're ready, I'll go with you. Which Pole do you propose to start from?"

"The North Pole," said the Professor, quietly, as though he were uttering the merest commonplace, "although still undiscovered, is getting a little bit hackneyed.

I propose that we shall start from the South Pole. It is very good of you to be so generous in the way of finances. Of course, you understand that you cannot hope for any monetary return, and it is also quite possible that we may both lose our lives."

"People who stick at small things never do great ones," replied Princeps. "As for the money, it doesn't matter. I have too much—more than anyone ought to have. Besides, we might find oceans of half-molten gold inside—who knows? Anyhow, when you're ready to start, I am."

II

Nearly two months after this conversation had taken place, something else happened. The Professor's niece, the only blood-relation he had in the world, came back from Heidelberg with her degree of Doctor of Philosophy. She was "a daughter of the Gods, divinely tall and most divinely fair," as became one in whose veins ran both the Norse and the Anglo-Saxon blood. Certain former experiences had led Princeps to the opinion that she liked him exceedingly for himself, and disliked him almost as much for his money—a fact which somehow made the possession of millions seem very unprofitable in his eyes.

Brenda Haffkin happened to get back to London the day after everything had been arranged for the most amazing and seemingly impossible expedition that two human beings had ever decided to attempt.

The British Government and the Royal Geographical Society of London were sending out a couple of vessels—one a superannuated whaler, and the other a hopelessly obsolete cruiser, which had narrowly escaped experimental bombardment—to the frozen land of Antarctica. A splendid donation to the funds of the expedition had procured a passage in the cruiser for the adventurers and about ten tons of baggage, the ultimate use of which was little dreamt of by any other member of the expedition.

The great secret was broken to Brenda about a week before the starting of the expedition. Her uncle explained the theory of the project to her, and Arthur Princeps added the footnotes, as it were. Whatever she thought of it, she betrayed no sign either of belief or disbelief; but when the Professor had finished, she turned to Princeps and said very quietly, but with a most eloquent glow in those big, grey eyes into which he had often looked so longingly—

"And you are really going on this expedition, Mr. Princeps? You are going to run the risk of probable starvation and more than probable destruction; and, in addition to that, you must be spending a great deal of money to do it—you who have money enough to buy everything that the world can sell you?"

"What the world can sell, Miss Haffkin—or, in other words, what money can buy—has very little value beyond the necessaries of life. It is what money cannot buy, what the world has not got to sell, that is really precious. I suppose you know what I mean," he said, putting his hands into his pockets and turning to stare in an unmeaning way out of the window. "But I beg your pardon. I didn't mean to get back on to that old subject, I can assure you."

"And you really are going on this expedition?" she said, with a deliciously direct inconsequence which, in a beautiful Doctor of Philosophy, was quite irresistible.

"Of course I am. Why not? If we find that there really is a tunnel through the earth, and jump in at the South Pole and come out at the North, and take a series of electro-cinematograph photographs of the crust and core of the earth, we shall have done something that no one else has ever thought about. There ought to be some millions in it, too, besides the glory."

"And suppose you don't? Suppose this wonderful vessel of uncle's gets launched into this bottomless pit, and doesn't come out properly at the other end? Suppose your explosive just misses fire at the wrong moment, and when you've nearly reached the North Pole you go back again past the centre, and so on, and so on, until, perhaps, two or three centuries hence, your vessel comes to rest at the centre with a couple of skeletons inside it—what then?"

"We should take a medicine-chest with us, and I don't suppose we should wait for starvation."

"And so you seriously propose to stake your life and all your splendid prospects in the world on the bare chance of accomplishing an almost impossibly fantastic achievement?"

"That's about what it comes to, I suppose. I don't really see how a man in my position could spend his money and risk his life much better."

There was a little silence after this, and then Brenda said, in a somewhat altered voice—

"If you really are going, I should like to come, too."

"You could only do that, Miss Haffkin, on one condition."

"And that is?"

"That you say 'Yes' now to a question you said 'No' to nine months ago. You can call it bribery or corruption, or whatever you like; but there it is. On the other hand, as I have quite made up my mind about this expedition, I might as well tell you that if I don't get back, you will hear of something to your advantage by calling on my lawyers."

"I would rather go and work in a shop than do that!" she said. "Still, if you'll let me come with you, I will."

"Then the 'No' is 'Yes?' " he said, taking a half turn towards her and catching hold of her hand.

"Yes," she said, looking him frankly in the eyes. "You see, I didn't think you were in earnest about these things before; but now I see you are, and that makes you very different, you know, although you have such a horrible lot of money. Of course, it was my fault all the time, but still—"

She was in his arms by this time, and the; discussion speedily reached a perfectly satisfactory, if partially inarticulate, conclusion.

III

The quiet wedding by special licence at St. Martin's, Gower Street, and the voyage from Southampton to Victoria Land, were very much like other weddings and other voyages; but when the whaler *Australia* and His Majesty's cruiser *Beltona* dropped their anchors under the smoke-shadow of Mount Terror, the mysterious cases were opened, and the officers and crew began to have grave suspicions as to the sanity of their passengers.

The cases were brought up on deck with the aid of the derricks, and then they got unpacked. The ships were lying about a hundred yards off a frozen, sandy beach. Back of this rose a sheer wall of ice about eighteen hundred feet high. On this side lay all that was known of Antarctica. On the other was the Unknown.

The greater part of the luggage was very heavy. Many and wild were the guesses as to what the contents of these cases could possibly be used for at the uttermost ends of the earth.

The Handy Men only saw insanity—or, at least, a hopelessly impracticable kind of method—in the unloading of those strange-looking stores. There were little cylinders of a curiously light metal, with screw-taps on either end of them—about two thousand of them. There were also queer "fitments" which, when they were landed, somehow erected themselves into sledges with cog-wheels alongside them. There were also little balloons, filled out of the taps of the cylinders, which went up attached to big kites of the (quadrangular or box form. When the wind was sufficiently strong, and blowing in the right direction towards the Southern Pole, a combination of these kites took up Professor Haffkin and Mr. Arthur Princeps, and then, after a good many protestations, Mrs. Princeps. She, happening to get to the highest elevation, came down and reported that she had seen what no other Northernborn human being had ever seen.

She had looked over the great Ice Wall of the South, and from the summit of it she had seen nothing but an illimitable plain of snow-prairies, here and there broken up by a few masses of ice mountains, but, so far as she could see, intersected by snow-valleys, smooth and hard frozen, stretching away beyond the limit of vision to the South.

"Nothing," she said, "could have been better arranged, even if we had done it ourselves; and there is one thing quite certain—granted that that hole through the earth really exists, there oughtn't to be any difficulty in getting to the edge of it. The wind seems always blowing in the same direction, and with the sledges and the auxiliary balloons we ought to simply race along. It's only a little over twelve hundred miles, isn't it?"

"About that," said the Professor, opening his eyes a little wider than usual. "And now that we have got our stores all landed, and, as far as we can provide, everything that can stand between us and destruction, we may as well say 'Good-bye' to our friends and world. If we ever get back again, it will be *viâ* the North Pole, after we have accomplished what the sceptics call the impossible."

"But, Brenda, dear, don't you think you had better go back?" said her husband, laying his hands on her shoulders. "Why should you risk your life and all its possibilities in such an adventure as this?"

"If you risk it," she said, "I will. If you don't, I won't. You don't seem to have grasped the fact even yet that you and I are to all intents and purposes the same person. If you go, I go—through danger to death, or to glory such as human beings never won before. You asked me to choose, and that is what I have chosen. I will vanish with you into the Unknown, or I will come out with you at the North Pole in a blaze of glory that will make the *Aurora Borealis* itself look shabby. But whatever happens to you must happen to me as well, and the money in England must just take care of itself until we get back. That is all I have to say at present."

"And I wouldn't like you to hear you say one syllable more. You've said just what I wanted you to say, just what I thought you would say, and that's about good enough for me. We go from South to North through the core of the earth, or stop and be smashed up somewhere midway or elsewhere, but we'll do it together. If the inevitable happens, I will kill you first and then myself. If we get through, you will be, in the eyes of all men, just what I think you are now, and—well, that's about enough said, isn't it?"

"Almost," she said, "except——"

And then, reading what was plainly written in her eyes, he caught her closer to him.

Their lips met and finished the sentence more meaningly than any words could have done.

"I thought you'd say that," he said afterwards.

"I don't think you'd have asked me to marry you if you hadn't thought it," she said.

"No," he said. "I wouldn't. It seems a bit brutal to say so, but really I wouldn't."

"And if you hadn't asked like that," she said, once more looking him straight in the eyes, "I should have said 'No,' just as I did before."

She looked very tempting as she said this. He pulled her towards him; and as she turned her face up to his, he said—

"Has it ever struck you that there is infinitely more delight to a man in kissing lips which have once said 'No' to him, and then 'Yes,' than those which have only said 'Yes?' "

"What a very mean advantage to take of an unprotected female—"

A kiss ended the uncompleted sentence.

Then she began again—

"And when shall we start? "

"Seven to-morrow morning—that is to say, by our watches, not by the sun. Everything is on shore now, and we shouldn't make it later. I'm going to the Professor to help him up with the fixings, and I suppose you want to go into the tent and see after your domestic business. Good night for the present."

"Good night, dear, for the present."

And so was said the most momentous "Good night" that man and woman had ever said to each other since Adam kissed "Good night" to Eve in Eden.

IV

The next day—that is to say, a period of twelve hours later, measured according to the chronometers of the expedition (for the pale sun was only describing a little arc across the northern horizon, not to sink below it for another three months or so)— the members of the Pole to Pole Expedition said "Good-bye" to the companions with whom they had journeyed across the world.

There was a strong, steady breeze blowing directly from the northward. The great box-kites were sent up, six of them in all, and along the fine piano-wire cables which held them, the lighter portions of the stores were sent on carriers driven by smaller kites.

Princeps and Brenda had gone up first in the carrier-slings. The Professor remained on the beach with the bluejackets from the cruiser, who, with huge delight and no little mystification, were giving a helping hand in the strangest job that even British sailors had ever helped to put through. Their remarks to each other formed a commentary on the expedition as original as it was terse and to the point. It had, however, the disadvantage of being mostly unprintable.

It was twelve hours later when the Professor, having shaken hands all round, a process which came to between three and four hundred handshakes, took his seat in the sling of the last kite and went soaring up over the summit of the ice-wall. A hearty cheer from five hundred throats, and a rolling fire of blank cartridge from the cruiser, reverberated round the walls of everlasting ice which guarded the hitherto unpenetrated solitudes of Antarctica as the sling crossed the top of the wall, and a pull on the tiltingline bought the great kite slowly to the ground.

As the cable slackened, it was released from its moorings on the beach. A little engine, driven by liquid air, hauled it up on a drum. Three tiny figures appeared on the edge of the ice-cliff and waved their last adieus to the ships and the little crowd on the beach. Then they disappeared, and the last link between them and the rest of the world was cut, possibly—and, as every man of the Antarctic Expedition firmly believed, for ever.

The three members of the Pole to Pole Expedition bivouacked that night under a snow-knoll, and after a good twelve hours' sleep they set to work on the preparations for the last stage but one of their marvellous voyage. There were four sledges. One of these formed what might be called the baggage-wagon. It carried the gas-cylinders, the greater part of the provisions, and the vehicle which was to convey the three adventurers from the South Pole to the North through the centre of the earth, provided always that the Professor's theory as to the existence of the transterrestrial tunnel proved to be correct. It was packed in sections, to be put together when the edge of the great hole was reached.

The sledge could be driven by two means. As long as the north-to-south wind held good, it was dragged over the smooth, snow covered ice and land, which stretched away in an illimitable plain as far as the eye could reach from the top of the ice-wall towards the horizon behind which lay the South Pole and, perhaps, the tunnel. It was also furnished with sa liquid-air engine, which actuated four big, spiked wheels, two in front and two behind. These, when the wind failed, would grip the frozen snow or ice and drive the sledge-runners over it at a maximum speed of twenty miles an hour. The engine could, of course, be used in conjunction with the kites when the wind was light.

The other three sledges were smaller, but similar in construction and means of propulsion. Each had its drawing-kites and liquid-air engine. One carried a reserve of provisions, balloons, and basket-cars, with a dozen gas-cylinders. Another was loaded with the tents and cooking-apparatus, and the third carried the three passengers, with their immediate personal belongings, which, among other oddments, included a spirit-heater and a pair of curling-tongs and hair-wavers.

All the sledges were yoked together, the big one going first. Then came the passenger-car, and then the other two side by side. In case of accidents, there were contrivances which made it possible to cast any of the sledges loose at a moment's notice. The kites, if the wind got too high, could be emptied and brought down by means of tilting-lines.

There was a fine twenty-mile breeze blowing when the kites were sent up after breakfast. The yoked sledges were held by lines attached by pegs driven deeply into the frozen snow. The kites reached an altitude of about a thousand feet, and the sledges began to lift and strain at the mooring-lines as though they were living things. The Professor and Princeps cut all the lines but one before they took their places in the sledge beside Brenda. Then Princeps gave her a knife and said—

"Now start us."

She drew the keen edge backwards and forwards over the tautly stretched line. It parted with a springing jerk, and the next moment the wonderful caravan started forward with a jump which tilted them back into their seats.

The little snow-hills began to slip away behind them. The tracks left by the spring-runners tailed swiftly away into the distance, converging as railway-lines seem to do when you look down a long stretch of them. The keen, cold air bit hard on their flesh and soon forced them to protect their faces with the sealskin masks which let down from their helmets; but just before Brenda let hers down, she took a long breath of the icy air and said—

"Ah! That's just like drinking iced champagne. Isn't this glorious?"

Then she gasped, dropped her mask over her face, put one arm through her husband's and one through her uncle's, pulled them close to her, and from that moment she became all eyes, looking through the crystal plate in her mask at the strange, swiftly moving landscape and the great box-kites, high up in the air, dull white against the dim blue sky, which were dragging them so swiftly and so easily towards the Unknown and, perhaps, towards the impossible.

V

The expedition had been travelling for little more than six days, and so far the journey had been quite uneventful. The pale sun had swung six times round its oblique course without any intervention of darkness to break the seemingly endless polar day. At first they had travelled seventeen hours without halting. None of them could think of sleep amidst such novel surroundings, but the next day they were content with twelve, and this was agreed on as a day's journey.

They soon found that either their good fortune had given them a marvellously easy route, or else that the Antarctic continent was strangely different from the Arctic. Hour after hour their sledges, resting on rubber springs, spun swiftly over the undulating fields of snow-covered ice with scarcely a jog or a jar—in fact, as Brenda said at the end of the journey, it was more like a twelve-hundred mile switchback ride than a polar expedition.

So they travelled and slept and ate. Eight hours for sleep, two hours evening and morning for pitching and striking tents, supper and breakfast, and the stretching of limbs, and twelve hours' travel.

Lunch was eaten *en route,* because the lowering of the kites and the mooring of the sledges were a matter of considerable labour, and they naturally wanted to make the most of the wind while it lasted.

Every day, as the sun reached the highest point of its curved course along the horizon, the Professor took his latitude. Longitude, of course, there was practically none to take, since every day's travel took them so many hundred miles along the converging meridians, and east and west, with every mile they made, came nearer and nearer together.

On the seventh morning the kites were all lowered, taken to pieces, and packed up, with the exception of one which drew the big sledge.

They had calculated that they were now within about a hundred miles of the Pole—that is to say, the actual end of the earth's axis—and, according to the Professor's calculations (granted that the Pole to Pole tunnel existed) it would be about a hundred miles in diameter. At the same time, it might be a good deal more, and, therefore, it was not considered advisable to approach what would literally be the end of the earth at a speed of twenty miles an hour, driven by the strong, steady breeze which had remained with them from the top of the ice-wall. So the liquid-air engines were set to work, the spiked wheels bit into the hard-frozen snow, and the sledges, following the big one, and helped to a certain extent by its kite, began to move forward at about eight miles an hour.

The landscape did not alter materially as they approached the polar confines. On all sides was a vast plain of ice crossed in a generally southerly direction by long, broad snow-lanes. Here and there were low hills, mostly rounded domes of snow; but these were few and far between, and presented no obstacles to their progress.

A little before lunch-time the ground began to slope suddenly away to the southward to such an extent that the kite was hauled in, and the spiked wheels had to be used to check the increasing speed of the sledges. On either hand the slope extended in a perfectly uniform fashion, and after a descent of about an hour, they could see a vast curved ridge of snow stretching to right and to left behind them which shut out the almost level rays of the pale sun so that the semi-twilight in which they had been travelling was rapidly deepening into dusk.

What was it? Were they descending into a vast polar depression, to the shores of such an open sea as had often been imagined by geographers and explorers, or were they in truth descending towards the edge of the Arctic tunnel itself?

"I wonder which it is?" said Brenda, sipping her midday coffee. "Don't you think we'd better stop soon and do a little snowshoeing? I, for one, should object to beginning the journey by falling over the edge. Ugh! Fancy a fall of seven thousand miles into nowhere! And then falling back again another seven thousand miles and so for ever and ever, until your flesh crumbled off your bones and at last your skeleton came to a standstill exactly at the centre of the earth!"

"Not at all a pleasant prospect, I admit, my dear Brenda," said the Professor; "but, after all, I don't think you would be hurt much. You see, you would be dead in a very few seconds, and then think of the glory of having the whole world for your tomb."

"I don't like the idea," she replied. "A commonplace crematorium and a crystal urn afterwards will satisfy me completely. But don't you think we'd better stop and explore?"

"I certainly think Brenda's right," said Princeps. "If the tunnel is there, and the big sledge dragged us over into it—well, we needn't talk about that. I think we'd better do a little exploring, as she says."

The sledges were stopped, and the tilting-line of the great kite pulled so as to empty it of wind. It came gently to the earth, and then, rather to their surprise, disappeared completely.

"By Jove!" said Princeps. "I shouldn't be surprised if the tunnel is there, and the kite has fallen in. Brenda, I think it's just as well you spoke when you did. Fancy tobogganing into a hole like that at ten or fifteen miles an hour!"

"If that is the case," said the Professor, quietly ignoring the hideous suggestion, "the Axial Tunnel must be rather larger than I expected. I did not expect to arrive at the edge till late this afternoon."

When the sledges were stopped, they put on their snowshoes and followed the line of the kite-cable for about a mile and a half until they came to the edge of what appeared to be an ice-cliff. The cable hung over this, hanging down into a dusk which quickly deepened into utter darkness. They hauled upon it and found that there were only a few yards over the cliff, and presently they landed the great kite.

"I wonder if it really *is* the tunnel?" said Brenda, taking a step forward.

"Whatever it is, it's too deep for you to fall into with any comfort," said her husband, dragging her back almost roughly.

Almost at the same moment a mass of ice and snow on which they had been standing a few minutes before, hauling up the cable of the kite, broke away and disappeared into the void. They listened with all their ears, but no sound came back. The huge block had vanished in silence into nothingness, into a void which apparently had no bottom; for even if it had fallen a thousand feet, an echo would have come back to them up the wall.

"It *is* the tunnel," said Brenda, after a few moments' silence, during which they looked at each other with something like awe in their eyes. "Thank you, Arthur, I don't think I should have liked to have gone down, too. But, uncle," she went on, "if this is the tunnel, and that thing has gone on before us, won't it stop and come back when it gets near the North Pole? Suppose we were to meet it after we have passed the centre. A collision just there wouldn't be very pleasant, would it?"

"My dear Brenda," he replied, "there is really no fear of anything of that sort. You see, there is atmosphere in the tunnel, and long before it reaches the centre, friction will have melted the ice and dissipated the water into vapour."

"Of course. How silly of me not to have thought of that before! I suppose a piece of iron thrown over there would be melted to vapour, just as the meteorites are. Well now, If we've found the tunnel, hadn't we better go back and get ready to go through it?"

"We shall have to wait for the moon, I suppose," said Princeps, as they turned away towards the sledges.

"Yes," said the Professor. "We shall have plenty of moonlight to work by in about fifty-six hours. Meanwhile we can take a rest and do as Brenda says."

It was just fifty hours later when the moon, almost at the full, rose over the eastern edge of the snow-wall, casting a flood of white light over the dim, ghostly land of the World's End. As it rose higher and higher, they saw that the sloping plain ended in a vast semicircle of cliff, beyond which there was nothing. They went down towards it and looked beyond and across, but the curving ice-walls reached away on either hand until they were lost in the distance. They were standing literally on the end of the earth. No sound of water or of volcanic action came up out of the void. They brought down a couple of rockets and fired them from the edge at a downward angle of sixty degrees. The trail of sparks spread out with inconceivable rapidity, and then, when the rockets burst, two tiny blue stars shone out, apparently as far below them as the stars of heaven were above them.

"I don't think there's very much doubt about that," said the Professor. "We have found the Axial Tunnel; but, after all, if it is only a very deep depression, our balloons can take us out of it after we have touched the bottom. Still, personally, I believe it to be the tunnel."

"Oh, it must be!" said Brenda decisively. And so, in fact, it proved to be.

As the moon grew rounder and brighter, the work of preparation for the last stage of their amazing enterprise grew apace. Everything had, of course, been thought out to the minutest detail, and the transformation which came over their impedimenta was little short of magical.

The sledges dissolved into their component parts, and these came together again in the form of a big, conical, drum-like structure, with walls of thick *papier mâche*. It had four long plate-glass windows in the sides and a large round one top and bottom. It was ten feet in diameter and fifteen in height. The interior was plainly but snugly fitted up as a sitting-room by day and, by means of a movable partition, a couple of sleeping-berths by night.

The food and water were stowed away in cupboards and tanks underneath the seats, and the gas-cylinders, rockets, etc., were packed under the flooring, which had a round trap-door in the centre over the window.

The liquid air-engines and the driving apparatus of the sledges were strongly secured to the lower end with chains which, in case of emergency, could be easily released by means of slip-hooks operated from inside. There were also two hundred pounds of shot-ballast underneath the flooring.

Attached to the upper part of the structure were four balloons, capable at their full capacity of easily lifting it with its whole load on board. These were connected by tubes with the interior, and thus by means of pumps worked by a small liquid-air engine, the gas from the cylinders could either be driven up into them or drawn down and re-stored. In the centre of the roof was another cable, longer than those which held the balloons, and to this was attached a large parachute which could be opened or shut at will from inside.

VI

When the moment chosen for departure came, there remained no possible doubt as to the correctness of the Professor's hypothesis. The sun was dipping below the horizon and the long polar night was beginning. The full moon shone down from the zenith through a cloudless, mistless atmosphere. The sloping snow-field and the curved edge of the Axial Tunnel were brilliantly illuminated. They could see for miles along the ice-cliffs, far enough to make certain that they were part of a circle so vast that anything like an exact calculation of its circumference was impossible.

The breeze was still straight to the southward, to the centre of the tunnel. The balloons were inflated until the *Brenda*—as the strange vehicle had been named by a majority of two to one—began to pull at the ropes which held her down. Then, with a last look round at the inhospitable land they were leaving—perchance never to see land of any sort again—they went in through the curved sliding door to windward. Princeps started the engine, the balloons began to fill out, and three of the four mooring-ropes were cast off as the *Brenda* began to rock and swing like the car of a captive balloon.

"Once more," said Princeps, giving his wife the knife with which she had cut the sledges loose.

"And this time for good—or the North Pole—or—well, at any rate, this is the stroke of Fate."

She gave her left hand to her husband, knelt down on the threshold of the door, and made a sideward slash at the slender rope which was fastened just under it. The strands ripped and parted, the *Brenda* rocked twice or thrice and became motionless. The ice-cliffs slipped away from under them, the vast, unfathomed, and fathomless gulf spread out beneath them, and the voyage, either from Pole to Pole or from Time to Eternity, had begun.

The Professor, who was naturally in command, allowed the *Brenda* to drift for two and a half hours at a carefully calculated wind-speed of twenty miles an hour. Then he said to Princeps—

"You can deflate the balloons now, I think. We must be near the centre. I will see to the parachute."

They had been thinking and talking of this journey, with all its apparent impossibilities and terrific risks, until they had become almost commonplace to them. But for all that, they looked at each other as they had never done before, as the Professor gave the fateful order. Even his lips tightened and his brows came together a little as he turned to cast loose the fine wire cables which held the ribs of the parachute.

The powerful little engine got to work, and the gas from the balloons hissed back into the cylinders. Then the envelopes were hauled in and stowed away. Through the side windows, Brenda saw a dim, far-away horizon rise up all round, and through the top window and the circular hole in the parachute, she saw the full disc of the moon growing smaller and smaller, and so she knew that they had begun their fall of 41,708,711 feet.

Taking this at 7,000 miles, in round numbers, the Professor, reckoning on an average speed of fifty to sixty miles an hour, expected to make the passage from Pole to Pole in about six days, granted always that the tunnel was clear all through. If it wasn't, their fates were on the knees of the Gods, and there was nothing more to say. As events proved, they made it in a good deal less.

For the first thirty-six hours everything went with perfect smoothness. The wind gauges at each side showed a speed of fifty-one miles an hour, and the *Brenda* continued her fall with perfect steadiness.

Suddenly, just as they were about to say "Good night" for the second time, they heard a sharp snapping and rending sound break through the smooth swish of the air past the outer wall of their vehicle. The next instant it rocked violently from side to side, and the indicators of the gauges began to fly round into invisibility.

"Heavens, uncle! what has happened?" gasped Brenda, clinging to the seat into which she had been slung.

"It can only be one thing," replied the Professor, steadying himself against the opposite wall. "Some of the stays have given way, and the parachute has split or broken up. God forgive me! Why did I not think of that before?"

"Of what? "said Princeps, dropping into the seat beside Brenda and putting his arm round her.

"The increasing pull of gravitation as we get nearer to the earth's centre. I calculated for a uniform pull only. They must have been bearing a tremendous strain before they parted."

While he was speaking, the vehicle had become steady again. The wind-gauges whirled till the spindles screeched and smoked in their sockets. The rush of the wind past the outside wall deepened to a roar and then rose to a shrill, whistling scream. Long, uncounted minutes of sheer speechless, thoughtless terror passed. The inside air grew hot and stifling. Even the uninflammable walls began to crinkle and crack under the fearful heat developed by the friction of the rushing air.

Brenda gasped two or three times for breath, and then, slipping out of her husband's arms, fell fainting in a heap on the floor. Mechanically both he and the Professor stooped to lift her up. To their amazement, the effort they made to do so threw her unconscious form nearly to the top of the conical roof. She floated in mid-air for a moment and then sank gently back into their arms.

"The Centre of the Earth!" gasped the Professor. "The point of equal attraction! If we can breathe for the next hour, we have a chance. Quick, Arthur, give us more air! The evaporation will reduce the temperature."

Even in such an awful moment as this, Professor Haffkin could not quite forget his scientific phraseology.

He laid Brenda, still weighing only a few pounds, on one of the seats and went to the liqueur-case for some brandy. Princeps meanwhile turned the tap of a spare cylinder lying beside the air-engine which drove the little electric-light installation. The sudden conversion of the liquid atmosphere into the gaseous form brought the temperature down with a rush, and—as they thought afterwards, with a shudder—probably prevented all the cylinders from exploding.

The brandy and the sudden coolness immediately revived Brenda, and after the two men had taken a stiff glass to steady their shaken-up nerves, they sat down and began to consider their position as calmly as might be.

They had passed the centre of the earth at an enormous but unknown velocity, and they were, therefore, endowed with a momentum which would certainly carry them far towards the northern end of the Axial Tunnel; but how far, it was impossible to say, since they did not know their speed.

But, however great the speed, it was diminishing every second, and a time must come when it would be *nil*—and then the backward fall would begin. If they could not prevent this, they might as well put an end to everything at once.

Hours passed; uncounted, but in hard thinking, mingled with dumb apprehension. The rush of the wind outside began to slacken at last, and when Princeps at length managed to fit another wind-gauge in place of the one that had been smashed to atoms, it registered a little over two hundred miles an hour.

"Our only chance, as far as I can see," said the Professor at length, looking up from a writing-pad on which he had been making pages of calculations, "is this. We must watch that indicator; and when the speed drops, say, to ten miles an hour, we must inflate our balloons to the utmost, cut loose the engines and other gear, and trust to the gas to pull us out."

There was literally nothing else to be done, and so for the present they sat and watched the indicator, and, by the way of killing the weary hours, counted the possibilities and probabilities of their return to the civilised world should the *Brenda's* balloons succeed in lifting her out of the northern end of the Axial Tunnel.

Hour by hour the speed dropped. The fatal pull, which, unless the balloons were able to counteract it, would drag them back with a hand resistless as that of Fate itself, had got them in its grip. Somewhere, an unknown number of miles above them, were the solitudes of the Northern Pole, from which they might not get away even if they reached them. Below was the awful gulf through which they had already passed, and to fall back into that meant a fate so terrible that Brenda had already made her husband promise to shoot her, should the balloons fail to do their work.

The Professor passed most of his time in elaborate calculations, the object of which was the ascertaining, as nearly as possible, their distance from the centre of the earth, and, therefore, the number of miles which they would have to rise to reach the outer air again. There were other calculations which had relation to the lifting power of the balloons, the weight of the car and its occupants, and the amount of gas at their disposal, not only for the ascent to the Pole, but also for their flight southward, if happily they found favorable winds to carry them back to the confines of civilization. These he kept to himself. He had the best of reasons for doing so.

The hours went by, and the speed shown by the indicator dropped steadily. A hundred miles an hour had become fifty, fifty became forty, then thirty, twenty, ten.

"I think you can get your balloons out now, Arthur," said the Professor. "It's a very good thing we housed them in time, or they would have been torn to ribbons by this. If you'll cast them loose, I'll see to the gas apparatus. Meanwhile, Brenda, you may as well get dinner ready."

Within an hour the four balloons were cast loose through their portholes in the roof of the car and attached to their cables and supply pipes. Meanwhile the upward speed of the *Brenda* had dropped from ten to seven miles. The gas-cylinders were connected with the transmitters and apparatus which allowed the gas to return to a normal temperature before passing into the envelopes, and then the balloons began to fill.

For a few moments the indicator stopped and trembled as the cables tightened, then it went forward again. They saw that it was registering six and a half miles an hour. This rose to seven, eight, and nine. Presently it passed ten.

"We shall do it, after all," said Princeps. "You see, we're going faster every minute. I wonder what the reason of that check was?"

"Probably the increased atmospheric friction on the surface of the balloons," replied the Professor quietly, with his eyes fixed on the dial.

The indicator stopped again at ten, and then the little blue, steel hand, which to them was veritably the Hand of Fate, began to creep slowly backwards.

None of them spoke. They all knew what it meant. The upward pull of the balloons was not counteracting the downward pull exerted from the centre of the earth. In a few hours more they would come to a standstill, and then, when the two forces balanced, they would hang motionless in that awful gulf of everlasting night until the gas gave out, and then the backward plunge to perdition would begin.

"I don't like the look of that," said Princeps, keeping his voice as steady as he could. "Hadn't we better let the engines go?"

"I think we ought to throw away everything that we can do without," said Brenda, staring at the fateful dial with fixed, wide-open eyes. "What's the use of anything if we never get to the top of this horrible hole?"

"That's rather a disrespectful way in which to speak of the Axial Tunnel of the earth, Brenda," said the Professor, with the flicker of a smile. "But we won't get rid of the impedimenta just yet," he went on. "You see, as the mathematicians say, velocity is momentum multiplied into mass. Therefore, if we decrease our mass, we shall decrease our momentum. The engines and the other things are really helping us along now, though it doesn't seem so. When the indicator has nearly stopped, it will be time to cut the weight loose."

Then they had dinner, eaten with a mere pretence of appetite, assisted by a bottle of "Pol Roger '89." The speed continued to drop steadily during the night, though Princeps satisfied himself that the balloons were filled to the utmost limit consistent with safety, and at last, towards the middle of the conventional night, it hovered between one and zero.

"I think you may let the engines go now, Arthur," said the Professor, "It's quite evident that we're overweighted. Slip the hooks, and then go up and see if your balloons will stand any more."

He said this in a whisper, because Brenda, utterly worn out, had gone to lie down behind the partition.

The hooks were slipped, and the hand on the dial began to move again as the *Brenda,* released from about six hundred pounds' weight, began to ascend again. But the speed only rose to fifteen miles an hour, and that was eight miles short of the result the Professor had arrived at. The attractive force was evidently being exerted from the sides of the tunnel as well as from the centre of the earth. He looked at the dial and said to Princeps—

"I think you'd better go and lie down now. It's my watch on deck. We're doing nicely now. I want to run through my figures again."

"All right," said Princeps, yawning and shaking hands. "You'll call me in four hours, as usual, won't you?"

Professor Haffkin nodded and said: "Good night. I hope we shall be through our difficulties by the morning. Good night, Arthur."

He got out his papers again and once more went minutely through the maze of figures and formulas with which the sheets were covered. Then, when the sound of slow, deep breathing told him that Princeps was asleep, he opened the trap-door in the floor and counted the unexhausted cylinders of gas. When he had finished, he said to himself in a whisper—

"Barely enough to get them home, even with the best of luck; but still enough to prove that it is possible to make a journey through the centre of the earth from Pole to Pole. At least, that will be done and proved—and Karl Haffkin will live for ever."

There was the light of martyrdom in his eyes as he looked for the last time at the dial. Then he unscrewed the circular window from the bottom of the car, lowered himself through it, hung for a moment to the edge with his hands, and let go.

★ ★ ★

When Princeps and Brenda woke after several hours' sleep, they were astonished to find the windows of the car glowing with a strange, brilliant light—the light of the Northern Aurora. Princeps got out, saying: "Hurrah, Professor! we've got there! Daylight at last!"

But there was no Professor, and only the open trap-door and the window hanging on its hinges below told how an almost priceless life had been heroically sacrificed to make the way of life longer for two who had only just begun to tread it together through the golden gates of the Garden of Love. But Karl Haffkin's martyrdom meant even more than this. Without it, the great experiment must have failed, and three lives would have been lost instead of one; and so he chose to die the lesser death so that his comrades on that marvellous voyage might live out their own lives to Nature's limit, and that he himself might live for ever on the roll of honour which is emblazoned with the names of the noblest of all martyrs—those who have given their lives to prove that Truth is true.

Space

JOHN BUCHAN

Best known as the author of the classic mystery novel The Thirty-Nine
Steps, *John Buchan (1875–1940) wrote prolifically in a number of genres,
including fantasy. This story, first published in the May 1911 issue of the
British magazine* Blackwood's, *extrapolates a philosophical concept into
a science fiction scenario that is both fascinating and, to its protagonist's
thinking, terrifying in its alienness.*

"Est impossibile? Certum est."
—*Tertullian*

Leithen told me this story one evening in early September as we sat beside the pony
track which gropes its way from Glenvalin up the Correi na Sidhe. I had arrived that
afternoon from the south, while he had been taking an off-day from a week's stalking, so we had walked up the glen together after tea to get the news of the forest.
A rifle was out on the Correi na Sidhe beat, and a thin spire of smoke had risen from
the top of Sgurr Dearg to show that a stag had been killed at the burnhead. The
lumpish hill pony with its deer-saddle had gone up the Correi in a gillie's charge
while we followed at leisure, picking our way among the loose granite rocks and the
patches of wet bogland. The track climbed high on one of the ridges of Sgurr Dearg,
till it hung over a caldron of green glen with the Alt-na-Sidhe churning in its linn
a thousand feet below. It was a breathless evening, I remember, with a pale-blue sky
just clearing from the haze of the day. West-wind weather may make the North, even

in September, no bad imitation of the Tropics, and I sincerely pitied the man who all these stifling hours had been toiling on the screes of Sgurr Dearg. By-and-by we sat down on a bank of heather, and idly watched the trough swimming at our feet. The clatter of the pony's hoofs grew fainter, the drone of bees had gone, even the midges seemed to have forgotten their calling. No place on earth can be so deathly still as a deer-forest early in the season before the stags have begun roaring, for there are no sheep with their homely noises, and only the rare croak of a raven breaks the silence. The hillside was far from sheer—one could have walked down with a little care—but something in the shape of the hollow and the remote gleam of white water gave it an extraordinary depth and space. There was a shimmer left from the day's heat, which invested bracken and rock and scree with a curious airy unreality. One could almost have believed that the eye had tricked the mind, that all was mirage, that five yards from the path the solid earth fell away into nothingness. I have a bad head, and instinctively I drew farther back into the heather. Leithen's eyes were looking vacantly before him.

"Did you ever know Hollond?" he asked.

Then he laughed shortly. "I don't know why I asked that, but somehow this place reminded me of Hollond. That glimmering hollow looks as if it were the beginning of eternity. It must be eerie to live with the feeling always on one."

Leithen seemed disinclined for further exercise. He lit a pipe and smoked quietly for a little. "Odd that you didn't know Hollond. You must have heard his name. I thought you amused yourself with metaphysics."

Then I remembered. There had been an erratic genius who had written some articles in *Mind* on that dreary subject, the mathematical conception of infinity. Men had praised them to me, but I confess I never quite understood their argument. "Wasn't he some sort of mathematical professor?" I asked.

"He was, and, in his own way, a tremendous swell. He wrote a book on Number which has translations in every European language. He is dead now, and the Royal Society founded a medal in his honour. But I wasn't thinking of that side of him."

It was the time and place for a story, for the pony would not be back for an hour. So I asked Leithen about the other side of Hollond which was recalled to him by Correi na Sidhe. He seemed a little unwilling to speak. . . .

"I wonder if you will understand it. You ought to, of course, better than me, for you know something of philosophy. But it took me a long time to get the hang of it, and I can't give you any kind of explanation. He was my fag at Eton, and when I began to get on at the Bar I was able to advise him on one or two private matters, so that he rather fancied my legal ability. He came to me with his story because he

190

had to tell someone, and he wouldn't trust a colleague. He said he didn't want a scientist to know, for scientists were either pledged to their own theories and wouldn't understand, or, if they understood, would get ahead of him in his researches. He wanted a lawyer, he said, who was accustomed to weighing evidence. That was good sense, for evidence must always be judged by the same laws, and I suppose in the long-run the most abstruse business comes down to a fairly simple deduction from certain data. Anyhow, that was the way he used to talk, and I listened to him, for I liked the man, and had an enormous respect for his brains. At Eton he sluiced down all the mathematics they could give him, and he was an astonishing swell at Cambridge. He was a simple fellow, too, and talked no more jargon than he could help. I used to climb with him in the Alps now and then, and you would never have guessed that he had any thoughts beyond getting up steep rocks.

"It was at Chamonix, I remember, that I first got a hint of the matter that was filling his mind. We had been taking an off-day, and were sitting in the hotel garden, watching the Aiguilles getting purple in the twilight. Chamonix always makes me choke a little—it is so crushed in by those great snow masses. I said something about it—said I liked the open spaces like the Gornegrat or the Bel Alp better. He asked me why: if it was the difference of the air, or merely the wider horizon? I said it was the sense of not being crowded, of living in an empty world. He repeated the word 'empty' and laughed.

"'By "empty" you mean,' he said, 'where things don't knock up against you?'

"I told him No. I mean just empty, void, nothing but blank æther.

"'You don't knock up against things here, and the air is as good as you want. It can't be the lack of ordinary emptiness you feel.'

"I agreed that the word needed explaining. 'I suppose it is mental restlessness,' I said. 'I like to feel that for a tremendous distance there is nothing round me. Why, I don't know. Some men are built the other way and have a terror of space.'

"He said that that was better. 'It is a personal fancy, and depends on your *knowing* that there is nothing between you and the top of the Dent Blanche. And you know because your eyes tell you there is nothing. Even if you were blind, you might have a sort of sense about adjacent matter. Blind men often have it. But in any case, whether got from instinct or sight, the *knowledge* is what matters.'

"Hollond was embarking on a Socratic dialogue in which I could see little point. I told him so, and he laughed.

"'I am not sure that I am very clear myself. But yes—there *is* a point. Supposing you knew—not by sight or by instinct, but by sheer intellectual knowledge, as I know the truth of a mathematical proposition—that what we call empty space was full, crammed. Not with lumps of what we call matter like hills and houses, but with things as real—as real to the mind. Would you still feel crowded?'

" 'No,' I said, 'I don't think so. It is only what we call matter that signifies. It would be just as well not to feel crowded by the other thing, for there would be no escape from it. But what are you getting at? Do you mean atoms or electric currents or what?'

"He said he wasn't thinking about that sort of thing, and began to talk of another subject.

"Next night, when we were pigging it at the Geant cabane, he started again on the same tack. He asked me how I accounted for the fact that animals could find their way back over great tracts of unknown country. I said I supposed it was the homing instinct.

" 'Rubbish, man,' he said. 'That's only another name for the puzzle, not an explanation. There must be some reason for it. They must *know* something that we cannot understand. Tie a cat in a bag and take it fifty miles by train and it will make its way home. That cat has some clue that we haven't.'

"I was tired and sleepy, and told him that I did not care a rush about the psychology of cats. But he was not to be snubbed, and went on talking.

" 'How if Space is really full of things we cannot see and as yet do not know? How if all animals and some savages have a cell in their brain or a nerve which responds to the invisible world? How if all Space be full of these landmarks, not material in our sense, but quite real? A dog barks at nothing, a wild beast makes an aimless circuit. Why? Perhaps because Space is made up of corridors and alleys, ways to travel and things to shun? For all we know, to a greater intelligence than ours the top of Mont Blanc may be as crowded as Piccadilly Circus.'

"But at that point I fell asleep and left Hollond to repeat his questions to a guide who knew no English and a snoring porter.

"Six months later, one foggy January afternoon, Hollond rang me up at the Temple and proposed to come to see me that night after dinner. I thought he wanted to talk Alpine shop, but he turned up in Duke Street about nine with a kit-bag full of papers. He was an odd fellow to look at—a yellowish face with the skin stretched tight on the cheek-bones, clean-shaven, a sharp chin which he kept poking forward, and deep-set, greyish eyes. He was a hard fellow, too, always in pretty good condition, which was remarkable considering how he slaved for nine months out of the twelve. He had a quiet, slow-spoken manner, but that night I saw that he was considerably excited.

"He said that he had come to me because we were old friends. He proposed to tell me a tremendous secret. 'I must get another mind to work on it or I'll go crazy. I don't want a scientist. I want a plain man.'

"Then he fixed me with a look like a tragic actor's. 'Do you remember that talk we had in August at Chamonix—about Space? I daresay you thought I was playing the fool. So I was in a sense, but I was feeling my way towards something which has been in my mind for ten years. Now I have got it, and you must hear about it. You may take my word that it's a pretty startling discovery.'

"I lit a pipe and told him to go ahead, warning him that I knew about as much science as the dustman.

"I am bound to say that it took me a long time to understand what he meant. He began by saying that everybody thought of Space as an 'empty homogeneous medium.' 'Never mind at present what the ultimate constituents of that medium are. We take it as a finished product, and we think of it as mere extension, something without any quality at all. That is the view of civilised man. You will find all the philosophers taking it for granted. Yes, but every living thing does not take that view. An animal, for instance. It feels a kind of quality in Space. It can find its way over new country, because it perceives certain landmarks, not necessarily material, but perceptible, or if you like intelligible. Take an Australian savage. He has the same power, and, I believe, for the same reason. He is conscious of intelligible landmarks.'

" 'You mean what people call a sense of direction,' I put in.

" 'Yes, but what in Heaven's name is a sense of direction? The phrase explains nothing. However incoherent the mind of the animal or the savage may be, it is there somewhere, working on some data. I've been all through the psychological and anthropological side of the business, and after you eliminate the clues from sight and hearing and smell and half-conscious memory there remains a solid lump of the inexplicable.'

"Holland's eye had kindled, and he sat doubled up in his chair, dominating me with a finger.

" 'Here, then is a power which man is civilising himself out of. Call it anything you like, but you must admit that it is a power. Don't you see that it is a perception of another kind of reality that we are leaving behind us? Well, you know the way nature works. The wheel comes full circle, and what we think we have lost we regain in a higher form. So for a long time I have been wondering whether the civilised mind could not recreate for itself this lost gift, the gift of seeing the quality of Space. I mean that I wondered whether the scientific modern brain could not get to the stage of realising that Space is not an empty homogeneous medium, but full of intricate differences, intelligible and real, though not with our common reality.'

"I found all this very puzzling and he had to repeat it several times before I got a glimpse of what he was talking about.

" 'I've wondered for a long time,' he went on 'but now quite suddenly, I have begun to know.' He stopped and asked me abruptly if I knew much about mathematics.

" 'It's a pity,' he said, 'but the main point is not technical, though I wish you could appreciate the beauty of some of my proofs.'

"Then he began to tell me about his last six months' work. I should have mentioned that he was a brilliant physicist besides other things. All Hollond's tastes were on the borderlands of sciences, where mathematics fades into metaphysics and physics merges in the abstrusest kind of mathematics. Well, it seems he had been working for years at the ultimate problem of matter, and especially of that rarefied matter we call æther or space. I forget what his view was—atoms or molecules or electric waves. If he ever told me I have forgotten, but I'm not certain that I ever knew. However, the point was that these ultimate constituents were dynamic and mobile, not a mere passive medium but a medium in constant movement and change. He claimed to have discovered—by ordinary inductive experiment—that the constituents of æther possessed certain functions, and moved in certain figures obedient to certain mathematical laws. Space, I gathered, was perpetually 'forming fours' in some fancy way.

"Here he left his physics and became the mathematician. Among his mathematical discoveries had been certain curves or figures or something whose behaviour involved a new dimension. I gathered that this wasn't the ordinary Fourth Dimension that people talk of, but that fourth-dimensional inwardness or involution was part of it. The explanation lay in the pile of manuscripts he left with me, but though I tried honestly I couldn't get the hang of it. My mathematics stopped with desperate finality just as he got into his subject.

"His point was that the constituents of Space moved according to these new mathematical figures of his. They were always changing, but the principles of their change were as fixed as the law of gravitation. Therefore, if you once grasped these principles you knew the contents of the void. What do you make of that?"

I said that it seemed to me a reasonable enough argument, but that it got one very little way forward. "A man," I said, "might know the contents of Space and the laws of their arrangement and yet be unable to see anything more than his fellows. It is a purely academic knowledge. His mind knows it as the result of many deductions, but his senses perceive nothing."

Leithen laughed. "Just what I said to Hollond. He asked the opinion of my legal mind. I said I could not pronounce on his argument but that I could point out that he had established no trait d'union between the intellect which understood and the senses which perceived. It was like a blind man with immense knowledge but no eyes, and therefore no peg to hang his knowledge on and make it useful. He had not explained his savage or his cat. 'Hang it, man,' I said, 'before you can appreciate the existence of your Spacial forms you have to go through elaborate experiments and deductions. You can't be doing that every minute. Therefore you don't get any nearer to the *use* of the sense you say that man once possessed, though you can explain it a bit.'"

"What did he say?" I asked.

"The funny thing was that he never seemed to see my difficulty. When I kept bringing him back to it he shied off with a new wild theory of perception. He argued that the mind can live in a world of realities without any sensuous stimulus to connect them with the world of our ordinary life. Of course that wasn't my point. I supposed that this world of Space was real enough to him, but I wanted to know how he got there. He never answered me. He was the typical Cambridge man, you know—dogmatic about uncertainties, but curiously diffident about the obvious. He laboured to get me to understand the notion of his mathematical forms, which I was quite willing to take on trust from him. Some queer things he said, too. He took our feeling about Left and Right as an example of our instinct for the quality of Space. But when I objected that Left and Right varied with each object, and only existed in connection with some definite material thing, he said that that was exactly what he meant. It was an example of the mobility of the Spacial forms. Do you see any sense in that?"

I shook my head. It seemed to me pure craziness.

"And then he tried to show me what he called the 'involution of Space,' by taking two points on a piece of paper. The points were a foot away when the paper was flat, they coincided when it was doubled up. He said that there were no gaps between the figures, for the medium was continuous, and he took as an illustration the loops on a cord. You are to think of a cord always looping and unlooping itself according to certain mathematical laws. Oh, I tell you, I gave up trying to follow him. And he was so desperately in earnest all the time. By his account Space was a sort of mathematical pandemonium."

Leithen stopped to refill his pipe, and I mused upon the ironic fate which had compelled a mathematical genius to make his sole confidant of a philistine lawyer, and induced that lawyer to repeat it confusedly to an ignoramus at twilight on a Scotch hill. As told by Leithen it was a very halting tale.

"But there was one thing I could see very clearly," Leithen went on, "and that was Hollond's own case. This crowded world of Space was perfectly real to him. How he had got to it I do not know. Perhaps his mind, dwelling constantly on the problem, had unsealed some atrophied cell and restored the old instinct. Anyhow, he was living his daily life with a foot in each world.

"He often came to see me, and after the first hectic discussions he didn't talk much. There was no noticeable change in him—a little more abstracted perhaps. He would walk in the street or come into a room with a quick look round him, and sometimes for no earthly reason he would swerve. Did you ever watch a cat crossing a room? It sidles along by the furniture and walks over an open space of carpet as if it were picking its way among obstacles. Well, Hollond behaved like that, but he had always been counted a little odd, and nobody noticed it but me.

"I knew better than to chaff him, and had stopped argument, so there wasn't much to be said. But sometimes he would give me news about his experiences. The whole thing was perfectly clear and scientific and above board, and nothing creepy about it. You know how I hate the washy supernatural stuff they give us nowadays. Hollond was well and fit, with an appetite like a hunter. But as he talked, sometimes—well, you know I haven't much in the way of nerves or imagination—but I used to get a little eerie. Used to feel the solid earth dissolving round me. It was the opposite of vertigo, if you understand me—a sense of airy realities crowding in on you-crowding the mind, that is, not the body.

"I gathered from Hollond that he was always conscious of corridors and halls and alleys in Space, shifting, but shifting according to inexorable laws. I never could get quite clear as to what this consciousness was like. When I asked he used to look puzzled and worried and helpless. I made out from him that one landmark involved a sequence, and once given a bearing from an object you could keep the direction without a mistake. He told me he could easily, if he wanted, go in a dirigible from the top of Mont Blanc to the top of Snowdon in the thickest fog and without a compass, if he were given the proper angle to start from. I confess I didn't follow that myself. Material objects had nothing to do with the Spacial forms, for a table or a bed in our world might be placed across a corridor of Space. The forms played their game independent of our kind of reality. But the worst of it was, that if you kept your mind too much in one world you were apt to forget about the other and Hollond was always barking his shins on stones and chairs and things.

"He told me all this quite simply and frankly. Remember his mind and no other part of him lived in his new world. He said it gave him an odd sense of detachment to sit in a room among people, and to know that nothing there but himself had any relation at all to the infinite strange world of Space that flowed around them. He would listen, he said, to a great man talking, with one eye on the cat on the rug, thinking to himself how much more the cat knew than the man."

"How long was it before he went mad?" I asked.

It was a foolish question, and made Leithen cross. "He never went mad in your sense. My dear fellow, you're very much wrong if you think there was anything pathological about him—then. The man was brilliantly sane. His mind was as keen is a keen sword. I couldn't understand him, but I could judge of his sanity right enough."

I asked if it made him happy or miserable.

"At first I think it made him uncomfortable. He was restless because he knew too much and too little. The unknown pressed in on his mind as bad air weighs on the lungs. Then it lightened and he accepted the new world in the same sober practical way that he took other things. I think that the free exercise of his mind in a pure medium gave him a feeling of extraordinary power and ease. His eyes used to sparkle when he talked. And another odd thing he told me. He was a keen rock-climber, but, curiously enough, he had never a very good head. Dizzy heights always worried him, though he managed to keep hold on himself. But now all that had gone. The sense of the fulness of Space made him as happy—happier I believe—with his legs dangling into eternity, as sitting before his own study fire.

"I remember saying that it was all rather like the mediaeval wizards who made their spells by means of numbers and figures.

"He caught me up at once. 'Not numbers,' he said. "Number has no place in Nature. It is an invention of the human mind to atone for a bad memory. But figures are a different matter. All the mysteries of the world are in them, and the old magicians knew that at least, if they knew no more.'

"He had only one grievance. He complained that it was terribly lonely. 'It is the Desolation,' he would quote, 'spoken of by Daniel the prophet.' He would spend hours travelling those eerie shifting corridors of Space with no hint of another human soul. How could there be? It was a world of pure reason, where human personality had no place. What puzzled me was why he should feel the absence of this. One wouldn't you know, in an intricate problem of geometry or a game of chess. I asked him, but he didn't understand the question. I puzzled over it a good deal, for it seemed to me that if Hollond felt lonely, there must be more in this world of his than we imagined. I began to wonder if there was any truth in fads like psychical research. Also, I was not so sure that he was as normal as I had thought: it looked as if his nerves might be going bad.

"Oddly enough, Hollond was getting on the same track himself. He had discovered, so he said, that in sleep everybody now and then lived in this new world of his. You know how one dreams of triangular railway platforms with trains running simultaneously down all three sides and not colliding. Well, this sort of cantrip was 'common form,' as we say at the Bar, in Hollond's Space, and he was very curious about the why and wherefore of Sleep. He began to haunt psychological laboratories, where they experiment with the charwoman and the odd man, and he used to go up to Cambridge for seances. It was a foreign atmosphere to him, and I don't think he was very happy in it. He found so many charlatans that he used to get angry, and declare he would be better employed at Mother's Meetings!"

From far up the Glen came the sound of the pony's hoofs. The stag had been loaded up and the gillies were returning. Leithen looked at his watch. "We'd better wait and see the beast," he said.

". . . Well, nothing happened for more than a year. Then one evening in May he burst into my rooms in high excitement. You understand quite clearly that there was no suspicion of horror or fright or anything unpleasant about this world he had discovered. It was simply a series of interesting and difficult problems. All this time Hollond had been rather extra well and cheery. But when he came in I thought I noticed a different look in his eyes, something puzzled and diffident and apprehensive.

" 'There's a queer performance going on in the other world,' he said. 'It's unbelievable. I never dreamed of such a thing. I—I don't quite know how to put it, and I don't know how to explain it, but—but I am becoming aware that there are other beings—other minds—moving in Space besides mine.'

"I suppose I ought to have realised then that things were beginning to go wrong. But it was very difficult, he was so rational and anxious to make it all clear. I asked him how he knew.

"There could, of course, on his own showing be no *change* in that world, for the forms of Space moved and existed under inexorable laws. He said he found his own mind failing him at points. There would come over him a sense of fear— intellectual fear—and weakness, a sense of something else, quite alien to Space, thwarting him. Of course he could only describe his impressions very lamely, for they were purely of the mind, and he had no material peg to hang them on, so that I could realise them. But the gist of it was that he had been gradually becoming conscious of what he called 'Presences' in his world. They had no effect on Space—did not leave footprints in its corridors, for instance—but they affected his mind. There was some mysterious contact established between him and them.

I asked him if the affection was unpleasant and he said 'No, not exactly.' But I could see a hint of fear in his eyes.

"Think of it. Try to realise what intellectual fear is. I can't, but it is conceivable. To you and me fear implies pain to ourselves or some other, and such pain is always in the last resort pain of the flesh. Consider it carefully and you will see that it is so. But imagine fear so sublimated and transmuted as to be the tension of pure spirit. I can't realise it, but I think it possible. I don't pretend to understand how Hollond got to know about these Presences. But there was no doubt about the fact. He was positive, and he wasn't in the least mad—not in our sense. In that very month he published his book on Number, and gave a German professor who attacked it a most tremendous public trouncing.

"I know what you are going to say—that the fancy was a weakening of the mind from within. I admit I should have thought of that but he looked so confound-edly sane and able that it seemed ridiculous. He kept asking me my opinion, as a lawyer, on the facts he offered. It was the oddest case ever put before me, but I did my best for him. I dropped all my own views of sense and nonsense. I told him that, taking all that he had told me as fact, the Presences might be either ordinary minds traversing Space in sleep; or minds such as his which had independently captured the sense of Space's quality; or, finally, the spirits of just men made perfect, behaving as psychical researchers think they do. It was a ridiculous task to set a prosaic man, and I wasn't quite serious. But Hollond was serious enough.

"He admitted that all three explanations were conceivable, but he was very doubtful about the first. The projection of the spirit into Space during sleep, he thought, was a faint and feeble thing, and these were powerful Presences. With the second and the third he was rather impressed. I suppose I should have seen what was happening and tried to stop it; at least, looking back that seems to have been my duty. But it was difficult to think that anything was wrong with Hollond; indeed the odd thing is that all this time the idea of madness never entered my head. I rather backed him up. Somehow the thing took my fancy, though I thought it moonshine at the bottom of my heart. I enlarged on the pioneering before him. 'Think,' I told him, 'what may be waiting for you. You may discover the meaning of Spirit. You may open up a new world, as rich as the old one, but imperishable. You may prove to mankind their immortality and deliver them for ever from the fear of death. Why, man, you are picking at the lock of all the world's mysteries.'

"But Hollond did not cheer up. He seemed strangely languid and dispirited. 'That is all true enough,' he said, 'if you are right, if your alternatives are exhaustive.

But suppose they are something else, something . . .' What that 'something' might be he had apparently no idea, and very soon he went away.

"He said another thing before he left. We asked me if I ever read poetry, and I said, not often. Nor did he: but he had picked up a little book somewhere and found a man who knew about the Presences. I think his name was Traherne, one of the seventeenth-century fellows. He quoted a verse which stuck to my fly-paper memory. It ran something like

'Within the region of the air,
Compassed about with Heavens fair,
Great tracts of lands there may be found,
Where many numerous hosts,
In those far distant coasts,
For other great and glorious ends
Inhabit, my yet unknown friends.'

Hollond was positive he did not mean angels or anything of the sort. I told him that Traherne evidently took a cheerful view of them. He admitted that, but added: 'He had religion, you see. He believed that everything was for the best. I am not a man of faith, and can only take comfort from what I understand. I'm in the dark, I tell you . . .'

"Next week I was busy with the Chilian Arbitration case, and saw nobody for a couple of months. Then one evening I ran against Hollond on the Embankment, and thought him looking horribly ill. He walked back with me to my rooms, and hardly uttered one word all the way. I gave him a stiff whisky-and-soda, which he gulped down absent-mindedly. There was that strained, hunted look in his eyes that you see in a frightened animal's. He was always lean, but now he had fallen away to skin and bone.

" 'I can't stay long,' he told me, 'for I'm off to the Alps to-morrow and I have a lot to do.' Before then he used to plunge readily into his story, but now he seemed shy about beginning. Indeed I had to ask him a question.

" 'Things are difficult,' he said hesitatingly, and rather distressing. Do you know, Leithen, I think you were wrong about—about what I spoke to you of. You said there must be one of three explanations. I am beginning to think that there is a fourth.

"He stopped for a second or two, then suddenly leaned forward and gripped my knee so fiercely that I cried out. 'That world is the Desolation,' he said in a choking voice, 'and perhaps I am getting near the Abomination of the Desolation that the old prophet spoke of. I tell you, man, I am on the edge of a terror, a terror,' he almost screamed, 'that no mortal can think of and live.'

"You can imagine that I was considerably startled. It was lightning out of a clear sky. How the devil could one associate horror with mathematics? I don't see it yet. . . . At any rate, I—You may be sure I cursed my folly for ever pretending to take him seriously. The only way would have been to have laughed him out of it at the start. And yet I couldn't, you know—it was too real and reasonable. Anyhow, I tried a firm tone now, and told him the whole thing was arrant raving bosh. I bade him be a man and pull himself together. I made him dine with me, and took him home, and got him into a better state of mind before he went to bed. Next morning I saw him off at Charing Cross, very haggard still, but better. He promised to write to me pretty often. . . . "

The pony, with a great eleven-pointer lurching athwart its back, was abreast of us, and from the autumn mist came the sound of soft Highland voices. Leithen and I got up to go, when we heard that the rifle had made direct for the Lodge by a short cut past the Sanctuary. In the wake of the gillies we descended the Correi road into a glen all swimming with dim purple shadows. The pony minced and boggled; the stag's antlers stood out sharp on the rise against a patch of sky, looking like a skeleton tree. Then we dropped into a covert of birches and emerged on the white glen highway.

Leithen's story had bored and puzzled me at the start, but now it had somehow gripped my fancy. Space a domain of endless corridors and Presences moving in them! The world was not quite the same as an hour ago. It was the hour, as the French say, "between dog and wolf," when the mind is disposed to marvels. I thought of my stalking on the morrow, and was miserably conscious that I would miss my stag. Those airy forms would get in the way. Confound Leithen and his yarns!

"I want to hear the end of your story," I told him, as the lights of the Lodge showed half a mile distant.

"The end was a tragedy," he said slowly. "I don't much care to talk about it. But how was I to know? I couldn't see the nerve going. You see I couldn't believe it was all nonsense. If I could I might have seen. But I still think there was something in it—up to a point. Oh, I agree he went mad in the end. It is the only explanation. Something must have snapped in that fine brain, and he saw the little bit more which we call madness. Thank God, you and I are prosaic fellows. . . .

"I was going out to Chamonix myself a week later. But before I started I got a post-card from Hollond, the only word from him. He had printed my name and address, and on the other side had scribbled six words—'I know at last—God's mercy.—H.G.H' The handwriting was like a sick man of ninety. I knew that things must be pretty bad with my friend.

201

"I got to Chamonix in time for his funeral. An ordinary climbing accident— you probably read about it in the papers. The Press talked about the toll which the Alps took from intellectuals—the usual rot. There was an inquiry, but the facts were quite simple. The body was only recognised by the clothes. He had fallen several thousand feet.

"It seems that he had climbed for a few days with one of the Kronigs and Dupont, and they had done some hair-raising things on the Aiguilles. Dupont told me that they had found a new route up the Montanvert side of the Charmoz. He said that Hollond climbed like a 'diable fou' and if you know Dupont's standard of madness you will see that the pace must have been pretty hot. 'But monsieur was sick,' he added; 'his eyes were not good. And I and Franz, we were grieved for him and a little afraid. We were glad when he left us.'

"He dismissed the guides two days before his death. The next day he spent in the hotel, getting his affairs straight. He left everything in perfect order, but not a line to a soul, not even to his sister. The following day he set out alone about three in the morning for the Grepon. He took the road up the Nantillons glacier to the Col, and then he must have climbed the Mummery crack by himself. After that he left the ordinary route and tried a new traverse across the Mer de Glace face. Somewhere near the top he fell, and next day a party going to the Dent du Requin found him on the rocks thousands of feet below.

"He had slipped in attempting the most foolhardy course on earth, and there was a lot of talk about the dangers of guideless climbing. But I guessed the truth, and I am sure Dupont knew, though he held his tongue. . . ."

We were now on the gravel of the drive, and I was feeling better. The thought of dinner warmed my heart and drove out the eeriness of the twilight glen. The hour between dog and wolf was passing. After all, there was a gross and jolly earth at hand for wise men who had a mind to comfort.

Leithen, I saw, did not share my mood. He looked glum and puzzled, as if his tale had aroused grim memories. He finished it at the Lodge door.

". . . For, of course, he had gone out that day to die. He had seen the something more, the little bit too much, which plucks a man from his moorings. He had gone so far into the land of pure spirit that he must needs go further and shed the fleshly envelope that cumbered him. God send that he found rest! I believe that he chose the steepest cliff in the Alps for a purpose. He wanted to be unrecognisable. He was a brave man and a good citizen. I think he hoped that those who found him might not see the look in his eyes."

At the Earth's Core

EDGAR RICE BURROUGHS

In 1911, Edgar Rice Burroughs (1875–1950) gave the proto-science fiction story form known as the "scientific romance" an inventive spin with Under the Moons of Mars *(a.k.a.* A Princess of Mars*), the first of his tales of swashbuckling interplanetary warrior John Carter of Mars. The following year, he explored the primitive recesses of our world in his jungle adventure* Tarzan of the Apes. At the Earth's Core, *with its vividly imagined world of Pellucidar located at the center of our hollow Earth, can be read as something of a synthesis of these two story types. First serialized in four parts beginning with April 4, 1914 issue of* All-Story Weekly, *it inaugurated one of Burroughs' most popular and long-running sagas. Burroughs would publish another six adventures set in Pellucidar, and even merge it with his* Tarzan *series in the fourth novel,* Tarzan at the Earth's Core *(1929).*

Prologue

In the first place, please bear in mind that I do not expect you to believe this story. Nor could you wonder had you witnessed a recent experience of mine when, in the armor of blissful and stupendous ignorance, I gaily narrated the gist of it to a Fellow of the Royal Geological Society on the occasion of my last trip to London.

You would surely have thought that I had been detected in no less a heinous crime than the purloining of the Crown Jewels from the Tower, or putting poison in the coffee of His Majesty the King.

The erudite gentleman in whom I confided congealed before I was half through—it is all that saved him from exploding—and my dreams of an Honorary Fellowship, gold medals, and a niche in the Hall of Fame faded into the thin, cold air of his arctic atmosphere.

But I believe the story, and so would you, and so would the learned Fellow of the Royal Geological Society, had you and he heard it from the lips of the man who told it to me. Had you seen, as I did, the fire of truth in those gray eyes; had you felt the ring of sincerity in that quiet voice; had you realized the pathos of it all—you, too, would believe. You would not have needed the final ocular proof that I had—the weird rhamphorhynchus-like creature which he had brought back with him from the inner world.

I came upon him quite suddenly, and no less unexpectedly, upon the rim of the great Sahara Desert. He was standing before a goat-skin tent amidst a clump of date palms within a tiny oasis. Close by was an Arab douar of some eight or ten tents.

I had come down from the north to hunt lion. My party consisted of a dozen children of the desert—I was the only "white" man. As we approached the little clump of verdure I saw the man come from his tent and with hand-shaded eyes peer intently at us. At sight of me he advanced rapidly to meet us.

"A white man!" he cried. "May the good Lord be praised! I have been watching you for hours, hoping against hope that *this* time there would be a white man. Tell me the date. What year is it?"

And when I had told him he staggered as though he had been struck full in the face, so that he was compelled to grasp my stirrup leather for support.

"It cannot be!" he cried after a moment. "It cannot be! Tell me that you are mistaken, or that you are but joking."

"I am telling you the truth, my friend," I replied. "Why should I deceive a stranger, or attempt to, in so simple a matter as the date?"

For some time he stood in silence, with bowed head.

"Ten years!" he murmured, at last. "Ten years, and I thought that at the most it could be scarce more than one!" That night he told me his story—the story that I give you here as nearly in his own words as I can recall them.

I

TOWARD THE ETERNAL FIRES

I was born in Connecticut about thirty years ago. My name is David Innes. My father was a wealthy mine owner. When I was nineteen he died. All his property was to be mine when I had attained my majority—provided that I had devoted the two years intervening in close application to the great business I was to inherit.

I did my best to fulfil the last wishes of my parent—not because of the inheritance, but because I loved and honored my father. For six months I toiled in the mines and in the counting-rooms, for I wished to know every minute detail of the business.

Then Perry interested me in his invention. He was an old fellow who had devoted the better part of a long life to the perfection of a mechanical subterranean prospector. As relaxation he studied paleontology. I looked over his plans, listened to his arguments, inspected his working model—and then, convinced, I advanced the funds necessary to construct a full-sized, practical prospector.

I shall not go into the details of its construction—it lies out there in the desert now—about two miles from here. Tomorrow you may care to ride out and see it. Roughly, it is a steel cylinder a hundred feet long, and jointed so that it may turn and twist through solid rock if need be. At one end is a mighty revolving drill operated by an engine which Perry said generated more power to the cubic inch than any other engine did to the cubic foot. I remember that he used to claim that that invention alone would make us fabulously wealthy—we were going to make the whole thing public after the successful issue of our first secret trial—but Perry never returned from that trial trip, and I only after ten years.

I recall as it were but yesterday the night of that momentous occasion upon which we were to test the practicality of that wondrous invention. It was near midnight when we repaired to the lofty tower in which Perry had constructed his "iron mole" as he was wont to call the thing. The great nose rested upon the bare earth of the floor. We passed through the doors into the outer jacket, secured them, and then passing on into the cabin, which contained the controlling mechanism within the inner tube, switched on the electric lights.

Perry looked to his generator; to the great tanks that held the life-giving chemicals with which he was to manufacture fresh air to replace that which we consumed in breathing; to his instruments for recording temperatures, speed, distance, and for examining the materials through which we were to pass.

He tested the steering device, and overlooked the mighty cogs which transmitted its marvelous velocity to the giant drill at the nose of his strange craft.

Our seats, into which we strapped ourselves, were so arranged upon transverse bars that we would be upright whether the craft were ploughing her way downward into the bowels of the earth, or running horizontally along some great seam of coal, or rising vertically toward the surface again.

At length all was ready. Perry bowed his head in prayer. For a moment we were silent, and then the old man's hand grasped the starting lever. There was a frightful roaring beneath us—the giant frame trembled and vibrated—there was a rush of sound as the loose earth passed up through the hollow space between the inner and outer jackets to be deposited in our wake. We were off!

The noise was deafening. The sensation was frightful. For a full minute neither of us could do aught but cling with the proverbial desperation of the drowning man to the handrails of our swinging seats. Then Perry glanced at the thermometer.

"Gad!" he cried, "it cannot be possible—quick! What does the distance meter read?"

That and the speedometer were both on my side of the cabin, and as I turned to take a reading from the former I could see Perry muttering.

"Ten degrees rise—it cannot be possible!" and then I saw him tug frantically upon the steering wheel.

As I finally found the tiny needle in the dim light I translated Perry's evident excitement, and my heart sank within me. But when I spoke I hid the fear which haunted me. "It will be seven hundred feet, Perry," I said, "by the time you can turn her into the horizontal."

"You'd better lend me a hand then, my boy," he replied, "for I cannot budge her out of the vertical alone. God give that our combined strength may be equal to the task, for else we are lost."

I wormed my way to the old man's side with never a doubt but that the great wheel would yield on the instant to the power of my young and vigorous muscles. Nor was my belief mere vanity, for always had my physique been the envy and despair of my fellows. And for that very reason it had waxed even greater than nature had intended, since my natural pride in my great strength had led me to care for and develop my body and my muscles by every means within my power. What with boxing, football, and baseball, I had been in training since childhood.

And so it was with the utmost confidence that I laid hold of the huge iron rim; but though I threw every ounce of my strength into it, my best effort was as unavailing as Perry's had been—the thing would not budge—the grim, insensate, horrible thing that was holding us upon the straight road to death!

At length I gave up the useless struggle, and without a word returned to my seat. There was no need for words—at least none that I could imagine, unless Perry desired to pray. And I was quite sure that he would, for he never left an opportunity neglected where he might sandwich in a prayer. He prayed when he arose in the morning, he prayed before he ate, he prayed when he had finished eating, and before he went to bed at night he prayed again. In between he often found excuses to pray even when the provocation seemed far-fetched to my worldly eyes—now that he was about to die I felt positive that I should witness a perfect orgy of prayer—if one may allude with such a simile to so solemn an act.

But to my astonishment I discovered that with death staring him in the face Abner Perry was transformed into a new being. From his lips there flowed—not prayer—but a clear and limpid stream of undiluted profanity, and it was all directed at that quietly stubborn piece of unyielding mechanism.

"I should think, Perry," I chided, "that a man of your professed religiousness would rather be at his prayers than cursing in the presence of imminent death."

"Death!" he cried. "Death is it that appalls you? That is nothing by comparison with the loss the world must suffer. Why, David within this iron cylinder we have demonstrated possibilities that science has scarce dreamed. We have harnessed a new principle, and with it animated a piece of steel with the power of ten thousand men. That two lives will be snuffed out is nothing to the world calamity that entombs in the bowels of the earth the discoveries that I have made and proved in the success-ful construction of the thing that is now carrying us farther and farther toward the eternal central fires."

I am frank to admit that for myself I was much more concerned with our own immediate future than with any problematic loss which the world might be about to suffer. The world was at least ignorant of its bereavement, while to me it was a real and terrible actuality.

"What can we do?" I asked, hiding my perturbation beneath the mask of a low and level voice.

"We may stop here, and die of asphyxiation when our atmosphere tanks are empty," replied Perry, "or we may continue on with the slight hope that we may later sufficiently deflect the prospector from the vertical to carry us along the arc of a great circle which must eventually return us to the surface. If we succeed in so doing before we reach the higher internal temperature we may even yet survive. There would seem to me to be about one chance in several million that we shall succeed—otherwise we shall die more quickly but no more surely than as though we sat supinely waiting for the torture of a slow and horrible death."

I glanced at the thermometer. It registered 110 degrees. While we were talking the mighty iron mole had bored its way over a mile into the rock of the earth's crust.

"Let us continue on, then," I replied. "It should soon be over at this rate. You never intimated that the speed of this thing would be so high, Perry. Didn't you know it?"

"No," he answered. "I could not figure the speed exactly, for I had no instrument for measuring the mighty power of my generator. I reasoned, however, that we should make about five hundred yards an hour."

"And we are making seven miles an hour," I concluded for him, as I sat with my eyes upon the distance meter. "How thick is the Earth's crust, Perry?" I asked.

"There are almost as many conjectures as to that as there are geologists," was his answer. "One estimates it thirty miles, because the internal heat, increasing at the rate of about one degree to each sixty to seventy feet depth, would be sufficient to fuse the most refractory substances at that distance beneath the surface. Another finds that the phenomena of precession and mutation require that the earth, if not entirely solid, must at least have a shell not less than eight hundred to a thousand miles in thickness. So there you are. You may take your choice."

"And if it should prove solid?" I asked.

"It will be all the same to us in the end, David," replied Perry. "At the best our fuel will suffice to carry us but three or four days, while our atmosphere cannot last to exceed three. Neither, then, is sufficient to bear us in the safety through eight thousand miles of rock to the antipodes."

"If the crust is of sufficient thickness we shall come to a final stop between six and seven hundred miles beneath the earth's surface; but during the last hundred and fifty miles of our journey we shall be corpses. Am I correct?" I asked.

"Quite correct, David. Are you frightened?"

"I do not know. It all has come so suddenly that I scarce believe that either of us realizes the real terrors of our position. I feel that I should be reduced to panic; but yet I am not. I imagine that the shock has been so great as to partially stun our sensibilities."

Again I turned to the thermometer. The mercury was rising with less rapidity. It was now but 140 degrees, although we had penetrated to a depth of nearly four miles. I told Perry, and he smiled.

"We have shattered one theory at least," was his only comment, and then he returned to his self-assumed occupation of fluently cursing the steering wheel. I once heard a pirate swear, but his best efforts would have seemed like those of a tyro alongside of Perry's masterful and scientific imprecations.

Once more I tried my hand at the wheel, but I might as well have essayed to swing the earth itself. At my suggestion Perry stopped the generator, and as we came to rest I again threw all my strength into a supreme effort to move the thing even a hair's breadth—but the results were as barren as when we had been traveling at top speed.

I shook my head sadly, and motioned to the starting lever. Perry pulled it toward him, and once again we were plunging downward toward eternity at the rate of seven miles an hour. I sat with my eyes glued to the thermometer and the distance meter. The mercury was rising very slowly now, though even at 145 degrees it was almost unbearable within the narrow confines of our metal prison.

About noon, or twelve hours after our start upon this unfortunate journey, we had bored to a depth of eighty-four miles, at which point the mercury registered 153 degrees F.

Perry was becoming more hopeful, although upon what meager food he sustained his optimism I could not conjecture. From cursing he had turned to sing-ing—I felt that the strain had at last affected his mind. For several hours we had not spoken except as he asked me for the readings of the instruments from time to time, and I announced them. My thoughts were filled with vain regrets. I recalled numer-ous acts of my past life which I should have been glad to have had a few more years to live down. There was the affair in the Latin Commons at Andover when Calhoun and I had put gunpowder in the stove—and nearly killed one of the masters. And then—but what was the use, I was about to die and atone for all these things and several more. Already the heat was sufficient to give me a foretaste of the hereafter. A few more degrees and I felt that I should lose consciousness.

"What are the readings now, David?" Perry's voice broke in upon my somber reflections.

"Ninety miles and 153 degrees," I replied.

"Gad, but we've knocked that thirty-mile-crust theory into a cocked hat!" he cried gleefully.

"Precious lot of good it will do us," I growled back.

"But my boy," he continued, "doesn't that temperature reading mean anything to you? Why it hasn't gone up in six miles. Think of it, son!"

"Yes, I'm thinking of it," I answered; "but what difference will it make when our air supply is exhausted whether the temperature is 153 degrees or 153,000? We'll be just as dead, and no one will know the difference, anyhow." But I must admit that for some unaccountable reason the stationary temperature did renew my waning hope. What I hoped for I could not have explained, nor did I try. The very fact, as Perry took pains to explain, of the blasting of several very exact and learned scientific hypotheses made it apparent that we could not know what lay before us within the bowels of the earth, and so we might continue to hope for the best, at least until we were dead—when hope would no longer be essential to our happiness. It was very good, and logical reasoning, and so I embraced it.

At one hundred miles the temperature had *dropped to 152½ degrees!* When I announced it Perry reached over and hugged me.

From then on until noon of the second day, it continued to drop until it became as uncomfortably cold as it had been unbearably hot before. At the depth of two hundred and forty miles our nostrils were assailed by almost overpowering ammonia fumes, and the temperature had dropped to *ten below zero!* We suffered nearly two hours of this intense and bitter cold, until at about two hundred and forty-five miles from the surface of the earth we entered a stratum of solid ice, when the mercury quickly rose to 32 degrees. During the next three hours we passed through ten miles of ice, eventually emerging into another series of ammonia-impregnated strata, where the mercury again fell to ten degrees below zero.

Slowly it rose once more until we were convinced that at last we were nearing the molten interior of the earth. At four hundred miles the temperature had reached 153 degrees. Feverishly I watched the thermometer. Slowly it rose. Perry had ceased singing and was at last praying.

Our hopes had received such a deathblow that the gradually increasing heat seemed to our distorted imaginations much greater than it really was. For another hour I saw that pitiless column of mercury rise and rise until at four hundred and ten miles it stood at 153 degrees. Now it was that we began to hang upon those readings in almost breathless anxiety.

One hundred and fifty-three degrees had been the maximum temperature above the ice stratum. Would it stop at this point again, or would it continue its merciless climb? We knew that there was no hope, and yet with the persistence of life itself we continued to hope against practical certainty.

Already the air tanks were at low ebb—there was barely enough of the precious gases to sustain us for another twelve hours. But would we be alive to know or care? It seemed incredible.

At four hundred and twenty miles I took another reading.

"Perry!" I shouted. "Perry, man! She's going down! She's going down! She's 152 degrees again."

"Gad!" he cried. "What can it mean? Can the earth be cold at the center?"

"I do not know, Perry," I answered; "but thank God, if I am to die it shall not be by fire—that is all that I have feared. I can face the thought of any death but that."

Down, down went the mercury until it stood as low as it had seven miles from the surface of the earth, and then of a sudden the realization broke upon us that death was very near. Perry was the first to discover it. I saw him fussing with the valves that regulate the air supply. And at the same time I experienced difficulty in breathing. My head felt dizzy—my limbs heavy.

I saw Perry crumple in his seat. He gave himself a shake and sat erect again. Then he turned toward me.

"Good-bye, David," he said. "I guess this is the end," and then he smiled and closed his eyes.

"Good-bye, Perry, and good luck to you," I answered, smiling back at him. But I fought off that awful lethargy. I was very young—I did not want to die.

For an hour I battled against the cruelly enveloping death that surrounded me upon all sides. At first I found that by climbing high into the framework above me I could find more of the precious life-giving elements, and for a while these sustained me. It must have been an hour after Perry had succumbed that I at last came to the realization that I could no longer carry on this unequal struggle against the inevitable.

With my last flickering ray of consciousness I turned mechanically toward the distance meter. It stood at exactly five hundred miles from the earth's surface—and then of a sudden the huge thing that bore us came to a stop. The rattle of hurtling rock through the hollow jacket ceased. The wild racing of the giant drill betokened that it was running loose in *air*—and then another truth flashed upon me. The point of the prospector was *above* us. Slowly it dawned on me that since passing through the ice strata it had been above. We had turned in the ice and sped upward toward the earth's crust. Thank God! We were safe!

I put my nose to the intake pipe through which samples were to have been taken during the passage of the prospector through the earth, and my fondest hopes were realized—a flood of fresh air was pouring into the iron cabin. The reaction left me in a state of collapse, and I lost consciousness.

II

A STRANGE WORLD

I was unconscious little more than an instant, for as I lunged forward from the cross-beam to which I had been clinging, and fell with a crash to the floor of the cabin, the shock brought me to myself.

My first concern was with Perry. I was horrified at the thought that upon the very threshold of salvation he might be dead. Tearing open his shirt I placed my ear to his breast. I could have cried with relief—his heart was beating quite regularly.

At the water tank I wetted my handkerchief, slapping it smartly across his forehead and face several times. In a moment I was rewarded by the raising of his lids. For a time he lay wide-eyed and quite uncomprehending. Then his scattered wits slowly foregathered, and he sat up sniffing the air with an expression of wonderment upon his face.

"Why, David," he cried at last, "it's air, as sure as I live. Why—why what does it mean? Where in the world are we? What has happened?"

"It means that we're back at the surface all right, Perry," I cried; "but where, I don't know. I haven't opened her up yet. Been too busy reviving you. Lord, man, but you had a close squeak!"

"You say we're back at the surface, David? How can that be? How long have I been unconscious?"

"Not long. We turned in the ice stratum. Don't you recall the sudden whirling of our seats? After that the drill was above you instead of below. We didn't notice it at the time; but I recall it now."

"You mean to say that we turned back in the ice stratum, David? That is not possible. The prospector cannot turn unless its nose is deflected from the outside—by some external force or resistance—the steering wheel within would have moved in response. The steering wheel has not budged, David, since we started. You know that."

I did know it; but here we were with our drill racing in pure air, and copious volumes of it pouring into the cabin.

"We couldn't have turned in the ice stratum, Perry, I know as well as you," I replied; "but the fact remains that we did, for here we are this minute at the surface of the earth again, and I am going out to see just where."

"Better wait till morning, David—it must be midnight now."

I glanced at the chronometer.

"Half after twelve. We have been out seventy-two hours, so it must be midnight. Nevertheless I am going to have a look at the blessed sky that I had given up all hope of ever seeing again," and so saying I lifted the bars from the inner door, and swung it open. There was quite a quantity of loose material in the jacket, and this I had to remove with a shovel to get at the opposite door in the outer shell.

In a short time I had removed enough of the earth and rock to the floor of the cabin to expose the door beyond. Perry was directly behind me as I threw it open. The upper half was above the surface of the ground. With an expression of surprise I turned and looked at Perry—it was broad daylight without!

"Something seems to have gone wrong either with our calculations or the chronometer," I said. Perry shook his head—there was a strange expression in his eyes.

"Let's have a look beyond that door, David," he cried.

Together we stepped out to stand in silent contemplation of a landscape at once weird and beautiful. Before us a low and level shore stretched down to a silent sea. As far as the eye could reach the surface of the water was dotted with countless tiny isles—some of towering, barren, granitic rock—others resplendent in gorgeous trappings of tropical vegetation, myriad starred with the magnificent splendor of vivid blooms.

Behind us rose a dark and forbidding wood of giant arborescent ferns intermingled with the commoner types of a primeval tropical forest. Huge creepers depended in great loops from tree to tree, dense under-brush overgrew a tangled mass of fallen trunks and branches. Upon the outer verge we could see the same splendid coloring of countless blossoms that glorified the islands, but within the dense shadows all seemed dark and gloomy as the grave.

And upon all the noonday sun poured its torrid rays out of a cloudless sky.

"Where on earth can we be?" I asked, turning to Perry.

For some moments the old man did not reply. He stood with bowed head, buried in deep thought. But at last he spoke.

"David," he said, "I am not so sure that we are *on* earth."

"What do you mean Perry?" I cried. "Do you think that we are dead, and this is heaven?" He smiled, and turning, pointing to the nose of the prospector protruding from the ground at our backs.

"But for that, David, I might believe that we were indeed come to the country beyond the Styx. The prospector renders that theory untenable—it, certainly, could never have gone to heaven. However I am willing to concede that we actually may be in another world from that which we have always known. If we are not *on* earth, there is every reason to believe that we may be *in* it."

"We may have quartered through the earth's crust and come out upon some tropical island of the West Indies," I suggested. Again Perry shook his head.

"Let us wait and see, David," he replied, "and in the meantime suppose we do a bit of exploring up and down the coast—we may find a native who can enlighten us."

As we walked along the beach Perry gazed long and earnestly across the water. Evidently he was wrestling with a mighty problem.

"David," he said abruptly, "do you perceive anything unusual about the horizon?"

As I looked I began to appreciate the reason for the strangeness of the landscape that had haunted me from the first with an illusive suggestion of the bizarre and unnatural—*there was no horizon!* As far as the eye could reach out the sea continued and upon its bosom floated tiny islands, those in the distance reduced to mere specks; but ever beyond them was the sea, until the impression became quite real that one was *looking up* at the most distant point that the eyes could fathom—the distance was lost in the distance. That was all—there was no clear-cut horizontal line marking the dip of the globe below the line of vision.

"A great light is commencing to break on me," continued Perry, taking out his watch. "I believe that I have partially solved the riddle. It is now two o'clock. When we emerged from the prospector the sun was directly above us. Where is it now?"

I glanced up to find the great orb still motionless in the center of the heaven. And such a sun! I had scarcely noticed it before. Fully thrice the size of the sun I had known throughout my life, and apparently so near that the sight of it carried the conviction that one might almost reach up and touch it.

"My God, Perry, where are we?" I exclaimed. "This thing is beginning to get on my nerves."

"I think that I may state quite positively, David," he commenced, "that we are—" but he got no further. From behind us in the vicinity of the prospector there came the most thunderous, awe-inspiring roar that ever had fallen upon my ears. With one accord we turned to discover the author of that fearsome noise.

Had I still retained the suspicion that we were on earth the sight that met my eyes would quite entirely have banished it. Emerging from the forest was a colossal beast which closely resembled a bear. It was fully as large as the largest elephant and with great forepaws armed with huge claws. Its nose, or snout, depended nearly a foot below its lower jaw, much after the manner of a rudimentary trunk. The giant body was covered by a coat of thick, shaggy hair.

Roaring horribly it came toward us at a ponderous, shuffling trot. I turned to Perry to suggest that it might be wise to seek other surroundings—the idea had evidently occurred to Perry previously, for he was already a hundred paces away, and with each second his prodigious bounds increased the distance. I had never guessed what latent speed possibilities the old gentleman possessed.

I saw that he was headed toward a little point of the forest which ran out toward the sea not far from where we had been standing, and as the mighty creature, the sight of which had galvanized him into such remarkable action, was forging steadily toward me. I set off after Perry, though at a somewhat more decorous pace. It was evident that the massive beast pursuing us was not built for speed, so all that I considered necessary was to gain the trees sufficiently ahead of it to enable me to climb to the safety of some great branch before it came up.

Notwithstanding our danger I could not help but laugh at Perry's frantic capers as he essayed to gain the safety of the lower branches of the trees he now had reached. The stems were bare for a distance of some fifteen feet—at least on those trees which Perry attempted to ascend, for the suggestion of safety carried by the larger of the forest giants had evidently attracted him to them. A dozen times he scrambled up the trunks like a huge cat only to fall back to the ground once more, and with each failure he cast a horrified glance over his shoulder at the oncoming brute, simultaneously emitting terror-stricken shrieks that awoke the echoes of the grim forest.

At length he spied a dangling creeper about the bigness of one's wrist, and when I reached the trees he was racing madly up it, hand over hand. He had almost reached the lowest branch of the tree from which the creeper depended when the thing parted beneath his weight and he fell sprawling at my feet.

The misfortune now was no longer amusing, for the beast was already too close to us for comfort. Seizing Perry by the shoulder I dragged him to his feet, and rushing to a smaller tree—one that he could easily encircle with his arms and legs— I boosted him as far up as I could, and then left him to his fate, for a glance over my shoulder revealed the awful beast almost upon me.

It was the great size of the thing alone that saved me. Its enormous bulk rendered it too slow upon its feet to cope with the agility of my young muscles, and so I was enabled to dodge out of its way and run completely behind it before its slow wits could direct it in pursuit.

The few seconds of grace that this gave me found me safely lodged in the branches of a tree a few paces from that in which Perry had at last found a haven.

Did I say safely lodged? At the time I thought we were quite safe, and so did Perry. He was praying—raising his voice in thanksgiving at our deliverance—and had just completed a sort of paeon of gratitude that the thing couldn't climb a tree when without warning it reared up beneath him on its enormous tail and hind feet, and reached those fearfully armed paws quite to the branch upon which he crouched.

The accompanying roar was all but drowned in Perry's scream of fright, and he came near tumbling headlong into the gaping jaws beneath him, so precipitate was his impetuous haste to vacate the dangerous limb. It was with a deep sigh of relief that I saw him gain a higher branch in safety.

And then the brute did that which froze us both anew with horror. Grasping the tree's stem with his powerful paws he dragged down with all the great weight of his huge bulk and all the irresistible force of those mighty muscles. Slowly, but surely,

215

the stem began to bend toward him. Inch by inch he worked his paws upward as the tree leaned more and more from the perpendicular. Perry clung chattering in a panic of terror. Higher and higher into the bending and swaying tree he clambered. More and more rapidly was the tree top inclining toward the ground.

I saw now why the great brute was armed with such enormous paws. The use that he was putting them to was precisely that for which nature had intended them. The sloth-like creature was herbivorous, and to feed that mighty carcass entire trees must be stripped of their foliage. The reason for its attacking us might easily be accounted for on the supposition of an ugly disposition such as that which the fierce and stupid rhinoceros of Africa possesses. But these were later reflections. At the moment I was too frantic with apprehension on Perry's behalf to consider aught other than a means to save him from the death that loomed so close.

Realizing that I could outdistance the clumsy brute in the open, I dropped from my leafy sanctuary intent only on distracting the thing's attention from Perry long enough to enable the old man to gain the safety of a larger tree. There were many close by which not even the terrific strength of that titanic monster could bend.

As I touched the ground I snatched a broken limb from the tangled mass that matted the jungle-like floor of the forest and, leaping unnoticed behind the shaggy back, dealt the brute a terrific blow. My plan worked like magic. From the previous slowness of the beast I had been led to look for no such marvelous agility as he now displayed. Releasing his hold upon the tree he dropped on all fours and at the same time swung his great, wicked tail with a force that would have broken every bone in my body had it struck me; but, fortunately, I had turned to flee at the very instant that I felt my blow land upon the towering back.

As it started in pursuit of me I made the mistake of running along the edge of the forest rather than making for the open beach. In a moment I was knee-deep in rotting vegetation, and the awful thing behind me was gaining rapidly as I floundered and fell in my efforts to extricate myself.

A fallen log gave me an instant's advantage, for climbing upon it I leaped to another a few paces farther on, and in this way was able to keep clear of the mush that carpeted the surrounding ground. But the zigzag course that this necessitated was placing such a heavy handicap upon me that my pursuer was steadily gaining upon me.

Suddenly from behind I heard a tumult of howls, and sharp, piercing barks—much the sound that a pack of wolves raises when in full cry. Involuntarily I glanced backward to discover the origin of this new and menacing note with the result that I missed my footing and went sprawling once more upon my face in the deep muck.

My mammoth enemy was so close by this time that I knew I must feel the weight of one of his terrible paws before I could rise, but to my surprise the blow did not fall upon me. The howling and snapping and barking of the new element which had been infused into the melee now seemed centered quite close behind me, and as I raised myself upon my hands and glanced around I saw what it was that had distracted the *dyryth,* as I afterward learned the thing is called, from my trail.

It was surrounded by a pack of some hundred wolf-like creatures—wild dogs they seemed—that rushed growling and snapping in upon it from all sides, so that they sank their white fangs into the slow brute and were away again before it could reach them with its huge paws or sweeping tail.

But these were not all that my startled eyes perceived. Chattering and gibbering through the lower branches of the trees came a company of manlike creatures evidently urging on the dog pack. They were to all appearances strikingly similar in aspect to the Negro of Africa. Their skins were very black, and their features much like those of the more pronounced Negroid type except that the head receded more rapidly above the eyes, leaving little or no forehead. Their arms were rather longer and their legs shorter in proportion to the torso than in man, and later I noticed that their great toes protruded at right angles from their feet—because of their arboreal habits, I presume. Behind them trailed long, slender tails which they used in climbing quite as much as they did either their hands or feet.

I had stumbled to my feet the moment that I discovered that the wolf-dogs were holding the dyryth at bay. At sight of me several of the savage creatures left off worrying the great brute to come slinking with bared fangs toward me, and as I turned to run toward the trees again to seek safety among the lower branches, I saw a number of the man-apes leaping and chattering in the foliage of the nearest tree.

Between them and the beasts behind me there was little choice, but at least there was a doubt as to the reception these grotesque parodies on humanity would accord me, while there was none as to the fate which awaited me beneath the grinning fangs of my fierce pursuers.

And so I raced on toward the trees intending to pass beneath that which held the man-things and take refuge in another farther on; but the wolf-dogs were very close behind me—so close that I had despaired of escaping them, when one of the creatures in the tree above swung down headforemost, his tail looped about a great limb, and grasping me beneath my armpits swung me in safety up among his fellows.

There they fell to examining me with the utmost excitement and curiosity. They picked at my clothing, my hair, and my flesh. They turned me about to see if

I had a tail, and when they discovered that I was not so equipped they fell into roars of laughter. Their teeth were very large and white and even, except for the upper canines which were a trifle longer than the others—protruding just a bit when the mouth was closed.

When they had examined me for a few moments one of them discovered that my clothing was not a part of me, with the result that garment by garment they tore it from me amidst peals of the wildest laughter. Apelike, they essayed to don the apparel themselves, but their ingenuity was not sufficient to the task and so they gave it up.

In the meantime I had been straining my eyes to catch a glimpse of Perry, but nowhere about could I see him, although the clump of trees in which he had first taken refuge was in full view. I was much exercised by fear that something had befallen him, and though I called his name aloud several times there was no response.

Tired at last of playing with my clothing the creatures threw it to the ground, and catching me, one on either side, by an arm, started off at a most terrifying pace through the tree tops. Never have I experienced such a journey before or since— even now I oftentimes awake from a deep sleep haunted by the horrid remembrance of that awful experience.

From tree to tree the agile creatures sprang like flying squirrels, while the cold sweat stood upon my brow as I glimpsed the depths beneath, into which a single misstep on the part of either of my bearers would hurl me. As they bore me along, my mind was occupied with a thousand bewildering thoughts. What had become of Perry? Would I ever see him again? What were the intentions of these half-human things into whose hands I had fallen? Were they inhabitants of the same world into which I had been born? No! It could not be. But yet where else? I had not left that earth—of that I was sure. Still neither could I reconcile the things which I had seen to a belief that I was still in the world of my birth. With a sigh I gave it up.

III

A CHANGE OF MASTERS

We must have traveled several miles through the dark and dismal wood when we came suddenly upon a dense village built high among the branches of the trees. As we approached it my escort broke into wild shouting which was immediately answered from within, and a moment later a swarm of creatures of the same strange race as those who had captured me poured out to meet us. Again I was the center of a wildly chattering horde. I was pulled this way and that. Pinched, pounded, and thumped until I was black and blue, yet I do not think that their treatment was dictated by either cruelty or malice—I was a curiosity, a freak, a new plaything, and their childish minds required the added evidence of all their senses to back up the testimony of their eyes.

Presently they dragged me within the village, which consisted of several hundred rude shelters of boughs and leaves supported upon the branches of the trees.

Between the huts, which sometimes formed crooked streets, were dead branches and the trunks of small trees which connected the huts upon one tree to those within adjoining trees; the whole network of huts and pathways forming an almost solid flooring a good fifty feet above the ground.

I wondered why these agile creatures required connecting bridges between the trees, but later when I saw the motley aggregation of half-savage beasts which they kept within their village I realized the necessity for the pathways. There were a number of the same vicious wolf-dogs which we had left worrying the dyryth, and many goatlike animals whose distended udders explained the reasons for their presence.

My guard halted before one of the huts into which I was pushed; then two of the creatures squatted down before the entrance—to prevent my escape, doubtless. Though where I should have escaped to I certainly had not the remotest conception. I had no more than entered the dark shadows of the interior than there fell upon my ears the tones of a familiar voice, in prayer.

"Perry!" I cried. "Dear old Perry! Thank the Lord you are safe."

"David! Can it be possible that you escaped?" And the old man stumbled toward me and threw his arms about me.

He had seen me fall before the dyryth, and then he had been seized by a number of the ape-creatures and borne through the tree tops to their village. His captors had been as inquisitive as to his strange clothing as had mine, with the same result. As we looked at each other we could not help but laugh.

"With a tail, David," remarked Perry, "you would make a very handsome ape."

"Maybe we can borrow a couple," I rejoined. "They seem to be quite the thing this season. I wonder what the creatures intend doing with us, Perry. They don't seem really savage. What do you suppose they can be? You were about to tell me where we are when that great hairy frigate bore down upon us—have you really any idea at all?"

"Yes, David," he replied, "I know precisely where we are. We have made a magnificent discovery, my boy! We have proved that the earth is hollow. We have passed entirely through its crust to the inner world."

"Perry, you are mad!"

"Not at all, David. For two hundred and fifty miles our prospector bore us through the crust beneath our outer world. At that point it reached the center of gravity of the five-hundred-mile-thick crust. Up to that point we had been descending—direction is, of course, merely relative. Then at the moment that our seats revolved—the thing that made you believe that we had turned about and were speeding upward—we passed the center of gravity and, though we did not alter the direction of our progress, yet we were in reality moving upward—toward the surface of the inner world. Does not the strange fauna and flora which we have seen convince you that you are not in the world of your birth? And the horizon—could it present the strange aspects which we both noted unless we were indeed standing upon the inside surface of a sphere?"

"But the sun, Perry!" I urged. "How in the world can the sun shine through five hundred miles of solid crust?"

"It is not the sun of the outer world that we see here. It is another sun—an entirely different sun—that casts its eternal noonday effulgence upon the face of the inner world. Look at it now, David—if you can see it from the doorway of this hut—and you will see that it is still in the exact center of the heavens. We have been here for many hours—yet it is still noon.

"And withal it is very simple, David. The earth was once a nebulous mass. It cooled, and as it cooled it shrank. At length a thin crust of solid matter formed upon its outer surface—a sort of shell; but within it was partially molten matter and highly expanded gases. As it continued to cool, what happened? Centrifugal force hurled the particles of the nebulous center toward the crust as rapidly as they approached a solid state. You have seen the same principle practically applied in the modern cream separator. Presently there was only a small super-heated core of gaseous matter remaining within a huge vacant interior left by the contraction of the cooling gases. The equal attraction of the solid crust from all directions maintained this luminous core in the exact center of the hollow globe. What remains of it is the sun you saw today—a relatively tiny thing at the exact center of the earth. Equally to every part of this inner world it diffuses its perpetual noonday light and torrid heat.

"This inner world must have cooled sufficiently to support animal life long ages after life appeared upon the outer crust, but that the same agencies were at work here is evident from the similar forms of both animal and vegetable creation which we have already seen. Take the great beast which attacked us, for example. Unquestionably a counterpart of the Megatherium of the post-Pliocene period of the outer crust, whose fossilized skeleton has been found in South America."

"But the grotesque inhabitants of this forest?" I urged. "Surely they have no counterpart in the earth's history."

"Who can tell?" he rejoined. "They may constitute the link between ape and man, all traces of which have been swallowed by the countless convulsions which have racked the outer crust, or they may be merely the result of evolution along slightly different lines—either is quite possible."

Further speculation was interrupted by the appearance of several of our captors before the entrance of the hut. Two of them entered and dragged us forth. The perilous pathways and the surrounding trees were filled with the black ape-men, their females, and their young. There was not an ornament, a weapon, or a garment among the lot.

"Quite low in the scale of creation," commented Perry.

"Quite high enough to play the deuce with us, though," I replied. "Now what do you suppose they intend doing with us?"

We were not long in learning. As on the occasion of our trip to the village we were seized by a couple of the powerful creatures and whirled away through the tree tops, while about us and in our wake raced a chattering, jabbering, grinning horde of sleek, black ape-things.

Twice my bearers missed their footing, and my heart ceased beating as we plunged toward instant death among the tangled deadwood beneath. But on both occasions those lithe, powerful tails reached out and found sustaining branches, nor did either of the creatures loosen their grasp upon me. In fact, it seemed that the incidents were of no greater moment to them than would be the stubbing of one's toe at a street crossing in the outer world—they but laughed uproariously and sped on with me.

For some time they continued through the forest—how long I could not guess for I was learning, what was later borne very forcefully to my mind, that time ceases to be a factor the moment means for measuring it cease to exist. Our watches were gone, and we were living beneath a stationary sun. Already I was puzzled to compute the period of time which had elapsed since we broke through the crust of the inner world. It might be hours, or it might be days—who in the world could tell where it was always noon! By the sun, no time had elapsed—but my judgment told me that we must have been several hours in this strange world.

Presently the forest terminated, and we came out upon a level plain. A short distance before us rose a few low, rocky hills. Toward these our captors urged us, and after a short time led us through a narrow pass into a tiny, circular valley. Here they got down to work, and we were soon convinced that if we were not to die to make a Roman holiday, we were to die for some other purpose. The attitude of our captors altered immediately as they entered the natural arena within the rocky hills. Their laughter ceased. Grim ferocity marked their bestial faces—bared fangs menaced us.

We were placed in the center of the amphitheater—the thousand creatures forming a great ring about us. Then a wolf-dog was brought—*hyaenadon* Perry called it—and turned loose with us inside the circle. The thing's body was as large as that of a full-grown mastiff, its legs were short and powerful, and its jaws broad and strong. Dark, shaggy hair covered its back and sides, while its breast and belly were quite white. As it slunk toward us it presented a most formidable aspect with its upcurled lips baring its mighty fangs.

Perry was on his knees, praying. I stooped and picked up a small stone. At my movement the beast veered off a bit and commenced circling us. Evidently it had been a target for stones before. The ape-things were dancing up and down urging the brute on with savage cries, until at last, seeing that I did not throw, he charged us.

At Andover, and later at Yale, I had pitched on winning ball teams. My speed and control must both have been above the ordinary, for I made such a record during my senior year at college that overtures were made to me in behalf of one of the great major-league teams; but in the tightest pitch that ever had confronted me in the past I had never been in such need for control as now.

As I wound up for the delivery, I held my nerves and muscles under absolute command, though the grinning jaws were hurtling toward me at terrific speed. And then I let go, with every ounce of my weight and muscle and science in back of that throw. The stone caught the hyaenodon full upon the end of the nose, and sent him bowling over upon his back.

At the same instant a chorus of shrieks and howls arose from the circle of spectators, so that for a moment I thought that the upsetting of their champion was the cause; but in this I soon saw that I was mistaken. As I looked, the ape-things broke in all directions toward the surrounding hills, and then I distinguished the real cause of their perturbation. Behind them, streaming through the pass which leads into the valley, came a swarm of hairy men—gorilla-like creatures armed with spears and hatchets, and bearing long, oval shields. Like demons they set upon the ape-things, and before them the hyaenodon, which had now regained its senses and its feet, fled howling with fright. Past us swept the pursued and the pursuers, nor did the hairy ones accord us more than a passing glance until the arena had been emptied of its former occupants. Then they returned to us, and one who seemed to have authority among them directed that we be brought with them.

When we had passed out of the amphitheater onto the great plain we saw a caravan of men and women—human beings like ourselves—and for the first time hope and relief filled my heart, until I could have cried out in the exuberance of my happiness. It is true that they were a half-naked, wild-appearing aggregation; but they at least were fashioned along the same lines as ourselves—there was nothing grotesque or horrible about them as about the other creatures in this strange, weird world.

But as we came closer, our hearts sank once more, for we discovered that the poor wretches were chained neck to neck in a long line, and that the gorilla-men were their guards. With little ceremony Perry and I were chained at the end of the line, and without further ado the interrupted march was resumed.

Up to this time the excitement had kept us both up; but now the tiresome monotony of the long march across the sun-baked plain brought on all the agonies consequent to a long-denied sleep. On and on we stumbled beneath that hateful noonday sun. If we fell we were prodded with a sharp point. Our companions in chains did not stumble. They strode along proudly erect. Occasionally they would exchange words with one another in a monosyllabic language. They were a noble-appearing race with well-formed heads and perfect physiques. The men were heavily bearded, tall and muscular; the women, smaller and more gracefully molded, with great masses of raven hair caught into loose knots upon their heads. The features of both sexes were well proportioned—there was not a face among them that would have been called even plain if judged by earthly standards. They wore no ornaments; but this I later learned was due to the fact that their captors had stripped them of everything of value. As garmenture the women possessed a single robe of some light-colored, spotted hide, rather similar in appearance to a leopard's skin. This they wore either supported entirely about the waist by a leathern thong, so that it hung partially below the knee on one side, or possibly looped gracefully across one shoulder. Their feet were shod with skin sandals. The men wore loin cloths of the hide of some shaggy beast, long ends of which depended before and behind nearly to the ground. In some instances these ends were finished with the strong talons of the beast from which the hides had been taken.

Our guards, whom I already have described as gorilla-like men, were rather lighter in build than a gorilla, but even so they were indeed mighty creatures. Their arms and legs were proportioned more in conformity with human standards, but their entire bodies were covered with shaggy, brown hair, and their faces were quite as brutal as those of the few stuffed specimens of the gorilla which I had seen in the museums at home.

Their only redeeming feature lay in the development of the head above and back of the ears. In this respect they were not one whit less human than we. They were clothed in a sort of tunic of light cloth which reached to the knees. Beneath this they wore only a loin cloth of the same material, while their feet were shod with thick hide of some mammoth creature of this inner world.

Their arms and necks were encircled by many ornaments of metal—silver predominating—and on their tunics were sewn the heads of tiny reptiles in odd and rather artistic designs. They talked among themselves as they marched along on either side of us, but in a language which I perceived differed from that employed by our fellow prisoners. When they addressed the latter they used what appeared to be a third language, and which I later learned is a mongrel tongue rather analogous to the Pidgin-English of the Chinese coolie.

How far we marched I have no conception, nor has Perry. Both of us were asleep much of the time for hours before a halt was called—then we dropped in our tracks. I say "for hours," but how may one measure time where time does not exist! When our march commenced the sun stood at zenith. When we halted our shadows still pointed toward nadir. Whether an instant or an eternity of earthly time elapsed who may say. That march may have occupied nine years and eleven months of the ten years that I spent in the inner world, or it may have been accomplished in the fraction of a second—I cannot tell. But this I do know that since you have told me that ten years have elapsed since I departed from this earth I have lost all respect for time—I am commencing to doubt that such a thing exists other than in the weak, finite mind of man.

IV

DIAN THE BEAUTIFUL

When our guards aroused us from sleep we were much refreshed. They gave us food. Strips of dried meat it was, but it put new life and strength into us, so that now we too marched with high-held heads, and took noble strides. At least I did, for I was young and proud; but poor Perry hated walking. On earth I had often seen him call a cab to travel a square—he was paying for it now, and his old legs wobbled so that I put my arm about him and half carried him through the balance of those frightful marches.

The country began to change at last, and we wound up out of the level plain through mighty mountains of virgin granite. The tropical verdure of the lowlands was replaced by hardier vegetation, but even here the effects of constant heat and light were apparent in the immensity of the trees and the profusion of foliage and blooms. Crystal streams roared through their rocky channels, fed by the perpetual snows which we could see far above us. Above the snowcapped heights hung masses of heavy clouds. It was these, Perry explained, which evidently served the double purpose of replenishing the melting snows and protecting them from the direct rays of the sun.

By this time we had picked up a smattering of the bastard language in which our guards addressed us, as well as making good headway in the rather charming tongue of our co-captives. Directly ahead of me in the chain gang was a young woman. Three feet of chain linked us together in a forced companionship which I, at least, soon rejoiced in. For I found her a willing teacher, and from her I learned the language of her tribe, and much of the life and customs of the inner world—at least that part of it with which she was familiar.

She told me that she was called Dian the Beautiful, and that she belonged to the tribe of Amoz, which dwells in the cliffs above the Darel Az, or shallow sea.

"How came you here?" I asked her.

"I was running away from Jubal the Ugly One," she answered, as though that was explanation quite sufficient.

"Who is Jubal the Ugly One?" I asked. "And why did you run away from him?"

She looked at me in surprise.

"Why *does* a woman run away from a man?" she answered my question with another.

"They do not, where I come from," I replied. "Sometimes they run after them."

But she could not understand. Nor could I get her to grasp the fact that I was of another world. She was quite as positive that creation was originated solely to produce her own kind and the world she lived in as are many of the outer world.

"But Jubal," I insisted. "Tell me about him, and why you ran away to be chained by the neck and scourged across the face of a world."

"Jubal the Ugly One placed his trophy before my father's house. It was the head of a mighty *tandor*. It remained there and no greater trophy was placed beside it. So I knew that Jubal the Ugly One would come and take me as his mate. None other so powerful wished me, or they would have slain a mightier beast and thus have won me from Jubal. My father is not a mighty hunter. Once he was, but a *sadok* tossed him, and never again had he the full use of his right arm. My brother, Dacor the Strong One, had gone to the land of Sari to steal a mate for himself. Thus there was none, father, brother, or lover, to save me from Jubal the Ugly One, and I ran away and hid among the hills that skirt the land of Amoz. And there these Sagoths found me and made me captive."

"What will they do with you?" I asked. "Where are they taking us?"

Again she looked her incredulity.

"I can almost believe that you are of another world," she said, "for otherwise such ignorance were inexplicable. Do you really mean that you do not know that the Sagoths are the creatures of the Mahars—the mighty Mahars who think they own Pellucidar and all that walks or grows upon its surface, or creeps or burrows beneath, or swims within its lakes and oceans, or flies through its air? Next you will be telling me that you never before heard of the Mahars!"

I was loath to do it, and further incur her scorn; but there was no alternative if I were to absorb knowledge, so I made a clean breast of my pitiful ignorance as to the mighty Mahars. She was shocked. But she did her very best to enlighten me, though much that she said was as Greek would have been to her. She described the Mahars largely by comparisons. In this way they were like unto *thipdars,* in that to the hairless *lidi.*

About all I gleaned of them was that they were quite hideous, had wings, and webbed feet; lived in cities built beneath the ground; could swim under water for great distances, and were very, very wise. The Sagoths were their weapons of offense and defense, and the races like herself were their hands and feet—they were the slaves and servants who did all the manual labor. The Mahars were the heads—the brains—of the inner world. I longed to see this wondrous race of supermen.

Perry learned the language with me. When we halted, as we occasionally did, though sometimes the halts seemed ages apart, he would join in the conversation, as would Ghak the Hairy One, he who was chained just ahead of Dian the Beautiful. Ahead of Ghak was Hooja the Sly One. He too entered the conversation occasionally. Most of his remarks were directed toward Dian the Beautiful. It didn't take half an eye to see that he had developed a bad case; but the girl appeared totally oblivious to his thinly veiled advances. Did I say thinly veiled? There is a race of men in New Zealand, or Australia, I have forgotten which, who indicate their preference for the lady of their affections by banging her over the head with a bludgeon. By comparison with this method Hooja's lovemaking might be called thinly veiled. At first it caused me to blush violently although I have seen several Old Years out at Rectors, and in other less fashionable places off Broadway, and in Vienna, and Hamburg.

But the girl! She was magnificent. It was easy to see that she considered herself as entirely above and apart from her present surroundings and company. She talked with me, and with Perry, and with the taciturn Ghak because we were respectful; but she couldn't even see Hooja the Sly One, much less hear him, and that made him furious. He tried to get one of the Sagoths to move the girl up ahead of him in the slave gang, but the fellow only poked him with his spear and told him that he had selected the girl for his own property—that he would buy her from the Mahars as soon as they reached Phutra. Phutra, it seemed, was the city of our destination.

After passing over the first chain of mountains we skirted a salt sea, upon whose bosom swam countless horrid things. Seal-like creatures there were with long necks stretching ten and more feet above their enormous bodies and whose snake heads were split with gaping mouths bristling with countless fangs. There were huge tortoises too, paddling about among these other reptiles, which Perry said were Plesiosaurs of the Lias. I didn't question his veracity—they might have been most anything.

Dian told me they were *tandorazes,* or tandors of the sea, and that the other, and more fearsome reptiles, which occasionally rose from the deep to do battle with them, were *azdyryths,* or sea-dyryths—Perry called them Ichthyosaurs. They resembled a whale with the head of an alligator.

I had forgotten what little geology I had studied at school—about all that remained was an impression of horror that the illustrations of restored prehistoric monsters had made upon me, and a well-defined belief that any man with a pig's shank and a vivid imagination could "restore" most any sort of paleolithic monster he saw fit, and take rank as a first class paleontologist. But when I saw these sleek, shiny carcasses shimmering in the sunlight as they emerged from the ocean, shaking their giant heads; when I saw the waters roll from their sinuous bodies in miniature waterfalls as they glided hither and thither, now upon the surface, now half sub-merged; as I saw them meet, open-mouthed, hissing and snorting, in their titanic and interminable warring I realized how futile is man's poor, weak imagination by comparison with Nature's incredible genius.

And Perry! He was absolutely flabbergasted. He said so himself.

"David," he remarked, after we had marched for a long time beside that awful sea. "David, I used to teach geology, and I thought that I believed what I taught; but now I see that I did not believe it—that it is impossible for man to believe such things as these unless he sees them with his own eyes. We take things for granted, perhaps, because we are told them over and over again, and have no way of disprov-ing them—like religions, for example; but we don't believe them, we only think we do. If you ever get back to the outer world you will find that the geologists and paleontologists will be the first to set you down a liar, for they know that no such creatures as they restore ever existed. It is all right to *imagine* them as existing in an equally imaginary epoch—but now? poof!"

At the next halt Hooja the Sly One managed to find enough slack chain to permit him to worm himself back quite close to Dian. We were all standing, and as he edged near the girl she turned her back upon him in such a truly earthly feminine manner that I could scarce repress a smile; but it was a short-lived smile for on the instant the Sly One's hand fell upon the girl's bare arm, jerking her roughly toward him.

I was not then familiar with the customs or social ethics which prevailed within Pellucidar; but even so I did not need the appealing look which the girl shot to me from her magnificent eyes to influence my subsequent act. What the Sly One's intention was I paused not to inquire; but instead, before he could lay hold of her with his other hand, I placed a right to the point of his jaw that felled him in his tracks.

A roar of approval went up from those of the other prisoners and the Sagoths who had witnessed the brief drama; not, as I later learned, because I had championed the girl, but for the neat and, to them, astounding method by which I had bested Hooja.

And the girl? At first she looked at me with wide, wondering eyes, and then she dropped her head, her face half averted, and a delicate flush suffused her cheek. For a moment she stood thus in silence, and then her head went high, and she turned her back upon me as she had upon Hooja. Some of the prisoners laughed, and I saw the face of Ghak the Hairy One go very black as he looked at me searchingly. And what I could see of Dian's cheek went suddenly from red to white.

Immediately after we resumed the march, and though I realized that in some way I had offended Dian the Beautiful I could not prevail upon her to talk with me that I might learn wherein I had erred—in fact I might quite as well have been addressing a sphinx for all the attention I got. At last my own foolish pride stepped in and prevented my making any further attempts, and thus a companionship that without my realizing it had come to mean a great deal to me was cut off. Thereafter I confined my conversation to Perry. Hooja did not renew his advances toward the girl, nor did he again venture near me.

Again the weary and apparently interminable marching became a perfect nightmare of horrors to me. The more firmly fixed became the realization that the girl's friendship had meant so much to me, the more I came to miss it; and the more impregnable the barrier of silly pride. But I was very young and would not ask Ghak for the explanation which I was sure he could give, and that might have made everything all right again.

On the march, or during halts, Dian refused consistently to notice me—when her eyes wandered in my direction she looked either over my head or directly through me. At last I became desperate, and determined to swallow my self-esteem, and again beg her to tell me how I had offended, and how I might make reparation. I made up my mind that I should do this at the next halt. We were approaching another range of mountains at the time, and when we reached them, instead of winding across them through some high-flung pass we entered a mighty natural tunnel—a series of labyrinthine grottoes, dark as Erebus.

The guards had no torches or light of any description. In fact we had seen no artificial light or sign of fire since we had entered Pellucidar. In a land of perpetual noon there is no need of light above ground, yet I marveled that they had no means of lighting their way through these dark, subterranean passages. So we crept along at a snail's pace, with much stumbling and falling—the guards keeping up a singsong chant ahead of us, interspersed with certain high notes which I found always indicated rough places and turns.

Halts were now more frequent, but I did not wish to speak to Dian until I could see from the expression of her face how she was receiving my apologies. At last a faint glow ahead forewarned us of the end of the tunnel, for which I for one was devoutly thankful. Then at a sudden turn we emerged into the full light of the noonday sun.

But with it came a sudden realization of what meant to me a real catastrophe— Dian was gone, and with her a half-dozen other prisoners. The guards saw it too, and the ferocity of their rage was terrible to behold. Their awesome, bestial faces were contorted in the most diabolical expressions, as they accused each other of responsibility for the loss. Finally they fell upon us, beating us with their spear shafts, and hatchets. They had already killed two near the head of the line, and were like to have finished the balance of us when their leader finally put a stop to the brutal slaughter. Never in all my life had I witnessed a more horrible exhibition of bestial rage— I thanked God that Dian had not been one of those left to endure it.

Of the twelve prisoners who had been chained ahead of me each alternate one had been freed commencing with Dian. Hooja was gone. Ghak remained. What could it mean? How had it been accomplished? The commander of the guards was investigating. Soon he discovered that the rude locks which had held the neckbands in place had been deftly picked.

"Hooja the Sly One," murmured Ghak, who was now next to me in line. "He has taken the girl that you would not have," he continued, glancing at me.

"That I would not have!" I cried. "What do you mean?"

He looked at me closely for a moment.

"I have doubted your story that you are from another world," he said at last, "but yet upon no other grounds could your ignorance of the ways of Pellucidar be explained. Do you really mean that you do not know that you offended the Beautiful One, and how?"

"I do not know, Ghak," I replied.

"Then shall I tell you. When a man of Pellucidar intervenes between another man and the woman the other man would have, the woman belongs to the victor. Dian the Beautiful belongs to you. You should have claimed her or released her. Had you taken her hand, it would have indicated your desire to make her your mate, and had you raised her hand above her head and then dropped it, it would have meant that you did not wish her for a mate and that you released her from all obligation to you. By doing neither you have put upon her the greatest affront that a man may put upon a woman. Now she is your slave. No man will take her as mate, or may take her honorably, until he shall have overcome you in combat, and men do not choose slave women as their mates—at least not the men of Pellucidar."

"I did not know, Ghak," I cried. "I did not know. Not for all Pellucidar would I have harmed Dian the Beautiful by word, or look, or act of mine. I do not want her as my slave. I do not want her as my—" but here I stopped. The vision of that sweet and innocent face floated before me amidst the soft mists of imagination, and where I had on the second believed that I clung only to the memory of a gentle friendship I had lost, yet now it seemed that it would have been disloyalty to her to have said that I did not want Dian the Beautiful as my mate. I had not thought of her except as a welcome friend in a strange, cruel world. Even now I did not think that I loved her.

I believe Ghak must have read the truth more in my expression than in my words, for presently he laid his hand upon my shoulder.

"Man of another world," he said, "I believe you. Lips may lie, but when the heart speaks through the eyes it tells only the truth. Your heart has spoken to me. I know now that you meant no affront to Dian the Beautiful. She is not of my tribe; but her mother is my sister. She does not know it—her mother was stolen by Dian's father who came with many others of the tribe of Amoz to battle with us for our women—the most beautiful women of Pellucidar. Then was her father king of Amoz, and her mother was daughter of the king of Sari—to whose power I, his son, have succeeded. Dian is the daughter of kings, though her father is no longer king since the sadok tossed him and Jubal the Ugly One wrested his kingship from him. Because of her lineage the wrong you did her was greatly magnified in the eyes of all who saw it. She will never forgive you."

I asked Ghak if there was not some way in which I could release the girl from the bondage and ignominy I had unwittingly placed upon her.

"If ever you find her, yes," he answered. "Merely to raise her hand above her head and drop it in the presence of others is sufficient to release her; but how may you ever find her, you who are doomed to a life of slavery yourself in the buried city of Phutra?"

"Is there no escape?" I asked.

"Hooja the Sly One escaped and took the others with him," replied Ghak. "But there are no more dark places on the way to Phutra, and once there it is not so easy—the Mahars are very wise. Even if one escaped from Phutra there are the thipdars—they would find you, and then—" the Hairy One shuddered. "No, you will never escape the Mahars."

It was a cheerful prospect. I asked Perry what he thought about it; but he only shrugged his shoulders and continued a longwinded prayer he had been at for some time. He was wont to say that the only redeeming feature of our captivity was the ample time it gave him for the improvisation of prayers—it was becoming an obsession with him. The Sagoths had begun to take notice of his habit of declaiming throughout entire marches. One of them asked him what he was saying—to whom he was talking. The question gave me an idea, so I answered quickly before Perry could say anything.

"Do not interrupt him," I said. "He is a very holy man in the world from which we come. He is speaking to spirits which you cannot see—do not interrupt him or they will spring out of the air upon you and rend you limb from limb—like that," and I jumped toward the great brute with a loud "Boo!" that sent him stumbling backward.

I took a long chance, I realized, but if we could make any capital out of Perry's harmless mania I wanted to make it while the making was prime. It worked splendidly. The Sagoths treated us both with marked respect during the balance of the journey, and then passed the word along to their masters, the Mahars.

Two marches after this episode we came to the city of Phutra. The entrance to it was marked by two lofty towers of granite, which guarded a flight of steps leading to the buried city. Sagoths were on guard here as well as at a hundred or more other towers scattered about over a large plain.

V

SLAVES

As we descended the broad staircase which led to the main avenue of Phutra I caught my first sight of the dominant race of the inner world. Involuntarily I shrank back as one of the creatures approached to inspect us. A more hideous thing it

231

would be impossible to imagine. The all-powerful Mahars of Pellucidar are great reptiles, some six or eight feet in length, with long narrow heads and great round eyes. Their beak-like mouths are lined with sharp, white fangs, and the backs of their huge, lizard bodies are serrated into bony ridges from their necks to the end of their long tails. Their feet are equipped with three webbed toes, while from the fore feet membranous wings, which are attached to their bodies just in front of the hind legs, protrude at an angle of 45 degrees toward the rear, ending in sharp points several feet above their bodies.

I glanced at Perry as the thing passed me to inspect him. The old man was gazing at the horrid creature with wide astonished eyes. When it passed on, he turned to me.

"A rhamphorhynchus of the Middle Olitic, David," he said, "but, gad, how enormous! The largest remains we ever have discovered have never indicated a size greater than that attained by an ordinary crow."

As we continued on through the main avenue of Phutra we saw many thousand of the creatures coming and going upon their daily duties. They paid but little attention to us. Phutra is laid out underground with a regularity that indicates remarkable engineering skill. It is hewn from solid limestone strata. The streets are broad and of a uniform height of twenty feet. At intervals tubes pierce the roof of this underground city, and by means of lenses and reflectors transmit the sunlight, softened and diffused, to dispel what would otherwise be Cimmerian darkness. In like manner air is introduced.

Perry and I were taken, with Ghak, to a large public building, where one of the Sagoths who had formed our guard explained to a Maharan official the circumstances surrounding our capture. The method of communication between these two was remarkable in that no spoken words were exchanged. They employed a species of sign language. As I was to learn later, the Mahars have no ears, not any spoken language. Among themselves they communicate by means of what Perry says must be a sixth sense which is cognizant of a fourth dimension.

I never did quite grasp him, though he endeavored to explain it to me upon numerous occasions. I suggested telepathy, but he said no, that it was not telepathy since they could only communicate when in each others' presence, nor could they talk with the Sagoths or the other inhabitants of Pellucidar by the same method they used to converse with one another.

"What they do," said Perry, "is to project their thoughts into the fourth dimension, when they become appreciable to the sixth sense of their listener. Do I make myself quite clear?"

232

"You do not, Perry," I replied. He shook his head in despair, and returned to his work. They had set us to carrying a great accumulation of Maharan literature from one apartment to another, and there arranging it upon shelves. I suggested to Perry that we were in the public library of Phutra, but later, as he commenced to discover the key to their written language, he assured me that we were handling the ancient archives of the race.

During this period my thoughts were continually upon Dian the Beautiful. I was, of course, glad that she had escaped the Mahars, and the fate that had been suggested by the Sagoth who had threatened to purchase her upon our arrival at Phutra. I often wondered if the little party of fugitives had been overtaken by the guards who had returned to search for them. Sometimes I was not so sure but that I should have been more contented to know that Dian was here in Phutra, than to think of her at the mercy of Hooja the Sly One. Ghak, Perry, and I often talked together of possible escape, but the Sarian was so steeped in his lifelong belief that no one could escape from the Mahars except by a miracle, that he was not much aid to us—his attitude was of one who waits for the miracle to come to him.

At my suggestion Perry and I fashioned some swords of scraps of iron which we discovered among some rubbish in the cells where we slept, for we were permitted almost unrestrained freedom of action within the limits of the building to which we had been assigned. So great were the number of slaves who waited upon the inhabitants of Phutra that none of us was apt to be overburdened with work, nor were our masters unkind to us.

We hid our new weapons beneath the skins which formed our beds, and then Perry conceived the idea of making bows and arrows—weapons apparently unknown within Pellucidar. Next came shields; but these I found it easier to steal from the walls of the outer guardroom of the building.

We had completed these arrangements for our protection after leaving Phutra when the Sagoths who had been sent to recapture the escaped prisoners returned with four of them, of whom Hooja was one. Dian and two others had eluded them. It so happened that Hooja was confined in the same building with us. He told Ghak that he had not seen Dian or the others after releasing them within the dark grotto. What had become of them he had not the faintest conception—they might be wandering yet, lost within the labyrinthine tunnel, if not dead from starvation.

I was now still further apprehensive as to the fate of Dian, and at this time, I imagine, came the first realization that my affection for the girl might be prompted by more than friendship. During my waking hours she was constantly the subject of my thoughts, and when I slept her dear face haunted my dreams. More than ever was I determined to escape the Mahars.

"Perry," I confided to the old man, "if I have to search every inch of this diminutive world I am going to find Dian the Beautiful and right the wrong I unintentionally did her." That was the excuse I made for Perry's benefit.

"Diminutive world!" he scoffed. "You don't know what you are talking about, my boy," and then he showed me a map of Pellucidar which he had recently discovered among the manuscript he was arranging.

"Look," he cried, pointing to it, "this is evidently water, and all this land. Do you notice the general configuration of the two areas? Where the oceans are upon the outer crust, is land here. These relatively small areas of ocean follow the general lines of the continents of the outer world.

"We know that the crust of the globe is 500 miles in thickness; then the inside diameter of Pellucidar must be 7,000 miles, and the superficial area 165,480,000 square miles. Three-fourths of this is land. Think of it! A land area of 124,110,000 square miles! Our own world contains but 53,000,000 square miles of land, the balance of its surface being covered by water. Just as we often compare nations by their relative land areas, so if we compare these two worlds in the same way we have the strange anomaly of a larger world within a smaller one!

"Where within vast Pellucidar would you search for your Dian? Without stars, or moon, or changing sun how could you find her even though you knew where she might be found?"

The proposition was a corker. It quite took my breath away; but I found that it left me all the more determined to attempt it.

"If Ghak will accompany us we may be able to do it," I suggested.

Perry and I sought him out and put the question straight to him.

"Ghak," I said, "we are determined to escape from this bondage. Will you accompany us?"

"They will set the thipdars upon us," he said, "and then we shall be killed; but—" he hesitated—"I would take the chance if I thought that I might possibly escape and return to my own people."

"Could you find your way back to your own land?" asked Perry. "And could you aid David in his search for Dian?"

"Yes."

"But how," persisted Perry, "could you travel to strange country without heavenly bodies or a compass to guide you?"

Ghak didn't know what Perry meant by heavenly bodies or a compass, but he assured us that you might blindfold any man of Pellucidar and carry him to the farthermost corner of the world, yet he would be able to come directly to his own home again by the shortest route. He seemed surprised to think that we found anything wonderful in it. Perry said it must be some sort of homing instinct such as is possessed by certain breeds of earthly pigeons. I didn't know, of course, but it gave me an idea.

"Then Dian could have found her way directly to her own people?" I asked.

"Surely," replied Ghak, "unless some mighty beast of prey killed her."

I was for making the attempted escape at once, but both Perry and Ghak counseled waiting for some propitious accident which would insure us some small degree of success. I didn't see what accident could befall a whole community in a land of perpetual daylight where the inhabitants had no fixed habits of sleep. Why, I am sure that some of the Mahars never sleep, while others may, at long intervals, crawl into the dark recesses beneath their dwellings and curl up in protracted slumber. Perry says that if a Mahar stays awake for three years he will make up all his lost sleep in a long year's snooze. That may be all true, but I never saw but three of them asleep, and it was the sight of these three that gave me a suggestion for our means of escape.

I had been searching about far below the levels that we slaves were supposed to frequent—possibly fifty feet beneath the main floor of the building—among a network of corridors and apartments, when I came suddenly upon three Mahars curled up upon a bed of skins. At first I thought they were dead, but later their regular breathing convinced me of my error. Like a flash the thought came to me of the marvelous opportunity these sleeping reptiles offered as a means of eluding the watchfulness of our captors and the Sagoth guards.

Hastening back to Perry where he pored over a musty pile of, to me, meaningless hieroglyphics, I explained my plan to him. To my surprise he was horrified.

"It would be murder, David," he cried.

"Murder to kill a reptilian monster?" I asked in astonishment.

"Here they are not monsters, David," he replied. "Here they are the dominant race—we are the 'monsters'—the lower orders. In Pellucidar evolution has progressed along different lines than upon the outer earth. These terrible convulsions of nature time and time again wiped out the existing species—but for this fact some monster of the Saurozoic epoch might rule today upon our own world. We see here what might well have occurred in our own history had conditions been what they have been here.

"Life within Pellucidar is far younger than upon the outer crust. Here man has but reached a stage analogous to the Stone Age of our own world's history, but for countless millions of years these reptiles have been progressing. Possibly it is the sixth sense which I am sure they possess that has given them an advantage over the other and more frightfully armed of their fellows; but this we may never know. They look upon us as we look upon the beasts of our fields, and I learn from their written records that other races of Mahars feed upon men—they keep them in great droves, as we keep cattle. They breed them most carefully, and when they are quite fat, they kill and eat them."

I shuddered.

"What is there horrible about it, David?" the old man asked. "They understand us no better than we understand the lower animals of our own world. Why, I have come across here very learned discussions of the question as to whether *gilaks*, that is men, have any means of communication. One writer claims that we do not even reason—that our every act is mechanical, or instinctive. The dominant race of Pellucidar, David, have not yet learned that men converse among themselves, or reason. Because we do not converse as they do it is beyond them to imagine that we converse at all. It is thus that we reason in relation to the brutes of our own world. They know that the Sagoths have a spoken language, but they cannot comprehend it, or how it manifests itself, since they have no auditory apparatus. They believe that the motions of the lips alone convey the meaning. That the Sagoths can communicate with us is incomprehensible to them.

"Yes, David," he concluded, "it would entail murder to carry out your plan."

"Very well then, Perry." I replied. "I shall become a murderer."

He got me to go over the plan again most carefully, and for some reason which was not at the time clear to me insisted upon a very careful description of the apartments and corridors I had just explored.

"I wonder, David," he said at length, "as you are determined to carry out your wild scheme, if we could not accomplish something of very real and lasting benefit for the human race of Pellucidar at the same time. Listen, I have learned much of a most surprising nature from these archives of the Mahars. That you may not appreciate my plan I shall briefly outline the history of the race.

"Once the males were all-powerful, but ages ago the females, little by little, assumed the mastery. For other ages no noticeable change took place in the race of Mahars. It continued to progress under the intelligent and beneficent rule of the ladies. Science took vast strides. This was especially true of the sciences which we know as biology and eugenics. Finally a certain female scientist announced the fact that she had discovered a method whereby eggs might be fertilized by chemical means after they were laid—all true reptiles, you know, are hatched from eggs.

"What happened? Immediately the necessity for males ceased to exist—the race was no longer dependent upon them. More ages elapsed until at the present time we find a race consisting exclusively of females. But here is the point. The secret of this chemical formula is kept by a single race of Mahars. It is in the city of Phutra, and unless I am greatly in error I judge from your description of the vaults through which you passed today that it lies hidden in the cellar of this building.

"For two reasons they hide it away and guard it jealously. First, because upon it depends the very life of the race of Mahars, and second, owing to the fact that when it was public property as at first so many were experimenting with it that the danger of over-population became very grave.

"David, if we can escape, and at the same time take with us this great secret what will we not have accomplished for the human race within Pellucidar!" The very thought of it fairly overpowered me. Why, we two would be the means of placing the men of the inner world in their rightful place among created things. Only the Sagoths would then stand between them and absolute supremacy, and I was not quite sure but that the Sagoths owed all their power to the greater intelligence of the Mahars—I could not believe that these gorilla-like beasts were the mental superiors of the human race of Pellucidar.

"Why, Perry," I exclaimed, "you and I may reclaim a whole world! Together we can lead the races of men out of the darkness of ignorance into the light of advancement and civilization. At one step we may carry them from the Age of Stone to the twentieth century. It's marvelous—absolutely marvelous just to think about it."

"David," said the old man, "I believe that God sent us here for just that purpose—it shall be my life work to teach them His word—to lead them into the light of His mercy while we are training their hearts and hands in the ways of culture and civilization."

"You are right, Perry," I said, "and while you are teaching them to pray I'll be teaching them to fight, and between us we'll make a race of men that will be an honor to us both."

Ghak had entered the apartment some time before we concluded our conversation, and now he wanted to know what we were so excited about. Perry thought we had best not tell him too much, and so I only explained that I had a plan for escape. When I had outlined it to him, he seemed about as horror-struck as Perry had been; but for a different reason. The Hairy One only considered the horrible fate that would be ours were we discovered; but at last I prevailed upon him to accept my plan as the only feasible one, and when I had assured him that I would take all the responsibility for it were we captured, he accorded a reluctant assent.

VI

THE BEGINNING OF HORROR

Within Pellucidar one time is as good as another. There were no nights to mask our attempted escape. All must be done in broad daylight—all but the work I had to do in the apartment beneath the building. So we determined to put our plan to an immediate test lest the Mahars who made it possible should awake before I reached them; but we were doomed to disappointment, for no sooner had we reached the main floor of the building on our way to the pits beneath, than we encountered hurrying bands of slaves being hastened under strong Sagoth guard out of the edifice to the avenue beyond.

Other Sagoths were darting hither and thither in search of other slaves, and the moment that we appeared we were pounced upon and hustled into the line of marching humans.

What the purpose or nature of the general exodus we did not know, but presently through the line of captives ran the rumor that two escaped slaves had been recaptured—a man and a woman—and that we were marching to witness their punishment, for the man had killed a Sagoth of the detachment that had pursued and overtaken them.

At the intelligence my heart sprang to my throat, for I was sure that the two were of those who escaped in the dark grotto with Hooja the Sly One, and that Dian must be the woman. Ghak thought so too, as did Perry.

"Is there naught that we may do to save her?" I asked Ghak.

"Naught," he replied.

Along the crowded avenue we marched, the guards showing unusual cruelty toward us, as though we, too, had been implicated in the murder of their fellow. The occasion was to serve as an object-lesson to all other slaves of the danger and futility of attempted escape, and the fatal consequences of taking the life of a superior being, and so I imagine that Sagoths felt amply justified in making the entire proceeding as uncomfortable and painful to us as possible.

They jabbed us with their spears and struck at us with the hatchets at the least provocation, and at no provocation at all. It was a most uncomfortable half-hour that we spent before we were finally herded through a low entrance into a huge building the center of which was given up to a good-sized arena. Benches surrounded this open space upon three sides, and along the fourth were heaped huge bowlders which rose in receding tiers toward the roof.

At first I couldn't make out the purpose of this mighty pile of rock, unless it were intended as a rough and picturesque background for the scenes which were enacted in the arena before it, but presently, after the wooden benches had been pretty well filled by slaves and Sagoths, I discovered the purpose of the bowlders, for then the Mahars began to file into the enclosure.

They marched directly across the arena toward the rocks upon the opposite side, where, spreading their bat-like wings, they rose above the high wall of the pit, settling down upon the bowlders above. These were the reserved seats, the boxes of the elect.

Reptiles that they are, the rough surface of a great stone is to them as plush as upholstery to us. Here they lolled, blinking their hideous eyes, and doubtless conversing with one another in their sixth-sense-fourth-dimension language.

For the first time I beheld their queen. She differed from the others in no feature that was appreciable to my earthly eyes, in fact all Mahars look alike to me: but when she crossed the arena after the balance of her female subjects had found their bowlders, she was preceded by a score of huge Sagoths, the largest I ever had seen, and on either side of her waddled a huge thipdar, while behind came another score of Sagoth guardsmen.

At the barrier the Sagoths clambered up the steep side with truly apelike agility, while behind them the haughty queen rose upon her wings with her two frightful dragons close beside her, and settled down upon the largest bowlder of them all in the exact center of that side of the amphitheater which is reserved for the dominant race. Here she squatted, a most repulsive and uninteresting queen; though doubtless quite as well assured of her beauty and divine right to rule as the proudest monarch of the outer world.

And then the music started—music without sound! The Mahars cannot hear, so the drums and fifes and horns of earthly bands are unknown among them. The "band" consists of a score or more Mahars. It filed out in the center of the arena where the creatures upon the rocks might see it, and there it performed for fifteen or twenty minutes.

Their technic consisted in waving their tails and moving their heads in a regular succession of measured movements resulting in a cadence which evidently pleased the eye of the Mahar as the cadence of our own instrumental music pleases our ears. Sometimes the band took measured steps in unison to one side or the other, or backward and again forward—it all seemed very silly and meaningless to me, but at the end of the first piece the Mahars upon the rocks showed the first indications of enthusiasm that I had seen displayed by the dominant race of Pellucidar. They beat their great wings up and down, and smote their rocky perches with their mighty tails until the ground shook. Then the band started another piece, and all was again as silent as the grave. That was one great beauty about Mahar music—if you didn't happen to like a piece that was being played all you had to do was shut your eyes.

When the band had exhausted its repertory it took wing and settled upon the rocks above and behind the queen. Then the business of the day was on. A man and woman were pushed into the arena by a couple of Sagoth guardsmen. I leaned forward in my seat to scrutinize the female—hoping against hope that she might prove to be another than Dian the Beautiful. Her back was toward me for a while, and the sight of the great mass of raven hair piled high upon her head filled me with alarm.

Presently a door in one side of the arena wall was opened to admit a huge, shaggy, bull-like creature.

"A Bos," whispered Perry, excitedly. "His kind roamed the outer crust with the cave bear and the mammoth ages and ages ago. We have been carried back a million years, David, to the childhood of a planet—is it not wondrous?"

But I saw only the raven hair of a half-naked girl, and my heart stood still in dumb misery at the sight of her, nor had I any eyes for the wonders of natural history. But for Perry and Ghak I should have leaped to the floor of the arena and shared whatever fate lay in store for this priceless treasure of the Stone Age.

With the advent of the Bos—they call the thing a *thag* within Pellucidar—two spears were tossed into the arena at the feet of the prisoners. It seemed to me that a bean shooter would have been as effective against the mighty monster as these pitiful weapons.

As the animal approached the two, bellowing and pawing the ground with the strength of many earthly bulls, another door directly beneath us was opened, and from it issued the most terrific roar that ever had fallen upon my outraged ears. I could not at first see the beast from which emanated this fearsome challenge, but the sound had the effect of bringing the two victims around with a sudden start, and then I saw the girl's face—she was not Dian! I could have wept for relief.

And now, as the two stood frozen in terror, I saw the author of that fearsome sound creeping stealthily into view. It was a huge tiger—such as hunted the great Bos through the jungles primeval when the world was young. In contour and markings it was not unlike the noblest of the Bengals of our own world, but as its dimensions were exaggerated to colossal proportions so too were its colorings exaggerated.

Its vivid yellows fairly screamed aloud; its whites were as eider down; its blacks glossy as the finest anthracite coal, and its coat long and shaggy as a mountain goat. That it is a beautiful animal there is no gainsaying, but if its size and colors are magnified here within Pellucidar, so is the ferocity of its disposition. It is not the occasional member of its species that is a man hunter—all are man hunters; but they do not confine their foraging to man alone, for there is no flesh or fish within Pellucidar that they will not eat with relish in the constant efforts which they make to furnish their huge carcasses with sufficient sustenance to maintain their mighty thews.

Upon one side of the doomed pair the thag bellowed and advanced, and upon the other *tarag,* the frightful, crept toward them with gaping mouth and dripping fangs.

The man seized the spears, handing one of them to the woman. At the sound of the roaring of the tiger the bull's bellowing became a veritable frenzy of rageful noise. Never in my life had I heard such an infernal din as the two brutes made, and to think it was all lost upon the hideous reptiles for whom the show was staged!

The thag was charging now from one side, and the tarag from the other. The two puny things standing between them seemed already lost, but at the very moment that the beasts were upon them the man grasped his companion by the arm and together they leaped to one side, while the frenzied creatures came together like locomotives in collision.

There ensued a battle royal which for sustained and frightful ferocity transcends the power of imagination or description. Time and again the colossal bull tossed the enormous tiger high into the air, but each time that the huge cat touched the ground he returned to the encounter with apparently undiminished strength, and seemingly increased ire.

For a while the man and woman busied themselves only with keeping out of the way of the two creatures, but finally I saw them separate and each creep stealthily toward one of the combatants. The tiger was now upon the bull's broad back, clinging to the huge neck with powerful fangs while its long, strong talons ripped the heavy hide into shreds and ribbons.

For a moment the bull stood bellowing and quivering with pain and rage, its cloven hoofs widespread, its tail lashing viciously from side to side, and then, in a mad orgy of bucking it went careening about the arena in frenzied attempt to unseat its rending rider. It was with difficulty that the girl avoided the first mad rush of the wounded animal.

All its efforts to rid itself of the tiger seemed futile, until in desperation it threw itself upon the ground, rolling over and over. A little of this so disconcerted the tiger, knocking its breath from it I imagine, that it lost its hold and then, quick as a cat, the great thag was up again and had buried those mighty horns deep in the tarag's abdomen, pinning him to the floor of the arena.

The great cat clawed at the shaggy head until eyes and ears were gone, and naught but a few strips of ragged, bloody flesh remained upon the skull. Yet through all the agony of that fearful punishment the thag still stood motionless pinning down his adversary, and then the man leaped in, seeing that the blind bull would be the least formidable enemy, and ran his spear through the tarag's heart.

As the animal's fierce clawing ceased, the bull raised his gory, sightless head, and with a horrid roar ran headlong across the arena. With great leaps and bounds he came, straight toward the arena wall directly beneath where we sat, and then accident carried him, in one of his mighty springs, completely over the barrier into the midst of the slaves and Sagoths just in front of us. Swinging his bloody horns from side to side the beast cut a wide swath before him straight upward toward our seats. Before him slaves and gorilla-men fought in mad stampede to escape the menace of the creature's death agonies, for such only could that frightful charge have been.

Forgetful of us, our guards joined in the general rush for the exits, many of which pierced the wall of the amphitheater behind us. Perry, Ghak, and I became separated in the chaos which reigned for a few moments after the beast cleared the wall of the arena, each intent upon saving his own hide.

I ran to the right, passing several exits choked with the fear mad mob that were battling to escape. One would have thought that an entire herd of thags was loose behind them, rather than a single blinded, dying beast; but such is the effect of panic upon a crowd.

VII

FREEDOM

Once out of the direct path of the animal, fear of it left me, but another emotion as quickly gripped me—hope of escape that the demoralized condition of the guards made possible for the instant.

I thought of Perry, but for the hope that I might better encompass his release if myself free I should have put the thought of freedom from me at once. As it was I hastened on toward the right searching for an exit toward which no Sagoths were fleeing, and at last I found it—a low, narrow aperture leading into a dark corridor.

Without thought of the possible consequence, I darted into the shadows of the tunnel, feeling my way along through the gloom for some distance. The noises of the amphitheater had grown fainter and fainter until now all was as silent as the tomb about me. Faint light filtered from above through occasional ventilating and lighting tubes, but it was scarce sufficient to enable my human eyes to cope with the darkness, and so I was forced to move with extreme care, feeling my way along step by step with a hand upon the wall beside me.

Presently the light increased and a moment later, to my delight, I came upon a flight of steps leading upward, at the top of which the brilliant light of the noonday sun shone through an opening in the ground.

Cautiously I crept up the stairway to the tunnel's end, and peering out saw the broad plain of Phutra before me. The numerous lofty, granite towers which mark the several entrances to the subterranean city were all in front of me—behind, the plain stretched level and unbroken to the nearby foothills. I had come to the surface, then, beyond the city, and my chances for escape seemed much enhanced.

My first impulse was to await darkness before attempting to cross the plain, so deeply implanted are habits of thought; but of a sudden I recollected the perpetual noonday brilliance which envelopes Pellucidar, and with a smile I stepped forth into the daylight.

Rank grass, waist high, grows upon the plain of Phutra—the gorgeous flowering grass of the inner world, each particular blade of which is tipped with a tiny, five-pointed blossom—brilliant little stars of varying colors that twinkle in the green foliage to add still another charm to the weird, yet lovely, landscape.

But then the only aspect which attracted me was the distant hills in which I hoped to find sanctuary, and so I hastened on, trampling the myriad beauties beneath my hurrying feet. Perry says that the force of gravity is less upon the surface of the inner world than upon that of the outer. He explained it all to me once, but I was never particularly brilliant in such matters and so most of it has escaped me. As I recall it the difference is due in some part to the counter-attraction of that portion of the earth's crust directly opposite the spot upon the face of Pellucidar at which one's calculations are being made. Be that as it may, it always seemed to me that I moved with greater speed and agility within Pellucidar than upon the outer surface—there was a certain airy lightness of step that was most pleasing, and a feeling of bodily detachment which I can only compare with that occasionally experienced in dreams.

And as I crossed Phutra's flower-bespangled plain that time I seemed almost to fly, though how much of the sensation was due to Perry's suggestion and how much to actuality I am sure I do not know. The more I thought of Perry the less pleasure I took in my new-found freedom. There could be no liberty for me within Pellucidar unless the old man shared it with me, and only the hope that I might find some way to encompass his release kept me from turning back to Phutra.

Just how I was to help Perry I could scarce imagine, but I hoped that some fortuitous circumstance might solve the problem for me. It was quite evident however that little less than a miracle could aid me, for what could I accomplish in this strange world, naked and unarmed? It was even doubtful that I could retrace my steps to Phutra should I once pass beyond view of the plain, and even were that possible, what aid could I bring to Perry no matter how far I wandered?

The case looked more and more hopeless the longer I viewed it, yet with a stubborn persistency I forged ahead toward the foothills. Behind me no sign of pursuit developed, before me I saw no living thing. It was as though I moved through a dead and forgotten world.

I have no idea, of course, how long it took me to reach the limit of the plain, but at last I entered the foothills, following a pretty little cañon upward toward the mountains. Beside me frolicked a laughing brooklet, hurrying upon its noisy way down to the silent sea. In its quieter pools I discovered many small fish, of four-or five-pound weight I should imagine. In appearance, except as to size and color, they were not unlike the whale of our own seas. As I watched them playing about I discovered, not only that they suckled their young, but that at intervals they rose to the surface to breathe as well as to feed upon certain grasses and a strange, scarlet lichen which grew upon the rocks just above the water line.

It was this last habit that gave me the opportunity I craved to capture one of these herbivorous cetaceans—that is what Perry calls them—and make as good a meal as one can on raw, warm-blooded fish; but I had become rather used, by this time, to the eating of food in its natural state, though I still balked on the eyes and entrails, much to the amusement of Ghak, to whom I always passed these delicacies.

Crouching beside the brook, I waited until one of the diminutive purple whales rose to nibble at the long grasses which overhung the water, and then, like the beast of prey that man really is, I sprang upon my victim, appeasing my hunger while he yet wriggled to escape.

Then I drank from the clear pool, and after washing my hands and face continued my flight. Above the source of the brook I encountered a rugged climb to the summit of a long ridge. Beyond was a steep declivity to the shore of a placid, inland sea, upon the quiet surface of which lay several beautiful islands.

The view was charming in the extreme, and as no man or beast was to be seen that might threaten my new-found liberty, I slid over the edge of the bluff, and half sliding, half falling, dropped into the delightful valley, the very aspect of which seemed to offer a haven of peace and security.

The gently sloping beach along which I walked was thickly strewn with strangely shaped, colored shells; some empty, others still housing as varied a multitude of mollusks as ever might have drawn out their sluggish lives along the silent shores of the antediluvian seas of the outer crust. As I walked I could not but compare myself with the first man of that other world, so complete the solitude which surrounded me, so primal and untouched the virgin wonders and beauties of adolescent nature. I felt myself a second Adam wending my lonely way through the childhood of a world, searching for my Eve, and at the thought there rose before my mind's eye the exquisite outlines of a perfect face surmounted by a loose pile of wondrous, raven hair.

As I walked, my eyes were bent upon the beach so that it was not until I had come quite upon it that I discovered that which shattered all my beautiful dream of solitude and safety and peace and primal overlordship. The thing was a hollowed log drawn upon the sands, and in the bottom of it lay a crude paddle.

The rude shock of awakening to what doubtless might prove some new form of danger was still upon me when I heard a rattling of loose stones from the direction of the bluff, and turning my eyes in that direction I beheld the author of the disturbance, a great copper-colored man, running rapidly toward me.

There was that in the haste with which he came which seemed quite sufficiently menacing, so that I did not need the added evidence of brandishing spear and scowling face to warn me that I was in no safe position, but whither to flee was indeed a momentous question.

The speed of the fellow seemed to preclude the possibility of escaping him upon the open beach. There was but a single alternative—the rude skiff—and with a celerity which equaled his, I pushed the thing into the sea and as it floated gave a final shove and clambered in over the end.

A cry of rage rose from the owner of the primitive craft, and an instant later his heavy, stone-tipped spear grazed my shoulder and buried itself in the bow of the boat beyond. Then I grasped the paddle, and with feverish haste urged the awkward, wobbly thing out upon the surface of the sea.

A glance over my shoulder showed me that the copper-colored one had plunged in after me and was swimming rapidly in pursuit. His mighty strokes bade fair to close up the distance between us in short order, for at best I could make but slow progress with my unfamiliar craft, which nosed stubbornly in every direction but that which I desired to follow, so that fully half my energy was expended in turning its blunt prow back into the course.

I had covered some hundred yards from shore when it became evident that my pursuer must grasp the stern of the skiff within the next half-dozen strokes. In a frenzy of despair, I bent to the grandfather of all paddles in a hopeless effort to escape, and still the copper giant behind me gained and gained.

His hand was reaching upward for the stern when I saw a sleek, sinuous body shoot from the depths below. The man saw it too, and the look of terror that overspread his face assured me that I need have no further concern as to him, for the fear of certain death was in his look.

And then about him coiled the great, slimy folds of a hideous monster of that prehistoric deep—a mighty serpent of the sea, with fanged jaws, and darting forked tongue, with bulging eyes, and bony protuberances upon head and snout that formed short, stout horns.

As I looked at that hopeless struggle my eyes met those of the doomed man, and I could have sworn that in his I saw an expression of hopeless appeal. But whether I did or not there swept through me a sudden compassion for the fellow. He was indeed a brother-man, and that he might have killed me with pleasure had he caught me was forgotten in the extremity of his danger.

Unconsciously I had ceased paddling as the serpent rose to engage my pursuer, so now the skiff still drifted close beside the two. The monster seemed to be but playing with his victim before he closed his awful jaws upon him and dragged him down to his dark den beneath the surface to devour him. The huge, snakelike body coiled and uncoiled about its prey. The hideous, gaping jaws snapped in the victim's face. The forked tongue, lightning-like, ran in and out upon the copper skin.

Nobly the giant battled for his life, beating with his stone hatchet against the bony armor that covered that frightful carcass; but for all the damage he inflicted he might as well have struck with his open palm.

At last I could endure no longer to sit supinely by while a fellowman was dragged down to a horrible death by that repulsive reptile. Embedded in the prow of the skiff lay the spear that had been cast after me by him whom I suddenly desired to save. With a wrench I tore it loose, and standing upright in the wobbly log drove it with all the strength of my two arms straight into the gaping jaws of the hydrophidian.

With a loud hiss the creature abandoned its prey to turn upon me, but the spear, imbedded in its throat, prevented it from seizing me though it came near to overturning the skiff in its mad efforts to reach me.

VIII

THE MAHAR TEMPLE

The aborigine, apparently uninjured, climbed quickly into the skiff, and seizing the spear with me helped to hold off the infuriated creature. Blood from the wounded reptile was now crimsoning the waters about us and soon from the weakening struggles it became evident that I had inflicted a death wound upon it. Presently its efforts to reach us ceased entirely, and with a few convulsive movements it turned upon its back quite dead.

And then there came to me a sudden realization of the predicament in which I had placed myself. I was entirely within the power of the savage man whose skiff I had stolen. Still clinging to the spear I looked into his face to find him scrutinizing me intently, and there we stood for some several minutes, each clinging tenaciously to the weapon the while we gazed in stupid wonderment at each other.

What was in his mind I do not know, but in my own was merely the question as to how soon the fellow would recommence hostilities.

Presently he spoke to me, but in a tongue which I was unable to translate. I shook my head in an effort to indicate my ignorance of his language, at the same time addressing him in the bastard tongue that the Sagoths use to converse with the human slaves of the Mahars.

To my delight he understood and answered me in the same jargon.

"What do you want of my spear?" he asked.

"Only to keep you from running it through me," I replied.

"I would not do that," he said, "for you have just saved my life," and with that he released his hold upon it and squatted down in the bottom of the skiff.

"Who are you," he continued, "and from what country do you come?"

I too sat down, laying the spear between us, and tried to explain how I came to Pellucidar, and wherefrom, but it was as impossible for him to grasp or believe the strange tale I told him as I fear it is for you upon the outer crust to believe in the existence of the inner world. To him it seemed quite ridiculous to imagine that there was another world far beneath his feet peopled by beings similar to himself, and he laughed uproariously the more he thought upon it. But it was ever thus. That which has never come within the scope of our really pitifully meager world-experience cannot be—our finite minds cannot grasp that which may not exist in accordance with the conditions which obtain about us upon the outside of the insignificant grain of dust which wends its tiny way among the bowlders of the universe—the speck of moist dirt we so proudly call the World.

So I gave it up and asked him about himself. He said he was a Mezop, and that his name was Ja.

"Who are the Mezops?" I asked. "Where do they live?"

He looked at me in surprise.

"I might indeed believe that you were from another world," he said, "for who of Pellucidar could be so ignorant! The Mezops live upon the islands of the seas. In so far as I ever have heard no Mezop lives elsewhere, and no others than Mezops dwell upon islands, but of course it may be different in other far-distant lands. I do not know. At any rate in this sea and those near by it is true that only people of my race inhabit the islands.

"We are fishermen, though we be great hunters as well, often going to the mainland in search of the game that is scarce upon all but the larger islands. And we are warriors also," he added proudly. "Even the Sagoths of the Mahars fear us. Once, when Pellucidar was young, the Sagoths were wont to capture us for slaves as they do the other men of Pellucidar, it is handed down from father to son among us that this is so; but we fought so desperately and slew so many Sagoths, and those of us that were captured killed so many Mahars in their own cities that at last they learned that it were better to leave us alone, and later came the time that the Mahars became too indolent even to catch their own fish, except for amusement, and then they needed us to supply their wants, and so a truce was made between the races. Now they give us certain things which we are unable to produce in return for the fish that we catch, and the Mezops and the Mahars live in peace.

"The great ones even come to our islands. It is there, far from the prying eyes of their own Sagoths, that they practice their religious rites in the temples they have builded there with our assistance. If you live among us you will doubtless see the manner of their worship, which is strange indeed, and most unpleasant for the poor slaves they bring to take part in it."

As Ja talked I had an excellent opportunity to inspect him more closely. He was a huge fellow, standing I should say six feet six or seven inches, well developed and of a coppery red not unlike that of our own North American Indian, nor were his features dissimilar to theirs. He had the aquiline nose found among many of the higher tribes, the prominent cheek bones, and black hair and eyes, but his mouth and lips were better molded. All in all, Ja was an impressive and handsome creature, and he talked well too, even in the miserable makeshift language we were compelled to use.

During our conversation Ja had taken the paddle and was propelling the skiff with vigorous strokes toward a large island that lay some half-mile from the mainland.

The skill with which he handled his crude and awkward craft elicited my deepest admiration, since it had been so short a time before that I had made such pitiful work of it.

As we touched the pretty, level beach Ja leaped out and I followed him. Together we dragged the skiff far up into the bushes that grew beyond the sand.

"We must hide our canoes," explained Ja, "for the Mezops of Luana are always at war with us and would steal them if they found them," he nodded toward an island farther out at sea, and at so great a distance that it seemed but a blur hanging in the distant sky. The upward curve of the surface of Pellucidar was constantly revealing the impossible to the surprised eyes of the outer-earthly. To see land and water curving upward in the distance until it seemed to stand on edge where it melted into the distant sky, and to feel that seas and mountains hung suspended directly above one's head required such a complete reversal of the perceptive and reasoning faculties as almost to stupefy one.

No sooner had we hidden the canoe than Ja plunged into the jungle, presently emerging into a narrow but well-defined trail which wound hither and thither much after the manner of the highways of all primitive folk, but there was one peculiarity about this Mezop trail which I was later to find distinguished them from all other trails that I ever have seen within or without the earth.

It would run on, plain and clear and well defined to end suddenly in the midst of a tangle of matted jungle, then Ja would turn directly back in his tracks for a little distance, spring into a tree, climb through it to the other side, drop onto a fallen log, leap over a low bush and alight once more upon a distinct trail which he would follow back for a short distance only to turn directly about and retrace his steps until after a mile or less this new pathway ended as suddenly and mysteriously as the former section. Then he would pass again across some media which would reveal no spoor, to take up the broken thread of the trail beyond.

As the purpose of this remarkable avenue dawned upon me I could not but admire the native shrewdness of the ancient progenitor of the Mezops who hit upon this novel plan to throw his enemies from his track and delay or thwart them in their attempts to follow him to his deep-buried cities.

To you of the outer earth it might seem a slow and tortuous method of traveling through the jungle, but were you of Pellucidar you would realize that time is no factor where time does not exist. So labyrinthine are the windings of these trails, so varied the connecting links and the distances which one must retrace one's steps from the paths' ends to find them that a Mezop often reaches man's estate before he is familiar even with those which lead from his own city to the sea.

In fact three-fourths of the education of the young male Mezop consists in familiarizing himself with these jungle avenues, and the status of an adult is largely determined by the number of trails which he can follow upon his own island. The females never learn them, since from birth to death they never leave the clearing in which the village of their nativity is situated except they be taken to mate by a male from another village, or captured in war by the enemies of their tribe.

After proceeding through the jungle for what must have been upward of five miles we emerged suddenly into a large clearing in the exact center of which stood as strange an appearing village as one might well imagine.

Large trees had been chopped down fifteen or twenty feet above the ground, and upon the tops of them spherical habitations of woven twigs, mud covered, had been built. Each ball-like house was surmounted by some manner of carven image, which Ja told me indicated the identity of the owner.

Horizontal slits, six inches high and two or three feet wide, served to admit light and ventilation. The entrances to the house were through small apertures in the bases of the trees and thence upward by rude ladders through the hollow trunks to the rooms above. The houses varied in size from two to several rooms. The largest that I entered was divided into two floors and eight apartments.

All about the village, between it and the jungle, lay beautifully cultivated fields in which the Mezops raised such cereals, fruits, and vegetables as they required. Women and children were working in these gardens as we crossed toward the village. At sight of Ja they saluted deferentially, but to me they paid not the slightest attention. Among them and about the outer verge of the cultivated area were many warriors. These too saluted Ja, by touching the points of their spears to the ground directly before them.

Ja conducted me to a large house in the center of the village—the house with eight rooms—and taking me up into it gave me food and drink. There I met his mate, a comely girl with a nursing baby in her arms. Ja told her of how I had saved his life, and she was thereafter most kind and hospitable toward me, even permitting me to hold and amuse the tiny bundle of humanity whom Ja told me would one day rule the tribe, for Ja, it seemed, was the chief of the community.

We had eaten and rested, and I had slept, much to Ja's amusement, for it seemed that he seldom if ever did so, and then the red man proposed that I accompany him to the temple of the Mahars which lay not far from his village. "We are not supposed to visit it," he said; "but the great ones cannot hear and if we keep well out of sight they need never know that we have been there. For my part I hate them and always have, but the other chieftains of the island think it best that we continue to maintain the amicable relations which exist between the two races; otherwise I should like nothing better than to lead my warriors amongst the hideous creatures and exterminate them—Pellucidar would be a better place to live were there none of them."

I wholly concurred in Ja's belief, but it seemed that it might be a difficult matter to exterminate the dominant race of Pellucidar. Thus conversing we followed the intricate trail toward the temple, which we came upon in a small clearing surrounded by enormous trees similar to those which must have flourished upon the outer crust during the carboniferous age.

Here was a mighty temple of hewn rock built in the shape of a rough oval with rounded roof in which were several large openings. No doors or windows were visible in the sides of the structure, nor was there need of any, except one entrance for the slaves, since, as Ja explained, the Mahars flew to and from their place of ceremonial, entering and leaving the building by means of the apertures in the roof.

"But," added Ja, "there is an entrance near the base of which even the Mahars know nothing. Come," and he led me across the clearing and about the end to a pile of loose rock which lay against the foot of the wall. Here he removed a couple of large bowlders, revealing a small opening which led straight within the building, or so it seemed, though as I entered after Ja I discovered myself in a narrow place of extreme darkness.

"We are within the outer wall," said Ja. "It is hollow. Follow me closely."

The red man groped ahead a few paces and then began to ascend a primitive ladder similar to that which leads from the ground to the upper stories of his house. We ascended for some forty feet when the interior of the space between the walls commenced to grow lighter and presently we came opposite an opening in the inner wall which gave us an unobstructed view of the entire interior of the temple.

The lower floor was an enormous tank of clear water in which numerous hideous Mahars swam lazily up and down. Artificial islands of granite rock dotted this artificial sea, and upon several of them I saw men and women like myself.

"What are the human beings doing here?" I asked.

"Wait and you shall see," replied Ja. "They are to take a leading part in the ceremonies which will follow the advent of the queen. You may be thankful that you are not upon the same side of the wall as they."

Scarcely had he spoken than we heard a great fluttering of wings above and a moment later a long procession of the frightful reptiles of Pellucidar winged slowly and majestically through the large central opening in the roof and circled in stately manner about the temple.

There were several Mahars first, and then at least twenty awe-inspiring ptero-dactyls—thipdars, they are called within Pellucidar. Behind these came the queen, flanked by other thipdars as she had been when she entered the amphitheater at Phutra.

Three times they wheeled about the interior of the oval chamber, to settle finally upon the damp, cold bowlders that fringe the outer edge of the pool. In the center of one side the largest rock was reserved for the queen, and here she took her place surrounded by her terrible guard.

All lay quiet for several minutes after settling to their places. One might have imagined them in silent prayer. The poor slaves upon the diminutive islands watched the horrid creatures with wide eyes. The men, for the most part, stood erect and stately with folded arms, awaiting their doom; but the women and children clung to one another, hiding behind the males. They are a noble-looking race, these cave men of Pellucidar, and if our progenitors were as they, the human race of the outer crust has deteriorated rather than improved with the march of the ages. All they lack is opportunity. We have opportunity, and little else.

Now the queen moved. She raised her ugly head, looking about; then very slowly she crawled to the edge of her throne and slid noiselessly into the water. Up and down the long tank she swam, turning at the ends as you have seen captive seals turn in their tiny tanks, turning upon their backs and diving below the surface.

Nearer and nearer to the island she came until at last she remained at rest before the largest, which was directly opposite her throne. Raising her hideous head from the water she fixed her great, round eyes upon the slaves. They were fat and sleek, for they had been brought from a distant Mahar city where human beings are kept in droves, and bred and fattened, as we breed and fatten beef cattle.

The queen fixed her gaze upon a plump young maiden. Her victim tried to turn away, hiding her face in her hands and kneeling behind a woman; but the reptile, with unblinking eyes, stared on with such fixity that I could have sworn her vision pen-etrated the woman, and the girl's arms to reach at last the very center of her brain.

Slowly the reptile's head commenced to move to and fro, but the eyes never ceased to bore toward the frightened girl, and then the victim responded. She turned wide, fear-haunted eyes toward the Mahar queen, slowly she rose to her feet, and then as though dragged by some unseen power she moved as one in a trance straight toward the reptile, her glassy eyes fixed upon those of her captor. To the water's edge she came, nor did she even pause, but stepped into the shallows beside the little island. On she moved toward the Mahar, who now slowly retreated as though lead-ing her victim on. The water rose to the girl's knees, and still she advanced, chained by that clammy eye. Now the water was at her waist; now her armpits. Her fellows upon the island looked on in horror, helpless to avert her doom in which they saw a forecast of their own.

The Mahar sank now till only the long upper bill and eyes were exposed above the surface of the water, and the girl had advanced until the end of that repulsive beak was but an inch or two from her face, her horror-filled eyes riveted upon those of the reptile.

Now the water passed above the girl's mouth and nose—her eyes and forehead all that showed—yet still she walked on after the retreating Mahar. The queen's head slowly disappeared beneath the surface and after it went the eyes of her victim— only a slow ripple widened toward the shores to mark where the two vanished.

For a time all was silence within the temple. The slaves were motionless in terror. The Mahars watched the surface of the water for the reappearance of their queen, and presently at one end of the tank her head rose slowly into view. She was backing toward the surface, her eyes fixed before her as they had been when she dragged the helpless girl to her doom.

And then to my utter amazement I saw the forehead and eyes of the maiden come slowly out of the depths, following the gaze of the reptile just as when she had disappeared beneath the surface. On and on came the girl until she stood in water that reached barely to her knees, and though she had been beneath the surface sufficient time to have drowned her thrice over there was no indication, other than her dripping hair and glistening body, that she had been submerged at all.

Again and again the queen led the girl into the depths and out again, until the uncanny weirdness of the thing got on my nerves so that I could have leaped into the tank to the child's rescue had I not taken a firm hold of myself.

Once they were below much longer than usual, and when they came to the surface I was horrified to see that one of the girl's arms was gone—gnawed completely off at the shoulder—but the poor thing gave no indication of realizing pain, only the horror in her set eyes seemed intensified.

The next time they appeared the other arm was gone, and then the breasts, and then a part of the face—it was awful. The poor creatures on the islands awaiting their fate tried to cover their eyes with their hands to hide the fearful sight, but now I saw that they too were under the hypnotic spell of the reptiles, so that they could only crouch in terror with their eyes fixed upon the terrible thing that was transpiring before them.

Finally the queen was under much longer than ever before, and when she rose she came alone and swam sleepily toward her bowlder. The moment she mounted it seemed to be the signal for the other Mahars to enter the tank, and then commenced, upon a larger scale, a repetition of the uncanny performance through which the queen had led her victim.

Only the women and children fell prey to the Mahars—they being the weakest and most tender—and when they had satisfied their appetite for human flesh, some of them devouring two and three of the slaves, there were only a score of full-grown men left, and I thought that for some reason these were to be spared, but such was far from the case, for as the last Mahar crawled to her rock the queen's thipdars darted into the air, circled the temple once and then, hissing like steam engines, swooped down upon the remaining slaves.

There was no hypnotism here—just the plain, brutal ferocity of the beast of prey, tearing, rending, and gulping its meat, but at that it was less horrible than the uncanny method of the Mahars. By the time the thipdars had disposed of the last of the slaves the Mahars were all asleep upon their rocks, and a moment later the great pterodactyls swung back to their posts beside the queen, and themselves dropped into slumber.

"I thought the Mahars seldom, if ever, slept," I said to Ja.

"They do many things in this temple which they do not do elsewhere," he replied. "The Mahars of Phutra are not supposed to eat human flesh, yet slaves are brought here by thousands and almost always you will find Mahars on hand to consume them. I imagine that they do not bring their Sagoths here, because they are ashamed of the practice, which is supposed to obtain only among the least advanced of their race; but I would wager my canoe against a broken paddle that there is no Mahar but eats human flesh whenever she can get it."

"Why should they object to eating human flesh," I asked, "if it is true that they look upon us as lower animals?"

"It is not because they consider us their equals that they are supposed to look with abhorrence upon those who eat our flesh," replied Ja; "it is merely that we are warm-blooded animals. They would not think of eating the meat of a thag, which we consider such a delicacy, any more than I would think of eating a snake. As a matter of fact it is difficult to explain just why this sentiment should exist among them."

"I wonder if they left a single victim," I remarked, leaning far out of the opening in the rocky wall to inspect the temple better. Directly below me the water lapped the very side of the wall, there being a break in the bowlders at this point as there was at several other places about the side of the temple.

My hands were resting upon a small piece of granite which formed a part of the wall, and all my weight upon it proved too much for it. It slipped and I lunged forward. There was nothing to save myself and I plunged headforemost into the water below.

Fortunately the tank was deep at this point, and I suffered no injury from the fall, but as I was rising to the surface my mind filled with the horrors of my position as I thought of the terrible doom which awaited me the moment the eyes of the reptiles fell upon the creature that had disturbed their slumber.

As long as I could I remained beneath the surface, swimming rapidly in the direction of the islands that I might prolong my life to the utmost. At last I was forced to rise for air, and as I cast a terrified glance in the direction of the Mahars and the thipdars I was almost stunned to see that not a single one remained upon the rocks where I had last seen them, nor as I searched the temple with my eyes could I discern any within it.

For a moment I was puzzled to account for the thing, until I realized that the reptiles, being deaf, could not have been disturbed by the noise my body made when it hit the water, and that as there is no such thing as time within Pellucidar there was no telling how long I had been beneath the surface. It was a difficult thing to attempt to figure out by earthly standards—this matter of elapsed time—but when I set myself to it I began to realize that I might have been submerged a second or a month or not at all. You have no conception of the strange contradictions and impossibilities which arise when all methods of measuring time, as we know them upon earth, are non-existent.

I was about to congratulate myself upon the miracle which had saved me for the moment, when the memory of the hypnotic powers of the Mahars filled me with apprehension lest they be practicing their uncanny art upon me to the end that I merely imagined that I was alone in the temple. At the thought cold sweat broke out upon me from every pore, and as I crawled from the water onto one of the tiny islands I was trembling like a leaf—you cannot imagine the awful horror which even the simple thought of the repulsive Mahars of Pellucidar induces in the human mind, and to feel that you are in their power—that they are crawling, slimy, and abhorrent, to drag you down beneath the waters and devour you! It is frightful.

But they did not come, and at last I came to the conclusion that I was indeed alone within the temple. How long I should be alone was the next question to assail me as I swam frantically about once more in search of a means to escape.

Several times I called to Ja, but he must have left after I tumbled into the tank, for I received no response to my cries. Doubtless he had felt as certain of my doom when he saw me topple from our hiding place as I had, and lest he too should be discovered, had hastened from the temple and back to his village.

I knew that there must be some entrance to the building beside the doorways in the roof, for it did not seem reasonable to believe that the thousands of slaves which were brought here to feed the Mahars the human flesh they craved would all be carried through the air, and so I continued my search until at last it was rewarded by the discovery of several loose granite blocks in the masonry at one end of the temple.

A little effort proved sufficient to dislodge enough of these stones to permit me to crawl through into the clearing, and a moment later I had scurried across the intervening space to the dense jungle beyond.

Here I sank panting and trembling upon the matted grasses beneath the giant trees, for I felt that I had escaped from the grinning fangs of death out of the depths of my own grave. Whatever dangers lay hidden in this island jungle, there could be none so fearsome as those which I had just escaped. I knew that I could meet death bravely enough if it but came in the form of some familiar beast or man—anything other than the hideous and uncanny Mahars.

IX

THE FACE OF DEATH

I must have fallen asleep from exhaustion. When I awoke I was very hungry, and after busying myself searching for fruit for a while, I set off through the jungle to find the beach. I knew that the island was not so large but that I could easily find the sea if I did but move in a straight line, but there came the difficulty as there was no way in which I could direct my course and hold it, the sun, of course, being always directly above my head, and the trees so thickly set that I could see no distant object which might serve to guide me in a straight line.

As it was I must have walked for a great distance since I ate four times and slept twice before I reached the sea, but at last I did so, and my pleasure at the sight of it was greatly enhanced by the chance discovery of a hidden canoe among the bushes through which I had stumbled just prior to coming upon the beach.

I can tell you that it did not take me long to pull that awkward craft down to the water and shove it far out from shore. My experience with Ja had taught me that if I were to steal another canoe I must be quick about it and get far beyond the owner's reach as soon as possible.

I must have come out upon the opposite side of the island from that at which Ja and I had entered it, for the mainland was nowhere in sight. For a long time I paddled around the shore, though well out, before I saw the mainland in the distance. At the sight of it I lost no time in directing my course toward it, for I had long since made up my mind to return to Phutra and give myself up that I might be once more with Perry and Ghak the Hairy One.

I felt that I was a fool ever to have attempted to escape alone, especially in view of the fact that our plans were already well formulated to make a break for freedom together. Of course I realized that the chances of the success of our proposed venture were slim indeed, but I knew that I never could enjoy freedom without Perry so long as the old man lived, and I had learned that the probability that I might find him was less than slight.

Had Perry been dead, I should gladly have pitted my strength and wit against the savage and primordial world in which I found myself. I could have lived in seclusion within some rocky cave until I had found the means to outfit myself with the crude weapons of the Stone Age, and then set out in search of her whose image had now become the constant companion of my waking hours, and the central and beloved figure of my dreams.

But, to the best of my knowledge, Perry still lived and it was my duty and wish to be again with him, that we might share the dangers and vicissitudes of the strange world we had discovered. And Ghak, too; the great, shaggy man had found a place in the hearts of us both, for he was indeed every inch a man and king. Uncouth, perhaps, and brutal, too, if judged too harshly by the standards of effete twentieth-century civilization, but withal noble, dignified, chivalrous, and loveable.

Chance carried me to the very beach upon which I had discovered Ja's canoe, and a short time later I was scrambling up the steep bank to retrace my steps from the plain of Phutra. But my troubles came when I entered the cañon beyond the summit, for here I found that several of them centered at the point where I crossed the divide, and which one I had traversed to reach the pass I could not for the life of me remember.

It was all a matter of chance and so I set off down that which seemed the easiest going, and in this I made the same mistake that many of us do in selecting the path along which we shall follow out the course of our lives, and again learned that it is not always best to follow the line of least resistance.

By the time I had eaten eight meals and slept twice I was convinced that I was upon the wrong trail, for between Phutra and the inland sea I had not slept at all, and had eaten but once. To retrace my steps to the summit of the divide and explore another cañon seemed the only solution of my problem, but a sudden widening and levelness of the cañon just before me seemed to suggest that it was about to open into a level country, and with the lure of discovery strong upon me I decided to proceed but a short distance farther before I turned back.

The next turn of the cañon brought me to its mouth, and before me I saw a narrow plain leading down to an ocean. At my right the side of the cañon continued to the water's edge, the valley lying to my left, and the foot of it running gradually into the sea, where it formed a broad level beach.

Clumps of strange trees dotted the landscape here and there almost to the water, and rank grass and ferns grew between. From the nature of the vegetation I was convinced that the land between the ocean and the foothills was swampy, though directly before me it seemed dry enough all the way to the sandy strip along which the restless waters advanced and retreated.

Curiosity prompted me to walk down to the beach, for the scene was very beautiful. As I passed along beside the deep and tangled vegetation of the swamp I thought that I saw a movement of the ferns at my left, but though I stopped a moment to look it was not repeated, and if anything lay hid there my eyes could not penetrate the dense foliage to discern it.

Presently I stood upon the beach looking out over the wide and lonely sea across whose forbidding bosom no human being had yet ventured, to discover what strange and mysterious lands lay beyond, or what its invisible islands held of riches, wonders, or adventure. What savage faces, what fierce and formidable beasts were this very instant watching the lapping of the waves upon its farther shore! How far did it extend? Perry had told me that the seas of Pellucidar were small in comparison with those of the outer crust, but even so this great ocean might stretch its broad expanse for thousands of miles. For countless ages it had rolled up and down its countless miles of shore, and yet today it remained all unknown beyond the tiny strip that was visible from its beaches.

The fascination of speculation was strong upon me. It was as though I had been carried back to the birth time of our own outer world to look upon its lands and seas ages before man had traversed either. Here was a new world, all untouched. It called to me to explore it. I was dreaming of the excitement and adventure which lay before us could Perry and I but escape the Mahars, when something, a slight noise I imagine, drew my attention behind me.

As I turned, romance, adventure, and discovery in the abstract took wing before the terrible embodiment of all three in concrete form that I beheld advancing upon me.

A huge, slimy amphibian it was, with toad-like body and the mighty jaws of an alligator. Its immense carcass must have weighed tons, and yet it moved swiftly and silently toward me. Upon one hand was the bluff that ran from the cañon to the sea, on the other the fearsome swamp from which the creature had sneaked upon me, behind lay the mighty untracked sea, and before me in the center of the narrow way that led to safety stood this huge mountain of terrible and menacing flesh.

A single glance at the thing was sufficient to assure me that I was facing one of those long-extinct, prehistoric creatures whose fossilized remains are found within the outer crust as far back as the Triassic formation, a gigantic labyrinthodon. And there I was, unarmed, and, with the exception of a loin cloth, as naked as I had come into the world. I could imagine how my first ancestor felt that distant, prehistoric morn that he encountered for the first time the terrifying progenitor of the thing that had me cornered now beside the restless, mysterious sea.

Unquestionably he had escaped, or I should not have been within Pellucidar or elsewhere, and I wished at that moment that he had handed down to me with the various attributes that I presumed I have inherited from him, the specific application of the instinct of self-preservation which saved him from the fate which loomed so close before me today.

To seek escape in the swamp or in the ocean would have been similar to jumping into a den of lions to escape one upon the outside. The sea and swamp both were doubtless alive with these mighty, carnivorous amphibians, and if not, the individual that menaced me would pursue me into either the sea or the swamp with equal facility.

There seemed nothing to do but stand supinely and await my end. I thought of Perry—how he would wonder what had become of me. I thought of my friends of the outer world, and of how they all would go on living their lives in total ignorance of the strange and terrible fate that had overtaken me, or unguessing the weird surroundings which had witnessed the last frightful agony of my extinction. And with these thoughts came a realization of how unimportant to the life and happiness of the world is the existence of any one of us. We may be snuffed out without an instant's warning, and for a brief day our friends speak of us with subdued voices. The following morning, while the first worm is busily engaged in testing the construction of our coffin, they are teeing up for the first hole to suffer more acute sorrow over a sliced ball than they did over our, to us, untimely demise. The labyrinthodon was coming more slowly now. He seemed to realize that escape for me was impossible, and I could have sworn that his huge, fanged jaws grinned in pleasurable appreciation of my predicament, or was it in anticipation of the juicy morsel which would so soon be pulp between those formidable teeth?

He was about fifty feet from me when I heard a voice calling to me from the direction of the bluff at my left. I looked and could have shouted in delight at the sight that met my eyes, for there stood Ja, waving frantically to me, and urging me to run for it to the cliff's base.

I had no idea that I should escape the monster that had marked me for his breakfast, but at least I should not die alone. Human eyes would watch me end. It was cold comfort I presume, but yet I derived some slight peace of mind from the contemplation of it.

To run seemed ridiculous, especially toward that steep and unscalable cliff, and yet I did so, and as I ran I saw Ja, agile as a monkey, crawl down the precipitous face of the rocks, clinging to small projections, and the tough creepers that had found root-hold here and there.

The labyrinthodon evidently thought that Ja was coming to double his portion of human flesh, so he was in no haste to pursue me to the cliff and frighten away this other tidbit. Instead he merely trotted along behind me.

As I approached the foot of the cliff I saw what Ja intended doing, but I doubted if the thing would prove successful. He had come down to within twenty feet of the bottom, and there, clinging with one hand to a small ledge, and with his feet resting, precariously upon tiny bushes that grew from the solid face of the rock, he lowered the point of his long spear until it hung some six feet above the ground.

To clamber up that slim shaft without dragging Ja down and precipitating both to the same doom from which the copper-colored one was attempting to save me seemed utterly impossible, and as I came near the spear I told Ja so, and that I could not risk him to try to save myself.

But he insisted that he knew what he was doing and was in no danger himself.

"The danger is still yours," he called, "for unless you move much more rapidly than you are now, the *sithic* will be upon you and drag you back before ever you are halfway up the spear—he can rear up and reach you with ease anywhere below where I stand."

Well, Ja should know his own business, I thought, and so I grasped the spear and clambered up toward the red man as rapidly as I could—being so far removed from my simian ancestors as I am. I imagine the slow-witted sithic, as Ja called him, suddenly realized our intentions and that he was quite likely to lose all his meal instead of having it doubled as he had hoped.

When he saw me clambering up that spear he let out a hiss that fairly shook the ground, and came charging after me at a terrific rate. I had reached the top of the spear by this time, or almost; another six inches would give me a hold on Ja's hand, when I felt a sudden wrench from below and glancing fearfully downward saw the mighty jaws of the monster close on the sharp point of the weapon.

I made a frantic effort to reach Ja's hand, the sithic gave a tremendous tug that came near to jerking Ja from his frail hold on the surface of the rock, the spear slipped from his fingers, and still clinging to it I plunged feet foremost toward my executioner.

At the instant that he felt the spear come away from Ja's hand the creature must have opened his huge jaws to catch me, for when I came down, still clinging to the butt end of the weapon, the point yet rested in his mouth and the result was that the sharpened end transfixed his lower jaw.

With the pain he snapped his mouth closed. I fell upon his snout, lost my hold upon the spear, rolled the length of his face and head, across his short neck onto his broad back and from there to the ground.

Scarce had I touched the earth than I was upon my feet, dashing madly for the path by which I had entered this horrible valley. A glance over my shoulder showed me the sithic engaged in pawing at the spear stuck through his lower jaw, and so busily engaged did he remain in this occupation that I had gained the safety of the cliff top before he was ready to take up the pursuit. When he did not discover me in sight within the valley he dashed, hissing into the rank vegetation of the swamp and that was the last I saw of him.

X

PHUTRA AGAIN

I hastened to the cliff edge above Ja and helped him to a secure footing. He would not listen to any thanks for his attempt to save me, which had come so near miscarrying.

"I had given you up for lost when you tumbled into the Mahar temple," he said, "for not even I could save you from their clutches, and you may imagine my surprise when on seeing a canoe dragged up upon the beach of the mainland I discovered your own footprints in the sand beside it.

"I immediately set out in search of you, knowing as I did that you must be entirely unarmed and defenseless against the many dangers which lurk upon the mainland both in the form of savage beasts and reptiles, and men as well. I had no difficulty in tracking you to this point. It is well that I arrived when I did."

"But why did you do it?" I asked, puzzled at this show of friendship on the part of a man of another world and a different race and color.

"You saved my life," he replied; "from that moment it became my duty to protect and befriend you. I would have been no true Mezop had I evaded my plain duty; but it was a pleasure in this instance for I like you. I wish that you would come and live with me. You shall become a member of my tribe. Among us there is the best of hunting and fishing, and you shall have, to choose a mate from, the most beautiful girls of Pellucidar. Will you come?"

I told him about Perry then, and Dian the Beautiful, and how my duty was to them first. Afterward I should return and visit him—if I could ever find his island.

"Oh, that is easy, my friend," he said. "You need merely to come to the foot of the highest peak of the Mountains of the Clouds. There you will find a river which flows into the Lural Az. Directly opposite the mouth of the river you will see three large islands far out, so far that they are barely discernible, the one to the extreme left as you face them from the mouth of the river is Anoroc, where I rule the tribe of Anoroc."

"But how am I to find the Mountains of the Clouds?" I asked. "Men say that they are visible from half Pellucidar," he replied.

"How large is Pellucidar?" I asked, wondering what sort of theory these primitive men had concerning the form and substance of their world.

"The Mahars say it is round, like the inside of a tola shell," he answered, "but that is ridiculous, since, were it true, we should fall back were we to travel far in any direction, and all the waters of Pellucidar would run to one spot and drown us. No, Pellucidar is quite flat and extends no man knows how far in all directions. At the edges, so my ancestors have reported and handed down to me, is a great wall that prevents the earth and waters from escaping over into the burning sea whereon Pellucidar floats; but I never have been so far from Anoroc as to have seen this wall with my own eyes. However, it is quite reasonable to believe that this is true, whereas there is no reason at all in the foolish belief of the Mahars. According to them Pellucidarians who live upon the opposite side walk always with their heads pointed downward!" and Ja laughed uproariously at the very thought.

It was plain to see that the human folk of this inner world had not advanced far in learning, and the thought that the ugly Mahars had so outstripped them was a very pathetic one indeed. I wondered how many ages it would take to lift these people out of their ignorance even were it given to Perry and me to attempt it. Possibly we would be killed for our pains as were those men of the outer world who dared challenge the dense ignorance and superstitions of the earth's younger days. But it was worth the effort if the opportunity ever presented itself.

And then it occurred to me that here was an opportunity—that I might make a small beginning upon Ja, who was my friend, and thus note the effect of my teaching upon a Pellucidarian.

"Ja," I said, "what would you say were I to tell you that in so far as the Mahars' theory of the shape of Pellucidar is concerned it is correct?"

"I would say," he replied, "that either you are a fool, or took me for one."

"But, Ja," I insisted, "if their theory is incorrect how do you account for the fact that I was able to pass through the earth from the outer crust to Pellucidar. If your theory is correct all is a sea of flame beneath us, where in no peoples could exist, and yet I come from a great world that is covered with human beings, and beasts, and birds, and fishes in mighty oceans."

"You live upon the under side of Pellucidar, and walk always with your head pointed downward?" he scoffed. "And were I to believe that, my friend, I should indeed be mad."

I attempted to explain the force of gravity to him, and by the means of the dropped fruit to illustrate how impossible it would be for a body to fall off the earth under any circumstances. He listened so intently that I thought I had made an impression, and started the train of thought that would lead him to a partial under-standing of the truth. But I was mistaken.

"Your own illustration," he said finally, "proves the falsity of your theory." He dropped a fruit from his hand to the ground. "See," he said, "without support even this tiny fruit falls until it strikes something that stops it. If Pellucidar were not sup-ported upon the flaming sea it too would fall as the fruit falls—you have proven it yourself!" He had me, that time—you could see it in his eye.

It seemed a hopeless job and I gave it up, temporarily at least, for when I con-templated the necessity explanation of our solar system and the universe I realized how futile it would be to attempt to picture to Ja or any other Pellucidarian the sun, the moon, the planets, and the countless stars. Those born within the inner world could no more conceive of such things than can we of the outer crust reduce to factors appreciable to our finite minds such terms as space and eternity.

"Well, Ja," I laughed, "whether we be walking with our feet up or down, here we are, and the question of greatest importance is not so much where we came from as where we are going now. For my part I wish that you could guide me to Phutra where I may give myself up to the Mahars once more that my friends and I may work out the plan of escape which the Sagoths interrupted when they gathered us together and drove us to the arena to witness the punishment of the slaves who killed the guardsman. I wish now that I had not left the arena for by this time my friends and I might have made good our escape, whereas this delay may mean the wrecking of all our plans, which depended for their consummation upon the con-tinued sleep of the three Mahars who lay in the pit beneath the building in which we were confined."

"You would return to captivity?" cried Ja.

"My friends are there," I replied, "the only friends I have in Pellucidar, except yourself. What else may I do under the circumstances?"

He thought for a moment in silence. Then he shook his head sorrowfully.

"It is what a brave man and a good friend should do," he said; "yet it seems most foolish, for the Mahars will most certainly condemn you to death for running away, and so you will be accomplishing nothing for your friends by returning. Never in all my life have I heard of a prisoner returning to the Mahars of his own free will. There are but few who escape them, though some do, and these would rather die than be recaptured."

"I see no other way, Ja," I said, "though I can assure you that I would rather go to Sheol after Perry than to Phutra. However, Perry is much too pious to make the probability at all great that I should ever be called upon to rescue him from the former locality."

Ja asked me what Sheol was, and when I explained, as best I could, he said, "You are speaking of Molop Az, the flaming sea upon which Pellucidar floats. All the dead who are buried in the ground go there. Piece by piece they are carried down to Molop Az by the little demons who dwell there. We know this because when graves are opened we find that the bodies have been partially or entirely borne off. That is why we of Anoroc place our dead in high trees where the birds may find them and bear them bit by bit to the Dead World above the Land of Awful Shadow. If we kill an enemy we place his body in the ground that it may go to Molop Az."

As we talked we had been walking up the cañon down which I had come to the great ocean and the sithic. Ja did his best to dissuade me from returning to Phutra, but when he saw that I was determined to do so, he consented to guide me to a point from which I could see the plain where lay the city. To my surprise the distance was but short from the beach where I had again met Ja. It was evident that I had spent much time following the windings of a tortuous canon, while just beyond the ridge lay the city of Phutra near to which I must have come several times.

As we topped the ridge and saw the granite gate towers dotting the flowered plain at our feet Ja made a final effort to persuade me to abandon my mad purpose and return with him to Anoroc, but I was firm in my resolve, and at last he bid me good-bye, assured in his own mind that he was looking upon me for the last time.

I was sorry to part with Ja, for I had come to like him very much indeed. With his hidden city upon the island of Anoroc as a base, and his savage warriors as escort Perry and I could have accomplished much in the line of exploration, and I hoped that were we successful in our effort to escape we might return to Anoroc later.

There was, however, one great thing to be accomplished first—at least it was the great thing to me—the finding of Dian the Beautiful. I wanted to make amends for the affront I had put upon her in my ignorance, and I wanted to—well, I wanted to see her again, and to be with her.

Down the hillside I made my way into the gorgeous field of flowers, and then across the rolling land toward the shadowless columns that guard the ways to buried Phutra. At a quarter-mile from the nearest entrance I was discovered by the Sagoth guard, and in an instant four of the gorilla-men were dashing toward me.

Though they brandished their long spears and yelled like wild Comanches I paid not the slightest attention to them, walking quietly toward them as though unaware of their existence. My manner had the effect upon them that I had hoped, and as we came quite near together they ceased their savage shouting. It was evident that they had expected me to turn and flee at sight of them, thus presenting that which they most enjoyed, a moving human target at which to cast their spears.

"What do you here?" shouted one, and then as he recognized me, "Ho! It is the slave who claims to be from another world—he who escaped when the thag ran amuck within the amphitheater. But why do you return, having once made good your escape?"

"I did not 'escape,' " I replied. "I but ran away to avoid the thag, as did others, and coming into a long passage I became confused and lost my way in the foothills beyond Phutra. Only now have I found my way back."

"And you come of your free will back to Phutra!" exclaimed one of the guardsmen.

"Where else might I go?" I asked. "I am a stranger within Pellucidar and know no other where than Phutra. Why should I not desire to be in Phutra? Am I not well fed and well treated? Am I not happy? What better lot could man desire?"

The Sagoths scratched their heads. This was a new one on them, and so being stupid brutes they took me to their masters whom they felt would be better fitted to solve the riddle of my return, for riddle they still considered it.

I had spoken to the Sagoths as I had for the purpose of throwing them off the scent of my purposed attempt at escape. If they thought that I was so satisfied with my lot within Phutra that I would voluntarily return when I had once had so excellent an opportunity to escape, they would never for an instant imagine that I could be occupied in arranging another escape immediately upon my return to the city.

So they led me before a slimy Mahar who clung to a slimy rock within the large room that was the thing's office. With cold, reptilian eyes the creature seemed to bore through the thin veneer of my deceit and read my inmost thoughts. It heeded the story which the Sagoths told of my return to Phutra, watching the gorilla-men's lips and fingers during the recital. Then it questioned me through one of the Sagoths.

"You say that you returned to Phutra of your own free will, because you think yourself better off here than elsewhere—do you not know that you may be the next chosen to give up your life in the interests of the wonderful scientific investigations that our learned ones are continually occupied with?"

I hadn't heard of anything of that nature, but I thought best not to admit it.

"I could be in no more danger here," I said, "than naked and unarmed in the savage jungles or upon the lonely plains of Pellucidar. I was fortunate, I think, to return to Phutra at all. As it was I barely escaped death within the jaws of a huge sithic. No, I am sure that I am safer in the hands of intelligent creatures such as rule Phutra. At least such would be the case in my own world, where human beings like myself rule supreme. There the higher races of man extend protection and hospitality to the stranger within their gates, and being a stranger here I naturally assumed that a like courtesy would be accorded me."

The Mahar looked at me in silence for some time after I ceased speaking and the Sagoth had translated my words to his master. The creature seemed deep in thought. Presently he communicated some message to the Sagoth. The latter turned, and motioning me to follow him, left the presence of the reptile. Behind and on either side of me marched the balance of the guard.

"What are they going to do with me?" I asked the fellow at my right.

"You are to appear before the learned ones who will question you regarding this strange world from which you say you come."

After a moment's silence he turned to me again.

"Do you happen to know," he asked, "what the Mahars do to slaves who lie to them?"

"No," I replied, "nor does it interest me, as I have no intention of lying to the Mahars."

"Then be careful that you don't repeat the impossible tale you told Sol-to-to just now—another world, indeed, where human beings rule!" he concluded in fine scorn.

"But it is the truth," I insisted. "From where else then did I come? I am not of Pellucidar. Anyone with half an eye could see that."

"It is your misfortune then," he remarked dryly, "that you may not be judged by one with but half an eye."

"What will they do with me," I asked, "if they do not have a mind to believe me?"

"You may be sentenced to the arena, or go to the pits to be used in research work by the learned ones," he replied.

"And what will they do with me there?" I persisted.

"No one knows except the Mahars and those who go to the pits with them, but as the latter never return, their knowledge does them but little good. It is said that the learned ones cut up their subjects while they are yet alive, thus learning many useful things. However I should not imagine that it would prove very useful to him who was being cut up; but of course this is all but conjecture. The chances are that ere long you will know much more about it than I," and he grinned as he spoke. The Sagoths have a well-developed sense of humor.

"And suppose it is the arena," I continued; "what then?"

"You saw the two who met the tarag and the thag the time that you escaped?" he said.

"Yes."

"Your end in the arena would be similar to what was intended for them," he explained, "though of course the same kinds of animals might not be employed."

"It is sure death in either event?" I asked.

"What becomes of those who go below with the learned ones I do not know, nor does any other," he replied; "but those who go to the arena may come out alive and thus regain their liberty, as did the two whom you saw."

"They gained their liberty? And how?"

"It is the custom of the Mahars to liberate those who remain alive within the arena after the beasts depart or are killed. Thus it has happened that several mighty warriors from far distant lands, whom we have captured on our slave raids, have battled the brutes turned in upon them and slain them, thereby winning their freedom. In the instance which you witnessed the beasts killed each other, but the result was the same—the man and woman were liberated, furnished with weapons, and started on their homeward journey. Upon the left shoulder of each a mark was burned—the mark of the Mahars—which will forever protect these two from slaving parties."

"There is a slender chance for me then if I be sent to the arena, and none at all if the learned ones drag me to the pits?"

"You are quite right," he replied; "but do not felicitate yourself too quickly should you be sent to the arena, for there is scarce one in a thousand who comes out alive."

To my surprise they returned me to the same building in which I had been confined with Perry and Ghak before my escape. At the doorway I was turned over to the guards there.

"He will doubtless be called before the investigators shortly," said he who had brought me back, "so have him in readiness."

The guards in whose hands I now found myself, upon hearing that I had returned of my own volition to Phutra evidently felt that it would be safe to give me liberty within the building as had been the custom before I had escaped, and so I was told to return to whatever duty had been mine formerly.

My first act was to hunt up Perry; whom I found poring as usual over the great tomes that he was supposed to be merely dusting and rearranging upon new shelves.

As I entered the room he glanced up and nodded pleasantly to me, only to resume his work as though I had never been away at all. I was both astonished and hurt at his indifference. And to think that I was risking death to return to him purely from a sense of duty and affection!

"Why, Perry!" I exclaimed, "haven't you a word for me after my long absence?"

"Long absence!" he repeated in evident astonishment. "What do you mean?"

"Are you crazy, Perry? Do you mean to say that you have not missed me since that time we were separated by the charging thag within the arena?"

" 'That time,' " he repeated. "Why man, I have but just returned from the arena! You reached here almost as soon as I. Had you been much later I should indeed have been worried, and as it is I had intended asking you about how you escaped the beast as soon as I had completed the translation of this most interesting passage."

"Perry, you *are* mad," I exclaimed. "Why, the Lord only knows how long I have been away. I have been to other lands, discovered a new race of humans within Pellucidar, seen the Mahars at their worship in their hidden temple, and barely escaped with my life from them and from a great labyrinthodon that I met afterward, following my long and tedious wanderings across an unknown world. I must have been away for months, Perry, and now you barely look up from your work when I return and insist that we have been separated but a moment. Is that any way to treat a friend? I'm surprised at you, Perry, and if I'd thought for a moment that you cared no more for me than this I should not have returned to chance death at the hands of the Mahars for your sake."

The old man looked at me for a long time before he spoke. There was a puzzled expression upon his wrinkled face, and a look of hurt sorrow in his eyes.

"David, my boy," he said, "how could you for a moment doubt my love for you? There is something strange here that I cannot understand. I know that I am not mad, and I am equally sure that you are not; but how in the world are we to account for the strange hallucinations that each of us seems to harbor relative to the passage of time since last we saw each other. You are positive that months have gone by, while to me it seems equally certain that not more than an hour ago I sat beside you in the amphitheater. Can it be that both of us are right and at the same time both are wrong? First tell me what time is, and then maybe I can solve our problem. Do you catch my meaning?"

I didn't and said so.

"Yes," continued the old man, "we are both right. To me, bent over my book here, there has been no lapse of time. I have done little or nothing to waste my energies and so have required neither food nor sleep, but you, on the contrary, have walked and fought and wasted strength and tissue which must needs be rebuilt by nutriment and food, and so, having eaten and slept many times since last you saw me you naturally measure the lapse of time largely by these acts. As a matter of fact, David, I am rapidly coming to the conviction that there is no such thing as time—surely there can be no time here within Pellucidar, where there are no means for measuring or recording time. Why, the Mahars themselves take no account of such a thing as time. I find here in all their literary works but a single tense, the present. There seems to be neither past nor future with them. Of course it is impossible for our outer-earthly minds to grasp such a condition, but our recent experiences seem to demonstrate its existence."

It was too big a subject for me, and I said so, but Perry seemed to enjoy nothing better than speculating upon it, and after listening with interest to my account of the adventures through which I had passed he returned once more to the subject, which he was enlarging upon with considerable fluency when he was interrupted by the entrance of a Sagoth.

"Come!" commanded the intruder, beckoning to me. "The investigators would speak with you."

"Good-bye, Perry!" I said, clasping the old man's hand. "There may be nothing but the present and no such thing as time, but I feel that I am about to take a trip into the hereafter from which I shall never return. If you and Ghak should manage to escape I want you to promise me that you will find Dian the Beautiful and tell her that with my last words I asked her forgiveness for the unintentional affront I put upon her, and that my one wish was to be spared long enough to right the wrong that I had done her."

Tears came to Perry's eyes.

"I cannot believe but that you will return, David," he said. "It would be awful to think of living out the balance of my life without you among these hateful and repulsive creatures. If you are taken away I shall never escape, for I feel that I am as well off here as I should be anywhere within this buried world. Good-bye, my boy, good-bye!" and then his old voice faltered and broke, and as he hid his face in his hands the Sagoth guardsman grasped me roughly by the shoulder and hustled me from the chamber.

XI

FOUR DEAD MAHARS

A moment later I was standing before a dozen Mahars—the social investigators of Phutra. They asked me many questions, through a Sagoth interpreter. I answered them all truthfully. They seemed particularly interested in my account of the outer earth and the strange vehicle which had brought Perry and me to Pellucidar. I thought that I had convinced them, and after they had sat in silence for a long time following my examination, I expected to be ordered returned to my quarters.

During this apparent silence they were debating through the medium of strange, unspoken language the merits of my tale. At last the head of the tribunal communicated the result of their conference to the officer in charge of the Sagoth guard.

"Come," he said to me, "you are sentenced to the experimental pits for having dared to insult the intelligence of the mighty ones with the ridiculous tale you have had the temerity to unfold to them."

"Do you mean that they do not believe me?" I asked, totally astonished.

"Believe you!" he laughed. "Do you mean to say that you expected any one to believe so impossible a lie?"

It was hopeless, and so I walked in silence beside my guard down through the dark corridors and runways toward my awful doom. At a low level we came upon a number of lighted chambers in which we saw many Mahars engaged in various occupations. To one of these chambers my guard escorted me, and before leaving they chained me to a side wall. There were other humans similarly chained. Upon a long table lay a victim even as I was ushered into the room. Several Mahars stood about the poor creature holding him down so that he could not move. Another, grasping a sharp knife with her three-toed fore foot, was laying open the victim's chest and abdomen. No anesthetic had been administered and the shrieks and groans of the tortured man were terrible to hear. This, indeed, was vivisection with a vengeance. Cold sweat broke out upon me as I realized that soon my turn would come. And to think that where there was no such thing as time I might easily imagine that my suffering was enduring for months before death finally released me!

The Mahars had paid not the slightest attention to me as I had been brought into the room. So deeply immersed were they in their work that I am sure they did not even know that the Sagoths had entered with me. The door was close by. Would that I could reach it! But those heavy chains precluded any such possibility. I looked about for some means of escape from my bonds. Upon the floor between me and the Mahars lay a tiny surgical instrument which one of them must have dropped. It looked not unlike a button-hook, but was much smaller, and its point was sharpened. A hundred times in my boyhood days had I picked locks with a buttonhook. Could I but reach that little bit of polished steel I might yet effect at least a temporary escape.

Crawling to the limit of my chain, I found that by reaching one hand as far out as I could my fingers still fell an inch short of the coveted instrument. It was tantalizing! Stretch every fiber of my being as I would, I could not quite make it.

At last I turned about and extended one foot toward the object. My heart came to my throat! I could just touch the thing! But suppose that in my effort to drag it toward me I should accidentally shove it still farther away and thus entirely out of reach! Cold sweat broke out upon me from every pore. Slowly and cautiously I made the effort. My toes dropped upon the cold metal. Gradually I worked it toward me until I felt that it was within reach of my hand and a moment later I had turned about and the precious thing was in my grasp.

Assiduously I fell to work upon the Mahar lock that held my chain. It was pitifully simple. A child might have picked it, and a moment later I was free. The Mahars were now evidently completing their work at the table. One already turned away and was examining other victims, evidently with the intention of selecting the next subject.

Those at the table had their backs toward me. But for the creature walking toward us I might have escaped that moment. Slowly the thing approached me, when its attention was attracted by a huge slave chained a few yards to my right. Here the reptile stopped and commenced to go over the poor devil carefully, and as it did so its back turned toward me for an instant, and in that instant I gave two mighty leaps that carried me out of the chamber into the corridor beyond, down which I raced with all the speed I could command.

Where I was, or whither I was going, I knew not. My only thought was to place as much distance as possible between me and that frightful chamber of torture.

Presently I reduced my speed to a brisk walk, and later realizing the danger of running into some new predicament, were I not careful, I moved still more slowly and cautiously. After a time I came to a passage that seemed in some mysterious way familiar to me, and presently, chancing to glance within a chamber which led from the corridor I saw three Mahars curled up in slumber upon a bed of skins. I could have shouted aloud in joy and relief. It was the same corridor and the same Mahars that I had intended to have lead so important a role in our escape from Phutra. Providence had indeed been kind to me, for the reptiles still slept.

My one great danger now lay in returning to the upper levels in search of Perry and Ghak, but there was nothing else to be done, and so I hastened upward. When I came to the frequented portions of the building, I found a large burden of skins in a corner and these I lifted to my head, carrying them in such a way that ends and corners fell down about my shoulders completely hiding my face. Thus disguised I found Perry and Ghak together in the chamber where we had been wont to eat and sleep.

Both were glad to see me, it was needless to say, though of course they had known nothing of the fate that had been meted out to me by my judges. It was decided that no time should now be lost before attempting to put our plan of escape to the test, as I could not hope to remain hidden from the Sagoths long, nor could I forever carry that bale of skins about upon my head without arousing suspicion. However it seemed likely that it would carry me once more safely through the crowded passages and chambers of the upper levels, and so I set out with Perry and Ghak—the stench of the illy cured pelts fairly choking me.

Together we repaired to the first tier of corridors beneath the main floor of the buildings, and here Perry and Ghak halted to await me. The buildings are cut out of the solid limestone formation. There is nothing at all remarkable about their architecture. The rooms are sometimes rectangular, sometimes circular, and again oval in shape. The corridors which connect them are narrow and not always straight. The chambers are lighted by diffused sunlight reflected through tubes similar to those by which the avenues are lighted. The lower the tiers of chambers, the darker. Most of the corridors are entirely unlighted. The Mahars can see quite well in semidarkness.

Down to the main floor we encountered many Mahars, Sagoths, and slaves; but no attention was paid to us as we had become a part of the domestic life of the building. There was but a single entrance leading from the place into the avenue and this was well guarded by Sagoths—this doorway alone were we forbidden to pass. It is true that we were not supposed to enter the deeper corridors and apartments except on special occasions when we were instructed to do so; but as we were considered a lower order without intelligence there was little reason to fear that we could accomplish any harm by so doing, and so we were not hindered as we entered the corridor which led below.

Wrapped in a skin I carried three swords, and the two bows, and the arrows which Perry and I had fashioned. As many slaves bore skin-wrapped burdens to and fro my load attracted no comment. Where I left Ghak and Perry there were no other creatures in sight, and so I withdrew one sword from the package, and leaving the balance of the weapons with Perry, started on alone toward the lower levels.

Having come to the apartment in which the three Mahars slept I entered silently on tiptoe, forgetting that the creatures were without the sense of hearing. With a quick thrust through the heart I disposed of the first but my second thrust was not so fortunate, so that before I could kill the next of my victims it had hurled itself against the third, who sprang quickly up, facing me with wide-distended jaws. But fighting is not the occupation which the race of Mahars loves, and when the thing saw that I already had dispatched two of its companions, and that my sword was red with their blood, it made a dash to escape me. But I was too quick for it, and so, half hopping, half flying, it scurried down another corridor with me close upon its heels.

Its escape meant the utter ruin of our plan, and in all probability my instant death. This thought lent wings to my feet; but even at my best I could do no more than hold my own with the leaping thing before me.

Of a sudden it turned into an apartment on the right of the corridor, and an instant later as I rushed in I found myself facing two of the Mahars. The one who had been there when we entered had been occupied with a number of metal vessels, into which had been put powders and liquids as I judged from the array of flasks standing about upon the bench where it had been working. In an instant I realized what I had stumbled upon. It was the very room for the finding of which Perry had given me minute directions. It was the buried chamber in which was hidden the Great Secret of the race of Mahars. And on the bench beside the flasks lay the skin-bound book which held the only copy of the thing I was to have sought, after dispatching the three Mahars in their sleep.

There was no exit from the room other than the doorway in which I now stood facing the two frightful reptiles. Cornered, I knew that they would fight like demons, and they were well equipped to fight if fight they must. Together they launched themselves upon me, and though I ran one of them through the heart on the instant, the other fastened its gleaming fangs about my sword arm above the elbow, and then with her sharp talons commenced to rake me about the body, evidently intent upon disemboweling me. I saw that it was useless to hope that I might release my arm from that powerful, viselike grip which seemed to be severing my arm from my body. The pain I suffered was intense, but it only served to spur me to greater efforts to overcome my antagonist.

Back and forth across the floor we struggled—the Mahar dealing me terrific, cutting blows with her fore feet, while I attempted to protect my body with my left hand, at the same time watching for an opportunity to transfer my blade from my now useless sword hand to its rapidly weakening mate. At last I was successful, and with what seemed to me my last ounce of strength I ran the blade through the ugly body of my foe.

Soundless, as it had fought, it died, and though weak from pain and loss of blood, it was with an emotion of triumphant pride that I stepped across its convulsively stiffening corpse to snatch up the most potent secret of a world. A single glance assured me it was the very thing that Perry had described to me.

And as I grasped it did I think of what it meant to the human race of Pellucidar—did there flash through my mind the thought that countless generations of my own kind yet unborn would have reason to worship me for the thing that I had accomplished for them? Did I? I did not. I thought of a beautiful oval face, gazing out of limpid eyes, through a waving mass of jet-black hair. I thought of red, red lips, God-made for kissing. And of a sudden, apropos of nothing, standing there alone in the secret chamber of the Mahars of Pellucidar, I realized that I loved Dian the Beautiful.

XII

PURSUIT

For an instant I stood there thinking of her, and then, with a sigh, I tucked the book in the thong that supported my loin cloth, and turned to leave the apartment. At the bottom of the corridor which leads aloft from the lower chambers I whistled in accordance with the prearranged signal which was to announce to Perry and Ghak that I had been successful. A moment later they stood beside me, and to my surprise I saw that Hooja the Sly One accompanied them.

"He joined us," explained Perry, "and would not be denied. The fellow is a fox. He scents escape, and rather than be thwarted of our chance now I told him that I would bring him to you, and let you decide whether he might accompany us."

I had no love for Hooja, and no confidence in him. I was sure that if he thought it would profit him he would betray us; but I saw no way out of it now, and the fact that I had killed four Mahars instead of only the three I had expected to, made it possible to include the fellow in our scheme of escape.

"Very well," I said, "you may come with us, Hooja; but at the first intimation of treachery I shall run my sword through you. Do you understand?"

He said that he did.

Some time later we had removed the skins from the four Mahars, and so succeeded in crawling inside of them ourselves that there seemed an excellent chance for us to pass unnoticed from Phutra. It was not an easy thing to fasten the hides together where we had split them along the belly to remove them from their carcasses, but by remaining out until the others had all been sewed in with my help, and then leaving an aperture in the breast of Perry's skin through which he could pass his hands to sew me up, we were enabled to accomplish our design to really much better purpose than I had hoped. We managed to keep the heads erect by passing our swords up through the necks, and by the same means were enabled to move them about in a life-like manner. We had our greatest difficulty with the webbed feet, but even that problem was finally solved, so that when we moved about we did so quite naturally. Tiny holes punctured in the baggy throats into which our heads were thrust permitted us to see well enough to guide our progress.

Thus we started up toward the main floor of the building. Ghak headed the strange procession, then came Perry, followed by Hooja, while I brought up the rear, after admonishing Hooja that I had so arranged my sword that I could thrust it through the head of my disguise into his vitals were he to show any indication of faltering.

As the noise of hurrying feet warned me that we were entering the busy corridors of the main level, my heart came up into my mouth. It is with no sense of shame that I admit that I was frightened—never before in my life, nor since, did I experience any such agony of soul-searing fear and suspense as enveloped me. If it be possible to sweat blood, I sweat it then.

Slowly, after the manner of locomotion habitual to the Mahars, when they are not using their wings, we crept through throngs of busy slaves, Sagoths, and Mahars. After what seemed an eternity we reached the outer door which leads into the main avenue of Phutra. Many Sagoths loitered near the opening. They glanced at Ghak as he padded between them. Then Perry passed, and then Hooja. Now it was my turn, and then in a sudden fit of freezing terror I realized that the warm blood from my wounded arm was trickling down through the dead foot of the Mahar skin I wore and leaving its tell-tale mark upon the pavement, for I saw a Sagoth call a companion's attention to it.

The guard stepped before me and pointing to my bleeding foot spoke to me in the sign language which these two races employ as a means of communication. Even had I known what he was saying I could not have replied with the dead thing that covered me. I once had seen a great Mahar freeze a presumptuous Sagoth with a look. It seemed my only hope, and so I tried it. Stopping in my tracks I moved my sword so that it made the dead head appear to turn inquiring eyes upon the gorilla-man. For a long moment I stood perfectly still, eyeing the fellow with those dead eyes. Then I lowered the head and started slowly on. For a moment all hung in the balance, but before I touched him the guard stepped to one side, and I passed on out into the avenue.

On we went up the broad street, but now we were safe for the very numbers of our enemies that surrounded us on all sides. Fortunately, there was a great concourse of Mahars repairing to the shallow lake which lies a mile or more from the city. They go there to indulge their amphibian proclivities in diving for small fish, and enjoying the cool depths of the water. It is a fresh-water lake, shallow, and free from the larger reptiles which make the use of the great seas of Pellucidar impossible for any but their own kind.

In the thick of the crowd we passed up the steps and out onto the plain. For some distance Ghak remained with the stream that was traveling toward the lake, but finally, at the bottom of a little gully he halted, and there we remained until all had passed and we were alone. Then, still in our disguises, we set off directly away from Phutra.

The heat of the vertical rays of the sun was fast making our horrible prisons unbearable, so that after passing a low divide, and entering a sheltering forest, we finally discarded the Mahar skins that had brought us thus far in safety.

I shall not weary you with the details of that bitter and galling flight. How we traveled at a dogged run until we dropped in our tracks. How we were beset by strange and terrible beasts. How we barely escaped the cruel fangs of lions and tigers the size of which would dwarf into pitiful insignificance the greatest felines of the outer world.

On and on we raced, our one thought to put as much distance between ourselves and Phutra as possible. Ghak was leading us to his own land—the land of Sari. No sign of pursuit had developed, and yet we were sure that somewhere behind us relentless Sagoths were dogging our tracks. Ghak said they never failed to hunt down their quarry until they had captured it or themselves been turned back by a superior force.

Our only hope, he said, lay in reaching his tribe which was quite strong enough in their mountain fastness to beat off any number of Sagoths.

At last, after what seemed months, and may, I now realize, have been years, we came in sight of the dun escarpment which buttressed the foothills of Sari. At almost the same instant, Hooja, who looked ever quite as much behind as before, announced that he could see a body of men far behind us topping a low ridge in our wake. It was the long-expected pursuit.

I asked Ghak if we could make Sari in time to escape them.

"We may," he replied; "but you will find that the Sagoths can move with incredible swiftness, and as they are almost tireless they are doubtless much fresher than we. Then——" he paused, glancing at Perry.

I knew what he meant. The old man was exhausted. For much of the period of our flight either Ghak or I had half supported him on the march. With such a handicap, less fleet pursuers than the Sagoths might easily overtake us before we could scale the rugged heights which confronted us.

"You and Hooja go on ahead," I said. "Perry and I will make it if we are able. We cannot travel as rapidly as you two, and there is no reason why all should be lost because of that. It can't be helped—we have simply to face it."

"I will not desert a companion," was Ghak's simple reply. I hadn't known that this great, hairy, primeval man had any such nobility of character stowed away inside him. I had always liked him, but now to my liking was added honor and respect. Yes, and love.

But still I urged him to go on ahead, insisting that if he could reach his people he might be able to bring out a sufficient force to drive off the Sagoths and rescue Perry and myself.

No, he wouldn't leave us, and that was all there was to it, but he suggested that Hooja might hurry on and warn the Sarians of the king's danger. It didn't require much urging to start Hooja—the naked idea was enough to send him leaping on ahead of us into the foothills which we now had reached.

Perry realized that he was jeopardizing Ghak's life and mine and the old fellow fairly begged us to go on without him, although I knew that he was suffering a perfect anguish of terror at the thought of falling into the hands of the Sagoths. Ghak finally solved the problem, in part, by lifting Perry in his powerful arms and carrying him. While the act cut down Ghak's speed he still could travel faster thus than when half supporting the stumbling old man.

XIII

THE SLY ONE

The Sagoths were gaining on us rapidly, for once they had sighted us they had greatly increased their speed. On and on we stumbled up the narrow cañon that Ghak had chosen to approach the heights of Sari. On either side rose precipitous cliffs of gorgeous, parti-colored rock, while beneath our feet a thick mountain grass formed a soft and noiseless carpet. Since we had entered the cañon we had had no glimpse of our pursuers, and I was commencing to hope that they had lost our trail and that we would reach the now rapidly nearing cliffs in time to scale them before we should be overtaken.

Ahead we neither saw nor heard any sign which might betoken the success of Hooja's mission. By now he should have reached the outposts of the Sarians, and we should at least hear the savage cries of the tribesmen as they swarmed to arms in answer to their king's appeal for succor. In another moment the frowning cliffs ahead should be black with primeval warriors. But nothing of the kind happened— as a matter of fact the Sly One had betrayed us. At the moment that we expected to see Sarian spearmen charging to our relief at Hooja's back, the craven traitor was sneaking around the outskirts of the nearest Sarian village, that he might come up from the other side when it was too late to save us, claiming that he had become lost among the mountains.

Hooja still harbored ill will against me because of the blow I had struck in Dian's protection, and his malevolent spirit was equal to sacrificing us all that he might be revenged upon me.

As we drew nearer the barrier cliffs and no sign of rescuing Sarians appeared Ghak became both angry and alarmed, and presently as the sound of rapidly approaching pursuit fell upon our ears, he called to me over his shoulder that we were lost.

A backward glance gave me a glimpse of the first of the Sagoths at the far end of a considerable stretch of cañon through which we had just passed, and then a sudden turning shut the ugly creature from my view; but the loud howl of triumphant rage which rose behind us was evidence that the gorilla-man had sighted us.

Again the cañon veered sharply to the left, but to the right another branch ran on at a lesser deviation from the general direction, so that appeared more like the main cañon than the lefthand branch. The Sagoths were now not over two hundred and fifty yards behind us, and I saw that it was hopeless for us to expect to escape other than by a ruse. There was a bare chance of saving Ghak and Perry, and as I reached the branching of the cañon I took the chance.

Pausing there I waited until the foremost Sagoth hove into sight. Ghak and Perry had disappeared around a bend in the left-hand cañon, and as the Sagoth's savage yell announced that he had seen me I turned and fled up the right-hand branch. My ruse was successful, and the entire party of man-hunters raced headlong after me up one cañon while Ghak bore Perry to safety up the other.

Running has never been my particular athletic forte, and now when my very life depended upon fleetness of foot I cannot say that I ran any better than on the occasions when my pitiful base running had called down upon my head the rooter's raucous and reproachful cries of "Ice Wagon," and "Call a cab."

The Sagoths were gaining on me rapidly. There was one in particular, fleeter than his fellows, who was perilously close. The cañon had become a rocky slit, rising roughly at a steep angle toward what seemed a pass between two abutting peaks. What lay beyond I could not even guess—possibly a sheer drop of hundreds of feet into the corresponding valley upon the other side. Could it be that I had plunged into a cul-de-sac?

Realizing that I could not hope to outdistance the Sagoths to the top of the cañon I had determined to risk all in an attempt to check them temporarily, and to this end had unslung my rudely made bow and plucked an arrow from the skin quiver which hung behind my shoulder. As I fitted the shaft with my right hand I stopped and wheeled toward the gorilla-man.

In the world of my birth I never had drawn a shaft, but since our escape from Phutra I had kept the party supplied with small game by means of my arrows, and so, through necessity, had developed a fair degree of accuracy. During our flight from Phutra I had restrung my bow with a piece of heavy gut taken from a huge tiger which Ghak and I had worried and finally dispatched with arrows, spear, and sword. The hard wood of the bow was extremely tough and this, with the strength and elasticity of my new string, gave me unwonted confidence in my weapon.

Never had I greater need of steady nerves than then—never were my nerves and muscles under better control. I sighted as carefully and deliberately as though at a straw target. The Sagoth had never before seen a bow and arrow, but of a sudden it must have swept over his dull intellect that the thing I held toward him was some sort of engine of destruction, for he too came to a halt, simultaneously swinging his hatchet for a throw. It is one of the many methods in which they employ this weapon, and the accuracy of aim which they achieve, even under the most unfavorable circumstances, is little short of miraculous.

My shaft was drawn back its full length—my eye had centered its sharp point upon the left breast of my adversary; and then he launched his hatchet and I released my arrow. At the instant that our missiles flew I leaped to one side, but the Sagoth sprang forward to follow up his attack with a spear thrust. I felt the swish of the hatchet at it grazed my head, and at the same instant my shaft pierced the Sagoth's savage heart, and with a single groan he lunged almost at my feet—stone dead. Close behind him were two more—fifty yards perhaps—but the distance gave me time to snatch up the dead guardsman's shield, for the close call his hatchet had just given me had borne in upon me the urgent need I had for one. Those which I had purloined at Phutra we had not been able to bring along because their size precluded our concealing them within the skins of the Mahars which had brought us safely from the city.

With the shield slipped well up on my left arm I let fly with another arrow, which brought down a second Sagoth, and then as his fellow's hatchet sped toward me I caught it upon the shield, and fitted another shaft for him; but he did not wait to receive it. Instead, he turned and retreated toward the main body of gorilla-men. Evidently he had seen enough of me for the moment.

Once more I took up my flight, nor were the Sagoths apparently overanxious to press their pursuit so closely as before. Unmolested I reached the top of the cañon where I found a sheer drop of two or three hundred feet to the bottom of a rocky chasm; but on the left a narrow ledge rounded the shoulder of the over-hanging cliff. Along this I advanced, and at a sudden turning, a few yards beyond the cañon's end, the path widened, and at my left I saw the opening to a large cave. Before, the ledge continued until it passed from sight about another projecting but-tress of the mountain.

Here, I felt, I could defy an army, for but a single foeman could advance upon me at a time, nor could he know that I was awaiting him until he came full upon me around the corner of the turn. About me lay scattered stones crumbled from the cliff above. They were of various sizes and shapes, but enough were of handy dimensions for use as ammunition in lieu of my precious arrows. Gathering a number of stones into a little pile beside the mouth of the cave I waited the advance of the Sagoths.

As I stood there, tense and silent, listening for the first faint sound that should announce the approach of my enemies, a slight noise from within the cave's black depths attracted my attention. It might have been produced by the moving of the great body of some huge beast rising from the rock floor of its lair. At almost the same instant I thought that I caught the scraping of hide sandals upon the ledge beyond the turn. For the next few seconds my attention was considerably divided.

And then from the inky blackness at my right I saw two flaming eyes glaring into mine. They were on a level that was over two feet above my head. It is true that the beast who owned them might be standing upon a ledge within the cave, or that it might be rearing up upon its hind legs; but I had seen enough of the monsters of Pellucidar to know that I might be facing some new and frightful Titan whose dimensions and ferocity eclipsed those of any I had seen before.

Whatever it was, it was coming slowly toward the entrance of the cave, and now, deep and forbidding, it uttered a low and ominous growl. I waited no longer to dispute possession of the ledge with the thing which owned that voice. The noise had not been loud—I doubt if the Sagoths heard it at all—but the suggestion of latent possibilities behind it was such that I knew it would only emanate from a gigantic and ferocious beast.

As I backed along the ledge I soon was past the mouth of the cave, where I no longer could see those fearful flaming eyes, but an instant later I caught sight of the fiendish face of a Sagoth as it warily advanced beyond the cliff's turn on the far side of the cave's mouth. As the fellow saw me he leaped along the ledge in pursuit, and after him came as many of his companions as could crowd upon each other's heels. At the same time the beast emerged from the cave, so that he and the Sagoths came face to face upon that narrow ledge.

The thing was an enormous cave bear, rearing its colossal bulk fully eight feet at the shoulder, while from the tip of its nose to the end of its stubby tail it was fully twelve feet in length. As it sighted the Sagoths it emitted a most frightful roar, and with open mouth charged full upon them. With a cry of terror the foremost gorilla-man turned to escape, but behind him he ran full upon his on-rushing companions.

The horror of the following seconds is indescribable. The Sagoth nearest the cave bear, finding his escape blocked, turned and leaped deliberately to an awful death upon the jagged rocks three hundred feet below. Then those giant jaws reached out and gathered in the next—there was a sickening sound of crushing bones, and the mangled corpse was dropped over the cliff's edge. Nor did the mighty beast even pause in his steady advance along the ledge.

Shrieking Sagoths were now leaping madly over the precipice to escape him, and the last I saw he rounded the turn still pursuing the demoralized remnant of the man hunters. For a long time I could hear the horrid roaring of the brute intermingled with the screams and shrieks of his victims, until finally the awful sounds dwindled and disappeared in the distance.

Later I learned from Ghak, who had finally come to his tribesmen and returned with a party to rescue me, that the *ryth,* as it is called, pursued the Sagoths until it had exterminated the entire band. Ghak was, of course, positive that I had fallen prey to the terrible creature, which, within Pellucidar, is truly the king of beasts.

Not caring to venture back into the cañon, where I might fall prey either to the cave bear or the Sagoths I continued on along the ledge, believing that by following around the mountain I could reach the land of Sari from another direction. But

I evidently became confused by the twisting and turning of the cañons and gullies, for I did not come to the land of Sari then, nor for a long time thereafter.

XIV

THE GARDEN OF EDEN

With no heavenly guide, it is little wonder that I became confused and lost in the labyrinthine maze of those mighty hills. What, in reality, I did was to pass entirely through them and come out above the valley upon the farther side. I know that I wandered for a long time, until tired and hungry I came upon a small cave in the face of the limestone formation which had taken the place of the granite farther back.

The cave which took my fancy lay halfway up the precipitous side of a lofty cliff. The way to it was such that I knew no extremely formidable beast could frequent it, nor was it large enough to make a comfortable habitat for any but the smaller mammals or reptiles. Yet it was with the utmost caution that I crawled within its dark interior.

Here I found a rather large chamber, lighted by a narrow cleft in the rock above which let the sunlight filter in in sufficient quantities partially to dispel the utter darkness which I had expected. The cave was entirely empty, nor were there any signs of its having been recently occupied. The opening was comparatively small, so that after considerable effort I was able to lug up a bowlder from the valley below which entirely blocked it.

Then I returned again to the valley for an armful of grasses and on this trip was fortunate enough to knock over an *orthopi,* the diminutive horse of Pellucidar, a little animal about the size of a fox terrier, which abounds in all parts of the inner world. Thus, with food and bedding I returned to my lair, where after a meal of raw meat, to which I had now become quite accustomed, I dragged the bowlder before the entrance and curled myself upon a bed of grasses—a naked, primeval, cave man, as savagely primitive as my prehistoric progenitors.

I awoke rested but hungry, and pushing the bowlder aside crawled out upon the little rocky shelf which was my front porch. Before me spread a small but beautiful valley, through the center of which a clear and sparkling river wound its way down to an inland sea, the blue waters of which were just visible between the two mountain ranges which embraced this little paradise. The sides of the opposite hills were green with verdure, for a great forest clothed them to the foot of the red and yellow and copper green of the towering crags which formed their summit. The valley itself was carpeted with a luxuriant grass, while here and there patches of wild flowers made great splashes of vivid color against the prevailing green.

Dotted over the face of the valley were little clusters of palmlike trees—three or four together as a rule. Beneath these stood antelope, while others grazed in the open, or wandered gracefully to a nearby ford to drink. There were several species of this beautiful animal, the most magnificent somewhat resembling the giant eland of Africa, except that their spiral horns form a complete curve backward over their ears and then forward again beneath them, ending in sharp and formidable points some two feet before the face and above the eyes. In size they remind one of a pure bred Hereford bull, yet they are very agile and fast. The broad yellow bands that stripe the dark roan of their coats made me take them for zebra when I first saw them. All in all they are handsome animals, and added the finishing touch to the strange and lovely landscape that spread before my new home.

I had determined to make the cave my headquarters, and with it as a base make a systematic exploration of the surrounding country in search of the land of Sari. First I devoured the remainder of the carcass of the *orthopi* I had killed before my last sleep. Then I hid the Great Secret in a deep niche at the back of my cave, rolled the bowlder before my front door, and with bow, arrows, sword, and shield scrambled down into the peaceful valley.

The grazing herds moved to one side as I passed through them, the little orthopi evincing the greatest wariness and galloping to safest distances. All the animals stopped feeding as I approached, and after moving to what they considered a safe distance stood contemplating me with serious eyes and up-cocked ears. Once one of the old bull antelopes of the striped species lowered his head and bellowed angrily— even taking a few steps in my direction, so that I thought he meant to charge; but after I had passed, he resumed feeding as though nothing had disturbed him.

Near the lower end of the valley I passed a number of tapirs, and across the river saw a great sadok, the enormous double-horned progenitor of the modern rhinoceros. At the valley's end the cliffs upon the left ran out into the sea, so that to pass around them as I desired to do it was necessary to scale them in search of a ledge along which I might continue my journey. Some fifty feet from the base I came upon a projection which formed a natural path along the face of the cliff, and this I followed out over the sea toward the cliff's end.

Here the ledge inclined rapidly upward toward the top of the cliffs—the stratum which formed it evidently having been forced up at this steep angle when the mountains behind it were born. As I climbed carefully up the ascent my attention suddenly was attracted aloft by the sound of strange hissing, and what resembled the flapping of wings.

And at the first glance there broke upon my horrified vision the most frightful thing I had seen even within Pellucidar. It was a giant dragon such as is pictured in the legends and fairy tales of earth folk. Its huge body must have measured forty feet in length, while the batlike wings that supported it in midair had a spread of fully thirty. Its gaping jaws were armed with long, sharp teeth, and its claw equipped with horrible talons.

The hissing noise which had first attracted my attention was issuing from its throat, and seemed to be directed at something beyond and below me which I could not see. The ledge upon which I stood terminated abruptly a few paces farther on, and as I reached the end I saw the cause of the reptile's agitation.

Some time in past ages an earthquake had produced a fault at this point, so that beyond the spot where I stood the strata had slipped down a matter of twenty feet. The result was that the continuation of my ledge lay twenty feet below me, where it ended as abruptly as did the end upon which I stood.

And here, evidently halted in flight by this insurmountable break in the ledge, stood the object of the creature's attack—a girl cowering upon the narrow platform, her face buried in her arms, as though to shut out the sight of the frightful death which hovered just above her.

The dragon was circling lower, and seemed about to dart in upon its prey. There was no time to be lost, scarce an instant in which to weigh the possible chances that I had against the awfully armed creature; but the sight of that frightened girl below me called out to all that was best in me, and the instinct for protection of the other sex, which nearly must have equaled the instinct of self-preservation in primeval man, drew me to the girl's side like an irresistible magnet.

Almost thoughtless of the consequences, I leaped from the end of the ledge upon which I stood, for the tiny shelf twenty feet below. At the same instant the dragon darted in toward the girl, but my sudden advent upon the scene must have startled him for he veered to one side, and then rose above us once more.

The noise I made as I landed beside her convinced the girl that the end had come, for she thought I was the dragon; but finally when no cruel fangs closed upon her she raised her eyes in astonishment. As they fell upon me the expression that came into them would be difficult to describe; but her feelings could scarcely have been one whit more complicated than my own—for the wide eyes that looked into mine were those of Dian the Beautiful.

"Dian!" I cried. "Dian! Thank God that I came in time."

"You?" she whispered, and then she hid her face again; nor could I tell whether she were glad or angry that I had come.

Once more the dragon was sweeping toward us, and so rapidly that I had no time to unsling my bow. All that I could do was to snatch up a rock, and hurl it at the thing's hideous face. Again my aim was true, and with a hiss of pain and rage the reptile wheeled once more and soared away.

Quickly I fitted an arrow now that I might be ready at the next attack, and as I did so I looked down at the girl, so that I surprised her in a surreptitious glance which she was stealing at me; but immediately, she again covered her face with her hands.

"Look at me, Dian," I pleaded. "Are you not glad to see me?"

She looked straight into my eyes.

"I hate you," she said, and then, as I was about to beg for a fair hearing she pointed over my shoulder. "The thipdar comes," she said, and I turned again to meet the reptile.

So this was a thipdar. I might have known it. The cruel bloodhound of the Mahars. The long-extinct pterodactyl of the outer world. But this time I met it with a weapon it never had faced before. I had selected my longest arrow, and with all my strength had bent the bow until the very tip of the shaft rested upon the thumb of my left hand, and then as the great creature darted toward us I let drive straight for that tough breast.

Hissing like the escape valve of a steam engine, the mighty creature fell turning and twisting into the sea below, my arrow buried completely in its carcass. I turned toward the girl. She was looking past me. It was evident that she had seen the thipdar die.

"Dian," I said, "won't you tell me that you are not sorry that I have found you?"

"I hate you," was her only reply; but I imagined that there was less vehemence in it than before—yet it might have been but my imagination.

"Why do you hate me, Dian?" I asked, but she did not answer me.

"What are you doing here?" I asked, "and what has happened to you since Hooja freed you from the Sagoths?"

At first I thought that she was going to ignore me entirely, but finally she thought better of it.

"I was again running away from Jubal the Ugly One," she said. "After I escaped from the Sagoths I made my way alone back to my own land; but on account of Jubal I did not dare enter the villages or let any of my friends know that I had returned for fear that Jubal might find out. By watching for a long time I found that my brother had not yet returned, and so I continued to live in a cave beside a valley which my race seldom frequents, awaiting the time that he should come back and free me from Jubal.

"But at last one of Jubal's hunters saw me as I was creeping toward my father's cave to see if my brother had yet returned and he gave the alarm and Jubal set out after me. He has been pursuing me across many lands. He cannot be far behind me now. When he comes he will kill you and carry me back to his cave. He is a terrible man. I have gone as far as I can go, and there is no escape," and she looked hopelessly up at the continuation of the ledge twenty feet above us.

"But he shall not have me," she suddenly cried, with great vehemence. "The sea is there"—she pointed over the edge of the cliff—"and the sea shall have me rather than Jubal."

"But I have you now Dian," I cried; "nor shall Jubal, nor any other have you, for you are mine," and I seized her hand, nor did I lift it above her head and let it fall in token of release.

She had risen to her feet, and was looking straight into my eyes with level gaze.

"I do not believe you," she said, "for if you meant it you would have done this when the others were present to witness it—then I should truly have been your mate; now there is no one to see you do it, for you know that without witnesses your act does not bind you to me," and she withdrew her hand from mine and turned away.

I tried to convince her that I was sincere, but she simply couldn't forget the humiliation that I had put upon her on that other occasion.

"If you mean all that you say you will have ample chance to prove it," she said, "if Jubal does not catch and kill you. I am in your power, and the treatment you accord me will be the best proof of your intentions toward me. I am not your mate, and again I tell you that I hate you, and that I should be glad if I never saw you again."

Dian certainly was candid. There was no gainsaying that. In fact I found candor and directness to be quite a marked characteristic of the cave men of Pellucidar. Finally I suggested that we make some attempt to gain my cave, where we might escape the searching Jubal, for I am free to admit that I had no considerable desire to meet the formidable and ferocious creature, of whose mighty prowess Dian had told me when I first met her. He it was who, armed with a puny knife, had met and killed a cave bear in a hand-to-hand struggle. It was Jubal who could cast his spear entirely through the armored carcass of the sadok at fifty paces. It was he who had crushed the skull of a charging dyryth with a single blow of his war club. No, I was not pining to meet the Ugly One–and it was quite certain that I should not go out and hunt for him; but the matter was taken out of my hands very quickly, as is often the way, and I did meet Jubal the Ugly One face to face.

This is how it happened. I had led Dian back along the ledge the way she had come, searching for a path that would lead us to the top of the cliff, for I knew that we could then cross over to the edge of my own little valley, where I felt certain we should find a means of ingress from the cliff top. As we proceeded along the ledge I gave Dian minute directions for finding my cave against the chance of something happening to me. I knew that she would be quite safely hidden away from pursuit once she gained the shelter of my lair, and the valley would afford her ample means of sustenance.

Also, I was very much piqued by her treatment of me. My heart was sad and heavy, and I wanted to make her feel badly by suggesting that something terrible might happen to me—that I might, in fact, be killed. But it didn't work worth a cent, at least as far as I could perceive. Dian simply shrugged those magnificent shoulders of hers, and murmured something to the effect that one was not rid of trouble so easily as that.

For a while I kept still. I was utterly squelched. And to think that I had twice protected her from attack—the last time risking my life to save hers. It was incredible that even a daughter of the Stone Age could be so ungrateful—so heartless; but maybe her heart partook of the qualities of her epoch.

Presently we found a rift in the cliff which had been widened and extended by the action of the water draining through it from the plateau above. It gave us a rather rough climb to the summit, but finally we stood upon the level mesa which stretched back for several miles to the mountain range. Behind us lay the broad inland sea, curving upward in the horizonless distance to merge into the blue of the sky, so that for all the world it looked as though the sea lapped back to arch completely over us and disappear beyond the distant mountains at our backs—the weird and uncanny aspect of the seascapes of Pellucidar balk description.

At our right lay a dense forest, but to the left the country was open and clear to the plateau's farther verge. It was in this direction that our way led, and we had turned to resume our journey when Dian touched my arm. I turned to her, thinking that she was about to make peace overtures; but I was mistaken.

"Jubal," she said, and nodded toward the forest.

I looked, and there, emerging from the dense wood, came a perfect whale of a man. He must have been seven feet tall, and proportioned accordingly. He still was too far off to distinguish his features.

"Run," I said to Dian. "I can engage him until you get a good start. Maybe I can hold him until you have gotten entirely away," and then, without a backward glance, I advanced to meet the Ugly One. I had hoped that Dian would have a kind word to say to me before she went, for she must have known that I was going to my death for her sake; but she never even so much as bid me good-bye, and it was with a heavy heart that I strode through the flower-bespangled grass to my doom.

When I had come close enough to Jubal to distinguish his features I understood how it was that he had earned the sobriquet of Ugly One. Apparently some fearful beast had ripped away one entire side of his face. The eye was gone, the nose, and all the flesh, so that his jaws and all his teeth were exposed and grinning through the horrible scar.

Formerly he may have been as good to look upon as the others of his handsome race, and it may be that the terrible result of this encounter had tended to sour an already strong and brutal character. However this may be it is quite certain that he was not a pretty sight, and now that his features, or what remained of them, were distorted in rage at the sight of Dian with another male, he was indeed most terrible to see—and much more terrible to meet.

He had broken into a run now, and as he advanced he raised his mighty spear, while I halted and fitting an arrow to my bow took as steady aim as I could. I was somewhat longer than usual, for I must confess that the sight of this awful man had wrought upon my nerves to such an extent that my knees were anything but steady. What chance had I against this mighty warrior for whom even the fiercest cave bear had no terrors! Could I hope to best one who slaughtered the sadok and dyryth singlehanded! I shuddered; but, in fairness to myself, my fear was more for Dian than for my own fate.

And then the great brute launched his massive stone-tipped spear, and I raised my shield to break the force of its terrific velocity. The impact hurled me to my knees, but the shield had deflected the missile and I was unscathed. Jubal was rushing upon me now with the only remaining weapon that he carried—a murderous-looking knife. He was too close for a careful bowshot, but I let drive at him as he came, without taking aim. My arrow pierced the fleshy part of his thigh, inflicting a painful but not disabling wound. And then he was upon me.

My agility saved me for the instant. I ducked beneath his raised arm, and when he wheeled to come at me again he found a sword's point in his face. And a moment later he felt an inch or two of it in the muscles of his knife arm, so that thereafter he went more warily.

It was a duel of strategy now—the great, hairy man maneuvering to get inside my guard where he could bring those giant thews to play, while my wits were directed to the task of keeping him at arm's length. Thrice he rushed me, and thrice I caught his knife blow upon my shield. Each time my sword found his body—once penetrating to his lung. He was covered with blood by this time, and the internal hemorrhage induced paroxysms of coughing that brought the red stream through the hideous mouth and nose, covering his face and breast with bloody froth. He was a most unlovely spectacle, but he was far from dead.

As the duel continued I began to gain confidence, for, to be perfectly candid, I had not expected to survive the first rush of that monstrous engine of ungoverned rage and hatred. And I think that Jubal, from utter contempt of me, began to change to a feeling of respect, and then in his primitive mind there evidently loomed the thought that perhaps at last he had met his master, and was facing his end.

At any rate it is only upon this hypothesis that I can account for his next act, which was in the nature of a last resort—a sort of forlorn hope, which could only have been born of the belief that if he did not kill me quickly I should kill him. It happened on the occasion of his fourth charge, when, instead of striking at me with his knife, he dropped that weapon, and seizing my sword blade in both his hands wrenched the weapon from my grasp as easily as from a babe.

Flinging it far to one side he stood motionless for just an instant glaring into my face with such a horrid leer of malignant triumph as to almost unnerve me—then he sprang for me with his bare hands. But it was Jubal's day to learn new methods of warfare. For the first time he had seen a bow and arrows, never before that duel had he beheld a sword, and now he learned what a man who knows may do with his bare fists.

As he came for me, like a great bear, I ducked again beneath his outstretched arm, and as I came up planted as clean a blow upon his jaw as ever you have seen. Down went that great mountain of flesh sprawling upon the ground. He was so surprised and dazed that he lay there for several seconds before he made any attempt to rise, and I stood over him with another dose ready when he should gain his knees.

Up he came at last, almost roaring in his rage and mortification; but he didn't stay up—I let him have a left fair on the point of the jaw that sent him tumbling over on his back. By this time I think Jubal had gone mad with hate, for no sane man would have come back for more as many times as he did. Time after time I bowled him over as fast as he could stagger up, until toward the last he lay longer on the ground between blows, and each time came up weaker than before.

He was bleeding very profusely now from the wound in his lungs, and presently a terrific blow over the heart sent him reeling heavily to the ground, where he lay very still, and somehow I knew at once that Jubal the Ugly One would never get up again. But even as I looked upon that massive body lying there so grim and terrible in death, I could not believe that I, single-handed, had bested this slayer of fearful beasts—this gigantic ogre of the Stone Age.

Picking up my sword I leaned upon it, looking down on the dead body of my foeman, and as I thought of the battle I had just fought and won a great idea was born in my brain—the outcome of this and the suggestion that Perry had made within the city of Phutra. If skill and science could render a comparative pygmy the master of this mighty brute, what could not the brute's fellows accomplish with the same skill and science. Why all Pellucidar would be at their feet—and I would be their king and Dian their queen.

Dian! A little wave of doubt swept over me. It was quite within the possibilities of Dian to look down upon me even were I king. She was quite the most superior person I ever had met—with the most convincing way of letting you know that she was superior. Well, I could go to the cave, and tell her that I had killed Jubal, and then she might feel more kindly toward me, since I had freed her of her tormentor. I hoped that she had found the cave easily—it would be terrible had I lost her again, and I turned to gather up my shield and bow to hurry after her, when to my astonishment I found her standing not ten paces behind me.

"Girl!" I cried, "what are you doing here? I thought that you had gone to the cave, as I told you to do."

Up went her head, and the look that she gave me took all the majesty out of me, and left me feeling more like the palace janitor—if palaces have janitors.

"As you told me to do!" she cried, stamping her little foot. "I do as I please. I am the daughter of a king, and furthermore, I hate you."

I was dumbfounded—this was my thanks for saving her from Jubal! I turned and looked at the corpse. "May be that I saved you from a worse fate, old man," I said, but I guess it was lost on Dian, for she never seemed to notice it at all.

"Let us go to my cave," I said, "I am tired and hungry."

She followed along a pace behind me, neither of us speaking. I was too angry, and she evidently didn't care to converse with the lower orders. I was mad all the way through, as I had certainly felt that at least a word of thanks should have rewarded me, for I knew that even by her own standards, I must have done a very wonderful thing to have killed the redoubtable Jubal in a hand-to-hand encounter.

We had no difficulty in finding my lair, and then I went down into the valley and bowled over a small antelope, which I dragged up the steep ascent to the ledge before the door. Here we ate in silence. Occasionally I glanced at her, thinking that the sight of her tearing at raw flesh with her hands and teeth like some wild animal would cause a revulsion of my sentiments toward her; but to my surprise I found that she ate quite as daintily as the most civilized woman of my acquaintance, and finally I found myself gazing in foolish rapture at the beauties of her strong, white teeth. Such is love.

After our repast we went down to the river together and bathed our hands and faces, and then after drinking our fill went back to the cave. Without a word I crawled into the farthest corner and, curling up, was soon asleep.

When I awoke I found Dian sitting in the doorway looking out across the valley. As I came out she moved to one side to let me pass, but she had no word for me. I wanted to hate her, but I couldn't. Every time I looked at her something came up in my throat, so that I nearly choked. I had never been in love before, but I did not need any aid in diagnosing my case—I certainly had it and had it bad. God, how I loved that beautiful, disdainful, tantalizing, prehistoric girl!

After we had eaten again I asked Dian if she intended returning to her tribe now that Jubal was dead, but she shook her head sadly, and said that she did not dare, for there was still Jubal's brother to be considered—his oldest brother.

"What has he to do with it?" I asked. "Does he too want you, or has the option on you become a family heirloom, to be passed on down from generation to generation?"

She was not quite sure as to what I meant.

"It is probable," she said, "that they all will want revenge for the death of Jubal—there are seven of them—seven terrible men. Someone may have to kill them all, if I am to return to my people."

It began to look as though I had assumed a contract much too large for me—about seven sizes, in fact.

"Had Jubal any cousins?" I asked. It was just as well to know the worst at once.

"Yes," replied Dian, "but they don't count—they all have mates. Jubal's brothers have no mates because Jubal could get none for himself. He was so ugly that women ran away from him—some have even thrown themselves from the cliffs of Amoz into the Darel Az rather than mate with the Ugly One."

"But what had that to do with his brothers?" I asked.

"I forget that you are not of Pellucidar," said Dian, with a look of pity mixed with contempt, and the contempt seemed to be laid on a little thicker than the circumstance warranted—as though to make quite certain that I shouldn't overlook it. "You see," she continued, "a younger brother may not take a mate until all his older brothers have done so, unless the older brother waives his prerogative, which Jubal would not do, knowing that as long as he kept them single they would be all the keener in aiding him to secure a mate."

Noticing that Dian was becoming more communicative I began to entertain hopes that she might be warming up toward me a bit, although upon what slender thread I hung my hopes I soon discovered.

"As you dare not return to Amoz," I ventured, "what is to become of you since you cannot be happy here with me, hating me as you do?"

"I shall have to put up with you," she replied coldly, "until you see fit to go elsewhere and leave me in peace, then I shall get along very well alone."

I looked at her in utter amazement. It seemed incredible that even a prehistoric woman could be so cold and heartless and ungrateful. Then I arose.

"I shall leave you *now*," I said haughtily, "I have had quite enough of your ingratitude and your insults," and then I turned and strode majestically down toward the valley. I had taken a hundred steps in absolute silence, and then Dian spoke.

"I hate you!" she shouted, and her voice broke—in rage, I thought.

I was absolutely miserable, but I hadn't gone too far when I began to realize that I couldn't leave her alone there without protection, to hunt her own food amid the dangers of that savage world. She might hate me, and revile me, and heap indignity after indignity upon me, as she already had, until I should have hated her; but the pitiful fact remained that I loved her, and I couldn't leave her there alone.

The more I thought about it the madder I got, so that by the time I reached the valley I was furious, and the result of it was that I turned right around and went up that cliff again as fast as I had come down. I saw that Dian had left the ledge and gone within the cave, but I bolted right in after her. She was lying upon her face on the pile of grasses I had gathered for her bed. When she heard me enter she sprang to her feet like a tigress.

"I hate you!" she cried.

Coming from the brilliant light of the noonday sun into the semidarkness of the cave I could not see her features, and I was rather glad, for I disliked to think of the hate that I should have read there.

I never said a word to her at first. I just strode across the cave and grasped her by the wrists, and when she struggled, I put my arm around her so as to pinion her hands to her sides. She fought like a tigress, but I took my free hand and pushed her head back—I imagine that I had suddenly turned brute, that I had gone back a thousand million years, and was again a veritable cave man taking my mate by force—and then I kissed that beautiful mouth again and again.

"Dian," I cried, shaking her roughly, "I love you. Can't you understand that I love you? That I love you better than all else in this world or my own? That I am going to have you? That love like mine cannot be denied?"

I noticed that she lay very still in my arms now, and as my eyes became accustomed to the light I saw that she was smiling—a very contented, happy smile. I was
thunderstruck. Then I realized that, very gently, she was trying to disengage her arms,
and I loosened my grip upon them so that she could do so. Slowly they came up and
stole about my neck, and then she drew my lips down to hers once more and held
them there for a long time. At last she spoke.

"Why didn't you do this at first, David? I have been waiting so long."

"What!" I cried. "You said that you hated me!"

"Did you expect me to run into your arms, and say that I loved you before
I knew that you loved me?" she asked.

"But I have told you right along that I love you," I said. "Love speaks in acts,"
she replied. "You could have made your mouth say what you wished it to say, but
just now when you came and took me in your arms your heart spoke to mine in the
language that a woman's heart understands. What a silly man you are, David?"

"Then you haven't hated me at all, Dian?" I asked.

"I have loved you always," she whispered, "from the first moment that I saw you,
although I did not know it until that time you struck down Hooja the Sly One, and
then spurned me."

"But I didn't spurn you, dear," I cried. "I didn't know your ways—I doubt if
I do now. It seems incredible that you could have reviled me so, and yet have cared
for me all the time."

"You might have known," she said, "when I did not run away from you that
it was not hate which chained me to you. While you were battling with Jubal,
I could have run to the edge of the forest, and when I learned the outcome of the
combat it would have been a simple thing to have eluded you and returned to my
own people."

"But Jubal's brothers—and cousins—" I reminded her, "how about them?"

She smiled, and hid her face on my shoulder.

"I had to tell you *something*, David," she whispered. "I must needs have *some*
excuse for remaining near you."

"You little sinner!" I exclaimed. "And you have caused me all this anguish
for nothing!"

"I have suffered even more," she answered simply, "for I thought that you did
not love me, and *I* was helpless. I couldn't come to you and demand that my love be
returned, as you have just come to me. Just now when you went away hope went
with you. I was wretched, terrified, miserable, and my heart was breaking. I wept,
and I have not done that before since my mother died," and now I saw that there

was the moisture of tears about her eyes. It was near to making me cry myself when I thought of all that poor child had been through. Motherless and unprotected; hunted across a savage, primeval world by that hideous brute of a man; exposed to the attacks of the countless fearsome denizens of its mountains, its plains, and its jungles—it was a miracle that she had survived it all.

To me it was a revelation of the things my early forebears must have endured that the human race of the outer crust might survive. It made me very proud to think that I had won the love of such a woman. Of course she couldn't read or write; there was nothing cultured or refined about her as you judge culture and refinement; but she was the essence of all that is best in woman, for she was good, and brave, and noble, and virtuous. And she was all these things in spite of the fact that their observance entailed suffering and danger and possible death.

How much easier it would have been to have gone to Jubal in the first place! She would have been his lawful mate. She would have been queen in her own land—and it meant just as much to the cave woman to be a queen in the Stone Age as it does to the woman of today to be a queen now; it's all comparative glory any way you look at it, and if there were only half-naked savages on the outer crust today, you'd find that it would be considerable glory to be the wife a Dahomey chief.

I couldn't help but compare Dian's action with that of a splendid young woman I had known in New York—I mean splendid to look at and to talk to. She had been head over heels in love with a chum of mine—a clean, manly chap—but she had married a broken-down, disreputable old debauchee because he was a count in some dinky little European principality that was not even accorded a distinctive color by Rand McNally.

Yes, I was mighty proud of Dian.

After a time we decided to set out for Sari, as I was anxious to see Perry, and to know that all was right with him. I had told Dian about our plan of emancipating the human race of Pellucidar, and she was fairly wild over it. She said that if Dacor, her brother, would only return he could easily be king of Amoz, and that then he and Ghak could form an alliance. That would give us a flying start, for the Sarians and the Amozites were both very powerful tribes. Once they had been armed with swords, and bows and arrows, and trained in their use we were confident that they could overcome any tribe that seemed disinclined to join the great army of federated states with which we were planning to march upon the Mahars.

I explained the various destructive engines of war which Perry and I could construct after a little experimentation—gunpowder, rifles, cannon, and the like, and Dian would clap her hands, and throw her arms about my neck, and tell me what a wonderful thing I was. She was beginning to think that I was omnipotent although I really hadn't done anything but talk—but that is the way with women when they love. Perry used to say that if a fellow was one-tenth as remarkable as his wife or mother thought him, he would have the world by the tail with a downhill drag.

The first time we started for Sari I stepped into a nest of poisonous vipers before we reached the valley. A little fellow stung me on the ankle, and Dian made me come back to the cave. She said that I mustn't exercise, or it might prove fatal—if it had been a full-grown snake that struck me she said, I wouldn't have moved a single pace from the nest—I'd have died in my tracks, so virulent is the poison. As it was I must have been laid up for quite a while, though Dian's poultices of herbs and leaves finally reduced the swelling and drew out the poison.

The episode proved most fortunate, however, as it gave me an idea which added a thousand-fold to the value of my arrows as missiles of offense and defense. As soon as I was able to be about again, I sought out some adult vipers of the species which had stung me, and having killed them, I extracted their virus, smearing it upon the tips of several arrows. Later I shot a hyaenodon with one of these, and though my arrow inflicted but a superficial flesh wound the beast crumpled in death almost immediately after he was hit.

We now set out once more for the land of the Sarians, and it was with feelings of sincere regret that we bade good-bye to our beautiful Garden of Eden, in the comparative peace and harmony of which we had lived the happiest moments of our lives. How long we had been there I did not know, for as I have told you, time had ceased to exist for me beneath that eternal noonday sun—it may have been an hour, or a month of earthly time; I do not know.

XV

BACK TO EARTH

We crossed the river and passed through the mountains beyond, and finally we came out upon a great level plain which stretched away as far as the eye could reach. I cannot tell you in what direction it stretched even if you would care to know, for all the while that I was within Pellucidar I never discovered any but local methods of indicating direction—there is no north, no south, no east, no west. *Up* is about the only direction which is well defined, and that, of course, is *down* to you of the outer crust. Since the sun neither rises nor sets there is no method of indicating direction beyond visible objects such as high mountains, forests, lakes, and seas.

The plain which lies beyond the white cliffs which flank the Darel Az upon the shore nearest the Mountains of the Clouds is about as near to any direction as any Pellucidarian can come. If you happen not to have heard of the Darel Az, or the white cliffs, or the Mountains of the Clouds you feel that there is something lacking, and long for the good old understandable northeast and southwest of the outer world.

We had barely entered the great plain when we discovered two enormous animals approaching us from a great distance. So far were they that we could not distinguish what manner of beasts they might be, but as they came closer, I saw that they were enormous quadrupeds, eighty or a hundred feet long, with tiny heads perched at the top of very long necks. Their heads must have been quite forty feet from the ground. The beasts moved very slowly—that is their action was slow—but their strides covered such a great distance that in reality they traveled considerably faster than a man walks.

As they drew still nearer we discovered that upon the back of each sat a human being. Then Dian knew what they were, though she never before had seen one.

"They are lidis from the land of the Thorians," she cried. "Thoria lies at the outer verge of the Land of Awful Shadow. The Thorians alone of all the races of Pellucidar ride the lidi, for nowhere else than beside the dark country are they found."

"What is the Land of Awful Shadow?" I asked.

"It is the land which lies beneath the Dead World," replied Dian; "the Dead World which hangs forever between the sun and Pellucidar above the Land of Awful Shadow. It is the Dead World which makes the great shadow upon this portion of Pellucidar."

I did not fully understand what she meant, nor am I sure that I do yet, for I have never been to that part of Pellucidar from which the Dead World is visible; but Perry says that it is the moon of Pellucidar—a tiny planet within a planet—and that it revolves around the earth's axis coincidently with the earth, and thus is always above the same spot within Pellucidar.

I remember that Perry was very much excited when I told him about this Dead World, for he seemed to think that it explained the hitherto inexplicable phenomena of nutation and the precession of the equinoxes.

When the two upon the lidis had come quite close to us we saw that one was a man and the other a woman. The former had held up his two hands, palms toward us, in sign of peace, and I had answered him in kind, when he suddenly gave a cry of astonishment and pleasure, and slipping from his enormous mount ran forward toward Dian, throwing his arms about her.

In an instant I was white with jealousy, but only for an instant; since Dian quickly drew the man toward me, telling him that I was David, her mate.

"And this is my brother, Dacor the Strong One, David," she said to me.

It appeared that the woman was Dacor's mate. He had found none to his liking among the Sari, nor farther on until he had come to the land of the Thoria, and there he had found and fought for this very lovely Thorian maiden whom he was bringing back to his own people.

When they had heard our story and our plans they decided to accompany us to Sari, that Dacor and Ghak might come to an agreement relative to an alliance, as Dacor was quite as enthusiastic about the proposed annihilation of the Mahars and Sagoths as either Dian or I.

After a journey which was, for Pellucidar, quite uneventful, we came to the first of the Sarian villages which consists of between one and two hundred artificial caves cut into the face of a great cliff. Here to our immense delight, we found both Perry and Ghak. The old man was quite overcome at sight of me for he had long since given me up as dead.

When I introduced Dian as my wife, he didn't quite know what to say, but he afterward remarked that with the pick of two worlds I could not have done better.

Ghak and Dacor reached a very amicable arrangement, and it was at a council of the head men of the various tribes of the Sari that the eventual form of government was tentatively agreed upon. Roughly, the various kingdoms were to remain virtually independent, but there was to be one great overlord, or emperor. It was decided that I should be the first of the dynasty of the emperors of Pellucidar.

We set about teaching the women how to make bows and arrows, and poison pouches. The young men hunted the vipers which provided the virus, and it was they who mined the iron ore, and fashioned the swords under Perry's direction. Rapidly the fever spread from one tribe to another until representatives from nations so far distant that the Sarians had never even heard of them came in to take the oath of allegiance which we required, and to learn the art of making the new weapons and using them.

We sent our young men out as instructors to every nation of the federation, and the movement had reached colossal proportions before the Mahars discovered it. The first intimation they had was when three of their great slave caravans were annihilated in rapid succession. They could not comprehend that the lower orders had suddenly developed a power which rendered them really formidable.

In one of the skirmishes with slave caravans some of our Sarians took a number of Sagoth prisoners, and among them were two who had been members of the guards within the building where we had been confined at Phutra. They told us that the Mahars were frantic with rage when they discovered what had taken place in the cellars of the buildings. The Sagoths knew that something very terrible had befallen their masters, but the Mahars had been most careful to see that no inkling of the true nature of their vital affliction reached beyond their own race. How long it would take for the race to become extinct it was impossible even to guess; but that this must eventually happen seemed inevitable.

The Mahars had offered fabulous rewards for the capture of any one of us alive, and at the same time had threatened to inflict the direst punishment upon whomever should harm us. The Sagoths could not understand these seemingly paradoxical instructions, though their purpose was quite evident to me. The Mahars wanted the Great Secret, and they knew that we alone could deliver it to them.

Perry's experiments in the manufacture of gunpowder and the fashioning of rifles had not progressed as rapidly as we had hoped—there was a whole lot about these two arts which Perry didn't know. We were both assured that the solution of these problems would advance the cause of civilization within Pellucidar thousands of years at a single stroke. Then there were various other arts and sciences which we wished to introduce, but our combined knowledge of them did not embrace the mechanical details which alone could render them of commercial, or practical value.

"David," said Perry, immediately after his latest failure to produce gunpowder that would even burn, "one of us must return to the outer world and bring back the information we lack. Here we have all the labor and materials for reproducing anything that ever has been produced above—what we lack is knowledge. Let us go back and get that knowledge in the shape of books—then this world will indeed be at our feet."

And so it was decided that I should return in the prospector, which still lay upon the edge of the forest at the point where we had first penetrated to the surface of the inner world. Dian would not listen to any arrangement for my going which did not include her, and I was not sorry that she wished to accompany me, for I wanted her to see my world, and I wanted my world to see her.

With a large force of men we marched to the great iron mole, which Perry soon had hoisted into position with its nose pointed back toward the outer crust. He went over all the machinery carefully. He replenished the air tanks, and manufactured oil for the engine. At last everything was ready, and we were about to set out when our pickets, a long, thin line of which had surrounded our camp at all times, reported that a great body of what appeared to be Sagoths and Mahars were approaching from the direction of Phutra.

Dian and I were ready to embark, but I was anxious to witness the first clash between two fair-sized armies of the opposing races of Pellucidar. I realized that this was to mark the historic beginning of a mighty struggle for possession of a world, and as the first emperor of Pellucidar I felt that it was not alone my duty, but my right, to be in the thick of that momentous struggle.

As the opposing army approached we saw that there were many Mahars with the Sagoth troops—an indication of the vast importance which the dominant race placed upon the outcome of this campaign, for it was not customary with them to take active part in the sorties which their creatures made for slaves—the only form of warfare which they waged upon the lower orders.

Ghak and Dacor were both with us, having come primarily to view the prospector. I placed Ghak with some of his Sarians on the right of our battle line. Dacor took the left, while I commanded the center. Behind us I stationed a sufficient reserve under one of Ghak's head men. The Sagoths advanced steadily with menacing spears, and I let them come until they were within easy bowshot before I gave the word to fire.

At the first volley of poison-tipped arrows the front ranks of the gorilla-men crumpled to the ground; but those behind charged over the prostrate forms of their comrades in a wild, mad rush to be upon us with their spears. A second volley stopped them for an instant, and then my reserve sprang through the openings in the firing line to engage them with sword and shield. The clumsy spears of the Sagoths were no match for the swords of the Sarian and Amozite, who turned the spear thrusts aside with their shields and leaped to close quarters with their lighter, handier weapons.

Ghak took his archers along the enemy's flank, and while the swordsmen engaged them in front, he poured volley after volley into their unprotected left. The Mahars did little real fighting, and were more in the way than otherwise, though occasionally one of them would fasten its powerful jaw upon the arm or leg of a Sarian.

The battle did not last a great while, for when Dacor and I led our men in upon the Sagoth's right with naked swords they were already so demoralized that they turned and fled before us. We pursued them for some time, taking many prisoners and recovering nearly a hundred slaves, among whom was Hooja the Sly One.

He told me that he had been captured while on his way to his own land; but that his life had been spared in hope that through him the Mahars would learn the whereabouts of their Great Secret. Ghak and I were inclined to think that the Sly One had been guiding this expedition to the land of Sari, where he thought that the book might be found in Perry's possession; but we had no proof of this and so we took him in and treated him as one of us, although none liked him. And how he rewarded my generosity you will presently learn.

There were a number of Mahars among our prisoners, and so fearful were our own people of them that they would not approach them unless completely covered from the sight of the reptiles by a piece of skin. Even Dian shared the popular superstition regarding the evil effects of exposure to the eyes of angry Mahars, and though I laughed at her fears I was willing enough to humor them if it would relieve her apprehension in any degree, and so she sat apart from the prospector, near which the Mahars had been chained, while Perry and I again inspected every portion of the mechanism.

At last I took my place in the driving seat, and called to one of the men without to fetch Dian. It happened that Hooja stood quite close to the doorway of the prospector, so that it was he who, without my knowledge, went to bring her; but how he succeeded in accomplishing the fiendish thing he did, I cannot guess, unless there were others in the plot to aid him. Nor can I believe that, since all my people were loyal to me and would have made short work of Hooja had he suggested the heartless scheme, even had he had time to acquaint another with it. It was all done so quickly that I may only believe that it was the result of sudden impulse, aided by a number of, to Hooja, fortuitous circumstances occurring at precisely the right moment.

All I know is that it was Hooja who brought Dian to the prospector, still wrapped from head to toe in the skin of an enormous cave lion which covered her since the Mahar prisoners had been brought into camp. He deposited his burden in the seat beside me. I was all ready to get under way. The good-byes had been said. Perry had grasped my hand in the last, long farewell. I closed and barred the outer and inner doors, took my seat again at the driving mechanism, and pulled the starting lever.

As before on that far-gone night that had witnessed our first trial of the iron monster, there was a frightful roaring beneath us—the giant frame trembled and vibrated—there was a rush of sound as the loose earth passed up through the hollow space between the inner and outer jackets to be deposited in our wake. Once more the thing was off.

But on the instant of departure I was nearly thrown from my seat by the sudden lurching of the prospector. At first I did not realize what had happened, but presently it dawned upon me that just before entering the crust the towering body had fallen through its supporting scaffolding, and that instead of entering the ground vertically we were plunging into it at a different angle. Where it would bring us out upon the upper crust I could not even conjecture. And then I turned to note the effect of this strange experience upon Dian. She still sat shrouded in the great skin.

"Come, come," I cried, laughing, "come out of your shell. No Mahar eyes can reach you here," and I leaned over and snatched the lion skin from her. And then I shrank back upon my seat in utter horror.

The thing beneath the skin was not Dian—it was a hideous Mahar. Instantly I realized the trick that Hooja had played upon me, and the purpose of it. Rid of me, forever as he doubtless thought, Dian would be at his mercy. Frantically I tore at the steering wheel in an effort to turn the prospector back toward Pellucidar; but, as on that other occasion, I could not budge the thing a hair.

It is needless to recount the horrors or the monotony of that journey. It varied but little from the former one which had brought us from the outer to the inner world. Because of the angle at which we had entered the ground the trip required nearly a day longer, and brought me out here upon the sand of the Sahara instead of in the United States as I had hoped.

For months I have been waiting here for a white man to come. I dared not leave the prospector for fear I should never be able to find it again—the shifting sands of the desert would soon cover it, and then my only hope of returning to my Dian and her Pellucidar would be gone forever.

That I ever shall see her again seems but remotely possible, for how may I know upon what part of Pellucidar my return journey may terminate—and how, without a north or south or an east or a west may I hope ever to find my way across that vast world to the tiny spot where my lost love lies grieving for me?

That is the story as David Innes told it to me in the goat-skin tent upon the rim of the great Sahara Desert. The next day he took me out to see the prospector—it was precisely as he had described it. So huge was it that it could have been brought to this inaccessible part of the world by no means of transportation that existed there— it could only have come in the way that David Innes said it came—up through the crust of the earth from the inner world of Pellucidar.

I spent a week with him, and then, abandoned my lion hunt, returned directly to the coast and hurried to London where I purchased a great quantity of stuff which he wished to take back to Pellucidar with him. There were books, rifles, revolvers, ammunition, cameras, chemicals, telephones, telegraph instruments, wire, tool and more books—books upon every subject under the sun. He said he wanted a library with which they could reproduce the wonders of the twentieth century in the Stone Age and if quantity counts for anything I got it for him.

I took the things back to Algeria myself, and accompanied them to the end of the railroad; but from here I was recalled to America upon important business. However, I was able to employ a very trustworthy man to take charge of the caravan—the same guide, in fact, who had accompanied me on the previous trip into the Sahara—and after writing a long letter to Innes in which I gave him my American address, I saw the expedition head south.

Among the other things which I sent to Innes was over five hundred miles of double, insulated wire of a very fine gauge. I had it packed on a special reel at his suggestion, as it was his idea that he could fasten one end here before he left and by paying it out through the end of the prospector lay a telegraph line between the outer and inner worlds. In my letter I told him to be sure to mark the terminus of the line very plainly with a high cairn, in case I was not able to reach him before he set out, so that I might easily find and communicate with him should he be so fortunate as to reach Pellucidar.

I received several letters from him after I returned to America—in fact he took advantage of every northward-passing caravan to drop me word of some sort. His last letter was written the day before he intended to depart. Here it is.

My dear friend:

Tomorrow I shall set out in quest of Pellucidar and Dian. That is if the Arabs don't get me. They have been very nasty of late. I don't know the cause, but on two occasions they have threatened my life. One, more friendly than the rest, told me today that they intended attacking me tonight. It would be unfortunate should anything of that sort happen now that I am so nearly ready to depart.

However, maybe I will be as well off, for the nearer the hour approaches, the slenderer my chances for success appear.

Here is the friendly Arab who is to take this letter north for me, so good-bye, and God bless you for your kindness to me.

The Arab tells me to hurry, for he sees a cloud of sand to the south— he thinks it is the party coming to murder me, and he doesn't want to be found with me. So good-bye again.

Yours,
David Innes

A year later found me at the end of the railroad once more, headed for the spot where I had left Innes. My first disappointment was when I discovered that my old guide had died within a few weeks of my return, nor could I find any member of my former party who could lead me to the same spot.

For months I searched that scorching land, interviewing countless desert sheiks in the hope that at last I might find one who had heard of Innes and his wonderful iron mole. Constantly my eyes scanned the blinding waste of sand for the ricky cairn beneath which I was to find the wires leading to Pellucidar—but always was I unsuccessful.

And always do these awful questions harass me when I think of David Innes and his strange adventures.

Did the Arabs murder him, after all, just on the eve of his departure? Or, did he again turn the nose of his iron monster toward the inner world? Did he reach it, or lies he somewhere buried in the heart of the great crust? And if he did come again to Pellucidar was it to break through into the bottom of one of her great island seas, or among some savage race far, far from the land of his heart's desire?

Does the answer lie somewhere upon the bosom of the broad Sahara, at the end of two tiny wires, hidden beneath a lost cairn? I wonder.

The Moon Pool

A. MERRITT

In the pulp fiction magazines of the early twentieth century, Abraham Merritt (1884–1943) rivaled Edgar Rice Burroughs for popularity with readers. Merritt's specialty was the lost world fantasy, which shone a light on forgotten civilizations where science and the supernatural were indistinguishable from one another. This story, first published in the June 22, 1918 issue of All-Story Weekly, *proved so popular with readers that the following year Merritt wrote a novel-length sequel,* Conquest of the Moon Pool, *in which he elaborated an entire fantasy world to explain the mystery of the moon pool. For book publication, Merritt totally rewrote this introductory novelette to incorporate it into his longer tale. The story's narrator, Walter Goodwin, played a minor role in Merritt's next novel,* The Metal Monster.

I

THE THROCKMARTIN MYSTERY

I am breaking a long silence to clear the name of Dr. David Throckmartin and to lift the shadow of scandal from that of his wife and of Dr. Charles Stanton, his assistant. That I have not found the courage to do so before, all men who are jealous of their scientific reputations will understand when they have read the facts entrusted to me alone.

I shall first recapitulate what has actually been known of the Throckmartin expedition to the island of Ponape in the Carolines—the Throckmartin Mystery, as it is called.

Dr. Throckmartin set forth, you will recall, to make some observations of Nan-Matal, that extraordinary group of island ruins, remains of a high and prehistoric civilization, that are clustered along the vast shore of Ponape. With him went his wife to whom he had been wedded less than half a year. The daughter of Professor Frazier-Smith, she was as deeply interested and almost as well informed as he upon these relics of a vanished race that titanically strew certain islands of the Pacific and form the basis for the theory of a submerged Pacific continent.

Mrs. Throckmartin, it will be recalled, was much younger, fifteen years at least, than her husband. Dr. Charles Stanton, who accompanied them as Dr. Throckmartin's assistant, was about her age. These three and a Swedish woman, Thora Helversen, who had been Edith Throckmartin's nurse in babyhood and who was entirely devoted to her, made up the expedition.

Dr. Throckmartin planned to spend a year among the ruins, not only of Ponape, but of Lele—the twin centers of that colossal riddle of humanity whose answer has its roots in immeasurable antiquity; a weird flower of man-made civilization that blossomed ages before the seeds of Egypt were sown; of whose arts we know little and of whose science and secret knowledge of nature nothing.

He carried with him complete equipment for his work and gathered at Ponape a dozen or so natives for laborers. They went straight to Metalanim harbor and set up their camp on the island called Uschen-Tau in the group known as the Nan-Matal. You will remember that these islands are entirely uninhabited and are shunned by the people on the main island.

Three months later Dr. Throckmartin appeared at Port Mooresby, Papua. He came on a schooner manned by Solomon Islanders and commanded by a Chinese half-breed captain. He reported that he was on his way to Melbourne for additional scientific equipment and whites to help him in his excavations, saying that the superstition of the natives made their aid negligible. He went immediately on board the steamer Southern Queen which was sailing that same morning. Three nights later he disappeared from the Southern Queen and it was officially reported that he had met death either by being swept overboard or by casting himself into the sea.

A relief-boat sent with the news to Ponape found the Throckmartin camp on the island Uschen-Tau and a smaller camp on the island called Nan-Tanach. All the equipment, clothing, supplies were intact. But of Mrs. Throckmartin, of Dr. Stanton, or of Thora Helversen they could find not a single trace!

The natives who had been employed by the archeologist were questioned. They said that the ruins were the abode of great spirits—*ani*—who were particularly powerful when the moon was at the full. On these nights all the islanders were doubly careful to give the ruins wide berth. Upon being employed, they had demanded leave from the day before full moon until it was on the wane and this had been granted them by Dr. Throckmartin. Thrice they had left the expedition alone on these nights. On their third return they had found the four white people gone and they "knew that the *ani* had eaten them." They were afraid and had fled.

That was all.

The Chinese half caste was found and reluctantly testified at last that he had picked Dr. Throckmartin up from a small boat about fifty miles off Ponape. The scientist had seemed half mad, but he had given the seaman a large sum of money to bring him to Port Moresby and to say, if questioned, that he had boarded the boat at Ponape harbor.

That is all that has been known to anyone of the fate of the Throckmartin expedition.

Why, you will ask, do I break silence now; and how, came I in possession of the facts I am about to set forth?

To the first I answer: I was at the Geographical Club recently and I overheard two members talking. They mentioned the name of Throckmartin and I became an eavesdropper. One said:

"Of course what probably happened was that Throckmartin killed them all. It's a dangerous thing for a man to marry a woman so much younger than himself and then throw her into the necessarily close company of exploration with a man as young and as agreeable as Stanton was. The inevitable happened, no doubt. Throckmartin discovered; avenged himself. Then followed remorse and suicide."

"Throckmartin didn't seem to be that kind," said the other thoughtfully.

"No, he didn't," agreed the first. "Isn't there another story?" went on the second speaker. "Something about Mrs. Throckmartin running away with Stanton and taking the woman, Thora, with her? Somebody told me they had been recognized in Singapore recently."

"You can take your pick of the two stories," replied the other man. "It's one or the other I suppose."

It was neither one nor the other of them. I know—and I will answer now the second question—because I was with Throckmartin when he—vanished. I know what he told me and I know what my own eyes saw. Incredible, abnormal, against all the known facts of our science as it was, I testify to it. And it is my intention, after this is published, to sail to Ponape, to go to the Nan-Matal and to the islet beneath whose frowning walls dwells the mystery that Throckmartin sought and found—and that at the last sought and found Throckmartin!

I will leave behind me a copy of the map of the islands that he gave me. Also his sketch of the great courtyard of Nan-Tanach, the location of the moon door, his indication of the probable location of the moon pool and the passage to it and his approximation of the position of the shining globes. If I do not return and there are any with enough belief, scientific curiosity and courage to follow, these will furnish a plain trail.

I will now proceed straightforwardly with my narrative.

For six months I had been on the d'Entrecasteaux Islands gathering data for the concluding chapters of my book upon "Flora of the Volcanic Islands of the South Pacific." The day before, I had reached Port Moresby and had seen my specimens safely stored on board the Southern Queen. As I sat on the upper deck that morning I thought, with home-sick mind, of the long leagues between me and Melbourne and the longer ones between Melbourne and New York.

It was one of Papua's yellow mornings, when she shows herself in her most somber, most baleful mood. The sky was a smoldering ocher. Over the island brooded a spirit sullen, implacable and alien; filled with the threat of latent, malefic forces waiting to be unleashed. It seemed an emanation from the untamed, sinister heart of Papua herself—sinister even when she smiles. And now and then, on the wind, came a breath from unexplored jungles, filled with unfamiliar odors, mysterious, and menacing.

It is on such mornings that Papua speaks to you of her immemorial ancientness and of her power. I am not unduly imaginative but it is a mood that makes me shrink—I mention it because it bears directly upon Dr. Throckmartin's fate. Nor is the mood Papua's alone. I have felt it in New Guinea, in Australia, in the Solomons and in the Carolines. But it is in Papua that it seems most articulate. It is as though she said: "I am the ancient of days: I have seen the earth in the throes of its shaping; I am the primeval; I have seen races born and die and, lo, in my breast are secrets that would blast you by the telling, you pale babes of a puling age. You and I ought not be in the same world; yet I am and I shall be! Never will you fathom me and you I hate though I tolerate I tolerate—but how long?"

And then I seem to see a giant paw that reaches from Papua toward the outer world, stretching and sheathing monstrous claws.

All feel this mood of hers. Her own people have it woven in them, part of their web and woof; flashing into light unexpectedly like a soul from another universe; masking itself as swiftly.

I fought against Papua as every white man must on one of her yellow mornings. And as I fought I saw a tall figure come striding down the pier. Behind him came a

Kapa-Kapa boy swinging a new valise. There was something familiar about the tall man. As he reached the gangplank he looked up straight into my eyes, stared at me for a moment and waved his hand. It was Dr. Throckmartin!

Coincident with my recognition of him there came a shock of surprise that was definitely—unpleasant. It was Throckmartin—but there was something disturbingly different about him and the man I had known so well and had bidden farewell less than a year before. He was then, as you know, just turned forty, lithe, erect, muscular; the face of a student and of a seeker. His controlling expression was one of enthusiasm, of intellectual keenness, of—what shall I say—expectant search. His ever eagerly questioning brain had stamped itself upon his face.

I sought in my mind for an explanation of that which I had felt on the flash of his greeting. Hurrying down to the lower deck I found him with the purser. As I spoke he turned and held out to me an eager hand—and then I saw what the change was that had come over him!

He knew, of course, by my face the uncontrollable shock that my closer look had given me. His eyes filled and he turned briskly to the purser; then hurried off to his stateroom, leaving me standing, half dazed. At the stair he half turned. "Oh, Goodwin," he said. "I'd like to see you later. Just now—there's something I must write before we start—"

He went up swiftly.

" 'E looks rather queer—eh?" said the purser. "Know 'im well, sir? Seems to 'ave given you quite a start, sir."

I made some reply and went slowly to my chair. I tried to analyze what it was that had disturbed me so; what profound change in Throckmartin that had so shaken me. Now it came to me. It was as though the man had suffered some terrific soul searing shock of rapture and horror combined; some soul cataclysm that in its climax had remolded his face deep from within, setting on it the seal of wedded joy and fear. As though indeed ecstasy supernal and terror infernal had once come to him hand in hand, taken possession of him, looked out of his eyes and, departing, left behind upon him ineradicably their shadow.

Alternately I looked out over the port and paced about the deck, striving to read the riddle; to banish it from my mind. And all the time still over Papua brooded its baleful spirit of ancient evil, unfathomable, not to be understood; nor had it lifted when the "Southern Queen" lifted anchor and steamed out into the gulf.

II

DOWN THE MOON PATH

I watched with relief the shores sink down behind us; welcomed the touch of the free sea wind. We seemed to be drawing away from something malefic; something that lurked within the island spell I have described, and the thought crept into my mind, spoke—whispered rather—from Throckmartin's face.

I had hoped—and within the hope was an inexplicable shrinking, an unexpressed dread—that I would meet Throckmartin at lunch. He did not come down and I was sensible of a distinct relief within my disappointment. All that afternoon I lounged about uneasily but still he kept to his cabin. Nor did he appear at dinner.

Dusk and night fell swiftly. I was warm and went back to my deckchair. The *Southern Queen* was rolling to a disquieting swell and I had the place to myself.

Over the heavens was a canopy of cloud, glowing faintly and testifying to the moon riding behind it. There was much phosphorescence. Now and then, before the ship and at the sides, arose those strange little swirls of mist that steam up from the Southern Ocean like the breath of sea monsters, whirl for a moment and disappear. I lighted a cigarette and tried once more to banish Throckmartin's face from my mind.

Suddenly the deck door opened and through it came Throckmartin himself. He paused uncertainly, looked up at the sky with a curiously eager, intent gaze, hesitated, then closed the door behind him.

"Throckmartin," I called. "Come sit with me. It is Goodwin."

Immediately he made his way to me, sitting beside me with a gasp of relief that I noted curiously. His hand touched mine and gripped it with tenseness that hurt. His hand was icelike. I puffed up my cigarette and by its glow scanned him closely. He was watching a large swirl of the mist that was passing before the ship. The phosphorescence beneath it illumined it with a fitful opalescence. I saw fear in his eyes. The swirl passed; he sighed, his grip relaxed and he sank back.

"Throckmartin," I said, wasting no time in preliminaries. "What's wrong? Can I help you?"

He was silent.

"Is your wife all right and what are you doing here when I heard you had gone to the Carolines for a year?" I went on.

I felt his body grow tense again. He did not speak for a moment and then:

"I'm going to Melbourne, Goodwin," he said. "I need a few things—need them urgently. And more men—white men."

His voice was low; preoccupied. It was as though the brain that dictated the words did so perfunctorily, half impatiently; aloof, watching, strained to catch the first hint of approach of something dreaded.

"You are making progress then?" I asked. It was a banal question. Put forth in a blind effort to claim his attention.

"Progress?" he repeated. "Progress—"

He stopped abruptly; rose from his chair, gazed intently toward the north. I followed his gaze. Far, far away the moon had broken through the clouds. Almost on the horizon, you could see the faint luminescence of it upon the quiet sea. The distant patch of light quivered and shook. The clouds thickened again and it was gone. The ship raced southward, swiftly.

Throckmartin dropped into his chair. He lighted a cigarette with a hand that trembled. The flash of the match fell on his face and I noted with a queer thrill of apprehension that its unfamiliar expression had deepened; become curiously intensified as though a faint acid had passed over it, etching its lines faintly deeper.

"It's the full moon tonight, isn't it?" he asked, palpably with studied inconsequence.

"The first night of full moon," I answered. He was silent again. I sat silent too, waiting for him to make up his mind to speak. He turned to me as though he had made a sudden resolution.

"Goodwin," he said. "I do need help. If ever man needed it, I do, Goodwin— can you imagine yourself in another world, alien, unfamiliar, a world of terror, whose unknown joy is its greatest terror of all; you all alone there; a stranger! As such a man would need help, so I need—"

He paused abruptly and arose to his feet stiffly; the cigarette dropped from his fingers. I saw that the moon had again broken through the clouds, and this time much nearer. Not a mile away was the patch of light that it threw upon the waves. Back of it, to the rim of the sea was a lane of moonlight; it was a gleaming gigantic serpent racing over the rim of the world straight and surely toward the ship.

Throckmartin gazed at it as though turned to stone. He stiffened to it as a pointer does to a hidden covey. To me from him pulsed a thrill of terror—but terror tinged with an unfamiliar, an infernal joy. It came to me and passed away—leaving me trembling with its shock of bitter sweet.

He bent forward, all his soul in his eyes. The moon path swept closer, closer still. It was now less than half a mile away. From it the ship fled; almost it came to me, as though pursued. Down upon it, swift and straight, a radiant torrent cleaving the waves, raced the moon stream. And then—

"Good God!" breathed Throckmartin, and if ever the words were a prayer and an invocation they were.

And then, for the first time—I saw—*it!*

The moon path, as I have said, stretched to the horizon and was bordered by darkness. It was as though the clouds above had been parted to form a lane—drawn aside like curtains or as the waters of the Red Sea were held back to let the hosts of Israel through. On each side of the stream was the black shadow cast by the folds of the high canopies. And straight as a road between the opaque walls gleamed, shimmered and danced the shining, racing, rapids of moonlight.

Far, it seemed immeasurably far, along this stream of silver fire I sensed, rather than saw, something coming. It drew into sight as a deeper glow within the light. On and on it sped toward us—an opalescent mistiness that swept on with the suggestion of some winged creature in darting flight. Dimly there crept into my mind memory of the Dyak legend of the winged messenger of Buddha—the Akla bird whose feathers are woven of the moon rays, whose heart is a living opal, whose wings in flight echo the crystal clear music of the white stars—but whose beak is of frozen flame and shreds the souls of the unbelievers. Still it sped on, and now there came to me sweet, insistent tinklings—like a pizzicati on violins of glass, crystalline, as purest, clearest glass transformed to sound. And again the myth of the Akla bird came to me.

But now it was close to the end of the white path; close up to the barrier of darkness still between the ship and the sparkling head of the Moon stream. And now it beat up against that barrier as a bird against the bars of its cage. And I knew that this was no mist born of sea and air. It whirled with shimmering plumes, with swirls of lacy light, with spirals of living vapor. It held within it odd, unfamiliar gleams as of shifting mother-of-pearl. Coruscations and glittering atoms drifted through it as though it drew them from the rays that bathed it.

Nearer and nearer it came, borne on the sparkling waves, and less and less grew the protecting wall of shadow between it and us. The crystalline sounds were louder—rhythmic as music from another planet.

Now I saw that within the mistiness was a core, a nucleus of intenser light-veined, opaline, effulgent, intensely alive. And above it, tangled in the plumes and spirals that throbbed and whirled were seven glowing lights.

Through all the incessant but strangely ordered movement of the—*thing*—these lights held firm and steady. They were seven—like seven little moons. One was of a pearly pink, one of delicate nacreous blue, one of lambent saffron, one of the emerald you see in the shallow waters of tropic isles; a deathly white; a ghostly amethyst; and one of the silver that is seen only when the flying fish leap beneath the moon.

There they shone—these seven little varicolored orbs within the opaline mistiness of whatever it was that, poised and expectant, waited to be drawn to us on the light filled waves.

The tinkling music was louder still. It pierced the ears with a shower of tiny lances; it made the heart beat jubilantly—and checked it dolorously. It closed your throat with a throb of rapture and gripped it tight like the hand of infinite sorrow!

Came to me now a murmuring cry, stilling the crystal clear notes, it was articulate—but as though from something utterly foreign to this world. The ear took the cry and translated with conscious labor into the sounds of earth. And even as it compassed, the brain shrank from it irresistibly and simultaneously it seemed, reached toward it with irresistible eagerness.

"Av-o-lo-ha! Av-o-lo-ha!" So the cry seemed to throb. The grip of Throckmartin's hand relaxed. He walked stiffly toward the front of the deck, straight toward the vision, now but a few yards away from the bow. I ran toward him and gripped him—and fell back. For now his face had lost all human semblance. Utter agony and utter ecstasy—there they were side by side, not resisting each other; unholy inhuman companions blending into a look that none of God's creatures should wear—and deep, deep as his soul! A devil and a god dwelling harmoniously side by side! So must Satan, newly fallen, still divine, seeing heaven and contemplating hell, have looked.

And then—swiftly the moon path faded! The clouds swept over the sky as though a hand had drawn them together. Up from the south came a roaring squall. As the moon vanished what I had seen vanished with it—blotted out as an image on a magic lantern; the tinkling ceased abruptly—leaving a silence like that which follows an abrupt and stupendous thunder clap. There was nothing about us but silence and blackness!

Through me there passed a great trembling as one who had stood on the very verge of the gulf wherein the men of the Louisades say lurks the fisher of the souls of men, and has been plucked back by sheerest chance.

Throckmartin passed an arm around me.

"It is as I thought," he said. In his voice was a new note; of the calm certainty that has swept aside a waiting terror of the unknown. "Now I know! Come with me to my cabin, old friend. For now that you too have seen I can tell you"—he hesitated—"what it was you saw," he ended.

As we passed through the door we came face to face with the ship's first officer. Throckmartin turned quickly, but not soon enough for the mate not to see and stare with amazement. His eyes turned questioningly to me.

With a strong effort of will Throckmartin composed his face into at least a semblance of normality. "Are we going to have much of a storm?" he asked.

"Yes," said the mate. Then the seaman, getting the better of his curiosity, added, profanely: "We'll probably have it all the way to Melbourne."

Throckmartin straightened as though with a new thought. He gripped the officer's sleeve eagerly.

"You mean at least cloudy weather—for"—he hesitated—"for the next three nights, say?"

"And for three more," replied the mate.

"Thank God!" cried Throckmartin, and I think I never heard such relief and hope as was in his voice.

The sailor stood amazed. "Thank God?" he repeated. "Thank—what d'ye mean?"

But Throckmartin was moving onward to his cabin. I started to follow. The first officer stopped me. "Your friend," he said, "Is he ill?"

"The sea!" I answered hurriedly. "He's not used to it. I am going to look after him."

I saw doubt and disbelief in the seaman's eyes but I hurried on. For I knew now that Throckmartin was ill indeed—but that it was a sickness neither the ship's doctor nor any other could heal.

III

"DEAD! ALL DEAD!"

Throckmartin was sitting on the side of his berth as I entered. He had taken off his coat. He was leaning over, face in hands.

"Lock the door," he said quietly, not raising his head. "Close the port-holes and draw the curtains—and—have you an electric flash in your pocket—a good, strong one?"

He glanced at the small pocket flash I handed him and clicked it on. "Not big enough I'm afraid," he said. "And after all"—he hesitated—"it's only a theory."

"What's only a theory?" I asked in astonishment.

"Thinking of it as a weapon against—what saw," he said, with a wry smile.

"Throckmartin," I cried. "What was it? Did I really see—that thing—there in the moon path? Did I really hear——"

"This for instance," he interrupted.

Softly he whispered: "Av-o-lo-ha!" With the murmur I seemed to hear again the crystalline unearthly music; an echo of it, faint, sinister, mocking, jubilant.

"Throckmartin," I said. "What was it? What are you flying from, man? Where is your wife—and Stanton?"

"Dead!" he said monotonously. "Dead! All dead!" Then as I recoiled in horror—"All dead. Edith, Stanton, Thora—dead or worse. And Edith in the moon pool—with them—drawn by what you saw on the moon path—and that wants me—and that has put its brand upon me—and pursues me."

With a vicious movement he ripped open his shirt.

"Look at this," he said. I gazed. Around his chest, an inch above his heart, the skin was white as pearl. The whiteness was sharply defined against the healthy tint of the body. He turned and I saw it ran around his back. It circled him. The band made a perfect cincture about two inches wide.

"Burn it!" he said, and offered me his cigarette. I drew back. He gestured—peremptorily. I pressed the glowing end of the cigarette into the ribbon of white flesh. He did not flinch nor was there odor of burning nor, as I drew the little cylinder away, any mark upon the whiteness.

"Feel it!" he commanded again. I placed my fingers upon the band. It was cold—like frozen marble. He handed me a small penknife. "Cut!" he ordered. This time, my scientific interest fully aroused, I did so without reluctance. The blade cut into flesh. I waited for the blood to come. None appeared. I drew out the knife and thrust it in again, fully a quarter of an inch deep. I might have been cutting paper so far as any evidence followed that what I was piercing was human skin and muscle. Another thought came to me and I drew back, revolted.

"Throckmartin," I whispered. "Not leprosy!"

"Nothing so easy," he said. "Look again and find the places you cut."

I looked, as he bade me, and in the white ring there was not a single mark. Where I had pressed the blade there was no trace. It was as though the skin had parted to make way for the blade and closed. Throckmartin arose and drew his shirt about him.

"Two things you have seen," he said. "It—and its mark—the seal it placed on me that gives it, I think, the power to follow me. Seeing, you must believe my story. Goodwin, I tell you again that my wife is dead—or worse—I do not know; the prey of—what you saw; so, too, is Stanton; so Thora. How—" He stopped for a moment. Then continued:

"And I am going to Melbourne for the things to empty its den and its shrine; for dynamite to destroy it and its lair—if anything made on earth will destroy it, and for white men with courage to use them. Perhaps—perhaps after you have heard, you will be one of these men?" He looked at me a bit wistfully. "And now do not interrupt me. I beg of you, till I am through—for"—he smiled wanly—"the mate may be wrong. And if he is"—he arose and paced twice about the room—"if he is I may not have time to tell you."

"Throckmartin," I answered. "I have no closed mind. Tell me—and if I can I will help."

He took my hand and pressed it.

"Goodwin," he began, "if I have seemed to take the death of my wife lightly— or rather"—his face contorted—"or rather—if I have seemed to pass it by as something not of first importance to me—believe me it is not so. If the rope is long enough—if what the mate says is so—if there is cloudy weather until the moon begins to wane—I can conquer—that I know. But if it does not—if the dweller in the moon pool gets me—then must you or some one avenge my wife—and me— and Stanton. Yet I cannot believe that God would let a thing like that conquer! But why did He then let it take my Edith? And why does He allow it to exist? Are there things stronger than God, do you think, Goodwin?"

He turned to me feverishly. I hesitated.

"I do not know just how you define God," I said. "If you mean the will to know, working through science—"

He waved me aside impatiently.

"Science," he said. "What is our science against—that? Or against the science of whatever cursed, vanished race that made it—or made the way for it to enter this world of ours?"

With an effort he regained control of himself.

"Goodwin," he said, "do you know at all of the ruins on the Carolines, the cyclopean, megolithic cities and harbors of Ponape and Lele, of Kusaie, of Ruk and Hogolu, and a score of other islets there? Particularly, do you know of the Nan-Matal and Metalanim?"

"Of the Metalanim I have heard and seen photographs," I said. "They call it don't they, the Lost Venice of the Pacific?"

"Look at this map," said Throckmartin. He handed me the map. "That," he went on, "is Christian's map of Metalanim harbor and the Nan-Matal. Do you see the rectangles marked Nan-Tanach?"

"Yes," I said.

"There," he said, "under those walls is the moon pool and the seven gleaming lights that raise the dweller in the pool and the altar and shrine of the dweller. And there in the moon pool with it lie Edith and Stanton and Thora."

"The dweller in the moon pool?" I repeated half-incredulously.

"The thing you saw," said Throckmartin solemnly.

A solid sheet of rain swept the ports, and the *Southern Queen* began to roll on the rising swells. Throckmartin drew another deep breath of relief, and drawing aside a curtain peered out into the night. Its blackness seemed to reassure him. At any rate, when he sat again he was calm.

"There are no more wonderful ruins in the world than those of the island Venice of Metalanim on the east shore of Ponape," he said almost casually. "They take in some fifty islets and cover with their intersecting canals and lagoons about twelve square miles. Who built them? None knows! When were they built? Ages before the memory of present man, that is sure. Ten thousand, twenty thousand, a hundred thousand years ago—the last more likely.

"All these islets, Goodwin, are squared, and their shores are frowning sea-walls of gigantic basalt blocks hewn and put in place by the hands of ancient man. Each inner water-front is faced with a terrace of those basalt blocks which stand out six feet above the shallow canals that meander between them. On the islets behind these walls are cyclopean and time-shattered fortresses, palaces, terraces, pyramids; immense court-yards, strewn with ruins—and all so old that they seem to wither the eyes of those who look on them.

"There has been a great subsidence. You can stand out of Metalanim harbor for three miles and look down upon the tops of similar monolithic structures and walls twenty feet below you in the water.

"And all about, strung on their canals, are the bulwarked islets with their enigmatic giant walls peering through the dense growths of mangroves—dead, deserted for incalculable ages; shunned by those who live near.

"You as a botanist are familiar with the evidence that a vast shadowy continent existed in the Pacific—a continent that was not rent asunder by volcanic forces as was that legendary one of Atlantis in the Eastern Ocean. My work in Java, in Papua, and in the Ladrones had set my mind upon this Pacific lost land. Just as the Azores are believed to be the last high peaks of Atlantis, so evidence came to me steadily that Ponape and Lele and their basalt bulwarked islets were the last points of the slowly sunken western land clinging still to the sunlight, and had been the last refuge and sacred places of the rulers of that race which had lost their immemorial home under the rising waters of the Pacific.

"I believed that under these ruins I might find the evidence of what I sought. Time and again I had encountered legends of subterranean networks beneath the Nan-Matal, of passages running back into the main island itself; basalt corridors that followed the lines of the shallow canals and ran under them to islet after islet, linking them in mysterious chains.

"My—my wife and I had talked before we were married of making this our great work. After the honeymoon we prepared for the expedition. It was to be my monument. Stanton was as enthusiastic as ourselves. We sailed, as you know, last May in fulfilment of our dreams.

"At Ponape we selected, not without difficulty, workmen to help us—diggers. I had to make extraordinary inducements before I could get together my force. Their beliefs are gloomy, these Ponapeans. They people their swamps, their forests, their mountains and shores with malignant spirits—*ani* they call them. And they are afraid—bitterly afraid of the isles of ruins and what they think the ruins hide. I do not wonder—now! For their fear has come down to them, through the ages, from the people 'before their fathers,' as they call them, who, they say, made these mighty spirits their slaves and messengers.

"When they were told where they were to go, and how long we expected to stay, they murmured. Those who, at last, were tempted made what I thought then merely a superstitious proviso that they were to be allowed to go away on the three nights of the full moon. If only I had heeded them and gone, too!"

He stopped and again over his face the lines etched deep.

"We passed," he went on, "into Metalanim harbor. Off to our left—a mile away arose a massive quadrangle. Its walls were all of forty feet high and hundreds of feet on each side. As we passed it our natives grew very silent; watched it furtively, fearfully. I knew it for the ruins that are called Nan-Tanach, the 'place of frowning walls.' And at the silence of my men I recalled what Christian had written of this place; of how he had come upon its ancient platforms and tetragonal enclosures of stonework; its wonder of tortuous alleyways and labyrinth of shallow canals; grim masses of stonework peering out from behind verdant screens; cyclopean barricades. And now, when we had turned into its ghostly shadows, straightaway the merriment of our guides was hushed and conversation died down to whispers. For we were close to Nan-Tanach—the place of lofty walls, the most remarkable of all the Metalanim ruins." He arose and stood over me.

"Nan-Tanach. Goodwin," he said solemnly—"a place where merriment is hushed indeed and words are stifled; Nan-Tanach—where the moon pool lies hidden—lies hidden behind the moon rock, but sends its diabolic soul out—even through the prisoning stone." He raised clenched hands. "Oh, Heaven," he breathed, "grant me that I may blast it from earth!"

He was silent for a little time.

"Of course I wanted to pitch our camp there," he began again quietly, "but I soon gave up that idea. The natives were panic-stricken—threatened to turn back. 'No,' they said. 'too great *ani* there. We go to any other place—but not there.' Although, even then, I felt that the secret of the place was in Nan-Tanach. I found it necessary to give in. The laborers were essential to the success of the expedition, and I told myself that after a little time had passed and I had persuaded them that there was nothing anywhere that could molest them, we would move our tents to it. We finally picked for our base the islet called Uschen-Tau—you see it here—" He pointed to the map. "It was close to the isle of desire, but far enough away from it to satisfy our men. There was an excellent camping-place there and a spring of fresh water. It offered, besides, an excellent field for preliminary work before attacking the larger ruins. We pitched our tents, and in a couple of days the work was in full swing."

IV

THE MOON ROCK

"I do not intend to tell you now," Throckmartin continued, "the results of the next two weeks, Goodwin, nor of what we found. Later—if I am allowed I will lay all that before you. It is sufficient to say that at the end of those two weeks I had found confirmation of many of my theories, and we were well under way to solve a mystery of humanity's youth—so we thought. But enough. I must hurry on to the first stirrings of the inexplicable thing that was in store for us.

"The place, for all its decay and desolation, had not infected us with any touch of morbidity—that is not Edith, Stanton or myself. My wife was happy—never had she been happier. Stanton and she, while engrossed in the work as much as I, were of the same age, and they frankly enjoyed the companionship that only youth can give youth. I was glad—never jealous.

"But Thora was very unhappy. She was a Swede, as you know, and in her blood ran the beliefs and superstitions of the Northland—some of them so strangely akin to those of this far southern land; beliefs of spirits of mountain and forest and water—werewolves and beings malign. From the first she showed a curious sensitivity to what, I suppose, may be called the 'influences' of the place. She said it 'smelled' of ghosts and warlocks.

"I laughed at her then—but now I believe that this sensitivity of what we call primitive people is perhaps only a clearer perception of the unknown which we, who deny the unknown, have lost.

"A prey to these fears, Thora always followed my wife about like a shadow; carried with her always a little sharp hand-ax, and although we twitted her about the futility of chopping fantoms with such a weapon she would not relinquish it.

"Two weeks slipped by, and at their end the spokesman for our natives came to us. The next night was the full of the moon, he said. He reminded me of my promise. They would go back to their village next morning; they would return after the third night, as at that time the power of the *ani* would begin to wane with the moon. They left us sundry charms for our 'protection,' and solemnly cautioned us to keep as far away as possible from Nan-Tanach during their absence—although their leader politely informed us that, no doubt, we were stronger than the spirits. Half-exasperated, half-amused I watched them go.

"No work could be done without them, of course, so we decided to spend the days of their absence junketing about the southern islets of the group. Under the moon the ruins were inexpressibly weird and beautiful. We marked down several spots for subsequent exploration, and on the morning of the third day set forth along the east face of the breakwater for our camp on Uschen-Tau, planning to have everything in readiness for the return of our men the next day.

"We landed just before dusk, tired and ready for our cots. It was only a little after ten o'clock when Edith awakened me.

"'Listen!' she said. 'Lean over with your ear close to the ground!' I did so, and seemed to hear, far, far below, as though coming up from great distances, a faint chanting. It gathered strength, died down, ended, began, gathered volume, faded away into silence.

"'It's the waves rolling on rocks somewhere,' I said. 'We're probably over some ledge of rock that carries the sound.'

"'It's the first time I've heard it,' replied my wife doubtfully. We listened again. Then through the dim rhythms, deep beneath us, another sound came. It drifted across the lagoon that lay between us and Nan-Tanach in little tinkling waves. It was music—of a sort, I won't describe the strange effect it had upon me. You've felt it—"

"You mean on the deck?" I asked. Throckmartin nodded.

"I went to the flap of the tent," he continued, "and peered out. As I did so Stanton lifted his flap and walked out into the moonlight, looking over to the other islet and listening. I called to him.

"'That's the queerest sound!' he said. He listened again. 'Crystalline! Like little notes of translucent glass. Like the bells of crystal on the sistrums of Isis at Dendarah Temple,' he added half-dreamily. We gazed intently at the island. Suddenly, on the gigantic sea-wall, moving slowly, rhythmically, we saw a little group of lights. Stanton laughed.

"'The beggars!' he exclaimed. 'That's why they wanted to get away, is it? Don't you see, Dave, it's some sort of a festival—rites of some kind that they hold during the full moon! That's why they were so eager to have us *keep* away, too.'

"I felt a curious sense of relief, although I had not been sensible of any oppression. The explanation seemed good. It explained the tinkling music and also the chanting—worshipers, no doubt, in the ruins—their voices carried along passages I now knew honeycombed the whole Nan-Matal.

"'Let's slip over,' suggested Stanton—but I would not.

"'They're a difficult lot as it is,' I said. 'If we break into one of their religious ceremonies they'll probably never forgive us. Let's keep out of any family party where we haven't been invited.'

"'That's so,' agreed Stanton.

"The strange tinkling music, if music it can be called, rose and fell, rose and fell—now laden with sorrow, now filled with joy.

"'There's something—something very unsettling about it,' said Edith at last soberly. 'I wonder what they make those sounds with. They frighten me half to death, and, at the same time, they make me feel as though some enormous rapture was just around the corner.'

"I had noted this effect, too, although I had said nothing of it. And at the same time there came to me a clear perception that the chanting which had preceded it had seemed to come from a vast multitude—thousands more than the place we were contemplating could possibly have held. Of course, I thought, this might be due to some acoustic property of the basalt; an amplification of sound by some gigantic sounding-board of rock; still—

"'It's devilish uncanny!' broke in Stanton, answering my thought.

"And as he spoke the flap of Thora's tent was raised and out into the moonlight strode the old Swede. She was the great Norse type—tall, deep-breasted, molded on the old Viking lines. Her sixty years had slipped from her. She looked like some ancient priestess of Odin." He hesitated. "She knew," he said slowly, "something more far-seeing than my science had given her sight. She warned me—she warned me! Fools and mad that we are to pass such things by without heed!" He brushed a hand over his eyes.

"She stood there," he went on, "Her eyes were wide, brilliant, staring. She thrust her head forward toward Nan-Tanach, regarding the moving lights; she listened. Suddenly she raised her arms and made a curious gesture to the moon. It was—an archaic—movement; she seemed to drag it from remote antiquity—yet in it was a strange suggestion of power.

"Twice she repeated this gesture and—the tinkling died away! She turned to us.

"'Go,' she said, and her voice seemed to come from far distances. 'Go from here—and quickly! Go while you may. They have called—' She pointed to the islet. 'They know you are here. They wait.' Her eyes widened further. 'It is there,' she wailed. 'It beckons—the—the—'

"She fell at Edith's feet, and as she fell over the lagoon came again the tinklings, now with a quicker note of jubilance—almost of triumph.

"We ran to Thora, Stanton and I, and picked her up. Her head rolled and her face, eyes closed, turned as though drawn full into the moonlight. I felt in my heart a throb of unfamiliar fear—for her face had changed again. Stamped upon it was a look of mingled transport and horror—alien, terrifying, strangely revolting. It was"—he thrust his face close to my eyes—"what you see in mine!"

For a dozen heart-beats I stared at him, fascinated; then he sank back again into the half-shadow of the berth.

"I managed to hide her face from Edith," he went on. "I thought she had suffered some sort of a nervous seizure. We carried her into her tent. Once within the unholy mask dropped from her, and she was again only the kindly, rugged old woman. I watched her throughout the night. The sounds from Nan-Tanach continued until about an hour before moon-set. In the morning Thora awoke, none the worse, apparently. She had had bad dreams, she said. She could not remember what they were—except that they had warned her of danger. She was oddly sullen, and I noted that throughout the morning her gaze returned again half-fascinatedly, half-wonderingly to the neighboring isles.

"That afternoon the natives returned. They were so exuberant in their apparent relief to find us well and intact that Stanton's suspicions of them were confirmed. He slyly told their leader that 'from the noise they had made on Nan-Tanach the night before they must have thoroughly enjoyed themselves.'

"I think I never saw such stark terror as the Ponapean manifested at the remark! Stanton himself was so plainly startled that he tried to pass it over as a jest. He met poor success! The men seemed panic-stricken, and for a time I thought they were about to abandon us—but they did not. They pitched their camp at the western side of the island out of sight of Nan-Tanach. I noticed that they built large fires, and whenever I awoke that night I heard their voices in slow, minor chant—one of their song 'charms.' I thought drowsily, against evil *ani*. I heard nothing else; the place of frowning walls was wrapped in silence—no lights showed. The next morning the men were quiet, a little depressed, but as the hours wore on they regained their spirits, and soon life at the camp was going on just as it had before.

"You will understand, Goodwin, how the occurrences I have related would excite the scientific curiosity. We rejected immediately, of course, any explanation admitting the supernatural. Why not? Except the curiously disquieting effects of the tinkling music and Thora's behavior there was nothing to warrant any such fantastic theories—even if our minds had been the kind to harbor them.

"We came to the conclusion that there must be a passageway between Ponape and Nan-Tanach, known to the natives—and used by them during their rites. Ceremonies were probably held in great vaults or caverns beneath the ruins.

"We decided at last that on the next departure of our laborers we would set forth immediately to Nan-Tanach. We would investigate during the day, and at evening my wife and Thora would go back to camp, leaving Stanton and me to spend the night on the island, observing from some safe hiding-place what might occur.

"The moon waned, appeared crescent in the west; waxed slowly toward the full. Before the men left us they literally prayed us to accompany them. Their importunities only made us more eager to see what it was that, we were now convinced, they wanted to conceal from us. At least that was true of Stanton and myself. It was not true of Edith. She was thoughtful, abstracted—reluctant. Thora, on the other hand, showed an unusual restlessness, almost an eagerness to go. Goodwin"—he paused—"Goodwin, I know now that the poison was working in Thora—and that women have perceptions that we men lack—forebodings, sensings. I wish to Heaven I had known it then—Edith!" he cried suddenly. "Edith—come back to me! Forgive me!"

I stretched the decanter out to him. He drank deeply. Soon he had regained control of himself.

"When the men were out of sight around the turn of the harbor," he went on, "we took our boat and made straight for Nan-Tanach. Soon its mighty sea-wall towered above us. We passed through the water-gate with its gigantic hewn prisms of basalt and landed beside a half-submerged pier. In front of us stretched a series of giant steps leading into a vast court strewn with fragments of fallen pillars. In the center of the court, beyond the shattered pillars, rose another terrace of basalt blocks, concealing, I knew, still another enclosure.

"And now, Goodwin, for the better understanding of what follows and to guide you, should I—not be able—to accompany you when you go there, listen carefully to my description of this place: Nan-Tanach is literally three rectangles. The first rectangle is the sea-wall, built up of monoliths. Gigantic steps lead up from the landing of the sea-gate through the entrance to the courtyard.

"This courtyard is surrounded by another, inner basalt wall.

"Within the courtyard is the second enclosure. Its terrace, of the same basalt as the outer walls, is about twenty feet high. Entrance is gained to it by many breaches which time has made in its stonework. This is the inner court, the heart of Nan-Tanach! There lies the great central vault with which is associated the one name of living being that has come to us out of the mists of the past. The natives say it was the treasure-house of Chau-te-leur, a mighty king who reigned long 'before their fathers.' As Chau is the ancient Ponapean word both for sun and king, the name means 'place of the sun king.'

"And opposite this place of the sun king is the moon rock that hides the moon pool.

"It was Stanton who first found what I call the moon rock. We had been inspecting the inner courtyard, Edith and Thora were getting together our lunch. I forgot to say that we had previously gone all over the islet and had found not a trace of living thing. I came out of the vault of Chau-te-leur to find Stanton before a part of the terrace studying it wonderingly.

" 'What do you make of this?' he asked me as I came up, He pointed to the wall. I followed his finger and saw a slab of stone about fifteen feet high and ten wide. At first all I noticed was the exquisite nicety with which its edges joined the blocks about it. Then I realized that its color was subtly different—tinged with gray and of a smooth, peculiar—deadness.

" 'Looks more like calcite than basalt,' I said. I touched it and withdrew my hand quickly, for at the contact every nerve in my arm tingled as though a shock of frozen electricity had passed through it. It was not cold as we know cold that I felt. It was a chill force—the phrase I have used—frozen electricity—describes it better than anything else. Stanton looked at me oddly.

" 'So you felt it, too,' he said. 'I was wondering whether I was developing hallucinations like Thora. Notice, by the way, that the blocks beside it are quite warm beneath the sun.'

"I felt them and touched the grayish stone again. The same faint shock ran through my hand—a tingling chill that had in it a suggestion of substance, of force. We examined the slab more closely. Its edges were cut as though by an engraver of jewels. They fitted against the neighboring blocks in almost a hair-line. Its base, we saw, was slightly curved, and fitted as closely as top and sides upon the huge stones on which it rested. And then we noted that these stones had been hollowed to follow the line of the gray stone's foot. There was a semicircular depression running from one side of the slab to the other. It was as though the gray rock stood in the center of a shallow cup—revealing half, covering half. Something about this hollow attracted me. I reached down and felt it. Goodwin, although the balance of the stones that formed it, like all the stones of the courtyard, were rough and age-worn—this was as smooth, as even surfaced as though it just left the hands of the polisher.

" 'It's a door!' exclaimed Stanton. 'It swings around in that little cup. That's what make the hollow so smooth.'

" 'Maybe you're right,' I replied. 'But how the devil can we open it?'

"We went over the slab again—pressing upon its edges, thrusting against its sides. During one of those efforts I happened to look up—and cried out. For a foot above and even each side of the corner of the gray rock's lintel I had seen a slight convexity, visible only from the angle at which my gaze struck it. These bosses on the basalt were circular, eighteen inches in diameter, as we learned later, and at the center extended two inches only beyond the face of the terrace. Unless one looked directly up at them while leaning against the moon rock—for this slab, Goodwin, is the moon rock—they were invisible. And none would dare stand there!

"We carried with us a small scaling-ladder, and up this I went. The bosses were apparently nothing more than chiseled curvatures in the stone. I laid my hand on the one I was examining, and drew it back so sharply I almost threw myself from the ladder. In my palm, at the base of my thumb, I had felt the same shock that I had in touching the slab below. I put my hand back. The impression came from a spot not more than an inch wide. I went carefully over the entire convexity, and six times more the chill ran through my arm. There were, Goodwin, seven circles an inch wide in the curved place, each of which communicated the precise sensation I have described. The convexity on the opposite side of the slab gave precisely the same results. But no amount of touching or of pressing these spots singly or in any combination gave the slightest promise of motion to the slab itself.

" 'And yet—they're what open it,' said Stanton positively.

" 'Why do you say that?' I asked.

" 'I—don't know,' he answered hesitatingly. 'But something tells me so. Throck,' he went on half earnestly, half laughingly, 'the purely scientific part of me is fighting the purely human part of me. The scientific part is urging me to find some way to get that slab either down or open. The human part is just as strongly urging me to do nothing of the sort and get away while I can!'

"He laughed again—shamefacedly.

" 'Which will it be?' he asked—and I thought that in his tone the human side of him was ascendant.

" 'It will probably stay as it is—unless we blow it to bits.' I said.

" 'I thought of that,' he answered, 'and—I wouldn't dare,' he added somberly enough. And even as I had spoken there came to me the same feeling that he had expressed. It was as though something passed out of the gray rock that struck my heart as a hand strikes an impious lip. We turned away—uneasily, and faced Thora coming through a breach in the terrace.

"'Miss Edith wants you quick,' she began—and stopped. I saw her eyes go past me and widen. She was looking at the gray rock. Her body grew suddenly rigid; she took a few stiff steps forward and ran straight to it. We saw her cast herself upon its breast, hands and face pressed against it; heard her scream as though her very soul was being drawn from her—and watched her fall at its foot. As we picked her up I saw steal from her face the look I had observed when I first heard the crystal music of Nan-Tanach—that unhuman mingling of opposites!"

V

AV-O-LO-HA

"We carried Thora back down to where Edith was waiting. We told her what had happened and what we had found. She listened gravely, and as we finished Thora sighed and opened her eyes.

"'I would like to see the stone,' she said. 'Charles, you stay here with Thora.' We passed through the outer court silently—and stood before the rock. She touched it, drew back her hand as I had; thrust it forward again resolutely and held it there. She seemed to be listening. Then she turned to me.

"'David,' said my wife, and the wistfulness in her voice hurt me—'David, would you be very very disappointed if we went from here—without trying to find out any more about it—would you?'

"Goodwin, I never wanted anything so much in my life as I wanted to learn what that rock concealed. You will understand—the cumulative curiosity that all the happenings had caused, the certainty that before me was an entrance to a place that, while known to the natives—for I still clung to that theory—was utterly unknown to any man of my race, that within, ready for my finding, was the answer to the stupendous riddle of these islands and a lost chapter in the history of humanity. There before me—and was I asked to turn away, leaving it unread!

"Nevertheless. I tried to master my desire. and I answered—'Edith, not a bit if you want us to do it.'

"She read my struggle in my eyes. She looked at me searchingly for a moment and then turned back toward the gray rock. I saw a shiver pass through her. I felt a tinge of remorse and pity!

"'Edith,' I exclaimed, 'we'll go!'

"She looked at me hard. 'Science is a jealous mistress,' she quoted. 'No, after all it may be just fancy. At any rate, you can't run away. No! But, Dave, I'm going to stay too!'

" 'You are not!' I exclaimed. 'You're going back to the camp with Thora. Stanton and I will be all right.'

" 'I'm going to stay,' she repeated. And there was no changing her decision. As we neared the others she laid a hand on my arm.

" 'Dave,' she said. 'If there should be something—well—inexplicable tonight—something that seems—too dangerous—will you promise to go back to our own islet tomorrow, or, while we can, and wait until the natives return?'

"I promised eagerly—for the desire to stay and see what came with the night was like a fire within me.

"And would to Heaven I had not waited another moment, Goodwin; would to Heaven I had gathered them all together then and sailed back on the instant through the mangroves to Uschen-Tau!

"We found Thora on her feet again and singularly composed. She claimed to have no more recollection of what had happened after she had spoken to Stanton and to me in front of the gray rock than she had after the seizure on Uschen-Tau. She grew sullen under our questioning, precisely as she had before. But to my astonishment, when she heard of our arrangements for the night, she betrayed a febrile excitement that had in it something of exultance.

"We had picked a place about five hundred feet away from the steps leading into the outer court.

"We settled down just before dusk to wait for whatever might come. I was nearest the giant steps; next to me Edith; then Thora, and last Stanton. Each of us had with us automatic pistols, and all, except Thora, had rifles.

"Night fell. After a time the eastern sky began to lighten, and we knew that the moon was rising; grew lighter still, and the orb peeped over the sea; swam suddenly into full sight. Edith gripped my hand, for, as though the full emergence into the heavens had been a signal, we heard begin beneath us the deep chanting. It came from illimitable depths.

"The moon poured her rays down upon us, and I saw Stanton start. On the instant I caught the sound that had roused him. It came from the inner enclosure. It was like a long, soft sighing. It was not human; seemed in some way—mechanical. I glanced at Edith and then at Thora. My wife was intently listening. Thora sat, as she had since we had placed ourselves, elbows on knees, her hands covering her face.

"And then suddenly from the moonlight flooding us there came to me a great drowsiness. Sleep seemed to drip from the rays and fall upon my eyes, closing them—closing them inexorably. I felt Edith's hand relax in mine, and under my own heavy lids saw her nodding. I saw Stanton's head fall upon his breast and his body sway drunkenly. I tried to rise—to fight against the profound desire for slumber that pressed in on me.

"And as I fought I saw Thora raise her head as though listening; saw her rise and turn her face toward the gateway. For a moment she gazed, and my drugged eyes seemed to perceive within it a deeper, stronger radiance. Thora looked at us. There was infinite despair in her face—and expectancy. I tried again to rise—and a surge of sleep rushed over me. Dimly, as I sank within it, I heard a crystalline chiming; raised my lids once more with a supreme effort, saw Thora, bathed in light, standing at the top of the stairs, and then—sleep took me for its very own—swept me into the very heart of oblivion!

"Dawn was breaking when I wakened. Recollection rushed back on me and I thrust a panic-stricken hand out toward Edith; touched her and felt my heart give a great leap of thankfulness. She stirred, sat up, rubbing dazed eyes. I glanced toward Stanton. He lay on his side, back toward us, head in arms.

"Edith looked at me laughingly. 'Heavens! what sleep!' she said. Memory came to her. Her face paled. 'What happened?' she whispered. 'What made us sleep like that?' She looked over to Stanton, sprang to her feet, ran to him, shook him. He turned over with a mighty yawn, and I saw relief lighten her face as it had lightened my heart.

"Stanton raised himself stiffly. He looked at us. 'What's the matter?' he exclaimed. 'You look as though you've seen ghosts!'

"Edith caught my hands. 'Where's Thora?' she cried. Before I could answer she ran out into the open calling: 'Thora! Thora!'

"Stanton stared at me. 'Taken!' was all I could say. Together we went to my wife, now standing beside the great stone steps, looking up fearfully at the gateway into the terraces. There I told them what I had seen before sleep had drowned me. And together then we ran up the stairs, through the court and up to the gray rock.

"The gray rock was closed as it had been the day before, nor was there trace of its having opened. No trace! Even as I thought this Edith dropped to her knees before it and reached toward something lying at its foot. It was a little piece of gray silk. I knew it for part of the kerchief Thora wore about her hair. Edith took the fragment; hesitated. I saw then that it had been *cut* from the kerchief as though by a razor-edge; I saw, too, that a few threads ran from it—down toward the base of the slab; ran to the base of the gray rock and—under it! The gray rock was a door! And it had opened and Thora had passed through it!

"I think, Goodwin, that for the next few minutes we all were a little insane. We beat upon that diabolic entrance with our hands, with stones and clubs. At last reason came back to us. Stanton set forth for the camp to bring back blasting powder and tools. While he was gone Edith and I searched the whole islet for any other clue. We found not a trace of Thora nor any indication of any living being save ourselves. We went back to the gateway to find Stanton returned.

"Goodwin, during the next two hours we tried every way in our power to force entrance through the slab. The rock within effective blasting radius of the cursed door resisted our drills. We tried explosions at the base of the slab with charges covered by rock. They made not the slightest impression on the surface beneath, expending their force, of course, upon the slighter resistance of their coverings.

"Afternoon found us hopeless, so far as breaking through the rock was concerned. Night was coming on and before it came we would have to decide our course of action. I wanted to go to Ponape for help. But Edith objected that this would take hours and after we had reached there it would be impossible to persuade our men to return with us that night, if at all. What then was left? Clearly only one of two choices: to go back to our camp and wait for our men to return and on their return try to persuade them to go with us to Nan-Tanach. But this would mean the abandonment of Thora for at least two days. We could not do it; it would have been too cowardly.

"The other choice was to wait where we were for night to come; to wait for the rock to open as it had the night before, and to make a sortie through it for Thora before it could close again. With the sun had come confidence; at least a shattering of the mephitic mists of superstition with which the strangeness of the things that had befallen us had clouded for a time our minds. In that brilliant light there seemed no place for fantoms.

"The evidence that the slab had opened was unmistakable, but might not Thora simply have *found* it open through some mechanism, still working after ages, and dependent for its action upon laws of physics unknown to us upon the full light of the moon? The assertion of the natives that the *ani* had greatest power at this time might be a far-flung reflection of knowledge which had found ways to use forces contained in moonlight, as we have found ways to utilize the forces in the sun's rays. If so, Thora was probably behind the slab, sending out prayers to us for help.

"But how explain the sleep that had descended upon us? Might it not have been some emanation from plants or gaseous emanations from the island itself? Such things were far from uncommon, we agreed. In some way, the period of their greatest activity might coincide with the period of the moon, but if this were so why had not Thora also slept?

"As dusk fell we looked over our weapons. Edith was an excellent shot with both rifle and pistol. With the idea that the impulse toward sleep was the result either of emanations such as I have described or man made, we constructed rough-and-ready but effective neutralizers, which we placed over our mouths and nostrils. We had decided that my wife was to remain in the hollow spot. Stanton would take up a station on the far side of the stairway and I would place myself opposite him on the side near Edith. The place I picked out was less than five hundred feet from her, and I could reassure myself now as to her safety, as I looked down upon the hollow wherein she crouched. As the phenomena had previously synchronized with the risings of the moon, we had no reason to think they would occur any earlier this night.

"A faint glow in the sky heralded the moon. I kissed Edith, and Stanton and I took our places. The moon dawn increased rapidly; the disk swam up, and in a moment it seemed was shining in full radiance upon ruins and sea.

"As it rose there came as on the night before the curious little sighing sound from the inner terrace. I saw Stanton straighten up and stare intently through the gateway, rifle ready. Even at the distance he was from me, I discerned amazement in his eyes. The moonlight within the gateway thickened, grew stronger. I watched his amazement grow into sheer wonder.

"I arose.

"'Stanton, what do you see?' I called cautiously. He waved a silencing hand. I turned my head to look at Edith. A shock ran through me. She lay upon her side. Her face was turned full toward the moon. She was in deepest sleep!

"As I turned again to call to Stanton, my eyes swept the head of the steps and stopped, fascinated. For the moonlight had thickened more. It seemed to be— curdled—there; and through it ran little gleams and veins of shimmering white fire. A languor passed through me. It was not the ineffable drowsiness of the preceding night. It was a sapping of all will to move. I tore my eyes away and forced them upon Stanton. I tried to call out to him. I had not the will to make my lips move! I had struggled against this paralysis and as I did so I felt through me a sharp shock. It was like a blow. And with it came utter inability to make a single motion. Goodwin, I could not even move my eyes!

"I saw Stanton leap upon the steps and move toward the gateway. As he did so the light in the courtyard grew dazzlingly brilliant. Through it rained tiny tinklings that set the heart to racing with pure joy and stilled it with terror.

"And now for the first time I heard that cry '*Av-o-lo-ha! Av-o-lo-ha!*' the cry you heard on deck. It murmured with the strange effect of a sound only partly in our own space—as though it were part of a fuller phrase passing through from another dimension and losing much as it came; infinitely caressing, infinitely cruel!

"On Stanton's face I saw come the look I dreaded—and yet knew would appear; that mingled expression of delight and fear. The two lay side by side as they had on Thora, but were intensified. He walked on up the stairs; disappeared beyond the range of my fixed gaze. Again I heard the murmur—'*Av-o-lo-ha!*' There was triumph in it now and triumph in the storm of tinklings that swept over it.

"For another heart-beat there was silence. Then a louder burst of sound and ringing through it Stanton's voice from the courtyard—a great cry—a scream—filled with ecstasy insupportable and horror unimaginable! And again there was silence. I strove to burst the invisible bonds that held me. I could not. Even my eyelids were fixed. Within them my eyes, dry and aching, burned.

"Then, Goodwin—I first saw the inexplicable! The crystalline music swelled. Where I sat I could take in the gateway and its basalt portals, rough and broken, rising to the top of the wall forty feet above, shattered, ruined portals—unclimbable. From this gateway an intenser light began to flow. It grew, it gushed, and into it, into my sight, walked Stanton.

"Stanton! But—Goodwin! What a vision!" He ceased. I waited—waited.

VI

INTO THE MOON POOL

"Goodwin," Throckmartin said at last. "I can describe him only as a thing of living light. He radiated light; was filled with light, overflowed with it. Around him was a shining cloud that whirled through and around him in radiant swirls, shimmering tentacles, luminescent, coruscating spirals.

"I saw his face. It shone with a rapture too great to be borne by living men, and was shadowed with insuperable misery. It was as though his face had been remolded by the hand of God and the hand of Satan, working together and in harmony. You have seen it on my face. But you have never seen it in the degree that Stanton bore it. The eyes were wide open and fixed, as though upon some inward vision of hell and heaven! He walked like the corpse of a man damned who carried within him an angel of light.

"The music swelled again. I heard again the murmuring—'*Av-o-lo-ha!*' Stanton turned, facing the ragged side of the portal. And then I saw that the light that filled and surrounded him had a nucleus, a core—something shiftingly human shaped—

that dissolved and changed, gathered itself, whirled through and beyond him and back again. And as this shining nucleus passed through him Stanton's whole body pulsed with light. As the luminescence moved, there moved with it, still and serene always, seven tiny globes of light like seven little moons.

"So much I saw and then swiftly Stanton seemed to be lifted—levitated—up the unscalable wall and to its top. The glow faded from the moonlight, the tinkling music grew fainter. I tried again to move. The spell still held me fast. The tears were running down now from my rigid lids and brought relief to my tortured eyes.

"I have said my gaze was fixed. It was. But from the side, peripherally, it took in a part of the far wall of the outer enclosure. Ages seemed to pass and I saw a radiance stealing along it. Soon there came into sight the figure that was Stanton. Far away he was—on the gigantic wall. But still I could see the shining spirals whirling jubilantly around and through him; felt rather than saw his tranced face beneath the seven lights. A swirl of crystal notes, and he had passed. And all the time, as though from some opened well of light, the courtyard gleamed and sent out silver fires that dimmed the moon-rays, yet seemed strangely to be a part of them.

"Ten times he passed before me so. The luminescence came with the music; swam for a while along the man-made cliff of basalt and passed away. Between times eternities rolled and still I crouched there, a helpless thing of stone with eyes that would not close!

"At last the moon neared the horizon. There came a louder burst of sound; the second, and last, cry of Stanton, like an echo of the first! Again the soft sigh from the inner terrace. Then—utter silence. The light faded; the moon was setting and with a rush life and power to move returned to me. I made a leap for the steps, rushed up them. through the gateway and straight to the gray rock. It was closed—as I knew it would be. But did I dream it or did I hear, echoing through it as though from vast distances a triumphant shouting—'Av-o-lo-ha! Av-o-lo-ha!'?

"I remembered Edith. I ran back to her. At my touch she wakened; looked at me wonderingly; raised herself on a hand.

"'Dave!' she said. 'I slept—after all.' She saw the despair on my face and leaped to her feet. 'Dave!' she cried. 'What is it? Where's Charles?'

"I lighted a fire before I spoke. Then I told her. And for the balance of that night we sat before the flames, arms around each other—like two frightened children.

Suddenly Throckmartin held his hands out to me appealingly.

"Goodwin, old friend!" he cried. "Don't look at me as though I were mad. It's truth, absolute truth. Wait"—I comforted him as well as I could. After a little time he took up his story.

"Never," he said, "did man welcome the sun as we did that morning. As soon as it was light we went back to the courtyard. The basalt walls whereon I had seen Stanton were black and silent. The terraces were as they had been. The gray slab was in its place. In the shallow hollow at its base was—nothing. Nothing—nothing was there anywhere on the islet of Stanton—not a trace, not a sign on Nan-Tanach to show that he had ever lived.

"What were we to do? Precisely the same arguments that had kept us there the night before held good now—and doubly good. We could not abandon these two; could not go as long as there was the faintest hope of finding them—and yet for love of each other how could we remain? I loved my wife, Goodwin—how much I never knew until that day; and she loved me as deeply.

" 'It takes only one each night,' she said. 'Beloved, let it take me.'

"I wept, Goodwin. We both wept.

" 'We will meet it together,' she said. And it was thus at last that we arranged it."

"That took great courage indeed, Throckmartin," I interrupted. He looked at me eagerly.

"You do believe then?" he exclaimed.

"I believe," I said. He pressed my hand with a grip that nearly crushed it.

"Now," he told me. "I do not fear. If I—fail, you will prepare and carry on the work."

I promised. And—Heaven forgive me—that was three years ago.

"It did take courage," he went on, again quietly. "More than courage. For we knew it was renunciation. Each of us in our hearts felt that one of us would not be there to see the sun rise. And each of us prayed that the death, if death it was, would not come first to the other.

"We talked it all over carefully, bringing to bear all our power of analysis and habit of calm, scientific thought. We considered minutely the time element in the phenomena. Although the deep chanting began at the very moment of moonrise, fully five minutes had passed between its full lifting and the strange sighing sound from the inner terrace. I went back in memory over the happenings of the night before. At least fifteen minutes had intervened between the first heralding sigh and the intensification of the moonlight in the courtyard. And this glow grew for at least ten minutes more before the first burst of the crystal notes.

"The sighing sound—of what had it reminded me? Of course—of a door revolving and swishing softly along its base.

" 'Edith' I cried. 'I think I have it! The gray rock opens five minutes after upon the moonrise. But whoever or whatever it is that comes through it must wait until the moon has risen higher, or else it must come from a distance. The thing to do is not to wait for it, but to surprise it before it passes out the door. We will go into the inner court early. You will take your rifle and pistol and hide yourself where you can command the opening—if the slab does open. The instant it moves I will enter. It's our best chance, Edith. I think it's our only one.

"My wife demurred strongly. She wanted to go with me. But I convinced her that it was better for her to stand guard without, prepared to help me if I were forced from what lay behind the rock again into the open.

"The day passed too swiftly. In the face of what we feared our love seemed stronger than ever. Was it the flare of the spark before extinguishment? I wondered. We prepared and ate a good dinner. We tried to keep our minds from anything but scientific aspect of the phenomena. We agreed that whatever it was its cause must be human, and that we must keep that fact in mind every second. But what kind of men could create such prodigies? We thrilled at the thought of finding perhaps the remnants of a vanished race, living perhaps in cities over whose rocky skies the Pacific rolled, exercising there the lost wisdom of the half-gods of earth's youth.

"At the half-hour before moonrise we two went into the inner courtyard. I took my place at the side of the gray rock. Edith crouched behind a broken pillar twenty feet away, slipped her rifle-barrel over it so that it would cover the opening.

"The minutes crept by. The courtyard was very quiet. The darkness lessened and through the breaches of the terrace I watched the far sky softly lighten. With the first pale flush the stillness became intensified. It deepened—became unbearably— expectant. The moon rose, showed the quarter, the half, then swam up into full sight like a great bubble.

"Its rays fell upon the wall before me and suddenly upon the convexities I have described seven little circles of light sprang out. They gleamed, glimmered, grew brighter—shone. The gigantic slab before me turned as though on a pivot, sighing softly as it moved.

"For a moment I gasped in amazement. It was like a conjurer's trick. And the moving slab I noticed was also glowing, becoming opalescent like the little shining circles above.

"Only for a second I gazed and then with a word to Edith flung myself through the opening which the slab had uncovered. Before me was a platform and from the platform steps led downward into a smooth corridor. This passage was not dark, it glowed with the same faint silvery radiance as the door. Down it I raced. As I ran, plainer than ever before, I heard the chanting. The passage turned abruptly, passed parallel to the walls of the outer courtyard and then once more led abruptly downward. Still I ran, and as I ran I looked at the watch on my wrist. Less than three minutes had elapsed.

"The passage ended. Before me was a high vaulted arch. For a moment I paused. It seemed to open into space; a space filled with lambent, coruscating, many-colored mist whose brightness grew even as I watched. I passed through the arch and stopped in sheer awe!

"In front of me was a pool. It was circular, perhaps twenty feet wide. Around it ran a low, softly curved lip of glimmering silvery stone. Its water was palest blue. The pool with its silvery rim was like a great blue eye staring upward.

"Upon it streamed seven shafts of radiance. They poured down upon the blue eye like cylindrical torrents; they were like shining pillars of light rising from a sapphire floor.

"One was the tender pink of the pearl; one of the aurora's green; a third a deathly white; the fourth the blue in mother-of-pearl: a shimmering column of pale amber: a beam of amethyst: a shaft of molten silver. Such are the colors of the seven lights that stream upon the moon pool. I drew closer, awestricken. The shafts did not illumine the depths. They played upon the surface and seemed there to diffuse, to melt into it. The pool drank them!

"Through the water tiny gleams of phosphorescence began to dart, sparkles and coruscations of pale incandescence. And far, far below I sensed a movement, a shifting glow, as of something slowly rising.

"I looked upward, following the radiant pillars to their source. Far above were seven shining globes, and it was from these that the rays poured. Even as I watched their brightness grew. They were like seven moons set high in some caverned heaven. Slowly their splendor increased, and with it the splendor of the seven beams streaming from them. It came to me that they were crystals of some unknown kind set in the roof of the moon pool's vault and that their light was drawn from the moon shining high above them. They were wonderful, those lights—and what must have been the knowledge of those who set them there!

"Brighter and brighter they grew as the moon climbed higher, sending its full radiance down through them. I tore my gaze away and stared at the pool. It had grown milky, opalescent. The rays gushing into it seemed to be filling it; it was alive with sparkling scintillations, glimmerings. And the luminescence I had seen rising from its depths was larger, nearer!

"A swirl of mist floated up from its surface. It drifted within the embrace of the rosy beam and hung there for a moment. The beam seemed to embrace it, sending through it little shining corpuscles, tiny rosy spiralings. The mist absorbed the rays, was strengthened by it, gained substance. Another swirl sprang into the amber shaft, clung and fed there, moved swiftly toward the first and mingled with it. And now other swirls arose, here and there, too fast to be counted, hung poised in the embrace of the light streams; flashed and pulsed into each other.

"Thicker and thicker still they arose until the surface of the pool was a pulsating pillar of opalescent mist; steadily growing stronger; drawing within it life from the seven beams falling upon it, drawing to it from below the darting red atoms of the pool. Into its center was passing the luminescence I had sensed rising from the far depths. And the center glowed, throbbed—began to send out questing swirls and tendrils.

"There forming before me was *that* which had walked with Stanton, which had taken Thora—the thing I had come to find!

"With the shock of realization my brain sprang into action. My hand fell to my pistol and I fired shot after shot into its radiance. The place rang with the explosions and there came to me a sense of unforgivable profanation. Devilish as I knew it to be, that chamber of the moon pool seemed also—in some way—holy. As though a god and a demon dwelt there, inextricably commingled.

"As I shot the pillar wavered; the water grew more disturbed. The mist swayed and shook; gathered itself again. I slipped a second clip into the automatic and, another idea coming to me, took careful aim at one of the globes in the roof. From thence I knew scame the force that shaped the dweller in the pool. From the pouring rays came its strength. If I could destroy them I could check its forming. I fired again and again. If I hit the globes I did no damage. The little motes in their beams danced with the motes in the mist, troubled. That was all.

"Up from the pool like little bells, like bubbles of crystal notes rose the tinklings. Their notes were higher, had lost their sweetness, were angry, as it were, with themselves.

"And then out from the inexplicable, hovering over the pool, swept a shining swirl. It caught me above the heart; wrapped itself around me. I felt an icy coldness and then there rushed over me a mingled ecstasy and horror. Every atom of me quivered with delight and at the same time shrank with despair. There was nothing loathsome in it. But it was as though the icy soul of evil and the fiery soul of good had stepped together within me. The pistol dropped from my hand.

"So I stood while the pool gleamed and sparkled; the streams of light grew more intense and the mist glowed and strengthened. I saw that its shining core had shape—but a shape that my eyes and brain could not define. It was as though a being of another sphere should assume what it might of human semblance, but was not able to conceal that what human eyes saw was but a part of it. It was neither man nor woman; it was unearthly and androgynous. Even as I found its human semblance it changed. And still the mingled rapture and terror held me. Only in a little corner of my brain dwelt something untouched; something that held itself apart and watched. Was it the soul? I have never believed—and yet—

"Over the head of the misty body there sprang suddenly out seven little lights. Each was the color of the beam beneath which it rested. I knew now that the dweller was—complete!

"And then—behind me I heard a scream. It was Edith's voice. It came to me that she had heard the shots and followed me. I felt every faculty concentrate into a mighty effort. I wrenched myself free from the gripping tentacle and it swept back. I turned to catch Edith, and as I did so slipped—fell. As I dropped I saw the radiant shape above the pool leap swiftly for me!

"There was the rush past me and as the dweller paused, straight into it raced Edith, arms outstretched to shield me from it!"

He trembled.

"She threw herself squarely within its diabolic splendor," he whispered.

"She stopped and reeled as though she had encountered solidity. And as she faltered it wrapped its shining self around her. The crystal tinklings burst forth jubilantly. The light filled her, ran through and around her as it had with Stanton, and I saw drop upon her face—the look. From the pillar came the murmur—'*Av-o-lo-ha!*' The vault echoed it.

" 'Edith!' I cried. 'Edith!' I was in agony. She must have heard me, even through the—thing. I saw her try to free herself. Her rush had taken her to the very verge of the moon pool. She tottered; and in an instant—she fell—with the radiance still holding her, still swirling and winding around and through her—into the moon pool! She sank, Goodwin, and with her went—the dweller!

"I dragged myself to the brink. Far down I saw a shining, many-colored nebulous cloud descending; caught a glimpse of Edith's face, disappearing; her eyes stared up to me filled with supernal ecstasy and horror. And—vanished!

"I looked about me stupidly. The seven globes still poured their radiance upon the pool. It was pale-blue again. Its sparklings and coruscations were gone. From far below there came a muffled outburst of triumphant chanting!

" 'Edith!' I cried again. 'Edith, come back to me!' And then a darkness fell upon me. I remember running back through the shimmering corridors and out into the courtyard. Reason had left me. When it returned I was far out at sea in our boat wholly estranged from civilization. A day later I was picked up by the schooner in which I came to Port Moresby.

"I have formed a plan, you must hear it, Goodwin—" He fell upon his berth. I bent over him. Exhaustion and the relief of telling his story had been too much for him. He slept like the dead.

VII

THE DWELLER COMES

All that night I watched over him. When dawn broke I went to my room to get a little sleep myself. But my slumber was haunted.

The next day the storm was unabated. Throckmartin came to me at lunch. He looked better. His strange expression had waned. He had regained much of his old alertness.

"Come to my cabin," he said. There, he stripped his shirt from him. "Something is happening," he said. "The mark is smaller." It was as he said.

"I'm escaping," he whispered jubilantly. "Just let me get to Melbourne safely, and then we'll see who'll win! For, Goodwin, I'm not at all sure that Edith is dead— as we know death—nor that the others are. There was something outside experience there—some great mystery."

And all that day he talked to me of his plans.

"There's a natural explanation, of course," he said. "My theory is that the moon rock is of some composition sensitive to the action of moon rays; somewhat as the metal selenium is to sun rays. There is a powerful quality in moonlight, as both science and legends can attest. We know of its effect upon the mentality, the nervous system, even upon certain diseases.

"The moon slab is of some material that reacts to moonlight. The circles over the top are, without doubt, its operating agency. When the light strikes them they release the mechanism that opens the slab, just as you can open doors with sunlight by an ingenious arrangement of selenium-cells. Apparently it takes the strength of the full moon to do this. We will first try a concentration of the rays of the nearly full moon upon these circles to see whether that will open the rock. If it does we will be able to investigate the pool without interruption from—from—what emanates.

"Look, here on the chart are their locations. I have made this in duplicate for you in the event of something happening to me."

He worked upon the chart a little more.

"Here," he said, "is where I believe the seven great globes to be. They are probably hidden somewhere in the ruins of the islet called Tau, where they can catch the first moon rays. I have calculated that when I entered I went so far this way—here is the turn; so far this way, took this other turn and ran down this long, curving corridor to the hall of the moon pool. That ought to make lights, at least approximately here." He pointed.

"They are certainly cleverly concealed, but they must be open to the air to get the light. They should not be too hard to find. They must be found." He hesitated again. "I suppose it would be safer to destroy them, for it is clearly through them that the phenomenon of the pool is manifested; and yet, to destroy so wonderful a thing! Perhaps the better way would be to have some men up by them, and if it were necessary to protect those below, to destroy them on signal. Or they might simply be covered. That would neutralize them. To destroy them—" He hesitated again. "No, the phenomenon is too important to be destroyed without fullest investigation." His face clouded again. "But it is not human; it can't be," he muttered. He turned to me and laughed. "The old conflict between science and too frail human credulity!" he said.

Again—"We need half a dozen diving-suits. The pool must be entered and searched to its depths. That will indeed take courage, yet in the time of the new moon it should be safe, or perhaps better after the dweller is destroyed or made safe."

We went over plans, accepted them, rejected them, and still the storm raged—and all that day and all that night.

I hurry to the end. That afternoon there came a steady lightening of the clouds which Throckmartin watched with deep uneasiness. Toward dusk they broke away suddenly and soon the sky was clear. The stars came twinkling out.

"It will be tonight," Throckmartin said to me. "Goodwin, friend, stand by me. Tonight it will come, and I must fight."

I could say nothing. About an hour before moonrise we went to his cabin. We fastened the port-holes tightly and turned on the lights. Throckmartin had some queer theory that the electric rays would be a bar to his pursuer. I don't know why. A little later he complained of increasing sleepiness.

"But it's just weariness." he said. "Not at all like that other drowsiness. It's an hour till moonrise still," he yawned at last. "Wake me up a good fifteen minutes before."

He lay upon the berth. I sat thinking. I came to myself with a start. What time was it? I looked at my watch and jumped to the port-hole. It was full moonlight; the orb had been up for fully half an hour. I strode over to Throckmartin and shook him by the shoulder.

"Up, quick. man!" I cried. He rose sleepily. His shirt fell open at the neck and I looked, in amazement, at the white band around his chest. Even under the electric light it shone softly, as though little flecks of light were in it.

Throckmartin seemed only half-awake. He looked down at his breast, saw the glowing cincture, and smiled.

"Oh, yes," he said drowsily, "it's coming—to take me back to Edith! Well, I'm glad."

"Throckmartin," I cried. "Wake up! Fight!"

"Fight!" he said. "No use; keep the maps; come after us."

He went to the port and drowsily drew aside the curtain. The moon traced a broad path of light straight to the ship. Under its rays the band around his chest gleamed brighter and brighter, shot forth little rays; seemed to move.

He peered out intently and, suddenly, before I could stop him. threw open the port. I saw a glimmering presence moving swiftly along the moon path toward us, skimming over the waters.

And with it raced little crystal tinklings and far off I heard a long-drawn murmuring cry.

On the instant the lights went out in the cabin, evidently throughout the ship, for I heard shouting above. I sprang back into a corner and crouched there. At the port-hole was a radiance: swirls and spirals of living white cold fire. It poured into the cabin and it was filled with dancing motes of light, and over the radiant core of it shone seven little lights like tiny moons. It gathered Throckmartin to it. Light pulsed through and from him. I saw his skin turn to a translucent, shimmering whiteness like illumined porcelain. His face became unrecognizable, inhuman with the monstrous twin expressions. So he stood for a moment. The pillar of light seemed to hesitate and the seven lights to contemplate me. I shrank further down into the corner. I saw Throckmartin drawn to the port. The room filled with murmuring. I fainted.

When I awakened the lights were burning again.

But of Throckmartin there was no trace!

There are some things that we are bound to regret all our lives. I suppose I was unbalanced by what I had seen. I could not think clearly. But there came to me the sheer impossibility of telling the ship's officers what I had seen; what Throckmartin had told me. They would accuse me, I felt, of his murder. At neither appearance of the phenomenon had any save our two selves witnessed it. I was certain of this because they would surely have discussed it. Why none had seen it I do not know.

The next morning when Throckmartin's absence was noted. I merely said that I had left him early in the evening. It occurred to no one to doubt me, or to question me further. His strangeness had caused much comment; all had thought him half-mad. And so it was officially reported that he had fallen or jumped from the ship during the failure of the lights, the cause of which was another mystery of that night.

Afterward, the same inhibition held me back from making his and my story known to my fellow scientists.

But this inhibition is suddenly dead, and I am not sure that its death is not a summons from Throckmartin.

And now I am going to Nan-Tanach to make amends for my cowardice by seeking out the dweller. So sure am I that all I have written here is absolutely true.

Unseen, Unfeared

FRANCIS STEVENS

Francis Stevens was the pen name employed by Gertrude Barrows Bennett (1883–1948), who specialized in tales of fantasy and mystery in the pulp magazines of the early twentieth century, notably the lost race adventure The Citadel of Fear *(1918), the alternate world science fiction novel* The Heads of Cerberus *(1919), and the Atlantean fantasy* Claimed *(1920). This story, from the February 10, 1919 issue of* People's Favorite Magazine, *elaborates a theme similar to that found in J.H. Rosny's "The Sixth Sense, or Another World," but Stevens presents her wonders of the invisible world with much more horror than humor.*

I

I had been dining with my ever-interesting friend, Mark Jenkins, at a little Italian restaurant near South Street. It was a chance meeting. Jenkins is too busy, usually, to make dinner engagements. Over our highly seasoned food and sour, thin, red wine, he spoke of little odd incidents and adventures of his profession. Nothing very vital or important, of course. Jenkins is not the sort of detective who first detects and then pours the egotistical and revealing details of achievement in the ears of every acquaintance, however appreciative.

But when I spoke of something I had seen in the morning papers, he laughed. "Poor old 'Doc' Holt! Fascinating old codger, to anyone who really knows him. I've had his friendship for years—since I was first on the city force and saved a young assistant of his from jail on a false charge. And they had to drag him into the poisoning of this young sport, Ralph Peeler!"

"Why are you so sure he couldn't have been implicated?" I asked.

But Jenkins only shook his head, with a quiet smile. "I have reasons for believing otherwise," was all I could get out of him on that score, "But," he added, "the only reason he was suspected at all is the superstitious dread of these ignorant people around him. Can't see why he lives in such a place. I know for a fact he doesn't have to. Doc's got money of his own. He's an amateur chemist and dabbler in different sorts of research work, and I suspect he's been guilty of 'showing off.' Result, they all swear he has the evil eye and holds forbidden communion with invisible powers. Smoke?"

Jenkins offered me one of his invariably good cigars, which I accepted, saying thoughtfully: "A man has no right to trifle with the superstitions of ignorant people. Sooner or later, it spells trouble."

"Did in his case. They swore up and down that he sold love charms openly and poisons secretly, and that, together with his living so near to—somebody else—got him temporarily suspected. But my tongue's running away with me, as usual!"

"As usual," I retorted impatiently, "you open up with all the frankness of a Chinese diplomat."

He beamed upon me engagingly and rose from the table, with a glance at his watch. "Sorry to leave you, Blaisdell, but I have to meet Jimmy Brennan in ten minutes."

He so clearly did not invite my further company that I remained seated for a little while after his departure; then took my own way homeward. Those streets always held for me a certain fascination, particularly at night. They are so unlike the rest of the city, so foreign in appearance, with their little shabby stores, always open until late evening, their unbelievably cheap goods, displayed as much outside the shops as in them, hung on the fronts and laid out on tables by the curb and in the street itself. Tonight, however, neither people nor stores in any sense appealed to me. The mixture of Italians, Jews and a few Negroes, mostly bareheaded, unkempt and generally unhygienic in appearance, struck me as merely revolting. They were all humans, and I, too, was human. Some way I did not like the idea.

Puzzled a trifle, for I am more inclined to sympathize with poverty than accuse it, I watched the faces that I passed. Never before had I observed how bestial, how brutal were the countenances of the dwellers in this region. I actually shuddered when an old-clothes man, a gray-bearded Hebrew, brushed me as he toiled past with his barrow.

There was a sense of evil in the air, a warning of things which it is wise for a clean man to shun and keep clear of. The impression became so strong that before I had walked two squares I began to feel physically ill. Then it occurred to me that the one glass of cheap Chianti I had drunk might have something to do with the feeling. Who knew how that stuff had been manufactured, or whether the juice of the grape entered at all into its ill-flavored composition? Yet I doubted if that were the real cause of my discomfort.

By nature I am rather a sensitive, impressionable sort of chap. In some way tonight this neighborhood, with its sordid sights and smells, had struck me wrong.

My sense of impending evil was merging into actual fear. This would never do. There is only one way to deal with an imaginative temperament like mine— conquer its vagaries. If I left South Street with this nameless dread upon me, I could never pass down it again without a recurrence of the feeling. I should simply have to stay here until I got the better of it—that was all.

I paused on a corner before a shabby but brightly lighted little drug store. Its gleaming windows and the luminous green of its conventional glass show jars made the brightest spot on the block. I realized that I was tired, but hardly wanted to go in there and rest. I knew what the company would be like at its shabby, sticky soda fountain. As I stood there, my eyes fell on a long white canvas sign across from me, and its black-and-red lettering caught my attention.

SEE THE GREAT UNSEEN!
COME IN! THIS MEANS YOU!
FREE TO ALL!

A museum of fakes, I thought, but also reflected that if it were a show of some kind I could sit down for a while, rest, and fight off this increasing obsession of non-existent evil. That side of the street was almost deserted, and the place itself might well be nearly empty.

II

I walked over, but with every step my sense of dread increased. Dread of I knew not what. Bodiless, inexplicable horror had me as in a net, whose strands, being intangible, without reason for existence, I could by no means throw off. It was not the people now. None of them were about me. There, in the open, lighted street, with no sight nor sound of terror to assail me, I was the shivering victim of such fear as I had never known was possible. Yet still I would not yield.

Setting my teeth, and fighting with myself as with some pet animal gone mad, I forced my steps to slowness and walked along the sidewalk, seeking entrance. Just here there were no shops, but several doors reached in each case by means of a few iron-railed stone steps. I chose the one in the middle beneath the sign. In that neighborhood there are museums, shops and other commercial enterprises conducted in many shabby old residences, such as were these. Behind the glazing of the door I had chosen I could see a dim, pinkish light, but on either side the windows were quite dark.

Trying the door, I found it unlocked. As I opened it a party of Italians passed on the pavement below and I looked back at them over my shoulder. They were gayly dressed, men, women and children, laughing and chattering to one another; probably on their way to some wedding or other festivity.

In passing, one of the men glanced up at me and involuntarily I shuddered back against the door. He was a young man, handsome after the swarthy manner of his race, but never in my life had I see a face so expressive of pure, malicious cruelty, naked and unashamed. Our eyes met and his seemed to light up with a vile gleaming, as if all the wickedness of his nature had come to a focus in the look of concentrated hate he gave me.

They went by, but for some distance I could see him watching me, chin on shoulder, till he and his party were swallowed up in the crowd of marketers farther down the street.

Sick and trembling from that encounter, merely of eyes though it had been, I threw aside my partly smoked cigar and entered. Within there was a small vestibule, whose ancient tesselated floor was grimy with the passing of many feet. I could feel the grit of dirt under my shoes, and it rasped on my rawly quivering nerves. The inner door stood partly open, and going on I found myself in a bare, dirty hallway, and was greeted by the sour, musty, poverty-stricken smell common to dwellings of the very ill-to-do. Beyond there was a stairway, carpeted with ragged grass matting. A gas jet, turned low inside a very dusty pink globe, was the light I had seen from without.

Listening, the house seemed entirely silent. Surely, this was no place of public amusement of any kind whatever. More likely it was a rooming house, and I had, after all, mistaken the entrance.

To my intense relief, since coming inside, the worst agony of my unreasonable terror had passed away. If I could only get in some place where I could sit down and be quiet, probably I should be rid of it for good. Determining to try another entrance, I was about to leave the bare hallway when one of several doors along the side of it suddenly opened and a man stepped out into the hall.

"Well?" he said, looking at me keenly, but with not the least show of surprise at my presence.

I beg your pardon," I replied. "The door was unlocked and I came in here, thinking it was the entrance to the exhibit—what do they call it?—the 'Great Unseen.' The one that is mentioned on that long white sign. Can you tell me which door is the right one?"

"I can."

With that brief answer he stopped and stared at me again. He was a tall, lean man, somewhat stooped, but possessing considerable dignity of bearing. For that neighborhood, he appeared uncommonly well dressed, and his long, smooth-shaven face was noticeable because, while his complexion was dark and his eyes coal-black, above them the heavy brows and his hair were almost silvery-white. His age might have been anything over the threescore mark.

I grew tired of being stared at. "If you can and—won't, then never mind," I observed a trifle irritably, and turned to go. But his sharp exclamation halted me.

"No!" he said. "No—no! Forgive me for pausing—it was not hesitation, I assure you. To think that one—one, even, has come! All day they pass my sign up there—pass and fear to enter. But you are different. *You* are not of these timorous, ignorant foreign peasants. You ask me to tell you the right door? Here it is! Here!"

And he struck the panel of the door, which he had closed behind him, so that the sharp yet hollow sound of it echoed up through the silent house.

Now it may be thought that after all my senseless terror in the open street, so strange a welcome from so odd a showman would have brought the feeling back, full force. But there is an emotion stronger, to a certain point, than fear. This queer old fellow aroused my curiosity. What kind of museum could it be that he accused the passing public of fearing to enter? Nothing really terrible, surely, or it would have been closed by the police. And normally I am not an unduly timorous person. "So it's in there, is it?" I asked, coming toward him. "And I'm to be sole audience? Come, that will be an interesting experience." I was half laughing now.

"The most interesting in the world," said the old man, with a solemnity which rebuked my lightness.

With that he opened the door, passed inward and closed it again—in my very face. I stood staring at it blankly. The panels, I remember, had been originally painted white, but now the paint was flaked and blistered, gray with dirt and dirty finger marks. Suddenly it occurred to me that I had no wish to enter there. Whatever was behind it could be scarcely worth seeing, or he would not choose such a place for its exhibition. With the old man's vanishing my curiosity had cooled, but just as I again turned to leave, the door opened and this singular showman stuck his white-eyebrowed face through the aperture. He was frowning impatiently. "Come in—come in!" he snapped, and promptly withdrawing his head, once more closed the door.

"He has something there he doesn't want should get out," was the very natural conclusion which I drew. "Well, since it can hardly be anything dangerous, and he's so anxious I should see it—here goes!"

With that I turned the soiled white porcelain handle, and entered.

The room I came into was neither very large nor very brightly lighted. In no way did it resemble a museum or lecture room. On the contrary, it seemed to have been fitted up as a quite well-appointed laboratory. The floor was linoleum-covered, there were glass cases along the walls whose shelves were filled with bottles, specimen jars, graduates, and the like. A large table in one corner bore what looked like some odd sort of camera, and a larger one in the middle of the room was fitted with a long rack filled with bottles and test tubes, and was besides littered with papers, glass slides, and various paraphernalia which my ignorance failed to identify. There were several cases of books, a few plain wooden chairs, and in the corner a large iron sink with running water.

My host of the white hair and black eyes was awaiting me, standing near the larger table. He indicated one of the wooden chairs with a thin forefinger that shook a little, either from age or eagerness. "Sit down—sit down! Have no fear but that you will be interested, my friend. Have no fear at all—of anything!"

As he said it he fixed his dark eyes upon me and stared harder than ever. But the effect of his words was the opposite of their meaning. I did sit down, because my knees gave under me, but if in the outer hall I had lost my terror, it now returned twofold upon me. Out there the light had been faint, dingily roseate, indefinite. By it I had not perceived how this old man's face was a mask of living malice—of cruelty, hate and a certain masterful contempt. Now I knew the meaning of my fear, whose warning I would not heed. Now I knew that I had walked into the very trap from which my abnormal sensitiveness had striven in vain to save me.

III

Again I struggled within me, bit at my lip till I tasted blood, and presently the blind paroxysm passed. It must have been longer in going than I thought, and the old man must have all that time been speaking, for when I could once more control my attention, hear and see him, he had taken up a position near the sink, about ten feet away, and was addressing me with a sort of "platform" manner, as if I had been the large audience whose absence he had deplored.

"And so," he was saying, "I was forced to make these plates very carefully, to truly represent the characteristic hues of each separate organism. Now, in color work of every kind the film is necessarily extremely sensitive. Doubtless you are familiar in a general way with the exquisite transparencies produced by color photography of the single-plate type."

He paused, and trying to act like a normal human being, I observed: "I saw some nice landscapes done in that way—last week at an illustrated lecture in Franklin Hall."

He scowled, and made an impatient gesture at me with his hand. "I can proceed better without interruptions," he said. "My pause was purely oratorical."

I meekly subsided, and he went on in his original loud, clear voice. He would have made an excellent lecturer before a much larger audience—if only his voice could have lost that eerie, ringing note. Thinking of that I must have missed some more, and when I caught it again he was saying:

"As I have indicated, the original plate is the final picture. Now, many of these organisms are extremely hard to photograph, and microphotography in color is particularly difficult. In consequence, to spoil a plate tries the patience of the photographer. They are so sensitive that the ordinary darkroom ruby lamp would instantly ruin them, and they must therefore be developed either in darkness or by a special light produced by interposing thin sheets of tissue of a particular shade of green and of yellow between lamp and plate, and even that will often cause ruinous fog. Now I, finding it hard to handle them so, made numerous experiments with a view of discovering some glass or fabric of a color which should add to the safety of the green, without robbing it of all efficiency. All proved equally useless, but intermittently I persevered—until last week."

His voice dropped to an almost confidential tone, and he leaned slightly toward me. I was cold from my neck to my feet, though my head was burning, but I tried to force an appreciative smile.

"Last week," he continued impressively, "I had a prescription filled at the corner drug store. The bottle was sent home to me wrapped in a piece of what I first took to be whitish, slightly opalescent paper. Later I decided that it was some kind of membrane. When I questioned the druggist, seeking its source, he said it was a sheet of 'paper' that was around a bundle of herbs from South America. That he had no more, and doubted if I could trace it. He had wrapped my bottle so, because he was in haste and the sheet was handy.

I can hardly tell you what first inspired me to try that membrane in my photographic work. It was merely dull white with a faint hint of opalescence, except when held against the light. Then it became quite translucent and quite brightly prismatic. For some reason it occurred to me that this refractive effect might help in breaking up the actinic rays—the rays which affect the sensitive emulsion. So that night I inserted it behind the sheets of green and yellow tissue, next the lamp prepared my trays and chemicals laid my plate holders to hand, turned off the white light and—turned on the green!

There was nothing in his words to inspire fear. It was a wearisomely detailed account of his struggles with photography. Yet, as he again paused impressively, I wished that he might never speak again. I was desperately, contemptibly in dread of the thing he might say next.

Suddenly, he drew himself erect, the stoop went out of his shoulders, he threw back his head and laughed. It was a hollow sound, as if he laughed into a trumpet. "I won't tell you what I saw! Why should I? Your own eyes shall bear witness. But this much I'll say, so that you may better understand—later. When our poor, faultily sensitive vision can perceive a thing, we say that it is visible. When the nerves of touch can feel it, we say that it is tangible. Yet I tell you there are beings intangible to our physical sense, yet whose presence is felt by the spirit, and invisible to our eyes merely because those organs are not attuned to the light as reflected from their bodies. But light passed through the screen, which we are about to use has a wave length novel to the scientific world, and by it you shall see with the eyes of the flesh that which has been invisible since life began. Have no fear!"

He stopped to laugh again, and his mirth was yellow-toothed—menacing.

"*Have no fear!*" he reiterated, and with that stretched his hand toward the wall, there came a click and we were in black, impenetrable darkness. I wanted to spring up, to seek the door by which I had entered and rush out of it, but the paralysis of unreasoning terror held me fast.

I could hear him moving about in the darkness, and a moment later a faint green glimmer sprang up in the room. Its source was over the large sink, where I suppose he developed his precious "color plates."

Every instant, as my eyes became accustomed to the dimness, I could see more clearly. Green light is peculiar. It may be far fainter than red, and at the same time far more illuminating. The old man was standing beneath it, and his face by that ghastly radiance had the exact look of a dead man's. Besides this, however, I could observe nothing appalling.

"That," continued the man, "is the simple developing light of which I have spoken—now watch, for what you are about to behold no mortal man but myself has ever seen before."

For a moment he fussed with the green lamp over the sink. It was so constructed that all the direct rays struck downward. He opened a flap at the side, for a moment there was a streak of comforting white luminance from within, then he inserted something, slid it slowly in—and closed the flap.

The thing he put in—that South American "membrane" it must have been—instead of decreasing the light increased it—amazingly. The hue was changed from green to greenish-gray, and the whole room sprang into view, a livid, ghastly chamber, filled with—overcrawled by—what?

My eyes fixed themselves, fascinated, on something that moved by the old man's feet. It writhed there on the floor like a huge, repulsive starfish, an immense, armed, legged thing, that twisted convulsively. It was smooth, as if made of rubber, was whitish-green in color; and presently raised its great round blob of a body on tottering tentacles, crept toward my host and writhed upward—yes, climbed up his legs, his body. And he stood there, erect, arms folded, and stared sternly down at the thing which climbed.

But the room—the whole room was alive with other creatures than that. Everywhere I looked they were—centipedish things, with yard-long bodies, detestable, furry spiders that lurked in shadows, and sausage-shaped translucent horrors that moved—and floated through the air. They dived—here and there between me and the light, and I could see its bright greenness through their greenish bodies.

Worse, though; far worse than these were the *things with human faces*. Mask-like, monstrous, huge gaping mouths and slitlike eyes—I find I cannot write of them. There was that about them which makes their memory even now intolerable.

The old man was speaking again, and every word echoed in my brain like the ringing of a gong. "Fear nothing! Among such as these do you move every hour of the day and night. Only you and I have seen, for God is merciful and has spared our race from sight. But I am not merciful! I loathe the race which gave these creatures birth—the race which might be so surrounded by invisible, unguessed but blessed beings—and chooses these for its companions! All the world shall see and know. One by one shall they come here, learn the truth, and perish. For who can survive the ultimate of terror? Then I, too, shall find peace, and leave the earth to its heritage of man-created horrors. Do you know what these are—whence they come?"

This voice boomed now like a cathedral bell. I could not answer, him, but he waited for no reply. "Out of the ether—out of the omnipresent ether from whose intangible substance the mind of God made the planets, all living things, and man—man has made these! By his evil thoughts, by his selfish panics, by his lusts and his interminable, never-ending hate he has made them, and they are everywhere! Fear nothing—but see where there comes to you, its creator, the shape and the body of your FEAR!"

And as he said it I perceived a great Thing coming toward me—a Thing—but consciousness could endure no more. The ringing, threatening voice merged in a roar within my ears, there came a merciful dimming of the terrible, lurid vision, and blank nothingness succeeded upon horror too great for bearing.

IV

There was a dull, heavy pain above my eyes. I knew that they were closed, that I was dreaming, and that the rack full of colored bottles which I seemed to see so clearly was no more than a part of the dream. There was some vague but imperative reason why I should rouse myself. I wanted to awaken, and thought that by staring very hard indeed I could dissolve this foolish vision of blue and yellow-brown bottles. But instead of dissolving they grew clearer, more solid and substantial of appearance, until suddenly the rest of my senses rushed to the support of sight, and I became aware that my eyes were open, the bottles were quite real, and that I was sitting in a chair, fallen sideways so that my cheek rested most uncomfortably on the table which held the rack.

I straightened up slowly and with difficulty, groping in my dulled brain for some clue to my presence in this unfamiliar place, this laboratory that was lighted only by the rays of an arc light in the street outside its three large windows. Here I sat, alone, and if the aching of cramped limbs meant anything, here I had sat for more than a little time.

Then, with the painful shock which accompanies awakening to the knowledge of some great catastrophe, came memory. It was this very room, shown by the street lamp's rays to be empty of life, which I had seen thronged with creatures too loathsome for description. I staggered to my feet, staring fearfully about. There were the glass-floored cases, the bookshelves, the two tables with their burdens, and the long iron sink above which, now only a dark blotch of shadow, hung the lamp from which had emanated that livid, terrifically revealing illumination. Then the experience had been no dream, but a frightful reality. I was alone here now. With callous indifference my strange host had allowed me to remain for hours unconscious, with not the least effort to aid or revive me. Perhaps, hating me so, he had hoped that I would die there.

At first I made no effort to leave the place. Its appearance filled me with reminiscent loathing. I longed to go, but as yet felt too weak and ill for the effort. Both mentally and physically my condition was deplorable, and for the first time

I realized that a shock to the mind may react upon the body as vilely as any debauch of self-indulgence.

Quivering in every nerve and muscle, dizzy with headache and nausea, I dropped back into the chair, hoping that before the old man returned I might recover sufficient self-control to escape him. I knew that he hated me, and why. As I waited, sick, miserable, I understood the man. Shuddering, I recalled the loathsome horrors he had shown me. If the mere desires and emotions of mankind were daily carnified in such forms as those, no wonder that he viewed his fellow beings with detestation and longed only to destroy them.

I thought, too, of the cruel, sensuous faces I had seen in the streets outside— seen for the first time, as if a veil had been withdrawn from eyes hitherto blinded by self-delusion. Fatuously trustful as a month-old puppy, I had lived in a grim, evil world, where goodness is a word and crude selfishness the only actuality. Drearily my thoughts drifted back through my own life, its futile purposes, mistakes and activities. All of evil that I knew returned to overwhelm me. Our gropings toward divinity were a sham, a writhing sunward of slime-covered beasts who claimed sunlight as their heritage, but in their hearts preferred the foul and easy depths.

Even now, though I could neither see nor feel them, this room, the entire world, was acrawl with the beings created by our real natures. I recalled the cringing, contemptible fear to which my spirit had so readily yielded, and the faceless Thing to which the emotion had given birth.

Then abruptly, shockingly, I remembered that every moment I was adding to the horde. Since my mind could conceive only repulsive incubi, and since while I lived I must think, feel, and so continue to shape them, was there no way to check so abominable a succession? My eyes fell on the long shelves with their many-colored bottles. In the chemistry of photography there are deadly poisons—I knew that. Now was the time to end it—now! Let him return and find his desire accomplished. One good thing I could do, if one only. I could abolish my monster-creating self.

V

My friend Mark Jenkins is an intelligent and usually a very careful man. When he took from "Smiler" Callahan a cigar which had every appearance of being excellent, innocent Havana, the act denoted both intelligence and caution. By very clever work he had traced the poisoning of young Ralph Peeler to Mr. Callahan's door, and he believed this particular cigar to be the mate of one smoked by Peeler just previous to his demise. And if, upon arresting Callahan, he had not confiscated this bit of evidence, it would have doubtless been destroyed by its regrettably uncon-scientious owner.

But when Jenkins shortly afterward gave me that cigar, as one of his own, he committed one of those almost inconceivable blunders which, I think, are occasion-ally forced upon clever men to keep them from overweening vanity. Discovering his slight mistake, my detective friend spent the night searching for his unintended victim, myself; and that his search was successful was due to Pietro Marini, a young Italian of Jenkins' acquaintance, whom he met about the hour of 2:00 A.M. returning from a dance.

Now, Marini had seen me standing on the steps of the house where Doctor Frederick Holt had his laboratory and living rooms, and he had stared at me, not with any ill intent, but because he thought I was the sickest-looking, most ghastly specimen of humanity that he had ever beheld. And, sharing the superstition of his South Street neighbors, he wondered if the worthy doctor had poisoned me as well as Peeler. This suspicion he imparted to Jenkins, who, however, had the best of reasons for believing otherwise. Moreover, as he informed Marini, Holt was dead, having drowned himself late the previous afternoon. An hour or so after our talk in the restaurant, news of his suicide reached Jenkins.

It seemed wise to search any place where a very sick-looking young man had been seen to enter, so Jenkins came straight to the laboratory. Across the fronts of those houses was the long sign with its mysterious inscription, "See the Great Unseen," not at all mysterious to the detective. He knew that next door to Doctor Holt's the second floor had been thrown together into a lecture room, where at certain hours a young man employed by settlement workers displayed upon a screen stereopticon views of various deadly bacilli, the germs of diseases appropriate to dirt and indifference. He knew, too, that Doctor Holt himself had helped the educational effort along by pro-viding some really wonderful lantern slides, done by micro-color photography.

On the pavement outside, Jenkins found the two-thirds remnant of a cigar, which he gathered in and came up the steps, a very miserable and self-reproachful detective. Neither outer nor inner door was locked, and in the laboratory he found me, alive, but on the verge of death by another means that he had feared.

In the extreme physical depression following my awakening from drugged sleep, and knowing nothing of its cause, I believed my adventure fact in its entirety. My mentality was at too low an ebb to resist its dreadful suggestion. I was searching among Holt's various bottles when Jenkins burst in. At first I was merely annoyed at the interruption of my purpose, but before the anticlimax of his explanation the mists of obsession drifted away and left me still sick in body, but in spirit happy as any man may well be who has suffered a delusion that the world is wholly bad—and learned that its badness springs from his own poisoned brain.

The malice which I had observed in every face, including young Marini's, existed only in my drug-affected vision. Last week's "popular-science" lecture had been recalled to my subconscious mind—the mind that rules dreams and delirium—by the photographic apparatus in Holt's workroom. "See the Great Unseen" assisted materially, and even the corner drug store before which I had paused, with its green-lit show vases, had doubtless played a part. But presently, following something Jenkins told me, I was driven to one protest. "If Holt was not here," I demanded, "if Holt is dead, as you say, how do you account for the fact that I, who have never seen the man, was able to give you an accurate description which you admit to be that of Doctor Frederick Holt?"

He pointed across the room. "See that?" It was a life-size bust portrait, in crayons, the picture of a white-haired man with bushy eyebrows and the most piercing black eyes I had ever seen—until the previous evening. It hung facing the door and near the windows, and the features stood out with a strangely lifelike appearance in the white rays of the arc lamp just outside. "Upon entering," continued Jenkins, "the first thing you saw was that portrait, and from it your delirium built a living, speaking man. So, there are your white-haired showman, your unnatural fear, your color photography and your pretty green golliwogs all nicely explained for you, Blaisdell, and thank God you're alive to hear the explanation. If you had smoked the whole of that cigar—well, never mind. You didn't. And now, my very dear friend, I think it's high time that you interviewed a real, flesh-and-blood doctor. I'll phone for a taxi."

"Don't," I said. "A walk in the fresh air will do me more good than fifty doctors."

"Fresh air! There's no fresh air on South Street in July," complained Jenkins, but reluctantly yielded.

I had a reason for my preference. I wished to see people, to meet face to face even such stray prowlers as might be about at this hour, nearer sunrise than midnight, and rejoice in the goodness and kindliness of the human countenance—particularly as found in the lower classes.

But even as we were leaving there occurred to me a curious inconsistency.

"Jenkins," I said, "you claim that the reason Holt, when I first met him in the hall, appeared to twice close the door in my face, was because the door never opened until I myself unlatched it."

"Yes," confirmed Jenkins, but he frowned, foreseeing my next question.

"Then why, if it was from that picture that I built so solid, so convincing a vision of the man, did I see Holt in the hall before the door was open?"

"You confuse your memories," retorted Jenkins rather shortly.

"Do I? Holt was dead at that hour, but—*I tell you I saw Holt outside the door!* And what was his reason for committing suicide?"

Before my friend could reply I was across the room, fumbling in the dusk there at the electric lamp above the sink. I got the tin flap open and pulled out the sliding screen, which consisted of two sheets of glass with fabric between, dark on one side, yellow on the other. With it came the very thing I dreaded—a sheet of whitish, parchmentlike, slightly opalescent stuff.

Jenkins was beside me as I held it at arm's length toward the windows. Through it the light of the arc lamp fell—divided into the most astonishingly brilliant rainbow hues. And instead of diminishing the light, it was perceptibly increased in the oddest way. Almost one thought that the sheet itself was luminous, and yet when held in shadow it gave off no light at all.

"Shall we—put it in the lamp again—and try it?" asked Jenkins slowly, and in his voice there was no hint of mockery.

I looked him straight in the eyes. "No," I said, "we won't. I was drugged. Perhaps in that condition I received a merciless revelation of the discovery that caused Holt's suicide, but I don't believe it. Ghost or no ghost, I refuse to ever again believe in the depravity of the human race. If the air and the earth are teeming with invisible horrors, they are *not* of our making, and—the study of demonology is better let alone. Shall we burn this thing, or tear it up?"

"We have no right to do either," returned Jenkins thoughtfully, "but you know, Blaisdell, there's a little too darn much realism about some parts of your 'dream.' I haven't been smoking any doped cigars; but when you held that up to the light, I'll swear I saw—well, never mind. Burn it—send it back to the place it came from. "

"South America?" said I.

"A hotter place than that. Burn it."

So he struck a match and we did. It was gone in one great white flash.

A large place was given by morning papers to the suicide of Doctor Frederick Holt, caused, it was surmised, by mental derangement brought about by his unjust implication in the Peeler murder. It seemed an inadequate reason, since he had never been arrested, but no other was ever discovered.

Of course, our action in destroying that "membrane" was illegal and rather precipitate, but, though he won't talk about it, I know that Jenkins agrees with me—doubt is sometimes better than certainty, and there are marvels better left unproved. Those, for instance, which concern the Powers of Evil.

In the
Penal Colony

Franz Kafka

Czech writer Franz Kafka (1883–1924) wrote bleak stories rich with philosophical and metaphysical insights whose characters and situations often seem as though drawn from nightmares. This story, first published in the May 1919 issue of Kurt Wolff Verlag *(under the title "In der Strafkolonie") is memorable for its depiction of a fiendish invention wrought by inhumane captors for the purported enforcement of justice.*

"It's an exceptional apparatus," the officer said to the world traveler and, with a certain admiration, surveyed the apparatus that was, after all, quite familiar to him. The traveler appeared to have accepted purely out of politeness the commandant's invitation to attend the execution of a soldier, who had been condemned for insubordination and insulting a superior officer. There did not seem to be much interest in the execution throughout the penal colony itself. In any event, the only other persons present besides the officer and the traveler in this small but deep and sandy valley, surrounded by barren slopes on all sides, were the condemned man—a dull, thick-lipped creature with a disheveled appearance—and a soldier, who held the heavy chain that controlled the smaller chains attached to the condemned man's ankles, wrists, and neck, chains that were also linked together. But the condemned man looked so submissively doglike that it seemed as if he ought to have been allowed to run free on the slopes and would only need to be whistled for when the execution was due to begin.

The traveler was not particularly enthralled by the apparatus and he paced back and forth behind the condemned man with almost visible indifference while the officer made the final preparations, one moment crawling beneath the apparatus that was deeply embedded in the ground, another climbing a ladder to inspect its uppermost parts. These were tasks that really could have been left to a mechanic, but the officer performed them with energetic eagerness, perhaps because he was a devoted admirer of the apparatus or because, for whatever other reasons, the work be entrusted to no one else. "Now everything's ready" he called out at last, and climbed down from the ladder. He had worked up a sweat and was breathing with his mouth wide open; he had also tucked two very fine ladies' handkerchiefs under the collar of his uniform. "Surely these uniforms are too heavy for the tropics," said the traveler instead of inquiring, as the officer had expected, about the apparatus. "Of course," the officer said, washing the oil and grease from his hands in a nearby bucket of water, "but they represent home for us; we don't want to forget about our homeland—but now just take a look at this machine," he immediately added, drying his hands on a towel and simultaneously indicating the apparatus. "Up to this point I have to do some of the operations by hand, but from now on the apparatus works entirely by itself." The traveler nodded and followed the officer. Then the officer, seeking to prepare himself for all eventualities, said: "Naturally, there are sometimes problems; I hope of course there won't be any problems today, but one must allow for the possibility. The apparatus should work continually for twelve hours, but even if anything does go wrong, it will be something minor and easy to repair at once."

"Won't you sit down?" he inquired at last, pulling out a cane chair from a whole heap of them and offering it to the traveler, who was unable to refuse. The traveler was now sitting at the edge of a pit, and he glanced cursorily in its direction. It was not very deep. On one side of the pit, the excavated earth had been piled up to form an embankment, on the other side of the pit stood the apparatus. "I don't know," said the officer, "whether the commandant has already explained the apparatus to you." The traveler made an vague gesture with his hand, and the officer could not have asked for anything better, for now he was free to explain the apparatus himself. "This apparatus," he said, grabbing hold of the crankshaft and leaning against it, "was the invention of our former commandant. I myself was involved in the very first experiments and also shared in the work all the way to its completion, but the credit for the invention belongs to him alone. Have you ever heard of our former commandant? No? Well, it wouldn't be too much to say that the organization of the entire penal colony is his work. We who were his friends knew long before his death that the organization of the colony was so perfectly self-contained that his successor, even if he had a thousand new schemes brewing in his head, would find it impossible to alter a thing from the old system, at least for many years to come. Our prediction has indeed come true, and the new commandant has had to acknowledge as much. It's too bad you never met the old commandant!—but," the officer interrupted himself, "I'm rambling, and here is his apparatus standing right in front of us. It consists, as you can see, of three parts. In the course of time each part has acquired its own nickname. The lower part is called the bed, the upper one is the designer, and this one in the middle here that hovers between them is called the harrow." "The harrow?" asked the traveler. He had not been listening very intently; the sun beat down brutally into the shadeless valley, and it was difficult to collect one's thoughts. He had to admire the officer all the more: he wore his snugly fitting dress uniform, hung with braiding and weighted with epaulettes; he expounded on his subject with zeal and tightened a few screws here and therewith a screwdriver while he spoke. As for the soldier, he seemed to be much the same condition as the traveler: He had wound the condemned man's chain around both his wrists and propped himself up with one hand on his rifle; his head hung down and he took no notice of anything. The traveler was not surprised by this, as the officer was speaking in French and certainly neither the soldier nor the condemned man understood French. It was therefore that much more remarkable that the condemned man nevertheless strove to follow the officer's explanations. With a drowsy sort of persistence he directed his gaze wherever the officer pointed, and when the traveler broke in with his question, he, like the officer, looked at the traveler.

"Yes, the harrow," answered the officer, "a perfect name for it. The needles are arranged similarly to the teeth in a harrow and the whole thing works something like a harrow, although it is stationary and performs with much more artistry. You'll soon understand it anyway. The condemned is laid here on the bed—you see, first I want to explain the apparatus first and then start it up, that way you'll be able to follow it better; besides, one of the gears in the designer is badly worn, it makes a horrible screeching noise when it's turning and you can hardly hear yourself speak; unfortunately spare parts are difficult to come by around here—well, so here is the bed, as I said before. It's completely covered with a layer of cotton wool, you'll find out what that's for later. The condemned man is laid facedown on the cotton wool, naked, of course; here are straps for the hands, the feet, and here for the neck, in order to hold him down. So, as I was saying, here at the head of the bed here, where the condemned man is at first laid facedown, is the little felt gag that can be adjusted easily to fit straight in the man's mouth. Its meant to keep him from screaming or biting his tongue. The man has to take the felt in his mouth since otherwise the neck straps would break his neck." "That's cotton wool?" asked the traveler, leaning forward. "It certainly is," the officer said with a smile, "feel for yourself." He grabbed hold of the traveler's hand and guided it over the surface. "It's specially prepared cotton wool, which is why you don't recognize it; I'll come to its purpose in a minute." The traveler was starting to feel the stirrings of interest in the apparatus; he gazed up at it with one arm raised to shield his eyes from the sun, he looked up at the height of the apparatus. It was a large structure. The bed and the designer were the same size and looked like two dark steamer trunks. The designer hung about two meters above the bed; they were joined at the corners by four brass rods that practically gleamed in the sunlight. The harrow was suspended on a steel band between the two trunks.

The officer had barely noticed the traveler's previous indifference but definitely sensed his burgeoning interest, so he paused in his explanation in order to give the traveler time for undisturbed observation. The condemned man imitated the traveler, but since he could not shield his eyes, he blinked up into the sun.

"So, the man lies down," said the traveler, leaning back in his chair and crossing his legs.

"Yes," said the officer, pushing his cap back a little and mopping his sweaty face with his hand, "now listen! Both the bed and the designer have their own electric battery; the bed needs one for itself and the designer needs one for the harrow. As soon as the man is strapped in the bed is set in motion. It quivers with tiny, rapid vibrations, both from side to side and up and down. You will have seen similar contraptions in sanitariums, but for our bed, all the movements are calibrated precisely, for they must correspond to movements of the harrow. But it is the harrow that actually carries out the sentence."

"And just what is the sentence?" inquired the traveler. "You don't know that either?" the officer said in astonishment, and bit his lip. "Excuse me if my explanation seems a bit incoherent, I beg your pardon. The commandant's always used to take care of the explanations, but new commandant seems to scorn this duty; but that such a distinguished visitor"—the traveler tried to wave this distinction away with both hands, but the officer insisted on the expression—"that such a distinguished visitor should not even be made aware of the form our sentencing takes is a new development, which"—another was about to pass his lips but he checked himself and said only: "I was not informed of this, it's not my fault. In any case, I'm certainly the man best equipped to explain our sentencing, since I have here"—he patted his breast pocket—"the relevant drawings by our former commandant."

"Drawings by the commandant himself?" the traveler asked. "Was he everything himself? He was a soldier, judge, engineer, chemist, draftsman?"

"Yes sir, he was," the officer answered, nodding his head with a remote, contemplative look. Then he examined his hands closely; they did not seem to be clean enough for him to handle the drawings, so he went over to the bucket and washed them again. Then he drew out a small leather folder and said: "The sentence does not sound severe. Whatever commandment the condemned man has transgressed is engraved on his body by the harrow. This man, for example"—the officer indicated the man—"will have inscribed on his body, 'Honor thy superiors!' "

The traveler briefly looked at the man who stood, as the officer pointed him out, with bowed head, apparently straining with all his might to catch something of what was said. But the movements of his thick, closed lips clearly showed that he understood nothing. There were a number of questions the traveler wanted to ask, but at the sight of the man he asked only: "Does he know his sentence?" "No," said the officer, eager to continue his explanations, but the traveler interrupted him: "He doesn't know his own sentence?" "No," repeated the officer, and paused for a moment, as if he were waiting for the Traveler to elaborate on the reason for his question, then said: "It would be pointless to tell him. He'll come to know it on his body." The traveler would not have spoken further, but he felt the condemned man's gaze trained on him; it seemed to be asking if the traveler approved of all this. So after having already leaned back in his chair, he bent forward again and asked another question: "But does he at least know that he's been sentenced?" "No, not that either," the officer replied, smiling at the traveler as if expecting him to make more strange statements. "Well" said the traveler, "then you mean to tell me that the man is also unaware of the results of his defense?" "He has had no opportunity to defend himself," said the officer, looking away as if talking to himself and trying to spare the traveler the embarrassment of having such self-evident matters explained to him. "But he must have had some opportunity to defend himself," the traveler said, and got up from his seat.

The officer realized that his explanations of the apparatus were in danger of being held up for quite some time, so he approached the traveler, put his arm through his, and gestured toward the condemned man, who was standing up straight now he was so obviously the center of attention—the soldier had also given the chain a jerk—and said, "Here's the situation. I have been appointed judge in this penal colony—despite my youth—as I was the previous commandant's assistant in all penal matters and know the apparatus better than anyone else. The guiding principle for my decisions is this: Guilt is unquestionable. Other courts can not follow that principle because they have more than one member and even have courts that are higher than themselves. That is not the case here, or at least it was not so during the time of the former commandant. Although the new one has shown signs of interfering with my judgment, but I have succeeded in fending him off so far and shall continue to do so—you wanted to have this case explained; it's quite simple, as they all are. A captain reported to me this morning and charged this man—who is assigned to him as an orderly and sleeps in front of his door—with sleeping on duty. You see, it is duty is to get up every time the hour strikes and salute the captain's door. This certainly not a tremendously difficult task but a necessary one, as he must be alert both to guard and wait on his master. Last night the captain wanted to find out whether the orderly was performing his duty. When the clock struck two, he opened the door and found the man curled up asleep. He took his horsewhip and lashed him across the face. Now instead of rising and begging for pardon, the man grabbed his master by the legs, shook him and cried: 'Throw away that whip or I'll swallow you whole'—those are the facts. The captain came to me an hour ago, I wrote down his statement and immediately followed it up with the sentence. Then I had the man put in chains. That was quite simple. If I had call for this man first and interrogated him, it would only have resulted in confusion. He would have lied, and had I been successful in exposing those lies, he would have replaced them with new ones, and so on. But as it stands now, I have him and I won't let him go—is everything clear now? But time's marching on, the execution ought to be starting and I haven't finished explaining the apparatus yet." He pressed the traveler back into his seat, returned to the apparatus, and began: "As you can see, the shape of the harrow corresponds to the human form; here is the harrow for the upper body, here are the harrows for the legs. For the head there is just this one small spike. Is that clear?" He bent forward toward the traveler amiably, eager to furnish the most comprehensive explanations.

With a furrowed brow the traveler examined the harrow. He was not satisfied with the explanation of the judicial process. Still, he had to remind himself, this was a penal colony, special measures were needed here, military procedures had to be adhered to up to the very end. He also placed some hope in the new commandant, who intended to introduce, albeit slowly, new procedures that the officer's could not conceive of. These thoughts led him to his next question: "Will the commandant attend the execution?" "It's not certain," the officer said, wincing at the question, and his friendly expression clouded over. "That is why we must hurry. As much as it pains me, I'll have to cut my explanations short. But of course tomorrow, after the apparatus has been cleaned—its only drawback is that it gets so messy—I can go into more detail. So for now, just the essentials. When the man is laid down on the bed and it has started vibrating, the harrow is lowered onto the body. It automatically adjusts itself so that the needles just graze the skin; once the adjustment is completed, the steel band promptly stiffens to form a rigid bar. And now the performance begins. An uninformed observer would not be able to differentiate between one punishment and another. The harrow appears to do its work in a uniform manner. As it quivers, its points pierce the body, which is itself quivering from the vibrations of the bed. So the progress of the sentencing can be seen, the harrow is made of glass. Securing the needles in the glass presented some technical difficulties, but after many attempts we were successful. We spared no effort, you understand. And now anyone can observe the sentence being inscribed on the body. Don't you want to come closer and examine the needles?"

The traveler rose to his feet slowly, walked across, and bent over the harrow. "You see," said the officer, "there are two types of needles arranged in various patterns. Each long needle has a short one adjacent to it. The long needle does the writing, and the short one flushes away the blood with water so that the writing is always clearly legible. The bloody water is then conducted through grooves and finally flows into this main pipe, which empties into the pit." With his finger the officer outlined the exact route the bloody water had to take. As he began formally to demonstrate with both hands at the mouth of the outlet pipe, in order to make the image as vivid as possible, he cupped his hands under the mouth of the pipe as if to catch the outflow. The traveler drew his head back and, groping with one hand, tried to return to his chair. To his horror, he then saw that the condemned man had also accepted the officer's invitation to examine the harrow. He had tugged the sleepy soldier forward a little and was leaning over the glass. One could see that he was searching, with a puzzled expression, for what the gentlemen had just observed, but since he had not heard the explanation he was not successful. He bent this way and that; he repeatedly ran his eyes over the glass. The traveler wanted to drive him back because what he was doing was probably a criminal offense, but the officer restrained the traveler with a firm hand and with the other hand picked up a lump of dirt from the embankment and threw it at the soldier. The soldier jerked awake and saw what the condemned man had dared to do; he dropped his rifle, dug in his heels, yanked the condemned man back so forcefully that he immediately fell, and then stood over him, watching him writhe around and rattle his chains. "Get him on his feet!," shouted the officer, for he noticed that the traveler was dangerously distracted by the condemned man. The traveler even leaned across the harrow, taking no notice of it, only concerned with what was happening to the condemned man. "Be careful with him!" the officer yelled again. He circled the apparatus and grasped the condemned man under the armpits himself; with the help of the soldier he hauled him to his feet, which kept slipping and sliding.

"Now I know all there is to know about it," the traveler said as the officer returned to his side. "All but the most important thing," he replied, seizing the traveler by the arm and pointing upward. "Up there in the designer is the machinery that controls the movements of the harrow, and this mechanism is then programmed to correspond with the drawing of the prescribed sentence. I am still using the former commandant's drawings. Here they are"—he pulled some sheets out of the leather folder—"unfortunately I can't let you touch them, they're my most prized and valuable possession. Just sit, and I'll show you them from here, and you'll be able to see everything perfectly." He held up the first drawing. The traveler would gladly have said something complimentary, but all he saw was a labyrinth of crisscrossing lines that covered the paper so thickly it was difficult discern the blank space between them. "Read it." "I can't," said the traveler. "Well, it's clear enough," said the officer." "It's very artistic," the traveler offered evasively, "but I can't make it out." "Sure," agreed the officer, with a laugh, and put away the folder, "it's not calligraphy for schoolchildren. It must be carefully studied. I'm sure you'd eventually understand it too. Of course the script can't be too simple: it's not meant to kill on first contact, but only after twelve hours, on average; but the turning point is calculated to come at the sixth hour. So the lettering itself must be surrounded by lots and lots of flourishes; the actual wording runs around the body only in a narrow strip, and the rest of the body is reserved for ornamentation. Now do you appreciate the work of the harrow and of the whole apparatus?—Just watch!" and he leaped up the ladder, rotated a wheel, and called out: "Look out, step to the side!" then everything started up. If it had not been for the screeching gear it would have been fantastic. As if he were surprised by the noisy gear, he shook his fist, then shrugged apologetically to the traveler and clambered down below. Something that only he could detect was still not in order to be heard above the din. "Are you following the process? First, the harrow begins to write, as soon it has finished the initial draft of the inscription on the man's back, the layer of cotton wool is set rolling and slowly turns the body onto its side, giving the harrow fresh room to write. Meanwhile, the raw flesh that has already been inscribed rests against the cotton wool, which is specially prepared to staunch the bleeding immediately and ready everything for a further deepening of the script. Then, as the body continues to turn, these teeth here at the edge of the harrow tear the cotton wool away from the wounds and toss it into the pit; now there is fresh work for the harrow. So it keeps on writing more and more deeply for all twelve hours. For the first six hours the condemned man is alive almost as before, he only suffers pain. The felt gag is removed after two hours, as he no longer has the strength to scream. The electrically heated bowl at the head of the bed is filled with warm rice gruel, and the man is welcome, should he so desire, to take as much as his tongue can reach. No one ever passes up the opportunity; I don't know of one, and my experience is vast. The man loses his pleasure in eating only around the sixth hour. At this point, I usually kneel down to observe the phenomenon. The man rarely swallows the last mouthful but merely rolls it around in his mouth and spits it into the pit. I have to duck just then, otherwise he would spit it in my face. But how still the man becomes in the sixth hour! Enlightenment comes to even the dimmest. It begins around the eyes, and it spreads outward from there—a sight that might tempt one to lie down under the harrow oneself. Nothing more happens, just that the man begins to interpret the writing, he screws up his mouth as if he were listening. You've seen yourself how difficult the writing is to decipher with your eyes, but our man deciphers it with his wounds. Of course, it is hard work and it takes him six hours to accomplish it. But the harrow pierces him clean through and throws him into the pit, where he's flung down onto the cotton wool and bloody water and cotton wool. This concludes the sentence and we, the soldier and I, bury him."

The traveler had his ear cocked towards the officer and, with his hands in his pockets, was watching the machine at work. The condemned man watched as well, but with no understanding. He bent slightly forward, watching the moving needles, when the soldier, at a sign from the officer, sliced through shirt and trousers from behind with a knife so that they slipped off him; he tried to grab at the falling clothes to cover his nakedness, but the soldier lifted him up in the air and shook off the last of his rags. The officer turned off the machine, and in the ensuing silence the condemned man was placed under the harrow. The chains were removed and the straps fastened in their stead; for a moment this almost seemed a relief to the condemned man. The harrow now lowered itself a bit farther—as this was a thin man. When the needle points reached his skin, a shudder ran through him; while the soldier was busy with the condemned man's right hand, he stretched the left one out in a random direction; it was, however, in the direction of the traveler. The officer kept glancing at the traveler out of the corner of his eye as if to ascertain from his face how the execution, which had been at least nominally explained to him by now, impressed him.

The wrist strap snapped. The soldier had probably pulled it too tight. The officer's help was required; the soldier showed him the frayed piece of strap. So the officer went over to him and said, still facing the traveler, "The machine is very complex, so something or other is bound to break down and tear, but one mustn't allow this to cloud one's overall judgment. Anyway, a substitute for the strap is easy to find: I will use a chain—of course the delicacy of the vibrations for the right arm will be adversely affected." And while he was arranging the chain he remarked further: "The resources for maintaining the machine are quite limited these days. Under the old commandant, I had unlimited access to a fund set aside for just this purpose. There was a store here that stocked all sorts of spare parts. I must confess I wasn't exactly frugal—I mean before, not now as the new commandant claims, but he uses everything as an excuse to fight the old ways. Now he's wrested control of the machine fund; if I request a new strap, the old one is required as evidence, and the new one takes ten days to arrive and is of inferior quality, not much use at all. But in the meantime, how I'm supposed to operate the machine without a strap—no one's worries about that."

The traveler reflected that it is always dicey to meddle decisively in the affairs of other people. He was neither a citizen of the penal colony nor a citizen of the state to which it belonged. If he were to condemn, to say nothing of prevent, the execution, they could say to him: "You are a foreigner, keep quiet." He could make no answer to that, he could only add that he himself didn't understand his actions, for he traveled solely as an observer and certainly had no intention of revamping other people's judicial systems. But in the present circumstances it was very tempting. The injustice of the process and the inhumanity of the execution were unquestionable. No one could assume any selfish interest on the traveler's part, as the condemned man was a complete stranger, not even a fellow countryman, and he certainly inspired no sympathy. The traveler himself had been recommended by men in high office and received here with great courtesy, and the very fact that he had been invited to attend this execution seemed to suggest that his views on the judicial process were being solicited. And this was all the more probable since the commandant, as had just now been made plain, was no fan of this procedure and was nearly hostile in his attitude toward the officer.

Jut then the traveler heard the officer howl in rage. He had just succeeded, and not without difficulty, in shoving the felt gag into the mouth of the condemned man who, in an incontrollable fit of nausea, squeezed his eyes shut and vomited. The officer rushed to pull him away from the gag his head toward the pit, but it was too late, the vomit was running down the machine. "It's all the commandant's fault!" he shouted, thoughtlessly shaking at the brass rods closest to him. "The machine is as filthy as a sty." With trembling hands, he showed the traveler what had happened. "Haven't I spent hours trying to explain to the commandant that no food should be given for a whole day preceding the execution? But there are other opinions in this new, permissive regime. The commandant's ladies stuff the man's gullet full of sweets before he's led away. He's lived on stinking fish his whole life and now he must dine on sweets! But that would be all right, I wouldn't object to it, but why can't they get me a new felt gag like I've been been asking for the last three months? How can a man not be sickened when the felt in his mouth has been gnawed and drooled on by more than a hundred men as they lay dying?"

The condemned man had laid his head down and looked quite peaceful; the soldier was busy cleaning the machine with the condemned man's shirt. The officer approached the Traveler, who stepped back a pace in some vague dread, but the officer grasped his hand and drew him aside. "I would like to speak to you confidentially," he said, "if I may." "Of course," said the traveler, and listened with his eyes cast down.

"The procedure and execution, which you now have an opportunity to admire, no longer have any supporters in our colony. I am their sole advocate and, at the same time, the sole advocate of our former commandant's legacy. No longer can I ponder possible developments for the system, I spend all my energy preserving what's left. When the old commandant was alive, the colony was full of his supporters; I do possess some of his strength of conviction, but I have none of his power, and consequently his supporters have drifted away; there are many of them left, but none will admit to it. If you went into the teahouse today, an execution day, and listened to what was being said, you'd probably hear only ambiguous remarks. They would all be made by supporters, but considering the present commandant and his current beliefs, they're completely useless to me. And now I ask you: Is a life's work such as this"—he indicated the machine—"to be destroyed because of the commandant and the influence his women have over him? Should this be allowed to happen? Even by a stranger who has only come to our island for a few days? But there's no time to lose, plans are being made to undermine my jurisdiction. Meetings that I am excluded from are already being held in the commandant's headquarters. Even your presence here today seems significant. They are cowards and send you ahead, you, a foreigner. Oh, how different an execution used to be in the old days! As much as a whole day before the event the valley would be packed with people. They lived just to see it. The commandant appeared early in the morning with his coterie of ladies; fanfares roused the entire camp; I reported that everything was ready; the assembly— no high official could be absent—arranged themselves around the machine. This stack of cane chairs is a pathetic leftover from that time. The machine was freshly cleaned and gleaming; for almost every execution I used new spare parts. Before hundreds of eyes—all the spectators would stand on tiptoe to the very rims of the slopes—the commandant himself installed the condemned man beneath the harrow. What today is left to a common soldier was performed by me, the presiding judge, at that time, and it was a great honor for me. And then the execution began! There were no discordant sounds to disturb the working of the machine. Many no longer watched but lay in the sand with their eyes closed; everyone knew. The wheels of justice were turning. In the silence nothing but the moaning of the condemned man could be heard, though his moans were muffled by the gag. These days the machine can induce no moan too loud for the gag to stifle; of course back then an acid we're no longer allowed to use dripped from the writing needles. Well, anyway—then came the sixth hour! It was not possible to grant every request to watch from close-up. In his wisdom, the commandant decreed that children should be given the first priority. By virtue of my office, of course, I was always nearby; often I was squatting there with a small child in either arm! How we drank in the transfigured look on the sufferer's face, how we bathed our cheeks in the warmth of that—achieved at long last and fading quickly! What times those were, my comrade!" The officer had evidently forgotten whom he was addressing; he had embraced the traveler and laid his head on his shoulder. The traveler was deeply embarrassed and stared impatiently past the officer's head. The soldier had ended finished cleaning by now and was pouring rice gruel into the bowl from a can. As soon as the condemned man, who seemed to be fully recovered, saw this, he began to lap after the gruel with his tongue. The soldier continually pushed him away, since it was certainly meant for another time, but it was equally unfair of the soldier to stick his dirty hands into the basin and eat in the condemned man's ravenous face.

The officer quickly recovered. "I did not want to upset you," he said. "I know it's impossible to make someone understand what it was like then. In any event, the machine still works and is effective in and of itself. It is effective even though it stands alone in this valley. And in the end, the corpse still slips unbelievably smoothly into the pit, even if there aren't, as there once were, hundreds gathered like flies all around it. At that time, we had to erect a sturdy fence around the pit. It was torn down long ago."

The traveler wanted to avert his face away from the officer and looked about aimlessly. The officer assumed that he was marking the desolation of the valley, so he seized his hands and turned him around to meet his gaze and asked, "Can't you just see the shame of it?"

But the traveler said nothing. The officer left him alone for a little while and stood absolutely still, his legs apart, his hands on his hips, staring at the ground, then he smiled encouragingly at the traveler and said: "I was right beside you yesterday when the commandant invited you. I heard him, I know the commandant, I immediately understood what his intentions were. Although he's powerful enough to move against me, he doesn't yet dare do it, but he intends to subject me to your judgment, the judgment of a respected foreigner. He has calculated carefully. This is your second day on the island, you didn't know the old commandant and his way, you're conditioned by European mores, perhaps on principle you object to the death penalty in general and such a mechanical method as this one in particular; besides, you can see that executions are pathetic and have no public support here, even the machine is badly worn—now, taking all this into consideration (so thinks the commandant), isn't it quite possible that you would disapprove of my methods? And if you do disapprove (I am still speaking as the commandant), you wouldn't conceal this fact, for certainly you have confidence in your own tried and true convictions. Of course you have learned to respect the peculiarities of many other peoples, and you probably would not condemn our proceedings as forcefully as you would in your own land. But the commandant has no need for all that. Just letting slip a casual little remark will suffice. It may not even reflect your true opinions, so long as it serves his purpose. He will be very clever in his interrogation, of that I am sure, and his ladies will circle around you and prick up their ears. You might just say, 'Our judicial system is quite different,' or 'The defendant is questioned before he is sentenced in our country,' or 'In our country the condemned man is informed of his sentence' or 'We haven't used torture since the Middle Ages'—all of which are statements that are as true as they seem self-evident to you, innocent enough remarks that don't malign my methods in any way. But how will the commandant take them? I can picture him, the good commandant, hastily shoving his chair aside and rushing the balcony. I can see his ladies streaming about after him, I can hear his voice—the ladies call it a booming, thunderous voice—and so now he speaks: 'A renowned scholar from the West, charged with investigating the judicial systems of all the countries in the world, has just pronounced our traditional system of administering justice inhumane. After receiving the verdict of such a distinguished person, I can naturally no longer tolerate this procedure. Effective immediately I therefore ordain. . . ,' and so on and so forth. You would like to recant: You never said what he is asserting; you never called my methods inhumane, on the contrary you regard them, in keeping with your insight, as the most humane and worthy of humanity; you also admire this machinery—but it's too late; you'll never get to the balcony, which is already crowded with the ladies; you'll try to draw attention to yourself; you'll want to shout but your mouth will be covered by a lady's hand—and both I and the work of the old commandant will be finished."

The traveler had to suppress a smile; the task that he thought would be so difficult was now so easy. He evasively said: "You overestimate my influence; the commandant has read my letters of recommendation and knows that I am no expert in legal matters. If I were to express an opinion, it would be the opinion of a private individual, with no more weight than anyone else's, and in any case far less influential than the opinion of the commandant, who, as I understand it, has very extensive powers in this penal colony. If he is as decidedly against you as you believe, then I fear that the end of your procedure is indeed near—without any modest assistance on my part."

Did the officer finally understand? No, he still didn't understand. He shook his head firmly, glanced at the condemned man and the soldier, who both flinched and abruptly abandoned their rice, came right up to the traveler, and instead of looking him in the eye, addressed some spot of his coat and said in a lower voice:"You don't know the commandant, you believe your position in regard and the rest of us is somewhat—please pardon the expression—ineffectual, but trust me, your influence cannot be rated too highly. I was overjoyed when I heard that you would attend the execution alone. This decision of the commandant's was intended as a blow to me, but I shall now turn it to my advantage. Without the distraction of whispered lies and scornful glances—which would have been unavoidable with a large crowd of spectators—you have heard my explanations, seen the machine, and are now on the verge of watching the execution. I'm sure you've already formed an opinion; if you still have any niggling doubts left, the sight of the execution will eliminate them. And now I put this request to you: Help me defeat the commandant!"

The traveler allowed him to speak no further."How can I do that?"he exclaimed. "It's absolutely impossible. I can help you any more than I can hinder you."

"Yes, you can," replied the officer. With some alarm, the traveler noticed that the officer was clenching his fists. "Yes, you can," the officer repeated more urgently. "I have a plan that is bound to succeed. You don't believe that you have sufficient influence, but I know that you do. However, even granting that you're right, isn't it necessary for the sake of the old system's preservation that we try everything, even things that are potentially ineffective So listen to my plan. In order for it to succeed, it is extremely important that you say as little as possible in the colony today concerning the conclusions you've drawn about the procedure. Unless asked directly, you should on no account comment. What you do say, however, must be brief and noncommittal, it should appear that you find the matter difficult to speak about, that you're embittered over it, that, if you were to speak freely you would almost be tempted to curse. I'm not asking you to lie, by any means; you should just answer curtly, 'Yes, I have seen the execution' or 'Yes, it was all explained to me.' Just that, nothing more. Your bitterness, which should be made obvious, is sufficiently justified, although not in the way the commandant imagines. He will completely misunderstand its meaning of course and interpret it to suit his own needs. My plan's success hinges on this. Tomorrow there's to be a large conference of all the high administrative officials at the commandant's headquarters, presided over by the commandant himself. Naturally the commandant has turned these meetings into public exhibitions. He has built a gallery that is always packed with spectators. I am compelled to participate in these meetings, though they sicken and disgust me. No matter what the case, you are sure to be invited to this meeting: if you behave today as outlined, the invitation will become an urgent request. But if you are not invited for some obscure reason, you'll have to ask for an invitation—that will ensure you're getting one without a doubt. So now tomorrow you're sitting in the commandant's box with the ladies. He keeps looking up to make sure you are there. After discussing various ludicrous and unimportant issues, introduced solely for the benefit of the audience—usually it's some harbor works, it's always harbor works!—our judicial procedure is brought to the agenda. If the commandant fails to introduce it, or fails to do so soon enough, I'll make it my business to get it mentioned. I'll stand up and report on today's execution. A very brief statement: only that it has taken place. A statement of this sort is not quite standard at these meetings, but I will make it anyhow. The commandant thanks me, as always, with a friendly smile, and then can't restrain himself; he seizes the fortunate opportunity. 'It has just been reported,' he will say, or words to that effect, 'that there has been an execution. I should merely like to add that this execution was witnessed by the great scholar who as you all know has done our colony an immense honor by his visit. His presence here today lends further importance to this occasion. Shouldn't we now ask the great scholar his opinion of our traditional mode of execution and the whole process surrounding it?' Of course there's applause and general approval all around, of which mine is the loudest. The commandant bows to you and says, 'Then I put the question to you in the name of all assembled here.' And now you step up to the balustrade—keep your hands where everyone can see them, otherwise the ladies will press them and play with your fingers—and now you can speak out at last. I don't know how I'll be able to endure the tension while waiting for that moment. You mustn't put any restrictions on yourself in your speech, let the truth be heard out loud, lean over the railing and roar, yes, roar your judgment, your immutable judgment, down on the commandant. But perhaps that is not what you wish to do, it's not keeping with your character; perhaps in your country one behaves differently in such situations. That's fine, that'll work just as well. Don't stand up at all, just say a few words, in a whisper so that only those officials below you can hear. That will be enough. You don't even have to mention the lack of public support, the screeching gear, the torn strap, the repulsive felt; no, I'll take care of all that, believe me, if my speech does not hound him from the hall, it will force him to his knees in confession: 'Old commandant, I bow down before you. . . .' That is my plan, will you help me carry it out? But of course you will, what's more, you must." And the officer seized the traveler by the arms and, breathing heavily, stared into his face. He had shouted his last sentences so loudly that even the soldier and the condemned man were paying attention; though they couldn't understand a word, they stopped eating for a moment and looked over, still chewing at the traveler.

The answer that he was obliged to give was absolutely clear to the traveler from the very beginning. He had experienced too much in his lifetime to falter here; at heart he was honorable and without fear, all the same he did hesitate now for a beat, in the face of the officer and the condemned man. But at last he said what he had to: "No." The officer blinked several times, but kept his eyes locked on the traveler's. "Would you like an explanation," asked the traveler. The officer nodded dumbly. "I am opposed to this procedure," the traveler then continued, "even before you confided in me—and naturally under no circumstances would I ever betray your confidence. I had already been considering whether I would be justified in intervening and whether any such intervention on my part would have the slightest chance of success. It was clear to me whom I had to turn to first: the commandant, of course. You helped make this even clearer, although you did not strengthen my resolve; on the contrary, your sincere conviction has moved me, even though it cannot influence my judgment."

The officer remained mute, turned and approached the machine, took hold of one of the brass rods, and leaning back a little, gazed up at the designer as if to check that all was in order. The soldier and the condemned man seemed to have become quite friendly; the condemned man was gesturing to the soldier, though movement was difficult for him due to the tightly binding straps; the soldier bent down to him and the condemned man whispered something in his ear; the soldier nodded.

The traveler followed the officer and said: "You don't know what I plan to do yet. I'll certainly tell the commandant my thoughts on the procedure, but I will do so privately, not in a public meeting. Nor will I be here long enough to attend any such meeting; I'm sailing early tomorrow morning, or boarding my ship at the least."

It did not look as if the officer had been listening. "So you weren't convinced by the procedure," he muttered to himself, smiling the smile of an old man listening to a child's nonsense while pursuing thoughts of his own.

"Well then, the time has come," he said at last, and looked at the traveler suddenly with bright, somewhat challenging, apparently appealing for some kind of cooperation.

"Time for what?" the traveler inquired uneasily, but got no answer.

"You are free," the officer said to the condemned man in his own language. He did not believe this at first. "You are free now," repeated the officer. For the first time the face of the condemned man was truly animated. Was it the true? Was it just a whim of the officer's that might pass? Had the foreigner obtained his reprieve? What was it? His face seemed to be asking these questions. But not for long. Whatever the reason might be, he wanted to be really free if he could, and he began to thrash about as far as the Harrow would allow.

"You'll tear my straps," barked the officer. "Be still! We'll undo them." He signaled to the soldier, and they both set about doing so. The condemned man laughed quietly to himself without a word, turning his head first to the officer on his left, then to the soldier on his right.

"Pull him out," ordered the officer. This required a certain amount of care because of the harrow. Through his own impatience, the condemned man had already sliced up his back a little.

But from here on the officer paid little attention to him. He went up to the traveler, drew out his small leather folder again, thumbed through the pages, finally finding the one he wanted, and showed it to the traveler. "Read it," he said. "I can't," said the traveler. "I already told you that I can't read these scripts." "Take a closer look," the officer insisted, stepping around next to the traveler so that they could read it together. When that proved just as futile, he tried helping the traveler read by tracing the script with his little finger, though he held it far away from the paper as if that must never be touched. The traveler did make every effort in an attempt to please the officer at least in this respect, but it was impossible. Now the officer began to spell it out letter by letter, and then he read it altogether. "'Be just!' it says," he explained. "Surely you can read it now." The traveler bent so close to the paper that the officer, fearing he would touch it, pulled it farther away; the traveler said nothing more, but it was clear that he still could not decipher it. "'Be just!' it says," the officer repeated. "That may be," said the traveler, "I'm prepared to take your word for it." "Well then," said the officer, at least partially satisfied, and climbed the ladder with the sheet; he inserted the sheet into the designer with great care and seemed to completely rearrange all the gears; it was very difficult and intricate work that involved even the smallest gears, for the officer's head sometimes disappeared into the designer entirely, so precisely did he have to examine the mechanism.

The traveler followed this activity closely from below; his neck grew stiff and his eyes ached from the blaze of sunlight glaring across the sky. The soldier and the condemned man were absorbed with each other. The condemned man's shirt and trousers, which had already been dumped in the pit, were fished out by the soldier with the point of his bayonet. The shirt was filthy beyond belief, and the condemned man washed it in the bucket of water. When the condemned man donned the shirt and trousers, neither of the men could help bursting out laughing because the garments had been slit up up the back. Perhaps the condemned man felt obliged to amuse the soldier, he twirled around again and again in his slashed clothes while the soldier squatted on the ground, laughed, slapped his knees in merriment. They did, however, control themselves somewhat out of consideration for the gentlemen's presence.

When at long last the officer had finished his work up above, he surveyed each part of the entire machine with a smile and closed the cover of the designer, which had remained open until now. He climbed down, looked into the pit and then at the condemned man, noting with satisfaction that he had taken back his clothes, then went over to wash his hand in the water bucket, realizing only too late how revoltingly dirty it was, and disheartened that he could no longer wash his hands, he ultimately thrust them—this alternative did not please him, but he had to accept it—into the sand. He then rose and began to unbutton his tunic. As he did this, the two ladies' handkerchiefs that he had tucked behind his collar fell into his hands. "Here, take your handkerchiefs," he said and tossed them over to the condemned man. And to the traveler he said by way of an explanation: "Presents from the ladies."

Despite the obvious haste with which he removed the tunic and then the rest of his clothing, he handled each garment with the utmost care, even running his fingers over the tunic's silver braid and shaking a tassel into place. But all this care was in direct contrast with the fact that no sooner was he finished removing a garment than he hurled it unceremoniously into the pit with an indignant jerk. The last thing left to him was his short sword and its belt. He drew the sword out of its scabbard and broke it, then gathered it all up, the pieces of sword, the scabbard, the belt, and threw them into the pit so violently they clanked against each other.

Now he stood there naked. The traveler chewed his lip and said nothing. He knew without a doubt what was going to happen, but he had no right to prevent the officer from doing anything. If the judicial procedure that was so dear to the officer was truly near its end—possibly due to the traveler's intervention, to which he felt quite committed—then the officer's actions were proper; the traveler would have done the same in his place.

The soldier and the condemned man understood nothing at first, they weren't even watching. The condemned man was delighted to have his handkerchiefs returned, but he was not allowed to enjoy them for long as the soldier snatched them with a sudden unexpected motion. Now the condemned man tried in turn to grab at all the handkerchiefs, which the soldier had tucked under his belt for safe-keeping, but the soldier was on his guard. So they half jokingly wrestled with each other. Only when the officer was totally naked did they begin to pay attention. The notion that some drastic reversal was about to take place seemed to have struck the condemned man in particular. What had happened to him was now happening to the officer. Perhaps it would be seen through to the end. The foreign traveler had probably ordered it. This then was revenge. Without having suffered to the end him-self, nonetheless he would be avenged to the end. A broad, silent grin now appeared on his face and stayed there.

The officer, however, had turned to the machine. It had previously been clear that he understood the machine well, but now it was almost mind-boggling to see how he handled it and how it obeyed him. He had only to reach out a hand toward the harrow for it to raise and lower itself several times until it found the proper posi-tion to receive him; he merely nudged the edge of the bed and it started to vibrate; it was plain that he was rather reluctant, when the felt gag came to meet his mouth, to receive it, but his hesitation only lasted a moment; he promptly submitted and received it. Everything was ready; only the straps still hung down on the sides, but they were evidently superfluous; the officer did not need to be strapped in. But the condemned man noticed the loose straps, and in his opinion the execution was not complete unless the straps were fastened; he eagerly beckoned to the soldier and they both ran over to strap the officer down. The latter had already stretched out one foot to push the crank that would start the designer, then he saw the two men approaching; he withdrew his foot back and allowed himself to be strapped in. But now he could no longer reach the crank; neither the soldier nor the condemned man would be able to find it, and the Traveler was determined not to lift a finger. It wasn't necessary; hardly were the straps in place when the machine started to oper-ate. The bed shook, the needles danced over the flesh, the harrow gently bobbed up and down. The traveler had already been staring at it for some time before remem-bering that a gear in the designer should be screeching, but everything was still, not even the slightest whirring could be heard.

Because the machine was working so silently, it became virtually unnoticeable. The traveler looked over at the soldier and the condemned man. The condemned was the livelier of the two, every facet of the machine interested him—one moment he was bending down, the next reaching up his forefinger always extended to point something out to the soldier. This made the traveler extremely uncomfortable. He was determined to stay here till the end, but he couldn't bear the sight of those two for long. "Go on home," he said. The soldier might have been willing to do so, but the condemned man considered the order a punishment. With clasped hands he begged to be allowed to stay, and when the traveler, shaking his head, did not relent, he even went down on his knees. The Traveler realized that giving orders was useless and was at the point of going over to chase the pair away. Just then he heard a noise in the designer above him. He looked up. Was it that troublesome gear after all? But it was something else. The cover of the designer rose slowly and then fell completely open. The teeth of a gear wheel emerged and rose higher, soon the whole wheel could be seen. It was as if some monumental force was compressing the designer so that there was no more room for this wheel—the wheel spun to the edge of this designer, fell, and rolled a little ways in before it toppled onto its side. But a second wheel was already following it, with many others rolling after it—large ones, small ones, some so tiny they were hard to see; the same thing happened with all of them. One kept imagining that the designer was finally empty, but then a fresh, particularly numerous group would come into view, climb out, fall, spin in the sand, and lie still. In the thrall of this spectacle, the condemned man completely forgot the traveler's order. He was fascinated by the wheels and kept trying to catch one, urging the soldier at the same time to help him; but he always drew back his hand in alarm, for another wheel would immediately come speeding along and frighten him, at least when it started to roll.

The traveler on the other hand was deeply troubled—the machine was obviously falling apart—its silent operation was an illusion. He had the feeling that it was now his duty to take care of the officer, since he was no longer capable of looking after himself. However, while the chaos of the gear wheels claimed all his attention, he had failed to keep an eye on the rest of the machine; now that the last wheel had left the designer, he went over to the harrow and had a new and less welcome surprise. The harrow wasn't writing at all but just stabbing, and the bed wasn't rolling the body over but just thrusting it up, quivering, into the needles. The traveler wanted to do something, bring the whole machine to a stop if possible, because this was not the exquisite torture the officer had wished for; this was out-and-out murder. He reached out, but at that moment the harrow rose with the body already spitted upon it and swung to the side as it usually did only in the twelfth hour. Blood flowed in a hundreds of streams—not mixed with water, the water jets had also failed to work this time—and the last function failed to complete itself, the body did not drop from the long needles: It hung over the pit, streaming with blood, without falling. The harrow tried to return to its original position, but as if it also noticed that it had not unloaded its burden, it stayed where it was, suspended over the pit. "Come and help," the traveler shouted to the soldier and the condemned man, and grabbed the officer by the feet. He wanted to push against the feet from this side while the others two took hold of the head from the other side, so the officer could gently be removed from the needles. But the other couldn't make up their minds to come right away; the condemned man had even turned away. The traveler was compelled to go over to them and force them to get into position by the officer's head. And from this vantage point he had to look, almost against his will, at the face of the corpse. It was as it had been in life (no sign of the promised deliverance could be detected). What all the others had found in the machine, the officer had not; his lips were clamped together, his eyes were open and bore the same expression as in life, a quiet convinced look; and through the forehead was the point of the great iron spike.

As the traveler, with the soldier and the condemned man following, reached the first houses in the colony, the soldier pointed to one of them and said: "That's the teahouse."

On the ground floor of this house was a deep, low, cavernous room whose walls and ceiling were blackened with smoke. It was open to the street along the whole of its width width. Although the teahouse differed very little from other houses in the colony, which, except for the palatial buildings of the commandant's headquarters, were all dilapidated, it gave the traveler the impression of being a historic landmark, and he felt the power of earlier times. Followed by his companions, he went closer, passed between the empty tables that stood on the street in front of the teahouse, and breathed in the damp, cool air that came from the interior. "The old man is buried here," said the soldier. "The priest wouldn't allow him in the cemetery. For a while no one knew where to bury him, they ended up burying him here. The officer didn't tell you about it because, naturally, it's what he's most ashamed of. A few times he even tried to dig the old man up at night, but he was always chased away." "Where's the grave?" asked the traveler, finding it impossible to believe the soldier. Both the soldier and the condemned man immediately ran in front of him, pointing with outstretched hands to where the grave was. They led the traveler to the far wall, where several customers were sitting at tables. They were apparently dock workers, strong men with black, glistening, full beards. They were all in their shirt-sleeves and their shirts were raggedy: These were poor, humble people. As the traveler approached, some of them rose and edged back against the wall, staring at him. "He's a foreigner" was whispered around him, "he wants to see the grave." They pushed one of the tables aside, under it there was actually a gravestone. It was a simple stone, low enough to be hidden beneath a table. It bore an inscription in very small lettering; the traveler had to kneel down in order to read it. It read: "Here lies the old commandant. His followers, who must now remain nameless, have dug this grave and set this stone. It has been prophesied that after a certain number of years he will rise again and lead his followers out of this house to reclaim the colony. Have faith and wait!" When the traveler read this he rose to his feet. He saw the men surrounding him and smile, as if they had read the inscription with him, found it absurd, and were inviting him to agree with them. The traveler pretended not to notice, distributed a few coins among them, and waiting until the table was pushed back over the grave, left the teahouse, and made for to the harbor.

The soldier and the condemned man were detained in the teahouse by some acquaintances. But they must have broken away from them relatively quickly because the traveler had only descended half the long flight of stairs that led to the boats when they came running after him. They probably wanted to force the traveler to take them with him at the last minute. While he was down below negotiating with a ferryman to take him to the steamer, the two men charged down the steps in silence, as they did not dare shout. But by the time they arrived at the foot of the steps, the traveler was already in the boat and the ferryman was casting off. They could still have jumped aboard, but the traveler hoisted a heavy, knotted rope from the floor of the boat and threatened them with it, thereby preventing them from attempting to leap.

The Thing
from Outside

George Allan England

George Allan England (1877–1937) was an American pulpsmith, much of whose work, including his apocalyptic Darkness and Dawn *trilogy (1912–1914), was enthusiastically embraced by science fiction readers. This story, first published in the April 1923 issue of the technical journal* Science and Invention, *takes its cue from Charles Fort's theories of unexplained phenomena to develop a plot regarding invisible alien entities ravenously scavenging the earth for sustenance. The magazine's editor, Hugo Gernsback, liked the story so much that he reprinted it in the April 1926 issue of* Amazing Stories, *the first issue of the first science fiction magazine.*

They sat about their campfire, that little party of Americans retreating southward from Hudson Bay before the oncoming menace of great cold. Sat there, stolid under the awe of the North, under the uneasiness that the day's trek had laid upon their souls. The three men smoked. The two women huddled close to each other. Fire-glow picked their faces from the gloom of night among the dwarf firs. A splashing murmur told of the Albany River's haste to escape from the wilderness, and reach the Bay.

"I don't see what there was in a mere circular print on a rock ledge to make our guides desert," said Professor Thorburn. His voice was as dry as his whole personality. "Most extraordinary!"

377

"*They* knew what it was, all right," answered Jandron, geologist of the party. "So do I." He rubbed his cropped mustache. His eyes glinted grayly. "I've seen prints like that before. That was on the Labrador. And I've seen things happen, where they were."

"Something surely happened to our guides, before they'd gotten a mile into the bush," put in the professor's wife; while Vivian, her sister, gazed into the fire that revealed her as beauty, not to be spoiled even by a tam and a rough-knit sweater. "Men don't shoot wildly, and scream like that, unless—"

"They're all three dead now, anyhow," put in Jandron. "So they're out of harm's way. While we—well, we're two hundred and fifty wicked miles from the C.P.R. rails."

"Forget it, Jandy!" said Marr, the journalist. "We're just suffering from an attack of nerves, that's all. Give me a fill of 'baccy. Thanks. We'll all be better in the morning. Ho-hum! Now, speaking of spooks and such—"

He launched into an account of how he had once exposed a fraudulent spiritu-alist, thus proving—to his own satisfaction—that nothing existed beyond the scope of mankind's everyday life. But nobody gave him much heed. And silence fell upon the little night encampment in the wilds; a silence that was ominous.

Pale, cold stars watched down from spaces infinitely far beyond man's trivial world.

Next day, stopping for chow on a ledge miles upstream, Jandron discovered another of the prints. He cautiously summoned the other two men. They exam-ined the print, while the womenfolk were busy by the fire. A harmless thing the markings seemed: only a ring about four inches in diameter, a kind of cup-shaped depression with a raised center. A sort of glaze coated it, as if the granite had been fused by heat.

Jandron knelt, a well knit figure in a bright mackinaw and canvas leggings, and with a shaking finger explored the smooth curve of the print in the rock. His brows contracted as he studied it.

"We'd better get along out of this as quick as we can," he said in an unnatu-ral voice. "You've got your wife to protect, Thorburn, and I—well, I've got Vivian. And—"

"You have?" nipped in Marr. The light of an evil jealousy gleamed in his heavy-lidded look. "What you need is an alienist."

"Really, Jandron," the professor admonished, "you mustn't let your imagination run away with you."

"I suppose it's imagination that keeps this print cold!" the geologist reported. His breath made faint, swirling coils of vapor above it.

"Nothing but a pot-hole," judged Thorburn, bending his spare, angular body to examine the print. The professor's vitality all seemed centered in his big-bulged skull that sheltered a marvelous thinking machine. Now he put his lean hand to the base of his brain, rubbing the back of his head as if it ached. Then, under what seemed some powerful compulsion, he ran his bony finger around the print in the rock.

"By Jove, but it is cold!" he admitted. "And looks as if it had been stamped right out of the stone. Extraordinary!"

"Dissolved out, you mean," corrected the geologist. "By cold."

The journalist laughed mockingly.

"Wait till I write this up," he sneered. " 'Noted Geologist Declares Frigid Ghost Dissolves Granite!' "

Jandron ignored him. He fetched a little water from the river and poured it into the print.

"Ice!" ejaculated the professor. "Solid ice!"

"Frozen in a second," added Jandron, while Marr frankly stared. "And it'll never melt, either. I tell you, I've seen some of these rings before; and every time, horrible things have happened. Incredible things! Something burned this ring out of the stone—burned it out with the cold of interstellar space. Something that can impart cold as a permanent quality of matter. Something that can kill matter, and totally remove it."

"Of course that's all sheer poppycock," the journalist tried to laugh, but his brain felt numb.

"This something, this Thing," continued Jandron, "is a Thing that can't be killed by bullets. It's what caught our guides on the barrens, as they ran away—poor fools!"

A shadow fell across the print in the rock. Mrs. Thorburn had come up, was standing there. She had overheard a little of what Jandron had been saying.

"Nonsense!" she tried to exclaim, but she was shivering so she could hardly speak.

That night, after a long afternoon of paddling and portaging—laboring against inhibitions like those in a nightmare—they camped on shelving rocks that slanted toward the river.

"After all," said the professor, when supper was done, "we mustn't get into a panic. I know extraordinary things are reported from the wilderness, and more than one man has come out raving. But we, by Jove!, with our superior brains—we aren't going to let Nature play us any tricks!"

"And of course," added his wife, her arm about Vivian, "everything in the universe *is* a natural force. There's really no supernatural at all."

"Admitted," Jandron replied. "But how about things outside the universe?"

"And they call you a scientist," gibed Marr; but the professor leaned forward, his brows knit.

"Hm!" he grunted. A little silence fell.

"You don't mean, really," asked Vivian, "that you think there's life and intelligence—Outside?"

Jandron looked at the girl. Her beauty, haloed with ruddy gold from the firelight, was a pain to him as he answered.

"Yes, I do. And dangerous life, too. I know what I've seen in the North Country. I know what I've seen!"

Silence again, save for the crepitation of the flames, the fall of an ember, the murmur of the current. Darkness narrowed the wilderness to just that circle of flickering light ringed by the forest and the river, brooded over by the pale stars.

"Of course, you can't expect a scientific man to take you seriously," commented the professor.

"I know what I've seen! I tell you there's Something entirely outside man's knowledge."

"Poor fellow!" scoffed the journalist; but even as he spoke his hand pressed his forehead.

"There are Things at work," Jandron affirmed, with a dogged persistence. He lighted his pipe with a balzing twig. Its flame revealed his face drawn, lined. "Things. Things that reckon with us no more than we do with ants. Less, perhaps."

The flame of the twig died. Night stood closer, watching.

"Suppose there are?" the girl asked. "What's that got to do with these prints in the rock?"

"They," answered Jandron, "are marks left by one of those Things. Footprints, maybe. That This is near us, here and now!"

Marr's laugh broke a long stillness.

"And you," he exclaimed, "with an A.M. and a B.S. to write after your name."

"If you knew more," retorted Jandron, "you'd know a devilish sight less. It's only ignorance that's cock-sure."

"But," dogmatized the professor, "no scientist of any standing has ever admitted any outside interference with this planet."

"No, and for thousands of years nobody ever admitted that the world was round, either. What I've seen, I know."

"Well, what have you seen?" asked Mrs. Thorburn, shivering.

"You'll excuse me, please, for not going into that just now."

"You mean," the professor demanded, dryly, "if the—hm!—this supposed Thing wants to—?"

"It'll do any infernal thing it takes a fancy to, yes! If it happens to want us—"

"But what could Things like that want of us? Why should they come here at all?"

"Oh, for various things. For inanimate objects, at times, and then again for living beings. They've come here lots of times, I tell you," Jandron asserted with strange irritation, "and got what They wanted, and then gone away to—Somewhere. If one of Them happens to want us, for any reason, It will take us, that's all. If It doesn't want us, It will ignore us, as we'd ignore gorillas in Africa if we were looking for gold. But if it was gorilla fur we wanted, that would be different for gorillas, wouldn't it?"

"What in the world," asked Vivian, "could a—well, a Thing from Outside want of us?"

"What do men want, say, of guinea pigs? Men experiment with 'em, of course. Superior beings use inferior, for their own ends. To assume that man is the supreme product of evolution is gross self-conceit. Might not some superior Thing want to experiment with human beings, what?"

"But how?" demanded Marr.

"The human brain is the most highly organized form of matter known to this planet. Suppose, now—"

"Nonsense!" interrupted the professor. "All hands to the sleeping bags, and no more of this. I've got a wretched headache. Lets anchor in Blanket Bay!"

He, and both the women, turned in. Jandron and Marr sat a while longer by the fire. They kept plenty of wood piled on it, too, for an unnatural chill transfixed the night-air. The fire burned strangely blue, with greenish flicks of flame.

At length, after the vast acerbities of disagreement, the geologist and the newspaperman sought their sleeping bags. The fire was a comfort. Not that a fire could avail a pin's weight against a Thing from interstellar space, but subjectively it was a comfort. The instincts of a million years, centering around protection by fire, cannot be obliterated.

After a time—worn out by a day of nerve strain and of battling with swift currents, of flight from Something invisible, intangible—they all slept.

The deeps of space, star-sprinkled, hung above them with vastness immeasurable, cold beyond all understanding of the human mind.

Jandron woke first, in a red dawn.

He blinked at the fire as he crawled from his sleeping bag. The fire was dead, and yet it had not burned out. Much wood remained unconsumed, charred over, as if some gigantic extinguisher had in the night been lowered over it.

"Hmmm!" growled Jandron. He glanced about him on the ledge. "Prints, too. I might have known!"

He aroused Marr. Despite all the journalist's mocking hostility, Jandron felt more in common with this man of his own age than with the professor, who was close to sixty.

"Look here, now!" said he. "It has been all around here. See. It put out our fire—maybe the fire annoyed It, some way—and It walked around us, everywhere." His gray eyes smoldered. "I guess, by gad, you've got to admit facts now!"

The journalist could only shiver and stare.

"Lord what a head I've got on me this morning!" he chattered. He rubbed his forehead with a shaking hand, and started for the river. Most of his assurance vanished. He looked badly done up.

"Well, what say?" demanded Jandron. "See these fresh prints?"

"Damn the prints!" retorted Marr, and fell to grumbling some unintelligible thing. He washed unsteadily, and remained crouching at the river's lip, inert, numbed.

Jandron, despite a gnawing at the base of his brain, carefully examined the ledge. He found prints scattered everywhere, and some even on the river bottom near the shore. Wherever water had collected in the prints on the rock, it had frozen hard. Each print in the river-bed, too, was white with ice. Ice that the rushing current could not melt.

"Well, by gad!" he exclaimed. He lighted his pipe and tried to think. Horribly afraid—yes, he felt horribly afraid, but determined. Presently, as a little power of concentration came back, he noticed that all the prints were in straight lines, each mark about two feet from the next.

"It was observing us while we slept," said Jandron.

"What nonsense are you talking, eh?" demanded Marr. His dark, heavy face sagged. "Fire, now, and grub!"

He got up and shuffled unsteadily away from the river. Then he stopped with a jerk, staring.

"Look, look a' that ax!" he gulped, pointing.

Jandron picked up the ax, by the handle, taking good care not to touch the steel. The blade was white-furred with frost. And deep into it, punching out part of the edge, one of the prints was stamped.

"This metal," said he, "is clean gone. It's been absorbed. The Thing doesn't recognize any difference in materials. Water and steel and rock are all the same to It."

"You're crazy!" snarled the journalist. "How could a Thing travel on one leg, hopping along, making marks like that?"

"It could roll, if it was disk-shaped. And—"

A cry from the professor turned them. Thorburn was stumbling toward them, hands out and tremulous.

"My wife—!" he choked.

Vivian was kneeling beside her sister, frightened, dazed.

"Something's happened!" stammered the professor. "Here—come here—!"

Mrs. Thorburn was beyond any power of theirs to help. She was still breathing, but her respirations were stertorous, and a complete paralysis had stricken her. Her eyes, half-open and expressionless, showed pupils startlingly dilated. No resources of the party's drug kit produced the slightest effect on the woman.

The next half-hour was a confused panic—breaking camp, getting Mrs. Thorburn into a canoe, and leaving that accursed place, with a furious energy of terror that could no longer reason. Upstream, ever up against the swirl of current the party fought, driven by horror. With no thought of food or drink, paying no heed to landmarks, lashed forward only by the mad desire to be gone, the three men and the girl flung every ounce of their energy into the paddles. Their panting breath mingled with the sound of swirling eddies. A mist-blurred sun brooded over the northern wilds. Unheeded, hosts of black flies sang high-pitched keenings all about the fugitives. On either hand the forest waited, watched.

Only after two hours of sweating toil had brought exhaustion did they stop, in the shelter of a cove where black waters circled, foam-flecked. There they found the professor's wife was dead.

Nothing remained to do but bury her. At first Thorburn would not hear of it. Like a madman he insisted that through all hazards he would fetch the body out. But no—impossible. So, after a terrible time, he yielded.

In spite of her grief, Vivian was admirable. She understood what must be done. It was her voice that said the prayers, her hand that—lacking flowers—laid the fir boughs on the cairn. The professor was dazed past doing anything, saying anything.

Toward mid-afternoon, the party landed again, many miles upriver. Necessity forced them to eat. Fire would not burn. Every time they light it, it smoldered and went out with a heavy, greasy smoke. The fugitives ate cold food and drank water, then shoved off in two canoes and once more fled.

In the third canoe, hauled to the edge of the forest, lay all the rock specimens, data and curios, scientific instruments. The party kept only Mary's diary, a compass, supplies, firearms, and medicine kit.

"We can find the things we've left—sometime," said Jandron, nothing the place well. "Sometime—after It has gone."

"And bring the body out," added Thorburn. Tears, for the first time, wet his eyes. Vivian said nothing. Marr tried to light his pipe. He seemed to forget that nothing, not even tobacco, would burn now.

Vivian and Jandron occupied one canoe. The other carried the professor and Marr. Thus the power of the two canoes was about the same. They kept well together, upstream.

The fugitives paddled and portaged with a dumb, desperate energy. Toward evening they struck into what they believed to be the Mamattawan. A mile up this, as the blurred sun faded beyond a wilderness of ominous silence, they camped. Here they made determined efforts to kindle fire. Not even alcohol from the drug kit would start it. Cold, they nibbled a little food; cold, they huddled into their sleeping bags, there to lie with darkness leaden on their fear. After a long time, up over a world void of all sound save the river flow, slid an amber moon notched by the ragged tops of the conifers. Even the wail of a timber wolf would have come as welcome relief; but no wolf howled.

Silence and night enfolded them. And everywhere they felt that *It* was watching.

Foolishly enough, as a man will do foolish things in a crisis, Jandron laid his revolver outside his sleeping bag, in easy reach. His thought—blurred by a strange, drawing headache—was: "If It touches Vivian, I'll shoot!"

He realized the complete absurdity of trying to shoot a visitant from interstellar space; from the fourth dimension, maybe. But Jandron's ideas seemed tangled. Nothing would come right. He lay there, absorbed in a kind of waking nightmare. Now and then, rising on an elbow, he hearkened; all in vain. Nothing so much as stirred.

His thoughts drifted to better days, when all had been health, sanity, optimism; when nothing except jealousy of Marr, as concerned Vivian, had troubled him. Days when the sizzle of the frying pan over friendly coals had made friendly wilderness music; when the wind and the northern stars, the whir of the reel, the whispering vortex of the paddle in clear water had all been things of joy. Yes, and when a certain happy moment had, through some word or look of the girl, seemed to promise his heart's desire. But now—

"Damn it, I'll save her anyhow!" he swore with savage intensity, knowing all the while that what was to be, would be, immitigably. Do ants, by any waving of antennae, stay the down-crushing foot of man?

Next morning, and the next, no sign of the Thing appeared. Hope revived that possibly It might have flitted away elsewhere; back, perhaps, to outer space. Many were the miles the urging paddles spurred behind. The fugitives calculated that a week more would bring them to the railroad. Fire burned again. Hot food and drink helped, wonderfully. But where were the fish?

"Most extraordinary," all at once said the professor, at noon-day camp. He had become quite rational again. "Do you realize, Jandron, we've seen no traces of life in some time?"

The geologist nodded. Only too clearly he had noted just that, but he had been keeping still about it.

"That's so, too!" chimed in Marr, enjoying the smoke that some incomprehensible turn of events was letting him have. "Not a muskrat or a beaver. Not even a squirrel or a bird."

"Not so much as a gnat or a black fly!" the professor added. Jandron suddenly realized that he would have welcomed even those.

That afternoon Marr fell into a suddenly vile temper. He mumbled curses against the guides, the current, the portages, everything. The professor seemed more cheerful. Vivian complained of an oppressive headache. Jandron gave her the last of the aspirin tablets, and, as he gave them, took her hand in his.

"I'll see you through, anyhow," said he. "I don't count, now. Nobody counts, only you!"

She gave him a long, silent look. He saw the sudden glint of tears in her eyes; felt the pressure of her hand, and knew they two had never been so near each other as in that moment under the shadow of the Unknown.

Next day—or it may have been two days later, for none of them could be quite sure about the passage of time—they came to a deserted lumber camp. Even more than two days might have passed, because now their bacon was all gone, and only coffee, tobacco, beef-cubes, and pilot-bread remained. The lack of fish and game had cut alarmingly into the duffelbag. That day—whatever day it may have been— all four of them suffered teirrbly from headaches of an odd, ring-shaped kind, as if something circular were being pressed down about their heads. The professor said it was the sun that made his head ache. Vivian laid it to the wind and the gleam of the swift water, while Marr claimed it was the heat. Jandron wondered at all this, inasmuch as he plainly saw that the river had almost stopped flowing, and the day had become still and overcast.

They dragged their canoes upon a rotting stage of fir poles and explored the lumber camp, a mournful place set back in an old "slash," now partly overgrown with scrub poplar, maple, and birch. The log buildings covered with tarpaper partly torn from the pole roofs, were of the usual North Country type. Obviously the place had not been used for years. Even the landing stage where once logs had been rolled into the stream had sagged to decay.

"I don't quite get the idea of this," Marr exclaimed. "Where did the logs go to? Downstream, of course. But that would take 'em to Hudson Bay, and there's no market for spruce timber or pulpwood at Hudson Bay." He pointed down the current.

"You're entirely mistaken," put in the professor. "Any fool could see this river runs the other way. A log thrown in here would go down toward the St. Lawrence!"

"But then," asked the girl, "why can't we drift back to civilization?"

The professor retorted: "Just what we have been doing, all along! Extraordinary that I have to explain the obvious!" He walked away in a huff.

"I don't know but he's right, at that," half-admitted the journalist. "I've been thinking almost the same thing, myself, the past day or two—that is, ever since the sun shifted."

"What do you mean shifted?" from Jandron.

"You haven't noticed it?"

"But there's been no sun at all for the last two days!"

"Hanged if I'll waste time arguing with a lunatic!" Marr growled. He vouchsafed no explanation of what he meant by the sun's having "shifted," but wandered off, grumbling.

"What are we going to do?" the girl appealed to Jandron. The sight of her solemn, frightened eyes, of her palm-outward hands and (at last) her very feminine fear, constricted Jandron's heart.

"We're going through, you and I," he answered simply. "We've got to save them from themselves, you and I have."

Their hands met again, and for a moment held. Despite the dead calm, a fir tip at the edge of the clearing suddenly flicked aside, shriveled as if frozen. But neither of them saw it.

The fugitives, badly spent, established themselves in the "barroom" or sleeping shack of the camp. They wanted to feel a roof over them again, if only a broken one. The traces of men comforted them—a couple of broken peavies, a pair of snowshoes with the thongs all gnawed off, a cracked bit of mirror, a yellowed alamanac dated 1899.

Jandron called the professor's attention to this almanac, but the professor thrust it aside.

"What do I want of a Canadian census report?" he demanded, and fell to counting the bunks, over and over again. The big bulge of his forehead, that housed the massive brain of his, was oozing sweat. Marr cursed what he claimed was sunshine through the holes in the roof, though Jandron could see none; claimed the sunshine made his head ache.

"But it's not a bad place," he added. "We can make a blaze in that fireplace and be comfy. I don't like that window, though."

"What window," asked Jandron. "Where?"

Marr laughed, and ignored him. Jandron turned to Vivian, who had sunk down on the "deacon seat" and was staring at the stove.

"Is there a window?" he demanded.

"Don't ask me," she whispered. "I—I don't know."

With a very thriving fear in his heart, Jandron peered at her a moment. He fell to muttering: "I'm Wallace Jandron. Wallace, Jandron, 37 Ware Street, Cambridge, Massachusetts. I'm quite sane. And I'm going to stay so. I'm going to save her! I know perfectly well what I'm doing. And I'm sane. Quite, quite sane!"

After a time of confused and purposeless wrangling, they got a fire going and made coffee. This, and cube boullion with hardtack, helped considerably. The camp helped, too. A house, even a poor and broken one, is a wonderful barrier against a Thing from—Outside.

Presently darkness folded down. The men smoked, thankful that tobacco still held out. Vivian lay in a bunk that Jandron had piled with spruce boughs for her, and seemed to sleep. The professor fretted like a child over the blisters his paddle had made upon his hands. Marr laughed, now and then; though what he might be laughing at was not apparent.

Suddenly he broke out: "After all, what should It want of us?"

"Our brains, of course," the professor answered, sharply.

"That lets Jandron out," the journalist mocked.

"But," added the professor, "I can't imagine a Thing callously destroying human beings. And yet—"

He stopped short, with surging memories of his dead wife.

"What was it," Jandron asked, "that destroyed all those people in Vallodolid, Spain, that time so many of them died in a few minutes after having been touched by an invisible Something that left a slight red mark on each? The newspapers were full of it."

"Piffle!" yawned Marr.

"I tell you," insisted Jandron, "there are forms of life as superior to us as we are to ants. We can't see 'em. No ant ever saw a man. And did any ant ever form the least conception of a man? These things have left thousands of traces, all over the world. If I had my reference books—"

"Tell that to the marines!"

387

"Charles Fort, the greatest authority in the world on unexplained phenomena," persisted Jandron, "gives innumerable cases of happenings that science can't explain, in his *Book of the Damned*. He claims this Earth was once a No-Man's Land where all kinds of things explored and colonized and fought for possession. And he says that now everybody's warned off, except the Owners. I happen to remember a few sentences of his: 'In the past, inhabitants of a host of worlds have dropped here, hopped here, wafted, sailed, flown, motored, walked here; have come singly, have come in enormous numbers; have visited for hunting, trading, mining. They have been unable to stay here, have made colonies here, have been lost here.'"

"Poor fish, to believe that!" mocked the journalist, while the professor blinked and rubbed his bulging forehead.

"I do believe it," insisted Jandron. "The world is covered with relics of dead civilizations that have mysteriously vanished, leaving nothing but their temples and monuments."

"Rubbish!"

"How about Easter Island? How about all the gigantic works there and in a thousand other places—Peru, Yucatán, and so on—which certainly no primitive race ever built?"

"That's thousands of years ago," said Marr, "and I'm sleepy. For heaven's sake, can it!"

"Oh, all right. But how to explain things, then!"

"What the devil could one of those Things want of our brains?" suddenly put in the professor. "After all, what?"

"Well, what do we want of lower forms of life? Sometimes food. Again, some product or other. Or just information. Maybe It is just experimenting with us, the way we poke an anthill. There's always this to remember, that the human brain tissue is the most highly organized form of matter in this world."

"Yes," admitted the professor, but what—?"

"It might want brain tissue for food, for experimental purposes, for lubricant—how do I know?"

Jandron fancied he was still explaining things, but all at once he found himself waking up in one of the bunks. He felt terribly cold, stiff, sore. A sift of snow lay here and there on the camp floor, where it had fallen through holes in the roof.

"Vivian," he croaked hoarsely. "Thorburn! Marr!"

Nobody answered. There was nobody to answer. Jandron crawled with immense pain out of his bunk, and blinked round with bleary eyes. All of a sudden, he saw the professor and gulped.

The professor was lying stiff and straight in an other bunk, on his back. His waxen face made a mask of horror. The open, staring eyes, with pupils immensely dilated, sent Jandron shuddering back. A livid ring marked the forehead that now sagged inward as if empty.

"Vivian!" croaked Jandron, staggering away from the body. He fumbled to the bunk where the girl had lain. The bunk was quite deserted.

On the stove, in which lay half-charred wood—wood smothered out as if by some noxious gas—still stood the coffee pot. The liquid in it was frozen solid. Of Vivian and the journalist, no trace remained.

Along one of the sagging beams that supported the roof, Jandron's horror-blasted gaze perceived a straight line of frosted prints, ring-shaped, bitten deep.

"Vivian! Vivian!"

No answer.

Shaking, sick, gray, half-blind with a horror not of this world, Jandron peered slowly round. The duffelbag and supplies were gone. Nothing was left but the coffee pot and the revolver at Jandron's hip.

Jandron turned then. A-stare, his skull feeling empty as a burst drum, he crept lamely to the door and out—out into the snow.

Snow. It came slanting down. From a gray sky it steadily filtered. The tree showed no leaf. Birches, poplars, rock maples all stood naked. Only the conifers drooped sickly green. In a little shallow across the river snow lay white on thin ice.

Ice? Snow? Rapt with terror, Jandron stared. Why, then, he must have been unconscious three or four weeks? But how—?

Suddenly, all along the upper branches of trees that edged the clearing, puffs of snow flicked down. The geologist shuffled after two half-obliterated sets of foot-prints that wavered toward the landing.

His body was leaden. He wheezed as he reached the river. The light, dim as it was, hurt his eyes. He blinked in a confusion that could just perceive one canoe was gone. He pressed a hand to his head, where an iron band seemed screwed up tight, tighter.

"Vivian! Marr! Haalloooo!"

Not even an echo. Silence clamped the world; silence, and a cold that gnawed. Everything had gone a sinister gray.

After a certain time—though time now possessed neither reality nor dura-tion—Jandron dragged himself back to the camp and stumbled in. Heedless of the staring corpse he crumpled down by the stove and tried to think, but his brain had been emptied of power. Everything blended to a gray blur. Snow kept slithering in through the roof.

"Well, why don't you come and get me, Thing?" suddenly snarled Jandron. "Here I am. Damn you, come and get me!"

Voices. Suddenly he heard voices. Yes, somebody was outside, there. Singularly aggrieved, he got up and limped to the door. He squinted out into the gray; saw two figures down by the landing. With numb indifference he recognized the girl and Marr.

"Why should they bother me again?" he nebulously wondered. "Can't they go away and leave me alone?" He felt peevish irritation.

Then, a modicum of reasoning returning, he sensed that they were arguing. Vivian, beside a canoe freshly dragged from thin ice, was pointing; Marr was gesticulating. All at once Marr snarled, turned from her, plodded with bent back toward the camp.

"But listen!" she called, her rough-knot sweater all powdered with snow. "That's the way!" She gestured downstream.

"I'm not going either way!" Marr retorted. "I'm going to stay right here!" He came on, bareheaded. Snow grayed his stubble of beard, but on his head it melted as it fell, as if some fever there had raised the brain stuff to improbable temperatures. "I'm going to stay right here, all summer." His heavy lids sagged. Puffy and evil, his lips showed a glint of teeth. "Let me alone!"

Vivian lagged after him, kicking up the ash-like snow. With indifference, Jandron watched them. Trivial human creatures!

Suddenly Marr saw him in the doorway and stopped short. He drew his gun; he aimed at Jandron.

"You get out!" he mouthed. "Why in—can't you stay dead?"

"Put that gun down, you idiot!" Jandron managed to retort.

The girl stopped and seemed trying to understand. "We can get away yet, if we all stick together."

"Are you going to get out and leave me alone?" demanded the journalist, holding his gun steadily enough.

Jandron, wholly indifferent, watched the muzzle. Vague curiosity possessed him. Just what, he wondered, did it feel like to be shot?

Marr pulled the trigger.

Snap!

The cartridge missed fire. Not even powder would burn.

Marr laughed, horribly, and shambled forward.

"Serves him right!" he mouthed. "He'd better not come back again!"

Jandron understood that Marr had seen him fall. Still, he felt himself standing there, alive. He shuffled away from the door. No matter whether he was alive or dead, there was always Vivian to be saved.

The journalist came to the door, paused, looked down, grunted, and passed into the camp. He shut the door. Jandron heard the rotten wooden bar of the latch drop. From within echoed a laugh, monstrous in its brutality.

Then, quivering, the geologist felt a touch on his arm.

"Why did you desert us like that?" he heard Vivian's reproach. "Why?"

He turned, hardly able to see her at all.

"Listen," he said, thickly. "I'll admit anything. It's all right. But just forget it, for now. We've got to get out of here. The professor is dead, in there, and Marr's gone mad and barricaded himself in there. So there's no use staying. There's a chance for us yet. Come along!"

He took her by the arm and tried to draw her toward the river, but she held back. The hate in her face sickened him. He shook in the grip of a mighty chill.

"Go, with—you?" she demanded.

"Yes, by God!" he retorted, in a swift blaze of anger, "or I'll kill you where you stand. It shan't get you, anyhow!"

Swiftly piercing, a greater cold smote to his inner marrows. A long row of the cup-shaped prints had just appeared in the snow beside the camp. And from these marks wafted a faint, bluish vapor of unthinkable cold.

"What are you staring at," the girl demanded.

"Those prints! In the snow, there—see?" He pointed a shaking finger.

"How can there be snow at this season?"

He could have wept for the pity of her, the love of her. On her red tam, her tangle of rebel hair, her sweater, the snow came steadily drifting; yet, there she stood before him and prated of summer. Jandron heaved himself out of a very slough of down-dragging lassitudes. He whipped himself into action.

"Summer, winter—no matter!" he flung at her. "You're coming along with me!" He seized her arm with the brutality of desperation that must hurt to save. And murder, too, lay in his soul. He knew that he would strangle her with his naked hands, if need were, before he would ever leave her there, for *It* to work Its horrible will upon.

"You come with me," he mouthed "or by the Almighty—!"

Marr's scream in the camp whirled him toward the door. That scream rose higher, higher, ever more and more piercing, just like the screams of the runaway Indian guides in what now appeared the infinitely long ago. It seemed to last hours;

and always it rose, rose, as if being wrung out of a human body by some kind of agony not conceivable in this world. Higher, higher——

Then it stopped.

Jandron hurled himself against the plank door. The bar smashed; the door shivered inward.

With a cry, Jandron recoiled. He covered his eyes with a hand that quivered, claw-like.

"Go away, Vivian! Don't come here—don't look——"

He stumbled away, babbling.

Out of the door crept something like a man. A queer, broken, bent-over thing; a thing crippled, shrunken, and flabby, that whined.

This thing—yes, it was still Marr—crouched down at one side, quivering, whimpering. It moved its hands as a crushed ant moves its antennae, jerkily, without significance.

All at once Jandron no longer felt afraid. He walked quite steadily to Marr, who was breathing in little gasps. From the camp issued an odor unlike anything terrestrial. A thin, grayish grease covered the sill.

Jandron caught hold of the crumpling journalist's arm. Marr's eyes leered, filmed, unseeing. He gave the impression of a creature whose back has been broken, whose whole essence and energy have been wrenched asunder, yet in which life somehow clings, palpitant. A creature vivisected.

Away through the snow Jandron dragged him. Marr made no resistance; just let himself be led, whining a little, palsied, rickety, shattered. The girl, her face whitely cold as the snow that fell on it, came after.

Thus they reached the landing at the river.

"Come now, let's get away!" Jandron made an effort to articulate. Marr said nothing. But when Jandron tried to bundle him into a canoe, something in the journalist revived with swift, mad hatefulness. That something lashed him into a spasm of wiry, incredibly venomous resistance. Slavers of blood and foam streaked Marr's lips. He made horrid noises, like an animal. He howled dismally, and bit, clawed, writhed, and groveled! He tried to sink his teeth into Jandron's leg. He fought appallingly, as men must have fought in the inconceivably remote days even before the Stone Age. And Vivian helped him. Her fury was a tiger-cat's.

Between the pair of them, they almost did him in. They almost dragged Jandron down—and themselves, too—into the black river that ran swiftly sucking under the ice. Not till Jandron had flung off all vague notions and restraints of gallantry, not till he struck from the shoulder—to kill, if need were—did he best them.

He beat the pair of them unconscious, trussed them hand and foot with the painters of the canoes, rolled them into the larger canoe, and shoved off.

After that, the blankness of a measureless oblivion descended.

Only from what he was told, weeks after, in the Royal Victoria Hospital at Montreal, did Jandron ever learn how and when a field squad of Dominion Foresters had found them drifting in Lake Moosawamkeag. And that knowledge filtered slowly into his brain during a period inchoate as Iceland fogs. That Marr was dead and the girl alive—that much, at all events, was solid. He could hold to that; he could climb back, with that, to the real world again.

Jandron climbed back came back. Time healed him, as it healed the girl. After a long, long while, they had speech together. Cautiously he sounded her wells of memory. He saw that she recalled nothing. So he told her white lies about capsized canoes and the sad death—in realistically described rapids—of all the party except herself and him.

Vivian believed. Fate, Jandron knew, was being very kind to both of them.

But Vivian could never understand in the least why her husband, not very long after marriage, asked her not to wear a wedding ring or any ring whatever.

"Men are so queer!" covers a multitude of psychic agonies.

Life, for Jandron—life, softened by Vivian—knit itself up into some reasonable semblance of a normal pattern. But when, at lengthening intervals, memories even now awake—memories crawling amid the slime of cosmic mysteries that it is madness to approach—or when at certain times Jandron sees a ring of any sort, his heart chills with a cold that reeks of the horrors of Infinity.

And from shadows past the boundaries of our universe seem to beckon Things that, God grant, can never till the end of time be known on Earth.

The Colour
out of Space

H.P. LOVECRAFT

In stories gathered as his tales of the Cthulhu Mythos, H.P. Lovecraft (1890–1937) writes of otherworldly entities so incomprehensible to human understanding that humans speak of them in terms of gods and super-natural beings. Much of Lovecraft's fiction is a skillful fusion of horror and science fiction, including this story, first published in the September 1927 issue of Amazing Stories, *in which the malignant influence from a meteorite that strikes the earth constitutes a type of alien invasion.*

West of Arkham the hills rise wild, and there are valleys with deep woods that no axe has ever cut. There are dark narrow glens where the trees slope fantastically, and where thin brooklets trickle without ever having caught the glint of sunlight. On the gentler slopes there are farms, ancient and rocky, with squat, moss-coated cottages brooding eternally over old New England secrets in the lee of great ledges; but these are all vacant now, the wide chimneys crumbling and the shingled sides bulging perilously beneath low gambrel roofs.

The old folk have gone away, and foreigners do not like to live there. French-Canadians have tried it, Italians have tried it, and the Poles have come and departed. It is not because of anything that can be seen or heard or handled, but because of something that is imagined. The place is not good for the imagination, and does not bring restful dreams at night. It must be this which keeps the foreigners away, for old Ammi Pierce has never told them of anything he recalls from the strange days.

Ammi, whose head has been a little queer for years, is the only one who still remains, or who ever talks of the strange days; and he dares to do this because his house is so near the open fields and the travelled roads around Arkham.

There was once a road over the hills and through the valleys, that ran straight where the blasted heath is now; but people ceased to use it and a new road was laid curving far toward the south. Traces of the old one can still be found amidst the weeds of a returning wilderness, and some of them will doubtless linger even when half the hollows are flooded for the new reservoir. Then the dark woods will be cut down and the blasted heath will slumber far below blue waters whose surface will mirror the sky and ripple in the sun. And the secrets of the strange days will be one with the deep's secrets; one with the hidden lore of old ocean, and all the mystery of primal earth.

When I went into the hills and vales to survey for the new reservoir they told me the place was evil. They told me this in Arkham, and because that is a very old town full of witch legends I thought the evil must be something which grandams had whispered to children through centuries. The name "blasted heath" seemed to me very odd and theatrical, and I wondered how it had come into the folklore of a Puritan people. Then I saw that dark westward tangle of glens and slopes for myself, and ceased to wonder at anything besides its own elder mystery. It was morning when I saw it, but shadow lurked always there. The trees grew too thickly, and their trunks were too big for any healthy New England wood. There was too much silence in the dim alleys between them, and the floor was too soft with the dank moss and mattings of infinite years of decay.

In the open spaces, mostly along the line of the old road, there were little hillside farms; sometimes with all the buildings standing, sometimes with only one or two, and sometimes with only a lone chimney or fast-filling cellar. Weeds and briers reigned, and furtive wild things rustled in the undergrowth. Upon everything was a haze of restlessness and oppression; a touch of the unreal and the grotesque, as if some vital element of perspective or chiaroscuro were awry. I did not wonder that the foreigners would not stay, for this was no region to sleep in. It was too much like a landscape of Salvator Rosa; too much like some forbidden woodcut in a tale of terror.

But even all this was not so bad as the blasted heath. I knew it the moment I came upon it at the bottom of a spacious valley; for no other name could fit such a thing, or any other thing fit such a name. It was as if the poet had coined the phrase from having seen this one particular region. It must, I thought as I viewed it, be the outcome of a fire; but why had nothing new ever grown over those five acres of grey desolation that sprawled open to the sky like a great spot eaten by acid in the woods and fields? It lay largely to the north of the ancient road line, but encroached a little on the other side. I felt an odd reluctance about approaching, and did so at last only because my business took me through and past it. There was no vegetation of any kind on that broad expanse, but only a fine grey dust or ash which no wind seemed ever to blow about. The trees near it were sickly and stunted, and many dead trunks stood or lay rotting at the rim. As I walked hurriedly by I saw the tumbled bricks and stones of an old chimney and cellar on my right, and the yawning black maw of an abandoned well whose stagnant vapours played strange tricks with the hues of the sunlight. Even the long, dark woodland climb beyond seemed welcome in contrast, and I marvelled no more at the frightened whispers of Arkham people. There had been no house or ruin near; even in the old days the place must have been lonely and remote. And at twilight, dreading to repass that ominous spot, I walked circuitously back to the town by the curving road on the south. I vaguely wished some clouds would gather, for an odd timidity about the deep skyey voids above had crept into my soul.

In the evening I asked old people in Arkham about the blasted heath, and what was meant by that phrase "strange days" which so many evasively muttered. I could not, however, get any good answers, except that all the mystery was much more recent than I had dreamed. It was not a matter of old legendry at all, but something within the lifetime of those who spoke. It had happened in the 'eighties, and a family had disappeared or was killed. Speakers would not be exact; and because they all told me to pay no attention to old Ammi Pierce's crazy tales, I sought him out the next morning, having heard that he lived alone in the ancient tottering cottage where the trees first begin to get very thick. It was a fearsomely archaic place, and had begun to exude the faint miasmal odour which clings about houses that have stood too long. Only with persistent knocking could I rouse the aged man, and when he shuffled timidly to the door I could tell he was not glad to see me. He was not so feeble as I had expected; but his eyes drooped in a curious way, and his unkempt clothing and white beard made him seem very worn and dismal. Not knowing just how he could best be launched on his tales, I feigned a matter of business; told him of my surveying, and asked vague questions about the district. He was far brighter and more educated than I had been led to think, and before I knew it had grasped quite as much of the subject as any man I had talked with in Arkham. He was not like other rustics I had known in the sections where reservoirs were to be. From him there were no protests at the miles of old wood and farmland to be blotted out, though perhaps there would have been had not his home lain outside the bounds of the future lake. Relief was all that he shewed; relief at the doom of the dark ancient valleys through which he had roamed all his life. They were better under water now—better under water since the strange days. And with this opening his husky voice sank low, while his body leaned forward and his right forefinger began to point shakily and impressively.

It was then that I heard the story, and as the rambling voice scraped and whispered on I shivered again and again despite the summer day. Often I had to recall the speaker from ramblings, piece out scientific points which he knew only by a fading parrot memory of professors' talk, or bridge over gaps where his sense of logic and continuity broke down. When he was done I did not wonder that his mind had snapped a trifle, or that the folk of Arkham would not speak much of the blasted heath. I hurried back before sunset to my hotel, unwilling to have the stars come out above me in the open; and the next day returned to Boston to give up my position. I could not go into that dim chaos of old forest and slope again, or face another time that grey blasted heath where the black well yawned deep beside the tumbled bricks and stones. The reservoir will soon be built now, and all those elder secrets will be safe forever under watery fathoms. But even then I do not believe I would like to visit that country by night—at least, not when the sinister stars are out; and nothing could bribe me to drink the new city water of Arkham.

It all began, old Ammi said, with the meteorite. Before that time there had been no wild legends at all since the witch trials, and even then these western woods were not feared half so much as the small island in the Miskatonic where the devil held court beside a curious stone altar older than the Indians. These were not haunted woods, and their fantastic dusk was never terrible till the strange days. Then there had come that white noontide cloud, that string of explosions in the air, and that pillar of smoke from the valley far in the wood. And by night all Arkham had heard of the great rock that fell out of the sky and bedded itself in the ground beside the well at the Nahum Gardner place. That was the house which had stood where the blasted heath was to come—the trim white Nahum Gardner house amidst its fertile gardens and orchards.

Nahum had come to town to tell people about the stone, and had dropped in at Ammi Pierce's on the way. Ammi was forty then, and all the queer things were fixed very strongly in his mind. He and his wife had gone with the three professors from Miskatonic University who hastened out the next morning to see the weird visitor from unknown stellar space, and had wondered why Nahum had called it so large the day before. It had shrunk, Nahum said as he pointed out the big brownish mound above the ripped earth and charred grass near the archaic well-sweep in his front yard; but the wise men answered that stones do not shrink. Its heat lingered persistently, and Nahum declared it had glowed faintly in the night. The professors tried it with a geologist's hammer and found it was oddly soft. It was, in truth, so soft as to be almost plastic; and they gouged rather than chipped a specimen to take back to the college for testing. They took it in an old pail borrowed from Nahum's kitchen, for even the small piece refused to grow cool. On the trip back they stopped at Ammi's to rest, and seemed thoughtful when Mrs. Pierce remarked that the fragment was growing smaller and burning the bottom of the pail. Truly, it was not large, but perhaps they had taken less than they thought.

The day after that—all this was in June of '82—the professors had trooped out again in a great excitement. As they passed Ammi's they told him what queer things the specimen had done, and how it had faded wholly away when they put it in a glass beaker. The beaker had gone, too, and the wise men talked of the strange stone's affinity for silicon. It had acted quite unbelievably in that well-ordered laboratory; doing nothing at all and shewing no occluded gases when heated on charcoal, being wholly negative in the borax bead, and soon proving itself absolutely non-volatile at any producible temperature, including that of the oxy-hydrogen blowpipe. On an anvil it appeared highly malleable, and in the dark its luminosity was very marked. Stubbornly refusing to grow cool, it soon had the college in a state of real excitement; and when upon heating before the spectroscope it displayed shining bands unlike any known colours of the normal spectrum there was much breathless talk of new elements, bizarre optical properties, and other things which puzzled men of science are wont to say when faced by the unknown.

Hot as it was, they tested it in a crucible with all the proper reagents. Water did nothing. Hydrochloric acid was the same. Nitric acid and even aqua regia merely hissed and spattered against its torrid invulnerability. Ammi had difficulty in recalling all these things, but recognised some solvents as I mentioned them in the usual order of use. There were ammonia and caustic soda, alcohol and ether, nauseous carbon disulphide and a dozen others; but although the weight grew steadily less as time passed, and the fragment seemed to be slightly cooling, there was no change in the solvents to shew that they had attacked the substance at all. It was a metal, though, beyond a doubt. It was magnetic, for one thing; and after its immersion in the acid solvents there seemed to be faint traces of the Widmannstätten figures found on meteoric iron. When the cooling had grown very considerable, the testing was carried on in glass; and it was in a glass beaker that they left all the chips made of the original fragment during the work. The next morning both chips and beaker were gone without trace, and only a charred spot marked the place on the wooden shelf where they had been.

All this the professors told Ammi as they paused at his door, and once more he went with them to see the stony messenger from the stars, though this time his wife did not accompany him. It had now most certainly shrunk, and even the sober professors could not doubt the truth of what they saw. All around the dwindling brown lump near the well was a vacant space, except where the earth had caved in; and whereas it had been a good seven feet across the day before, it was now scarcely five. It was still hot, and the sages studied its surface curiously as they detached another and larger piece with hammer and chisel. They gouged deeply this time, and as they pried away the smaller mass they saw that the core of the thing was not quite homogeneous.

They had uncovered what seemed to be the side of a large coloured globule imbedded in the substance. The colour, which resembled some of the bands in the meteor's strange spectrum, was almost impossible to describe; and it was only by analogy that they called it colour at all. Its texture was glossy, and upon tapping it appeared to promise both brittleness and hollowness. One of the professors gave it a smart blow with a hammer, and it burst with a nervous little pop. Nothing was emitted, and all trace of the thing vanished with the puncturing. It left behind a hollow spherical space about three inches across, and all thought it probable that others would be discovered as the enclosing substance wasted away.

Conjecture was vain; so after a futile attempt to find additional globules by drilling, the seekers left again with their new specimen—which proved, however, as baffling in the laboratory as its predecessor had been. Aside from being almost plastic, having heat, magnetism, and slight luminosity, cooling slightly in powerful acids, possessing an unknown spectrum, wasting away in air, and attacking silicon compounds with mutual destruction as a result, it presented no identifying features whatsoever; and at the end of the tests the college scientists were forced to own that they could not place it. It was nothing of this earth, but a piece of the great outside; and as such dowered with outside properties and obedient to outside laws.

That night there was a thunderstorm, and when the professors went out to Nahum's the next day they met with a bitter disappointment. The stone, magnetic as it had been, must have had some peculiar electrical property; for it had "drawn the lightning", as Nahum said, with a singular persistence. Six times within an hour the farmer saw the lightning strike the furrow in the front yard, and when the storm was over nothing remained but a ragged pit by the ancient well-sweep, half-choked with caved-in earth. Digging had borne no fruit, and the scientists verified the fact of the utter vanishment. The failure was total; so that nothing was left to do but go back to the laboratory and test again the disappearing fragment left carefully cased in lead. That fragment lasted a week, at the end of which nothing of value had been learned of it. When it had gone, no residue was left behind, and in time the professors felt scarcely sure they had indeed seen with waking eyes that cryptic vestige of the fathomless gulfs outside; that lone, weird message from other universes and other realms of matter, force, and entity.

As was natural, the Arkham papers made much of the incident with its collegiate sponsoring, and sent reporters to talk with Nahum Gardner and his family. At least one Boston daily also sent a scribe, and Nahum quickly became a kind of local celebrity. He was a lean, genial person of about fifty, living with his wife and three sons on the pleasant farmstead in the valley. He and Ammi exchanged visits frequently, as did their wives; and Ammi had nothing but praise for him after all these years. He seemed slightly proud of the notice his place had attracted, and talked often of the meteorite in the succeeding weeks. That July and August were hot, and Nahum worked hard at his haying in the ten-acre pasture across Chapman's Brook; his rattling wain wearing deep ruts in the shadowy lanes between. The labour tired him more than it had in other years, and he felt that age was beginning to tell on him.

Then fell the time of fruit and harvest. The pears and apples slowly ripened, and Nahum vowed that his orchards were prospering as never before. The fruit was growing to phenomenal size and unwonted gloss, and in such abundance that extra barrels were ordered to handle the future crop. But with the ripening came sore disappointment; for of all that gorgeous array of specious lusciousness not one single jot was fit to eat. Into the fine flavour of the pears and apples had crept a stealthy bitterness and sickishness, so that even the smallest of bites induced a lasting disgust. It was the same with the melons and tomatoes, and Nahum sadly saw that his entire crop was lost. Quick to connect events, he declared that the meteorite had poisoned the soil, and thanked heaven that most of the other crops were in the upland lot along the road.

Winter came early, and was very cold. Ammi saw Nahum less often than usual, and observed that he had begun to look worried. The rest of his family, too, seemed to have grown taciturn; and were far from steady in their churchgoing or their attendance at the various social events of the countryside. For this reserve or melancholy no cause could be found, though all the household confessed now and then to poorer health and a feeling of vague disquiet. Nahum himself gave the most definite statement of anyone when he said he was disturbed about certain footprints in the snow. They were the usual winter prints of red squirrels, white rabbits, and foxes, but the brooding farmer professed to see something not quite right about their nature and arrangement. He was never specific, but appeared to think that they were not as characteristic of the anatomy and habits of squirrels and rabbits and foxes as they ought to be. Ammi listened without interest to this talk until one night when he drove past Nahum's house in his sleigh on the way back from Clark's Corners. There had been a moon, and a rabbit had run across the road, and the leaps of that rabbit were longer than either Ammi or his horse liked. The latter, indeed, had almost run away when brought up by a firm rein. Thereafter Ammi gave Nahum's tales more respect, and wondered why the Gardner dogs seemed so cowed and quivering every morning. They had, it developed, nearly lost the spirit to bark.

In February the McGregor boys from Meadow Hill were out shooting wood-chucks, and not far from the Gardner place bagged a very peculiar specimen. The proportions of its body seemed slightly altered in a queer way impossible to describe, while its face had taken on an expression which no one ever saw in a woodchuck before. The boys were genuinely frightened, and threw the thing away at once, so that only their grotesque tales of it ever reached the people of the countryside. But the shying away of the horses near Nahum's house had now become an acknowl-edged thing, and all the basis for a cycle of whispered legend was fast taking form.

People vowed that the snow melted faster around Nahum's than it did any-where else, and early in March there was an awed discussion in Potter's general store at Clark's Corners. Stephen Rice had driven past Gardner's in the morning, and had noticed the skunk-cabbages coming up through the mud by the woods across the road. Never were things of such size seen before, and they held strange colours that could not be put into any words. Their shapes were monstrous, and the horse had snorted at an odour which struck Stephen as wholly unprecedented. That afternoon several persons drove past to see the abnormal growth, and all agreed that plants of that kind ought never to sprout in a healthy world. The bad fruit of the fall before was freely mentioned, and it went from mouth to mouth that there was poison in Nahum's ground. Of course it was the meteorite; and remembering how strange the men from the college had found that stone to be, several farmers spoke about the matter to them.

One day they paid Nahum a visit; but having no love of wild tales and folklore were very conservative in what they inferred. The plants were certainly odd, but all skunk-cabbages are more or less odd in shape and odour and hue. Perhaps some mineral element from the stone had entered the soil, but it would soon be washed away. And as for the footprints and frightened horses—of course this was mere country talk which such a phenomenon as the aërolite would be certain to start. There was really nothing for serious men to do in cases of wild gossip, for supersti-tious rustics will say and believe anything. And so all through the strange days the professors stayed away in contempt. Only one of them, when given two phials of dust for analysis in a police job over a year and a half later, recalled that the queer colour of that skunk-cabbage had been very like one of the anomalous bands of light shewn by the meteor fragment in the college spectroscope, and like the brittle globule found imbedded in the stone from the abyss. The samples in this analysis case gave the same odd bands at first, though later they lost the property.

The trees budded prematurely around Nahum's, and at night they swayed ominously in the wind. Nahum's second son Thaddeus, a lad of fifteen, swore that they swayed also when there was no wind; but even the gossips would not credit this. Certainly, however, restlessness was in the air. The entire Gardner family developed the habit of stealthy listening, though not for any sound which they could consciously name. The listening was, indeed, rather a product of moments when consciousness seemed half to slip away. Unfortunately such moments increased week by week, till it became common speech that "something was wrong with all Nahum's folks." When the early saxifrage came out it had another strange colour; not quite like that of the skunk-cabbage, but plainly related and equally unknown to anyone who saw it. Nahum took some blossoms to Arkham and shewed them to the editor of the Gazette, but that dignitary did no more than write a humorous article about them, in which the dark fears of rustics were held up to polite ridicule. It was a mistake of Nahum's to tell a stolid city man about the way the great, overgrown mourning-cloak butterflies behaved in connexion with these saxifrages.

April brought a kind of madness to the country folk, and began that disuse of the road past Nahum's which led to its ultimate abandonment. It was the vegetation. All the orchard trees blossomed forth in strange colours, and through the stony soil of the yard and adjacent pasturage there sprang up a bizarre growth which only a botanist could connect with the proper flora of the region. No sane wholesome colours were anywhere to be seen except in the green grass and leafage; but everywhere those hectic and prismatic variants of some diseased, underlying primary tone without a place among the known tints of earth. The Dutchman's breeches became a thing of sinister menace, and the bloodroots grew insolent in their chromatic perversion. Ammi and the Gardners thought that most of the colours had a sort of haunting familiarity, and decided that they reminded one of the brittle globule in the meteor. Nahum ploughed and sowed the ten-acre pasture and the upland lot, but did nothing with the land around the house. He knew it would be of no use, and hoped that the summer's strange growths would draw all the poison from the soil. He was prepared for almost anything now, and had grown used to the sense of something near him waiting to be heard. The shunning of his house by neighbours told on him, of course; but it told on his wife more. The boys were better off, being at school each day; but they could not help being frightened by the gossip. Thaddeus, an especially sensitive youth, suffered the most.

In May the insects came, and Nahum's place became a nightmare of buzzing and crawling. Most of the creatures seemed not quite usual in their aspects and motions, and their nocturnal habits contradicted all former experience. The Gardners took to watching at night—watching in all directions at random for something . . . they could not tell what. It was then that they all owned that Thaddeus had been right about the trees. Mrs. Gardner was the next to see it from the window as she watched the swollen boughs of a maple against a moonlit sky. The boughs surely moved, and there was no wind. It must be the sap. Strangeness had come into everything growing now. Yet it was none of Nahum's family at all who made the next discovery. Familiarity had dulled them, and what they could not see was glimpsed by a timid windmill salesman from Bolton who drove by one night in ignorance of the country legends. What he told in Arkham was given a short paragraph in the Gazette; and it was there that all the farmers, Nahum included, saw it first. The night had been dark and the buggy-lamps faint, but around a farm in the valley which everyone knew from the account must be Nahum's the darkness had been less thick. A dim though distinct luminosity seemed to inhere in all the vegetation, grass, leaves, and blossoms alike, while at one moment a detached piece of the phosphorescence appeared to stir furtively in the yard near the barn.

The grass had so far seemed untouched, and the cows were freely pastured in the lot near the house, but toward the end of May the milk began to be bad. Then Nahum had the cows driven to the uplands, after which the trouble ceased. Not long after this the change in grass and leaves became apparent to the eye. All the verdure was going grey, and was developing a highly singular quality of brittleness. Ammi was now the only person who ever visited the place, and his visits were becoming fewer and fewer. When school closed the Gardners were virtually cut off from the world, and sometimes let Ammi do their errands in town. They were failing curiously both physically and mentally, and no one was surprised when the news of Mrs. Gardner's madness stole around.

It happened in June, about the anniversary of the meteor's fall, and the poor woman screamed about things in the air which she could not describe. In her raving there was not a single specific noun, but only verbs and pronouns. Things moved and changed and fluttered, and ears tingled to impulses which were not wholly sounds. Something was taken away—she was being drained of something—something was fastening itself on her that ought not to be—someone must make it keep off—nothing was ever still in the night—the walls and windows shifted. Nahum did not send her to the county asylum, but let her wander about the house as long as she was harmless to herself and others. Even when her expression changed he did nothing. But when the boys grew afraid of her, and Thaddeus nearly fainted at the way she made faces at him, he decided to keep her locked in the attic. By July she had ceased to speak and crawled on all fours, and before that month was over Nahum got the mad notion that she was slightly luminous in the dark, as he now clearly saw was the case with the nearby vegetation.

It was a little before this that the horses had stampeded. Something had aroused them in the night, and their neighing and kicking in their stalls had been terrible. There seemed virtually nothing to do to calm them, and when Nahum opened the stable door they all bolted out like frightened woodland deer. It took a week to track all four, and when found they were seen to be quite useless and unmanageable. Something had snapped in their brains, and each one had to be shot for its own good. Nahum borrowed a horse from Ammi for his haying, but found it would not approach the barn. It shied, balked, and whinnied, and in the end he could do nothing but drive it into the yard while the men used their own strength to get the heavy wagon near enough the hayloft for convenient pitching. And all the while the vegetation was turning grey and brittle. Even the flowers whose hue had been so strange were greying now, and the fruit was coming out grey and dwarfed and tasteless. The asters and goldenrod bloomed grey and distorted, and the roses and zinneas and hollyhocks in the front yard were such blasphemous-looking things that Nahum's oldest boy Zenas cut them down. The strangely puffed insects died about that time, even the bees that had left their hives and taken to the woods.

By September all the vegetation was fast crumbling to a greyish powder, and Nahum feared that the trees would die before the poison was out of the soil. His wife now had spells of terrific screaming, and he and the boys were in a constant state of nervous tension. They shunned people now, and when school opened the boys did not go. But it was Ammi, on one of his rare visits, who first realised that the well water was no longer good. It had an evil taste that was not exactly foetid nor exactly salty, and Ammi advised his friend to dig another well on higher ground to use till the soil was good again. Nahum, however, ignored the warning, for he had by that time become calloused to strange and unpleasant things. He and the boys continued to use the tainted supply, drinking it as listlessly and mechanically as they ate their meagre and ill-cooked meals and did their thankless and monotonous chores through the aimless days. There was something of stolid resignation about them all, as if they walked half in another world between lines of nameless guards to a certain and familiar doom.

Thaddeus went mad in September after a visit to the well. He had gone with a pail and had come back empty-handed, shrieking and waving his arms, and sometimes lapsing into an inane titter or a whisper about "the moving colours down there." Two in one family was pretty bad, but Nahum was very brave about it. He let the boy run about for a week until he began stumbling and hurting himself, and then he shut him in an attic room across the hall from his mother's. The way they screamed at each other from behind their locked doors was very terrible, especially to little Merwin, who fancied they talked in some terrible language that was not of earth. Merwin was getting frightfully imaginative, and his restlessness was worse after the shutting away of the brother who had been his greatest playmate.

Almost at the same time the mortality among the livestock commenced. Poultry turned greyish and died very quickly, their meat being found dry and noisome upon cutting. Hogs grew inordinately fat, then suddenly began to undergo loathsome changes which no one could explain. Their meat was of course useless, and Nahum was at his wit's end. No rural veterinary would approach his place, and the city veterinary from Arkham was openly baffled. The swine began growing grey and brittle and falling to pieces before they died, and their eyes and muzzles developed singular alterations. It was very inexplicable, for they had never been fed from the tainted vegetation. Then something struck the cows. Certain areas or sometimes the whole body would be uncannily shrivelled or compressed, and atrocious collapses or disintegrations were common. In the last stages—and death was always the result—there would be a greying and turning brittle like that which beset the hogs. There could be no question of poison, for all the cases occurred in a locked and undisturbed barn. No bites of prowling things could have brought the virus, for what live beast of earth can pass through solid obstacles? It must be only natural disease—yet what disease could wreak such results was beyond any mind's guessing. When the harvest came there was not an animal surviving on the place, for the stock and poultry were dead and the dogs had run away. These dogs, three in number, had all vanished one night and were never heard of again. The five cats had left some time before, but their going was scarcely noticed since there now seemed to be no mice, and only Mrs. Gardner had made pets of the graceful felines.

On the nineteenth of October Nahum staggered into Ammi's house with hideous news. The death had come to poor Thaddeus in his attic room, and it had come in a way which could not be told. Nahum had dug a grave in the railed family plot behind the farm, and had put therein what he found. There could have been nothing from outside, for the small barred window and locked door were intact; but it was much as it had been in the barn. Ammi and his wife consoled the stricken man as best they could, but shuddered as they did so. Stark terror seemed to cling round the Gardners and all they touched, and the very presence of one in the house was a breath from regions unnamed and unnamable. Ammi accompanied Nahum home with the greatest reluctance, and did what he might to calm the hysterical sobbing of little Merwin. Zenas needed no calming. He had come of late to do nothing but stare into space and obey what his father told him; and Ammi thought that his fate was very merciful. Now and then Merwin's screams were answered faintly from the attic, and in response to an inquiring look Nahum said that his wife was getting very feeble. When night approached, Ammi managed to get away; for not even friendship could make him stay in that spot when the faint glow of the vegetation began and the trees may or may not have swayed without wind. It was really lucky for Ammi that he was not more imaginative. Even as things were, his mind was bent ever so slightly; but had he been able to connect and reflect upon all the portents around him he must inevitably have turned a total maniac. In the twilight he hastened home, the screams of the mad woman and the nervous child ringing horribly in his ears.

Three days later Nahum lurched into Ammi's kitchen in the early morning, and in the absence of his host stammered out a desperate tale once more, while Mrs. Pierce listened in a clutching fright. It was little Merwin this time. He was gone. He had gone out late at night with a lantern and pail for water, and had never come back. He'd been going to pieces for days, and hardly knew what he was about. Screamed at everything. There had been a frantic shriek from the yard then, but before the father could get to the door, the boy was gone. There was no glow from the lantern he had taken, and of the child himself no trace. At the time Nahum thought the lantern and pail were gone too; but when dawn came, and the man had plodded back from his all-night search of the woods and fields, he had found some very curious things near the well. There was a crushed and apparently somewhat melted mass of iron which had certainly been the lantern; while a bent bail and twisted iron hoops beside it, both half-fused, seemed to hint at the remnants of the pail. That was all. Nahum was past imagining, Mrs. Pierce was blank, and Ammi, when he had reached home and heard the tale, could give no guess. Merwin was gone, and there would be no use in telling the people around, who shunned all Gardners now. No use, either, in telling the city people at Arkham who laughed at everything. Thad was gone, and now Mernie was gone. Something was creeping and creeping and waiting to be seen and felt and heard. Nahum would go soon, and he wanted Ammi to look after his wife and Zenas if they survived him. It must all be a judgment of some sort; though he could not fancy what for, since he had always walked uprightly in the Lord's ways so far as he knew.

For over two weeks Ammi saw nothing of Nahum; and then, worried about what might have happened, he overcame his fears and paid the Gardner place a visit. There was no smoke from the great chimney, and for a moment the visitor was apprehensive of the worst. The aspect of the whole farm was shocking—greyish withered grass and leaves on the ground, vines falling in brittle wreckage from archaic walls and gables, and great bare trees clawing up at the grey November sky with a studied malevolence which Ammi could not but feel had come from some subtle change in the tilt of the branches. But Nahum was alive, after all. He was weak, and lying on a couch in the low-ceiled kitchen, but perfectly conscious and able to give simple orders to Zenas. The room was deadly cold; and as Ammi visibly shivered, the host shouted huskily to Zenas for more wood. Wood, indeed, was sorely needed; since the cavernous fireplace was unlit and empty, with a cloud of soot blowing about in the chill wind that came down the chimney. Presently Nahum asked him if the extra wood had made him any more comfortable, and then Ammi saw what had happened. The stoutest cord had broken at last, and the hapless farmer's mind was proof against more sorrow.

Questioning tactfully, Ammi could get no clear data at all about the missing Zenas. "In the well—he lives in the well—" was all that the clouded father would say. Then there flashed across the visitor's mind a sudden thought of the mad wife, and he changed his line of inquiry. "Nabby? Why, here she is!" was the surprised response of poor Nahum, and Ammi soon saw that he must search for himself. Leaving the harmless babbler on the couch, he took the keys from their nail beside the door and climbed the creaking stairs to the attic. It was very close and noisome up there, and no sound could be heard from any direction. Of the four doors in sight, only one was locked, and on this he tried various keys on the ring he had taken. The third key proved the right one, and after some fumbling Ammi threw open the low white door.

It was quite dark inside, for the window was small and half-obscured by the crude wooden bars; and Ammi could see nothing at all on the wide-planked floor. The stench was beyond enduring, and before proceeding further he had to retreat to another room and return with his lungs filled with breathable air. When he did enter he saw something dark in the corner, and upon seeing it more clearly he screamed outright. While he screamed he thought a momentary cloud eclipsed the window, and a second later he felt himself brushed as if by some hateful current of vapour. Strange colours danced before his eyes; and had not a present horror numbed him he would have thought of the globule in the meteor that the geologist's hammer had shattered, and of the morbid vegetation that had sprouted in the spring. As it was he thought only of the blasphemous monstrosity which confronted him, and which all too clearly had shared the nameless fate of young Thaddeus and the livestock. But the terrible thing about this horror was that it very slowly and perceptibly moved as it continued to crumble.

Ammi would give me no added particulars to this scene, but the shape in the corner does not reappear in his tale as a moving object. There are things which cannot be mentioned, and what is done in common humanity is sometimes cruelly judged by the law. I gathered that no moving thing was left in that attic room, and that to leave anything capable of motion there would have been a deed so monstrous as to damn any accountable being to eternal torment. Anyone but a stolid farmer would have fainted or gone mad, but Ammi walked conscious through that low doorway and locked the accursed secret behind him. There would be Nahum to deal with now; he must be fed and tended, and removed to some place where he could be cared for.

Commencing his descent of the dark stairs, Ammi heard a thud below him. He even thought a scream had been suddenly choked off, and recalled nervously the clammy vapour which had brushed by him in that frightful room above. What presence had his cry and entry started up? Halted by some vague fear, he heard still further sounds below. Indubitably there was a sort of heavy dragging, and a most detestably sticky noise as of some fiendish and unclean species of suction. With an associative sense goaded to feverish heights, he thought unaccountably of what he had seen upstairs. Good God! What eldritch dream-world was this into which he had blundered? He dared move neither backward nor forward, but stood there trembling at the black curve of the boxed-in staircase. Every trifle of the scene burned itself into his brain. The sounds, the sense of dread expectancy, the darkness, the steepness of the narrow steps—and merciful heaven! . . . the faint but unmistakable luminosity of all the woodwork in sight; steps, sides, exposed laths, and beams alike!

Then there burst forth a frantic whinny from Ammi's horse outside, followed at once by a clatter which told of a frenzied runaway. In another moment horse and buggy had gone beyond earshot, leaving the frightened man on the dark stairs to guess what had sent them. But that was not all. There had been another sound out there. A sort of liquid splash—water—it must have been the well. He had left Hero untied near it, and a buggy-wheel must have brushed the coping and knocked in a stone. And still the pale phosphorescence glowed in that detestably ancient woodwork. God! how old the house was! Most of it built before 1670, and the gambrel roof not later than 1730.

A feeble scratching on the floor downstairs now sounded distinctly, and Ammi's grip tightened on a heavy stick he had picked up in the attic for some purpose. Slowly nerving himself, he finished his descent and walked boldly toward the kitchen. But he did not complete the walk, because what he sought was no longer there. It had come to meet him, and it was still alive after a fashion. Whether it had crawled or whether it had been dragged by any external force, Ammi could not say; but the death had been at it. Everything had happened in the last half-hour, but collapse, greying, and disintegration were already far advanced. There was a horrible brittleness, and dry fragments were scaling off. Ammi could not touch it, but looked horrifiedly into the distorted parody that had been a face. "What was it, Nahum—what was it?" he whispered, and the cleft, bulging lips were just able to crackle out a final answer.

"Nothin' . . . nothin' . . . the colour . . . it burns . . . cold an' wet . . . but it burns . . . it lived in the well . . . I seen it . . . a kind o' smoke . . . jest like the flowers last spring . . . the well shone at night . . . Thad an' Mernie an' Zenas . . . everything alive . . . suckin' the life out of everthing . . . in that stone . . . it must a' come in that stone . . . pizened the whole place . . . dun't know what it wants . . . that round thing them men from the college dug outen the stone . . . they smashed it . . . it was that same colour . . . jest the same, like the flowers an' plants . . . must a' ben more of 'em . . . seeds . . . seeds . . . they growed . . . I seen it the fust time this week . . . must a' got strong on Zenas . . . he was a big boy, full o' life . . . it beats down your mind an' then gits ye . . . burns ye up . . . in the well water . . . you was right about that . . . evil water . . . Zenas never come back from the well . . . can't git away . . . draws ye . . . ye know summ'at's comin', but 'tain't no use . . . I seen it time an' agin senct Zenas was took . . . whar's Nabby, Ammi? . . . my head's no good . . . dun't know how long senct I fed her . . . it'll git her ef we ain't keerful . . . jest a colour . . . her face is gettin' to hev that colour sometimes towards night . . . an' it burns an' sucks . . . it come from some place whar things ain't as they is here . . . one o' them professors said so . . . he was right . . . look out, Ammi, it'll do suthin' more . . . sucks the life out. . . ."

But that was all. That which spoke could speak no more because it had completely caved in. Ammi laid a red checked tablecloth over what was left and reeled out the back door into the fields. He climbed the slope to the ten-acre pasture and stumbled home by the north road and the woods. He could not pass that well from which his horse had run away. He had looked at it through the window, and had seen that no stone was missing from the rim. Then the lurching buggy had not dislodged anything after all—the splash had been something else—something which went into the well after it had done with poor Nahum. . . .

409

When Ammi reached his house the horse and buggy had arrived before him and thrown his wife into fits of anxiety. Reassuring her without explanations, he set out at once for Arkham and notified the authorities that the Gardner family was no more. He indulged in no details, but merely told of the deaths of Nahum and Nabby, that of Thaddeus being already known, and mentioned that the cause seemed to be the same strange ailment which had killed the livestock. He also stated that Merwin and Zenas had disappeared. There was considerable questioning at the police station, and in the end Ammi was compelled to take three officers to the Gardner farm, together with the coroner, the medical examiner, and the veterinary who had treated the diseased animals. He went much against his will, for the afternoon was advancing and he feared the fall of night over that accursed place, but it was some comfort to have so many people with him.

The six men drove out in a democrat-wagon, following Ammi's buggy, and arrived at the pest-ridden farmhouse about four o'clock. Used as the officers were to gruesome experiences, not one remained unmoved at what was found in the attic and under the red checked tablecloth on the floor below. The whole aspect of the farm with its grey desolation was terrible enough, but those two crumbling objects were beyond all bounds. No one could look long at them, and even the medical examiner admitted that there was very little to examine. Specimens could be analysed, of course, so he busied himself in obtaining them—and here it develops that a very puzzling aftermath occurred at the college laboratory where the two phials of dust were finally taken. Under the spectroscope both samples gave off an unknown spectrum, in which many of the baffling bands were precisely like those which the strange meteor had yielded in the previous year. The property of emitting this spectrum vanished in a month, the dust thereafter consisting mainly of alkaline phosphates and carbonates.

Ammi would not have told the men about the well if he had thought they meant to do anything then and there. It was getting toward sunset, and he was anxious to be away. But he could not help glancing nervously at the stony curb by the great sweep, and when a detective questioned him he admitted that Nahum had feared something down there—so much so that he had never even thought of searching it for Merwin or Zenas. After that nothing would do but that they empty and explore the well immediately, so Ammi had to wait trembling while pail after pail of rank water was hauled up and splashed on the soaking ground outside. The men sniffed in disgust at the fluid, and toward the last held their noses against the foetor they were uncovering. It was not so long a job as they had feared it would be, since the water was phenomenally low. There is no need to speak too exactly of what they found. Merwin and Zenas were both there, in part, though the vestiges were mainly skeletal. There were also a small deer and a large dog in about the same state, and a number of bones of smaller animals. The ooze and slime at the bottom seemed inexplicably porous and bubbling, and a man who descended on hand-holds with a long pole found that he could sink the wooden shaft to any depth in the mud of the floor without meeting any solid obstruction.

Twilight had now fallen, and lanterns were brought from the house. Then, when it was seen that nothing further could be gained from the well, everyone went indoors and conferred in the ancient sitting-room while the intermittent light of a spectral half-moon played wanly on the grey desolation outside. The men were frankly nonplussed by the entire case, and could find no convincing common element to link the strange vegetable conditions, the unknown disease of livestock and humans, and the unaccountable deaths of Merwin and Zenas in the tainted well. They had heard the common country talk, it is true; but could not believe that anything contrary to natural law had occurred. No doubt the meteor had poisoned the soil, but the illness of persons and animals who had eaten nothing grown in that soil was another matter. Was it the well water? Very possibly. It might be a good idea to analyse it. But what peculiar madness could have made both boys jump into the well? Their deeds were so similar—and the fragments shewed that they had both suffered from the grey brittle death. Why was everything so grey and brittle?

It was the coroner, seated near a window overlooking the yard, who first noticed the glow about the well. Night had fully set in, and all the abhorrent grounds seemed faintly luminous with more than the fitful moonbeams; but this new glow was something definite and distinct, and appeared to shoot up from the black pit like a softened ray from a searchlight, giving dull reflections in the little ground pools where the water had been emptied. It had a very queer colour, and as all the men clustered round the window Ammi gave a violent start. For this strange beam of ghastly miasma was to him of no unfamiliar hue. He had seen that colour before, and feared to think what it might mean. He had seen it in the nasty brittle globule in that aërolite two summers ago, had seen it in the crazy vegetation of the springtime, and had thought he had seen it for an instant that very morning against the small barred window of that terrible attic room where nameless things had happened. It had flashed there a second, and a clammy and hateful current of vapour had brushed past him—and then poor Nahum had been taken by something of that colour. He had said so at the last—said it was like the globule and the plants. After that had come the runaway in the yard and the splash in the well—and now that well was belching forth to the night a pale insidious beam of the same daemoniac tint.

411

It does credit to the alertness of Ammi's mind that he puzzled even at that tense moment over a point which was essentially scientific. He could not but wonder at his gleaning of the same impression from a vapour glimpsed in the daytime, against a window opening on the morning sky, and from a nocturnal exhalation seen as a phosphorescent mist against the black and blasted landscape. It wasn't right—it was against Nature—and he thought of those terrible last words of his stricken friend, "It come from some place whar things ain't as they is here . . . one o' them professors said so. . . ."

All three horses outside, tied to a pair of shrivelled saplings by the road, were now neighing and pawing frantically. The wagon driver started for the door to do something, but Ammi laid a shaky hand on his shoulder. "Dun't go out thar," he whispered. "They's more to this nor what we know. Nahum said somethin' lived in the well that sucks your life out. He said it must be some'at growed from a round ball like one we all seen in the meteor stone that fell a year ago June. Sucks an' burns, he said, an' is jest a cloud of colour like that light out thar now, that ye can hardly see an' can't tell what it is. Nahum thought it feeds on everything livin' an' gits stronger all the time. He said he seen it this last week. It must be somethin' from away off in the sky like the men from the college last year says the meteor stone was. The way it's made an' the way it works ain't like no way o' God's world. It's some'at from beyond."

So the men paused indecisively as the light from the well grew stronger and the hitched horses pawed and whinnied in increasing frenzy. It was truly an awful moment; with terror in that ancient and accursed house itself, four monstrous sets of fragments—two from the house and two from the well—in the woodshed behind, and that shaft of unknown and unholy iridescence from the slimy depths in front. Ammi had restrained the driver on impulse, forgetting how uninjured he himself was after the clammy brushing of that coloured vapour in the attic room, but perhaps it is just as well that he acted as he did. No one will ever know what was abroad that night; and though the blasphemy from beyond had not so far hurt any human of unweakened mind, there is no telling what it might not have done at that last moment, and with its seemingly increased strength and the special signs of purpose it was soon to display beneath the half-clouded moonlit sky.

All at once one of the detectives at the window gave a short, sharp gasp. The others looked at him, and then quickly followed his own gaze upward to the point at which its idle straying had been suddenly arrested. There was no need for words. What had been disputed in country gossip was disputable no longer, and it is because of the thing which every man of that party agreed in whispering later on that the strange days are never talked about in Arkham. It is necessary to premise that there was no wind at that hour of the evening. One did arise not long afterward, but there was absolutely none then. Even the dry tips of the lingering hedge-mustard, grey and blighted, and the fringe on the roof of the standing democrat-wagon were unstirred. And yet amid that tense, godless calm the high bare boughs of all the trees in the yard were moving. They were twitching morbidly and spasmodically, clawing in convulsive and epileptic madness at the moonlit clouds; scratching impotently in the noxious air as if jerked by some alien and bodiless line of linkage with subterrene horrors writhing and struggling below the black roots.

Not a man breathed for several seconds. Then a cloud of darker depth passed over the moon, and the silhouette of clutching branches faded out momentarily. At this there was a general cry; muffled with awe, but husky and almost identical from every throat. For the terror had not faded with the silhouette, and in a fearsome instant of deeper darkness the watchers saw wriggling at that treetop height a thousand tiny points of faint and unhallowed radiance, tipping each bough like the fire of St. Elmo or the flames that came down on the apostles' heads at Pentecost. It was a monstrous constellation of unnatural light, like a glutted swarm of corpse-fed fireflies dancing hellish sarabands over an accursed marsh; and its colour was that same nameless intrusion which Ammi had come to recognise and dread. All the while the shaft of phosphorescence from the well was getting brighter and brighter, bringing to the minds of the huddled men a sense of doom and abnormality which far outraced any image their conscious minds could form. It was no longer shining out, it was pouring out; and as the shapeless stream of unplaceable colour left the well it seemed to flow directly into the sky.

The veterinary shivered, and walked to the front door to drop the heavy extra bar across it. Ammi shook no less, and had to tug and point for lack of a controllable voice when he wished to draw notice to the growing luminosity of the trees. The neighing and stamping of the horses had become utterly frightful, but not a soul of that group in the old house would have ventured forth for any earthly reward. With the moments the shining of the trees increased, while their restless branches seemed to strain more and more toward verticality. The wood of the well-sweep was shining now, and presently a policeman dumbly pointed to some wooden sheds and bee-hives near the stone wall on the west. They were commencing to shine, too, though the tethered vehicles of the visitors seemed so far unaffected. Then there was a wild commotion and clopping in the road, and as Ammi quenched the lamp for better seeing they realised that the span of frantic greys had broke their sapling and run off with the democrat-wagon.

The shock served to loosen several tongues, and embarrassed whispers were exchanged. "It spreads on everything organic that's been around here," muttered the medical examiner. No one replied, but the man who had been in the well gave a hint that his long pole must have stirred up something intangible. "It was awful," he added. "There was no bottom at all. Just ooze and bubbles and the feeling of something lurking under there." Ammi's horse still pawed and screamed deafeningly in the road outside, and nearly drowned its owner's faint quaver as he mumbled his formless reflections. "It come from that stone . . . it growed down thar . . . it got everything livin' . . . it fed itself on 'em, mind and body . . . Thad an' Mernie, Zenas an' Nabby . . . Nahum was the last . . . they all drunk the water . . . it got strong on 'em . . . it come from beyond, whar things ain't like they be here . . . now it's goin' home. . . ."

At this point, as the column of unknown colour flared suddenly stronger and began to weave itself into fantastic suggestions of shape which each spectator later described differently, there came from poor tethered Hero such a sound as no man before or since ever heard from a horse. Every person in that low-pitched sitting room stopped his ears, and Ammi turned away from the window in horror and nausea. Words could not convey it—when Ammi looked out again the hapless beast lay huddled inert on the moonlit ground between the splintered shafts of the buggy. That was the last of Hero till they buried him next day. But the present was no time to mourn, for almost at this instant a detective silently called attention to something terrible in the very room with them. In the absence of the lamplight it was clear that a faint phosphorescence had begun to pervade the entire apartment. It glowed on the broad-planked floor and the fragment of rag carpet, and shimmered over the sashes of the small-paned windows. It ran up and down the exposed corner-posts, coruscated about the shelf and mantel, and infected the very doors and furniture. Each minute saw it strengthen, and at last it was very plain that healthy living things must leave that house.

Ammi shewed them the back door and the path up through the fields to the ten-acre pasture. They walked and stumbled as in a dream, and did not dare look back till they were far away on the high ground. They were glad of the path, for they could not have gone the front way, by that well. It was bad enough passing the glowing barn and sheds, and those shining orchard trees with their gnarled, fiendish contours; but thank heaven the branches did their worst twisting high up. The moon went under some very black clouds as they crossed the rustic bridge over Chapman's Brook, and it was blind groping from there to the open meadows.

When they looked back toward the valley and the distant Gardner place at the bottom they saw a fearsome sight. All the farm was shining with the hideous unknown blend of colour; trees, buildings, and even such grass and herbage as had not been wholly changed to lethal grey brittleness. The boughs were all straining skyward, tipped with tongues of foul flame, and lambent tricklings of the same monstrous fire were creeping about the ridgepoles of the house, barn, and sheds. It was a scene from a vision of Fuseli, and over all the rest reigned that riot of luminous amorphousness, that alien and undimensioned rainbow of cryptic poison from the well—seething, feeling, lapping, reaching, scintillating, straining, and malignly bubbling in its cosmic and unrecognisable chromaticism.

Then without warning the hideous thing shot vertically up toward the sky like a rocket or meteor, leaving behind no trail and disappearing through a round and curiously regular hole in the clouds before any man could gasp or cry out. No watcher can ever forget that sight, and Ammi stared blankly at the stars of Cygnus, Deneb twinkling above the others, where the unknown colour had melted into the Milky Way. But his gaze was the next moment called swiftly to earth by the crackling in the valley. It was just that. Only a wooden ripping and crackling, and not an explosion, as so many others of the party vowed. Yet the outcome was the same, for in one feverish, kaleidoscopic instant there burst up from that doomed and accursed farm a gleamingly eruptive cataclysm of unnatural sparks and substance; blurring the glance of the few who saw it, and sending forth to the zenith a bombarding cloudburst of such coloured and fantastic fragments as our universe must needs disown. Through quickly re-closing vapours they followed the great morbidity that had vanished, and in another second they had vanished too. Behind and below was only a darkness to which the men dared not return, and all about was a mounting wind which seemed to sweep down in black, frore gusts from interstellar space. It shrieked and howled, and lashed the fields and distorted woods in a mad cosmic frenzy, till soon the trembling party realised it would be no use waiting for the moon to shew what was left down there at Nahum's.

Too awed even to hint theories, the seven shaking men trudged back toward Arkham by the north road. Ammi was worse than his fellows, and begged them to see him inside his own kitchen, instead of keeping straight on to town. He did not wish to cross the nighted, wind-whipped woods alone to his home on the main road. For he had had an added shock that the others were spared, and was crushed forever with a brooding fear he dared not even mention for many years to come. As the rest of the watchers on that tempestuous hill had stolidly set their faces toward the road, Ammi had looked back an instant at the shadowed valley of desolation so lately sheltering his ill-starred friend. And from that stricken, far-away spot he had seen something feebly rise, only to sink down again upon the place from which the great shapeless horror had shot into the sky. It was just a colour—but not any colour of our earth or heavens. And because Ammi recognised that colour, and knew that this last faint remnant must still lurk down there in the well, he has never been quite right since.

Ammi would never go near the place again. It is over half a century now since the horror happened, but he has never been there, and will be glad when the new reservoir blots it out. I shall be glad, too, for I do not like the way the sunlight changed colour around the mouth of that abandoned well I passed. I hope the water will always be very deep—but even so, I shall never drink it. I do not think I shall visit the Arkham country hereafter. Three of the men who had been with Ammi returned the next morning to see the ruins by daylight, but there were not any real ruins. Only the bricks of the chimney, the stones of the cellar, some mineral and metallic litter here and there, and the rim of that nefandous well. Save for Ammi's dead horse, which they towed away and buried, and the buggy which they shortly returned to him, everything that had ever been living had gone. Five eldritch acres of dusty grey desert remained, nor has anything ever grown there since. To this day it sprawls open to the sky like a great spot eaten by acid in the woods and fields, and the few who have ever dared glimpse it in spite of the rural tales have named it "the blasted heath".

The rural tales are queer. They might be even queerer if city men and college chemists could be interested enough to analyse the water from that disused well, or the grey dust that no wind seems ever to disperse. Botanists, too, ought to study the stunted flora on the borders of that spot, for they might shed light on the country notion that the blight is spreading—little by little, perhaps an inch a year. People say the colour of the neighbouring herbage is not quite right in the spring, and that wild things leave queer prints in the light winter snow. Snow never seems quite so heavy on the blasted heath as it is elsewhere. Horses—the few that are left in this motor age—grow skittish in the silent valley; and hunters cannot depend on their dogs too near the splotch of greyish dust.

They say the mental influences are very bad, too. Numbers went queer in the years after Nahum's taking, and always they lacked the power to get away. Then the stronger-minded folk all left the region, and only the foreigners tried to live in the crumbling old homesteads. They could not stay, though; and one sometimes wonders what insight beyond ours their wild, weird stores of whispered magic have given them. Their dreams at night, they protest, are very horrible in that grotesque country; and surely the very look of the dark realm is enough to stir a morbid fancy. No traveller has ever escaped a sense of strangeness in those deep ravines, and artists shiver as they paint thick woods whose mystery is as much of the spirit as of the eye. I myself am curious about the sensation I derived from my one lone walk before

Ammi told me his tale. When twilight came I had vaguely wished some clouds would gather, for an odd timidity about the deep skyey voids above had crept into my soul.

Do not ask me for my opinion. I do not know—that is all. There was no one but Ammi to question; for Arkham people will not talk about the strange days, and all three professors who saw the aërolite and its coloured globule are dead. There were other globules—depend upon that. One must have fed itself and escaped, and probably there was another which was too late. No doubt it is still down the well—I know there was something wrong with the sunlight I saw above that miasmal brink. The rustics say the blight creeps an inch a year, so perhaps there is a kind of growth or nourishment even now. But whatever daemon hatchling is there, it must be tethered to something or else it would quickly spread. Is it fastened to the roots of those trees that claw the air? One of the current Arkham tales is about fat oaks that shine and move as they ought not to do at night.

What it is, only God knows. In terms of matter I suppose the thing Ammi described would be called a gas, but this gas obeyed laws that are not of our cosmos. This was no fruit of such worlds and suns as shine on the telescopes and photographic plates of our observatories. This was no breath from the skies whose motions and dimensions our astronomers measure or deem too vast to measure. It was just a colour out of space—a frightful messenger from unformed realms of infinity beyond all Nature as we know it; from realms whose mere existence stuns the brain and numbs us with the black extra-cosmic gulfs it throws open before our frenzied eyes.

I doubt very much if Ammi consciously lied to me, and I do not think his tale was all a freak of madness as the townfolk had forewarned. Something terrible came to the hills and valleys on that meteor, and something terrible—though I know not in what proportion—still remains. I shall be glad to see the water come. Meanwhile I hope nothing will happen to Ammi. He saw so much of the thing—and its influence was so insidious. Why has he never been able to move away? How clearly he recalled those dying words of Nahum's—"can't git away . . . draws ye . . . ye know summ'at's comin', but 'tain't no use. . . ." Ammi is such a good old man—when the reservoir gang gets to work I must write the chief engineer to keep a sharp watch on him. I would hate to think of him as the grey, twisted, brittle monstrosity which persists more and more in troubling my sleep.